KU-008-064

Bellagrand

Paullina Simons was born in Leningrad and emigrated to the United States in 1973. She has lived in Italy, England, Kansas, and Texas, and now lives close to New York, with her husband and most of her children. Go to her website www.paullinasimons. com, for more information on her novels.

By the same author

PAULLINA SIMONS

Bellagrand

HARPER

Harper
An imprint of HarperCollins*Publishers*
77–85 Fulham Palace Road,
Hammersmith, London W6 8JB

www.harpercollins.co.uk

This paperback edition 2014
3

First published in Great Britain by
HarperCollins*Publishers* 2014

A catalogue record for this book is
available from the British Library

ISBN: 978-0-00-749371-5

Typeset in Goudy

Printed and bound in Great Britain by
Clays Ltd, St Ives plc

MIX
Paper from
responsible sources
FSC www.fsc.org **FSC™ C007454**

For my mother,
An engineer
A teacher
An immigrant
A romantic
A dreamer
A giver of life
Who looked for Paradise
Every place she lived.

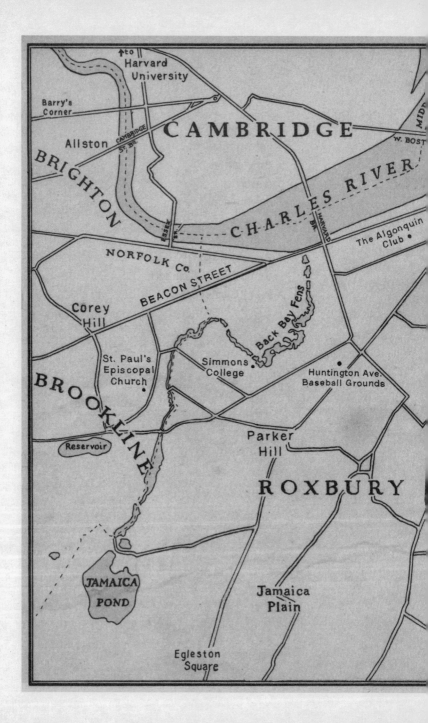

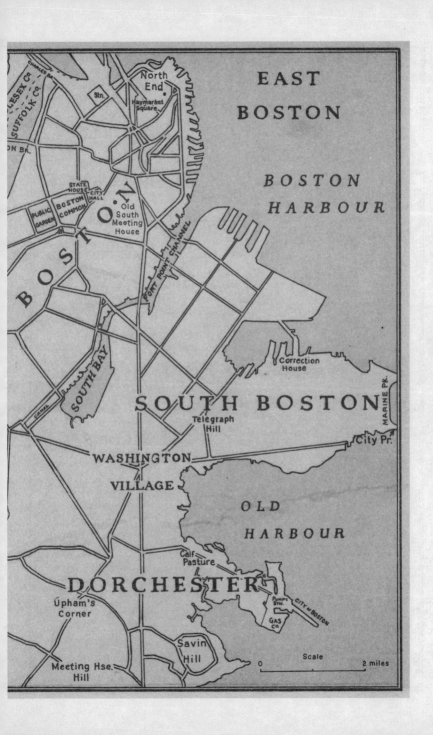

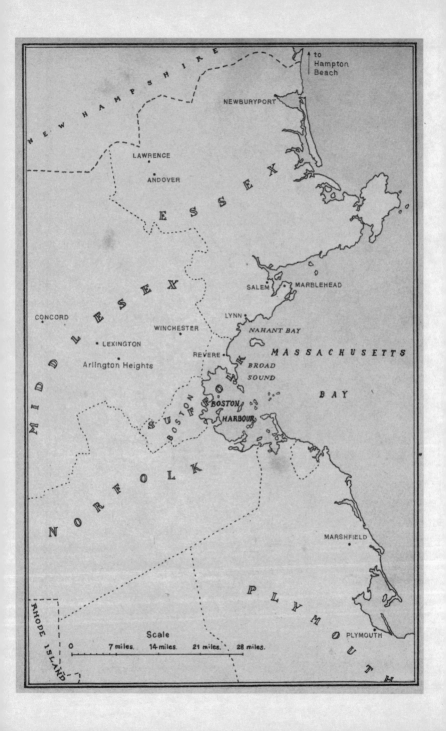

But heard are the Voices
Heard are the Sages,
The Worlds and the Ages:
Choose well; your choice is
Brief, and yet endless.
—Johann von Goethe

Prologue

1936

On a train a once beautiful woman sits shivering in an old coat. Next to her is a young man nearly at full bloom. He doesn't shiver. He stares straight ahead, stone cold, his face inscrutable. So is the woman's. Except for her shivering, neither of them moves. She wants to speak but has nothing to say. She glances at him. He has nothing to say either.

Their ride is long. Eight hundred kilometers. Five hundred miles through bleakest terrain. The rivers hardly move, the melting ice crushing down the flow, the waters heavy. The flattened fields are black, old speckled snow clinging to the trees gray and bare. It's grim, desolate, barren, and it's all flying by. *O World! O Life! O Time! On whose last steps I climb.*

The young man stares out the window purposefully, single-mindedly. A boy yet not a boy. His hair is black upon his head, his eyes the color of coffee. He wants nothing less than to discuss the unspeakable. The train car is almost empty. They deliberately took the later train, the one no one takes, because it gets in late at night. They don't want to be noticed.

The woman tries to take his hand. It's cold. He gives it, yet doesn't give it. He wants to be left alone. He wants to shout things he knows he can't, say things he knows he can't. He stops himself only because of her, because of his reverence for her—still and despite everything. The things he wants to whisper, she is not strong enough to hear and doesn't deserve to. How could you bring me here, he wants to ask her in

1

his most frightened voice. Knowing my life was at stake, how could you come here with me? It's too late now for if onlys. Why didn't you know enough back then?

Listen to me, she whispers intensely after the train screeches to a stop and the few remaining passengers shuffle out. There's nothing to be done. You can't think about what's past.

What else is there to think about? The future?

I want you to not look back. Forget where you came from. Forget everything, do you hear?

That's the opposite of what you've been telling me my whole life.

The train speeds on.

It's a long way between two metropolitan cities. They have ample time to sit, to stare speechlessly at the countryside.

He wants to know about only one thing. He wants to ask about the place he can't remember. She refuses to entertain his questions, hence her new commandment: stop looking back. His entire life, he has heard only: never forget where you came from. Suddenly she wants him to forget.

He asks her about the place he forgot. To help him remember what he can't remember.

Stop asking me about what's meaningless, she says.

The past is now meaningless? Why can't you answer me?

Why do you keep wanting to know? What does it matter? God, you've been on and on about it lately. Why?

Why can't you answer me?

She turns to him. Promise to remember about the money?

You just told me to forget everything. So that's what I'm going to do.

Remember only the money. Make sure you hide it again. Keep it secure. But don't forget where it is. Don't keep it in the house in case they come, but hide it somewhere close to you, somewhere safe, where you can easily get to it. Do you have such a place? If you don't, you'll need to find one.

The money! The money is what makes him want to rail at her more, not less. The money is the thing that brings cold to his heart, and cold toward her. The money is what screams to him the brutal truth: You did know what you were doing when you brought me here. That's why you saved the money, took it with you, hid it, kept it hidden all these years. Because you knew. You can't claim ignorance, which is what I want to believe in most of all, your ignorance of the way things might turn out for us. Turn out for me. But you keep reminding me about the money. Which reminds me that this act on your part—bringing me here—was for my destruction.

He says nothing.

Do you hear me?

I'm trying desperately not to.

Promise me you'll remember.

I thought you just told me to forget? Make up your mind.

It's not about the money.

You want me to remember it's not about the money?

Stop joking.

Who's joking? After what happened today, how do you think your money will help me?

Here not much, you're right. But elsewhere it might buy you another life. It might free you. It's not magic. You must participate in your own salvation. Strength. Resoluteness. Courage. Will they be the hallmarks of your character? I don't know. She shrugs her crumpled narrowing shoulders. I hope so.

He shrugs his widening ones. Perhaps instead I can misspend it. Drink it away, maybe? He stares—glares—at her. Buy myself fancy shoes and red wool overcoats?

Where are you going to get those here? she asks.

Anything is possible with money. You just said.

Please don't jest. This isn't the time.

They whisper under the relentless hum of the wheels, under the hiss of the steam engine.

Tell me about that place, he says. Tell me or I'll promise you nothing.

I know nothing about it.

The warm white place with the boats and the frogs. The carnival wheel across the blue water. What am I remembering?

3

I don't know, she says, letting go of his hand, falling back against the seat. A nightmare perhaps.

He shakes his head.

She closes her eyes.

Promise me you'll find a way to keep the money safe, she repeats in a breath. Everything else, including the marble palace with the white curtains, will one day be revealed.

Not today?

Nothing is clear today and won't be for a long time.

They sit so close. He is slumped down, deep in the crook of her arm. He turns his face to her, away from the icy window. Tell me honestly, do you think we'll be okay? His tremulous voice is too small for his body. Or do you think because of what we did we might be in danger?

She meets his eyes, a beat, another, a blink, and then she smiles. No, she says. We'll be fine. She kisses his forehead, his hair, his face. Don't worry. Everything is going to be all right. They sit with their heads pressed together.

Ti voglio bene, she says. You are what I love most in life.

Now maybe. Once you loved someone else too.

Yes, my son, and still do, she says, her voice trailing off, the marsh grasses outside, the taupe and gray towns flying by. Klin, Kalashnikovo, Okulovka, Luka. Once another Calais lay on my heart. Once I loved more than just one someone.

Sic Transit Gloria Mundi, she whispers. Thus passes the glory of the world.

Part One

BREAD AND ROSES

1911–1918

If you press me to say why I loved him,
I can say no more than because he was he,
and I was I.
—Michel de Montaigne

Love is not blind;
that is the last thing that it is.
Love is bound;
And the more it is bound
The less it is blind.
—GK Chesterton

Chapter 1

WINE INTO STONES

One

ALL LOVE STORIES END. Who said that? Gina heard it once years ago. But she didn't believe it. That hers never would is what she believed.

Gina set her internal clock by two things. One was the train schedule to Boston, a shining city on a hill if ever there was one. And the other was her monthly cycle. She'd been marking the calendar for the last three years. She'd been making the trip to Boston for twelve, and she was making it still, setting store by it, anticipating it. She would put her long-fingered hands in black silk gloves on the train window to touch the towns she passed and would dream about other cities and cradles, parks and prams, annual fairs and lullabies.

Her gauzy reflection in the glass returned curls and dark auburn hair, hastily piled up because she was always late, always running out of time. Returned translucent skin, full lips, bottomless coffee pools for eyes. Her rust-colored wool skirt and taupe blouse were not new but were clean and pressed and perfectly tailored, a custom fit for her tall, slender, slightly curvy figure. She always made sure, no matter how broke they were, that whenever she went out she was dressed as if she could run into her high society father-in-law and not look like an immigrant, could run into her husband's ditched and furious former fiancée and not look like steerage, could run into the King of England himself and curtsy like a lady.

Where else besides Boston might the train take her? If she stayed on past North Station, where might she ride to? Where would she *want* to ride to in her velvet hat and leather shoes? If the train could take her anywhere, where would it be? She spent Monday mornings imagining where she might ride to.

Every Monday but today.

Everything was different today, and was going to be different from now on. Everything had changed.

Gina was running down Salem Street past the lunchtime peddlers, breathing through her mouth to avoid the pervasive odor of the North End—fish and molasses—that today was making her subtly queasy. The train had been delayed and she knew her brother would be upset because until she arrived to look after his little girl, he couldn't go to work.

By the time she got to his cold-water flat, all the way in the upper-north corner of Charter and Snow Hill, he was fit to be tied, pacing about the tiny living room like a caged lion, carrying Mary, who was cooing merrily. She clearly thought it was all in good fun, daddy carrying her back and forth, back and forth, rocking her in his arms as if he were a swing.

"I'm sorry," Gina said, extending her arms to the child. Salvo had dressed her, but like a dad would. Not only did nothing match, but he had dressed the child in shorts—in December.

He didn't want to hear it. "You're always sorry." He swung the baby upside down. She squealed more more and then cried when he handed her over. Not to be outdone, Gina held the girl upside down by her ankles. Mary chortled, and this allowed Gina to speak.

"I have to talk to you, Salvo."

"You've made that impossible. Should've thought of that before you sauntered in two hours late."

"It's not my fault."

"Nothing is ever your fault."

"The train was late."

"Should've taken an earlier train."

"Salvo, *basta*."

There was no more talking after that. He left, after kissing Mary's feet.

"Let's re-dress you, angel, shall we? What was your daddy thinking?" Gina dressed the girl warmly and wrapped her snug, then took her out in the carriage so they wouldn't be cooped up all afternoon playing patty cake and staring out onto Copp's Old Burying Ground. "At least in the graveyard there are trees she can look at," Salvo would say. "Anywhere else, poor thing would just be looking at a tenement."

Trees and graves.

They walked slowly to Prince Park, with Mary suddenly deciding she wanted to push her own carriage, which added nine to thirteen years to their already lengthy excursion. They got a sandwich they split in half, caught the end of a late afternoon Mass at St. Leonard's and then bought a few gifts for Christmas. Money was tighter than ever. Gina didn't know how they would manage. Even the holiday ham was too much. She bought new knitting needles for her mother and a scarf for her cousin Angela, a beautiful red silk she spied in a tailor's window. It was damaged on one side and imperfectly loomed, but the craftsmanship on the rest of it was superb. It was a real find.

She returned with Mary after six, fed her some cheese on a piece of bread, stacked blocks on the floor, waited. Salvo wasn't back. Was this revenge for her own inadvertent lateness? He often did this. Stayed out knowing she absolutely *had* to catch the train home. She would be late returning to Lawrence, and then Harry would be upset with her.

Did her brother do this so her husband would be upset with her?

Mary's mother finally strolled in around seven. She was a piece of work, that one. God knows what she got up to, out all hours day and night.

"What, he's not back yet? Typical." Phyllis yanked Mary out of Gina's arms.

"He's working."

"Sure he is."

"Mama, we got you Christmas things!" the little girl said, clutching her mother's leg.

"You shouldn't have bothered," the blowsy, bedraggled young woman said rudely to Gina. "It's tough this year. Where's her coat? I have to go."

"Maybe you can speak to Salvo when he comes back …" Gina said.

"I'm not waiting. You can wait until a cold day in hell for him to grace this apartment. No, we're leaving. Come on, Marybeth, where's your coat?"

"Goodbye, Aunt Ginny," Mary said, hugging Gina around the neck. "Come tomorrow?"

"Not tomorrow, baby. Wednesday."

Phyllis pulled her daughter away from Gina and rushed out without a goodbye. Gina stared after mother and daughter with a sick longing. What must it be like to have the right to pull your own babies out of other people's arms. She stuck around for a few more minutes, hoping Salvo would return, and when he didn't, she put on her coat and went out to look for him.

She hated walking past the brick wall separating the burying grounds from the street. It made her heart cold knowing that though she couldn't see the gravestones, they were lurking there, behind a deliberately erected wall, as if they were so terrible that she shouldn't lay eyes on them.

She found her brother in a tavern down Hanover, shivering in a huddle with drunk men spilling their brew onto the sidewalk and blowing into their hands to keep warm.

"Salvo," she said, coming up behind him, prodding him with her hand. She pulled him away from the others, but saw he was in no condition to talk, or even listen. Gina didn't have the answer to the eternal question: did he drink *so* he could become unhappy? Or was he just an unhappy drunk?

Gina didn't have answers to many eternal questions.

"Where's the baby?"

That she knew. "With her mother."

Salvo spat.

"You were supposed to come back by five so we could talk."

"I got busy."

She saw that. She was cold. "I have to run now. I'll miss my train. I'll come back Wednesday."

"Come earlier. Please. I'll lose my job if I can't work lunch. How is Mimoo?"

Gina shrugged. "She lost another domestic job. She keeps dropping things. But Salvo …" She struggled with herself. This wasn't the time. But it was Christmas soon. "Will you come with Mary, spend Christmas with us? Please?"

Salvo shook his head. "You know I can't. Also her damn mother takes her."

"Don't talk like that about the mother of your baby."

"Have you met the beastly creature?"

"All the same. Just … swallow your pride, Salvo. For our mother. Bring Mary. Bring Phyllis too. One day a year, on Christmas, let's bury the hatchet."

"You know where I'd like to bury the hatchet," her brother said, lucid enough.

"Oh, Salvo … what are you going to do, be angry forever?"

"*Per sempre.*"

"Please. Mimoo cries every night. She wants to see her grandchild for Christmas."

"Her mother has her, I told you. Her mother, who, by the way, has found herself another fool to pay her rent." Salvo swore. "Instead of talking to me, why don't you tell that common-law husband of yours to go visit *his* family for Christmas? Tell him to go spend some time with them. Or tell him to go get a fucking job. Then I'll come."

"He is not my common-law husband."

"Did you get married in a church?"

"Salvo."

"Exactly."

"You know he can't," she finally said.

"Can't get a job? What a great country this is." Salvo laughed. "Where one can live without doing any fucking work whatsoever. Can the immigrants do this? How many generations must we toil before we're able to do nothing but sit around the table and pretend we're smart?"

"Stop it, Salvo, you know he's been working. He's trying hard. It's not easy for him. I mean, he can't visit his family."

"Oh, he can't, can he? Well, I can't either."

"He can't visit them because they don't want him. That's the difference. They want nothing to do with him. His father made that very clear. You know that."

Salvo sighed. His black eyes glistened. "I can never set foot in the house where that man resides."

"The man who's your sister's husband?"

"Whatever you call him." He blinked, shrugged, deflected as always. "Tell Mimoo I'm thinking of changing professions. Look at this." He showed his sister a pipe inlaid with intricate carving. "The Battle of Bunker Hill is carved on it," he said with incredulity. "Isn't it fantastic? I want to be a pipe carver. I know a guy. I'm trying to get in as an apprentice." He shook his head. "There's an idiotic rule, though, we're trying to get around. I have to apprentice for twenty-five years before I can become a carver. Can you imagine?"

She gazed at him fondly. "You gonna become a pipe carver, Salvo? Do you even hear yourself?"

They chuckled, they hugged. Turning her around, Salvo pointed her down the street. "Go. Quick. Or he'll think you're stepping out on him. Although maybe then he'll leave you and you'll finally be free like Papa wanted." He stuck some bills into her hand. "Kiss Mimoo for me. Tell her it's for Christmas. I'll have more on Wednesday. I'm trying to get hired by the Purity Distilling Company. They make molasses here in the North End. I get a job there, I'd be set for life. Union and everything. Tell Mimoo that so she stops fretting. Now go."

Two

ON THE TRAIN BACK, Gina thought about Salvo's words. She didn't think Harry would interpret her lateness as faithlessness. He wasn't that kind.

14

Her hands were on the cold glass, her palms. The train was stopped in the well, waiting for a signal.

They tried hard to make the best of it. Did Gina ever complain? How could she complain when she had been given what her heart wanted most. You'd have to be an ingrate to complain after that, wouldn't you?

Mill workers were being laid off left and right, though it was nearing the holidays. Gina was lucky to have her job. Talent and style, Angela had said to her with approval. But how much style did Gina need to work in the mending room? She wore white to work, she didn't dye wool anymore. She worked with ladies at a table, dressed in a skirt in a room full of windows.

Then why did she sometimes wish the buildings would burn to the ground?

Once, in 1886, there had been a fire. Why did she recall that wistfully?

So many blessings. She sewed handmade costumes, walked in city parades, dressed the nurses, supported their floats.

She worked on Mill Island, but she wasn't a carpenter, wasn't a machinist. Her long curly hair didn't get tangled in heavy equipment. She wasn't hospitalized for months with a near-fatal injury like her friend Pamela.

She wasn't a child anymore. The child labor laws no longer applied to her.

Many things no longer applied to her.

For a time Gina had worked at Duck Mill, making cloth out of specialty cotton called canvas that was also used to make sails. Tonight on the train it came back to her. Making a sail. For a boat on the ocean. Having the wind take her away. In any direction. She dreamed about the sails as she spun the cotton. She worked blazing fast, as always, but dreamed languidly of warm water and boats and the wind grabbing hold of her with the sail up. Well, why not? Harry was such a dreamer. It's one of the things she loved most about him. Why shouldn't she allow herself a dream or two? What, only the young and the (formerly) wealthy were allowed to dream?

Things hadn't quite turned out as she thought they might, planned they would, dreamed they could. It was cold on the train. Like in their house. She closed the coat tighter around herself, breathed into her woolen scarf, curved into a ball.

For one, she truly had believed in her Italian, family-centered heart that after a few months Harry would make amends with his family.

They had spent the summer after they were married at her mother's house in Lawrence while they figured things out. She continued to work with Salvo in his restaurants. A few nights a week she helped out at St. Vincent de Paul's mending their donations. She had intended to return to Simmons College in the fall to finish her degree. She expected to move to Cambridge when Harry started teaching at Harvard again and to commute to classes from there.

It took him until the morning she was rushing off to register for her fall semester to show her the letter from the head of the economics department terminating Harry's relationship with Harvard University.

He said he didn't have all the answers. She hoped he had some. He had been reading so much, out on the porch in a rocking chair, his nose always buried inside one thick educational tome or another. Surely he could have read a morsel that would solve just one of their problems. But he couldn't solve her senior year in Simmons.

"What do you propose we do?" he had said. "Live apart? I live here with your mother, brother, cousin, while you live on campus close to Archer?" Archer was a boy who had liked Gina.

She suggested they both move to Boston.

"What would we live on? Your bookstore salary?"

Gina didn't know what to say. She cocked her head this way, that, looked out on to Summer Street, chewed her lip. "You could, oh, get a job."

"Doing what?"

Gina wanted to point out the sewing machine, the looms, St. Vincent's, St. Mary's, Salvo's restaurants, the houses Mimoo cleaned, the quarries, the lumber yards, the printing presses, the textile mills. She wanted to gently remind Harry of his black contempt for indolent Dyson, a boy proud of his desire to work only five hours a day. She wanted to tell him that Canney's, the basket-weaving factory, was hiring. She didn't say any of these things. Because you couldn't say them to a descendant of one of the Founding Fathers, an aristocrat. "How are we going to live?"

He shrugged and she saw in his face that he didn't have a plan. "I'll figure it out. This is new for me, uncharted. Give me time."

She stood in front of him in her smart coat and hat, her walkabout shoes. She had her green purse in her hands, that's how close she had been to going to the train station to catch the 9:45 to Boston to register for senior fall. Slowly she put down her purse and untied the ribbons of her hat.

That was six years ago.

"I was going to become even more politically active on campus," Gina told him when she still told him things. "I was going to form a club to advocate for women's suffrage. Perhaps other rights too. Advocate for women to be allowed to attend Harvard University one day. Maybe even teach there."

"Women teach at Harvard?" Harry laughed. "What are you saying? That's not a right, that's folly."

"I wanted to get my masters."

"I wanted things too," he said.

"Yes," she said. "They're sitting in front of you in a skirt and blouse."

"Indeed." The verbal conversation ended and another conversation, less verbal but no less intense began.

"I've already worked in Salvo's restaurant, Harry," she said, picking up the topic of work a few days, weeks, years later. "I kept books, hired and fired, hosted. Washed dishes. Made pizza. I did all that."

"So now you want me to take a job even *you* don't want?"

"You want to continue living with my mother?"

"You know I don't," Harry said quietly, in the little bedroom they shared, with her Shaker nightstand and dresser, her narrow wooden bed. "You're too quiet in your mother's house. As if you're afraid she'll hear us."

"I *am* afraid she'll hear us."

After they had tried hard to make sure Mimoo didn't hear them, Gina tried again. "We both want it, we have to find our own place, darling."

"Well, we can't find our own place," Harry said, "without money."

She hung her head. "Not money," she said. "Work. We can't find it without *work*."

He stared at her blankly. "That's what I said."

"No. You said ..."

"What's the difference?"

"Without work," Gina said, "there is no money."

"Oh the miseries of constantly toiling for a subsistence!" he exclaimed. "How does one ever have a *moment* to discover his path in the forest if one is always scrounging a penny or two for his next meal?"

"Immigrants don't have the luxury of paths in forests," Gina said. "They're too busy working."

"But I'm not an immigrant."

She didn't want to remind him he was also without luxuries.

The train ride was too long.

She would prefer not to be cold.

She would prefer not to have to work so long, so hard, so late that when she fell into bed she was too tired for dreams, for nightmares, for love.

Though in some ways raw exhaustion was preferable to having time to sit and think when the trains were stalled and the miseries multiplied.

Blessedly the train began moving. She would try again tonight. Everything had changed. He had to know that.

Three

GINA DIDN'T GET BACK to Lawrence until after nine and walked with her eyes averted past the establishment that used to be her brother's dream, where the crowds used to mob him for lunch because he made the most delicious pizza in town. She kept her eyes to the ground and rushed the mile across Haverhill, past the Common, to

Summer Street, a mile back to Mimoo's small folk Victorian home they had been renting since 1899.

Braced for questions about her late arrival, she climbed the porch stairs and opened the door. Harry was sitting at the kitchen table with his back to her, papers and maps in front of him, huddled over them with Angela, Joe and Arturo. He turned his head to her, smiled absent-mindedly, distant intimacy in his eyes, and turned back to the table. Indeed there were loud words, but they weren't for her. The four of them were animatedly discussing something problematic. But they always animatedly discussed something problematic.

"What is more important?" Arturo asked. "Freedom or equality?"

"Why can't we have both?" said Harry. "Why do we have to choose? I don't want to choose. And I want the people of Lawrence to have both. I want them to be free, to live in harmony, to be selfless and happy, and I want them to have economic, material equality. Not one or the other. First Lawrence, then everywhere. Right, Gia?" Harry wore a flannel shirt untucked and had a four-day growth on his face, there since Friday. His sandy hair was long, almost long enough to tie back. No one had hair like that, she kept telling him. That's why I like it, he told her. There is no one like me. His clear gray eyes were as lovely as ever, his voice strong, calm, droll.

She bent to kiss his cheek. "Right, *tesoro*."

Lightly he leaned his head into hers. "You're home late. Have you eaten?"

"I'm not hungry. Salvo was working and Phyllis didn't get the baby until after seven."

"Did you talk to Salvo, Gia?" Angela asked. "About Christmas?"

Gina hung up her coat and hat, put down her small purse. She took off her shoes, put on her slippers. She went to the cast-iron stove and lit the kettle. Then she spoke. "I did talk to him," she said. "Anyone for a cup of tea?"

But they were buried in the labor laws of Massachusetts. No one replied. She made one for Mimoo, and when it was steeped and sugared, she walked past the round table at which the radical knights sat, plotting and planning, and headed upstairs to her mother's bedroom.

"Arturo says *he'll* come for Christmas," said Angela, her hand over his.

"I'll come too," Joe said. "If I'm invited."

"Of course, Joe," said Harry. "The more the merrier. Gina, you're all right with Joe coming for Christmas dinner?"

"If he brings the turkey, why not?"

"Is your wife joking?" she heard Joe say. "Where am I going to get a turkey?"

"She's joking," said Harry. "She fancies herself as a bit of a comedienne."

Mimoo was lying on the bed, still in her street clothes. She was salt and pepper gray now, heavier than when she had first come to America, but no quieter.

"About time you came to see your mother after being gone all day. How is he?"

"Why don't you get under the covers, Mimoo?" Gina said, setting the cup of tea by the bedside.

"I'll get under the covers when I'm good and ready. What did he say?"

"Who? Joe?"

"Don't play dumb with me. What do I care what that fool has to say about anything? What did my son say?"

Gina sighed.

Mimoo turned away.

They sat for a few moments while downstairs boisterous voices planned unrest and street action.

"Help me get ready for bed," Mimoo said. "I'm tired."

Gina helped her mother up. "Don't worry," she said. "1912 will be better."

"You sure about that?"

"I am."

Mimoo laughed. "Do you not hear what's going on in your very own kitchen? What are they conspiring about? Mark my words, it will be the worst year yet."

"What are they always conspiring about? Strikes. Demonstrations. Petitions for better wages. It's all talk, don't worry." She squeezed her mother's hand. "I only know what I know. It'll be a good year. You'll see."

"You know what would make next year a better year? If my son and that no-good husband of yours made amends, put the past behind them, sat down at the same table."

"I'm working on that." Gina unhooked Mimoo's dress and underskirts, took off her stockings. She slipped the nightgown over her head and brought her a basin filled with water. When her mother was in bed, Gina laid Salvo's money on the nightstand beside the cup of tea.

"He thinks money is going to make up for it?" Mimoo said. "Tell him I don't want his money."

"We tried that," Gina said. "He didn't speak to us for a year. He had a baby and didn't tell us."

"The way your brother gets around, how do you know he had just the one?"

"Mimoo!" Gina covered up her mother and kissed her.

Mimoo took her daughter's hand, looked her over, touched her pale face, pushed the strands of her dark curls behind her ears.

"I'm good," Gina whispered. "Don't worry. Just tired."

"What else is new? Did you hear? Your friend Verity is with child again."

"*Dio mio*, no. How do you know this?"

"I play bingo with her mother every Saturday. She told me. What is that, her sixth baby now?"

"Fifth, Mimoo. Stop it." Gina rubbed her eyes. "How does she do it?"

"Clearly you haven't taught Verity your foolproof methods of family planning," Mimoo said. "Someone should tell her that human beings in many ways are like vegetables: quality and not quantity is what counts."

Gina smiled, leaning down again to kiss her mother. "I learned that well," she said. "No one can accuse me of disastrous overbreeding."

"*Mia figlia*, no one can accuse you of any breeding at all."

The smile gone from her face, Gina stepped away to the door.

"Tell them to keep it down," Mimoo said, clutching her rosary beads. "Some of us have to get up in the morning."

Four

HARRY WAS TRYING TO sleep, but she wasn't having any of it.

"Don't give me this tired business," she whispered. "You weren't too tired for revolutionary blather."

He put his hand over her mouth. "It was just blather. I'm exhausted." He kissed her. "Tomorrow we'll talk. As long as it's not your usual Christmas sermon."

"Which is …"

He mimicked her. "Harry, when oh when are you going to make amends with your family?"

"What a good question."

"I'm sleeping. I can't hear a word you're saying. I'm dreaming you're quiet."

She shook him.

He groaned.

"Shh," she said. "Or Mimoo will think we're up to no good."

"If only," said Harry, his fingers pressing into her.

"First we talk, then we'll see about other things." They were conjoined under the covers of their small bed. It was cold. They pressed against each other to stay warm.

"I won't be awake for the other things."

But something was signaling to Gina that he might be.

"Why aren't you nicer to Arturo?" Harry murmured into her neck. "Angela feels deeply wronged that you and Mimoo aren't more friendly to him."

"I'm friendly." But it was true her mother was intractable when it came to Arturo. As if she saw black ravens above his head.

"American polite. Not Italian friendly."

"I'm trying to be more American and less Italian in all my ways."

His hands were over her body, under her nightgown, his mouth finding her mouth. "Please don't. Anything but that. Be Italian, I beg you."

"Italian then in *all* ways," she murmured back. "Not just in this one way you love."

"I'll take the baby with the bathwater." The blankets came

off slightly as he clung to her, his mouth on her bare shoulders, the nightgown pulled away. She squirmed away from his mouth, she was hypersensitive, and what to say about that? Nothing really, except …

"Speaking of babies … um, listen … I wouldn't mind a little baby, Harry."

"What?"

"You mentioned babies."

"I didn't mention babies. I mentioned a metaphor."

"I was thinking of an actual baby."

"Since when?"

She didn't want to confess that for a long time she had been counting out her days, crossing them off her womb's relentless calendar. "For a little while now."

"I thought we agreed no. We both said no."

"We did agree this," she said into the pillow.

He had been lying on top of her back. Now he climbed off. "Well, then."

"Well, then nothing. I changed my mind. That's the prerogative of being a woman."

Harry sat up. He was perplexed in expression and body. Gina had to suppress an affectionate laugh. "How can that be?" he asked. "Every other week you're distributing illicit pamphlets about some reproductive freedom thing or other. Just this morning I saw in your bag an article from Lucifer the Lightbearer."

"Okay …" she drew out an answer. "Reproductive freedom also means *having* a baby, does it not?"

"Not according to your pamphlets. Have you read them?"

She didn't want to admit she had stopped reading them. "I don't know what to tell you. I want a baby."

"So sudden?"

"We're married six years. That seems sudden to you?"

"It doesn't seem *un*-sudden," Harry said. "Besides, you expressly told me no babies. Remember Chicago?"

"Yes, I remember Chicago. Our few brief days of rainy honeymoon bliss." The only honeymoon they'd had, she wanted to add, but didn't.

"I was twenty! You can't imagine that at twenty and still in college I would not want a child?"

"I thought it spoke to a larger state of your independent character."

"It spoke to me being twenty and in college."

"And going to hear Emma Goldman sermonize every week? Did you not hear her say babies are slavery?"

"Like I pay attention. She also says God is slavery. And marriage is slavery. And work is slavery. We must choose carefully what to agree with."

"Oh goodness, but is the bloom off the rose!" Harry half-feigned shock. "Quite frightening. Is this what's ahead for me, too?"

"No, I'm still fond of you. Do you want me to show you how fond?"

"Kill me if I ever say no."

He took from her some sweet, not so quiet love, and afterward in the dark, in bed, held her close, caressed her face, her body, and softly whispered to her, as confounded as before. "I simply don't understand your precipitous change of heart."

"Yes, it's like falling off a cliff," she whispered, tired herself, relaxed, sated, happy, and yet still needing to say what had to be said.

"Are you being facetious again? I can't tell with you."

"Me? Never." She half-listened, gently rubbing the arm that embraced her. "But Harry, in our current circumstance, Mother Jones may be right. *You* can't have a baby. Only me. That's the law of the prophets. I can't do what I do now and take care of a baby."

Mary Harris Jones, or Mother Jones, was one of the co-founders of the Industrial Workers of the World and a tireless labor union organizer. She was also detested by most of the prominent women of the day for being vehemently opposed to abortion and women's rights. She told everyone who would listen that the main reason for juvenile delinquency was mothers working outside the home. This endeared her to no one.

"I suppose *I* could take care of it," Harry said, in the tone of someone who might say, I guess I can try making ice cream.

"I don't want you to take care of it. I want to have a baby because I want to be a mother. I don't want to be *called* a mother. I want to *be* a mother. I want to *mother* a child. I want that to be the work of my life."

24

With an everlasting sigh, he kissed her lips, kissed her between her swollen breasts, kissed her head, closed his eyes, breathed deeply. "Tell you what," he said. "How about we cross that bridge when we get to it?"

He settled in for sleep. Gina was quiet, lying in his arms, barely breathing, listening for the rhythmic rising and falling of his heart.

"Harry," she whispered at last. "*Amore mio*, I think we're about to cross that bridge."

Lightly he laughed, squeezing her. "Why don't we give our coupling a few weeks to seed, sugarplum."

She raised her head from his chest, looked up at him in the dark. "Crossing that bridge now, *mio marito*."

Finally he understood.

For a long while didn't speak, his back to her. She stroked him. He didn't move away.

"Why didn't you tell me?"

"I *am* telling you. This is what I'm doing right now."

He put on his overshirt and slumped on his side of the bed. "Gina, what are we going to do?"

"We'll be fine. Isn't that what you always say about everything? We'll be fine."

"You're not worried?"

"Are *you* worried?" She ran her fingernails down his back tapping and scraping her fingers over him to rile him. "*Caro*, you're not ready to move out of my mother's house, you're not ready to get a job, you're not ready for a baby. Before me you weren't ready to be married. You're thirty-four years old. It's time. Time to take your one life by its unformed horns. You aren't going to get another chance to swim in this river again."

"I thought you were happy with us, with the way things are."

She didn't want to pause, but couldn't help an ever so slight hesitation. "I'm not *un*happy. But I wouldn't mind not living with my mother. I wouldn't mind a little privacy with you, just you and me and our baby. I wouldn't mind not having to work two jobs, be away from you all these hours during the day."

"One of us would still have to be away," he said. "If I was working."

She nodded in quiet non-judgmental agreement. "*Ti amo*. But I would like for that person to now be you."

"Gina ... we agreed."

"Okay. We agreed."

"And then you went to hear one feminist after another talk about free love, birth control, women behaving like men, and so on."

"I did."

"And?"

"And what? I got tired of it."

"You didn't tell me."

"You got tired of it so long ago, you haven't come with me for years. Which is why I've had to keep dragging Angela with me to all those meetings. Which is why she met Arturo. Which is why my mother blames me for Angela's current predicament."

"What predicament? Love?"

"Something like that."

"My point is," he said, "we never talked about *having* babies. We only talked about *not* having babies."

Gina sighed. "When was the last time we talked about not having a baby?"

She saw by his silence he couldn't remember. And he usually remembered everything.

"In any case," she continued, "what would you like me to do about it?"

"Nothing, clearly."

"All right then."

"Where are we going to live? We're still at your mother's house."

"I can't make enough, that's true," she said. "I'm not a man. But you are. And you can."

"Did you do this to force me to get some menial job?"

"No, Harry," said Gina. "I just want a baby. I wish you still had your father's bank accounts to fall back on. I know things were easier for you when you could just buy what you wanted and send on the bill to your father's accountant. I won't object if you decide to get in touch with him."

"You know that will never happen. Not after what he did, what he said."

"You can tell them about their grandchild. Esther—"

"Never."

"Your sister might be happy to hear from you, no?"

"I don't know. I don't care."

"Babies smooth over a lot of things."

"Not this."

"Mimoo says ..."

"I don't care. Baby, no baby, my father, my sister are gone from my life. Just like they wanted."

She fell back on the bed. "Why are you pushing them away, *caro*? Your family, my brother. Your friend Ben. You used to be so close. Why have you not written to him? You don't even know if he's still in Panama."

"If I don't know where he is, how can I write to him?"

"I bet your sister knows. You could ask her."

"Stop it."

"His mother must know. You could get in touch with her. You got along with his mother so well."

"Yes, but she gets along too well with my father. I'm not going to reach out to her, Gia. Besides, I don't think Ben wants to hear from me anyway."

"You can't be on the outs with everyone, Harry."

"Salvo hates me so much he won't step foot in his own mother's house. How is this my fault?"

Gina said nothing, biting her lip, *forcing* herself to say nothing. Why did she have to be a Sicilian? They always blurted out every damn fool thing on their minds.

"Do you know what Mimoo says?"

He fell back on the bed too. His hand went over her belly. He spun toward her, bent over her, kissed her. "No. Tell me what Mimoo says."

"She says the baby brings his own food."

"Mmm." He kissed her bare stomach, caressed her hips, fondled her breasts. "You know who brings her own food? You."

27

Five

SHE MAKES HER OWN tomato paste. She is dressed in some shimmering gauzy summery thing, and her hair is tied up. The dress has to be loose and sheer because she is about to undertake heavy physical labor. She might perspire. All he does is sit and watch her, his mouth slightly open, his whole soul short of breath. He has watched her make the paste so many times. He never gets tired of it.

She has been simmering tomatoes all morning, boiling them down. She has strained all the pulp, removed their seeds, their skin. She has undressed the tomatoes.

Now she needs his help, and that's why he's been sitting at the kitchen table gaping at her.

They drag two plywood boards from the porch down the stairs and to the back. The boards take up nearly the whole overgrown yard. But that's where the sunshine is. It's late summer and warm, and it's the only way to make enough paste to last the winter. The tomatoes she grows are always splendid. In his father's house he never ate tomatoes the way he eats them now, raw, cooked, boiled, steamed, fried. Any which way he relishes the tomatoes. It's the fruit from the Sicilian tree of life.

They carry the two pots of stewed tomatoes to the boards. She spreads the thick messy pulp over the boards, tilting them slightly to drain off any remaining liquid. There is much liquid. They set the tomato boards in the sunshine to dry.

Mimoo is cleaning houses, Salvo is sweeping the streets. Harry and Gina make love all afternoon, as the sun moves forty-five degrees in the August sky. They can barely stumble down the stairs to bring her boards back inside. All he wants *now* is to take a long nap, but it's almost dinnertime, and she is forcing him to help her. But now, *after*, he doesn't want to.

They roll the dried-out paste into large balls. He tries not to make any off-color jokes, but fails. He doesn't particularly want to make jokes. What he wants is to nap and then make love to her again. Their hands are sticky with gooey sickly sweet paste, red and overripe.

They clean their hands as best they can. Sometimes they make love again, with all their clothes on to save time, though it's so late, and any minute everyone else will come home—Angela, Mimoo, Salvo, Rita for Saturday night dinner. Panting and disheveled, with the hands that just loved one another, they coat the balls of tomato paste with a layer of olive oil, cover them tightly with cheesecloth and pack them into large glass jars. It's work for a whole Saturday afternoon. She grows enough tomatoes to feed them the whole winter. They never have to worry about sauce for anything they cook. They always have plenty.

Harry associates tomatoes with love. He gets a physical throb in the pit of the place that makes him a man, a flame of fire about two pounds large whenever she opens one of those jars, whenever she feeds him from them, when she asks him what he wants for dinner. What springs to his mind is the heady, acidic sweetness of their sweltering summer afternoons.

Six

IF HARRY EXPRESSED BOTH inwardly and outwardly a certain quarrelsome ambivalence about the regeneration of his future, no one had any doubt how Mimoo felt about it. It was as if all her ailments had left her bones. After Gina told her mother the blessed news, she jumped out of bed, threw on nice clothes and *ran* through the streets of Lawrence, carrying candles to the church and chocolates to her friends. "Finally she's having a baby! She's having a baby!" Mimoo bought flowers, went to the market, made a feast, had a celebration to which she invited what seemed like half of Lawrence. "You didn't give me a chance to celebrate your pretend wedding. At the very least I can rejoice in the fruit of it."

Harry leaned into Gina's neck. "Why does your dear mother insist on calling it pretend? Does she want to see the judge's papers?"

Gina kissed his nose. "I think she'd prefer to see the priest's papers."

He grabbed her around her still slender waist and pulled her out onto the porch. "So she thinks we're improperly married." He laughed. "Does that mean you're a kept woman?" He kissed her. "Why do I find that *so* enticing?"

True to her roots as a good wife and true woman, Gina returned his open-mouthed kiss and tamped down the other Sicilian part of herself and didn't say what she was ashamed to be thinking when he was being all flirty with her and kind, which was: of all the things I am, and I am many things, one of the things I'm absolutely not is a *kept* woman.

"Go to Boston, you two," Mimoo ordered them, not a day later. "You tell your family, Harry, and you, Gia, go tell your brother."

Gina agreed. Harry amiably shook his head.

"Salvo will come around, Harry."

"He won't, Mimoo."

"He will."

"He won't."

"God, why are you such a stubborn mule?"

"*He* won't come back and *I'm* the mule?"

Mimoo pressed her son-in-law: "Salvo is waiting for you to beg his forgiveness. He just needs to hear repentance from you."

Harry shook his head. "I've tried already. It's no use."

"How many years ago did you try?"

"Your son has too much pride," Harry said.

"And you?"

"I'm not your son."

"Charming, Harry," whispered Gina, sitting nearby, listening.

Mimoo bristled. "You're my daughter's so-called husband."

"I'm actually her husband."

"In our country, husbands, even such as you are, are considered family. Not in your country?"

Harry said nothing.

"Like I was saying. Besides, you're still somebody's son, aren't you?"

"Not anymore."

Seven

HALF-HEARTEDLY HARRY SEARCHED THROUGH the job ads in the paper. "What a burden it is," he exclaimed one night, "to keep needing paid work."

"Welcome to real life," Gina said. "Not the pretend one you've been living."

She was right, of course, and he didn't like to argue with her. He certainly wasn't going to argue that he did indeed once live what had seemed to him a fake life. To fall in love was one thing. But to *choose* her was another. He married her because she was the realest thing he had ever found. There was no calibration in his life with her. There was no pretense and no temperance. Every ball was up in the air at once. It was always too hot or too cold; there was too much wine or not enough. His bed was never empty, and that made up for many other missing things—the conjugal union of two kindred spirits, two poles apart when it came to their station in life, but one in the only way it counted. One of body, one of soul.

Still … unmitigated smells and labor, constant labor. There was no time to ever think, make long-term plans, figure things out, barely even read!

"Perhaps you'd like to move to Kalamazoo, Michigan?" Harry asked Gina. "So I could work on Henry Ford's assembly line."

"The man will pay you five dollars a day, Harry," Gina said. "That's ransom for a prince."

"Five dollars?"

"A day!"

"Florenz Ziegfeld spends three hundred dollars on stage pillows!" Harry said. "Three hundred dollars *each*."

"Perhaps then you should be the one selling him these magical pillows."

"There you go, always turning every conversation back to money."

"I don't do that."

"Yes, you do."

"You mean lack of money?"

"Whatever you want to call it."

And just like that, another casual spousal back-and-forth turned into intemperance. No calibration ever.

Harry found a day job that lasted a week, delivering paper goods to local restaurants. He drove a small truck, picking up supplies from Weston and delivering them to Lawrence and Andover. The job ended a week before Christmas. Gina said nothing. He said nothing, but went out looking again. A few days later he returned home excited, and told her he had found work. She was still in her first trimester and throwing up all the time.

"Full-time work?" Gina tried to sound excited herself.

"Absolutely," he said, getting the corkscrew for the celebratory red wine.

"That's wonderful! With who?"

"Bill Haywood."

Gina stepped back from the table at which she had been about to sit. "Big Bill Haywood?" she repeated incredulously.

"Is there another?"

She fell quiet. Bile came up in her throat.

"I already help Joe and Arturo with organization, ideas, planning. I'm always helping them with this speech and that. Now I'll be paid for it. Better than doing it *pro bono*, no?"

"I don't know how to answer that," Gina said. "What could one-eyed Bill possibly want with you, Harry?"

"Why wouldn't he want something to do with me?"

"What's the job?"

"I don't know. He needs something, I do it."

"See, *that's* the part that worries me."

"It shouldn't worry you." He opened the wine and fetched two glasses. "It should make you happy."

"Big Bill!" she exclaimed again. "You do know that he recently stood trial for blowing up a man with a bomb, right?"

"Come on, you know he wasn't convicted."

She shook her head, but not hard; the nausea was making it difficult to react properly. "This is a terrible omen. Why is he in town? What is he planning here? This isn't a mining town." Bill Haywood had been the president of the Miners Federation before it joined with the Socialists to become the Industrial Workers of the World. "The man's had nothing but trouble with the law, and has wreaked nothing but havoc every place he's been. Every town he goes to, someone dies, gets shot, stampeded, beaten, bombed. Every single one! He has never passed through a town without taking half a dozen scalps with him. You want to get involved with that?"

"It's not his fault he's hated by the police. It's because he's so effective. And you told me to get a job."

"Harry," said Gina. "There are a number of jobs I could get that might not be palatable from your perspective, if you know what I mean. If you said to me, get a job, and I came back with something less than maritally appropriate, would you be blasé about it?"

"Okay, you're comparing Bill Haywood to Miss Camilla's merry girls by the railroad tracks?"

"A man acquitted on a technicality for murdering another man in front of his own home is going to pay you for doing whatever he tells you?" Gina tightened her grip on the chair. "Yeah, I'd say it's worse."

Harry put down the wine glasses without pouring.

"Since when did you become so fastidious?" he asked coldly. "I don't recall you turning up your nose at your radical anarchist Emma Goldman whose speeches inspired a man to assassinate a president."

"Emma Goldman is all talk," said Gina. "Bill Haywood is violent action. He calls it direct action. But we know what he means, don't we?" She put her hands together in supplication. "We're having a baby. We have to think about these fine distinctions."

"Did you think about those distinctions as you illegally distributed Goldman's pamphlets on birth control in felonious violation of the Comstock Act?"

"That was obviously a major failure," she said, placing her hands on her churning and twisting abdomen. She didn't have the stomach for a fight.

"On her part or yours?"

"On mine."

He watched her warily for a few moments. "Don't be upset," he said. "We need the work. I don't want to disappoint you. It'll be all right. I'll stay with Bill just until something better comes along. He gave me a small advance for Christmas. At least we'll be all right until the new year."

Grabbing the bottle, Gina poured the wine herself. "Better count your Advent blessings now, Bill Haywood's flunky," she said, raising her glass to her husband. "If I've read about him correctly, there'll be precious few of them soon."

They clinked, drank their wine. The fight always fizzled out of the both of them. Intimacy was a salve to smooth the sharpest edges.

"Big Bill thinks I'm too involved with you," Harry said that night in bed. "He says I can't be of help to him if my allegiance is divided."

Gina wrapped her arms, her legs around her husband. "Did you tell him your allegiance isn't divided at all? It is wholly to me."

"You're just making his point. Bill told me that great men cannot be great or become great when they are surrounded"—he groaned—"by their women."

She did not unwrap herself. "And you believe him?"

"Right now, I can't think straight."

The covers went over their heads. The covers flew off their overheated bodies.

Afterward: "Can you think straight now?"

"I fear he may be right."

Gina shook her head in exasperation, in muted affection. "Truly," she said, "and in this case literally, in the kingdom of the blind, the one-eyed man is king."

Chapter 2

ANNIE LoPIZO

One

FROM CHILDHOOD, GINA ALWAYS hated it when her mother was right. Now that she was an adult, she liked it even less. And what was worse was the number of things Mimoo was right about, and what was even more infuriating was the way her mother always knew it. Her powers of observation unabated despite faltering eyesight, onslaught of age, and general indifference, Mimoo continued to call them as she saw them.

So when Mimoo heard about the job Harry finally found, the only thing she said was, "I pray that Bill doesn't make you his financial secretary, Harry."

Gina glared at her impervious-to-glares mother.

When Angela had first brought Arturo home in the palm of her hand like a shiny display of male greatness, Mimoo took one look at him and barely waiting until he had left, said to her niece, "Angie, are you a fool? Do you not see that awful man is no good for you?" With Angela's immediate family back in Sicily, Mimoo had taken it upon herself to be a surrogate mother to the young woman.

Angela kissed her. "You think no one is good enough for me, Mimoo. I love you."

"No," Mimoo said calmly. "Just him."

"But he is wonderful! He writes poetry. He studied to be a seminarian …"

"Is he in the seminary now?"

"Well, no …"

"Exactly."

In 1908 Emma Goldman had been scheduled to speak on the Revolutionary Spirit in Modern Drama. Gina had asked Harry if he wanted to go and he said, "I don't want to go to Boston right now. Or possibly ever again. Anarchism and socialism are like two magnetic norths. You go. Take Angela with you."

"You never want to come with me anywhere anymore," Gina said. "You used to come to all my meetings before we were married."

"That was courtship," Harry replied. "Listening to anarchic blather equating marriage to slavery. Nodding my head at sermons against subjugated women. That's the way I got you to marry me."

"You're teasing me, *mio sposo.*"

"Am I? Are you married to me or no?"

Angela started going with Gina instead, like Verity once used to. Together they listened to "The Economic Crisis: Its Cause and Remedy," "Syndicalism: A New Phase of the Labor Struggle," "Woman Under Anarchism," and "The Relation of Anarchism to Trade Unionism."

The last was the speech that changed Angela's life, though according to Mimoo not for the better, because that's when she met Arturo Giovannitti.

Arturo had emigrated from Naples in 1901, barely speaking English. He was tall, good-looking, arrogant, loud. He had indeed studied briefly at the Theological Seminary. Heavy-set, thick-browed Angela, friendly, happy, for years waiting for a suitable man, was smitten. She never had a chance. "Like me, Harry," Gina had said, nonplussed when he didn't reply right away. "You mean like me," he said to her, upon further nudging.

Arturo described himself as a union leader, a socialist, a poet, and he brought with him to the conference center his friend, Joe Ettor, "Smiling Joe" of the Industrial Workers of the World. Joe cast his eyes on the dark-haired, tall and dramatic Gina, who flashed her wedding ring and invited him back to Lawrence to meet her husband. Joe got the hint, but came for dinner anyway. He and Harry hit it off—that evening and many evenings that followed expounding on Marx's dialectical materialism and on economic development being the foundation of all life. Evening after joyful inebriated evening they played cards, told jokes and dreamed of a true socialist state, one that didn't yet exist, where money, prices and markets were abolished, and all capitalist property confiscated and divided among the people.

Joe and Arturo became fascinated by Lawrence, the woolen and worsted production center of the world, a flourishing yet deeply troubled textile town. Joe had worked as a waterboy on railroads, filed saws at lumber mills, was a barrel maker, a shipyard worker, and had been last employed at a cigar factory. He began his work with the IWW as a community organizer and became an outstanding public speaker. He spent years taking Arturo with him, traveling the country and organizing miners, migrant laborers and foreign-born workers. Twice he had persuaded Harry, who just happened to be in between jobs, to go with him and Arturo to help them write their speeches. Both men looked up to Harry, revering his contemplative bookishness. Where they were brash, he was quiet, where they shouted, he spoke softly, where they were full of rhetorical passions, he engaged coolly in reasoned argument.

Aided by Harry's speechwriting, they had put together the Brooklyn shoe factory strike earlier in 1911. Buoyed by the success in Brooklyn, Joe and Arturo returned to Lawrence, rented two rooms off Lowell Street, close to where Angela now lived with her friend Pamela, and settled into intoxicated vigilance. They were convinced something big was going to happen in Lawrence, and they wanted to be there when it did.

And so during Christmas of 1911, Arturo huddled with Angela, Harry and Joe at the little round table like battle headquarters in the kitchen of Mimoo's rented house on Summer Street and tried to make heads or tails of American Woolen's recent actions. Gina stood by the kitchen sink and watched warily, nervous before, nauseated now. Why was she agreeing with Mimoo? Why did this agitation around Christmastime smell like nothing but a pot of trouble?

The Lawrence mills were the world's largest producers of textile products and needed vast numbers of laborers, mostly unskilled and underage women. After the invention of the two-loom system, the pace became grueling, the repetition and boredom dangerous, and the frequent injuries job-and-family-destroying. So after the textile union vigorously lobbied for two fewer hours of work a week, the Massachusetts legislature cut maximum hours from fifty-six to fifty-four. Fred Ayer and his son-in-law William Wood of American Woolen, who owned and operated all the mills in Lawrence, said with nary a complaint: ladies, you wanted it? It is done. Merry Christmas.

American Woolen's instant agreement prompted a sudden and direct action of the entire cauldron's brew of the IWW to descend onto Lawrence in December of 1911 like it was Paris in 1789. The main question on every socialist's mind was: why would American Woolen give in to the demands so quickly? This puzzled the four heads on Summer Street, and unsettled Gina.

Salvo didn't come home for Christmas, his absence a black sore at the table. Mimoo and Gina didn't discuss it. Mimoo prayed more than usual, which is to say, nearly all day. It was Christmas, after all, she said. Prayers were in order. But on Christmas Eve she couldn't help herself, she accused Harry of heartlessness in abandoning his family.

"Do you not see me?" she said to him, having had too much holiday cheer in the form of red port. "I don't have my son on Christmas. I weep with despair. You don't think your father and your sister feel the same about not having you with them on Christmas?"

"No, I don't think they do."

"You're blind inside your soul!"

"Mimoo, they threw me out," Harry said in self-defense. "I didn't leave like Salvo, of my own free will. They forced me out, told me I would never be welcome in their home again. My father disowned me. He stopped my access to our family accounts. They did this because I had the gall to marry your daughter."

Mimoo harrumphed in agreement. "He felt betrayed by you. He lost his temper."

"My father never loses his temper. He said exactly what he meant. He did exactly what he intended. He told me he didn't have a son anymore."

"You're a fool, Harry. Gina, you married a fool. Do you know how impossible what you're saying is? A father can*not* abandon his children."

Gina tried to comfort her mother. "Mimoo, they're not like us," she said. "They don't feel the same way about their children."

Mimoo staggered from the table. "You don't think a man feels most deeply about his only son?" she said. "Are you even my daughter? Think what you're saying. His only son!"

"Honestly, Mimoo, believe him."

"A man who doesn't feel deeply about his son feels deeply about nothing."

"Well, then, Mimoo," said Harry, "perhaps you've answered your own question."

Holding on to the railing, the old woman slowly climbed the stairs, refusing Gina's help. "You are both blind. Because you haven't had children. Just you wait. Wait till August. Then you'll understand."

They rang in the New Year of 1912 with champagne and roast pig. Arturo told Angela that maybe this summer, if all went well, they could be married.

Mimoo snorted all the way up the stairs, loudly enough for everyone to hear.

"Mimoo, you're embarrassing him," said Angela after the men had left. "You know he can hear you, right?"

"I hope the dead can hear me. *Madre di Dio.* Do *you* hear me? Did he give you a ring?"

"He doesn't have the money right now."

"He has money to spend on his cigarettes and train rides all across the country, doesn't he? And every time I see him he's wearing a new suit."

"Rings are expensive," Angela said, calling downstairs to her cousin. "Gina, how much was your ring?"

In the kitchen cleaning up the wine glasses, Gina inquisitively tapped at Harry, reading the paper. "How should I know?" he said with

39

a shrug. "I walked into the jewelers and picked out the largest stone. My father got the bill."

Gina stared at the fourth finger on her left hand. The two-karat princess-cut diamond sparkled. She cleaned it every morning, even before she cleaned her teeth. It was like something out of someone else's life.

"He says it wasn't that expensive, Mimoo," Gina yelled up to the bedroom.

"Is he going to lure you into a pretend marriage," Mimoo asked Angela, "like that Harry with my daughter?"

"Mimoo, we are not in a pretend marriage!" Gina called from downstairs. "And also, Harry can hear you."

"No, Mimoo," said Angela, sitting on the corner of the bed and smiling. "Unlike Harry with Gina, Arturo is going to marry me properly, in a church. Because as you know, the Italian atheist rhetoric is all for show. There is no such thing as an Italian atheist."

Downstairs, Harry glanced up from his newspaper to catch Gina's eye for a reply to the truth of that. She crossed herself and bowed in assent before kissing him with champagne on her lips.

"There is also no ring," an implacable Mimoo pointed out upstairs.

Gina waved her ring hand at Harry, wondering how much her rock was worth and if she pawned it, would she ever be able to get together the money to buy it back.

Two

RIGHT AFTER THE HOLIDAYS, in the first week in January, the Lawrence women returned to work. Five days later, when they received their paychecks, they discovered there had been a small error. They got paid half a dollar less than the previous week.

Arturo asked Angela to perform some simple math. And lo! It turned out that, yes indeed, they were working two hours less a week, just as they had requested. But now they were getting two hours less pay.

That Friday night Arturo paced around the Summer Street parlor like a self-satisfied peacock, saying, "I told you. I told you. I knew they were up to no good, and I was right."

Two hundred women, Angela at the forefront, dragging with her a desperately reluctant Gina, showed up the next Monday in front of the red doors of Wood Mill at the T-junction of Union and Essex, loudly demanding that the accounting error be corrected immediately since they were not returning to work until it was.

The manager of American Woolen, Lester Evans, a small polite man, came outside to talk to Angela and Gina.

"Why are you ladies upset?" he asked calmly, dressed in his tailored finery. "Stop shouting. What is the problem? Do you think you should be getting paid the same for less work?"

"YES!" came the defiant cries. Gina stayed quiet.

"But you all received a generous raise when you negotiated your last contract barely four months ago. Are you saying it's not enough?"

"SHORT PAY!"

"Why would we pay you more for working less? *That* hardly seems fair."

"NO CUT IN PAY! NO CUT IN PAY!"

"What's not fair is the cut in pay," Angela shouted into Lester's face, strengthened by the yelling women at her back, like a sail in the tail winds.

"But you didn't receive a cut in pay," Lester said amiably.

"Yes, a cut in pay!"

"You're playing with the big boys now, Annie LoPizo," Lester told her. "In the real world you get paid for the hours you work. You don't work, you don't get paid."

The women had no strategy but to continue shouting. Lester had had enough. Before he left he pointed a finger at Gina. "You have a good job," he said to her. "You get paid well for the work you do. Don't ruin your life by involving yourself in this malarkey. Stay away. I've seen this before. It's nothing but trouble."

All the nerve endings in Gina's body agreed.

*　*　*

That evening when he heard what had happened, Arturo ordered Angela and Gina to march right back to the mill doors the following morning and make clear to this Mr. Evans that not a single worker was returning to the looms until the "accounting error" was rectified. "Not a single one."

Shaking his head, Harry got up from the table. "Angie, you do what you want," he said. "Listen to Arturo, don't listen to him, it's no difference to me. You're a grown woman. But don't involve my wife in this."

"She is also a grown woman! She also got paid two hours less."

"Yes, Harry, what are you talking about?" Arturo said, frowning. "You're involved in this."

"I didn't say me. I said her."

"What could you be thinking?"

"You know what I'm thinking," Harry said, pulling Gina by her wrist from the table, nudging her up the stairs, away, away. "Because I just told you. I'll do what I have to, but keep her out of it."

Angela followed Gina upstairs behind a shut bedroom door. "Are you really not going to come with me?" she asked disbelievingly.

"I can't, Ange. We're having a baby. We need the money."

"What money? There *is* no money. Gina, if there is a strike, no one will get paid."

Gina turned jelly-legged. She sat on the bed. "Maybe it'll all be over by tomorrow."

"How in the world …"

"Maybe cooler heads will prevail."

"Are you saying I'm not in my right mind?"

"I'm saying we need the money. Don't you?"

"I need justice more."

"Harry doesn't want me involved. What am I going to do? Go against his wishes?"

"I'm family!" yelled Angela. "You're not going to stand by your own family?"

42

"Angie, don't go! He's my family, too. And we're having a baby. Why can't you understand?"

"Oh, I understand. I understand being pushed away."

"Ask Pam to go."

"Lester hates Pam after she nearly lost her hand at the double loom and made such a stink about it. But he likes *you*. He's apt to give in to you."

"Did he give in to me this morning?" Gina shook her head. "Harry said no."

"Look at you, all your feminist virtues into the trash as soon as there's a hint of trouble!"

"It's because there's trouble that he's telling me to keep out of it."

"And you're listening. What happened to the right to your own soul?"

"We're having a baby!"

"This is social change. Progress! The revolution. It's all the things we've been talking about finally carried into action. Are you really going to stand idly by while the blood of other men and women is spilled onto your sidewalk?"

"Angela, maybe you don't hear yourself, but you're making my argument for me. The time for radical action is not when I'm pregnant."

"History is not going to stand still for your baby, Gina."

"Well, then, I'll just hop on the next train if it's all the same to you. There seems to be a revolution every year."

They stopped speaking. Angela stormed out, and Gina didn't go with her the next morning. In a crowd of women, Angela went by herself to confront Lester Evans.

It couldn't have gone less well. The manager fired Angela then and there. He told her that if she ever harassed him in front of his mill again, he'd have her arrested and thrown in jail. Through a megaphone he informed the fifty women shouting behind her that unless they showed up for work the following morning, they would also be fired. "And Miss LoPizo, please tell Miss Attaviano," he added, "that unless *she* shows up for work, she too will be fired with all the rest."

"She's a married woman, now, Mr. Evans," shouted Angela. "She doesn't answer to you or to me. She answers to her husband. And he works for Bill Haywood."

"Then too bad for her being associated with all those filthy Wobblies," said Evans. "Too bad for all of you. Now get away from my factory."

Gina was outraged. "I didn't go with you and that's how you punish me?" she said to Angela. "By making me lose my job? I'm going to work. I don't know how *you're* planning to pay your rent, but in this house we work for a living."

"Gina, this isn't punishment. It's war. We have to fight."

"I can't and I won't."

"You can either stand with your family and your women and your fellow workers fighting for your wages, or you can break the line, but then no one in this town will ever speak to you again. Because we don't talk to scabs," Angela said. "Not even family scabs. Tell her, Arturo."

"We don't talk to scabs," said Arturo.

"Get out of my house," said Gina. "Where is Harry?"

"Striking!"

"How can he strike? He doesn't work at the mills!"

"Organizing the strikers then," Arturo said. "Going door to door with Joe. Wiring telegrams to Big Bill telling him he's urgently needed in Lawrence. Calling Mother Jones. Calling Emma Goldman. Your husband," he went on with pomposity, "is fighting for our side. Like you should be doing."

"I thought I told you to get out of my house, Arturo."

"Gina, this strike is for you, too. The full-time wages of mill employees are inadequate for a family."

Gina pointedly said nothing. Angela cleared her throat. "Actually, Arturo," she said, "Gina makes quite a decent wage working in the mending room." She averted her eyes. "Yes, a generous wage for skilled labor. But even you, Gia, are now making less because they cut your salary."

"They didn't cut my salary. They cut my hours."

"You were working too much."

"Who decides this—you? I needed the money," Gina said. "I didn't want to work less, and I don't want what's not due me. I'm a grown-up." She felt weak, she needed to lie down. "I'm responsible for my own choices. I want to work."

"The IWW will fully support your efforts for larger pay and fewer hours."

"Arturo, I thought I told you to leave!"

"If he goes, I go," said Angela.

Folding her arms, Gina stared them both down.

"Wait till Mimoo hears about this!"

"You don't want to know what Mimoo thinks about this, Angie," said Gina.

"I can't wait to ask her. She always supports me."

"Not in folly."

"This isn't folly!"

"Well, too bad she can't hear about it because, oh, that's right—she's still at work."

"Wait till Salvo hears."

"He's also working. And staying far away."

"Sometimes," Arturo said, "you've got to *not* work to fight for what is right."

"Get out!"

"Let's go, Arturo," said Angela. "I know where we're not wanted."

That night Harry told Gina what happened when he spoke with Mother Jones. Harry and Joe made a personal plea to the woman to join the coming strike, but she, despite being co-president and co-founder of the IWW with Big Bill, refused to stand with her own fair sex, pronouncing Lawrence a city headed for disaster. She would not support the women's right not to return to their slave wages. She said all her life she had petitioned for men, not women. "Men work," she told Harry. "Women work for the family." Before she ended the conversation she said that Big Bill, whom she had known for years, was a cheap tightfist of a man, but Harry should ask him for a raise so his wife, too, could stay at home.

Gina was pretending to read and only half-listening. "Oh yeah? What did Bill say about that?"

"Publicly, not a word," Harry replied. "But to us he said he will not rest until that traitor is purged from the IWW for good."

"I mean about the raise."

"I didn't ask him."

Gina shrugged her indifference. "Then all I want to know is whether come seven-thirty tomorrow morning I'm going to the mending room."

Harry sat quietly. "No," he said at last. "You aren't."

"So we're deciding to lose me my job? My easy, well-paying, skilled-labor job that other women wait years to get?"

"I don't want you to lose it," he said. "But you were going to quit anyway when the baby came …"

"Seven months from now."

"So, it'll be a little sooner than we planned. The baby came a little sooner than we planned. It'll all work out. You'll see."

"If I can't work, then I'm going on the streets, Harry. With Angela, Pam, Dona, Elda. I have to, or they'll never forgive me."

"You can't," he said. "Gestation keeps you from other activities ending in *tion*. Like demonstration. It's pandemonium out there."

"It's chaos in here, too. How do you propose we pay the rent? Buy food? Put money into the electric lamp you're sitting by as you write your slogans and glue your pamphlets?"

"Mimoo is working," Harry said.

"Don't even think about my money," Mimoo bellowed from upstairs. "Pretend it doesn't exist." How did her mother have such good hearing now, and yet was deaf when you tried to ask her all the important questions?

They lowered their voices.

"We'll use kerosene if we can't afford the electricity," Harry said. "And Big Bill pays me."

"Are you sure about that? I haven't seen anything since before Christmas."

"Yes. We'll be fine. The strike will last but a few days. A week at most. I know how these things shake out. The factory will cave. William

Wood needs to make money. The mill must operate. Production can't stop. They always cave when somebody has to make money."

"No kidding," said Gina. "Someone like me. Can I cave?"

Three

AFTER GINA LOST HER JOB, she went to work with her mother cleaning houses in Prospect Hill while Arturo and Joe organized rolling walkouts across the mills to disrupt operations as much as possible. They knew the looms needed (wo)manning, and without an adequate workforce, fabrics would not be made, and 600,000 pounds of sheep fleece would remain unspun.

Smiling Joe, no stranger to oratory, collected a thousand women right on the Common, hopped up on a soggy bench, and started shouting Harry-written bromides. *"If one man has a dollar he didn't work for, another man has a dollar he didn't get!"* One minute it was about two unpaid hours, the next it was about equality and economic freedom and brotherhood of man.

The ladies got revved up like little runarounds after hearing Joe yell for an hour. The next morning, two thousand women descended on Essex and Union. By the third morning, there were three thousand women on the streets. They interlocked arms and paraded on Merrimack and Water, across the bridges, and down Broadway. They hurled stones through mill windows, chanted and yelled, and exhorted *all* the workers to walk off their jobs.

Big Bill arrived for a brief visit. He praised Joe's and Arturo's efforts, commended Harry's speechifying, approved of the protesting women, advised Joe and Arturo to urge them to be louder and more violent, and went on a speaking tour around the country lauding the IWW's efforts in the Lawrence strike.

The walkouts rolled on through all eight mills in Lawrence. By the end of the second week, ten thousand people, mostly women and their children, were on the streets. The looms stopped spinning completely.

When Joe saw how many women were in his corner, he raised his demands, calling for a blanket fifteen percent increase in wages, double overtime pay, and a fifty-three-hour week. It wasn't just about American Woolen anymore.

Harry built Joe a special platform, four feet off the ground, which he and Arturo set up on the Common. Arturo extravagantly praised Harry's work. "You write speeches *and* build platforms? Where did you learn to do that, Harvard man? You're like the future hero Engels was talking about. You can be architect for an hour, but also push a wheelbarrow, if need be. I'm looking at you, Harold Barrington, and the future is here."

Onto Harry's platform, Joe hopped every day and denounced the mill owners, shouting Harry's penned words until he was hoarse.

"*Labor produces all wealth! All wealth belongs to the producer thereof!*"

The mills shuttered their doors. No one was reporting to work. Other businesses were forced to close. The unstoppable mobs frightened the shop owners. Now that the women weren't working and weren't getting paid, no one was buying things.

"*Complete demolition of social and economic conditions is the only salvation of the working classes!*"

In desperation, American Woolen and the Lawrence Association of Businesses called on Mayor Scanlon to resolve things. The mayor did the only thing he could think of: he brought in additional police protection. The chief of police himself showed up on Union Street and warned the women that if they didn't get off the streets and stop loitering, they'd be arrested, "each and every bloody one of you," and dispersed through the minimum-security prisons of Massachusetts. The women nearly trampled him to death. Afterward, Angela ran to City Hall's research room to look up "loitering" in the legal code. It was defined as "standing still in the public square." In defiance, the women began to march back and forth on Union Street in the reformed *moving* picket line. The police had to devise another way to get the ladies off the streets.

Lawrence brought in another reinforcement division from nearby Andover and arrested thousands of strikers, most of them kicking and screaming, for disturbing the peace. The city didn't have the space to jail three hundred women, much less ten thousand livid women. The clogging up of the courts was prohibitively expensive and socially debilitating. As soon as they were released, the women returned to the picket lines, parading and chanting in a sing-song day in and day out, "We want bread, but we want roses too!"

All women, that is, but an anxious and defenseless Gina, who, wishing only for bread, bowed her head and walked the other way to St. Vincent de Paul's to spin for pennies or up to Prospect Hill with Mimoo to dust for the affluent.

Emma Goldman, not to remain in the shadows of Mother Jones's limelight, decided to come to Lawrence and weigh in on her nemesis's well-publicized comments by giving her own impassioned speech atop Harry's platform. Of *course*, she said, the most prominent woman socialist in the country wanted ever stronger chains of bondage for women. In the middle of freezing January, Goldman yelled that free love was the *only* way out for women because freedom and equality and justice for women were utterly incompatible with marriage. Goldman declared that unlike certain others she would not mention by name, she would gladly stand in the cold with the Lawrence strikers.

When Big Bill, over in Montana, heard what Emma Goldman was saying, he telegraphed Harry to inform him that if he ever saw Emma Goldman on the streets of Lawrence he would suffocate her with his bare hands. The last thing the IWW wanted was Goldman in the middle of a striking city advocating for freedom *from* state regulation! The IWW advocated total state control, not freedom from it. Like Mother Jones, though for different reasons, Emma Goldman was detrimental to the strikers' cause.

"Gina, my faithful wife, tell me something," Harry said after he related the day's events. "Your beloved Emma Goldman was yelling in the freezing rain, yet I couldn't help but notice that you were nowhere to be found."

"You told me to stay inside," she replied, arranging a white poster board on the dining table. "I'm being a good wife." Lightly she smiled. "I have no time for free love in the freezing rain."

49

"Very wise. What in the world are you doing?"

She had been making placards. EQUALITY NOW! JUSTICE NOW! FAIR WAGES NOW!

"I'm helping Angie."

"I know why you're doing it." He took away her black paintbrush. "I don't want you to appease her."

"I told her I would." She reached for the brush. "Make amends for before."

"Tell her you'll make amends by feeding her. Because it all starts with the placards. The next thing you know you're marching to 'The Marseillaise' and defeating Britain. It's dangerous out there."

She took the brush from him. "I'm not going out, *tesoro*. I'm just making signs."

"You're going to St. Vincent's, aren't you?"

"It's on Haverhill. The other way." She didn't want to remind him, as if he needed reminding, that their Victorian on Summer Street was just half a block from the Common where Joe Ettor shouted twice a day every day, and four blocks from Essex and Union, a long lobbed softball away from *all* the trouble. She had no business being out, and they both knew it. But what choice did she have? Mimoo's seven houses to clean were not enough to cover their bills, and new cleaning work was scarce with so many women competing for the only viable employment. At least St. Vincent's paid her a tiny wage for sewing, ironing, sorting donations, and spinning, and they gave her food from their pantry, as if she herself were now one of the people in desperate need of help.

Harry stood close, twisting the curls of her hair around his fingers. "I'm glad we don't meet here anymore," he said. "Now we go to talk nonsense at Arturo's. It's better. Our house is quieter. Nicer."

"Yes, here is quieter. Because you're never here. You're always *there*, on Lowell, in that boiling cauldron of plotting. How is that better?"

"We have to keep planning. But when I come home, it's quiet." He bent to her cheek.

She raised her face to him. "If you're just planning, I'm just making art."

Harry watched her paint in block letters. "I *have* to go out there," he said. "I'm on the strike committee. And Bill's paying me. I have to go out there so you don't have to. Just like Mother Jones said."

"Oh, so *now* we listen to her. Some feminist I am."

"Some feminist indeed." Leaning down, he patted her belly.

She kissed him. "I won't go out there, *mio amore*. Only to clean and spin."

"Promise?" He blinked anxiously.

"Of course." She blinked anxiously back.

She prayed for her child, for her husband, for her mother, for the strike to be over. Sometimes not in that order. Angela barely spoke to her. The placards weren't sufficient atonement.

Gina hated being broke, hated having no money. The bills piled up. Rent was coming due in February, the light bill. Food needed to be bought. They could eat her stewed tomatoes for only so long. Eventually they'd need bread, pasta. Harry might not care about mundane things like food on the table, but Gina did. She was too poor for idealism.

Four

THE LAWRENCE TEXTILE BOARD of directors brought in Floyd Russell, a whip-smart lawyer from Boston, to defend themselves against an association with police brutality. Apparently it was bad publicity to spray women with fire hoses to disperse them. A no-nonsense man, Floyd said, "Brutality? But they're still on the street! This ridiculous mess should've been stopped weeks ago. The police should've been instructed to shoot. That's how *successful* leaders handle things."

But the police didn't shoot. They only threatened to shoot. The state militia arrived to boost their numbers because the striking crowds kept swelling, to fifteen thousand, to twenty.

"Twenty thousand angry screaming women," Harry said to Gina over one tense dinner of boiled beans and artichokes. "I can barely handle just one."

"When have I screamed at you, *marito*?"

"Once you wanted to."

She remembered that one time. "Not the same."

He agreed that it wasn't.

Gina tried hard to keep her Italian self concealed from him, hidden behind pressed-together teeth, a composed smile, half-hooded eyes, clenched fists as he spooned her in bed. She didn't want to have loud words and prove Mimoo right. Her mother kept saying to her, "Who are you putting on airs for? You don't think sooner or later he'll notice the hot Sicilian blood that runs through your deepest veins straight into your heart?"

"The ladies he was used to before me didn't hector their men about desperately unsuitable employment."

"Is he married to them? As I recall, he deliberately discarded one of those prissy debutantes for you, or am I wrong?"

"I don't want to discuss this with you, Mimoo. I'm glad at the very least you're acknowledging our nuptials."

"Only to make my point."

"Which is?"

"You're like Pompeii. You keep hissing, letting out steam. When he least expects it, and least wants it, you're going to erupt. It'll be judgment day for him and he won't even know why he's up in flames. You should give him fair warning, daughter."

"Mother, I'm going to prove you wrong. I'm an American lady now. We keep our boiling on the inside where it belongs."

"Why is he out every night?"

"He's with Joe at their place. I didn't want them here anymore, you know that."

"So your husband you accept on any terms, but our poor Angela you won't speak to?"

"She won't speak to *me*!"

"She's right not to."

"Is she? Do you want me to go out and picket with her? Because that's what she wants."

Mimoo put her hand on her daughter's face. "No, *mia figlia*. I want you to be careful most of all."

* * *

Sam Gompers and his American Federation of Labor were called to Lawrence to negotiate a settlement and act as the voice of reason against the IWW. "It takes a man like Bill Haywood to make Gompers, of all people, look like an angel," remarked the District Attorney. But as soon as Gompers was called to the table and it looked as if a deal might be struck, Big Bill promptly returned to Lawrence, this time for good.

To ingratiate himself with the strikers and to push the AFL out of Lawrence, Haywood warned American Woolen that they could not weave their cloth with bayonets. An AFL negotiator accused Haywood of having no interest in industrial peace. He said that for the last ten years Big Bill's actions screamed from the streets that what he wanted was the creation of a proletarian impulse that would do nothing less than revolutionize society. To this Big Bill happily replied by hopping up onto Harry's podium—though he didn't need to, being over six feet tall—that the AFL drudge was right. *"The complete DEMOLITION of social and economic conditions is the only salvation of the working classes!"* he shouted. He turned his left side to the cheering women to hide his empty right eye socket. Harry stood nearby and watched him. *"The mine owners did not find the gold, did not mine the gold, did not mill the gold. Yet all the gold belongs to them! How can this be? It can't be! It won't do, ladies, it simply will. Not. Do."*

Under Haywood's direction, it didn't take long for the Bread and Roses women to gain notoriety as radicals of the worst sort. Big Bill wanted the women front and center every day as if on a stage, harassing the factories in their bonnets, hitching up their long skirts to wade over the mud, shouting down men, waving American flags and placards in the men's faces. He exhorted the women to speak their mind, to bravely bear the cold, to nag the men into submission. When the strident tactics resulted in shoving, falls, broken noses, visible and copious blood, Bill became even more excited. Women bleeding on the streets of Lawrence to defend their principles against the brutality of the capitalists, who employed them, and the police, who tried to subdue them, was far better than meekly marching down the streets, singing songs and carrying signs.

The women were accused of having "lots of cunning" and "bad temper."

"*One police officer can handle ten men,*" the District Attorney was quoted as saying in *The Evening Tribune.* "*But it takes ten police officers to handle one woman.*"

"Ain't that the truth," echoed Harry, closing the newspaper. His one woman was sitting at her workbench in the corner of their living room, stitching a roomy panel into a cotton skirt to allow for her expanding belly.

"What is it about me," Gina wanted to know without turning around, "that requires ten men to handle and my husband to make such a comment?"

He came over to her chair, pushed her loose bun to the side, and pressed his lips deeply into the slope of her bare neck. "Husband is trying to be funny."

"*Divertente?* Trying and failing."

Five

IN AN UNPRECEDENTED MOVE, Haywood arranged for six hundred children of the striking women to be publicly taken away from their mothers (he called it being taken out of "harm's way") and bussed south to New York City to stay with some well-to-do families for the duration of the strike. The women that agreed to this became even more violent after their children left them.

Crying children separated from their howling mothers was a public relations disaster for American Woolen and for Lawrence. Mayor Scanlon was urged to break the strike, and though he stated that his aim was "to break the strikers' head," it was nothing but grandstanding, for he did nothing. An incredulous Floyd Russell raged against the mayor's impotent response. "How long are you going to let this continue? Your city is going bust! No one is working! No one is making any money.

You've got millions of dollars' worth of international contracts going unfulfilled because of what's happening under your fucking windows. You're destroying Lawrence with your inaction!"

"Not my inaction—*their* action!" Scanlon shouted back. "They won't compromise! You heard Haywood. What am I supposed to do? Shoot the women?"

"Yes," Floyd said instantly. "That's how Napoleon did it."

"He *shot* the women?"

"He ordered the strikers to be shot, yes."

"Not *women*!"

"Listen," the lawyer said defiantly, "they want to work like men, live like men, get paid like men? Fuck like men? Then they should accept being shot like men."

American Woolen tried again to negotiate. With Gompers and his AFL long gone, William Wood came to the table with Haywood and offered 54 hours and $8.76 a week. Big Bill walked out. He loved the attention. He refused to let the women back down. Though he said the fight was about wages and hours, it was a well-known fact, which he didn't attempt to hide, that his IWW held union-written contracts in disdain because they encouraged workers to become complacent and abandon the class struggle. He and Smiling Joe continued to advocate for violence as a means to an end, supporting not only a general strike, but the overthrow of American capitalism itself. "*Let the workers own the textile mills and set their own wages and hours*," Joe yelled from the podium when Bill grew tired in the late afternoons and Harry stood and watched nearby. "*Until that happens, nothing is going to do the trick!*"

With Harry's help, Haywood raised the funds to feed the strikers. Gina volunteered at the soup kitchen. As long as she didn't leave the basement of the Corpus Christi Church where she prepared the food, Harry agreed to accept her mild contribution to the war effort. Not Angela. "What do you expect?" Mimoo said to Harry. "Two Sicilian women butting heads like mules. Cooler heads can't prevail because no one in this town's got one."

Gina baked bread and cooked beans in molasses while the law enforcement and business heavyweights of Lawrence joined in daily condemnation of Big Bill.

Haywood kept his demands deliberately outrageous and William Wood continued to respond in kind: he said he would go broke before he was blackmailed.

"Behind raised wages, resumed work, vanished militia and the whirring looms is the most revolutionary organization in the history of American industry," thundered the District Attorney on the pages of the *Tribune*. Floyd Russell, having given up, left town like Gompers.

The mayor was staying quiet. He was running for reelection the following November. He didn't want to further incense the public.

"*First in violence, deepest in dirt, lawless, unlovely, ill-smelling, irreverent, new; an overgrown gawk of a village, the 'tough' among cities, a spectacle for the nation,*" wrote Lincoln Steffens, a reporter, in *The Shame of the Cities*.

The town of Lawrence was crumbling—no work, no orders filled by American Woolen, no retail sales. The town was sliding into anarchy and bankruptcy, with no end to the impasse.

Something had to give. But what Gina felt as she cooked the beans, and begged Angela to stop marching in the streets, and accompanied Mimoo on the bus to clean their few remaining homes, was that nothing good could possibly come from this.

Six

LATE ONE MORNING, at the end of January, Gina was helping the Sodality sisters at St. Vincent's organize the incoming donations when Big Bill walked into their little mission house across from St. Mary's rectory. He frightened the nuns and they wouldn't glance up at him. It took a lot to frighten the nuns. In their spare time they cared for lepers. He scared Gina too, but she was the one he addressed, so she had no choice but to respond. He said it was freezing outside and the marching women were so miserable they were thinking of packing it in for the day and heading home. He couldn't allow that. Were there any coats or waterproof shoes he could take to keep the women warm and keep them on the streets?

Gina and the sisters hurried to collect a few dozen warm coverings. It wasn't enough, but it was a start.

"Can you help me cart them?" Bill asked. "You're Harry's wife, aren't you?" He brazenly appraised her with his one good eye.

She nodded as she helped him put the coats and boots into a wheelbarrow.

"Why is he hiding you? Why are you never by his side? He's out there every day busting his hide, helping the righteous cause. Why aren't you supporting the women?"

Gina didn't want to tell him the truth. She wanted to tell him nothing.

"I work here," she replied tersely. If Harry hadn't told Bill about the baby, she certainly wasn't going to. If Harry hadn't told Bill she worked in the soup kitchen making lunch for the strikers, she wasn't going to.

"Are you not on our side?" He glared at her with his one eye.

"I'm on your side," she replied in her smallest voice.

He forgot to turn his good profile to her, such as it was, and left her staring at him full on. She muttered something vapid about looms and missions and her work for the church. All her bravado had left her. She began to understand why her husband couldn't say no to this man. She was pregnant. She was hardly going to provoke him into argument. He was completely intimidating.

"Come and help me," he said. "It's nearly lunchtime."

"Yes, I know," she said. "I make the food. Hot beans. Bread."

"Ah. Very good. But today you can help me serve them."

"I can't."

"You have to. My regular girl is out sick. The nuns can spare you for an hour or two, can't they?"

"They can't."

The sisters assured Gina they could.

"I have to speak to Harry first," Gina muttered.

"Come, we'll find him together. Put on your coat."

She left with Bill, trying very hard not to stare into the vacant horror show of a socket that once housed his eye. Rumor had it that he had punctured it with a knife while whittling a slingshot when he was eight. She tried to walk on his right side, so he would walk closer to the curb, but Bill had suddenly become less self-conscious about his ocular deficiency. It was windy and cold and ice was falling. Bill wore a tailored gray wool overcoat and didn't want the mud and slush to spatter it as cars and horses passed by. He kept talking to Gina in an endless harangue, but she pulled her hat over her ears and eyes so she wouldn't hear him or be forced to look up into his dead milky deformity. She was drowning in her anxiety over heading straight to Union Street after promising Harry she would keep away. Surely he wouldn't be upset when he learned his boss made her do it. Madame Camilla indeed! The only real money they had was the money this man was paying her husband. From blocks away she could hear the mob, even through her hat and over Bill's booming voice.

The crowds were impassable; it was only because she was with him that they were able to push through. He could push through a stone barricade. They distributed the meager coat donations to some women in the picket line in front of Wood Mill and walked through the low iron fence of the Corpus Christi church to the lunch tent.

"Bill, I really need to speak to my husband," Gina said. "You said you would go find him?"

"I said I would go find him," he repeated to mock her. "Yes, I'm now your fetch boy."

"I'll be glad to go myself. I'll be right back."

He put his hand out. "Stay here. Serve the women. I'll find him."

Her hands were shaking so bad she could barely ladle out the beans into bowls. The gruel kept spilling from the sides, upsetting the women.

No sooner had Bill left than a dozen or so state troopers appeared out of the human sea to confront her at the cast-iron pot, telling her that if she didn't want to be arrested for aiding and abetting the criminal elements out and about on the street, she'd better stop what she was doing, and head on home and out of trouble. Finding this to be eminently and blessedly sensible advice, Gina moved away, planning to rush through the back streets to Summer Street. But a hundred shouting women in front of her hot beans ordered her not to move, but to feed them as she had come to do, feed those who were fighting for *her* rights. The police again commanded her to leave.

Tempers got short, bodies inched closer.

Within moments it got so pulsing loud that Gina could scarcely think for the din of enraged noise. All she knew was she wanted out—not now, not later, but thirty minutes ago. She cursed the day Harry ever shook Big Bill's hand. She cursed the day she took Angela to see Emma Goldman, the fateful day she introduced her to Arturo.

There was a wall of people between her and anywhere. Big Bill was nowhere to be seen. In the near distance, across Union Street near the red doors of the factory, Gina spotted Angela. She thought she heard Angela's strident voice, frenzied above the rest. Helplessly Gina looked around for Harry. She wouldn't be able to explain to him how she had ended up here, in the worst possible place at the worst possible time with cold faces and empty stomachs and flared rage all around. She tried to hide near the police, but most of the direct action was aimed at them. They were the frontline.

The iron pot was flipped over—by the police? By the protesters?—and hot beans dripped onto the wet slushy pavement, onto her boots and the police boots and the battered footwear of the strikers. There was nowhere for her to run, nowhere to move. No one was going to part the red irate crowd for her so she could run to safety through the alleys.

Someone grabbed her arm from behind, yanked her sideways. She spun around. It was Harry.

She started to cry.

"What are you doing?" he shouted because she wouldn't have heard him otherwise, although he was standing in front of her. "What the hell are you doing here? I told you ..."

"I want to go home!"

"Gina! God, why did you come here?" They were surrounded on all sides. The tent was shaking on its supports, any minute it was going to come down. He pulled her close for the briefest of moments, then yelled to her to crawl under the table. She saw Angela thirty heads away getting trampled, screaming, shoving, slapping somebody, in desperate trouble herself.

"Harry, look, Angela …"

"Can't help her now," he said, pulling Gina under the table.

"Angela!" Gina shouted, hoarse, out of breath. Angela didn't hear.

Big Bill reappeared with great force. He pushed his way past the sticks of the police and confronted Harry. "Come with me," he yelled, grabbing Harry's arm. "We need your help."

"I can't, Bill," Harry shouted back, pulling away. "My wife."

Bill didn't even glance at Gina. "She'll be fine. She's safer than the rest of us. Come quick. Vandalism in the grocery store—the coppers are about to arrest Arturo. I need your silver tongue. Come! Quick."

Harry stared desperately at Gina. "Go, Harry," she said. "Go with Bill. Go help Angie."

"I'll be right back," he said—and was swallowed up by Big Bill and the mob.

Under the table she curled into a ball, covered her head and closed her eyes. She lay on the dead January grass in a fetal position, facing away from the mob, facing toward the church, praying it would help, that anything would. A gaggle of people caught in the clash barreled in under the table after her. The narrow table was knocked over, the legs broke apart, it fell on their heads, on Gina's. There was only screaming.

Behind her there was the sound of assault, fists meeting faces, sticks meeting bodies, black panic, wild confusion. She imagined Milan, long ago, her revered brother Alessandro, hot-headed, impulsive, mule-stubborn, beautiful, dead, vile unrest, horses, policemen, stampede, a knife flying out, a life snuffed out, one life, then another. For who could live bearing the weight of your child's last moment. Her father couldn't.

Popping sounds. Shots? Everybody *really* screamed. She kept her head covered. More firecracker noise, perhaps return fire? Gina squeezed shut her eyes. Harry, Harry, come back to me, please. Legs, boots, feet, bottoms of coats whooshing by, people falling. She was shoved hard in the back by someone trying to get up, someone else stepped on her ankle trying to get away. Still in a fetal position, she put one hand on her head and the other on her stomach to protect the fragile life barely forming. Another boot landed on her head, on her knuckles. Man, woman? She couldn't even stand up in her blind terror.

"Get your fucking head off the ground, lady! Or you'll get your skull bashed in! Get off the ground!"

Harry, Harry?

It wasn't Harry. She was yanked into a standing position by a man. People running everywhere. Tent stakes violently pulled from the ground. People tripping over them, heavy gray canvas falling on their heads. The man who helped her up looked down at the ground at her feet and said, "Lady, are you shot? You're bleeding!" The last thing she thought before fainting was that Harry was going to be so upset she hadn't stayed under the table.

Seven

WHEN SHE CAME TO, she was in her bed. No Harry, no Arturo, no Joe, no Angela. Only her mother sitting by her side, silently crying. Her mother and Salvo!

"Salvo?" Gina was so happy for a moment. She raised her hand to reach for him.

"Why doesn't anybody *ever* listen to me?" Mimoo said, sobbing into her rosary beads. Her arthritis and tears prevented her from counting them properly. She kept rolling them around between her barely mobile fingers.

"How are you feeling, *sorella*?" Salvo said, the hat in his hands twitching.

"Where's Harry?" Gina reached down to touch her stomach. "Is he all right? What's happened?"

Salvo got up and left the bedroom before Mimoo could speak.

Mimoo shook her head. "He's not all right," she said. "Things are as bad as can be, child. Harry, Arturo, Joe have all been arrested. Along with dozens of others." She sobbed in a prayer. "They're about to be charged with murder."

"Murder? What murder? Harry too?"

Mimoo cried louder. "Our precious angel, Angela. Your cousin. Like your sister. Gone. Struck down. Stray bullet. Right to the heart. Oh!"

Santa Maria, prega per noi peccattori.

Gina tried to stand up.

"Stop it, lie down," Mimoo said. "You're still bleeding, it's not safe for you, you're sick, lie down."

She would not lie down. "Bleeding, why?"

Her mother wouldn't answer her.

"Mimoo? Salvo!"

"Don't call him. He can't speak to you."

"Salvo!"

"You lost your baby, Gia, my child. *Nessuna sofferenza, ma la vita eterna.*"

Now Gina didn't want to speak to anyone. Clutching her stomach, she turned away. *Where is Harry*, she whispered, but no one heard. *I need my husband.*

Salvo was so upset, he couldn't come back into the room to comfort her. Mumbling a few indecipherables from the door, he left, ran.

No one knew what had happened. In the commotion, shots ringing out, Angela was dragged inside a shop, everyone thought for safety. The police opened fire, fearing they had been fired upon. Perhaps she had already been shot before she was pulled inside the grocery store. No one could say for certain, but when the crowd had dispersed, Angela's blood flowed in the streets and Arturo and Joe had been arrested. They had been nowhere near Essex Street, nowhere near Angela. But because they were Wobblies, they were charged with conspiracy to incite a riot—in other words with a felony that resulted in a woman's death. That was murder. If convicted they faced execution.

No one saw Angela get hit or fall. No one heard the shot that pierced her heart. There were dozens of injured people on the ground, but only one of them lay dead, shot through the chest. Angela was twenty-eight years old, though all the papers later said Annie LoPizo was thirty, not knowing that Angela Tartaro had long ago lied about her age when she first came to America from Sicily so she could get the job that eventually claimed her life.

Angela's life wasn't the only one claimed. For days blood seeped out onto the starched white sheets of Gina's bed.

Bill kept the strike going as long as he could, but a few weeks after Angela's death, it ended. It took sixty-three days, fifty thousand women, one dead woman and one lost baby. American Woolen agreed to all the demands, and the women returned to work without a contract in mid-March.

Everybody but Angela.

Eight

JOE AND ARTURO WERE held without bail. Because Harry was not a member of the IWW, he was charged with a lesser crime of assault and destruction of private property. Bail was set against him, bail that no one could pay.

It took Gina a little while to get herself together to go see Harry in the Lawrence city jail. She couldn't face him. She finally went because she dreaded the questions he might otherwise ask. What took you so long to get here? You're my wife, why didn't you come?

He said nothing. He couldn't look at her. He didn't reach for her across the table, he didn't speak to her, offered no words of comfort or remonstration. He just sat, and she sat. She was too afraid she would cry so she held her tongue and kept her mouth shut. His inscrutable gray eyes were focused on anything but her.

"Are you all right?" he finally said. His voice was raspy.

Shrugging, she nodded, but didn't trust her voice.

"Can I get out?"

"I don't know how," she said. "We don't have the money for bail."

"Can we collect some? It's just a loan."

"It's five hundred dollars, Harry."

"It's temporary. Just get me out of here."

"How do you propose I do this?" She squeezed her hands together.

"I don't know," he said. "But I don't want to be in jail. I can't stay in jail."

"Harry, *please* can you call your father?"

His gray eyes froze over. He blinked in judgment. "No." He stood up.

"Harry, please. He can help you. He *will* help you."

"I went to him once, when he called in the money he had lent to your brother. Do you remember how he treated me?"

"But what if you get convicted? What if you go to prison?"

"I'll rot before I *ever* ask him for a single thing."

Gina did not understand. "Mimoo is right," she said. "What father would turn away a son in such trouble?"

"Herman Barrington, that's who. I see, so you refuse to get me out? When is my trial?"

"In the fall. And I don't refuse—"

"What month is it now?"

"March."

"March! Gina!"

"What would you like me to do, Harry?" She paused. "Perhaps Big Bill can help you, lend you what you need? Surely he can help. You're here because of him."

"I don't think he sees it that way."

"Really? Big Bill is the one you trust to interpret *visual* stimuli?"

"Very good, why don't you try your *ad hominem* tack on him. I don't see how it could fail."

They didn't and couldn't speak about the unspeakable. They quarreled about only what could be quarreled about.

Right before time was up, they stared at each other mutely, hiding behind the veil of their blank eyes and cold words.

"Why didn't you stay under the table, like I told you?" he finally asked.

"I did. The table fell. The tent fell. I fell."

"Why did you go there at all? I told you not to go to Essex Street."

"Your all-seeing boss commanded me to. What choice did I have? I tried to find you. Maybe if you had listened to me and stayed away from that man …"

Harry stood up abruptly. "Are we done? I guess so."

"You wouldn't be in jail, is how I wanted to finish," finished Gina.

"Yes, of course that's how you wanted to finish."

"Would you like me to call him for you? Ask him for five hundred dollars?"

"No, Gina."

She stood up too. "I didn't think so. I guess I'll see you next Sunday."

At his arraignment, Harry went before a judge and said he was not a paying member of the IWW but would join as soon as he was freed. The judge said, "Well, then, Mr. Barrington, we had better make sure you don't go free."

Elston Purdy, the lousy public defender assigned to Harry, though overworked and indifferent, was sharp enough to question why bail had been set so uncommonly high. It seemed unduly punitive, Purdy said to the judge. It took a while to get a straight answer. Bail was set high, the judge finally admitted, because Harry was Herman Barrington's son. The customary low bail wasn't the impediment to the likes of the Barringtons that it was to the ordinary folk of Lawrence, who couldn't raise fifty dollars, much less ten times that. The public defender proceeded to successfully argue that a son should not be penalized for the inaccessible wealth of his estranged father. That fell under cruel and unusual detainment. "It's like setting bail high because John Paul Getty is a wealthy man, your Honor. My client and his father have not spoken to each other in seven years. He has no more right to Herman Barrington's accounts than he does to Mr. Getty's is what I'm trying to say."

The judge considered the motion for two days.

Harry was released without any bail at all, on his own recognizance.

At the end of September, despite Gina's volcanic imprecations, Harry marched in support of Joe and Arturo. "They're being railroaded, Gina, and you know it. The charges against them are bogus. They're now being implicated in the planting of those undetonated bombs found at Wood Mill. You know they weren't involved in that. They're being set up. I won't stand for it. And you shouldn't either. They're our friends."

"Angela is dead," Gina said. "They're not my friends."

There were no American flags at the parade, but many red flags and banners that proclaimed the anarchist slogan, NO GOD NO MASTER. Harry's involvement was duly noted by the District Attorney's office.

A few weeks later, in October, a hundred thousand people watched and participated in the Columbus Day Parade to demonstrate Lawrence's faith in democracy and the American way. Harry was conspicuously absent from these festivities, a fact that was also duly noted by the authorities.

Joe and Arturo remained locked up until November 1912, when their trial finally got underway, right after their old friend Eugene Debs kicked Big Bill Haywood out of the Socialist Party and received a million votes for president of the United States. *"An elective office is only one step toward a revolution,"* Debs said in his concession speech to Woodrow Wilson.

During the trial Joe and Arturo were locked in metal cages in the courtroom. With the stakes being execution, the two men had the temerity to represent themselves against the charge of murder.

Arturo protested his innocence eloquently as only a poet could. "I loved her," he said of Angela. "I would never kill her. I would never put her in danger. She was my good and true friend. I love life, I would never risk life and my soul by committing murder. Ask my loved ones, ask my family. Out in the free world waits a fine woman whom I love and who loves me. I have parents who are praying for my release. My dear friend Joe Ettor and I, we are nothing more than foot soldiers in the mighty army we call the working class of the world."

The prosecutor told him that he was deliberately misunderstanding the charges brought against him. He was on trial for murder, not his political beliefs.

"No! It is communism itself that is on trial," cried Arturo in the courtroom, arguing for his very life. "It has nothing to do with that poor girl's death. Does the District Attorney really believe that the gallows can settle an idea? If the idea lives, it's because history judges it right. Joe and I, and our friend Harry too, ask only for justice. Whatever my social views are, they are. I am an immigrant. I came to this country for freedom. Like my religion, my politics cannot be tried in this courtroom."

Smiling Joe, in his own impassioned plea to the jury, argued not only for the morality of a general strike, but for the very overthrow of capitalism because it was intrinsically immoral. "You cannot argue with immorality as if it has a voice, a reason, you cannot argue with it as with an equal partner in a discussion between men! It will not stand. We are not guilty. We are communists! And being a communist is not yet a crime in this country, is it?"

An electrified Harry sat in the courtroom and soaked it all in. Gina was deeply unimpressed with Harry's demeanor. Mimoo was deeply unimpressed with Arturo's oratory. "I told you, Gia," she said, "that man was no good. Did you hear him say he had another woman waiting for him, another woman he loved? Poor Angela! Poor girl."

"Mimoo, is that *all* you took away from their closing arguments?" Gina tried to suppress the anger Arturo's revelation sparked in her.

"I took away the most important part," Mimoo said. "He never loved our sainted, beautiful, martyred child, while she ran around after him like a schoolgirl, and for what? He left the entire jury in tears after that fine and fraudulent soliloquy! But where is our Angela? St. Mary's Cemetery, that's where. How many times did I tell her to listen to me? I know everything." Mimoo cried and prayed.

"It wasn't fraudulent, Mimoo." Harry, who didn't usually argue with Mimoo, argued that day. "It was a sincere effort to protest their innocence."

"They do too much protesting if you ask me," Mimoo said. "The protesting is what got them into this mess to begin with, and our Angela killed."

"Mimoo, you and your daughter are immigrants," said Harry. "They were fighting for your rights, her rights. They were on your side against the greed of capitalists, who care nothing for your well-being, only for making a dollar. How can you not respect what they did?"

Mimoo laughed. She said a few choice words in Italian, which she didn't translate for him even when asked. "Harry, you are a learned man," Mimoo said, "and a well-read man, I know that. You're always buried in some book. Our electric bill is proof of how much you read. You have many fine qualities. But there are things you are completely ignorant about, and I don't mind telling you what some of them are."

"Please tell me, Mimoo, what I'm ignorant about."

"One is how fathers feel about their sons."

As soon as she said it, all three of them, sitting on a bench outside the courtroom while court was in recess, bowed their heads. August had come and gone, and with it Harry and Gina's chance to find out how parents felt about their own children.

"What's the second thing, Mimoo?" said Harry, hurrying on.

"Do you know who Guilherme Medeiros Silva is?"

"I don't believe I do."

"That's why," said Mimoo, "you are ignorant."

Harry waited. He turned to Gina. "Do you know who that is?"

Gina sighed. "Mimoo, leave him alone. What do you hope to achieve?"

"Do I *want* to know who it is?"

"No," said Gina. "You don't."

"Guilherme Jr. was born in this country," Mimoo said, "in a hut off Martha's Vineyard, but he was the son of Portuguese immigrants from the Azores. His father worked as a crewman on a whaling ship. He was killed when the boy was twelve."

Harry opened his hands. "Okay."

"That's when Guilherme left school and went to work to support his mother and younger sisters. He took a job at the cotton mill in New Bedford. He worked very hard and was noticed by his employer. He got promoted. He learned everything about manufacturing and production and costs. When he was eighteen years old he went to Philadelphia to study stocks and bonds. After he came back he took a job at a factory, turned that factory around, saved it from bankruptcy, made it profitable. That's when he was asked to save another mill in trouble. He not only saved it, but saved eight other nearly bankrupt mills around it. In 1899, the year your wife, her brother and I came to America, he started to build the largest textile mill in the world. The one that produces twenty percent of all the woolens and worsteds in the United States."

"Wood Mill?" Harry said.

"Yes. He named it after himself. William Madison Wood is the American name of little Guilherme Silva, born in a shack, son of a deckhand. An immigrant like your wife. That's your greedy capitalist whose business rebuilt this town and whose business you brought to its knees. Go picket against him."

The jury delivered its verdict: the two Italian men were acquitted of all charges. Two weeks later, however, Harry, facing a lesser charge of felonious public disturbance, was sentenced to eighteen months in prison, commuted to two months followed by two years probation.

While Harry served out his sentence in January and February of 1913, Big Bill stopped paying his wages. "But tell him that I'm organizing another project," Bill said to Gina when she called to collect, "even bigger than Lawrence, and as soon as he gets out, he's right back on the payroll because I need his help. This one is at the silk factories in Paterson, New Jersey. We're mobilizing now."

When Gina protested the lack of wages, Bill patiently explained to her that a man could not be paid for hours he didn't work. "That way anarchy lies," Bill said. "And we are not anarchists, are we? Well, maybe you are. I know most women are. No, we are communists."

A year after the Lawrence strike, the agreements Big Bill had hastily set up with Wood Mill had all but collapsed and most of the gains the women paid for with Angela's blood and Gina's baby's blood had all but vanished. It took the town many years to recover from the damaging effects of the strike. Some say it never recovered. When the textile mills in the Carolinas started to make the worsteds and woolens at a fraction of the northern price, American Woolen went out of business and Lawrence with it.

Certainly Gina felt that she and Harry had never recovered.

Chapter 3

A SERVANT OF RELIEF

One

To HIDE WAS EVERYTHING. In 1905, in the immediate aftermath of her and Harry's elopement, Gina could hardly hide from herself, but she took some comfort in being anonymous to others. She didn't want to face the questions she couldn't answer, not in Lawrence, nor in Boston.

Why aren't you back in school? Why isn't he working? Why didn't you have a proper wedding? Where is his family? What happened to all his money? Wasn't he about to marry someone else?

When she went to visit her old friend Verity, they barely talked about the past, Verity's hands full and eyes myopic of the current chaotic present.

For the most part, Gina could hide from the dreadful things.

But not all dreadful things.

To get Verity out of her narrow flat on the fifth floor of a brownstone in Back Bay, Gina had persuaded her friend to leave her four children with her husband and help her with some of the Sodality tasks she volunteered for on the weekends. She took Verity with her to a hospital ward for terminally ill women at Massachusetts General, and then to the Boston Library where they sorted through boxes of donated books. They visited an ice cream shop and finally headed to Holy Lazarus on Clarendon. A soup kitchen had been recently set up in the basement, and on late Saturday afternoons, before evening Mass, Gina would feed the poor. She liked to do it before she received Communion.

When they had almost finished ladling out the grits and beans and bread, a petite blonde woman and a tall, imperious-looking woman walked in from the back stairs with the parish priest.

"Oh my God," whispered Gina to Verity, her hands going numb. "That's Esther. And *Alice*!" Frantically she glanced around for a door to escape through, a pantry to hide inside.

"Who are Esther and Alice?" Verity said in her normal voice.

"Harry's sister and his former fiancée!"

"Oh, of course. That's why I recognize—"

"Shh! Look down!"

Gina couldn't follow her own advice. Father Gabriel held the blonde's elbow deferentially, as he showed the two women the meager facilities, the few beds in the corner. He brought them to the food line. Gina thought her insides would fall out. Why did she have to wear a happy floral peasant dress, why was her hair so loosely piled atop her head, falling down, curling all over the place, why did she have to come today of all days? There was a fair by the Charles River that night, she and Verity planned to go there with the kids; still, why couldn't she have been more tailored, ironed, polished? She lowered her head and continued serving the grits, missing the plates, making a mess, not looking up. They passed right in front of her.

And stopped.

Ah, Father Gabriel. Sweet, oblivious, well-meaning Father Gabriel. "Ladies, these two girls are Verity and Gina. They volunteer for us, help us prepare the food, serve it, clean up. Gina especially is very dedicated. She is a Sicilian immigrant and lives thirty miles away in some town near Andover—Gina, where do you live again?—but she's here every Saturday, helping us. Isn't that right, Gina?"

"That's right, Father."

"Look up, child, be polite."

Gina couldn't. All the blood had drained from her face into the heart that was about to fly from her chest.

"Gina speaks good English, I know she does. What's your name now? She recently got married and changed her name to something American. I can never remember. What is it?"

Gina said nothing—as if she could speak! Even Verity next to her mishandled a serving.

The only sound came from Alice—a sharp intake of a much-needed breath.

In the crashing heart attack silence of the next few seconds, it was Esther who spoke, never forgetting her impeccable breeding that dictated you must never make a kindly priest feel uncomfortable by keeping silent when a word would do.

"Barrington," Esther said, in her ice-cold polite contralto, perhaps foggy on some of the other tenets of her exalted education pertaining to tact. "I believe it is Barrington. Isn't it?"

Was that last question addressed to her? Gina couldn't tell, because she was never lifting her head again as long as she lived.

Father Gabriel laughed amiably. "No, dearest Esther, I don't mean *your* last name. I mean *her* last name. Girls, these ladies are two of our most generous benefactors. They're the reason the indigent men have food to eat and a bed to sleep in."

"Speaking of somewhere to be, Father," Alice said, "Esther and I must run. Mustn't we, Esther?"

"Oh, Alice, we're well past the time we must be running. Father, will you please excuse us?"

"Lord Jesus, have mercy!" cried Verity after the priest and the women had barely walked away.

"Shh!"

"I'm going to faint!"

"*You*? Verity, shh! Don't look up, just—"

When Gina glanced up, Father Gabriel was blessing the two women by the back door.

Gina watched Alice tie her bonnet under her throat, close her light silk coat. A silk coat, how beautiful, how elegant. Not homespun rough Sicilian cotton, but cream silk. She watched the slender woman's squared back, her proud shoulders, not a blonde strand out of place. Gina straightened up, certain that before she left, Alice would turn and fix her with a wintry stare. As Esther was doing. Gina steeled her spine, ready for it, deserving it.

But Alice didn't. She took her umbrella, smiled at the priest, took Esther's arm, and vanished through the doors without a single glance back.

Gina was stunned. Invisible despite her height, insignificant despite her straight stature, humbled by Alice's mute contempt, she realized Alice's not turning around was worse than Esther's blatant confrontation.

She took off her apron, wiped her hands on a rag. "Excuse me, Verity, I'll be right back."

"Where are you going?"

"Right back." Gina ran after Alice.

What did she want, a Sicilian scene? Did she want Alice to scratch out her eyes, rend her garments, to hue and cry, to *stürm und drang*? She didn't know what she wanted.

She caught up with them, running—ladies didn't run—a block down Commonwealth, disheveled, shoes muddy, her hair out of place. Alice and Esther stopped walking and stood, arm in arm, Alice in her perfect bonnet, exquisite gloves, and maroon silk scarf that brought out the blondeness of her features. She was a pristine pool of clear water.

"Alice," said Gina, panting. "Can I have a word?"

"Please step away from us," said Esther, almost touching Gina with the back of her hand as if to swat her away. "We never want to speak to you."

It was Alice who stopped Esther. "It's all right. Excuse us for a moment, Esther. It'll take but a minute."

How Gina wished she were dressed better. At this moment of all moments what she would give not to be judged for her old shoes, a frayed dress two years out of fashion. What she would give for these women not to think that Harry deserved much better.

"Tell me why you do it," Alice said.

73

"I don't know what you mean." Gina's voice trembled. She wasn't afraid of Alice, she was sad for Alice, and the sorrow prevented her mouth from forming the simplest words of remorse.

"Your name appears on the Sodality lists all over Boston. Why? Why do you go to hospitals I am the benefactor of, libraries to which I donate books, churches to which I give alms? What is the profit in it for you? Do you think that if you do this, I will hate you less?"

Gina shook her head, nodded her head, stupefied, shamed.

"Do you do it for some twisted sense of penance? Like if you feed the poor the food I buy them, you won't be as contemptible in God's eyes?"

"Maybe that," whispered Gina inaudibly.

Alice's voice was strong. She hardly blinked, her blue-eyed stare condemning and unafraid. "You're wasting your time. Nothing is going to make me hate him less or hate you less. Nothing. You tell him that. Nothing you will ever do will change what you did."

To this Gina could respond. "I'm so sorry," she said.

"He never even came to tell me he wasn't going to marry me. The flowers were being carried into the church when I found out about you and him."

"Please forgive us."

Alice leaned in before she left to catch up with Esther. "You think God could ever bless a union that began in such dishonor?" She laughed. "Esther is right. Please," she added, turning her back on Gina, "make sure we never see you again."

That's when Gina stopped visiting Verity, going to demonstrations, working at soup kitchens and hospitals. No more parade grounds, or parks, or dreams of boat rides in spring on the Charles.

Her beloved Boston relegated to the stuff of nightmares, she stayed in Lawrence and willed herself not to think about the past, the future, the present. Not to think about anything as she waited out the black doom of Alice's words. She prayed Alice was wrong, she hoped Alice was wrong, she believed Alice was wrong.

Until the Bread and Roses strike.

Two

IN MID-SPRING OF 1913, Gina took a train and a bus to the Wayside in Concord to see her old friend and mentor Rose Hawthorne. Nathaniel Hawthorne's youngest daughter was devoting the last half of her life to ministering after the needy and desperate, and Gina desperately needed to be ministered to. She knew Rose back from her high school days when she and other students from Notre Dame had traveled to Salem and Concord to work for Rose's Home for the Sick as part of their Sodality service.

"Child, I'm so happy to see you," Rose said smiling, diminutive but solid, dressed as always in a nun's habit. "I haven't seen you since the night many years ago that you came to introduce to me your intended betrothed. How is Harry?"

For many minutes Gina sat in the chair in the front hall and wept into Rose's sleeve. Rose, full of compassion, said nothing. She didn't need to. Only her palm that patted Gina's back spoke. There, there, the palm said. There, there. "Come with me to the kitchen. I'll make you some tea. You'll have to walk past the beds of the terminally sick. You won't mind, will you?"

"I lost my baby, Rose," Gina said when they sat down at the kitchen table.

"God keep you. I'm sorry. I know it's a terrible pain."

Gina nodded, thinking those were just words from Rose. For what did Rose know of this pain?

Rose with her kind and round face leaned over and whispered, "I know what it is to lose a soul you love. As your husband lost his mother, I lost my beloved father at thirteen. He was too young to die."

"Mine too, mine too. I lost my father at fifteen," said Gina. "I miss him every day."

"As your husband misses his mother?"

"I can't say. He never speaks of her."

"Still waters run deep, my child."

Gina wiped her face, pulled herself up in her chair.

"First my father," said Rose, "then my sister, then my mother. And then my husband. Yes, Gina, I had a husband. I lost him"—she continued—"because he couldn't bear the grief we both shared." She paused. "The grief of losing our four-year-old boy to the diphtheria that took him as suddenly as he had appeared in our life."

Now it was Gina's hand that reached out to pat Rose's black vestments. Was that presumptuous? There, there. So she did know everything.

"I suffered as you suffer," Rose said. "All possibilities were extinguished with Frankie's last breath."

"That's exactly what I feel," whispered Gina.

"Except you're still young, you can have another baby, with the blessing of the Lord. I was nearly forty. I couldn't. My poor George, he was just bent in half by it. He took to drink to drown himself, and soon the drink obliged." Tears came to Rose's eyes and she made a clucking sound, crossing herself with a shudder. "Whatever you do, my girl, keep yourself away from the liquid sorrows. They have a way of swallowing up everything, like the highest tides."

"Don't worry about me on that score," Gina said. "I don't have a taste for it." They sat. "Rose, I'm sorry," she whispered. "I came because I don't know how to help myself anymore. Or my husband."

"That's how I was, too," Rose said. "But then I opened a home for dying, cast-out women. I got busy with other people's suffering. Sometimes, during the day, it helps me forget."

"Yes," Gina said. "You think that's what I should do? Open a home for the dying?"

Rose chuckled. "No. But tell me, how is Harry? He must also be struggling terribly through the loss of your baby."

Gina clenched her fists, unclenched them, folded them into a prayer.

"We never speak of it." She lifted her hand to stop Rose from repeating herself. "There's been … I don't know how to put it … a divvying up of blame."

"He blames you?"

"I think he might."

"Do you blame him?"

She didn't want to lie to a nun. "I don't *not* blame him." It was like the sacrament of reconciliation coming here to talk to Rose.

Rose shook her head. "That's a slow poison. Like rot."

Gina hung her head. "I know. I tried to move past it." Her mouth twisted, got tight. "But he hasn't made it easy for me. He was just in jail for the problems during the Bread and Roses strike. Have you heard about that?"

"I'm afraid I haven't. Sorrows are so abundant here, I have no time to read the papers."

"I understand. Well, I thought when he was released we'd begin our life again, try again maybe … but as soon as he was released, he packed his bags and left."

"Left you?"

"Not left me, but …" She didn't know what to say, how to put it. "He asked me to go with him. He's at another strike at the moment, in Paterson, New Jersey."

"New Jersey?"

"The man who pays his salary organized that one, too." Gina sighed. "Harry says we need the money. And we do. But I can't leave my mother, my job. I'm lucky to have a job. So now he sends me his money, but hasn't been home in weeks." Her lips trembled. She didn't want to tell Rose what Alice had said long ago that had tattooed fear into her heart because it sounded too much like the unwanted truth. Was it wrong to build a house like marriage, even a mansion like their marriage, on the ashes of someone else's devastated heart?

The money trickled in with the mail. Instead of being in the thick of her bed, Harry was once again in the thick of trouble. And the silk strike in Paterson was violent and unending and destined for failure. No. It was Big Bill and his radicalism that was responsible for the gradual dissolution of her marriage.

Rose watched her conflicted face. "If you have the time, on Saturdays or Sundays, why don't you come and help me here? I can't pay you, as you know. We never pay, but we could definitely use a pair of good hands. I can feed you. You can sleep at the Wayside if you need a place to stay."

"What about my mother?"

"Don't you have a brother?"

"Yes, but ..."

"A boy also can be a good child to his mother. Ask your brother to be a good son while you help me."

Gina took off her coat. "No use in fretting," she said. "How about I help you now?"

Three

"THINGS ARE STILL QUITE SPARTAN," Rose said to Gina as she took her around the ward, a long annex attached to the Wayside, and showed her where they kept the salves, the bandages, the sponges, the bedpans. "Please stay away if you become with child again. Just in case. Sometimes we have lepers staying with us. They are highly infectious. There is bacteria in the air from all sorts of sickness. If you're blessed enough to fall pregnant, don't breathe in the air of the dying. Promise me?"

"The danger of that while the strike continues," said Gina, "is slim. But how do you not get sick?"

Smiling, Rose raised her eyes and palms to the ceiling. "The God of all comfort comforts us in our tribulation so that we may give comfort to those who are in any trouble." Rose put her arm through Gina's. "You are a good girl, and you're going to be just fine." She leaned in for a confidence. "You know, I had no nursing experience before I started caring for the incurably sick. Oh, yes. Don't be so surprised. But like my dear father, I have always been fascinated by medicine. He wanted to be a doctor before he became a writer, did you know that? Not a lot of people do. What do you think? Did he make the right choice in his life's path?"

"Hard to say no to that, isn't it, Rose? His books bless the future generations."

"I suppose they do. But look, please don't tell anyone else that I have no nursing training. They'll close me down for sure. Come with me—I hear Alice."

Gina blanched.

78

"Not *that* Alice," Rose said gently. "My Alice. She must be back from her walkabout. She goes around Concord twice a week, in the afternoons. Visits the sick in their homes." The nun paused. "Though I must say, I'm surprised the other Alice is still so top of mind for you."

"What can I say?" Gina nodded. "She left me with a few parting words I haven't been able to shake from my heart. Her valedictory salvo, so to speak. When things aren't going well, her words are all I can think about."

"Clearly what catches seed is the grain of truth, no matter how small."

"Not even that small." Gina pointed to the door. "Let's go say hello."

In the front hall they were greeted by a plump serious woman. "Gina," Rose said, "you remember my friend and colleague Alice Huber, don't you?"

Nodding, Gina shook Alice's hand.

"Alice used to be a portrait painter," Rose told Gina with a proud smile.

"I'll tell my own story, Rose, dearest." Alice took Gina's other arm. Flanked by the petite sisters, the towering Gina walked through the ward between the beds of the dying. "It's true I used to be a portrait painter," Alice concurred. "But my heart wasn't in it. I was looking for something else. I said that when I found a work of perfect charity, I would join it. And so I did."

"It's not for everyone, Alice," Rose said. "Don't judge people." She looked up at Gina. "My friend can be too critical sometimes, God love her. I tell her all the time—people are the keepers of their own souls, not you."

"And do I listen, Rose?"

"Hardly ever."

"Exactly. Do you know, Gina," Alice continued, "that before we built this small annex, we housed the sick right in Rose's Wayside?"

"And it wasn't even my Wayside anymore." Rose laughed. "Imagine how my dear Harriet felt about it." The Wayside was the only home Nathaniel Hawthorne had ever owned. In 1879, many years after his death, Rose and George bought the beloved house to keep it in the family. Financial hardship forced them to sell it just four years later to George's publisher and his wife, Harriet Stone, also known as Margaret Sidney, the writer of children's books.

"We bathed them and changed their dressings right in the parlor room."

Rose nodded. "In the summers we used the front porch for their beds. My father used to sit and have his morning tea on that porch."

"And in New York we collected the sick into three cold-water flats on the Lower East Side," said Alice. "We managed. They managed."

"Well, yes," Rose said. "Because our goal wasn't convenience. It was to do something to comfort other hearts than ours. To take the lowest rank of human beings—both in poverty and in suffering—and put them in such a condition that if our Lord knocked on our door, we would not be ashamed to let Him in."

"Let's go then and comfort other hearts than ours," said Gina, rolling up her sleeves. "Perhaps we can make our Lord proud."

Eighteen months went by.

Four

IN OCTOBER 1914, GINA was in the kitchen at the Wayside making chicken soup for the annex patients and mopping the floor when there was a knock on the glass pane of the back door. She had been thinking about the lateness of the hour and her long trip home to Lawrence when the soft knock startled her out of her musings. She opened the door and in front of her stood Ben Shaw. He took off his hat, bowed to her slightly, and smiled.

"Ben?" She almost didn't recognize him, having not seen him in nearly fifteen years. They hugged like the old friends they were, kissed each other on both cheeks like Europeans. Instinctively Gina's hands lifted to adjust and pin up her always falling-down hair. She smiled with joy at seeing his kind, familiar face, fleetingly wishing she looked less grubby.

"Benjamin, I am *stunned* to see you!"

"Why?" he asked cheerfully. "Did you think I'd be dead by now?"

Ben had been in Panama, engineering and building the Panama Canal. His modulated tenor hadn't changed, his amiable face was as handsome as ever. His dark eyes sparkled, the expression in them when he looked at her familiar and welcome and true, but in all else he was hardly the same person. He was a grown man now, not an eager, smitten boy. His dark hair was clipped short and graying above his ears. He had an impeccably groomed salt-and-pepper goatee, was thin like a steel pole, and extremely tanned. So tanned that if Gina hadn't known better, she would've guessed he was of Mediterranean or South American stock. Lines had gathered under his friendly eyes and around his burned-by-the-sun mouth. He wore thin-wire glasses that made him look like a solemn scientist. Yet he was still inimitably Ben when he smiled.

He walked in, placed his sharply structured hat on the entry table, hung up his wool coat. He wore a smart gray serge suit, a white shirt, a silk tie. He looked modern. He looked successful. His black shoes had been recently shined. He looked as if *he* had been recently shined. A seamstress, a textile expert, a dreamer of high fashion, Gina knew about such things. He was put together well. Like Harry had been once, before he married her.

She was disappointed in herself, at how happy she was to see him again, to see a familiar face that belonged to a man who had once gazed upon her with unreturned affection. She put on a kettle to make him some tea, and then puttered around feeling flustered, not knowing what to ask him first or what to get hold of next. She was all too aware of her drab brown dress, the stains of her difficult work on it, the labor-scratched hands, the short unpolished nails.

She saw herself as if through a looking glass, a reflected plain Gina, not the blaze she had once been, but a working woman wan of face and devoid of makeup, with no embellishments in her skirt or sparkles in her auburn hair. Deeply self-conscious, she busied herself with their cups of tea. They sat down at the tiny table in the corner by the window, where she sat by herself during the brief breaks in her day.

"You're dressed too well for someone who's been digging in mud for a decade," said Gina.

"Digging is a weak word for what we've been doing. I won't miss that part."

"So tell me everything—where to start—what in the world are you doing here?"

"Here in Boston or here at Rose's?"

"Yes!"

"I could ask the same of you."

"I help out on the weekends. They're always short-staffed."

"I thought you had to be a nun to work here?" he said, teasing her.

She chuckled at the memory of her silly fifteen-year-old self being mortified once by that question, but she was not discomfited anymore, not blushing. "Well and truly, the time for the nunnery has passed," Gina said. "But don't change the subject. What are you doing here?"

"I came to pay Rose a visit. She told me you were here, in the back. It would've been rude not to stop by and say hello."

"Pay Rose a visit?" Gina was flustered. "How could you possibly know her?"

Ben smiled. "Have you forgotten? My family knows her because of you." He reminded her that it was through her intervention that Rose had come to Boston and ministered to his aunt Josephine Shaw Lowell who had been terminally ill with cancer. "Months after you brought them together, Aunt Effie died with Rose at her side."

So much had happened, Gina had forgotten indeed. She nearly cried at the sharp, stinging memory of that awful night, when she first discovered what a torment it was for Harry to face up to the truth of immutable things.

"Aunt Effie left a good portion of her estate to Rose's Home, here and in New York," Ben told her. "Twice a year, still, the Shaws and the Lowells do a blowout charity bash for Rose and Alice." When Gina winced at the sound of the name *Alice*, he frowned. "I meant Alice Huber."

"I know," Gina said. "Who else could you possibly be fundraising for?"

"Quite right." Ben tilted his head sympathetically. "Listen, you must feel bad about the way things turned out. Don't. This is what was meant to be."

"Who says I feel bad?"

Ben smiled. "Unlike your husband, I'm not the black sheep. *I* still keep in touch with everyone. I hear certain things."

"Oh. Like what? What did Esther tell you?"

"Nothing. What I'm trying to say is, don't worry about Alice. She is fine."

Gina sniffed skeptically. "If you say so."

"I say so because it's true. She married a rancher from Texas a few years back."

"No!"

"Yes. When her father died, she sold his lumber company and took his money and her mother with her. She now runs a four hundred-acre cattle spread somewhere near Austin. Has two little ones. Is completely happy from what Esther tells me."

"Texas!" Marveling, Gina stared out the window at the sugar maples and the elms framing the green clearing.

"That's the only part you heard? Texas?"

"Texas is just shorthand for what I'm feeling." She sat for a moment, hand on her heaving chest, trying to squeeze relief from her repentant heart. She took a deep breath. "And Harry's family is well, I hope? Herman, Esther?"

"Yes, everyone's all right now."

Gina perked up. "Now?"

"Harry's father had a heart attack a few years ago. In 1912." Ben paused for meaning or maybe for a reaction from Gina.

Gina lost her baby in 1912. She shuddered. "But he's better?"

"Yes. Of course now Esther is out of sorts."

"Why? She must be happy you're back home."

"I don't know about that. Elmore, her husband, just left for England."

"What on earth for?"

"Some archduke got shot in Bosnia."

"Ah, yes. The pesky archduke." She sounded exhausted even to herself.

"Dr. Lassiter went with the Red Cross as a medic. Esther is not pleased with him, to say the least."

"I know how she feels."

"Why?" Ben asked. "Has Harry become an army medic and gone to England?"

"Sure." Gina stared out the window. "Something like that. And your mother?" Ellen Shaw had quite a reputation around Boston, demonstrating day and night against each affront to the independence of women and every encroachment against the isolationism of the United States.

He nodded agreeably. "Fine. Militant as ever."

"Tell her to be careful," Gina said. "Or she'll be sharing a cell with Harry."

"So I keep telling her. What did *he* do?"

"Which time? I don't know. Kept arguing?"

Ben whistled in fond amazement. "Don't they know he is the original objection-maker? They can't punish him for his essential nature. But seriously, what did he do?"

"Broke the terms of his probation by inciting a riot in Paterson during the silk strike. Have you heard about that?"

"Yes," Ben said. "I heard something about that. Where is he?"

"Nearby. Up in the Massachusetts Correctional Institution near Warner's Pond. That's why I'm here every weekend. I work Saturdays and take the bus to visit him on Sundays."

"Prison!" Ben looked disbelieving. "That doesn't seem like the Harry I knew."

"It's really been an unending smorgasbord of humiliation." Gina almost cried. "No, no," she quickly said, catching herself, keeping away the hand that reached across to her. "My own life is the last thing I want to talk about. I am, however, *completely* enthralled by your wonderful reappearance. Tell me really why you're back." She made an effort to smile. "Who's getting married this time?" Ten years ago Ben had sailed home from Panama to be best man at Harry and Alice's wedding.

"Just like last time," he said. "Nobody."

They sat cupping their tea, warming their hands on it. The New England flaming fall was on full display; inside and outside glowed with light like fire.

"The papers have been writing about nothing but your canal." Gina smiled with pride. "You always said the impossible was possible. And you were right."

"You mean I was a lunatic. I looked at nothing but mountains and mud and said we would build a fifty-mile waterway above sea level with concrete dams to push giant ships through."

If she could whistle and she weren't a lady, she would have. "It's extraordinary."

"It's madness."

"It's a phenomenon! They're calling it the engineering wonder of the modern world. Just like you said it would be."

"It was nothing like I thought it would be." He shrugged. "I said a lot of things when I was young and foolish. I received a healthy dose of reality in Panama."

"Did you get yellow fever, too?" Gina asked, appraising him. He seemed toughened, but somehow worn-out. He looked as if he needed a juicy steak, a stiff drink.

"Yes. Washed my face in the river. Teaches me."

"Well, you don't need to go all the way to Panama to catch yellow fever," said Gina. "Mother Jones's husband and four of her children died of it somewhere in Tennessee."

"It was touch and go for me, too, for a while. Though now I'm immune for life."

"Really? From malaria, too?"

"No, but do I carry a small bottle of quinine with me everywhere I go."

"I don't think there's much risk of malaria in Concord, Ben."

"One can never be too careful against that wretched blight."

"That's true." Her elbows were on the table, her head resting between her hands. "So they didn't need you in Panama anymore?"

"I don't know. All I know is that in August we finally had our first ship navigate through. I stayed until mid-September to make sure there were no irrecoverable disasters, and at first sign of trouble, when one of the levees failed to open, I sailed home." He laughed. "I told them I was testing the time of travel through the canal instead of around Cape Horn."

"How did you get here?"

"The liner took me to Key West where a railroad met me."

"A railroad in Key West? Isn't it an island?"

"So you would think. Little did I know that in the last ten years, some man named Henry Flagler was bringing a railroad over one hundred and fifty miles of sea to Key West, precisely because of our canal. He thought the United States could use a southernmost port connected by rail to the mainland."

"Oh, that is amazing! So many amazing things everywhere. People working, making things." She shook off her words, coughed. Why were the simplest things so hard to talk about? "Are you home for good?"

"We'll see." He smiled, slightly rueful. "I'm afraid I still miss it terribly, against all reason. Why in the world would I miss the sandflies and what they do to my body? What if I discover I can't make a life anywhere else but in the infested malarian tropics?"

"Hmm. You look like you adjusted well." She appraised his tailored suit, his crisp white shirt. "Are you working here?"

"As opposed to what? Of course I'm working. Still and ever with the Army Corps. Headquartered in Boston, but constantly out on civil engineering projects."

"Oh, Ben." She sighed, remembering the past, gazing at him fondly. "So how was it? Where did you live? What did you eat? Did you work long days? Did you get hurt? Was there any fun?"

He smiled, with amusement, with pleasure. "That's a mouthful of questions."

"I know. I'm sorry!"

He got a look in his eyes as if he were recalling a lost lover. "It's like nothing I've ever imagined."

"Aren't most things?"

"I don't know," said Ben. "Depends on the things." Without a blink, he continued. "Panama is more mountainous than I expected.

More dramatically landscaped. Rocky. It's nearly completely covered by impenetrable forest. Dissected with rivers, streams, deep gorges. It's tropically hot, it pours rain like you've never seen, and then is dry like the desert. The fish is good." He smiled broadly. "The women are very friendly."

"Well, who wouldn't be friendly to a handsome American man like you," Gina said, just as Rose stuck her head in, reminding her that the patients were still not fed, and it was well past six. But there was still so much to talk about! Gina jumped up with regret and hurried to the stove, organizing the tray with the stacked soup bowls and bread.

"Here," Ben said. "Let me help." He took off his suit jacket, unbuttoned his vest, rolled up his white sleeves, and carried the soup tureen into the annex.

It was after seven and dark when they were finished with the feeding and the cleaning up.

"Sorry you spent such a long time helping me," said Gina. "I thought we might have time to go for a walk. Concord is lovely in the fall."

He chuckled.

"What?"

"Nothing. I'm trying to remember what Louisa May Alcott wrote about Concord. As I recall, it wasn't very complimentary."

"It couldn't have been that bad," Gina said. "She lived and died in Orchard House, just down the road. But …"

"Another time perhaps."

"Yes." She mulled things over quickly, chewing her lip. "Could you maybe take me back to Lawrence? I don't like to travel alone. You could keep me company, we could finish our catch-up and I'll make you dinner for your trouble." She smiled. "What do you say? I have a recipe for mustard chicken."

He nodded. "I'd be happy to take you home. You shouldn't travel alone this late. But let's not wait until Lawrence. How about dinner first? You must be hungry after a full day's work. Let's go to Wright's Tavern."

"Go where?" She glanced at her skirt. "I can't … I'm not dressed for dinner. I can't show myself in a nice restaurant."

"Who said anything about nice? Wright's Tavern, I told you. You'll be the best dressed woman in the place. Possibly the only woman."

She laughed. "Ben, what could you possibly know about taverns in Concord?"

"It's the only thing I know about Concord. Except what Louisa May Alcott wrote."

She chewed her lip, curious, ambivalent, hungry.

Ben must have been reading her thoughts. He leaned closer to her. "You're worried about propriety?"

She nodded.

"Manners do dictate that a woman cannot be seen out and about with a man alone unless she is married."

"That's what I feared, I mean, um, *thought*."

"But Gina, do I need to remind you that you *are* married?" Ben straightened up. "In every way, even this one, we can be proper Bostonians."

She laughed happily, she couldn't help herself. "Please, another time?" She really wasn't dressed to go out. Ladies didn't go out in stained clothing in public. She pulled out a train schedule from her purse.

"I tell you what," Ben said, taking the booklet out of her hands. "How about we take my car." He led her outside.

"You have a car?"

"Why are you surprised? Everybody has one."

"We don't," Gina said. "We can't afford it. Harry says only rich people have cars."

"That may have been true in 1905 when Bill Haywood was yelling that only oppressors like Harry had cars. But now, thanks to Mr. Ford and his assembly line, there are two million cars on the road. He has transformed the United States. A nation of toilers is fast becoming a nation of consumers."

"Not me," Gina said. "I'm still a toiler. You must make a good living if you can afford a car." She said this with a feeling approaching envy.

"Not really. I just make a living. But I will say that in Panama"—he smiled—"they paid us engineers as if we were kings. They paid us more than they paid the doctors! Can you imagine? And they paid the chief engineers most of all. I saved all my money. I had nothing to spend it on. All I did was work. The housing was paid for and the Canal Commissary fed tens of thousands of workers for free."

Gina could tell he was trying to make her feel better. Someone else to pay for her food and housing? What would that be like?

Rose walked out to say goodbye. "Ben, come again. You're always welcome."

"Maybe next time I could help a bit more?"

"Help do what?" asked Gina.

"I don't know. This place is run by women. There must be something a man could do. Fix a window? Repair a door knob?"

Rose put her grateful hand on Ben's. "You know one of my deepest regrets is that no matter how I try I can never get good devoted men to come and shoulder the burden of this work, care for the sick men the way we attend to sick women."

Ben lowered his head to her. "I don't know about attending to the sick, Sister Alphonsa," he said, using the name Rose had adopted when she joined the convent. "But I'll fix your windows and patch your doors."

"Oh!" Gina said. "We have dozens of projects like that."

"We certainly do," said Rose. "Our Ben can also be a servant of relief."

After they passed Andover and neared Lawrence, Ben slowed down his vehicle. Gina hadn't nearly finished her story of the last ten years of her life.

"Since he got mixed up with that horrible Cyclops of a man," Gina was telling Ben, "it's been nothing but trouble. And do you know why?"

"Because wherever that man goes, trouble follows?"

"Exactly. Lawrence strike, people dead. Paterson strike, people dead." Gina shook her head. "Do you know who else Harry met in Paterson? John Reed. Have you heard of him?"

"No, I'm afraid not. Should I have? I haven't been following the strikes and the radicals."

"And Elizabeth Gurley Flynn. She is quite the inspired feminist, that one." Gina's mouth tightened in flagrant disapproval. "He was gone for months gallivanting with them, carousing ..."

"Not Harry, not carousing."

"And then they all got arrested."

"For carousing? Or gallivanting?"

"For conspiracy to incite riots. And this time he was a member of the IWW. He broke the terms of his parole five ways to Sunday. John Reed and Max Eastman bailed him out. Someone had to. His bail was set at a thousand dollars!"

Ben tightened his grip on the wheel.

"But now he's in union with the Greenwich Village radicals. He calls himself a revolutionary. Harry, your oldest friend, my bookish quiet husband, a revolutionary! Can you believe it?"

"No. Perhaps just a drawing-room revolutionary?"

Gina shook her head. "He keeps talking of moving to New York when he gets out."

"When is he getting out?"

"Not sure. He served a reduced sentence for the Paterson strike, six months or so, and not long after he got out, in May, the archduke got shot! So Harry started protesting a war that hadn't begun. This time there wasn't even a trial." Gina sighed, deeply weary. "He received a mandatory five-year sentence that for a reason I can't fathom got reduced to two. Can't be Elston Purdy, Harry's public defender, as he is awful. But Purdy assures me Harry will be out in time for Christmas. Apparently he's a model prisoner." She swallowed. "Between the arrests and the strikes, I can't help but think he wants to be away."

Ben made an incredulous sound as he drove on. "It can't be that."

"You don't think so? Then why would he, knowing he's out on probation, be charging an army recruiting station, blocking the entrance, yelling, 'Commercial rivals are having a fight and for *that* our young boys are going to die?'"

Ben shook his head.

"While you were building and opening the engineering wonder of the modern world," said Gina, "some man named Franz Ferdinand was murdered in Bosnia and because of a random death half a world away, my husband is once again in prison."

She didn't speak again until they were back in Lawrence.

*   *   *

They got home around nine. No one was in. Saturday nights Mimoo went to vespers and played bingo. Salvo was out God knows where. He told his sister he served beer in a saloon on Friday and Saturday nights. Gina and Mimoo never saw a penny of that money.

Ben sat down at Gina's formerly revolutionary table while she put together some potatoes with cold mustard chicken and opened a bottle of red wine. They sat down together and broke bread.

"This is very good," he said, eating hungrily. "But you don't make Italian food anymore? Your brother was such a good cook."

"After what happened to his restaurants, no, we don't make Italian food like we used to. No one wants to cook it, no one wants to eat it."

"You know, Gina," Ben said, "years ago when I learned that Harry helped Salvo, everybody thought I was upset because of *you*, but really I was just jealous because I thought he'd be having Italian food every night."

Flushing at Ben's casual admission that once there was a time when he might have been upset over her, Gina tried to respond in kind—lightly. "Well, Harry did have it every night," she said lowering her eyes. "Now he has it sporadically."

"That's a real shame," said Ben. "So where's your brother?"

"During the week he works at Purity in the North End. On the weekends he's back home. We see him much more now that Harry's away. Mimoo is happy. It's quite a predicament. On the one hand, my husband is in prison, on the other hand, my brother is home."

Ben finished eating. "So what happened?" he asked quietly, wiping his mouth on a napkin. "I thought the restaurants were doing so well." He poured Gina more wine.

"Esther didn't tell you?"

"Esther doesn't know what happened. She just knows they were sold. Tell me. We have time. When is Mimoo coming home?"

"Eleven. And she'll be delighted to find you here."

Ben smiled. "Just like old times."

They sat at the table as Gina poured out her life to Ben, all the Salvo, Harry and Angela miseries of it.

Five

AFTER THE ELOPEMENT SALVO invites Harry, who's "between jobs" to come work at the family's two restaurants. Harry says, "Doing what? I can't make pizza."

They laugh. "Of course you can't." Because he isn't Italian.

Harry mopes for days, and only when Gina presses him does he reveal to her the contents of the letter he recently received from Herman Barrington calling in the mortgage on Salvo's two restaurants. Salvo has been slow in making the payments, and after what has transpired, Herman has no interest in remaining flexible. "I'm sorry. I didn't know how to tell you what a vindictive, cruel son of a bitch my father is. I know I should have said something sooner. Please don't be upset with me. I tried to make it right. I even went to see him." Harry can't look at Gina's dumbstruck face. "Do you know how hard that was? I went to him for help, to ask him to reconsider, to give Salvo a little more time to pay, and he wouldn't let me in, wouldn't come out to speak to me! Sent his lackey instead."

Herman's letter about duties, responsibilities, betrayal, wrath, finalities, hangs from Gina's hands.

Salvo reluctantly agrees to the solution Harry proposes and meets with Ervin Cassidy, the manager of the local First National Bank of Lawrence. After much back and forth, the bank manager offers Salvo a painful compromise: a payoff to Herman's bank to settle the loans, and then a new mortgage. But the price of that transaction will be one of the restaurants.

Salvo has no choice but to agree.

The bank sells off the less profitable one, the upscale Alessandro's, and leaves Salvo with a hefty mortgage for the bustling Antonio's by the railroad. He makes lots of pizza to please the crowds and hopes in a few years to perhaps turn a profit.

Harry doesn't have a choice after that. The Attavianos need his help if they're going to make it. Harry goes to work with Salvo in his one remaining restaurant.

That's the good news.

The bad news: Harry goes to work with Salvo in his one remaining restaurant.

It isn't that Harry is a slow learner. It's that he can't find a role for himself in the many-spoked wheel that is the smooth operation of a family business. He tries ordering supplies, but gets bored. He tries maintaining the equipment. Tedium. Writing advertising copy isn't for him—too facile. Neither is placing ads in the local newspaper (too pushy) or coming up with ideas to draw more people in (really too pushy). He isn't adept at running the weekly management meetings and has no idea how to solve the many petty but constant problems that crop up in a workplace with twenty-two employees and seventy-seven suppliers. He certainly doesn't want to learn how to cook. Counting money at the end of the night makes him ornery. Walking to the bank, making deposits, paying the bills, calling in accounts—all grate on him.

A tense year passes. And another.

One fateful day in 1908, Angela comes to Salvo in confusion. She says she ran into the bank manager walking his dog on the Common, and the man told her that despite a dozen notices there has not been a mortgage payment in over three months and Antonio's is five minutes away from going into default.

Salvo and Gina go to the bank to clear up the mistake because they know, *know*, that Harry has been making deposits *and* telling Salvo everything is running like warm milk from morning cows. It's an oversight. It must be.

But apparently, as the meticulous bank records show, the flowing warm milk doesn't entail paying the mortgage.

The truth turns out to be worse than Salvo and Gina fear. How often does that happen? They are in the back office combing over the books, with Harry once again conveniently not around, when Margaret, their seating hostess, comes in to inform them she has been underpaid for the previous week. She patiently explains that for the past six months, Harry has been doubling her salary, until last week, with no explanation, he went back to paying her the woefully inadequate original wage.

"The problem is, you see, we got quite used to the new salary and thought it was for keeps," Margaret says. "My husband and I moved to a larger home, we went to Ohio to visit his mother, took a few weeks for ourselves, and now with Christmas coming up … I'm sorry but we just can't afford a cut in pay."

Gina and Salvo sit like blackened statues. As she sits now in her dimly lit parlor room across from a stunned Ben as she recounts it. She doesn't want to recount it. She wishes there were music instead. She wishes she could forget, talk about something else, never speak of it again, never think of it again, like the Bread and Roses strike, like Angela. Why does it all keep coming back up like disagreeable food?

"Margaret," Gina says in an even voice, keeping her squeezing hand on Salvo, who is the master of raised voices, "you didn't get a cut in pay. You got an unauthorized and unapproved bonus, and the reason it stopped is because there is no extra money."

An unhappy Margaret, too broke to quit, says before walking out, "You're going to have a mutiny on your hands. Because all of us who are not family have been getting extra money. And it's Christmas for everybody, not just me. What are you going to do, not pay your staff extra on Christmas?"

Gina and Salvo sit, pods of salt.

"Don't say a word, Salvo," says Gina when Margaret leaves.

"I'm going to kill him."

"I told you not to say a word."

"One way or another he better make this right, or I swear on our mother …"

"Salvo!"

Gina, afraid for both men she loves, runs out looking for Harry. She finds him on a bench in the back of City Hall, handsome, absent-minded, detached yet affectionate, wrapped in a huge overcoat, serenely eating his lunch in the cold, immersed in his reading.

With the book still open, as if he doesn't want her to bother him too much during his daily break, he tells her that, yes, he has been feeling bad for the people who work for them because they are having so much trouble making ends meet and they never have any extra for birthdays, a

94

wedding, a vacation, a new house. One woman's mother is sick and the doctor's bills are large, one man's boat has sprung a leak and the baker's uncle died and the funeral expenses were a quarter of his annual salary. The dishwasher is having an unexpected third baby …

Harry tells Gina all this and then leans back against the bench, glancing down into his tome as if there is no need for further discussion. They needed extra so he gave them extra, that's all there is to it.

"Harry," Gina asks quietly, "you paid them out of what money?"

"Out of the money we make every night."

"But that's our operating money."

"Okay. Labor is part of the operating budget."

"But you already paid them a regular salary, yes? You paid them a fair wage for their labor?"

"How can it be a fair wage when Eddie's uncle needed to be buried?"

Gina clamps her hands on her chest as if she is having a heart attack. "Because you have been overpaying the payroll, we don't have enough to cover our mortgage. The note the bank holds against our restaurant is the one fixed capital expense we absolutely must pay."

"*Labor* is the one fixed capital expense we must pay."

"No, Harry. We can fire everyone and run the restaurant with just the family working for nothing, but if we don't pay the mortgage, there will be no restaurant to run."

"You're placing people below institutions, Gia," he says. "Always a mistake and unlike you. I thought you and I were sewn of the same cloth. The bank can wait for its money. The people can't."

"Harry, the bank *has* waited for its money. Over three months. Now we owe them not just next month's payment, but the last quarter besides. And we need to pay it in the next twenty days."

"So let's pay it."

"We don't have it. Had you *loaned* our employees the money instead of simply giving it to them, the bank could see those loans as an asset, but as it stands …"

"We'll have to get it." Harry is unconcerned. "It'll be fine. The bank will wait."

"They won't wait. They'll take Salvo's restaurant!"

"No, they won't. That's just to scare you. I know how this works. I'll go talk to them. Just … let me finish my lunch and this one chapter." He shows her the book he's reading: Lincoln Steffens, *The Shame of the Cities*. "Look what he writes, it's brilliant! *'Politics is business. That's what's the matter with politics. That's what's the matter with everything— art, literature, religion, journalism, law, medicine—they're all business. Make politics a sport, as they do in England, or a profession, as they do in Germany.'*" Harry clucks in deep approval. "Isn't he something?"

Gina has nothing to say.

"Just let me finish this chapter and then we'll go."

Harry goes to the bank. He goes with a barely contained Salvo and an overstrung Gina, who sits in the corner chair in Cassidy's office and wants to break her fingers as she listens.

Ervin Cassidy is a kindly man, but a stern one. His placid, portly demeanor belies a steely interior. "Mr. Barrington," he says, "we've been writing to you for three months, and you've been ignoring our letters and requests for payment. Our bylaws are our bylaws. Your loan is not coming from *my* pocket. This bank has investors it has to answer to. You have a collateralized note on which you cannot be more than ninety days in arrears. And you are currently at one hundred and seventeen. On top of that," he calmly continues, "you have been constantly, and I mean nearly every single month since we began servicing your loan, late with your payments. In the last forty-one months you have not paid your mortgage on time once. Sometimes you're eleven days late, sometimes forty-two, sometimes twenty-nine. But you're *always* late."

"We pay you eventually, don't we," Harry says sourly.

"Not for the last one hundred and seventeen days you haven't," Cassidy says. "A few months ago you asked me to extend you an overdraft, using the restaurant as collateral. This I did for you. That account is also thousands of dollars in arrears."

"Perhaps you can increase the overdraft," Harry says.

"Why would we do that?"

"So we can pay you back the money we owe you."

The bank manager laughs softly, almost benignly, as if he is dealing with an irrational child. "You want us to increase your overdraft so you can pay us the money you owe us? You're not even borrowing from Peter to pay Paul. You're borrowing from Peter to pay Peter."

"It's just accounting," Harry says. "Moving the debt from one place to another."

"Yes," Cassidy says. "But your debt has to be backed by the possibility of future earnings. The bank is not unreasonable, is it, to expect a small chance of being repaid?" Cassidy turns to Gina's brother. "Salvatore, when you owned two restaurants, it was possible to increase revenue above the operating expense line. But as it stands right now, your one business will barely break even in the next three to five years. You have nothing extra to pay back the bank with."

"We'll increase sales," says an unconcerned Harry.

"Mr. Barrington, let me explain to you how it works."

"I know how it works."

"The way it works," Cassidy continues, as if he hasn't been interrupted, "is first you increase sales and then you bring us your receipts and ask for a loan. Not vice versa. How would you increase your profits, may I ask? You've got two ovens and twenty tables. There is very little room for growth. You can increase your prices, but then you'll have fewer customers. It's a fine balance, running a business, which is why a high debt ratio breaks that balance, makes the whole equation untenable. I'm truly sorry."

"Mr. Cassidy," Harry says, "we don't have the money right now. But the bank has plenty of money. It's not as if you're going to go broke, or lose your business if you wait a little longer."

"That is where you're quite wrong, Mr. Barrington. Quite mistaken. If we did what you're proposing, we would indeed lose our business. And wait for what?"

Harry sighs, finally shaking his head in frustration. "Okay, fine. Go ahead and charge us a higher rate of interest on the overdraft."

"We already are. And you can't pay it. You know how I know? Because you haven't paid it. And besides, charging you more to provide you with a service that you already can't afford is doubly bad business. For you and for me. I've been doing this a long time, Mr. Barrington. Thirty-seven years. We are the First National Bank of Lawrence and we are very proud of our relationship with our customers, many of them immigrants, like your brother-in-law and your wife, who often fall on hard times. We help them as best we can—prudently. So that they don't feel overwhelmed by debt and we still make money."

"Making money is the important thing, it seems," Harry says. "That's first, isn't it?"

Ervin Cassidy ices over after hearing Harry's disrespectful tone. "Every single business in this town and in your father's town and in every town in the United States is built with bank loans that are given to families such as your own," he says, rising out of his chair. "We are the reason you have a restaurant in the first place. We are the reason your father has a thriving construction business, the reason there are roads and factories and carriages and horses. We are the reason the Panama Canal is being built. Where do you think this money comes from? The magic vault in the back? The bank has money because other people—not you, but other people—come to us and entrust it to us. They lend us *their* money for safekeeping, and then we turn around and lend their lifeblood to *you* so you can use their hard-earned savings to enrich your life. *That's* how it works. Perhaps you should take an economics class, Mr. Barrington, to acquaint yourself with the rudiments of basic business practice. In the meantime, if you'll excuse me, Mrs. Wagner is waiting outside my office. She has applied for a loan for a new ice cream stand."

"What, we're done here?" Salvo says, rising.

"Yes, Salvatore. I'm very sorry, but I'm afraid we are. If I don't see four months of mortgage payments on my desk in ten days, we will commence recovery of your business property. I will hold off calling in the overdraft to give you more time to pay, if that helps any."

The police have to be called to restrain Salvo in the public square on Essex Street. He attacks Harry, is arrested for assault and battery, and would be in jail, except Harry refuses to press charges. Salvo commands Harry to go to Herman Barrington and make it right. Harry says he will be damned before he ever shames himself again.

"You *are* damned and you have already shamed us—our entire family and my sister most of all for being the biggest fool in Lawrence."

Salvo tells his mother that he cannot live another second under the same roof as the man who has single-handedly destroyed the business he came from Sicily to build. Either Harry leaves or Salvo will. But Harry can't leave on his own. Gina has to go with him. So the choice is between Mimoo's only daughter and her one remaining son. Caught in the Gordian crossfire, she refuses to make the devil's choice. Salvo chooses for her. He packs his bags and leaves Lawrence for the North End.

That was 1908.

Antonio's was auctioned at gavel to Ned Rector, who sold it piece by piece, making off with the pizza ovens, the tables, and the silverware and reopened six months later as Ned's Mattresses and Beds, and six months after that as Ned's Burgers.

Six

"SALVO HAS NOT FORGIVEN Harry?" Ben asked. "To *this* day?"

Gina shook her head. "Would you?"

"Why didn't Salvo just partner with one of his friends in the North End?" Ben wanted to know. "It's been a few years. Banks are more forgiving than your brother. They'd lend to him again, I'm sure."

Gina shook her head. "It's unending work, running a business," she said. "Salvo learned it the hard way. To do it right, he has to do it himself. But he doesn't want to. Which is one of the reasons he gave so much control to Harry, who unfortunately happened to be the wrong man for the job. Besides, Salvo found out things about himself, too, during the fiasco. He doesn't like to be pinned down. He wants to be able to change jobs, like he changes women, and move on to the next flight of fancy. He continues to blame Harry, who certainly deserves a fair portion of the blame for what happened, but the truth is, Salvo himself is ill-suited to the daily grind of running a business. Or a marriage. He's too much of a wanderer."

"Oh, Gina."

"I know. Listen." She leaned closer. "Tell me, are they … his father and his sister … are they still upset with him over what happened? It's been so many years."

Ben also leaned forward, as if talking about difficult things required hushed voices. "All I know is that no one speaks of him. His name is never mentioned."

Gina sat back, exhaling with resignation and sadness.

The front door opened, they both turned and in the porch light stood Mimoo, helped up the stairs by Rita, the renter from the third floor.

"Who is this?" Mimoo said to Gina without preamble.

"Well, I'm going to head up," Rita said. "Your mother did well tonight. Won twenty dollars. Hit bingo three times."

"Who is this, Gina?" Mimoo repeated.

"It's Ben Shaw, Mimoo."

"Who?"

Ben stood up to greet Gina's mother. "Hello, Mrs. Attaviano."

"It's Harry's friend from years ago, Mimoo. Remember, Panama Canal?"

"I remember everything," said Mimoo, glaring at Gina and taking off her coat. "You're looking for Harry in the wrong place, young man. He's in the Correctional."

"Yes, I know," Ben said. "I drove your daughter home so she wouldn't have to take the train."

Mimoo walked past them, on her way upstairs. "Come help me," she said to Gina. "I'm going to fall down I'm so tired. Bingo this late doesn't come without a price."

Gina turned to Ben. "I have to run. Thank you so much for the ride. Sorry I kept you."

"It was my pleasure—" He was stopped by Mimoo's loud snort from the bottom of the stairs. "Nice to see you again, Mimoo. Please give my regards to Salvo."

Upstairs, the first thing Mimoo said was, "And you're doing what, exactly?"

"Harry's old friend, Mother," Gina said impatiently. "*Basta.*"

"Your brother is out gallivanting somewhere, rowdy in a roadhouse, I'm sure. Good thing he didn't come back early to see you gallivanting in your own house."

On Sunday, when Salvo did come back, barely making it in time for the start of the ten o'clock Mass, Gina leaned to her mother before the litany of supplication and whispered, "Oh, yes, Salvo is the one to judge *me*."

"Just because he lives in a glass house doesn't mean he won't throw stones."

And right after the service, barely out of St. Mary's doors, Mimoo turned to her hungover, rumpled son and said, "You'll never guess who drove your sister home from Concord yesterday."

"Do I dare guess?" said Salvo, squinting terribly in the morning sunshine and adjusting his gray serge cap so it covered his eyes.

"Ben Shaw. Remember him? Some Panama foolishness long ago. Was that boy sweet on your sister, or what?"

Salvo didn't even turn his head to Gina, who was standing tall and elegant near the entrance, saying hello to the other parishioners, smiling, friendly, cleaned up for church, in a blue gingham dress and a wool coat, both old but pressed and well kept. Salvo's parka coat was torn on one sleeve and stained with the revelry of many a Saturday night. "As long as it wasn't her suddenly sprung-from-jail husband, it's no never mind to me."

"Salvo, I don't know whether to thank you or to smack you," said Gina. "But what I must do is bid you both goodbye."

"Where are you off to?"

"Where I'm off to every Sunday," said Gina. "To visit my husband."

They sit across from each other. Roy, Harry's guard, a burly, very large black man, born and bred free in the north, and now a sentinel over the incarcerated white man, has taken a real shine to Gina, and sometimes, when he's the only one on duty, he lets Harry touch her across the partition. When she hands him the newspaper he takes it from her and then holds her hands until Roy clears his throat. They sit. Sometimes they don't say much.

Sometimes it's because there's nothing to say.

Sometimes it's because there's too much.

Today they speak almost as if there are no penumbras.

"What books did you bring me?" he asks. "I finished five days ago the two lousy ones you brought last week."

"Does lousy refer to the quantity of the books or their quality?"

"Both."

She laughs.

"They were terrible and there wasn't nearly enough of them. Why can't you bring me more? I've memorized the paper. It's gotten so desperate I actually opened the Bible Roy left on my table pretending he forgot."

"Oh, dear, things can't be that bad, *mio marito*," she says, "that you're reduced to reading the Bible."

"That's what I'm saying."

"What, you didn't like *Sons and Lovers*?"

"Not much. That Oedipal bullshit. Not for me."

"What's Oedipal?"

"Never mind."

"I never read it."

"That's fine. But just in case the rest of Lawrence's oeuvre is from the same cloth, don't bring him."

"How about *The Man Without a Country*?" she asks, teasing. "Can I bring that?"

"I know that idiot thing by heart," he says, frowning. "Why would you bring that to me here?"

"I'm joking."

"Oh."

"Has prison excised your sense of humor, Harry?"

"My irony meter is clearly down," he says. "Don't say things you don't mean. At the very least smile when you say them so I know to laugh myself."

"Okay, *tesoro*."

"And that other book you brought me, *The Seven Who were Hanged*, no more like that. I was *thisclose* to being the eighth by the time I'd finished it."

"But you asked me specifically to bring it for you!"

"Don't listen to me. The problem with it is built into the title. When you see a title like that, Gina, run the other way. The Russian angst is too depressing for a man in a cell. Everything is terrible and everyone is about to die. And then they do die. What's wrong with those Russians and their entire line of literature?"

"How about Chekhov?"

Harry is tepid toward Chekhov. "He is so tubercular. I never know when he's finished. Everything I read by him, it could all end a hundred pages earlier or a hundred later, I have no way of telling. It's like breathing."

"How about I bring you some Sherlock Holmes next week?"

"Yes," he says, brightening. "Excellent. Stay away from the melancholics. Hardy, Gide. All the Russians."

She looks down into her satchel.

"What did you bring me this week?"

"I brought you *Love Among the Chickens*."

He laughs. "I like it already," he says, taking Wodehouse from her hands. His fingers linger on hers.

"What about Oscar Wilde? *The Soul of Man Under Socialism*?" She smiles.

"You're teasing, right? Very good. But no, thank you. I've had quite enough of his anarchic blather, his and his mentor Kropotkin's. Nothing pleases them—"

"Well, Kropotkin *is* Russian."

"The least of his problems. They contradict themselves constantly. They make me pine for curfew, and we can't have that. What else?" He waits eagerly.

"Look—I sewed a new layette for one of Mimoo's housecleaning ladies who's having a baby, and with the money I made, I bought you three books you can actually keep."

He stands up with excitement, looking over the partition.

"Turgenev's *Fathers and Sons*," she says, handing the books over. "*Don Quixote*. It'll take you your full sentence to finish that one. And Joseph Conrad's *Heart of Darkness*."

He slumps back down. "I've read them all," he says. "Several times."

"They were on sale and available, and it's what I could afford."

He sighs. Minutes pass. His head tilts to stare at her as a lover might stare before a kiss.

"What are you up to this week?"

Gina opens her mouth to tell him about Ben, then closes it. Harry is chatty, more or less friendly, relaxed. His gray eyes look blue today and she knows they change color depending on his mood. Today his mood is easy. She can say many things to ruin it. Mentioning Ben would be one of those things.

"Is Salvo really back home?"

"Temporarily." She is glad for the diversion. "Until you come back."

"You smile as if it's a joke, but you and I know you're not joking."

"I'm not joking," agrees Gina, trying to suppress her smile.

When he quietly chuckles, she is so happy, and glad she hasn't mentioned Ben.

"So how is it out there?"

"The leaves are changing. It's like you love it."

"Yes. I do love the New England autumn."

They clear their throats. "Purdy says you should be out in a month or two. Definitely by Christmas."

He can barely look at her when he says, "So far away." His blinking eyes are deep with remorse. "I'm sorry I'm in here again," he says. "I've really done it this time, haven't I?"

She says nothing.

"I didn't think I was doing anything wrong. I thought I was exercising my First Amendment rights. Voicing my disapproval. What's more American than dissent?"

She wavers.

"How did I know," he continues, "that it's against the law to flaunt your free speech by blocking entrances to army recruitment stations? Who made that cretinous law?"

She keeps quiet.

"Even that would've been okay if I weren't on probation."

To that she has something to say. "You were already on probation when you went to Paterson. You should've never gone."

"Bill was paying me," Harry says, immediately less nice. "We talked about this. What did you want me to do?"

"Not go." She is also less nice. "Get another job. Tell him to stuff it. I could think of about five minutes worth of things I would have told him had he asked *me*." She pauses. "Hasn't he done enough to hurt us?"

They don't even glance at each other when she says this.

"Okay, okay." His tone softens. "Clearly I need to find other employment when I'm back outside."

That part is a fact. One of the conditions of his release that the District Attorney and Purdy have been going back and forth on is that Harry will not be allowed to come within a quarter mile of Big Bill Haywood or the IWW. Harry has been resistant, not because he wants to work for Big Bill, but because he doesn't want the government telling him where he can and can't work. No matter how many times Gina mentions it's only temporary, Harry doesn't care and doesn't want to hear it.

They change the subject. They always do. They have to. They have only two hours a week together and Gina will be damned before she ruins it with lectures and nagging. She has a lot going on in her life, but Harry only has these two hours. No point making him feel worse, when all he's got is his own thoughts and her words until the following Sunday.

"Anything special you want me to get for you next week?" she asks.

He thinks. "Maybe you can bring me some pumpkin pie."

"Some what?"

"Pumpkin pie. It's the season for pumpkins."

They don't have pumpkins in Italy. Gina's never had a pumpkin or made a pie out of it. She smiles. "Sure, *mio amore*," she says. "Anything you want. Next time I come I'll bring you pumpkin pie."

"Bring one for Roy, too," he tells her. "The other week when you brought *biscotti*, he raved to everyone how good they were. And he let me keep my light on an hour past curfew because he knows I like to read in bed."

"Okay, *tesoro*. I'll bring one for Roy, too. He's a nice man. He likes me."

"A little too much if you ask me."

She wants to touch him to reassure him, hold his hand, press his head to hers. Other things.

"Do you know," Harry says, "when I was, I don't know, eleven, twelve maybe, my father took my sister and me to a pumpkin farm, and we brought these great big pumpkins home and carved them."

"Why would you do this?"

"Carve pumpkins? I don't know. The inside of the pumpkin is what you make the pie with. It's messy, though. You'd like it." He inhales. "It's messy, just like your tomatoes."

They can barely speak after that or look at each other. Short of breath, he can't go on with his story. Somehow he does.

"After we removed the flesh from inside and carved the pumpkins, Esther decided she wanted to give me a fright, play a practical joke on me. So she cut one pumpkin in half, and placed it on top of our huge black tomcat sleeping on the grass, covering him as if he were in a clamshell and leaving him holes for eyes. We were sitting in our backyard that night, and through the eyeholes, the tomcat sees a squirrel and takes off like a horse, with the pumpkin still on top of him." He laughs as he recalls it. "It was dark, and I wasn't expecting it, everything had been so quiet, and this giant pumpkin just up and gallops across the yard, a pumpkin running after a squirrel. I must have screamed for five minutes, it was so startling and unexpected."

Gina laughs.

Harry leans back. "I don't think I ever heard my sister and my father laugh harder. My father actually cried. I had never seen that. Before or since. And then he kissed my sister and said, 'You've outdone yourself, Esther. Well played.'" Harry shrugged. "Since he never praised her for anything, she nearly cried herself. We kept trying to do it again, stage a prank that would make him laugh. But ..." he trails off. "You know."

Gina leans closer to the partition, her heart opening, squeezing shut.

"You said you were only eleven or twelve?"

"Yes."

"So your mother was still alive? Where was she?"

Harry looks down at the table, then up at the hands of the clock above Gina's head. "I don't know where she was," he says, his eyes opaque. "Not with us."

When it is time to go, she stands with the books to be returned in one hand.

"Lean forward," he says. She obeys. Harry glances behind her at Roy, reaches out and strokes her cheek, her hair, cups her face. Gina presses his fingers against her lips as they pass over her mouth.

"I'll see you next Sunday, *il mio delitto*."

"I'll see you next Sunday, my wife."

Chapter 4

THE LOVE OF AN AMERICAN GIRL

One

"I ADORE THIS HOUSE," Rose was saying to Gina about the Wayside. "Sometimes I half-wish it were still mine, still in my family. I told everyone we sold it because we couldn't stand living in it after my son died, but the truth is, George couldn't keep up with the mortgage payments, no matter how hard he worked. We *had* to sell it."

Gina listened half-attentively, one spiritual part of her listening, one mechanical part washing the floor, and one female part lamenting the sorry state of her dress.

The last part was the loudest of all.

"Did he"—she thought hard to recall Rose's words—"work hard?" Her question less to do with Rose than with her own self, her own life.

"Yes. He was a professor, he corrected other people's manuscripts on the side, he edited books, he wrote columns. He was a genius, and he never stopped working. But it just wasn't enough for this summer home and a place in Boston." Rose sighed and crossed herself. "It's better this way. I chose this—not just to serve the poor, but to be *of* the poor. And I'm still here in my beloved Wayside, where I can sleep and yet continue to do the work of the Lord." Rose gazed at Gina, scrutinized her. "In my past life when I thought I also could be a writer, like my father, I penned a story called 'The Love of an American Girl.' Have you heard of it?"

With her bare hands Gina was wringing the mop of all debris, filth, waste, medicines. "I haven't heard of it, no."

Rose followed her outside while Gina changed the water in the bucket. "Not many people have. I'm not my father, I soon learned. I don't have his gifts. In any case, in my story, the heroine is dazzling and full of virtue. But the crux of any story is to *know* when one is loved." Rose paused. Waited. When there was no response from Gina, she nudged further. "Don't you agree?"

"I don't know," Gina said, full of hesitation. "What if one thinks one is loved, but one is not?"

"I think what often happens," Rose said, "is one is loved differently from the way one expects, and it's this false judgment and subsequent disillusion that leads to so much trouble in life. Wouldn't you agree?"

Gina didn't answer. What Rose was saying didn't apply either to her physical activity or to her spiritual distance. She was rushing to finish mopping because she wanted desperately to change her dress before she had to cook and serve lunch and Ben came.

At 11 a.m. every day the bell rang five times in the tiny makeshift chapel to commemorate the five wounds of the Lord, followed by an hour of silence, during which Gina washed and cleaned and prepared food for the sick. Psalms were recited before and after meals, starting with Psalm 1, ending with Psalm 150, repeating every three days.

Have mercy on me, o God, and hide thy face from my sins.

"Gina, you know how I feel about you," Rose was saying. "You are like a divine child. But you also know how I feel about the work we do. It's uncompromising. And I'm unyielding when it comes to maintaining a very high level of servitude. The sicker our patients, the poorer and more wretched, the more I expect from the women who minister to them."

"I know that, Rose."

"I cannot force anyone to be good, it is not my inclination nor my desire. But any hint of laziness, frivolity or self-indulgence and I must ask them to seek service elsewhere."

Gina tried hard not to bow her head. "I understand."

Rose kissed her. "Do you remember you once told me you were too fond of dancing and ice cream to be a nun?"

"I don't remember saying that." It did sound like her, though.

Rose smiled. "Do you still feel that way?"

Gina frowned, slightly puzzled. "I'm married, Rose. I can hardly become a nun now."

"Are you too fond of dancing and ice cream to be a wife?"

Letting go of Rose's hands, Gina stepped away. She tried not to stagger away. "No. But I must run, I have much to do."

"This may surprise you to hear, Gina, but I myself am not a merciful woman." Rose crossed herself. "What I do is bountifully preach mercy." She paused. "And by mercy I don't mean forgiveness. I mean care for life's poorest of the poor and its most abandoned."

He drew me out of deep waters, he brought me out into a spacious place, he rescued me because he delighted in me according to the cleanness of my hands in his sight.

Rose's patients *were* the poorest of the poor, life's most abandoned. At death's door, they required nothing more than compassion and kindness. They were kept clean to the best of the nuns' abilities. Rose insisted that whatever one may have felt about the state of the sick, the only face one was allowed to show them was one of mercy and goodness, because that was what the dying required. But sometimes even the priests who came to administer last rites or to offer Communion would turn their heads and vomit before they continued to walk between the beds, so overpowering were the physical conditions that surrounded the sick.

For many months Gina had immersed herself in the works of God, as an offering, as repentance, praying for Harry to be released early, for a baby to bless their life, for a bit more money, to struggle less, to want less, to be happier. But something happened to her after Ben returned to her life. Whereas before, all she had noted about herself was her inner life, she was now made unduly conscious of the outer Gina. The woman who sewed her own clothes, who had once saved money for silk and chiffon, for lace gloves, for patent leather shoes, for bobbles and beads, gave herself a withering once-over and concluded that no woman who worked in a ward of humans that made priests retch and men faint could make herself outwardly attractive to anyone. Holiness was wonderful but did nothing for vanity. Holiness was beautiful but not externally.

Yet Ben came. He came like the professed, the novices, and the postulants. He came wearing his most dispensable clothing, calling himself Gina's orderly. Sometimes he drove up to Concord so early on Saturday morning, he got to the Wayside even before Gina. He was always full of good cheer and happy stories of Panamanian feasts and fevers. He worked side by side with her among the oppressed, carrying her pails of dirty water, searching for potatoes in the earth, taking her to a market in Lexington so she could buy vegetables and bread for dinner. He never fainted and he never retched. When one day she asked him how he did it, how he stopped himself from reacting to what even the men of the cloth could not ignore, he said he had seen things in Panama, lived through things in Panama that had given him a permanently altered outlook on life.

"I'm not a debutante, Gina," he said.

"Me either."

"That I know. But even Alice, who was one, was not one. Do you know what I mean?"

Ben often brought up Alice. As if he were trying to make Gina feel better about the road her life had taken.

"Marriage must be socially and economically endogamous," Ben said. They were cleaning the soiled pails outside in the cold brook at the back of the house.

"Excuse me? Are you allowed to say that word to women?"

He laughed. He laughed often and openly when he was with her. "It means marrying only within one's own social stratum. Alice, released from the burden of that suffocating duty by Harry's rejection, found herself a man and a life much better suited to her."

"A Texan?"

"A rancher, yes. He traveled north to her lumber mill to buy a quality haul for his ranch in Abilene. She advised him on what kind and how much. A month later he was back. He said he needed more for his stables and paddocks. She advised him on what kind and how much. A month later he was back for lumber for his rodeo. Apparently it was all too subtle for Alice. Finally he asked her to travel south with him—with her mother as chaperone, of course—so she could advise him a little more specifically." Ben laughed. "At the wedding reception, he told everyone he nearly bankrupted his father's business pretending to procure enough lumber until the girl of his dreams married him."

Gina still could not believe it. "How could Alice, the women's club, parlor lounge, piano-playing, drawing-room social debutante, marry a horseman from Texas?"

"Some pairings make no sense to the outside world, it's true."

Gina turned red and away. Harry was a dreamer, a reader. He was all head and no hands. He was unsturdy, un-Italian, but so American. It's what she loved most about him outside of their bed.

Ben continued. "The outdoors was always what Alice loved best. So she chose a life that had most of what she loved in it. Wide open spaces, horses, and a man who worked all day with his hands."

Gina was thoughtful, listening, pondering, daydreaming, even as Ben was talking.

"Excuse me, what?"

"What do you think?" Ben asked. "Do *you* have a life that has most of what you love in it?"

"I don't know." She mulled it over. "I don't own a lumber yard like Alice, so I don't keep a ledger of such things. My life has many things that I love in it." But her brow tightened across her strong forehead, a darkness shadowed her happy eyes. She wanted to push the curls away from her perspiring face, but her hands weren't clean. She would not admit to Ben that her life had things she did not like in it. Lawrence. Missing pennies. Missing husband. And it sorely and gapingly lacked the one thing she wanted most. A tiny child so she could be a mother.

"What about you?"

"What about me?"

"Is Panama what you love most?"

Ben shrugged as if he didn't want to answer, didn't want to tell her the truth. "The work is what I love the most. I might like Panama better if it were a suburb of Boston and didn't give me muscle tremors, a vicious rash, and life-ending fevers."

"Yes, that's hardly appealing."

"A suburb of Boston," Ben added slowly, "perhaps like Concord."

The valleys of the sea were exposed and the foundations of the earth laid bare at the blast of breath, O Lord, from your nostrils.

At the Massachusetts Correctional, Gina wants to tell Harry about Alice, about the horses and the prairie, but doesn't know how to bring up or explain the provenance of this newfound knowledge. So she doesn't.

She wants to ask Harry if his life contains most of what he loves in it, but she doesn't know how to ask. It seems cruel to ask him this while he chafes in prison, thin, drawn, pale, with a distant look in his rainy gray eyes, a man physically there but a million miles away in his soul. She wants to ask him where he wants to be, but doesn't dare. She is afraid. What if his answer is, not with you? Because she is right here, yet his eyes are glazed, as if they're recalling another time, another place.

She thinks this as they sit. But what he says to her confounds her, makes her doubt her own perception of everything.

"What's wrong with you? Why do you seem as if you're a million miles away?" asks Harry.

"I'm here, *tesoro*," she hastens to assure him, her eyes clearing, smiling at him. "Right here."

She hands him the newspaper and watches him as he leafs through it.

"In 1911," Harry says, "Max Eastman was asked to help restore a nearly defunct political magazine. He turned it around, and is now releasing an issue a month. You should take a look at it. It's called *The Masses*."

"Why would I want to take a look at it?"

"It's good. It's political. It's funny. John Reed, Sherwood Anderson, Lincoln Steffens write for it."

She waits. She knows him well, she knows more is coming.

"In Paterson," he goes on, "I wrote some speeches and articles for the strike pamphlets. Max liked them. He said I had a gift. This week I got a letter from him. He said when I get out he'd like to get me on board. As an editor or a writer. Better than working for Bill, no? From *your* perspective, I mean."

From her perspective, Gina sits on the side of the table from which, come two o'clock, she can get up, walk through the doors and out into the blinding sunshine. That's *her* perspective. She can take a bus and go to the sea, she can buy gloves, listen to the radio, drink a cold beer, go to the library to borrow a book and to the butcher to buy a sausage. She can take a train to anywhere in the country.

"Yes," Gina says. "From my perspective anything is better than working for Big Bill."

"Anything?" He smiles. She wonders what else he's got in store for her. Instead of telling her, he lowers his head into the newspaper, and reads to her stories weaved from fine print as she listens and watches him.

"Why do you read so much?" she asks in the lull. "What are you looking for?"

"The meaning of life," he replies. "Isn't that what everyone is looking for? Isn't that what you're looking for?"

Gina doesn't reply. She wants to tell him that she thought she had found hers, but doesn't. Until she becomes a mother, she can no longer answer. Immigrants don't usually ask themselves these questions. They haven't the time. Yet her father who brought her to America by the sheer force of his longing and his passion demands nothing less from her. For her dead father she will ask herself this question over and over until the answer comes to her by the awful grace of God.

"Like many men," Harry says, "Henry David Thoreau included, I wish to discover the essential parts of life."

"Me too," says Gina.

"I don't want to miss them while I'm toiling like the worker bees in the mills."

Is there much danger of that kind of toil, she wants to ask, but doesn't. "Are you looking for the essential parts while you're on the picket lines in New Jersey?" she asks instead.

"Clearly. I don't want to discover when it comes time for me to die that I haven't lived."

Me neither, Gina thinks, but doesn't say, doesn't dare say.

"But you live in prison," she says quietly. "Away from me." Even quieter.

"Here I am simplicity itself," he says. "I have so few needs, so few wants." He catches his breath when he says it, almost as if to stop himself. She waits. He is silent. "I have *some* wants," he says, almost whispers.

"Me too," she says, almost whispers.

"But I am pared down to my most basic elements. I've got to rise above the purely elemental, don't you agree?"

She doesn't know if she agrees. She fears she doesn't. She tries not to glance above his head where the hands of the clock are stopped motionless, as if dead.

May the Lord remember all your sacrifices and accept your burnt offerings. May he give you the desire of your heart.

Two

GINA HAD NEVER SEEN anyone get as animated and lost in the topic of conversation as Ben when he was talking about his years in Panama.

No, that wasn't entirely true. Harry would get the same intense, far-away look, maintain the same consuming focus when they would talk about harmonizing the world, remaking it into the image of what he thought it should be and not what it was. And though she still, as always, admired Harry's learned passion, she had heard all she could stand for the time being about the Reeds and the Debs and the Haywoods. What she wanted to hear about was Panama.

"All forest and mountains. Impassable forest combined with tropical temperatures. And mountains like a spine. I should've just thrown up my hands. We couldn't get a canal from north to south to connect. We excavated, we dammed off the Chagres, we built a lake. We worked from two seas inland, from Cristobal to Miraflores into the center of the country, we were diligent as beavers, and when we designed and built the concrete locks that moved the sea levels up and down, I thought there was nothing harder than that or more accomplished than that. Until we got to the Continental Divide. There was no river, no water, no field, no stream. It was just mountain." Ben shook his head.

Gina shook hers. "I don't know how you did it. I still don't understand it."

"Me neither."

"But seriously."

"We blew it up."

She laughed.

"I'm not being metaphorical. Or rhetorical. We actually blew it up."

"You blew up a mountain?"

"We drilled holes, placed explosives in the holes, and detonated the mountain, yes. After the rubble settled, we used enormous steam-powered shovels to load the loose rock onto freight trains which carted it away to landfills."

Gina exclaimed in frightened but impressed astonishment. "You must have had to drill a lot of holes to make a valley in a mountain, no?"

"Six hundred holes a day," Ben said. "We drilled the holes and detonated twice a day. Then the trains would come. So we had to build a railroad and lay new tracks constantly as the valley got longer and wider."

"Oh, my word. How long did this valley become?" It was called the Culebra Cut.

"Nine miles."

"Ben!"

"What? Too long or too short?"

"Impossible!"

"That's what everyone said to my boss, Colonel Gaillard, the most gallant and patient of men. What you're doing, it will never work, they said to him. It had been my honor to work with that dedicated, quiet man side by side, but I can't tell you how often he expressed his doubts to me, how often he would say, This is just a fool's errand, isn't it, Mr.

116

Shaw, what we're attempting here? To move a mountain to let ships pass through? And I would reply, despite my gravest doubts, no, Colonel Gaillard. We must succeed, and so we shall."

"The newspapers were merciless," Gina said. "It will never work, they wrote, just like it didn't with the French. It will cost tens of thousands of lives, like it did with the French. This is a waste of human and material resources."

Ben sighed, as if even success in the present was not sufficient to gloss over the monumental crises in the past. "It was the Culebra Cut that had felled the French." He shrugged. "They were trying to excavate too high. Sixty meters above sea level was too high for the valley. We made it only twelve feet above. That was better."

"Not good, but better?"

"Not good, but better. This is one of the reasons I'm cautious and not yet fully optimistic. I know what it took. And that was before the landslides."

"The what?"

"Oh, yes," Ben said. "We at Army Corps told everyone to beware of the landslides. Gaillard was very afraid of them. But the International Board of Engineers overseeing the project decreed we had nothing to worry about. They had deemed the Divide sufficiently stable. Except they didn't count on water from the rains infiltrating a previously impregnable mountain. This, of course, caused a weakening and then a mass wasting of half a million cubic yards of clay."

"Ben!"

"Oh yes. And this clay was too soft to be excavated by our steam shovels."

"Like a mud volcano." Gina recalled the mighty and fearsome Etna, what it was like living under the volcanic threat her entire childhood. Yet she didn't feel as afraid then as she sometimes felt now in her folk Victorian on Summer Street.

Ben glanced at her approvingly. "Except we can't have a tropical glacier made of mud lying in the path of our ocean liners, can we?"

"Mud lying in the path of civilization? Certainly not. So what did you do?"

"Nothing." He shrugged. "What could we do? We climbed the mountain, sluiced the clay down with water from great heights, and continued detonating."

She was thoughtful. "But won't water keep getting into the rock? How are you going to keep the torrential rains from coming? Are you going to control the skies as well as the seas?"

"Clearly we're not. This will continue to be a problem."

"I read that just last month the canal closed for a week because of another landslide."

"Yes, the canal will continue to close intermittently so the falling debris can be cleared. No way around it."

She patted his arm affectionately, and quickly withdrew when she realized that etiquette had been breached.

"I heard the valley is going to be renamed after your general?"

"Colonel."

"What's the difference?"

Ben laughed. "Right. But yes, next year it'll be called the Gaillard Cut."

"Such a shame he didn't live long enough to see the canal completed," Gina said. David Gaillard died of a brain tumor in 1913.

Ben stopped smiling. "I even grew a bushy mustache in his honor. I shaved it before I returned home," he added when she stared at the smooth skin between his nose and mouth. "He was a West Point man. Which may explain why he succeeded where others had failed."

She resisted the impulse to touch him again, though he looked exhausted by the exertions of his memories. "You certainly did make the dirt fly, didn't you?"

They walked on, lost in their thoughts. They were headed back to the Wayside after a three-mile excursion to buy a few apples.

"So was it worth it?" she asked.

"Was what worth it?"

"The toil, the sacrifice of blood and men, time away from home, sickness, misery. Are you crowned in glory? I mean, from my perspective, it seems a monumental achievement, almost like a miracle. But what do you think?"

"From an engineering and technological standpoint, without a doubt," he said. "And no one but us could've done it, by the way. It was the American heavy machinery that made it happen, and we only had the steam shovels and the trains and the excavators because we spent the last sixty years building railroads across this nation. So in that regard, to build the canal through fog and mountain, to dam rivers, to raise the seas, to divide the Divide, it *is* a feast of civilization. But we didn't build it just to build it. We built it so it could change the path of mankind. And perhaps it's too soon to answer your question—was it worth it? First we must gauge the impact it'll have on the world, on war, on the world at war, on the economies and standard of living of distant countries, on the living conditions and life span of sailors and navies. Clearly I hope that the answer is yes. But ask me again in fifteen years. If I haven't keeled over by then from the mosquitoes and the sandflies."

"Let's shake on it," said Gina. But she did not extend her roughened hand, even in jest. And he knew she wouldn't, for he made no movement toward her. Only his eyes gleamed at the possibility of being in touch with her in fifteen years. Well, why not, reasoned Gina. It was over fifteen years ago when they had first met, and here they were, though under vastly different circumstances.

"Why don't we take a drive to a pumpkin farm next Sunday afternoon?"

"Why would I want to go there?"

"Because it might be an enjoyable way to spend a few hours. We can go pumpkin picking. There might be hot mulled cider. Sometimes they have sack races. We could race and beat the very small children. You get to weave your own basket. You learn to make pumpkin butter."

"Ugh."

"Apple butter?"

"Better."

"There is a corn maze."

"I don't like mazes. I always get lost."

"I never get lost. You can come with me."

She shook her head. "I don't know. I have so much work at Rose's. We've taken too long today as it is. We walked nearly to Walden Pond! We haven't been very good workers on Sundays, I'm afraid."

"You're right. But even the good Lord rested on Sunday."

Feebly she protested. "But even on the Sabbath you have to take care of the sick. The Lord didn't rest when there was work to be done, did He? And … Rose has been chiding me for my absent-mindedness, for my derelictions. I don't want to displease her. It's like displeasing God."

"Come on," Ben said. "The world is not a sad and solemn place." He took hold of her calloused hand. "Don't fret. Be glad like the belle of Belpasso. Be glad in the trees and the silence. Come to the maze with me."

"You know there is nothing like that we can do except dream it." She had been soaking her hands in milk every night to lessen the visible hurt of her work. Perhaps Ben didn't notice they still felt like sandpaper.

"We can do anything," he said. "For a few hours on Sunday, even the weary can sing in the trees. Even monkeys eat red bananas and have bliss."

"Ben …"

"Don't Ben me. Just say you'll come with me."

Three

SUNDAY FROM NOON TO TWO.

Harry asks if she brought him the newspaper.

Gina hands him the newspaper.

He leafs through it purposefully. He is clean-shaven. When she asks why he always shaves, he says they make him shave on Sundays. It's God's day, they tell him. It's also visitors' day. They want me to look my best for you, with my prison pajamas and my clean-shaven face.

She wants to ask if she looks her best for him. She wears a white crepe de chine blouse and a plaid fitted skirt. He likes it best when she wears fitted styles to emphasize on her the things that he used to murmur he loved. Her tapered waist. Her long arms and legs. Her slender hips. Her high breasts. Her smooth neck like royalty's, the throat he loves to lay his lips upon.

His gray eyes are not full of bliss. They're sad and solemn, and they barely glance at her as he reads, as he holds out his hand for a smoke, the ring gone from his finger a long time. There are scrapes and scratches on his knotted knuckles she hasn't seen before. She wants to reach across the partition and take his hand, but he is holding the newspaper.

The hour passes. Another conjugal Sunday with Harry. Like Mass earlier in the day: the liturgy, the supplication, the sermon, the presentation of gifts, the laments. The dry Communion. The guard calls time. Gina stands for Harry, as earlier she stood for Jesus, and collects her bag.

He stares at the newspaper for another moment. Then he gets up too.

I'll see you next Sunday, okay, *mio marito*? she says. Be well. She bows her head.

Don't forget to bring me the newspaper.

Of course. I won't forget.

Last week you forgot.

Ah. Yes. I'm sorry. I won't forget.

Is it cold out? He glances at the light coat she has put on, the thin crepe beige wool.

It's crisp. Not too cold yet.

The leaves?

They're falling.

Mimoo?

She is good.

Are you still with Rose?

On the weekends, yes.

He is silent for just one moment too long. You don't work in these clothes, do you? he says. His eyes are on her white silk blouse.

No, I change to come see you.

121

He nods. You always look so fresh, as if you just ran in from outside.

I did, she says, run in from outside.

They stand face to face, the table, the barrier between them. They blink at each other, wary, affectionate, sorrowful.

Have you heard from Purdy?

Not yet, she says. But last time I saw him, he said it all looked good for Christmas.

Now it's really time for her to go. His hand squeezes into a fist.

So what words of wisdom does our holy Rose have for me this week?

Gina puts on her hat, ties the silk ribbons under her chin. He doesn't take his eyes off her.

There can be art and love, Rose says, *but art and economics are mutually exclusive.*

Harry nods, as if he approves. But not economics and war, he says. Because millions of boys are about to be slaughtered for economics. Perhaps someone will draw a picture of the carnage. Then they can call it art.

She turns to leave. He turns to leave. At the door she turns to glance at him one last time. He has already turned. She sees his eyes on her, profound, somber, unwilling to let her go. She raises her gloved fingers to her lips and blows him a lingering kiss. He disappears through the steel-reinforced door. Slowly she leaves too, flagellating herself with another thing Rose said: *Those whose hands are pure don't need to glove them.*

Because the pumpkin farm and the corn maze await.

Four

WHILE THE SUGAR MAPLES in Concord looked as if they were on fire under the sun, and Gina finished her Saturday duties at the Wayside, she changed into a slim, embroidered, above the ankle, rust-colored crepe day dress with a lace collar. It had a black velvet belt and silk appliqué. Her nails were painted a rust color also. Her wavy hair was piled expertly, fake-casually atop her head. She put on gold hoop earrings and wore bracelets on her wrists. She covered herself with a wool cape and walked out through the gate and into the street where Ben was waiting.

They went for an evening walk into town, where they found a small restaurant with hay bales at its doors. They walked in like a gentleman and a lady. He held the door open for her, took her cape, her hat, her gloves. Gina could not remember the last time she and Harry had the money to go out together for an evening. She didn't want to remember.

It couldn't be true, she thought, as the server pulled her chair away from the table to allow her to sit, that since Harry's all-consuming, life-transforming pursuit of her back in 1905, she had not been to a restaurant for dinner? She pressed her lips together to banish the memory and the tears of self-pity that weren't far behind.

There was candlelight and fine china. Voices were hushed and the laughter delicate. She wanted to tell Ben that no Italian she knew spoke so low and laughed so daintily, but didn't. When they ordered, she spoke so low, and when he made a joke, she laughed so daintily. During aperitifs Ben asked her why she kept herself in such check. "That's not how I remember you."

"I'm grown up now."

"Yes, but you were a girl on fire when I knew you. Where is the Sicilian?"

She didn't reply. She didn't want to tell him how hard she worked on herself to hide the Sicilian parts—the loud boisterous voice, the flailing gesticulations, the instant emotions, the lilting accent—lest they expose her to all the world as an immigrant. She didn't want to tell Ben how desperately she wished to be not an immigrant, but like the girls she envied, the girls from Harry and Ben's world.

Girls like Alice.

The way Ben knowingly blinked at her, it was as if he already knew.

"You've become so proper, why?"

She said nothing.

"You want to be like the girl he left behind, the girl he left—for you?"

She flushed. "It's not like that."

"What is it like then?"

"Not like that."

"So explain it to me, like I explained the Culebra Cut to you."

"I'm just grown up, that's all. Sicily is the child part of me."

He shook his head. "You've taken deportment and speech lessons. You've learned how to dress, how to laugh, how to speak. You did it all to hide who you are."

"Harry doesn't much care for the loud Italian," Gina told Ben. "For the flashes of my Old World self." Except for the times he wanted nothing from her *but* her Sicilian flame. Oh God! Could there be one exchange this entire evening, just a merciful *one*, when she wasn't recalling her husband after every sentence?

"I feel as if I should go visit him," Ben said. "It seems wrong not to. We were such good friends. I want him to know there are no hard feelings. Do you think I should?"

"It might make him feel worse," she said. "Point up the stark contrast between your freedom and his incarceration."

"That's true. But not to visit him even once …"

She agreed. "His mood is not great. It won't be like your old times."

"Few things are. And, why should he be in a swell mood? He's in prison." Ben sighed as they sipped their wine and buttered their bread. "What's he reading nowadays? Maybe I can get you a book to take to him."

"If it's in Russian, then yes."

"He's reading *Russian*? Good God of Jacob, why?"

"At first he wanted nothing to do with the Russian writers, but Max Eastman and John Reed have been in touch with him recently and now he's all about learning to speak Russian like them."

"Your husband is trying to be like John Reed?" Ben laughed. "So just like you, he's trying to become someone else?" He eyed her with affection. "Would you like Harry better if he were a Russian-speaking Bostonian? I've never heard of such a combination."

Gina laughed, too, and said she liked Harry just fine without his ever speaking a word of Russian. "But then I've never heard of an explosive-detonating Bostonian either, so there you have it."

"Ah, okay, but the question is, do you like me better now that I'm an explosive-detonating Bostonian?"

She knew it was a rhetorical question that didn't require an answer, but if she absolutely had to answer, she would admit that the answer was yes.

During peach cobbler, Ben brought up Lawrence.

"Gina, why do you always keep running somewhere else other than Lawrence when you're not working? From the beginning you'd sneak out on trains and come to Boston, first for my mother and her radicals, then for Eugene Debs and Emma Goldman. Now you come here to Concord. I'm not saying you don't work for a noble cause with Rose. All I'm saying is, isn't there a noble cause in Lawrence? Why are you always running somewhere else? Or am I plain wrong about this?"

She thought for a long time. She finished her cobbler before she spoke.

"You're not wrong," she said at last. "I used to fool myself into thinking it was for this reason, or that. And even to come here, I mean, Harry is here, and—"

"Gina, that's not why."

"No, it's not," she agreed. "Truth be told I want nothing to do with the immigrants. It's terrible to say."

"It's not."

"It is. Like I'm not grateful. But I'm just so bone-tired of them! I'd prefer to live anywhere but Lawrence. It is so ethnic—the stores, the smells. Like the North End, but worse. All I want is to live somewhere people aren't drying their washing outside their front windows and making their mozzarella fresh on the street. When I come to Concord it's so peaceful. Even robins don't sing too loud here. Everyone is polite, no one raises their voice, and on the benches in town men are reading calmly under the umbrellas, while nannies push the babies up and down. The women talk *sotto voce*, and the men take off their hats when a woman approaches. There is something classy about that. It's so staunchly American." She paused.

"And what else?"

"And ... you couldn't imagine twenty thousand women stampeding down the Concord streets, trampling each other without any regard for anyone's safety or security, could you? Spitting, hollering, breaking windows, kicking the men, flailing on the ground in a temper tantrum that lasts sixty-three days."

"No," Ben said. "I can't imagine it."

"That must be it." Gina took a long, lingering sip of her dessert wine. "I want to live in a place where Bread and Roses is as distant as the stars."

Ben stopped driving her back to Lawrence on Saturday nights. Their dinners would run too late, and she had to be back in Concord early the next morning for the ringing of the five bells and for Harry. It made no sense to do all that driving, her to Lawrence, Ben to Boston. She started staying regularly overnight at the Wayside and Ben rented a room at the Ridge Bed and Breakfast down Lexington Road as it wound down a steep hill, around a field, a stream and a meadow, away from town, from Rose, from Harry.

One Sunday in November Gina didn't visit Harry. The next Sunday she told him she had been sick, things weren't right, she hoped it would pass.

If October was a month for painted leaves, then November was a month for cloaking.

In December, Gina went to see Elston Purdy, and was shocked to learn that the judge presiding over Harry's case was adamant: his sentence having already been commuted from five years to two, Harry was not getting out early.

"But you said ..."

"That's what they told me. I think they changed their minds because of the war. They don't want troublemakers on the streets. Nothing but a headache for the police."

"Not even for Christmas?" She tried not to sound despondent. "What do I tell him? Oh God. Even the Germans and the French declared a ceasefire for Christmas."

"Perhaps your husband should've been a Frog or a Kraut then. His bad luck is to be an American who wants to wreak havoc *here* because the Frogs and the Krauts are having a fist-fight *there*."

"Are your loyalties divided?" Harry asks Gina on a cold December Sunday after she relates to him the awful news from Purdy about the parole. At first he is so upset he can't even talk about it.

"What?" She stumbles in her speech, trembles.

He stares at her petulantly. "What's the matter with you? I meant, do you wish your home country Italy was on Germany's side?"

"Why in the world would I wish this? I'm an American now. And we're not at war."

"Yet. Did you march against the war last Saturday as you promised me you would?"

"Quietly, but yes," she says. "I was a good anti-war American, me and Emma Goldman and fifteen hundred others. Do you care that you and she sound exactly the same when you talk about this war?"

"There are no anarchists or socialists when it comes to imperialist wars," he says. "Everyone should be on the same side."

"You're lucky I wasn't arrested like you," she tells him. "Then where would we be? Who'd visit us?"

"I don't know," he says. "You barely visit me."

She glides over his words as if she hasn't heard him.

"Apparently the arrests are getting more common and the convictions harsher. The constables were quite angry with us."

"How angry? ... Lawrence angry?"

They stop speaking, even looking at each other. What more is there to say after that? When the time comes, she leaves, almost runs, without telling him a single piece of Rose's wisdom for the week, and he doesn't ask her for one.

Five

"BEN, HOW IS IT that you didn't find yourself a nice Panamanian girl and settle down?"

127

"Who says I didn't?"

They were on Broadway in Lawrence walking between rows of Christmas trees. Gina was determined to make this a good Christmas for her mother. Salvo was in between girls, and the intemperate mother of his child had found a fisherman from Maine and moved to Acadia, taking Mary with her. Salvo was drowning his sorrows at the local tavern and with the local girls. Gina invited Ben for Christmas, but he had to spend it with his own mother. "If only to keep her from getting herself arrested for her anti-war fervor. I keep warning her they're about to pass the Espionage Act. No more small infractions for civil disobedience. Every cross word against the war is about to be called high treason. Does Mother listen to me? Never has, never will. I have to do what I can to save her from herself."

But Gina needed his help tonight carrying the tree, so Ben was helping her.

"Where is this girl?" she asked.

"Which girl are you talking about?"

"Ha!"

"Believe it or not, you have to be quite careful with the girls in Panama, too," Ben said. "Their fathers and brothers carry lethal weapons. It's almost like Sicily."

"Who would think?" she said with a delighted chortle. "Everywhere you go in the world, silly men keep trying to protect their daughters and sisters."

"Do you know why?"

"Because only men know so well what men are like?"

"Exactly!" They both laughed.

They found a tree, not too large, not too small, just right. Ben paid for it, and they each grabbed an end and walked from Essex to Summer Street carrying it between them through the twinkling evening. December was a good month to walk in Lawrence. There was no washing on the streets. It was crowded, the Christmas lights were up, music played from the open shops, people were happily buying gifts.

"There *is* a girl waiting for me back in Panama," Ben said. "But she doesn't want to live here, and I'm not sure I want to live there." He paused, catching a breath. Gina, too, was panting. The tree was heavy. "She still writes me."

"Why wouldn't she?"

They struggled to get the tree inside, broke off several of the branches, then trimmed it in her small parlor room near the porch window. "Is she a nice girl, Ben? What's her name?"

"Ingersol. She's nice."

"Is she pretty?"

"No, I prefer my women deeply unattractive," Ben said. "Of course she's pretty." Smiling, he recalled her. "In Panama the women have a very natural look to them. But they wear a lot of gold jewelry."

"Real gold?" She jangled the bracelets Harry had given her long ago.

"I don't know about that. But their dress, called the *pollera*, is all white, and has gold accents on the hem and around the puffy sleeves. It's very feminine. Different from here. The dress is always white, for purity, for innocence, I guess, but it's got ruffles everywhere, and gold buttons and in the back there's a train almost like a peacock tail." He shook his head in amusement. "So yes white, but a come-hither-and-marry-me white."

"So the best kind?"

"Not if you don't want to get married."

Gina nudged him lightly. "You're funny. So what do you eat for your Christmas meal in Panama? Maybe I can make it for you here next time you come."

"Can you make chicken *tamales*?"

She didn't know what those were.

"*Arroz con pollo*?" he asked. "Rice with chicken. *Pavo*? That's turkey. *Relleno*? Stuffing. Something called *Puerca asada pernil*, a meat dish? Eggnog. Lots of fruit." He grinned widely. "Bananas, red and yellow."

"You're funny with the bananas. Did you say eggnog?"

"Eggnog like you've never had in your life."

"Well, certainly, that's true, since I've never had eggnog."

They were done with the tree and with dinner. Mimoo was upstairs with Rita listening to the radio in Rita's attic apartment, and Gina and

Ben had a few moments to themselves with tea and honey cake before he had to drive back.

"You've never had *this* eggnog. It's called *ron ponche*. Rum punch."

She got up and went to the cupboard to get out a pitcher and two glasses. "Do I have any of the ingredients? Maybe I can make some for you tonight."

"Let's see." He went to stand by her at the counter. "Do you have sweetened condensed milk?"

"Yes."

"Evaporated milk?"

She pulled down three cans.

"Eggs? We'll need six of them."

She got out a half-dozen eggs.

"Nutmeg? We don't absolutely need it. I'll bring some next time I come. What about rum?"

She found some rum hiding in the back of a cupboard, from the old days of Joe and Arturo. And Angela. Days long passed. Nowadays Arturo was writing love poetry to another lucky girl in Washington State and Smiling Joe owned a fruit orchard in San Clemente, California. Angela was at St. Mary's.

Ben combined the ingredients together, stirred them vigorously, poured the concoction into the glasses. They clinked.

"Merry Christmas."

"Merry Christmas."

She drank.

"Ben," she said, pupils dilating, eyes widening. "I don't think you should drive home tonight after drinking this. You won't be able to see straight. I'll barely be able to make it upstairs to my bedroom."

"Yes, I know. I told you. Good, isn't it?"

"Quite good."

"But don't worry. If you fall I'll carry you upstairs."

"Upstairs to my bedroom?"

He said no more and she said no more. They stood quietly side by side, leaning against the counter, sipping their eggnog.

"Can I ask you something?" he said.

"Should we have more to drink before you do?"

"What do Salvo and Mimoo think of me picking you up, bringing you home, having dinner here, being around?"

Gina swayed a little.

"I ask because Salvo especially doesn't seem to mind. And Mimoo is crotchety, but she is like that even with you and we know she loves you, so …"

"Yes. You're right about Mimoo. And Salvo would prefer Harry stay in prison for life, so he's just peachy with it. But they do loudly judge me when you're not around."

"Tell them I'm your friend, Gia."

"They know. I told them. I like my friends, Ben."

"Yes, me too."

I need my friends, she wanted to tell him, having drunk too much eggnog, but didn't. "You're sure you can't spend Christmas with us?" She smiled. "I'll make you *tamale fritos chickita con flan* or whatever you said."

"What red-blooded man could say no to that? But my only living parent would disown me. I don't want Harry and me to have *that* in common, too."

They glanced at each other and away. Swaying, she held on to the counter. He didn't finish his drink. He left soon after, wisely, but not before he bent and kissed the palms of her hands, one after the other, pressing his warm, eggnog-moistened lips into them for a long moment.

Six

"FAIRYLAND POND HAS BEEN frozen solid over a month!" Ben exclaimed. "Want to go ice skating?"

"Go do what?"

January 1915 was cold like Gina didn't remember ever being cold. For many reasons told and untold she liked being in Concord on the weekends. Told: because Rose kept the house warm for her sick patients, while in Lawrence, she and Mimoo couldn't afford the heating bills. So unless the stove was on, there was no heat.

Reasons untold: "Ice skating!"

Ben smiled happily, showing her an open bag that contained two pairs of lace-up boots with blades on the bottom. It was a Saturday afternoon and they were done with Rose's work early.

"What are those?"

"Ice skates."

She took one skate out of the bag, examined it, frowned. "You want me to put these on and go stand on a pond?"

"Not stand, skate."

"Ben, there is something about me you probably don't know," Gina said, carefully replacing the skate in the bag. "I was born and raised in Sicily. You clearly have never heard of Sicily, but it's a very beautiful island in the *Mediterranean* Sea. The southern part of this sea borders *Africa*. I'm not sure how much you know about world geography, but Africa transects the *equator*. Italians don't have ice. Italians don't skate. We swim."

Ben was unperturbed. "Too cold for swimming."

"Yes," she agreed heartily. "Too cold to be outside at all. How about you wait fifteen minutes, let me finish up here, and we walk next door? I'll make a nice cup of mulled apple cider and we can sit by the fire, warm up, and talk about books?"

"We can do that after we skate." He took hold of her wrist, squeezing it lightly. "Come with me. It'll be fun."

"Nothing done in subfreezing temperatures on ice, wearing knives on your feet can ever be considered fun."

He parked his car on Walden Street and they inched their way down the steep woodsy paths of Hapgood-Wright Forest to Fairyland Pond. They stood for a moment and stared through the white-covered trees down deep into the clearing where dozens of children and couples glided on an icy shimmering oval.

"Told you," he said. "Fun."

"Look, that poor child just fell."

"And got back up again and skated."

Gina pretended to be trepidatious, but secretly she was thrilled.

"Is it really called Fairyland?" she asked as they made their way down the hill.

"Rumor is," Ben told her, "the Alcott and the Emerson children named it. Ask Rose later. She would know. She seems to know everything. Now come. Stop delaying. You're walking deliberately slow."

"It's steep. I'm being cautious. You don't want me to fall, do you?"

"I suppose not."

She mulled over his answer. "How thick is that ice?"

"Not at all," he replied. "On the plus side, it's not that deep."

"Ben!"

Getting the skates on her feet was an ordeal, but nothing compared to what it was like when she finally stepped out onto the ice. Instantly she went down, her feet sliding out from under her.

A laughing Ben helped her up, but as soon as he let go, she fell again. After that, she sat on a bench near an old toothless woman with a cane and watched Ben skate around the pond by himself waving to her as he spiraled in circles.

"Come on, try again," he kept calling.

She kept shaking her head. "When did you learn to skate like that?"

"I grew up in New England. Everybody skates."

"Not everybody. Not Harry."

Ben smiled. "Oh, indeed Harry. He's an excellent skater. Better than me. He and I played hockey together in Barrington when we were kids."

"Harry played *hockey*?" She was dumbfounded. "You are talking about Harry, my husband, right?"

"You think all he does is read books?" He helped her off the bench, leading her onto the ice.

"Ben, all he does *is* read books." She tried not to put too grim a point on it.

"Well, before he became a bookworm, he was quite the skater," said Ben, holding her hand tight. "Now, wait, wait—don't do what you're doing."

"What am I doing?" she said, falling.

"Falling." He picked her up again. "Wait! No, don't do that—Gina, look at me," he said, turning her to face him. "Keep your knees slightly

133

bent, you're not walking, you're gliding; tilt your body forward, arms at your sides, slightly out, and now ... bend and push, with alternating feet. Bend and push with your right, then bend and push with your left. Look at my feet."

"You just told me to look at *you*."

"Okay, but now look at my feet. Watch. Don't worry, if you fall, I'll catch you. On first bounce, promise. Come!"

He held her hand and she tried. After another half a dozen slips and falls, she almost succeeded in standing up on the ice for five or six seconds. Ben was so balanced, so graceful on his skates, and he laughed at her as if he didn't understand how someone couldn't instantly grasp gliding on a quarter-inch metal edge over a sheet of ice.

She clutched his hand and pretended it was for balance.

And he didn't let go and pretended it was for safety.

She did it! She moved one foot and slid forward and then the other and slid forward some more. She was so happy she clapped—and promptly fell again.

"I told you not to let go," Ben said, both arms under hers, helping her up.

They were on the ice for over two hours. He had to drag her away after it got dark. The town had strung up white lights on the bare trees around the pond, and Gina thought it was magical, like skating on white diamonds. She wished they could stay.

On the way to dinner, and at dinner, all Gina could talk about was the skating. "You were right. I admit that was a *lot* of fun. But I still don't understand how you do the things you do—how do you skate backward, without falling?" Her nose, her cheeks, her hands were still cold; she didn't care. "It's amazing. You're amazing on that ice. I like watching you." She became more sedate. "I had a good time. Where did you get the skates? Maybe ..." she broke off.

Ben watched her joyfully, from across the candlelit table, his head tilted forward. "Maybe what? We can go again? Maybe we can get you your own pair of skates?"

"How about tomorrow?"

She dreamed about the ice while they shared a slice of warm apple pie.

"What do you think the ice is doing when no one is on it? Like now?"

"What is the *ice* doing? I suppose it's just sitting there under the trees getting more icy."

"Do you think the lights are still on? Or does an orderly come around and turn them off?"

"I don't know." Ben thought for a moment, chewing his lip. "What are you asking me? After dinner, what? Do you want to go and see if the lights are still on?"

She almost clapped. "But no, no—I can't. I can't walk down those woods in the dark. We'll wait." She was disappointed. "But the lights won't be on in the daytime. We won't see them."

"So let's go now."

"Where does the electricity come from to light them?"

"I think they're kerosene lights."

"Oh." She deflated. "So they must burn out. When the kerosene oil runs out, the lights turn off." The secret of the magic lights revealed, she sank in her chair.

They went for a walk through the town park after dinner. The paths were still lit up by the kerosene lamps in the snow-covered trees.

"If only there were a small pond here," she said, "we wouldn't have to walk down deep into that grisly forest."

His hand on her forearm tightened. "There *is* a small pond here," he said.

"There isn't!"

Ben knew about these things, about taverns and ice rinks and ponds all over Concord, and of course he was right. It was a tiny pond, a glorified puddle, and the lights didn't twinkle, they were dim in the distance as he laced up her skates, laced up his, and led her onto the frozen milk. She laughed and glided. She couldn't believe she had joy again and at night-time too. They were alone. She stumbled and fell and he caught her, their woolen coats snowy and icy, with mittens on their hands and hats on their heads. He stood close while she was still laughing and then took off his hat and held it in his hand.

"Why did you take off your hat?" she asked.

"Because," he replied quietly, nearly whispering, "no gentleman can kiss a true lady without first taking off his hat."

"Oh," she breathed, inaudibly.

Bareheaded, Ben leaned forward and kissed her. Their lips weren't icy, their breath wasn't icy. Her legs went out from under her, she lost her balance and fell and he fell too, the hat slipping out of his gloved hands and rolling onto the ice like a wheel.

Gina didn't stay overnight at the Wayside that evening. Or again. She stayed at Ridge House with Ben.

Oh, to be touched, to be loved.

The pain will go away.

No it won't. But it will be hidden for a while.

What are we doing, what will become of us, what have we done.

Just planting flowers, gardening, weeding.

This is not that.

No, it's better. It's sweeter.

Do you know how long I have loved you, Ben whispered. How long I have longed for this.

Don't tell me. Don't ever tell me. Plant the violets, watch them grow, cut them down. Don't speak about the intervening years. Please.

This is so sweet.

Yes, it's like the syrup from the sugar maples.

And hills and streams, the wild, the swallow, the sparrow, it's aster, birch and pine. It's everything.

She didn't reply. It wasn't everything.

Can you believe, he whispered to her, that Louisa May Alcott thought Concord was the grayest of towns?

I don't believe it. She lived and died here.

Yes. But she said the last time the town saw a startling hue was when the redcoats were here.

Gina laughed, her breath so hot, it could have burned Ben's throat.

The red maple is the brightest scarlet, he whispered into her slick neck, into her parched mouth. It's the most vivid of all earthly things.

This she believed.

Oh, to be touched, to be loved.

They had a linen-colored room facing the morning sun. And on Sundays, after a night of love, a morning of tenderness, of kindness, they didn't want to venture out into the world of the sick and the downtrodden, and even the incarcerated. Leaving the room felt like torture.

Please don't ever be unhappy, she would say to him. What a blessing to wake up here and see your loving face. Every week I kiss it, I thank our gracious Lord for blessing me so bountifully.

You're not Salome, are you, Gina?

I don't know. She pondered. The name sounded vaguely familiar. It was precisely because the name was so unusual that it jogged her memory. The strict Catholic education came in handy when playing bedroom games with her Panamanian explosive-detonating lover.

Does Salome have something to do with John the Baptist?

Give this girl a prize! Ben grinned with pleasure. Not just beautiful, but smart too.

She pinched him lightly. If I'm Salome, are you equating yourself to John the Baptist, a messenger heralding the coming of Jesus?

Perhaps I'm King Herod instead, Ben said.

If you're Herod, then who do I ask you to behead, as I bask in my wickedness?

They dropped the analogy. I told you, you weren't Salome.

I'm not Cassia either, Gina said. Luke's repentant woman. All she wants is to be forgiven for her sins.

One day that will be you.

One day it will be me. Just not yet.

She raised her lips to him, her face, her long, bare arms, her hips. Not yet. Not yet.

You are red wine to me, to my mouth, he whispered, covering them, both man and woman, with the ardent white quilt, climbing, climbing.

They christened Macone's ice pond with kisses.

They drank beer at a small table at Wright's Tavern and pretended to be married. They walked arm in arm like lovers.

They went ice skating on all the Concord ponds, big Goose and little Goose, Crosby, White (that glistened like black diamonds). Warner's. Walden. And Fairyland hidden in the secret woods where the bears slept. He taught her how to skate backward and on one foot and do crossovers, spin fast with joy.

She stopped going to ring the bells for Jesus' five wounds on Sunday mornings. Stopped because she couldn't.

Stopped going regularly to visit Harry on Sunday afternoons.

Stopped because she couldn't.

The less she came, the more impersonal Harry became when she did visit. Smiling politely, trying to be warm, soliciting words she longed for but never heard, she instead let him regale her with the Russian he'd learned, listened to him read Marxist verse in Russian, from Lenin, from Trotsky, as if he were reading Lord Byron. He didn't want her to talk. He wanted to hear nothing about her family or Lawrence. He didn't care about Rose's Home. He no longer asked about Elston Purdy or his chance of parole. Mostly he talked about Lenin and Kerensky and the Romanovs, and she pretended to listen. He spoke about the political agitation happening in Russia the way other people talked about their children or their lovers.

She learned how to cook Panamanian rice with chicken for Ben, and *tamales*, to bake bread so sweet it tasted holy. Since she couldn't and didn't receive Communion on Sundays anymore, it was the only bread that crossed her lips.

When the snowbanks melted and lilac ornaments adorned the Concord paths, Ben took her to pick strawberries at Maplewood Farm. She made him warm strawberry jam. He took her rowing on Sudbury River. He taught her how to drive.

Chapter 5

MARBLE AND MUD

One

IT HAD RAINED AND SNOWED, and was now black and awful outside. As soon as Gina ran down the steps of her house and got into his car, she could tell Ben knew that something was wrong. It was the deep fall of 1915. The leaves were long off the trees. He picked her up on Saturday mornings now and drove her to Concord so she wouldn't have to take the train and bus.

"What's the matter?" he said, the smile of happy greeting wiped off his face. "You look like you've received the worst news. What is it?" He paled, couldn't continue driving. He pulled over. "Oh God, you're not …"

"Harry is coming home," she said. "For Christmas."

Ben got back on the road.

"When?" he said, after he'd been driving a while.

"Monday week."

"Just for Christmas? Like furlough?"

She was silent. "No."

Another twenty miles went by.

Then thirty.

Then they were in Concord.

For ten hours they worked side by side without saying much except to attend to the sick before them. She scrubbed, he carried. She changed dressings, made food. He cleaned pails and fixed locks. During their short breaks they drank tea in the kitchen, wordlessly.

At night in their little rented room in Ridge House down a steep hill through the fields and meadows and a stream away from the Wayside, they lay in the dark face to face. The fire had almost burned out in the stone enclosure, the candles had long dimmed, frost covered the night windows.

"What are we going to do?"

"I don't know," she said. "What can we do?"

"Come away with me," Ben said, staring intensely at her.

"Come away with you where?"

"Panama. We could have a wedding. The weather is great. There is no snow." He touched her fiery lips with the tips of his fingers.

"So no ice skating?"

"No, but swimming. Fishing. Lots of it. Rivers. Lakes. A mighty sea. An even mightier ocean."

Keeping her arms around him, Gina closed her eyes to hide her throbbing heart. They didn't want to speak too loud, wanted to stay quiet, silent, mute, oh, but to be able to read each other's thoughts. "I can't leave America, Ben," she finally said. "I *came* to America. I'm not like you. When you start here, it's true, you can go someplace else. But when you achieve America, when you receive it as a gift, it's unseemly to snub your nose at it."

"Well, it's not really a nose-snubbing," Ben said. "After all, if it weren't for America, there'd be no Panama Canal. So it would be an extension of your gratefulness."

She caressed his face. "*Vorrei poterlo fare*," she whispered inaudibly. "*Ma non posso*."

He spoke Spanish, not Italian. She whispered it to him in Spanish. *Ojalá pudiera. Pero no puedo.*

"You don't want to think about it? We don't have to leave. We could stay in Boston. I have my job. I would take good care of you. I would take care of everything. Wouldn't you like that?"

"More than I want to admit."

"You'd never have to work again, you could just do what you wanted, get your degree, become a professor, learn jazz on the piano. I hear it's becoming all the rage. Have babies …" He took a breath. "What I would give to have a baby with you."

Gina shuddered. What she would give to have a baby, period. But she couldn't bring a child into a miry bog such as this, no.

"I haven't been very good at the baby part," she said.

"You're extraordinary at everything, Gia," said Ben. "I've never met a more beautiful human being than you."

"Ben …" She trailed off, trying hard not to cry. "You make me so happy. I didn't realize how sad and lonely I had been until you reappeared in my life. You and me, we had such joy, didn't we?"

"We did."

"We picked berries and made eggnog."

"You made me *arroz con leche*."

"Yes."

"We ice skated and raced my car."

"We took care of sick people."

"And this."

"And this."

Afterward they clung to each other. "Ben Shaw!" she cried in the night. "Don't you understand? Don't you get it? He gave up *everything* to marry me." Gina almost couldn't continue. "Every single thing he ever had and valued, he gave up—to be with me. Turning my back on him would be like turning my back on America, wouldn't it?"

"Maybe he didn't value what he had," Ben said coolly. "Did you ever think of that? Does he value you?"

"Yes and yes, and I don't agree," said Gina. "You and he were inseparable. And his Harvard friends. His family, his sister, his house, his station, his purse! Everything. He had a whole life, Ben, that he threw away. I know something about this, what it means to leave behind the only life you know."

"Exactly. You leave because you think you're headed to something better."

"Right," whispered Gina. "And that something better would be me. That's what I'm saying."

Ben shook his head. "He wasn't that close to them. He had a terrible conflict with his father."

"That's normal father–son affairs. My own father and my oldest brother constantly butted heads." She tutted tearfully. "Until Antonio got stabbed and killed, but again, that was because he hadn't listened to Papa."

"Harry and Herman were not just butting heads."

"Herman lost his wife, Ben. That's not easy for anyone. A father left alone with two motherless children to raise. Herman is not Mimoo. It's tougher for men, especially busy, successful men like Herman. And Harry and Esther were permanently bonded by this unspeakable grief."

"How permanent can it be if he turned his back on her? Are you sure it's unspeakable?" Ben was skeptical even when naked.

"Yes," she replied. "You know how I know? Because he never speaks of it. To lose your mother, I can't even begin ..." She didn't want to continue that discussion. "I know how it is with me and my brother," Gina resumed. "I couldn't imagine my life if he weren't in it. And yet Harry ..."

"The Barringtons weren't that kind of family."

"Still family, though, Ben. Fractured, yes, but still father, son, daughter. And yet Harry surrendered his birthright, his inheritance, his place in the world. You think it's easy for him to live broke, to sleep in the small bedroom next to my mother? He did it for me."

"What I mean is ..." Ben searched for words. "Maybe saying he didn't value all the things you speak of is not quite correct, but now that I look back, I think Harry had always been looking for a way out."

"Out of what?"

"Out of that life. It was an ill-fitting suit. He didn't wear it well."

Gina pushed Ben away. "Why is it," she said, cooler and less teary, "that when men postulate about the motives of other men they forget that they're also talking about the women attached to them?"

"I remember the woman attached to Harry."

Because that woman was now attached to *him*.

"Yes, but what you're saying is, if his former life meant little to him, then the sacrifice of it wasn't so monumental. What you're saying is, the price for me was smaller than I led myself to believe. You are devaluing me, to *me*! In bed as we lie here together."

"I'm sorry, Gina. I didn't mean it." He faced away from her in contrition. "I'm drowning and grabbing on to anything to stay afloat. What can I say to persuade you?"

"You can't justify it away, Ben, Harry's sacrifice. I wasn't an *excuse* for him to run the other way. He didn't chance upon me like an object in the sand and say Eureka! Think about how long he spent hiding what he felt for me from you, from me, from his family, from himself. Years! From the very beginning when we met you on the Freedom Docks. And you also forget that in fateful 1905, he wasn't out looking for me. Just the opposite. He was ready to marry Alice. I was the one who was searching for *him*. I was the one who found *him*. Not the other way around."

"Forgive me." Ben pulled her to him, cradling her, his arms around her soft, bare back. "I don't know what I'm saying. I'm crazy, you are right. When I came back from Panama, I was the one who went out looking for you. What can *I* sacrifice? I'll give it all up—instantly."

"Ben … please. I don't need that. I didn't want it from Harry. I don't want it from you. Think what you're asking of me. I'll have to get a divorce …"

"Okay. You weren't even married in a church."

"Good thing, too," she returned, "since the Catholics wouldn't consider it."

He fell silent.

"And think about my mother. The government just established Mother's Day as a national holiday, and yet I'm going to sail off and leave her? What am I going to do with my mother, did you think of that?"

"We'll take her with us."

"She won't survive the trip. And she won't leave Salvo. She doesn't want to go. For the same reason I don't. She came to America, *this* is the promised land. Not Panama."

"Would you leave America for Harry? If he asked you?"

Gina breathed heavily, regretfully. "Let's hope we never get to find out the answer to your terrible question," she said.

"So let's stay here," Ben said. "With Mimoo. You love Boston. We'll move to Beacon Hill just like you dreamed when you were a young girl. We'll live in a big brownstone and we'll go skating on Frog Pond on the Common."

"Ben, *amico mio*," she whispered. "I would love that. But I'm married. I can't."

Minutes passed in mute darkness. Minutes or hours?

"I want to ask you a Rose Hawthorne question," he said. "*Let men tremble to win the hand of a woman, unless they win along with it the utmost passion of her heart.*" He swallowed as if reluctant to ask. "Does Harry have the utmost passion of your heart?"

She didn't answer.

"Does he still have it?"

She didn't answer.

No sound but Ben's wretched struggle for calm breath.

"I thought …" He almost cried. "I thought you loved me."

"I do," she said haltingly. "I still can't leave him."

"So what am I going to be to you? A chapter you've finished? A book you've thrown away?"

She said nothing. You don't throw away your favorite books, she wanted to say to him, but didn't.

She had never been treated as decently, as generously, with as much kindness as she had been by Ben. Why wasn't it enough?

"I am a Sicilian woman."

"I thought you were an American woman."

"I'm Sicilian where it counts. He is my husband. On the scales I weigh my life on, that outweighs everything else." Except maybe motherhood. But she wouldn't know. "When Sicilian women get married, they get married for life."

When they were alone, in bursts and glimmers, between strikes and subjugations, Harry still communed with her, still intimately adored her. She was bound by love.

"There is no way out of this for us, Ben," she whispered.

"Except out."

"Except out."

Purple petals have fallen into our ice pond, Ben whispered brokenly. I will write your name on it in violets.

She held Ben closer, until no closer was possible. What they had was a blissful interlude, a fairyland reverie between one life and another. But what kind of life waited for her on the other side? And what if Harry's once mystical love for her could not be roused from its deathlike slumber?

Two

BEN AND GINA PICKED UP Harry together from the Concord prison. They waited for him outside the gates on Elm Street, standing far apart, orienting themselves only toward the red brick building, and presently he appeared in the same suit and tie he had been sentenced in, carrying a black bag. He was thin, drawn, but clean-shaven and neatly trimmed. If he was surprised to see Ben, he did not show it, other than in a stiffening of his body. He and Ben shook hands, even hugged. Then Harry leaned coolly toward Gina. He didn't meet her eyes.

"Are you all right?" she asked, returning his near-formal embrace.

"I'm fine, why wouldn't I be?" He turned to Ben. "What are you doing back? Your work done?"

"Work's never done," Ben said. "In fact, I was thinking I might go back soon."

Gina sucked in her breath—but managed to stay quiet.

"How long have you been back?"

"Over a year now."

"Over a year, you don't say." Harry didn't so much as glance in Gina's direction. "So, the entire time I've been inside?"

"You're right, it couldn't be that long—let's go, my car's right over there."

Harry quickened his step to catch up to Ben. Gina lumbered behind them. "Nice car," he said. "Yours?"

"Want to drive?"

Harry stared at the keys in Ben's hand. "Probably shouldn't. I haven't driven in over a decade."

"Your wife drives now." Ben stretched out the hand with the keys to her. "Want to show him?" He didn't call her by name. Gina knew Ben couldn't say her name out loud without giving himself away in the caress of his throat.

"My wife drives now?" Harry climbed into the passenger seat. "Surprises all around." His deep gray eyes deepened to concrete.

Gina got behind the wheel. Her hands were unsteady. Ben sat silently in the back. They were on the road a while before Harry spoke. "Where are we going?"

"I thought home," said Gina. "Unless you have other plans." She wanted to ask if maybe there was a demonstration or a strike he would prefer to be driven to, but knew that Harry hated it when she was snide.

"Ben's coming too?"

"Well, it *is* his car. We'll give it back to him after he drops us off."

"Harry," Ben interjected, "you must be glad to be out."

Harry shrugged. "Are you glad you're out of Panama?"

A slight pause from Ben. "Are you equating Panama with prison?"

"Not in a negative way. I consider it a badge of honor to be in prison for the things I believe in."

"Ah. Well, in that case, me too."

Into minutes of strained silence Gina folded in a defeated thought about herself. There she was working at the mission, at Rose's, at the looms and the mending rooms, taking in sewing, helping clean Mimoo's houses, and here he was, her newly sprung husband mentioning offhandedly that he was proud to have been away for over a year from his young wife who desperately wanted to have a baby. Gina wanted to ask Harry if maybe he didn't believe in *her*. But again—no use saying things that would only incite trouble. She kept her mouth shut, inside the cauldron swirling, outside her eyes stinging from hurt.

* * *

Back in Lawrence, Mimoo was not especially elated to see her liberated son-in-law. Gina concluded this because her trouble-making mother asked Ben to stay for dinner.

"I should be getting back," Ben said. "But thank you, Mimoo."

"Won't hear of it," she said. "You stay."

"Yes, Ben, stay," Harry said. "Right, Gina?"

"He said he had to be getting back," Gina said, busying herself with setting the table. "I take him at his word. Would you like to put your things upstairs, Harry? Freshen up?"

"I'm fresh like a flower," said Harry, sitting at the round table in his customary seat. "Ben, sit. Please. We'll eat like we used to in Barrington on Sundays when Louis served us. Better. Because I don't know if you know this, but Gina is a wonderful cook. And we'll talk like we used to. Right?"

During dinner of mustard chicken and dill potatoes, Harry didn't ask Ben about Louis, or his father, or his sister, or his erstwhile betrothed, Alice. His interest seemed to be only in Ben. "Where are you working now?"

"Still with the Army Corps."

"What else is there for the Army Corps to do?" Harry poured himself more wine. "Is there another world-changing canal you can build?"

"No, but there are roads all over New England that need to be mapped and planned and paved. There were no cars on the road in 1900. Now there are hundreds of thousands."

"The car is folly," said Harry. "A plaything for the rich."

"Be that as it may, even playthings for the rich need new roads. Plus," Ben added, "the car is cheap now. It's not like it was. It costs a dollar for a pound of car. You can't get good steak that cheap."

"I'd rather have steak," Harry said.

"Gina is saving for a car," Mimoo piped up. "Aren't you, child?"

"Yes, Mimoo. Slowly."

"Well, perhaps we could go to the bank and borrow what you need," Harry said, getting up and going to the counter to open another bottle of red wine.

"No, we won't borrow," Gina said quickly. "We'll have enough for a car by next spring. If you get a job, we'll have it even sooner."

"I have a job," Harry said, downing his wine by the counter. "I work for Big Bill."

"Big Bill has long left these parts," Gina said. "After the failure of the Paterson strike he went out west."

"It didn't *fail*," Harry said, coming back to the table and sitting down with a sharp humph. "We couldn't raise enough money to feed the strikers."

"Right," Gina said. "They went without work until they couldn't anymore and then returned to their jobs. That's called a failed strike."

He waved to dismiss her. "I know Bill's people. I'll get in touch with him."

"He's busy," said Gina. "He is about to witness one of his other speechwriters, one Joe Hill, face the firing squad for murdering a cop and his son in Salt Lake City."

"A travesty," Harry said. "I read about it. Joe Hill was wrongly accused."

"Yes, I'm sure so are they all, all honorable men," said Gina. "But you still have to find work."

"Yes, yes," Harry said. "I heard. You want a car."

"Harry," Ben cut in, "I may be able to get you a job with the Road Works. They're always looking for people—"

"Thanks, but no. So tell me," he asked without pause, "you spent all these years building a canal for the capitalists on the back of slave labor. The capitalists are now getting richer. But the Panamanians are still poor as mud, right?"

"Who are these capitalists you speak of?" Calmly Ben continued to eat. "Just the opposite. The economy around the canal has pulled up all Panama by its shoelaces. New housing, new stores, a massive influx of foreign cash, of tourism, of consumer goods. There are schools and hospitals where before there weren't any. And there is an enormous amount of work. Everywhere. And because of the work, the standard of living has gone up."

"For none more so than the canal investors, right?"

"Well, yes," Ben said. "The people who risked their own money also benefit. Is it your position that they shouldn't?" When Harry said nothing, Ben continued. "Had the canal gone under, failed like the French canal efforts had failed, the investors would have been out three hundred and sixty-six million dollars. Your father would have lost his entire substantial investment. Instead he'll build a mill, pave a road, put up another residence. Everyone benefits."

"Not equally."

"Proportionately equally, yes. The pauper won't become a king," Ben said. "But he won't stay a pauper either."

"Capitalism means a few kings and a million paupers."

"Does socialism mean no kings and a million paupers?"

"No! Socialism means a million kings."

Ben took a breath. "A million kings. Your father's wealth creates wealth for others. He employs hundreds of people. Because of him, men support their families, buy food, build homes, eat, live."

"Wealth for others? He pays them a pittance."

"He pays them a living wage. But forget your father. What about Salvo?"

"What about him?" Harry glared at his wife. She looked away.

"Salvo employed twenty-two people when he owned Antonio's."

"Yes, and they couldn't pay their doctors' bills on the trifle he paid them."

"They can hardly afford even their rent now," said Ben.

"Clearly the solution is not Salvo's way or my father's way," Harry said. "But another way. They would get a decent wage from the start. I've seen the effects of these so-called free markets on human beings. It's not pretty."

"But the standard of living has risen for everyone. Wealth creation is an undeniable fact."

"I deny it."

"Look at Lawrence. People live better now than a hundred years ago. They live better than sixteen years ago when Mimoo and"—he couldn't say Gina's name—"your wife came to this country. They eat better, their children are healthier, die less in infancy, they dress better, they have cars, they take vacations. By every conceivable measure, their quality of life has risen."

"Quality of life is not measured *just* by the standard of living," Harry said. "Life is not all economics, you know. Only the naïve can make this conclusion."

Ben nodded. "You and I are in perfect agreement on that score, my friend. Because that's exactly what I believe. Life is not about how much your neighbor makes or has. Life is not about the paycheck. Life is about other things too."

Gina raised her hand. "Harry, Ben …"

They both ignored her.

"Ben, you're not blind," Harry said. "You must see that we're on the brink of a massive social transformation. Slavery is gone, feudalism is gone. Soon capitalism will be gone, left behind by progressive, educated people. Socialism is the wave of the future, it will come to wash everything away."

"Like a tidal wave," said a weary Gina.

"You don't believe that, do you?" asked Ben.

"With all my heart," Harry replied. "Instead of fighting a useless war abroad to overthrow the German government, I'd much rather petition my own government for its overthrow, to be blunt with you. With the ballot box *or* the bayonet, I'm not choosy."

Ben shook his head. "How precious can the right to overthrow your own government be if you won't even petition the Germans in support of it?"

"I would, I just don't want to petition them with bayonets!"

"You can try to petition them through the ballot box, but I don't think they'll listen."

"Just like this government."

A gust of wind flung the front door open, letting the chill in. Gina stood up to go close it, moved behind Harry, widening her pleading eyes at Ben, shaking her head.

She came back toward the table. "Ben, would you like something else to eat?"

"No, thank you. Overthrow it and what?"

"Build a new world order," Harry said. "A modern socialist utopia."

"A *utopia*?"

"Yes, because my idea hasn't failed," said Harry. "Unlike capitalism. I'm allowed to call it utopia until it does."

"Harry?" Gina held out the bowl of boiled potatoes.

"What?"

"Would you like something else to eat?"

"No!"

Mimoo and Gina exchanged a helpless glance.

"Men don't *believe* in free markets." Ben rolled his eyes. "They live them. And capitalism hasn't failed."

"No? Then why is there so much strife in the world?"

"I don't know," Ben said. "Perhaps it has something to do with the likes of Big Bill turning a smorgasbord of brotherly love into the battle-cry of a class fight. Sitting around the fireplace, holding hands, singing songs, and growing wheat together has become a robber raid and a land grab, the imposition of this pleasant utopian dream you talk about down unwilling throats. I can't imagine why there would be strife."

"If business were run on cooperative principles, life *would* be friendly and peaceful," Harry said. "We shouldn't strive to be ignorant and selfish. We should strive to be enlightened beings, to unite all interests and eventually remove this cause for conflict between men."

"And we're going to get this cooperation whether men want it or not?"

"Only the hopelessly bourgeois wouldn't want it." Harry shook his head. "I think you've worked too long digging a ditch, Ben. It's clouded your thinking."

"And you think Big Bill hasn't clouded yours?"

Harry turned his stone gaze to Gina.

Gina hung her head, hung it low.

"You're right," Harry said. "The ideal world of which Bill and I speak—and Max Eastman and John Reed—doesn't happen by itself. Equality and unity for all does require effort, hard work, and a transformation of our ingrained selfish principles. Every *man* can't be just for himself. Taking what he wants. Taking when he wants it."

Ben glanced at Gina and opened his mouth. She shook her head imperceptibly. He got up and, smiling, picked up his hat. "At the center of any economic theory, heck, of any theory at all, at the center of every question, every problem facing us, is *man*. Capitalism is not an idea. It's freedom. And without *man*, freedom is meaningless. Like air without us to breathe it."

"Capitalism is not freedom," Harry said. "It's usurping our earth's natural resources."

"What are these natural resources?" Ben asked. "Are you talking about a tree? So go cut it down. It still won't build you a house, a factory, buy your food, put bread on your table, or float a ship to bring your bride to you from a far-off land." He swallowed, but went on. "Those things didn't spring forth like gods from rocks, Harry. They were all *built*. By free *men*."

"No man who works for another man is truly free," said Harry.

Gina, Ben, and Mimoo all stared at Harry. A foreboding silence gathered in the parlor of their little house. "Well, then, my old friend," Ben said, "I guess that makes you the freest man of all." He put on his hat and took a short bow. "I must head back. Thank you, Mimoo, for a lovely dinner, and Harry, for a spirited conversation, as always. I miss our talks. You and I used to spend many a fine Sunday like this. Would you like me to give Esther and Herman your regards when I see them next?"

"Absolutely not," said Harry, stabbing his cold food.

Ben nodded, curt in return. "Understood." He allowed himself a gaze at Gina, one small, regretful smile. He shook Harry's barely proffered hand. The recently jailed man would not get up from the table.

Unsteadily, Gina walked Ben to the front door.

"Goodbye, Gina."

"Goodbye, Ben," she said, her voice giving out.

At the bottom of the porch steps, in the dark, he turned to her, looked up, took off his hat and took a deep last long bow.

Alone in bed, Gina waited for Harry to come, but he sat outside on the wet porch, reading, drinking his tea, his wine, smoking, staring into the darkness. By the time she felt him crawl in next to her, she had been asleep for hours.

His cold hand went around her. She was on her side. Her back was to him. He fitted in behind her and lifted her nightgown above her hips, pressing his trembling icy lips to her warm neck. She cried when she heard him whisper her name. *Oh Gina.*

Desperately, quickly, mutely it was over. But even after he was long asleep, Gina's hands continued to grip the sheet in her fists.

Three

THANK GOD FOR WORK. In the early morning she jumped out of bed, got dressed, made Mimoo toast with jam, herself a cup of tea, and ran to Wood Mill. At six when she was done and it was dark, she walked to St. Vincent's, all bundled up, shivering, her eyes to the ground. By the time she got home it was nearing nine.

"Is every day going to be like this?" Harry asked, standing by the sink as she sat by herself eating her cold dinner at the table. "You not coming home until all hours of the night?"

Gina wanted to remind him that's how every day was for her—or had he forgotten? Their house was too little for big words. "Some days are longer," she said, hiding behind little words. "Some days I also clean houses if Mimoo can't manage without me. And some days I go to Boston."

"What for?"

"To visit my brother in the North End. And on some weekends I'd still like to go to Concord to help Rose." At the mention of Rose, sudden tears sprang to her eyes. He didn't mention them. And she could not. "She needs my help," Gina whispered.

Harry's silence was his only response.

"I don't have to go," she said, wiping her face. "If you don't want me to."

"Why would I not want you to work with Rose?" he said, turning to the sink. "It's God's work, isn't it?"

Weeks crawled by. They talked around the borders of their life. They talked about the things they could talk about. Like current events. Joe Hill was put to death in Utah. Bill Haywood became the sole president of the IWW. And from Rose, Gina heard that Ben had sailed back to Panama just before Christmas. Not wanting Harry to see how upset she was, she didn't return home until late that Saturday night, her eyes red and puffy, but her demeanor finally composed by the time she walked through her front door.

"Must have been a late night in Concord," Harry said. "I'm surprised the trains are still running."

When she told Harry about Ben he shrugged indifferently.

"I thought you would want to know."

"It's no concern of mine," he said.

It became 1916. Now that Harry was back, Salvo didn't come for New Year's. Gina missed her brother, Mimoo missed her son. But one evening her mother's grumbling became too much. "Listen, Mimoo, Salvo has a choice, but Harry and I have none. You don't want Harry here? So go live with Salvo in Boston."

"I'm going to leave my own house because your husband won't leave mine?"

"You want us to move out, Mimoo? We'll find a room somewhere, like Angela did. You do understand that if he goes, I go, too, right? Say the word. Is that what you want? I'll do as you please. I've always been an obedient daughter."

Mimoo scoffed.

"Outwardly obedient."

"You're a mule," said Mimoo, relenting. "So now I'm not allowed to complain in my own house about your dirt-poor choices?"

"No," Gina said. "You're not."

"Your husband is home," Mimoo said. "He told me he got a job. I think he's already in bed. Even the interview tired him out."

"What did I say, Mimoo? *Basta!*" Gina went upstairs.

Apparently Max Eastman had hired Harry to be his New England contributing editor for *The Masses* magazine. He was going to help Floyd Dell edit the literary fiction column called "Books That Are Interesting." When Gina allowed herself to be excited and asked Harry how much he was going to be paid, he stared at her with what looked like contempt.

"What? Is this out of bounds to ask?"

"Max Eastman is the editor-in-chief of that historic publication," said Harry. "He doesn't get a penny."

She flung her cardigan on the bed with rank exasperation. "So how can it be called *work* then? You said *work*."

"I don't know, Gina," he said. "You spend all your weekends at the Wayside, and you don't get paid. Do you call *that* work?"

She sat down on the bed to take off her shoes.

"John Reed doesn't get paid," Harry continued. "Neither do Sherwood Anderson or Upton Sinclair. But you want *me* to get paid?"

"I wouldn't mind it if you got paid for something, yes," Gina said. "Like me. Find something to do that makes you money, not leaches money away from our family. I know—what a harpy I am."

"Did I say a word?"

She tried to remain calm and failed. There had been a countrywide depression the year before and it hit Lawrence hard. St. Vincent's had cut her hours. Wood Mill eliminated her overtime pay in the mending room. Fewer women asked her for custom-sewn dresses, layettes for their babies, the darning of their old skirts. The sewing machine stood in the corner unused. Mimoo lost two of her five domestic jobs. They barely had enough money for two meals a day. If Salvo didn't help with Mimoo's half of the rent, they would go under, for sure.

Gina force-fed herself a generous helping of constrained Methodist manners—not Catholic manners, not Italian manners, certainly not the histrionic, passionate bowl of Sicilian agitation that overflows from being constantly thwarted to bursting by the one she loved and had indulged beyond all reason.

"Well, Harry," she said through a tight and proper mouth. "Sherwood Anderson must be making a living some other way. As is Max Eastman, no?"

"I really don't know, Jane," Harry said, using her Anglicized name, as if to detach himself from her true self. Any more detached and they'd be on different continents. "What I *do* know is that this is an incredible opportunity for me, a tremendous opportunity, to be asked, to be invited to work with people, all of whom are striving to change the world for the better, while *you* are doing nothing but obsessing about money."

"That's what you think? That I do nothing but obsess over money?"

"You're always running from one place to another to make a buck. You're always lamenting the silence of your sewing machine because you can't make another dollar."

"But Harry," Gina said, "if you and Max Eastman are tirelessly changing the world for free, someone's got to pay our light bill, no?"

He waved at her dismissively as if both she and her comments were irrelevant. "Are you or are you not willing to move to Greenwich Village?"

"Will you get paid if we do?"

"Do you see what I mean? Are you willing to move even to Boston?"

"Will you get paid if we do?"

"Gina!"

Gina's meager wage started going not just toward the living expenses they could barely afford, but also toward Harry's train commute and money he needed in Boston, where he often stayed so late he started borrowing a couch at someone's apartment—Gina didn't know whose and Harry wouldn't say. When she complained about his hours, he said, "I thought you'd be happy. I'm trying to do what you want. Work."

"But you're not making any money!"

"I'm away from the house like you're away from the house with your nuns and your sewing circles."

"Except I make money. And I've stopped going to Rose's, haven't I?"

"Did I ask you to?"

"No, but—" Rose had told her not to come anymore in her condition. She bit her tongue.

"I'm working just like you and just as hard," Harry said. "I'm just not getting paid. By staying overnight in Boston, I'm saving money on my train fare. I thought you'd be happy. But no, you're never satisfied."

"Yes, that's me, I expect too much."

"Don't you, oh snide one?" He paused. "Don't you keep expecting from me what I cannot give you?"

She ran outside and threw up.

Mimoo consoled Gina after the argument subsided. "What's wrong with the both of you? Salvo promised he would give us extra until we get some of our work back. But you have to stop it. You have to take care of yourself this time."

"I'm doing my best, Mimoo. I don't feel good, but I can't rest, I can't lie down."

"I don't know why you won't just tell him."

"I want a little time to pass."

"Why?"

"In case I'm not lucky again."

"The first time it was that horrible man's fault. But now you have to be smarter. Don't scream and carry on like you do. Relax. Tell him. Make him happy. Let him help you."

"You think it will make him happy?" She hugged her mother. "I just want a little more time to pass. I want to be sure."

"Sure of what?"

Four

THEY SAT DOWN TO DINNER on a rare Saturday night when they were all home. Well, Harry and Gina sat down to dinner. Mimoo was in the back, in the washroom. They both heard her crying.

"What's the matter with your mother?" asked Harry, cutting the bread.

"I don't know."

"Why is she sobbing as if someone died?"

Gina's pale lips trembled. "She's just blowing her nose. Mimoo! Come!"

"She was so distraught today, you had to go and clean two of her houses."

"I don't mind helping. She's feeling poorly."

"I didn't go to Boston to work this weekend so we could spend the day together. I thought I was going to take you to the market."

"Maybe next week. Mimoo! Please come. Dinner's getting cold."

Her mother finally appeared at the table. She wouldn't look at either Harry or Gina. "I'm not feeling poorly," she said, sitting down. "*You're* feeling poorly."

Harry glanced at Gina, at her mother. "Have you two caught the flu or something? Gina, I heard you throwing up a few days ago. And you both look white."

Mimoo started to cry again, right at the table. Gina gave her mother a withering look. "*Basta!*" she mouthed as she served the rigatoni with mozzarella and garlic to a troubled husband and a disconsolate mother.

"Nice Saturday dinner we're having," Harry said. "Mimoo, why are you crying?"

"I'm not crying."

"Ah."

"That's right," said Gina. "She's not. Have some bread, Mimoo. Butter for you, Harry? A glass of wine?"

Harry studied Gina's wan face.

For a long time he was silent as the two women ate. He did not pick up his fork.

"Aren't you going to eat, *marito*?"

"How many weeks was it this time?" he asked.

No one spoke.

He raised his voice. "How many?"

"Just a few," said Gina.

"Twelve!" cried Mimoo.

"Mimoo!"

"Twelve …" Harry repeated, going pale himself.

"Does that seem like a few to you? A third of a baby! Gone, gone! *O forza mia, affretti ad aiutarmi!*"

Harry shot up. He wiped his mouth on a napkin, though he hadn't eaten a bite. "Will you please excuse me, Mimoo?" He did not forget his manners. "I'm not very hungry." He fled the house, taking care not to slam the door.

Gina threw down her napkin. "Why?" she cried. "Can't you help me once, just once, by not making *everything* harder?"

"I'm sorry! I can't help it."

"I wish you could help it, just once! I told you I didn't want him to know. Everything would have been all right if you had just kept your mouth shut."

The old woman was sobbing.

Gina grabbed her coat and, slamming the door, ran to follow him. He was halfway down the street.

"Harry."

He didn't stop, or answer her.

"Where are you going?" she panted, catching up.

"To clear my head."

"Please. Slow down. I can't keep up."

"So don't keep up."

"Please." She grabbed his arm, held on to him. Reluctantly he was forced to slow down. They crossed the street and entered the Common, smiling thinly at another couple passing them arm in arm. Gina liked this park. In late spring the ducks had babies, and dozens of them waddled after their mothers along the paths, over the lawns and among the flowers. Sometimes she would come here at lunchtime to watch them.

They found a quiet perch, sank onto it, and were themselves mute, like the bench, like the overhanging willows.

"Why didn't you tell me?" he asked.

"Tell you what?"

"Are there so many things to tell me that you honestly don't know what I'm talking about or are you just pretending to be dense?"

She suppressed a sigh. "I was going to tell you. I wanted to make sure everything was okay first. And then when it wasn't ... well, you were busy. I thought the less said the better."

"Really, you thought that. How many other pregnancies have you kept from me?"

"Harry, please."

"Please what?" He was staring straight ahead. "Tell me. How many?"

"What are you asking me? None, of course."

"Is that so? How many failed pregnancies did you keep from me while I was in prison for fifteen months?"

She jumped up, but couldn't face him.

"None," she breathed. "Stop it."

"Am I being irrational?"

"Yes. I'm sorry. I thought it was for the best. I just wanted to get on with things, that's why I didn't tell you."

"Is that right? So tell me now."

"What do you want to know? There's little to say at this point."

"Is there really little to say?"

"Yes." The less said the better. She crumpled back into the corner of the wet bench, away from him.

"Mimoo said twelve weeks."

Gina couldn't help it, she started to shake.

Harry pretended to count backward three months from March. "About December, then?"

She found her smallest voice. "You were home in December, were you not? In our bed?"

He said nothing. The unsaid was so crashingly loud that Gina put her mittened hands over her ears as if words were being screamed, as if the sound were deafening.

It was the end of March, and wet, and cold. It was so cold.

"What about the ice skates in your closet?"

Gina swallowed. "What about them?"

"I didn't know you knew how to skate."

"I didn't know *you* knew how to skate."

160

"How do you know now?" Harry said. "Did you find my skates in our closet?"

"No." She stared straight ahead, never looking at him. "What does this have to do with the baby?"

"You tell me. And why do I suspect everything?"

She was flush out of words and defenses.

"I don't care," he said. "But when you hide things so poorly it really makes me think you don't give a shit. I mean, if you didn't want me to know, you might have considered throwing out the skates. Doing with them what you're doing with the bloodied gauze. Putting them into the trash so I wouldn't find them."

"That's not what I'm doing. And … I'm not hiding anything. I have nothing to hide. You're busy. *Economic Interpretation of the Constitution, Winesburg, Ohio.* You have a lot to do. Buried in your books and pamphlets. I didn't want to disturb."

"I bury myself in what I can so I don't come home and see what rags of life you're scattering for me all over our house."

"Don't say that. It's not what you do."

"It is what I do."

"Harry, I'm sorry I didn't tell you."

He didn't look at her as he spoke, his eyes like windows paved over with cement to keep her out. "What do you want?" he said. "For me to weep?"

"No," she whispered.

"I will weep an eternity in hell before you take my pride from me too."

They sat, hollow and defeated.

The cold pierced her skin to the bone. The truth was Gina didn't know how to answer his questions. Had she kept the skates so he would find them? And could she say with certainty—absolute certainty—that the skates and *la piccola vita* had nothing to do with one another? Her knuckles were stiff, her barely beating heart felt faint and pallid.

He stared out at the pond.

"You need powers of second sight to figure out how I might feel about you not telling me you were pregnant?"

"It was a mistake not to tell you," she said. "I know that. I thought it would make you feel bad."

"You thought *that's* what would make me feel bad?"

On the frozen dead grass in front of them, the baby ducks were trying to keep up with their mother, but the last one was having trouble. The mother was not slowing down. Gina was about to get up and help the baby duckling, hurry it along.

"Sometimes it's really hard to tell what you feel, Harry," she said at last. "You tell me nothing, you keep it all so close to the vest. And you're busy, busy, busy. With strikes, with prison, *The Masses*. Busy, in other words," she added, "with anything and everything but me."

"I can hardly be busy with you when I'm in prison."

"Prison is a choice, though, isn't it?"

"Everything is a choice, Gina," he said. "Even ice skating."

She weighed her words. "I came to see you every Sunday."

"Not every Sunday. In the beginning, maybe. But not at the end. Not nearly."

"I came when I could. I brought you things you asked for. Had you asked me for other things, I would have brought you those. I brought you newspapers, books. You worked in the laundry. It must have been nice to work with your hands for once, not just your head. You had time to think about things, learn Russian. You had *time*. You didn't write letters, but then who writes anymore—oh, wait," Gina said, as if just remembering. "That's not *entirely* true. You didn't write to *me*. But apparently you did write *some* letters. You wrote to John Reed, and to Max Eastman, and to Big Bill, you wrote to Elizabeth Gurley Flynn—oh, and also to some woman named Mary Heaton Vorse, a poetess apparently, a suffragette."

Harry rubbed his eyes. "You have *seen* Mary Vorse, right? You and I went together to New York last month, you met everyone. You found Max Eastman very handsome, remember? Mary Vorse was by his side."

"She's quite the letter writer, no?"

"I don't know. Is she?"

"She is, yes. And I met the attractive Elizabeth Gurley Flynn. You and she were quite chummy in New York. You poured her drinks and held open her doors."

"Yours first."

"As long as we're in the right order then."

He said nothing.

"I don't sit in judgment of you, Harry," Gina said. "You cannot ask your lover to be your judge."

"You are not *my* lover," he said, bolting up and facing her. "You're my *wife*. You keep from me skates in your closet and lost babies. And you don't find it," he added, "even remotely ironic, Miss Lover of Irony, that you would go to *Nathaniel Hawthorne's* daughter's home to meet someone in secret?"

"Harry, I didn't meet anyone in secret at Rose's. I worked with many people, Ben included, in full view of everyone."

"He decided to come to Concord every weekend to work for free by your side?"

"Why not? You go to Boston every day including the weekends to work for free by Mary Vorse's side." How Gina kept herself from crying, she didn't know.

Shivering, Harry walked away.

She came after him. The ducks were forgotten, the freezing March evening unfelt. She was hot around the throat, hot in her eyes. "When your husband is in prison or on strike three and a half years out of the last four, someone has to pay the bills, no?"

"You weren't just paying the bills, were you? And we are not armchair debaters, Sunday dinner argumentarians like you and your ditch digger. We're remaking the world. You'd expect it to take some time, no?"

"I don't know how well you could be advocating for anything while sitting on your rump in prison throwing linen down laundry chutes."

"I'm not afraid of prison. Not anymore."

"Yes, but while you were there someone still had to buy food for Mimoo and me. Who do you think that was?"

"I don't know, Gina," Harry said. "Perhaps the ditch digger?"

"And who do you think feeds you now?"

He increased his pace until he was almost running. She increased hers to stay by his side. "Perhaps I should write to your father, ask him for a small monthly stipend for you?"

"Get away from me," he panted.

"Well, why not? The money to feed *you* has to come from somewhere."

He whirled to face her. "Change the subject all you wish," he said, grabbing her around the waist and pressing his fist hard to her chest. "But I *hear* the pounding of your telltale heart!"

Gasping, she recoiled from him, tried to free herself.

He wouldn't let her go, blazing and breathless. "Just like I suspected. The whole of Lawrence hears it. Like the fucking bells of Notre Dame."

"Why do you torture me," she exhaled, not even trying to push him away. She grabbed at his coat.

He ran off, leaving her with the mother ducks and their babies.

Five

SHE WAITED FOR HIM near the duck pond, leaning on a railing in Boston's Public Garden. They had agreed to meet at half-past one in the afternoon. Their overnight train to Chicago was leaving at five, and they wanted plenty of time to do everything properly. It was the end of June, and warm. She hadn't overdressed, but oh, had she dressed! She had packed her bag for the few days they were going to be away. She had to wear something simple enough for the secular registrar at City Hall, yet glamorous enough to mark this day as she would mark no other. With Harry's money she went to a fashion store on Newbury Street and bought herself a lawn dress *nonpareil*, in the lightest creamiest silk and lace, with short cap sleeves and an empire waist but no corset or petticoat because that was what he loved best. He said only the truly liberated woman was courageous enough to go without a corset. The dress fit her as though it were stitched onto her body, like a second skin. It sported large pearl buttons on a high bust bodice, like porcelain nipples on cotton milk breasts, and its slim slender train of cascading silk highlighted the length of her legs. The dress came with a short cream silk jacket. Gina added white patent leather pumps and long white gloves past her elbows. On her head was an exquisite wide-brim organza couture hat with wispy layers of tulle flowers and white ostrich feathers. She bought a few daisies and tucked them around her hat and into her hair. She expertly styled her curly hair around the hat to frame her eager face. As she waited for him, afraid to sit down on a bench lest she get dirty, she knew she was a vision, *knew* it. Well, if Harry was discarding his old life for her, changing his world order for her, she wanted to give him a picture of herself like an oil painting, so that he would always remember: her standing under the willows and the flowers in the Public Garden, indifferent to the falling rain, more beautiful than ever. At an instant he would be able to recall her and always know how much she loved him.

Are you sure you want to do this? she had asked him three days earlier when they were in bed with the covers over their heads, whispering as if they were hiding from God.

Never been more sure.

Are you sure about that?

What are you worried about?

That you're being impulsive. That you're being rash.

I am being rashly impulsive. That doesn't make my answer any less true.

What about your family?

What about them? He paused. What about *your* family?

Gina shrugged. Is it too impetuous? she asked. Are we being fools?

Fools for love.

Is it wise?

No, it's supremely foolish.

She asked if he sometimes thought it might be wiser for them to part.

You are mad.

Am I?

You are the greatest of all created things. The sweetest of all breathing women. You are exclamatory. If being naked were the fashion, you would be the best dressed woman in the United States. You are my dream, my soul, my life. Teach me to say it in Italian.

Mio diletto.

The other thing.

Tu sei il mio sogno, la mia anima, la mia vita.

La mia vita, Harry repeated. Why do even sweet nothings sound better in Italian?

Because it's the language of love. She smiled, stretching out her willing, impatient body to him. *Italiano è la lingua dell'amore.*

He touched her warm bare stomach with his fingertips. Do you know what the language of love is? He kissed her stomach with his moist and ravenous mouth. *Love.* Thou hast ravished my heart.

Tu mi hai rapito il cuore.

And now she was waiting and fretting, and suddenly it started to rain. It had been sunny a moment earlier.

When she was truly soaked, for she hadn't brought an umbrella—why would she, it had been a cloudless day when she woke up—that's when he showed up. He looked stressed, harried. But when he saw her he beamed with his whole tailored being. *He* had brought an umbrella.

That's Boston, he said and kissed her, holding the black umbrella over her white dress.

Look, she said, when his lips ceased, my dress is wet with rain.

He touched it with delight.

I have daisies in my hair.

He touched the daisies with delight. They're a little wilted after the downpour, he said. But you're glowing.

Did you bring the rings?

I forgot.

She knew he was joking. We have no witnesses, she said.

That's what happens when you elope. No one can bear witness to the secret truth.

She shivered all the while, but the smile didn't leave her face.

Arm in arm they walked down the flowered paths to Beacon Street. She was trying not to hurry. She didn't want to miss their train, but she didn't want to hurry a second of this day. It would be gone soon enough. Already so much of this day felt too rushed. Marry in haste, repent at leisure. What an idiotic saying. Why did she have to think of it just then. Their love wasn't in haste, was it? The love that consumed her since she set foot in the New World. *Amore il mio unico.*

What will your father say? she asked. Oh! I shudder when I think of him.

Harry stopped walking. He pulled her to him, held her around the waist, held her close. Propriety be damned. They were about to be married. But even married people didn't hold each other so intimately in public. It was like a photograph amid red roses of limbs in a rumpled bed.

My father will be upset no question, Harry said. He gave her another squeeze. He kissed her deeply. But I'm his only son. He'll have to get over it, won't he? They resumed walking, her arm threaded through his. The rain had stopped, the clouds vanished. It had poured just long enough to soak her.

But will he get over it?

Absolutely, Harry said. Let me tell you about my father. He is easily embarrassed by personal troubles, petty squabbles, little conflicts. You know how some people are squeamish about blood? My father is squeamish about melodrama. He kissed her silk-gloved hand. I see you're still worried, darling. Do you want me to tell you a little story while we're panting our way up to City Hall to make you feel better?

If you can walk uphill and tell comforting little stories at the same time, then yes.

Do you remember Billingsworth?

Remember? Harry, he still comes to Lawrence once a month to look over the books for Salvo's restaurants.

Ah. Of course. Well, one year he and my father were having a conversation about the budget allowances for the household for the coming year.

When was this?

They do this every year, but, in my story, it's the early 1890s. They were going over the list of expenditures and Billingsworth, as he's always done in the past, set aside a certain sum for my mother's household expenses.

My father stared at the ledger line. Billingsworth said, what is it, sir? Not enough? I can increase it if you wish; it won't be any trouble. My father blurted out to the man, Billingsworth, I'm so sorry, what an oversight on my part. He looked Billingsworth in the eye and said, Frances passed away. I can't believe I haven't told you. Please forgive my moral failing.

Harry emitted a short laugh, amused as he related the story to Gina.

How do you know this?

Billingsworth told me. It's the only time I've seen him do an animated spot-on impression of my father, of anyone, really. Complete with the jab in the forehead, the slapping, the tutting, the intonation.

Oh, Harry.

So Billingsworth said to my father, I'm ever so sorry, sir. Please accept my most sincere condolences, my deepest sympathies. Where is she being laid to rest? I'd like to send a bouquet, if I may. When did this terrible thing happen?

And my father, without missing a beat, said, six months ago.

Flabbergasted, Gina stared at Harry. Harry nodded. I told you. Our banker, our accountant, our family's chief financial officer, our business manager, the only man my father sees every single day of his life, was not informed of my mother's death for six months. Harry brought Gina's stunned hand to his lips. So don't worry, he said. If *that* could be swept under the rug, this most certainly will be.

He turned to her when they were breathless at the top of Beacon Street, near the side door of City Hall.

I want just one success in my life, he said, and that is to win *you*. I would walk with you soaked up a mountain of mud tireless and full of boundless joy as long as I walked it with you.

She stood pressed against him in the city clerk's office, in front of the justice of the peace, with a small bouquet of red roses in her hands and a ring on her finger. The stenographer and the prosecutor's secretary agreed to witness their vows. The justice made a little speech about uniting them in matrimony, about the commitment they were making to one another, about marriage being a journey, not a destination. Ironic, because it certainly felt like a destination to Gina. The journey had been just to get there.

I now introduce you to the world for the first time, the justice said, as Mr. and Mrs. Harold and Jane Barrington.

Then they were kissing and kissing. He held her to him, and she wasn't going to be the first to pull away. Her dress, still damp with rain, her hair curling extravagantly after being wet, her hands moist inside the silk gloves—she felt as if she were being spun around, as if on a merry-go-round, as if in a waltz.

Her eyes were closed to shut out the words of the justice of the peace to Harry. "Have you promised yourself to any other bride?"

"I have not, your Honor."

Have you promised yourself to any other bride?

I have not, your Honor.

Why of all things should she hone in on these thirteen words, the ones that stuck in her craw, as round and round they went, swirling like a small-cell hurricane. Was it a bad omen for newly wedded bliss to lie to an officer of the law?

The train to Chicago was interminable. They booked a private sleeper car. It was the only thing that saved her small-town Sicilian honor. She tried to stay quieter than the high-pitched caterwaul of the wheels against the rail, quieter than the intermittent ejaculation of the hissing steam engine. Their wedding night of consummated pyre was spread across a thousand miles and six states.

Love feels no burden, thinks nothing of trouble, attempts what is above its strength, pleads no excuse of impossibility; for it thinks all things lawful for itself, and all things possible was what the justice of the peace had said, quoting Thomas à Kempis.

Why did the quote that was meant to strengthen them, only weaken her?

Six

ARMS WRAPPED AROUND HERSELF, Gina walked beside the Lawrence canals and the Merrimack River until it got dark, and then went home. She was half-hoping Harry wouldn't be home; he often wasn't. But no such luck.

There he was on their porch, sitting, smoking. She walked past him, thought of saying something, thought better of it, and quietly went inside. Because it was Saturday night, Mimoo had somehow gotten herself together and gone to the bingo hall on Essex. The dinner dishes were still piled in the sink. Gina filled it up with water, dropped in a dollop of soap, and rolled up her long sleeves, made of black crepe as if she were a widow.

She heard him come in, shut the door, pace back and forth behind her. She heard his voice. "You know, I used to think Rose Hawthorne placed entirely too much importance on her father's favorite theme—sin. But now I'm beginning to wonder if perhaps what was required was more emphasis, not less. In any case, the lesson, weak or strong, seems to have been lost on you."

He didn't ask her a question, so she didn't reply. Her hands nearly broke the porcelain cup she was washing. She was afraid his words were true. Insufficient emphasis, lost lessons, lack of remorse.

"Tell me," he said, with fake calm, "how does *that* man of all the men out there jibe with your political awakening? Have you told him you're a feminist and an anarchist?"

"An armchair anarchist," she said. "In *your* derisive words. I won't go to jail for it." She continued to wash the dishes.

"You've never met a more free-market rationalist, a more anti-free-love traditionalist than him. Everything he believes, you pretend to me is anathema to you. I always thought you and I were of the same mind on these things, but perhaps *I'm* the one being pretended to."

"Perhaps you are."

He fell mute.

Her gaze was on the dishes. She struggled not to sigh. Not to cry.

He came up behind her, too close, not close enough.

"Did you do it to punish me?"

"I don't know what you mean." She squeezed shut her eyes.

"You explain nothing," Harry said, breathing hotly into the back of her head. "You just shop and cook and lie down with me."

"And work. Like a good wife."

170

"No one can accuse you of anything but. *All* in a day's work, in a day's life. But I need you to explain one thing to me."

She opened her eyes and swilled the plates in the soapy water. She heard him struggling with his words.

"Why didn't you just go with him?"

"Why would I?"

"Stop it!"

She was afraid he was going to shake her until the confessions tumbled out.

"Tell me. Why didn't you?"

She heaved out her sadness. "I didn't want to."

He heaved out a breath. "When? Then? Or now?"

"Harry, please."

"I'm asking you a fucking question. Then or now?"

"Then."

He exhaled his heartbreak behind her, right into her hair. She shut her eyes again, her hands hanging limply in the dishwater, her squared shoulders rounding.

"And now?"

Ben got married. He married Ingersol in Panama. Gina wanted to scream, to sob, to weep. Rose had told her that, and then Gina lost her baby.

"Then *and* now," she replied, her voice a vapor.

"Why don't you tell me I left you alone too long?"

"You left me alone too long."

"Why don't you tell me I'm not the man you thought I was."

She said nothing.

"Nothing more you will say?"

"There is nothing *to* say." Her head was lowered, as if she were praying, confessing, repenting.

"Tell me you don't love me," Harry whispered.

"I can't," she said. "*Ti amo.*"

He staggered away. "I wish I'd never come back," he said in a groan. "I wish I didn't get paroled early for good behavior."

"Not early enough," said Gina.

"Why did I work so hard for it?"

"I don't know," she said. "Why struggle for good behavior in prison ..."

"So I could come back to *you*!"

She raised her hand. The back of her hand was to him, as her back was to him. She wouldn't even turn around. "You didn't let me finish. Why struggle for good behavior in prison when there is no such compunction in your free life?"

"You're lecturing *me* about good behavior?"

"I haven't said a word to you, ever."

"Who can find a virtuous wife?" he asked desolately.

"A virtuous husband, that's who," she replied, never turning from the sink. She had the sheaf of letters to Harry from Reed and Haywood, from Elizabeth Flynn and Mary Vorse, forwarded from the prison after Harry had been released, letters opened and read by Gina, now lying deep in the closet, below her ice skates. She didn't know how he could have missed them. That's how she knew that Mary Vorse corresponded with her husband in ways that seemed too politically intimate, as if she were replying to his own intimate thoughts. She didn't have Harry's letters. Not to Mary Vorse, not to herself. He did not write to his wife, only to the woman who in her replies quoted Shelley. *And my heart ever gazes on the depth of thy deep mysteries,* Mary had written to Gina's husband.

They stopped talking. The tank was empty. They had run out of all fueling words. Gina finished cleaning up. Harry threw away the newspapers. Mimoo was still not home. Gina couldn't go to sleep until she helped her mother get ready for bed, and wished Mimoo could come home from bingo a little earlier just once.

Upstairs, she lay next to Harry for a few minutes listening to him breathe, hard and broken. "I thought we were so strong that nothing could touch us," he said.

"Oh God. We are. *Mi dispiace.* Forgive me, *marito* ..." With exhaustion she reached for him.

He jumped out of bed. Both his hands were up as if either to surrender or to shove her away. "Not a *word* more about it. Especially in our bed. I know I accused you of not explaining anything. Believe me, that's but a small mercy. We can do one of two things, you and I. We can talk about it and then part for good. And perhaps that's best and maybe it's what you want. *You* tell me. Or we can walk on and pretend it never happened. Pretend there's nothing to talk about, as if it doesn't exist between us. Those are our two choices. Rather, those are *your* two choices. What will it be?"

"Do you want to part with *me*?"

He blinked. His hands were still up. "You know I can't," he whispered, clawing at his chest as if he wished to rend it open like a cloak. "You are my only Calais."

Gina opened her arms. "As you are mine."

He came back to bed.

They walked on.

Except …

Gina had to stop working at Rose's Home, reluctantly, regretfully. Harry couldn't take it. He said nothing but she could tell it was impossible. She couldn't explain it to Rose, but Rose understood everything.

"You know what my father said about regret?" Rose said when Gina went one last time to say goodbye. "About choosing a path you later think has led you astray? He said there was a fatality to it, a feeling so irresistible it had the force of doom, which invariably compelled human beings—you, your husband—to linger around and haunt, ghostlike, the spot where some great and marked event had given the color to your lifetime; and the more irresistibly you returned to that spot, the darker the tinge that saddened it." She kissed Gina's crying face. "Every single thing in this world," Rose said, "is marble and mud, my darling child. The only thing you can do is make the best of it."

Chapter 6

TEN DAYS THAT SHOOK THE WORLD

One

"YOU WANT TO GO *where?*"

"Russia, I told you."

"But *why?*" It had begun as a normal Sunday afternoon. She had been about to start on an early dinner. It was April, and warm out. She had been thinking they could eat outside. Maybe amble down to the Common to see if the ducks had hatched more babies.

"Gina, have you been reading the papers? Or even the magazine I work for? Russia is about to have a bonafide revolution!"

"Didn't they just have a revolution last month?" It was 1917. "The Tsar abdicated, Kerensky is signing decrees with a gold pen in the Winter Palace. How many uprisings can they have in one year? But more to the point, what do their buffets of revolutions have to do with our business, yours and mine?"

"Only everything."

"Only nothing. Why would we go to Russia? The annual Boston spring fair is next month. I wouldn't mind going to that."

"Be serious."

"I am."

"Max said he would raise money for John Reed and me to go."

"Wonderful," she said. "He can't raise ten dollars to pay you for a week's work. But he's going to raise money to get you to Russia?"

"I desperately want to be part of something bigger, to be part of history. Don't you?"

"Um … no."

"You've become so provincial." Unamused, he returned to leafing through the paper. "I realize when it happened. The moment you became hell-bent on having a child, your concerns now begin and end with the bedroom. Shame, really. You used to have such an abundance of other passions."

"Funny that. There was once a time you used to have only one." She said it because she knew he would ignore her words, and true to himself, Harry didn't disappoint. He ignored them. She said quite a lot to him that he simply ignored.

"Louise Bryant is going." That was to bait her. Because he knew she ignored nothing. Louise was John Reed's wife. As if she were the perfect wife, this prize of a woman who married John Reed and immediately set up house with his best friend, the playwright. Gina wouldn't be baited. Not yet. He tap-tapped at the paper. "Lenin just returned to Petrograd from Geneva. A triumphant return to the country that exiled him. He's ready to overthrow Kerensky and the Mensheviks who have betrayed the communist cause by making devil's bargains with absolutely everyone."

"And is Lenin promising not to make devil's bargains with anyone?"

"Of course." He stood up to come near her.

"Well," Gina said, "if what you're saying is true, then Petrograd is the *last* place you and I want to be."

"No, please be serious." He took her by the arms and turned her to him.

"Do I seem facetious to you?" Her solemn brown unimpressed eyes met with his inflamed gray ones.

"We *must* go." He stopped. The look on her face must have been a sight. "*I* must go."

She shrugged as if to say, you do what you must do.

Harry continued his persuasion. "Your Emma Goldman is going."

"I care about this why?"

"Come on, princess. We will go for solidarity." He shook her a little. "Gina! I have been dreaming of this moment."

"You've always been a dreamer, that's true. But dreaming of going to Russia?"

"Yes!"

"Quietly, then, because this is the first *I'm* hearing of this particular dream."

"I have been talking about nothing but this moment for twenty years."

"About going to Russia?" She tried not to sound incredulous.

"I have to go ... to watch a new order be born. To stand shoulder to shoulder with giants. To bear witness to the most radical change your eyes will ever see."

"Radical change?" She emptied the dried dead flowers out of the grimy vase. She used to always have fresh flowers in the house. It had been weeks since these tulips had withered and died in a centerpiece on her table. "Harry, do you forget I'm an immigrant? I came from a volcanic town. My father cut hair for free for all the poor people in Belpasso and charged the rich people triple so he could save enough for me to come here." She laughed. "America *is* my radical change. I came here on a boat, remember? I told—" she broke off. It wasn't Harry she had told this. She blinked to shake off the past, the memories, everything. "And I will tell *you* again"—Oh, what an elision, what a fraud—"I have zero interest in leaving this country."

"Not forever," Harry said. "For a month. Maybe three."

"Last time I heard that, you were in prison fifteen months. And what do I do with my mother?"

"Stop hiding behind her, for once. You can't move to Boston, to New York, can't go to Russia. You might as well be in Belpasso for all the good America's doing you."

"What, I came to America to abandon my mother? My father would be well pleased."

"Can't Salvo take care of her?"

"What is it with you men?" She shook her head.

"What men?"

"Harry, Salvo has been paying half of the rent for three years, while you've been yodeling for *The Masses*."

"Max Eastman calls me indispensable to our publication!"

"Salvo pays Mimoo's doctor's bills. He comes to visit her on Sundays." Though not today because Harry was home. "He cooks for her when he comes. But he is not her daughter. He can't take care of her. He is a man." She wanted to ask if Harry could have taken care of his own mother, but she knew the conversation would then snap to an instant halt. Perhaps that was preferable.

"She'll be fine for a month. She's got a townful of friends. She knows every single person we pass on the street. Last time I took her shopping it took us forty-five minutes to walk two blocks! She's got more friends than I've had dinners. Come on, Gia. History!" Harry was beseeching, not authoritarian. "Aren't you the least bit excited?" He was turning forty in a few months. His hair was lightened a shade by the oncoming gray, but it didn't look gray, more like sand after rain. He was still slim and thoughtful, put-together and rumpled at the same time, as if the clothes fit or didn't, and he was all right either way. His eyes were sparkling clear. They weren't fog and they weren't slate. She hadn't seen him this animated in months, maybe years. It made her slightly happy to see him excited, but only slightly, and she wouldn't admit it to him.

"Not the least bit." She turned back to the sink. The dead tulips thrown away, she scrubbed the inside of the filthy vase. "Harry, you've been in constant trouble with the law. What if they don't let you come back?"

"Not constant. I've been careful lately."

"They're threatening to close down *The Masses* because of the stuff you write."

"I know," he said proudly. "I told you Max says I'm indispensable."

"Yes—to me, not to him."

Nicely true to form he ignored her. "And why wouldn't they let me come back? And who's they?"

"The Americans."

There was a silence from him as if he were speaking one step behind the beat of his thoughts.

Encouraged, she went on. "America has just entered the war …"

Unfortunately this sent him in another direction, an apoplexy of vitriol against Wilson. "The man got re-elected on one slogan!" he said. "One. Do you remember what it was?"

"I do," she replied, "but I don't care."

"He kept us out of war. That's it. Six words got him re-elected. That was what, four months ago?"

"He did keep us out of war—for almost three years. Maybe that's what he meant. He did use the past tense."

"You're joking, right? Hair-splitting over fraud perpetrated upon the American people?"

"Besides," Gina continued, calmer than her husband, "Wilson told us the war would be over in a flash. The most it would take, he said, is six weeks."

"Six weeks?" Harry sneered. "He also wants to sell you a bridge. Mark my words, the clang of noisome machines is about to be ousted by the clatter of even more noisome machine guns."

"Don't be such a pessimist, Harry," she said. "Dream bigger. Wilson thinks you can have both."

He laughed. "I'm not a pessimist," he said. "I'm an eternal optimist."

"I was joking. You did laugh, correct?"

"I always tell you not to worry about anything. I always tell you everything will turn out all right. This too." Turning her away from the vase and the dead flowers, he took her into his arms, toward himself and his agitation. "We'll go to Russia to get away from Wilson's foul oppression of lies and deceit."

"The laws have gotten so much stricter," said Gina, spooling her long arms around his neck. "You can't behave like you used to. They'll throw us both out of the country." She kissed him. "They'll say we were supporting the Bolsheviks."

"We *are* supporting the Bolsheviks." He kissed her back. "I'm an American citizen. They can't refuse me re-entry into my own country."

"Are you sure about that?"

He wavered. "Almost certain."

"It's dangerous out there," she said, trying a different tactic. When Harry wanted something this intensely, it had always been difficult to move his needle in a different direction. He was the same way with everything, whether or not it made sense, whether or not it was good for his life, for business, for his marriage. Sometimes that persistence was arousing. Sometimes it was exasperating. And sometimes it was frightening. This felt a little like all three. They were standing spousally close. She didn't want to move away. "The *Lusitania* was torpedoed, full of civilians," she said. "What if we won't be able to come back through the war-torn seas?"

"So we'll stay on for a few more months. Just you and me." He tilted his head.

Shaking hers, Gina kept silent. Bad portents flew like crows through her insides. She moved away from him, her attention back on the vase. The glass was permanently stained. It was not going to get crystal clean no matter how hard she scrubbed it.

He came up behind her, close, so close. His arms went around her waist, his face pressed into her hair. "Gia, what's really behind this?"

She didn't want to say. She didn't want to go, that was plain, this she told him. But she didn't want to say what was really behind this, not yet.

She changed the subject the only way she knew how. "Well, you're behind me for now." She wiped her hands dry and turned to him for good. She lured him away from Russia with her willing, receptive, vulnerable body, hoping it would be enough and he would let it go.

As always, Harry let the wrong thing go. A few days later he told her that Max Eastman couldn't raise enough money for Harry *and* for John Reed to travel to Russia. Harry asked her if they had enough money in the bank to pay for two third-class tickets to France. She showed him the bank ledger. They didn't have nearly enough for two sea passages, two train tickets, plus money to live in Petrograd. Gina closed the bank book with barely hidden satisfaction, hoping that would be the end of that, practical matters resolving his abundant enthusiasm.

But Harry had other ideas.

"Clearly both of us can't go," he said, pacing through the living room. "Your mother is not well anyway. You said so yourself. And you don't really want to go. You said so yourself. I'll go by myself. I'll be back for Christmas."

"As if Christmas has some kind of special significance for you!" Sicilian-like, not Boston-like. She wished she didn't feel so run over by the turn of this ludicrous conversation.

"I don't want to go without you," he said. "You know that. I don't want to be away from you. But I desperately want us to go. Please. Can we hock your wedding ring? We'll have enough for a trip around the world and back with the money we get from it."

She became so weak she had to sit down.

"You want me to sell my wedding ring?" she said in horror.

"Not sell, *pawn*."

"And how do you propose we will *ever* get it back? What's your plan for getting it out of hock? You're mad! You've lost your mind."

"What's gotten into you? Why are you snapping at me like a turtle?"

"Harry, we're not giving away my wedding ring. Never."

"I'll go by myself then. We have just enough for me to go."

Gina chewed her lip as if she were trying to chew it off.

"We don't have enough money for the Revolution *and* a baby," she said haltingly.

He was momentarily stunned into silence. "Who said anything about a baby?"

"I'm saying it now."

He was stunned into a longer silence.

"Oh, so this one you do bother to tell me about," he said dully, sounding defeated.

"You told me to tell you everything."

"You could've waited to tell me after I left."

"What?"

"Written me a letter. Sent me a telegram. Never mind."

"I'm telling you now because I don't want you to go. And we have good reason not to. *I* certainly can't go." She palmed her still flat stomach.

"How far along?"

"A few months. Around three."

He looked down on the table, at their bank book, at maps of Russia, newspapers of war and disaster, posters of proletarians.

"I'll be back before it's born," he said weakly.

"It's due in October 1917," she said. "What if you're not back? What if the Bolsheviks and the Mensheviks get into a scuffle and the upheaval continues until then? What if you get thrown into prison there, get sick, or … worse? You want your child to grow up without a father?"

"It's the revolution …" he said.

"*Mio amore*, the baby is also a revolution," said Gina.

Harry didn't go.

Two

SIX WEEKS LATER, in June 1917, just as *The Masses* was being shut down by the Espionage Act, Gina started to bleed. She stopped all work, all movement, lay in bed, and prayed, tried to save herself, save her child. No success, only sorrow.

There was no hiding this loss from him even for five minutes. She lay in her bed while a crying Mimoo changed her dressings, and a mute Harry slept sitting up on the couch. Both devastated, they took out their crushing disappointment on each other. He blamed her for forcing him "for no reason" to miss out on the greatest experience of his life. And she, beyond blaming anything or anyone, feeling responsible for everything, disappeared wholly inside herself. She became nearly mute, stopped speaking. She prayed only to become like Helen Keller before the water flowed into her palm, to live in a place inside her soul where no words, no symbols, no sounds had any meaning.

To get away from Lawrence, Harry scrambled to get his visa application approved for Russia, but was informed by the State Department it was already too late. With the war raging and the United States in the midst of it, only a few exit visas per year were currently allowed, and they had all been applied for and allotted until January 1918.

Harry was forced to read about the storming of the Winter Palace from John Reed's dispatches to Max Eastman and relate it to Gina with barely controlled hostility. And she, with barely controlled hostility, pretended to listen.

"Lenin has abolished all private property," said Harry. "One of his thirteen decrees upon taking power."

"Abolished," Gina repeated. "It's now illegal in Russia to own land?"

"Correct. All property finally belongs to the working man."

"Ah. What about all the men who presently own land or real estate in Russia?"

"They're out of bounds of the new law."

"So what happens to their property?"

"It will be confiscated, I guess."

"Nice," said Gina, going back to her sewing. The pedal went down, the machine resumed its rat-tat-tat sound. "Taking the pails from other kids in the sandbox. I'm sure that'll happen without a fight."

"What did you say?" The noise of the sewing machine partly covered her words.

"Nothing, nothing. I was being ironic. I almost smiled." There was not a glimmer of a smile on her face.

After the Bolshevik Revolution in October but no baby, Harry became even more vociferously anti-war. The more Gina implored him to stay quiet, the louder he railed. He fully supported Lenin's pledges to pull Russia out of the war. Russia was not only communist now, but pacifist; two ideals Harry fell firmly behind. Weeks after Lenin took power, Russia stopped fighting on the side of the Allies and brought its soldiers home. Trotsky started negotiating with Germany for a separate peace. Everywhere in the United States, in Britain, in France, Russia was condemned as a traitor. The war could be lost by the Allies because of Russia's actions, was what everyone wrote in their newspapers and editorials. But in Harry's circles, Russia was a heroine. They could not say or write enough about her bravery for *The Masses*. The magazine was shut down twice for seditionist prose, and its chief editors taken to court.

Once Harry was free of the burdens of editing literary and political criticism and had some time on his hands, he began to attend every anti-war rally, big and small, in the vicinity of Boston, many in the presence of Emma Goldman. "No one says things against the war as clearly and vigorously as she," Harry told Gina. "Why do you refuse to come with me, now that I'm starting to really respect her?"

"I can't imagine why," Gina replied, wishing for less cleverness from both Goldman and her husband, who with their public remonstrations were flying headlong like blind birds into the Espionage Act.

"Don't worry about that," Harry told an increasingly anxious Gina. "Worry only about what's right."

In March 1918, Leon Trotsky finally signed a separate peace with Germany, ceding to the Central Power two-thirds of Russia's territory and a quarter of her population.

"I see what you mean, Harry," said Gina, "about Lenin never making a devil's bargain with anyone like that snake Kerensky. You're right, he's nothing if not an honorable man."

They didn't speak for a week after she said that.

A month later, in April 1918, Harry and a hundred others were arrested at the ill-fated recruitment station near Faneuil Hall during a loud demonstration that had turned violent. He was arrested after a futile year of protesting an inevitable war, a war everyone knew with cloudless clarity that the United States, a new global power, must one day join and would one day join. There was brutal language and an assault on three police officers. But most damagingly, there was once again the willful obstruction of a recruiting enlistment station, an act that was suddenly, as Harry found out only after he was openly charged, punishable by *twenty years* in prison as per the newly enacted Sedition clauses of the Espionage Act.

Three

AT FIRST HARRY TOOK what he called his "bad fortune" in stride. Eugene Debs and Emma Goldman had also been arrested in other parts of the country for their protests against the war, as was Bill Haywood. Harry thought he was in good company. He told Gina the United States simply couldn't convict all those public figures at once. Gina thought Harry was wildly naïve and said so. "You pretend you want peace," she told him, "but all you do is foment strife. You, Big Bill, Emma, Eugene Debs. All you do is sow seeds of conflict and struggle. And then you lament why you don't have the two things you clearly do not want."

"Which are?"

"Peace," she said. "And freedom."

"Did you come to jail to visit me or to torment me?"

"Why do I have to choose?"

All their savings for a car that never happened were not enough to make his extortionate bail. She borrowed from a resentful Mimoo, from St. Vincent's, from Father O'Reilly, and from the First Savings Bank of Lawrence—and was still short by half.

"There is a tide in the affairs of men," Harry said to her in the city jail while she was battling to raise the money for his release, "which, taken at the flood, leads on to fortune; omitted, and all the voyage of your life is bound in shallows and miseries."

Gina bowed her head, pretending to agree with him, while bitter tears fell from her eyes.

"You have nothing to cry about. You're not in prison."

"I once wrapped you in myself," she said to him, "but you have wrapped me in your own shallows. And yet look how deep they are. If you're convicted, you could go away for twenty years! That's *your* choice, but I'm going to be thirty-three and without a husband. That's not *my* choice."

"Your choice was me. And this is who I am."

She struggled up. The visiting hours were over.

"Doesn't seem fair, does it," she said blackly, "that one wrong decision can thus lay waste my life."

Which wrong decision did she mean? His decision to parade against Faneuil Hall? Or her decision to marry him?

"Your life? What about my life? I could've gone to Russia and could right now be writing dispatches about it, like John Reed. It's all I wanted. Instead you forced my hand and kept me here, and now look at me. Look where I am."

"I didn't know you were so passionate a writer, Harry." Gina clutched her years-old frayed purse. "You're barely even a letter-writer. It's a lost art, I hear, letter-writing."

He was scarcely listening to her.

"Did you hear what John Reed wrote to Max Eastman?" He was red with his disappointment. "The people are crowding to his lectures by the hundreds, by the thousands!"

"That's because John Reed is wisely not in prison."

"They protest against the way things are! That's the now, the protest is the future. Did you read what he wrote? That people weep with joy when they hear him, knowing there is something so close to dreams coming true in Russia."

She was weeping too for a place where dreams came true.

Instead of going to Russia, Gina pawned Harry's two-karat diamond ring and paid his bail.

Four

RELEASED FROM PRISON, Harry returned to Lawrence and spent the summer of 1918 on pre-trial hearings and motions, preparing his defense and shuttling back and forth to Boston. They were completely broke, materially and emotionally, and had nothing to say. Despite Harry's casual apathy, they both feared the ominous tide that was coming, like a tsunami after an earthquake. They both understood the change in the American air. The country was at war, and Harry broke its laws shouting hate from the pedestals and throwing rocks. Gina ground out each day through sheer will: get up, work, clean, help Mimoo, pray, sleep.

But by the end of August she couldn't take it anymore. By the end of August she had something to say, having come to the end of her very long tether one broiling afternoon when she had returned home for lunch to find the house a wreck and Harry unshaven and insolent.

She glared at him, trying to calm herself before she spoke. She counted to ten, breathed deep. It didn't work.

"What?" he barked. "I'm trying to put together my defense. I have no time for women's work."

"Do you know what Nathaniel Hawthorne says?"

"I don't give a fig. Now is not the time for his pithy sayings."

"On the contrary, it's precisely the time. He says," Gina continued in a controlled eruption, "that even a *dull river has a deep religion of its own. So, let us trust, has the dullest human soul, though perhaps unconsciously.*"

"What does that have to do with me? Are you calling me dull?"

"No, no." She shook her head. "You're *far* beyond that. I don't agree with Nathaniel this time. I don't think you have religion running under the sludge. I think with you, it's just sludge."

Gone were the yesterdays of well-appointed drawing rooms and Harry in his gray waistcoat and white-pique trousers, entertaining by the fire with a cocktail in his hand. This Harry wore the same stained cotton trousers ironed by her last Sunday week and a brown shirt mis-buttoned and torn at the collar. She used to repair his old clothes, but when her sewing machine broke and they didn't have the money to repair it, she stopped. To think that Harry once wore lacquered shoes when he courted her in New Hampshire, dazzled her in silk morning shirts in Revere Beach, accompanied her on the ocean promenades in black swagger coats to contrast with her pink summer dresses.

"Oh, you're delightful this afternoon. Why in the world did you even come home for lunch if you're going to be like this?"

"Why in the world did I beg and borrow and pawn my diamond to get you out of jail if you're going to be both lazy and nasty? Look at our house! Look at you!"

"I'm nasty? Are you listening to yourself? I should've just stayed in jail."

"Perfect!"

"No one nags me there."

"I find that difficult to believe."

"Lots of things you have no clue about, sweetheart."

"Do you have a clue about how to be a good husband?"

"Oh, like you have about being a good wife?"

She gasped, let out a hiss of shallow air.

"God! Why didn't you just leave me three years ago?" she yelled, hurling his newspapers and cigarette butts at him.

"Why didn't you leave *me*?" He shot up out of his chair, the ashtrays, cups, papers falling to the floor.

"I should have! I'd rather be without a husband than live like this, unforgiven. Why did you bother to stay if you knew you couldn't forgive me?"

"Why are you so provincial? What does any of this have to do with you? Have you been stricken blind with brain fever? Is that why you can't see?"

"I see everything!"

"I'm about to lose my life!" he yelled. "I don't know what *you're* talking about. Forgiven you for what? That you fucked another man while you were married to me, pretending to love me? You aspire to be so bourgeois, Gina. You think your tawdry dalliance is what keeps me up at night?" He laughed. "I'm long past that. This has nothing to do with you, princess, what's happening now. So go put on your silk gloves and pretend you're a fine lady, go tend to your little business, whatever it is. I stopped thinking about you long ago. The world is in dire upheaval while you waltz around with your head in the clouds pretending what's happening with us is about some degrading personal bullshit! I don't give a shit about personal. Can't you see? The world is being turned upside down. I don't recognize the world anymore."

"Funny, that's what you said to me when you were falling in love with me on the beach in Hampton."

Caught sideways, he breathed out brine and regret before he spoke. "Yes," he said, panting through his clamped teeth. "And I was right. You turned me inside out, and since then my life has never been the same."

"Shut up! If I hear one more word about all you gave up for me, I will hang myself! You've held your sacrifice over me like a bludgeon for thirteen years so you don't have to do a single blessed thing you don't want to do. And every time I ask you for the smallest thing, the littlest thing, you beat me over the head with your fucking sacrifice! I'm sick and tired of it. I'm sick and tired of you. What favor do you think you've done me?" She was shaking, barely standing, grasping the back of a chair. "With or without you, my life is exactly the same. Worse with you. I'm still with my mother, in Lawrence, broke, without a baby—"

"And that's *my* fault?"

She burst into tears.

He took one step toward her. "I'm s—"

She put her hands up to stop him. "Get away from me. Even when you're here, you're not here, except to make a dire mess of all things."

He stepped away. "Don't worry, soon you'll be without me. So no more mess. All good?"

"It'll be better than this. Anything would be better than this."

"Right. And I won't fret about you. I know that while I'm in prison you'll find a way to comfort yourself."

She slapped him across the face. He let her. They stood glaring at each other, panting.

"You gave away your married body and *I'm* the one getting slapped?"

"I thought you didn't give a shit about it?"

"And you believed me?"

They made crashing savage piercing love with the doors closed, the windows shuttered, trying not to scream through their antagonism in the sweltering dog day afternoon.

"Why won't you leave me?" She breathed out, parched and spent. "You want to. You've wanted to for so long. You have friends that don't include me, a life that doesn't include me. You're fomenting trouble while I spin and toil. Why won't you go?"

"I'll ask you the same question. Why won't *you* go?"

"Where am I going to go? My life is here."

"Mine too."

They fell quiet, clammy with their exertions.

"You've really done it this time," she said. "Really done it. The Sedition Act is implacable and you've flagrantly transgressed it."

"I hate their laws, I find them loathsome. I fight on the side only of what's right."

"You're standing on a soapbox in the middle of war, supporting Lenin and yelling for the overthrow of the U.S. government."

"Yes. Like Lenin, I believe it's morally wrong to send young men to war to fight for a cause no one, not the President, not Congress, not the hawks, the economists or any of the politicians can even articulate. Imperial internationalist finance capital is as good a reason as any. No one can explain to anyone else why we are sending our young men to be slaughtered in Europe. Can you?"

"I don't care."

"Oh, you'd care if you had a son."

She tore away from him, but he grabbed her and bound her close.

"Nowhere to go," Harry whispered, holding her down, climbing on top of her. "Shackled together for life, you and I, and the chains are eating away into your lovely ankles."

Eventually when they were good and done, he released her, and she crawled to the edge of their small bed and curled into a ball, her back to him.

"We're done," he said.

"We've been done a long time." She emitted a shallow groan. "And we didn't even know it."

Five

A MONTH LATER, IN September 1918, Harry, Eugene Debs and Emma Goldman were convicted under the Sedition Act for hindering the recruitment at a military station, attacking a police officer and propagating vicious lies against the U.S. government. Their looming punishment was ten years without parole. It was better than the twenty-year sentence Bill Haywood received. Big Bill was found guilty of a total of ten thousand counts of sedition. Twenty years seemed a light penalty in his case.

Harry's sentencing was in December, but his bail in the meantime had been raised to an unattainable ten thousand dollars because the

District Attorney deemed Harry a flight risk, and this time, the judge agreed. They returned to Gina the original bail amount, and she paid everyone back except the pawnshop. She had ninety days to buy back her ring, and it had been one hundred and thirty-seven. There was no way she could pay the interest and storage charges on it past the ninety days to keep it in the shop indefinitely. She barely had enough money for the bus to Concord each week.

Gina had asked him last time he was incarcerated in Concord why he never wrote to her, and he said it was because she would find their visits a lot less interesting if he bombarded her with words in the in-between days, but she recalled their Sunday visits, him sitting across from her, peeking at her through the diamond mesh of the steel partition, reading the newspaper, commenting on the week's events, talking about the laundry, the awful food, and wondered if that was true.

Weeks into his imprisonment in October, Harry finally wrote to Gina.

> Don't come visit me. It's best you stay away. Don't take me too
> seriously, but no one writes letters anymore. It's becoming a
> lost art. We scribble now, dictate commands. I'm sorry I'm not
> more charming. But it's difficult to be amiable when around me
> everyone is falling like flies from the Spanish flu. If you come,
> you're sure to get sick. I don't want you to fall sick. I'm in a fog as
> to how you feel about me, after all the words you screamed at me
> in August, which sounded too much like the bitter truth. Perhaps
> I will get sick, and clarify your heart in the process. Maybe I'll
> drop dead. Would you find that appealing? Perhaps I'm not being
> artful enough, but what I'm trying to say is, then you won't
> even have to feel guilty about not visiting me. If the ditch digger
> perchance happens to return home again at the precise moment
> when I'm conveniently in prison, please give him my regards.

But Gina barely registered Harry's ill-tempered letter. She was worried about her mother.

Six

MIMOO COULDN'T GET OUT of bed. She kept vomiting, couldn't keep anything down, not even water. She couldn't move her frail body. Gina couldn't work the looms at the mission or the sewing machines at the mending room because she had to stay home to take care of her mother. Salvo took time off from Purity for a day here, a day there, but it wasn't enough. He couldn't take time off and be the only breadwinner for his sister and mother. The Sodality Sisters began a collection to help Gina pay the rent and buy food. But it wasn't enough. The mission got involved. Father O'Reilly got involved.

When it looked as if Mimoo had caught pneumonia, Gina borrowed money from Rita for a taxi and took her mother to the Lawrence hospital. She never left her side.

"Mimoo," Gina said on a dark and quiet evening, sitting by her mother. "You say you know everything—why haven't I been able to carry a baby? What's wrong with me?"

"Child, I don't have all the answers. Pray to the good Lord for guidance. I thought for a long time it was because you didn't want a child. You know that God in His infinite wisdom wouldn't want to give you something He knew you didn't want."

"You know I did, Mimoo," Gina whispered. "What you're saying is not true. I wanted one desperately. I still want one."

Mimoo leveled a weak look at her daughter. "Good luck with that, now that your husband is in prison for the rest of your child-bearing life."

Oh, Mimoo.

Oh, Harry.

"You and your Emma Goldman, you and your Margaret Sanger. They're in jail too, just like that husband of yours. None of you believe in children."

"I do. Maybe not they. But I do."

"Well," said Mimoo. She was wheezing, struggling to breathe. "No use talking about pointless things now. Your ship has sailed and is sitting in the pokey until 1928. Don't be glum. You'll have other joys."

Like what, Gina wanted to ask, but didn't.

"Don't leave me, Mama."

Mimoo placed her cold, worn-out hand on her daughter's wet face. Rales, abnormal sounds, rose from her chest. The skin was blue on her once olive face. "The greatest joy I have in my life is being your mother. Despite everything."

A few hours later Mimoo bled from her mouth, gasping for air, unable to breathe, suffocating, not breathing. From beginning to end, barely a week, a faint candle flame.

Seven

GINA WAS WRETCHEDLY THROWING up in the hospital lavatory, with her mother five doors away, untaken. She could hear her brother in the corridor sobbing. A nurse passing by said she should see a doctor. A mask was on her face. Gina put her own mask on. "What's happening?" she asked the doctor who came to record the time and cause of Maria Attaviano's death. Gina had been crying so hard and throwing up that her eyes were bloodshot. The doctor took one look at her and hurried to put his mask on. "No one is going to make it," he told her, "absolutely no one, if you don't get yourself into isolation immediately. You can't be in the hospital coughing like that. What are you doing, making yourself sick, vomiting everywhere? Get control of yourself! Your mother got the flu. Millions of people are infected all over the Eastern seaboard. Tens of thousands have already died. Stay away from hospitals. Hospitals are hotbeds of germ activity. And this germ travels fast and is lethal. Have you *not* been reading the papers?"

Newspapers brought her nothing but bad news. She had deliberately stopped reading them after Harry went away.

Half of Lawrence turned out for Mimoo's funeral. They all took up a collection for the priest and the cemetery. Luigi, the local coffin maker, made Mimoo a wooden casket free of charge for all the pasta sauce Gina had given him over the years. Father O'Reilly performed the service.

All the bingo ladies from the parish sat in the front pews weeping. But other people were sick, too. You couldn't miss the haunted faces, the translucent skin, the coughing. Something terrible was going around, something no one had seen before. Mimoo's multitude of friends memorialized her, buried her, all walked in a procession after the casket to St. Mary's Cemetery, all crossed themselves and sang *Ave Maria*, but Gina could tell that they were crying for Mimoo, while thinking, who's next? Do I have what she had? She worked last week, and five days later she's dead. What is happening? Will it happen to me?

And Father O'Reilly, as if picking up on the black mood, read from Matthew for the funeral sermon, the parable of the Ten Virgins.

"Five were wise, but five were foolish," he said. "The wise ones brought the oil for their lamps to meet the bridegroom, but the foolish ones left their oil behind. The bridegroom tarried. They slept. And then He came. The fools jumped up. Give us your oil, they said to the others, for our lamps are going out.

"Yet they failed. Not the humanity of those they asked, not the simplicity of their request, not their want, made them obtain what they wanted. Because no man can protect us if we are not ready," Father O'Reilly said. "Not because he will not, but because he cannot.

"They ran to buy the oil and missed the bridegroom. I know you not, He said to them when they finally knocked on His door.

"So brothers and sisters, servants of God, I beseech you, the good Lord beseeches you, carry oil in your lamps, for you know not the day nor the hour. How frequently our Lord adds this admonition to us concerning the terrible ignorance of our earthly departure. You know not the day nor the hour. Be ready."

Peculiarly the sermon had the opposite of its intended effect. The sobbing and coughing, the lack of comfort and the increase in fear became only more resounding after the priest had finished.

Salvo couldn't stop crying—before or after Father O'Reilly, as if the priest were incidental to Salvo's sorrow. He wasn't numb like Gina or unwell like her. He had been working and couldn't get to the hospital before Mimoo died. He was inconsolable about not saying goodbye. "Just last week I saw her," he kept repeating.

"She wasn't well last week either, Salvo. You kissed her goodbye when you left, didn't you?"

He wiped his nose in the wet windy weather. They were walking to the church reception hall after burying their mother. "I know," he said. "But she was better than this. She was alive."

They stayed together for a day or two afterward in their lonely house. Gina tried to talk to Salvo about Harry, but Salvo was an exceptionally hostile audience. She let it go.

"Come back, Salvo," Gina said to him. "I don't want to live alone. Stay with me."

"If I stay with you, we'll both be on the street because I'll be out of work. How can I pay your rent?"

"Get a job here. Luigi is hiring."

"I'm going to make caskets?"

"Is what you're doing now so much better?" She sneezed.

"I work three jobs. I cook at the tavern on the weekends. And nights I'm on the docks, unloading olive oil, tobacco. You want me to give that up?"

She said nothing.

"Soon when the war is over, *you* might have to come stay with me, *sorella*. Might have to come live with me in the North End, no matter how much you don't want to."

"*Is* the war going to be over?"

"Haven't you heard? The Germans are about to lose the battle of attrition because the flu is killing more of them than the British and French."

"The flu is on our side?" Gina said. "I don't believe it."

"The Germans are stronger and better trained. The strong die first."

"That's absurd!"

Salvo left after three days, after fifty of Mimoo's friends came to bring Gina platters of food. She had nowhere to put any of it. On the plus side, she didn't have to worry about shopping, buying, money, cooking.

On the minus side she had no appetite.

The weather didn't get better.

Gina didn't get better either. Many mornings she couldn't get out of bed. "It's normal," said Rita, who looked in on her. "You just lost your mother. Why would anyone want to get out of bed after that?"

That was true. Gina agreed. But this physical malaise was not normal: the low-grade fever, the lack of interest in food, the whole-body dire exhaustion.

Salvo paid her November rent.

And then Rita got a low-grade fever and stopped working. She stumbled down the stairs one evening and said she was taking herself to the hospital because her chest was hurting like there was a baby in it trying to get out. Gina didn't see Rita again. Two days later, Father O'Reilly buried Rita.

Gina was so afraid. She couldn't take another day of fever and vomiting. She decided not to go to the hospital. Was it just her imagination, or did everyone who went to the hospital die there? As she dragged her body along Randall Street on the way to their family physician, she overheard from two men smoking cigars and chatting on the street corner telling each other about their elderly fathers throwing up. As she walked past them too weak to button her overcoat, she thought, is that what I am, elderly? I'm throwing up because I've gotten so old?

Her doctor, with the alliterative and endearing name of Clifford Clyde, examined her but blessedly did not appear to be as panicked as she was. She was embarrassed because as always she couldn't remember which name was his first and which his last. Clifford or Clyde. She kept getting confused even after the receptionist behind the desk told her.

"My mother just died of the flu," Gina said, and started to cry.

"Yes, I know. I'm very sorry about Mimoo," said Clyde Clifford Clyde. "But I'm not sure *that's* what's troubling you. Is your husband sick?"

"I don't know. He's in prison."

"Again?" Through a stethoscope the doctor listened to her breathe. "He sure likes it there, doesn't he?"

"Well, there he doesn't have to worry about paying the rent," said Gina. Is that what happened to people who were born with a silver spoon in their mouth? Once the spoon is taken away, they don't know how to feed themselves.

"When did you last see him?"

"Two weeks ago at the jail."

"No. I mean ..."

"Oh. August. He was convicted in September."

Gina didn't want to tell the doctor that after their blistering August attack on each other, Harry had left Lawrence and stayed in Boston for three weeks until his trial date. And when his bail was denied, he was remanded to the medium security at Concord to await sentencing. She kept silent. "He told me not to come visit him because of the flu."

"He is very wise, your husband," Clifford Clyde Clifford said, pulling up her sleeve to draw some blood. "I'll have to take it to the lab," he told her when he was done. "Your blood pressure is too high, you're flushed. You're not normal."

"I know. I told you. How long before the results are in?"

"A few days. A week at most."

Gina stopped by two days later just in case the results had come in early. It was the middle of the day and the office was closed. Perhaps it was because of the snow. But there was a sign on the door telling her the doctor had died.

The doctor had *died*! Clifford Clyde. Died? What an anomaly!

The following day the receptionist was back at the desk, but no one could find Gina's lab results or even her chart. There was a new doctor, younger. She didn't even bother to ask for his name. He also took blood from her and told her to call in seven days for the results.

"The last doctor who told me that stood where you're standing today," Gina said. "And when I called two days later, he was dead."

"Do you think that was because of your blood work?" The doctor was deadpan. "Or because you didn't wait the requisite days?"

She stared at him blankly.

"I'll tell you right now what's the matter with you, if you want."

She held on to the arm of the patient's chair for strength.

"You most likely have the flu," he said.

She started to cry.

"Also, you're expecting a child."

"I'm *what*?" Swiping at her face, she slipped down to the medical gurney and dully watched his impassive face. "That can't be."

"Which part, the flu, or … are you married?"

"Well, yes …"

"So it *can* be."

"No, no, you don't understand."

"How old are you?"

"Thirty-four."

"That really is too old to have a baby. Why did you wait so long?"

"I didn't wait," she said weakly. "We had trouble."

"Conceiving or keeping?"

"Keeping."

He nodded. "Do your best with this one. Where is your husband?"

"Prison."

The doctor was quiet, not knowing what to say. Gina didn't help him find a way.

After leaving his office, she walked stoically back home through the freezing mud. How long would it take this time? They had blamed the Bread and Roses strike for their failures, Big Bill, sick people at Rose's Home, the Russian Revolution.

Who were they going to blame now? The Spanish?

Eight

GINA DIDN'T LEAVE THE house the next day. She simply didn't know how she would ever get up again or why she would want to. She had food she wasn't eating and Salvo had paid her rent. She would worry about December's rent in three weeks. But in the evening, the young doctor knocked on her door. She was too weak to go out and greet him. From the couch she motioned to him to come in.

"You don't look good," he said, sitting down at her kitchen table. He covered his mouth.

"You don't think? But I'm feeling so spry."

"I want to help you."

The lonely lamp on the end table burned dim. She didn't want to run out of kerosene oil because she had no money to get more.

"What am I going to do?" she said. "My mother died. I'm alone. I can't work, I have no money. My husband is in prison. And you just told me I'm having a baby."

"I told you because you are. I'm only the messenger."

"What am I going to do? How am I going to work and stay pregnant? How am I going to pay the rent? How am I going to take care of this baby?" She was weeping.

"Don't worry," he said, almost but not quite reaching out to pat her for comfort. "Don't worry about those things. The baby brings his own food. That's what the Persians say. I spent some time in Tehran."

"The baby brings his own food," she repeated like a distant echo. "That's what my mother once said. And she'd never been to Tehran."

"She must have been wise. But this thing that's going around, is really dangerous for young people like you."

"I thought you said I wasn't young?" She waved away his protest. "And yet my elderly mother is dead," she said, wiping her face. "Go figure."

"I didn't say it's *not* dangerous for older people. I said it's *most* dangerous for young people with strong immune systems. It's counter-intuitive, I know. But, and this is what I came to say, it's *most* dangerous for pregnant women."

"Why? Do pregnant women have strong immune systems?"

"Yes. Something happens to the body when it's fighting for two. It becomes like a warrior. The viral response rises in proportion. It's called a *cytokine storm*. Have you heard of that? No? Well, you're doubly vulnerable."

"Okay," she said. *Cytokine storms, violet catastrophes.* How did they come up with these pithy phrases to signify her implosion? She didn't want to speak aloud about how few wan illusions she held about this pregnancy. "What do you recommend?"

"Leave. Go someplace else. It's terrible here, this freezing rain, the drafts, the wind."

"Go where? Like a quarantine?"

"Exactly like a quarantine. But to protect *you*."

Gina almost laughed. If she had the strength, she would have. "Would that I had a place I could disappear to and gestate in privacy."

"You've got to do something. You and your baby are in mortal danger. Don't you want to save yourself, save your child?"

Gina blinked. "I've got nowhere to go," she inaudibly mouthed. "I barely have a husband."

She fell back on the couch after the doctor left. It was as if the good Lord came knocking on the door of her heart and said, you wanted it like this? Like this it is. When you were young, you kept praying to me over and over, *Dear God, the only thing I want is him*. You asked, and so you have been given.

The only thing you have is him.

Nine

SHE HAD MISSED THREE Sundays of going down to Concord to visit Harry. Last time she had gone was just after her mother died. The first thing he said to her this time was, "Are you sick?"

"No, I'm fine," she lied. She didn't want him to forbid her again to come see him. She wasn't going to listen to him anyway, but she didn't want to hear it.

"Oh. Because we've had a hundred unexplained deaths here. Big strong guys get a fever and three days later drop dead."

"I don't have a fever." Yet her malaise was unmistakable.

Harry seemed shocked by her haunted appearance.

"You look terrible," he said. "You've lost so much weight, and you're deathly pale. You *must* be sick."

They sat behind a table with no glass between them, just a wire cage. He moved slightly back. He looked like he might want to cover his mouth from her.

"I'll be fine," she said, chewing her lip. To look away from him, she glanced around at other families, other couples. The men who were not Harry were eagerly talking to their women, holding their hands through the steel diamonds of intimacy.

"Gina, have you heard? They took Jack Reed's papers! The man went to Russia, recorded every minute he spent there in his journals, and they took them."

"Who's they?"

"The Department of Justice."

"Really." She studied her short, unpolished nails, her fingers empty of rings. "Didn't they just give them back? I read something …"

"That's not the point. They had them for six months. Why would they take his personal notes? They'll stop at nothing! Department of Justice, indeed. All in the name of war. Have you heard your Emma on this?"

"No."

"She said that the military spirit is the most merciless, heartless and brutal in existence. There's not even a pretense of justification for it."

"Such a firecracker, that woman." When was the last time Gina had red polish on her nails? Could it be two years ago? Three? God! Well, who could afford nail polish now? She didn't care. Just something to think about. To not think about the unthinkable things. To hear him less well.

"The soldier, to quote Tolstoy, is a professional man-killer," Harry was saying. "He is a cold-blooded, mechanical tool of his military superiors. He is ready to cut throats at the first command of his ranking officer."

"Not all soldiers."

Harry was barely listening to her. "I believe that militarism," he said, "a standing army and navy in *any* country is indicative of the decay of liberty and the destruction of all that is finest in any nation."

That she heard. Finally she raised her head away from her white hands. "Does Russia have an army and a navy?"

"What?" He was as surprised she had asked him a question as she was by asking it.

"Does Russia have a standing army?" Gina repeated. "Does she have soldiers?"

"Out of necessity. What's your point?"

"That *some* wars are justified."

"Not this war."

"But other wars? Perhaps wars not yet fought? Or wars fought by countries other than this country?"

He grimaced. "What are you talking about? It's self-defense for Russia. They would never use their army to invade their neighbors, to attack a country thousands of miles away, to use another country for its natural resources. They just gave away most of their empire for peace."

"Ironic, that's what Goldman says." She had stopped being on first-name terms with Emma Goldman long ago.

"Yes, she and I both oppose the American nation soon being able to hurl dynamite bombs upon defenseless enemies from flying machines."

Gina looked down again, into the lines of her palms. There were some people who were palm readers. Gypsies maybe? Some old withered Sicilians. Were there any on the streets of sleepy Concord? It was so quiet here, so nice. She had forgotten how tranquil. Maybe she could move here now. If she weren't *incinta*, she could move into Rose's Home for the desperately afflicted. How was she ever going to tell Harry what was going on with her?

"This country's ship is down, Gina, it's floating sideways. We have to set it right."

"*We?*"

"Why are you judging me?"

"Did I say anything? Did I lay down one accusation?"

"Your averted eyes say it all."

"Harry, assaulting a police officer is not setting the ship right. That's also violence. Which you say you oppose."

"He was an instrument of the state. He was violating my civil rights. I was protesting an illegal war, trying to dissuade innocent ignorant boys from joining the armed forces. And he was trying to get them to join. He was basking in their ignorance."

"Got it. It's selective violence you oppose."

"What would make any young man join the army, especially for a war that is *so* pointless, so useless, so illegal, is just *beyond* me!" Harry had worked himself up into quite a lather.

She struggled up. How could she tell him? What was the point? He was stuck in here, mired in his militancy unabated, and she was stuck out there, clutching like she was drowning to the thin, living branch extended to her, yet swallowed by *La Pesadilla*.

He couldn't get out.

And she couldn't carry to term anyway. She left without telling him a thing except as an afterthought when she said over her shoulder, "Oh, you didn't hear? I would've thought for sure they'd tell you. War is over. Armistice Day was November 11. The flu has defeated the Germans. They conditionally surrendered. Until they get better, I suppose. Well, goodbye. See you next week, I hope."

Ten

DECEMBER, AND SHE WAS still alive.

And the baby was still alive.

During her many sleepless nights of lying in bed and studying the ceiling, and crying for her mother, Gina counted out on nine of her fingers the months forward from the end of August 1918, which was the last time Harry had loved her.

End of May 1919.

She didn't want to think about it. It might as well be a century away. So many things she couldn't think about, this at the top of her list. She'd been here before, and even heavier with child than now. Thirteen weeks. Sixteen. Seventeen. Every day was painful to live through, to count, to walk through. Every time she got up, she was afraid the blood would flow again. Any minute of any day it could come. Just like all the other times. Yet she had to work. Which meant she had to get up in the morning, get herself dressed and ready, and walk to Wood Mill to work from eight until six. So many people had died, there was overtime being offered again. She would take the overtime, but she was afraid to even get up out of her chair. She knew that gravity, her mortal enemy, would pull the baby from her. She wanted to lie in her bed until May. In what world could that ever be possible? Not in this one.

Gradually the fever left her body and the vomiting stopped. She got a little of her appetite back. She lay in bed, holding her stomach, looking up at the ceiling and praying for help, for salvation. Praying for a way out. *Unto thee O Lord, will I cry, and I will pray unto my God.*

She had enough energy for only one more commuting effort. She could go to Rose and beg for counsel. Or she could listen to Rose's voice clanging in her head like the five bells of the wounds of the Lord, and go where there remained the only glimmer of hope for her, her child, and her wayward foolish beloved husband.

Gina swallowed her pride and her fear and went to Barrington.

Chapter 7

BELLAGRAND

One

IT WAS AN ICY New England day, and black frozen mud covered the road and the sidewalks.

Gina took a train to Barrington on a late Tuesday afternoon after she had called in sick to Wood Mill but still dragged herself to St. Vincent's for a few hours to help them mend and sort their donations for the busy Christmas season.

At first she walked in the wrong direction from the Barrington train station, studying the map. It took her a while to find Cherry Street. All these years she had imagined Barrington as a smaller, fancier Lawrence, but it was nothing remotely like Lawrence. It was a hilly, white-washed tiny town with a pristine cobblestoned main street, two white spire churches bookending the winding avenue, quaint little shops with color-coordinated awnings, and multi-flashing Christmas lights strung from end to end. It was nested in the up and down hills and woods near Arlington Heights and Winchester, and if one drove too fast in a four-cylinder Model T, one could easily miss it.

Barrington was smaller than Concord, smaller than Hampton, smaller even than Revere. It was like a precious storybook oil painting.

There was something intimate about it, as if the painting wasn't meant for sale or for the eyes of the general public. If Gina were an artist and lived in New Guinea or the Philippines and dreamed about what small-town America might look like, and imagined the most idyllic scene, this is what she would paint. But it still wouldn't do the place justice, wouldn't show her what she saw now with wide-open eyes: the red-glow sign on the bakery window blinking the words in a red circle, *fresh hot donuts*. Gina didn't know what a donut was, but she was sure it was something exquisite because it smelled so good as she walked by slowly despite the wind and the rain.

Meandering, her heart aching, eventually she found Cherry Street and the expansive white colonial with sober black shutters. For a few minutes Gina stood in the sleet gazing at it. She could not believe that this was the house from which her husband came, where he was born and raised. She had never known anyone who lived in a home of such stature. In Belpasso, her mother cleaned houses for the wealthy dons, and her father made house calls to groom them, but the Attavianos remained stubbornly on the outside of that life. They may have had a dinghy on the ocean, but they were not *of* the ocean. Seeing this house, Gina at last fully understood that Harold Barrington, born 1877, class of Harvard 1900, a masters in economics, an almost PhD in economic theory, son of Herman Barrington, merchant, industrialist, investor, builder, son of Frances Barrington, the socialite Daughter of the Revolution, a direct descendant of Robert Treat Paine, a Founding Father, her husband Harry, a *Mayflower* pilgrim, once had been profoundly of the ocean.

It took Gina a while to get up the nerve to creak open the iron gate and walk up the brick path to the front door. After she knocked too softly, why did she stand and pray that no one was home?

The red door opened. An attractive plump brunette in her thirties appraised her. "May I help you? Are you collecting for the Sodality? I was expecting you. Let me get my purse."

"No, wait—" Gina stammered. "I'm … Mrs … Ba … I'm Ja … could I speak to Esther Barrington, please? Is she, um, in?"

The woman frowned. "I don't know if she is in. Who, may I say, is calling?"

"Gina Barrington."

The woman's entire demeanor changed. She stepped away. "Wait here."

The door closed. Five agonizing minutes floated by like icebergs. The door opened again. "I'm sorry," the plump woman said. "But Mrs. Barrington is *not* in."

"Please ..." whispered Gina, her voice breaking, her hand reaching out. "I desperately need her help. It's about her brother ..."

The woman blinked. "Wait here." The door slammed.

Another five minutes, her cheeks turning red from the cold.

The red door opened.

In front of Gina stood Esther. Gina hadn't seen Esther since running into her in the church basement in 1906, and she had aged considerably. Gina tried not to have her own face show the acknowledgement of time's merciless march upon Harry's sister. At forty-five, Esther looked much older than Harry despite his numerous stints in prison, which aged mortal men. Her lifelong thinness, once an elegant charm, now gave her a look of schoolmarmy, bony severity. Her hair had gone completely gray, her pale lined face had not a trace of makeup on it. With her sharp straight nose, chiseled cheeks and chin, and pronounced brows, she looked like a wizened flightless bird. She resembled Harry only in the eyes and the mouth. The eyes were deep-set and gray like his, and the mouth had the same dry sardonic twist to it, as if both brother and sister were constantly keeping caustic comments from tripping off their silver tongues. As always, Esther was impeccably dressed, in a two-piece fine-cloth twill black suit, gray stockings, and sharp, smart-heeled, closed-toe black pumps. The two tall women stood silent, warily eyeing each other, Gina vanquished, Esther cold. Her voice was harsh when she spoke. "What is it you want?"

"Esther ... may I come in for a few minutes?"

"What you have to say can't be said at the open door?"

"No," said Gina. "It can't."

Reluctantly, Esther pulled the door open. Gina stepped into a wide grand hall with a twenty-foot ceiling and a long-chain crystal chandelier. Everything was decorated, put away, shined, dusted. Heavy-framed oil paintings adorned the walls. It was warm. Through the door on Esther's right, Gina could see a reflection of a flickering amber flame, perhaps a fire.

They stood in the resounding hall. Esther sighed. "May I take your coat?"

"Yes, please." Gina handed Esther her velvet bonnet and the gray wool coat she had made herself. Under the coat she wore her finest olive green wool serge dress. It wasn't the quality of Esther's, but it was sophisticated and well made. Gina always received compliments when she wore it, and so she wore it today.

Esther stood with Gina's coat in her hands until the woman who had opened the door came back to the hall. "Rosa," said Esther, "this is Gina Barrington, Harry's wife. This is Rosa, my lady's maid."

"Oh," said Rosa, her mouth pursed, "nice to meet you," in a tone meant to convey that meeting Gina was the worst thing that had ever happened to her.

"Likewise," said Gina.

The three women stood. Esther sighed again. "Would you like some tea?"

"Yes, please."

Esther gestured to Rosa to go get on with it, but quickly. She showed Gina into the parlor room, where indeed there was a fire, and tall slender floor lamps, all lighted, and a wall full of books. A Persian rug covered the wide-plank parquet, cream-colored, comfortable Edwardian couches faced each other. Gina sank down at the edge of one. Esther sat primly across from her.

"Rosa will be here in a moment with the tea," Esther said. "But in the meantime, would you like to tell me what this impromptu visit is about?"

Gripping her hands together so tightly it caused her pain, Gina, through her distorted mouth, told Esther everything. In the middle of her squalid account, she started to cry, though she had tried really hard not to.

In the middle of it, Rosa entered with a tray of tea and biscuits. Gina wiped her face with her hand.

"Rosa, can you please get a handkerchief for ..." Esther stopped. She clearly didn't know what to call Gina, preferring to call her nothing. "She doesn't seem to be able to locate her own."

The handkerchief with the Barrington family crest on it was helpful, and while Gina wiped her face with it and blew her nose, Rosa critically poured the tea and arranged the biscuits. Gina stopped speaking until she was done and gone.

"Well, thank you for coming to see us. I've heard you out," Esther said calmly, as if they weren't talking about her only brother. "But I don't know what it is you want me to do."

"My child needs his father."

"His father has been convicted by a court of law. What can I possibly do about that?"

Gina's fingers were cracking under the tension. She wanted to drink something hot, but couldn't pick up her cup of tea. "His sentencing is in less than two weeks," she said feebly. "I know his father—your father—is a respected member of the community. He knows people, doesn't he? He knows judges, the District Attorney. Maybe he can do something. Talk to the prosecutor? Maybe there can be clemency?"

"For a felony?" Esther shook her head. "Only an outgoing president of the United States can issue a clemency, and Mr. Wilson is not due to leave office for another two years. Besides I'm not sure my brother would warrant a pardon from him."

"Perhaps your father can help work out a plea deal?"

"That's done before a conviction, not after."

"Maybe there is some way Mr. Barrington could intercede on behalf of his son, vouch for him?"

"Vouch for what?" asked Esther. "How can our father vouch for him? Harry is an incorrigible recidivist."

"Perhaps Harry could be paroled? Probationed?"

"He is about to be sentenced to a mandatory ten years without parole!" Esther exclaimed. "Isn't that what you just told me?"

"I don't know what I told you, Esther," Gina whispered. "I don't know anything anymore." The two women sat in the parlor room. The wood crackled in the fire. Gina finally picked up her cup of tea and drank from it.

"Why did you decide to have a baby now?" Esther asked. "You've been married for so long. You must be past your child-bearing years. What are you now, nearly forty?"

"I'm thirty-four."

"Ah." Esther nodded. "Yes, how could I forget. You're seven years younger than my brother."

"Yes."

"When he and Ben Shaw first met you, when you came to this country, you were just fourteen years old, isn't that right?"

"I was a month away from fifteen."

"So what I said was correct. You were fourteen years of age."

"Yes, that is correct."

"Indeed," said Esther, appraising her. "Indeed."

Gina wasn't meeting Esther's piercing gaze. She was holding her warm teacup.

"Why now?"

Gina stirred the sugar at the bottom of her tea. The shaking spoon jangled against the porcelain. "When we first got married, we didn't want children. Then we thought we had plenty of time. And when we wanted to, we couldn't. I couldn't." Gina didn't look at Esther. "We tried."

Esther was silent. Gina couldn't see her expression. Was it sympathy or contempt? "But you knew he was in the middle of a trial that could put him away for many years," Esther said. "Why didn't you wait at least until the jury finished deliberating?"

"That would have been prudent," said Gina. "We hadn't planned it."

"Have you or my brother planned a single thing in your life?"

"I don't know," said Gina. "I guess the answer to that is no." The tea was barely warm. She wanted a sweet biscuit, but didn't think it was ladylike to chew and cry at the same time. Esther herself wasn't drinking or eating.

Tears fell from Gina's eyes into her teacup. "I just want to give life to this one baby," she whispered. "I can't work anymore because when I'm rushing, carrying things, up and down, I start to bleed. This is my last chance, I know it. Please Esther. I don't know if you have any children ..."

Esther groaned under her breath, and in that brief anguished sound, Gina suddenly heard the parallel years, years with money and a husband, with a paid for house, and yet agony still, suffering still. She hadn't even asked how Esther had been, how she and her husband, the Red Cross medic, had managed through the war. Esther was wearing black. There was no wedding band on her finger, but that meant little. There was no wedding band on Gina's finger either. Gina dried her face, ashamed of her self-absorption.

"I'm sorry I can't help you," Esther said in a captured-bird stilted voice. "But thank you for coming to see us. I can't imagine it was easy."

"No."

"I wish you all the best with this pregnancy, and I mean that sincerely. I wish there were something I could do. But there is nothing. My father has not been well lately, he's had to restrict his numerous business activities on doctor's orders. He doesn't have the kind of influence you ascribe to him, the power to bend a judge to commute my brother's conviction."

Gina was quiet. "Are you absolutely sure?"

"Positive." Esther paused. "I can offer you some money ..."

Gina shot up, knees faulty, legs liquid. She felt unsteady, like all the blood had rushed to her head. "No, no." She put up her hands in stark refusal. "I really must run. I've imposed on you terribly with my visit. I truly apologize. I won't keep you a moment longer."

"Wait." Esther got up herself, much slower. "Did my brother send you?"

"No. He doesn't even know I'm pregnant."

"Because it would be just like him. To send you. All his life he could never face up to anything ..."

"Oh, you're quite wrong about him," said Gina. "Maybe he was like that before, but now ... he is stalwart. Yes, he faces up to things. He's accepted that he's done wrong, he is remorseful, but completely ready for his sentence. He is strong."

The women stood facing each other in the front hall.

Gina clenched her fists for strength.

"Esther, forgive me for barging in on you like this. And ask your father to forgive me. Forgive *us*. I know what Harry did ... back then ... was judged harshly by his family, because what he did was unforgivable. We loved each other very much, though that's not an excuse for bad behavior." She almost added how glad she was that Alice had found happiness in Texas, but remembered just in time that it was Ben who had told her this, and she didn't think it was a good idea to divulge that part to Esther. She was certain that Esther would not take kindly to learning that Ben of all people had been coming around, while Harry was in prison, to tell Gina things. "You've been very kind to listen to me," she said instead. "Please don't worry about us. We'll be fine. Really. We'll figure it out. Could you get my coat?"

Esther stood, chewing her lip, wanting to say something, unable to.

"You have a lovely home," said Gina. "Harry was blessed to have lived here."

"It's too late," Esther blurted out.

Gina lowered her head. "I know."

"No, what I mean is you can't go back to Lawrence now."

"Pardon?"

"Did you take the train? You can't go out there." Adamantly Esther shook her head. "It's been raining all day and now the ground has frozen. It's too dangerous."

"I'll be all right. What time is it? There's a train at quarter of nine. If I hurry I'll just make it. I did overstay, I'm afraid."

"Nonsense. No reason to canter out there like a gazelle. Be safe. You can go back tomorrow."

"I have to be at work at eight in the morning tomorrow."

"You just told me you couldn't work anymore."

"I can't work, but I *do* work."

"So call them, tell them you'll be an hour or two late. Better yet, call in sick. That's the truth, isn't it?"

Gina protested.

"I won't hear of it. I won't hear another word. Rosa, come! Quickly!"

Esther ordered an incredulous Rosa to make up the guestroom upstairs, and then called on Darryl, the butler, to organize Gina some dinner.

"My father likes to take his supper late in the dining room," Esther said apologetically, "and I don't want to upset him with your visit because it's very difficult to get him to eat as it is. Would you mind taking your dinner in your room?"

"Of course not."

And what a room it was.

Gina fell onto a plush four-poster bed with white sheets and down quilts, there was a fire, full and burning, the velvet draperies over the four tall windows were drawn, the ceilings were cathedral-high. Fresh pink flowers stood graceful in mosaic vases. Rosa brought her some food, but all Gina wanted to do was lie under the covers and dream about sleeping in this room, and when she woke up she wanted to wake in this bed, in Harry's house.

Two

AFTER SHE GOT GINA upstairs and settled, Esther came back down and found her father in the banquet-hall dining room, alone at the long table, in front of his filled plate and brimming glass.

"Well?" Herman said. "What did she say?"

Esther sat down next to him while Darryl poured her a glass of wine. "Would you like to have something to eat, Madam?" Darryl asked. Darryl, unlike Louis, was white, but like Louis, he was old.

"No, thank you, Darryl."

"Esther, I also asked you a question," said Herman, his deep voice as strong as ever. "The difference is I asked you first."

"She is having a baby."

Herman nodded, his jaw trembling involuntarily. His hair had thinned out, turned white. He himself had thinned out, didn't have quite the same ironing board posture of twenty years earlier. His hands shook slightly as he carefully took hold of his knife and fork. Age spots lined the stretched skin on his face. His own gray eyes, passed down to both of his children, were expressionless, nearly colorless. "Who's the father?"

"Daddy!"

"My son has not been out of prison long enough to father a child. Surely it can't be his."

"Can you be serious?"

"I don't seem serious to you? Does she want money?"

"She wouldn't hear of it." Esther took a sip of her wine. "I nearly lost her when I offered. She was ready to flee."

"Is her brother still at Purity?"

"I suppose. She might have to go live with him if things don't improve. He can't keep paying her rent. Their mother just died of the flu."

Herman clicked his teeth together, as he methodically, thoughtfully buttered his bread. "When is the sentencing?"

"Less than two weeks," she said.

They didn't speak while he took a few bites of his unwanted steak.

"The baby needs a father, Daddy," Esther said.

"I agree wholeheartedly," Herman said. "Perhaps we can introduce its mother to someone. Whom do we know?"

"Stop it!"

"What? It needs a better father than the one who's in prison."

"You have to help him."

"Do I now?"

"Yes. You simply have to."

"I can't. I'm all helped out. You know I can't."

"She read somewhere he could get a pardon. Is she right?"

"How in the world could he get a pardon?" exclaimed Herman.

"That's what *I* said to her. But she seemed sure. Something else perhaps?"

Herman shook his head. "Offer her some material assistance, Esther. She can't work like she's been working, the mill, housecleaning, the church, and carry a child. It's ruinous."

"I told you already, she won't hear of it."

"Offer again. Offer her enough so she doesn't have to worry."

"I'm going to force charity down her throat?"

"Offer her the penthouse apartment in our Back Bay building off Dartmouth."

"She won't take it. She won't accept."

"God, the pride! Why, tell me, do the poor have such a surfeit of it? It's unseemly."

"Because it's all they have," said Esther. "Now please. She doesn't want your money. She wants her husband."

"I refuse to believe that's true. He's been a terrible husband." He paused. "Where is she now?"

Esther looked stumped by the question. "In the guestroom upstairs, why?"

"You sent her up without dinner?"

"Of course not. I had Rosa take it to her."

Herman put down his fork and stared at his daughter. "Why invite her to stay if you're just going to insult her?"

"I did it for you. I didn't want to upset you."

"So show her the door. Escort her out. But if you're going to ask her to stay, why lock her up? What am I, Bluebeard? Where are your manners, Esther?"

Herman looked into his plate. Shamefaced, Esther didn't know what to say.

"Well?" he went on without looking up. "Are you going to sit there or are you going to ask her to come downstairs so I can finally meet her?"

Three

GINA STOOD ERECT IN the open double glass doors leading into the dining hall, watching Herman eat at the head of the table with the tall window to Cherry Street behind him. It was dark outside and the snow was falling, but the room was lit by table lamps and glowing candles. The fire was on. The house seemed to have a fireplace in every room. She wondered if the washrooms also had fireplaces, and nearly chuckled. It was incredibly comforting. She stood and waited, content to say nothing. Finally Harry's father looked up. For a few moments he also said nothing, as they studied each other.

"So you're Gina Barrington."

"Very nice to meet you, Mr. Barrington," she said. "I wish it were under different circumstances. Please call me Gina."

"Please call me Herman. Would you like to sit down?"

"Yes, thank you." Carefully she perched down next to him. She said no to Darryl's offer of wine and food, and remained stiffly sitting with her hands folded in her lap and her back straight like his.

"Why come to me now?" Herman asked. "Why didn't he come to me before when it could have done some good? He didn't come to me when he was arrested during Bread and Roses, or after Paterson, or after any of his other numerous violations. He didn't come to me even at the beginning of this current mess when he knew—knew—that he had transgressed an impregnable new Act and was facing a severe punishment."

Open-mouthed, Gina studied the table in astonishment.

But suddenly the world made sense again. Mimoo would be pleased. The father would not—could not—abandon his creation. She was always right, her mother. She had kept saying this. But no one believed her. Gina wanted to cry.

"He is still not coming to you," she said when she had cleared her creaking voice. "I am. He doesn't know I'm here. But ... how do you know so much about him?"

"He made it my business to know," said Herman, "by dragging my good name through the papers and the court records. Harold Barrington this, Harold Barrington that. I could hardly help knowing about it. Every person I met commiserated with me about my son and his unending quest for trouble. He's never made it easy for me, never."

"I wanted to come to you earlier. He forbid me. You had turned him away, and he learned his lesson. He has too much pride."

"And he's not the only one." Herman carefully considered her.

215

Across from her on the wall near the fireplace was a gilt-edged rectangular mirror. Catching her reflection, Gina sat up straighter, if that were possible, under Herman's solemn scrutiny, wanting to make a good impression. She was tall, slim, long-legged, wild-haired, passionate-looking, even as a grown woman. Hardship and anxiety had taken away the softer edges from her romantic face, and she acquired the suppressed tightness in her jaw and brow from keeping too many things hidden that were difficult to keep hidden. She knew that about herself. She called it her Protestant look. She would tell her mother that true Italians did not carry this feature because they never kept anything on the inside, and Mimoo had said, "*You're* Italian and yet you do. You've now become fully American. Congratulations."

"How have you been?" That was Gina asking after Herman.

"We've been fine, thank you."

He didn't say any more and after a few minutes of sitting by his side, she stood up to go, figuring she had been dismissed.

"Will you be staying with us?" he asked.

She tightened her jaw. "I don't know the answer to that question," she replied. "What about your son?"

Herman tightened his jaw. "I don't know the answer to that question."

When she turned from the table, she gasped, startled to see a whittled-down black man mutely encased in a wingback chair, concealed from view by the open double doors that partially obscured him. He sat silent and motionless. She would not have noticed him even now, except he raised his arm to scratch his cheek, displaying to her his animation.

Turning her head back to Herman, Gina whispered, "Who is that?"

"Better not to whisper," Herman replied loudly. "It's Louis. He is deaf. And almost nearly blind. But if you're not too frightened, approach him, and tell him you are Harry's wife. Maybe he'll hear. He used to be quite fond of my son. Knew him from the day he was born."

"That's Louis? Your old butler?"

"Harry told you about him? Yes. Been with our family since the war."

"Which one?"

Herman smiled. "Very good. The Civil War."

Carefully Gina approached the ancient black man. Pulling up a chair, she sat in front of him and leaning in, peered into his eyes. "Louis? Can you hear me?"

He sat.

"So you're the famous Louis." She took his dry old hands into hers. "Do you know who I am?" She squeezed his hands.

He sat.

"I'm Gina Barrington. I'm Harry's wife."

Louis blinked. A tear fell from his fogged-over glassy eye.

"Ah, so you *can* hear me." Rising, Gina leaned over and kissed him on his bald head. "I'll tell him you said hello when I see him next."

After Gina went upstairs, Herman disappeared into his study. Soon there was a knock on the door. "Come in, Esther. What do you want? I have to get some work done. Billingsworth is coming first thing tomorrow and all my papers need to be in order."

"What did you think?"

"What did I think of what? Your errant brother? He doesn't make it easy on anyone who has the bad judgment to care for him, does he?"

"She knows what she's doing, Father," said Esther. "Don't feel too bad for her. She's always known. Come hither, once said the lithe Italian spider to a fly."

"Your brother is solely responsible for his own actions, Esther. He is not the fly. He is a sentient human being. But what has she ever done to deserve him or his treatment of her?"

"You're already defending her?" Esther opened her arms. "You're making my case for me as we speak, Daddy," she said. "When even you, at seventy, don't stand a chance."

"I don't know what you're talking about."

"I guess I don't have to ask what you thought of her."

"You may ask. I'll tell you. She is remarkable," said Herman.

"Of course she is." Esther waved her hands in front of her in a web-like pattern.

"Remind me to apologize to her someday," Herman said. "I have gotten it exactly wrong. She is entirely too good for him."

"It's Harry who needs your help."

Herman's face was pale, his teeth were set. He motioned for Esther to close the study door. "What would you like me to do? He was convicted by a jury of his peers. His *minimum* sentence is ten years. Debs, the man who ran for president not too long ago, also received ten years. He's not getting out. Haywood, the IWW ringleader, got twenty!"

"Harry can't go to prison for ten years!" Esther cried.

Herman took a deep breath. For a few minutes they didn't speak.

"He can't go to prison ..." she repeated.

"I don't know what you want me to do," he said. "I called in the last of my favors to get his previous sentence reduced to a year instead of five. You remember that, don't you? When he was slapped with a mandatory five-year term for violating his easy parole with a felony? And the judge who helped me, a good friend of mine, has recently died! Who's left?" He breathed hard. "Do you think she'll want a divorce?"

Esther plied her hands together. "For God's sake, divorce? They're having a *baby*. They're having a *Barrington* child."

"I'll thank you not to remind me of this."

"She's had trouble carrying ..."

"Perhaps if your brother stopped shoving her in front of picket lines she might've had less trouble."

"You know it has nothing to do with that, Daddy," Esther said faintly, not looking at her father.

Herman blinked. A deep pool of lifelong compassion reflected on Esther, and for Esther. "Fine. Don't get so overwrought. Tell her to stay. Tell her to come live with us."

"Believe me when I tell you that this isn't about her. I have no fondness for that woman, as you well know. This is about the child. He needs his father."

Herman walked to the liquor cabinet to fix himself a drink. "Harry is not a child," he said. "No matter how much he acts like one."

"I'm talking about the *baby*, Daddy! Not Harry."

They fell silent. Herman's hands shook noticeably as he poured himself a whiskey, raised it to his lips, and drank it in one long, pained swallow.

"Esther, he has been convicted of inciting violence and of *actual* violence against our armed forces and law enforcement. He has been convicted of scurrilous and abusive language toward his government at war, convicted of aiding and abetting the enemy by willfully interfering with the operation and success of the United States armed forces by obstructing and preventing army recruitment. I mean, that's almost a high crime, is it not? Ten years seems woefully insufficient. Who do you think I could possibly know on the federal bench who can help us?"

Esther folded her arms. "I don't know. I don't care."

Herman sighed. "Let's say goodnight. He utterly exhausts me and I haven't seen him in years. Before he was charged I whispered in the DA's ear for weeks to persuade him to ask for a smaller sentence. He had wanted twenty! I have to sleep now. Tomorrow is another day. Though tomorrow I'm headed to Roxbury with Billingsworth. He wants me to look over some investment properties."

"No. Go to court with him instead. Billingsworth is always bragging about how many people he knows at the DA's office. And didn't you sponsor the DA's son through Yale? Doesn't that count for something?"

"I don't know how good a student he was, I can't say."

"All right. Joke. Do whatever you need to—just help my brother."

"Esther," said Herman, "that's the very DA who asked for ten years for Harry instead of twenty. That's the return favor we got for the Yale sponsorship. The well is dry."

"Draw one last bucket from it." She stood to go. "Remind all concerned that one, it's Christmas, and two, Harry's wife is expecting."

"On the first count, the DA, I believe, is Jewish. And the second one might not be a plus either," Herman said, putting down his empty highball and grabbing an inconspicuous cane near the corner bookshelf. "What if the DA stipulates that as one of the conditions of his release, Harold not procreate?"

Four

GINA REMAINED IN BARRINGTON. She barely got out of bed for the first few sleepy days, wishing that whatever was happening out of her line of sight with Herman and Esther would take just a little bit longer because it was a summer walk through a field to stay in a house this warm and comfortable in December. There was always hot water, and no drafts, and the towels were fresh and white, miraculously starched by someone other than her. She had brought no clothes with her, but as if by magic, the next afternoon new clothes appeared on her dresser; white undergarments, a navy wool dress, a plaid skirt, a cashmere shawl, a red scarf, new black boots with patent heels and in just the right size. Every few hours a woman came in, a maid, not Rosa, and inquired if Gina needed anything, anything at all. Some tea, a sandwich, a cake, another pillow, a book? Did she want to get dressed, did she want a bath? The woman offered to dress her, to bathe her. Her name was Donna. She cleaned up Gina's cups and plates and crumbs from the cake that fell from her mouth onto the floor. She opened the drapes, she drew them. Every time she walked into the room, Gina cried.

She slept like a male lion, twenty hours out of every twenty-four, praying to God that Herman would find a way to help them so she could find a way to be a better wife to her husband. She could not believe Harry would give up this life, even for a woman like her. And perhaps that was the source of his constant undercurrent of resentment toward her. Perhaps he realized early on she hadn't been worth it.

Could she give it all up for a man like Harry? Gina wanted to say yes. She remembered fondly their once unquenchable blaze, but as she, covered to her neck by a down quilt, lay in the soft white four-poster bed the few hours she was awake, weeping repentance for her weakness, her loneliness, for her fleeting joy with another soul, not Harry's, she couldn't say for sure.

Five

"DON'T STUDY ME, ESTHER, I'm not a textbook," Herman said after a week had passed. "No one wants to stick his neck out. The case is too high profile. He's been so publicly tried, so publicly convicted! All of his co-defendants are going away for decades. Oh, and by the way, Emma Goldman may be deported to Russia."

They were talking quietly in the library while taking their afternoon tea. They didn't want Gina to overhear.

"What? No!"

"That's the proposal. Two hundred convicted seditionists to be escorted on to a boat and shipped off to Russia as a present for Lenin and Trotsky. The reason I mention this is because that's what the DA has offered me. In lieu of his current sentence, Harry would be put on the Soviet Ark and shipped to Russia."

"Daddy, is this another joke? Because it's completely without humor."

Herman pointed to his face. "Do I look like I'm joking? Exactly. So don't judge me. I barely managed to reschedule his sentencing until early in the new year, to give me and Billingsworth a little more time to talk to the sentencing judge, to see if he has any leeway." Finished with his tea and requiring something stronger, Herman got up, poured himself a whiskey and sat back down on the couch next to his daughter. "Trouble is, the Red Scare is in full gale mode. No one wants to go on public record for supporting a communist, showing leniency to a Red."

"But the war ended! How can there *still* be sedition?"

"All right, my legal scholar daughter. Your brother committed his crimes when the war had *not* ended."

"You have to do something quick, Daddy. He is going to panic. She hasn't been to see him in weeks."

"So tell her to go and see him."

"And it's Christmas!"

"All the more reason to go."

"She doesn't know what to say to him."

"What does that have to do with me," Herman thundered, "that she doesn't know what to say to her own husband?"

They turned their heads to the door, and there was Gina standing in the entryway watching them.

"I am a terrible inconvenience," she said.

"Come in," said Herman, "sit down with us, have a drink. Esther, ring for Rosa, tell her to bring some more scones and jam." He turned to his daughter-in-law. "*You're* not the inconvenience here, Gina. This Sunday ask Clarence to drive you to Concord. Go visit him before Christmas. Bring him a small gift. Tell him you're expecting. Don't say anything else because there is a good chance I can't fix it."

But before Sunday there was a breakthrough of sorts, a small step forward. As always, when something was given, something had to be taken away. When Gina heard what was being proposed, she said she could not face Harry on her own. Herman and Esther reluctantly agreed to accompany her to Concord.

Six

ON SUNDAY ROY WENT into cell number 26694 and told Harry to get up.

"Has she come back?" was the first thing Harry asked when he saw Roy. That's the first thing he had been saying to Roy for four Sundays in a row since the last time he had seen her. He jumped down from his bunk.

Roy shook his head. Before Roy opened his mouth, Harry was already back in his bunk, his face turned to the wall. Roy started shaking him. "Get up, I said!"

"Forget it. Leave me alone." Harry closed his eyes.

"I don't know what you done to make that lovely woman so cross with you that she stopped visiting you in jail during Christmas season, only you knows that, you and God, but get up because you has new visitors. I has to dress you and shave you."

Harry turned to Roy. "What visitors?" He didn't get up. "As in plural? Who?"

222

"Do I know who? I do simple math, I count two, one of them is not your wife because I would know her anywhere, but I suggest you hurry or hours will be over. Don't make me regret I let you keep your light on so late. What could you possibly be reading? I bet it wasn't my Bible."

"I bet you're right," Harry said, closing the book he had fallen asleep on and reaching for his toothbrush. It was Ovid's *Metamorphoses*. What a perfect accompaniment to his current isolation. Sentencing for some reason postponed until after Christmas, the holiday in prison, in a cell by himself, alienated from everyone and everything. And Gina vanished through the haze. If Harry felt terror, he did not want to show it to his guard.

He got ready and clean in minutes.

In the visiting room behind a low partition of glass his father and his sister sat composed in the visitors' chairs. When Harry saw them, his knees buckled. Not because it was a shock to see them, whom he hadn't seen in over thirteen years, though it was that also. His knees gave out because he knew they were here for only one reason—to bring him bad news. Last time Gina had visited she looked like cold death. It was no secret that the flu was knocking them down in the cities and villages by the hundreds of thousands, that the flu was chiefly responsible for the sudden end to a world war. When Roy, holding Harry steady by his elbow, helped him into the metal chair, Harry couldn't speak because he feared the worst.

"Hello, Harry," said Esther.

"Is she all right?" was the only thing Harry could say.

Esther blinked as if just realizing what he must have been thinking about their inexplicable appearance. "Oh, yes, yes," she said quickly. "Gina is fine."

He relaxed just a little, but still gripped the metal chair rails. "She's not sick?"

"She was. She's better now."

Exhaling relief, Harry focused on his sister. He couldn't look at his father. He was afraid he would cry. He tightened his mouth and steeled his spine against the hard chair.

"Are you all right? How is everything? No one got sick?"

"No, we were lucky. Not out of the woods yet, though. What about here?"

Harry shrugged. "Eh. On the floor below me twenty out of thirty men died. But on our floor we only lost one. So … how's what's his name … Elmore?"

"What?" Esther paled, glancing sideways at her impassive father. Her hands clasped the edge of the table and then fell into her lap. "Elmore died in France, Harry." She frowned. "He went there with the Red Cross. He died in 1915. Typhus."

"I'm very sorry." Harry's mouth twisted. "I didn't know."

"How could you *not*? I asked Ben to tell you."

Now it was Harry's turn to frown. "How did you know I saw Ben?"

"He told us he was picking you up when you got out in 1915."

"Ah." Harry nodded. "That part he told you. Good."

"As opposed to what other part?"

"Nothing. Where is he now? Still back in Panama?" Harry almost added *I hope* but stopped himself.

Esther nodded. "He married his long-time sweetheart in 1916. He invited me to his wedding. In Panama," she said, shaking her disillusioned head. "As you can imagine, I politely declined. He has children now. Three girls. We write. He sends me photographs of his family. Would you like me to bring some with me next time I come?"

"No, thank you." Harry took the deepest breath. Finally he turned his eyes to his father. "Hello, Father."

"Hello, son."

They both blinked, were both silent. Harry had been right. Herman did have tears in his eyes.

"How've you been?"

"Can't complain."

"How is the business?"

"Good. I had to retire from active construction. The advancing years didn't permit me to keep to my punishing schedule." Herman's hands lay folded on the table. "I sold my half of the business to my brother. He passed away five years ago. His three sons now run it, very successfully, I might add."

Harry nodded, without comment, for he couldn't find anything to say and couldn't bear to say anything.

"So where's my wife?" he asked when he found his voice to speak again. "I figure her disappearance has something to do with your appearance."

"She's been staying with us," Esther said.

"Why?"

"She needed our help."

"What kind of help?"

"She is expecting."

"Expecting what?" And then Harry exhaled, pushing back against the chair. For a few difficult moments he had to hastily think back to a time when that would've been possible. They had so few opportunities for successful conjugation. It seemed as if all there had been in the last months was fights and arrests. "I wouldn't get your hopes up, if I were you," he said at last.

Herman and Esther became grim, appraising him with condemnation.

"She doesn't ... we've had some trouble." Harry turned to Esther. "Do you have children?"

"I haven't been blessed with any, no," she replied quietly. "But your wife is almost four months along."

Harry tried to hide his skeptical face. He showed them his poker face instead, his inscrutable face. He didn't want to tell them that he and Gina had gotten to this point time and again only to be bitterly disappointed. He changed the subject. "Why was my sentencing postponed? Did you have something to do with that?"

"Yes," said Herman.

"Father postponed the sentencing," Esther said, "to give himself time to talk to the judge."

"Why would Father need to talk to the judge?"

Herman and Esther were silent.

"Father?"

"He has persuaded the judge to commute your sentence!" Esther said in a thrilled breath. "It's nothing less than a Christmas miracle."

"Really?" Harry sat back. "How in the world did you manage to do that? In September the judge told me that even if the DA recommended a shorter sentence, he wouldn't allow it."

"Yes, Judge Rosen is not happy with you," said Herman. "I traded in every bit of goodwill I ever had anywhere with anyone. Never mind. It's the result that's important."

"Does this mean I'm free?"

"Uh—not quite."

"Ah," said Harry.

"You're under house arrest until 1922 and then on probation until 1925."

"House arrest? What does that mean? Like *your* house?"

"That can and will *never* happen," said Herman.

"Exactly. So where then? My house in Lawrence?"

Herman shook his head. "Lawrence is perceived as the nexus of the worst kind of trouble—social, political, financial. It is at the root of all discontent and upheaval. You will not be allowed to return there in the foreseeable future."

"So where then?" Harry asked, exasperated.

"The terms of your house arrest and probation are not easy. Any violation during the three-year period, any at all, and you're back in prison for the remainder of your ten-year sentence. This means no demonstrations, no strikes, no protests, no assaults on the police, no writing for new radical magazines, no joining Communist Labor Parties, no incitement, no slogans, no political books, no meetings, public or private, no telegrams or cables to Russia, probably best not even to wear red, just to be on the safe side."

Harry sat motionless. "Please can I choose the lady instead of the tiger?"

"Oh, most certainly," Herman replied. "The District Attorney of Boston, in coordination with Mitchell Palmer, the Attorney General of the United States, has offered me to send you permanently to Russia, since that's clearly where you want to be. Did you try to get a visa to go there for the revolution? They're offering you safe passage. They're working on commissioning a ship, perhaps the *Buford*, to deport you and a legion of your seditious compatriots. Palmer told me to tell you, you can bunk with Emma Goldman. When she leaves prison next year that's precisely where she is heading: Russia. They've reserved a special place for her on this ocean liner."

"Father, are you joking with me?"

"Have you known me to be a joker, Harry?"

"No, but this seems preposterous. Is this a real thing?"

"Palmer is very keen on making it happen, on making it real. As I just told you, he is looking into the mighty *Buford*. It's anchored in New York Harbor, ready to steam out. A few months, I'd say. Six maybe."

They sat.

"Will Gina come with me?" asked Harry.

"No," Esther replied. "Gina is due in May. She is not going to get on a ship in her condition or with a brand-new infant and be deported anywhere. That's lunacy."

Harry looked up at the clock in sour resignation. Time was ticking away. "Where is this proposed house arrest to be?" His shoulders slumped.

"I had to offer the judge a place for your exile he would deem acceptable, away from Boston, from New York, from all urban or industrial centers where you could get into trouble. Away from coal mines and factories and textile mills."

Harry waited silently.

"I offered him Bellagrand."

Harry sat.

Esther sat.

Herman sat.

"I don't know what you just said."

"In her will," said Herman, "your mother left you the only piece of property that belonged solely to her. She stipulated that it be placed in irrevocable trust, to be managed by me, but to become yours upon my death. Since inconveniently for you I am still alive, ownership can't yet transfer to you." Herman paused, having difficulty continuing. "Bellagrand has been unoccupied since your mother's death, but will be made available for your use should you choose to accept the terms of your conditional release."

"My mother left me a *house*?" Harry glanced at Esther, astonished. It was all he could do to sit straight, to not fall down.

"Don't look at *me*, Harry," his sister said. "She just left me her jewelry. I knew nothing about a house until a few days ago when Father told me."

"I don't know what I'm more shocked by—her leaving me a house or you not telling me," Harry said to his father. "What house? Why didn't you ever say anything? She died twenty-eight years ago. Why would you keep this from me all this time?"

"You're asking the wrong questions, Harry," said Herman. "And you know the answers to some of them. For the last thirteen years, you and I have had no contact. So I couldn't have possibly told you. And before that, I didn't feel you were ready to hear it. What you should be asking, or thinking about," he continued, "is why your mother, after everything that transpired between her and me, did not leave her beloved Bellagrand to you outright."

"All right, Dad," said Esther, placing a calming hand on her father's arm.

"I don't know what you're talking about," said Harry. "Why *beloved* Bellagrand? I've never heard of this place."

Herman withdrew his arm from his daughter's hold. Esther had no power to calm a cat. "What I'm saying is, it should tell you volumes about the confidence your mother had in your decision-making abilities."

"I see. So after all these years you come to visit me in prison to make *more* conflict?"

"Dad, please!" That was Esther, voice rising shrilly to calm the seas.

"It's fine, Esther," said Herman. "Harry, I'm following your mother's wishes, not my own."

"You've made that abundantly clear."

"She wanted you to use the property for a rightful purpose. This seems as rightful a purpose as there is."

Weakened, depleted, Harry fought the impulse to squeeze his eyes shut so he wouldn't have to look at his family. "I'm supposed to stay for three years in some place I've never heard of? Where did Mother get this house from, anyway?"

Herman was mute. Not like he wouldn't say. Like he couldn't say.

"Henry Flagler," Esther quietly replied for him.

"Oh my God!" Harry exclaimed. "Bellagrand is the *Florida* house?"

"Jupiter Island house to be precise."

Now all three of them sat lost in the fog of their black understanding. "She left *that* to me?" Harry covered his face, losing control of his fake-calm demeanor. He groaned. "Why punish *me*? Why torment *me*?" He struggled to pull himself together. "No. I might as well stay here. Why trade one cell for another? Why trade this for *that*? What, I don't have enough misery?"

"Your wife is having a *baby*!" Esther hissed like a locomotive.

"Do you really *need* to keep reminding him of that, Esther?" Herman banged his fist on the table. "Why does he keep acting like someone who doesn't know?"

"Or doesn't care."

Harry shrugged, tapping out his tension with anxious and impatient fingers. He glanced up again at the merciless hands of the clock, wishing desperately this visit would be over and he could go back to his cell. Better no visitors than this. Better anything than this. The *Buford* was preferable, infinitely. Gina's short-lived pregnancies had kept him from moving to New York, from leaving Lawrence, from going to Russia with John Reed, from pursuing his political future. And now the worst thing imaginable. He felt like he was being strangled.

Esther was staring at him coldly, glancing at Herman, looking down into her white hands.

"Daughter," Herman said, "are you wondering why we bother?"

"I'm no longer wondering. I don't know what to say."

Harry waved to them. "The man you're speaking about as if he doesn't exist is right here."

"We know where you are," said Herman. "In a jail cell, pursuing your political future."

229

"Okay. Yes," Harry said. "Because unlike this, it's some kind of *honor* being released into your dead mother's den of shame riding the shallow wake of your wife's fleeting pregnancy." He didn't look at anyone, his father most of all.

Hawthorne was right, Harry thought. *What other dungeon is so dark as one's own heart! What jailer so inexorable as one's own self!*

Big Bill was right, too. A man could never become great when he kept taking a woman, any woman, even one as compelling as Gina, into consideration about his path in life.

"Harry," Esther breathed out. "When did you become so callous?"

"Esther, when did you become so bourgeois?"

"We were born to the same parents."

"That's the *one* good thing about America," Harry snapped. "No one is limited to the station of one's birth."

Herman stood up, straightened out the best he could, and slowly took hold of his umbrella which he used as his cane in public. He was thin like his umbrella. "And you are certainly a fine example of the American dream, son," he said. "How does he do this? I'm absolutely drained. Come, Esther. His wife is downstairs waiting to see him."

"Not a lot of time left for her," Harry said, glancing at the clock.

"There's not been a lot of time for her all these years while you've been radicalizing yourself into prison. Come, Esther!"

Harry had five minutes with Gina before the visiting hours ended. The first minute they didn't know what to say.

"Are you angry?" she asked.

"No." He sighed. "How are you feeling?"

"Not too bad. You?"

"Why didn't you tell me?" *Again*, he wanted to add, but didn't. "Last time you came you looked so sick. I thought you had the flu."

She bowed her head. "I wanted to tell you but you were so full of anger about the war …" She shrugged. "I didn't want to interrupt."

"This is what you want? To leave Boston, your life here, all your friends, and spend three years cooped up in a *house*?"

"Many of my friends have died. And who said *I'm* going to be cooped up?" She tried to smile. "*I'm* not under house arrest." She paused. "What choice do we have? It's a way out of this. I *do* want that."

"What about your brother?"

"He can come visit."

"It sounds like hell to me, frankly. Utter torture."

Gina's lip trembled. "I'm going to have a baby," she whispered.

"I'll believe it when I see it," said Harry.

Gina's hands shook as she stood up, supporting herself against the table. "What is it about you," she said, "that you bend in half all the people who love you?"

He stood up, but couldn't think straight.

"Time, Barrington!" Roy yelled. "Wrap it up!"

Gina picked up her purse. "Harry, you tell me what you'd like to do. Stay here? Have me live with Esther? I'll do as you wish. I don't want to spring you from prison, if this is where you'd prefer to spend the next ten years of your life. Or perhaps Russia? Deportation? While there is still time, just give the word. The *Buford* is waiting. Bellagrand is supposed to be deliverance, not submission. Should I tell your father to forget the whole thing?"

"Stop being so Italian and melodramatic. I said I was sorry."

"Yes, and meant it."

"Look, I'm just dreaming of a time when you and I will once again see eye to eye on the important things. Like before. Remember?"

"Well, that's just it. You've always been *such* a dreamer, Harry."

"It's what you used to say you loved best about me."

"Must have been a long time ago," she said, turning away. "Perhaps it was when you and I saw eye to eye on the important things."

"Barrington, time!"

"Look, I want to get out, I do," he said.

"I'm sure."

"For the third time, I'm *sorry*—"

She left, she didn't even turn around. She barely managed to square her shoulders so he wouldn't see her cry. She was too proud to let him see the heartbreak in her humbled spine.

Seven

WHEN GINA WAS PACKING up their Lawrence house, throwing out twenty years of life, hoping she was leaving and never coming back, she found a letter Harry had written to her in June of 1905, barely three weeks before they were married.

> *My dearest Gia,*
> *I'm writing you this letter as you slumber curled up on your*
> *side in front of me. We haven't even parted, yet I'm sitting here*
> *watching you, missing you unbearably already, because I know*
> *what's coming in such a short while. You will go your way, and*
> *I will go mine, if only for this Wednesday. I wish you knew how*
> *desperately I don't want to spend a moment apart from you. I feel*
> *physical anguish as I write this, knowing how soon we will have*
> *to part.*
>
> *These stolen Wednesday afternoons are not enough for me.*
> *Crawling to you on Thursdays just to watch you for two hours*
> *sell books to strangers is not enough for me.*
>
> *I want nothing in my life as much as you. You are the whole*
> *reason for my breathing, for opening my eyes every morning. I*
> *can exhale because I know there is a chance I might see you this*
> *day if only for a few moments. You must be studying so hard into*
> *the late hours of night to fall asleep this soundly in the middle of*
> *the day, in the middle of our precious stolen afternoon. We've*
> *gotten it all backward, my heart. You should be studying in the*
> *middle of the day and staying awake into the witching hours with*
> *me. Look at this—I'm even jealous of your studying.*
>
> *I will confess, I am jealous of every single thing you do that*
> *does not include me. I'm on the rack of jealousy about everything*
> *you lay your exquisite eyes upon that's not me.*
>
> *Has anyone ever told you that you are a beautiful girl?*
> *You are a vision to look at, you are a Raphael work of art,*
> *a rare Caravaggio. If you saw what I see now, you would know*
> *that what I want to say is, you are a Modigliani singularis, but I*

don't want to make you blush, even in your sweet repose.

I hope you will not show this letter to anyone; how could I ever look them in the eye after these romantic ramblings, all the more awkward because they're so keenly heartfelt.

But you are the muse to my every insipid utterance.

Soon you will open your eyes, your mouth—O Lord, deliver me from this madness!

I can't imagine anyone feeling this way about anyone.

Can I write something and have you promise you won't laugh when you read it? I want to say that no one has ever loved as much as I adore you, as much as I worship you. You have taken me by fiercest storm. You've left me nothing of my former self, my former life. I cannot imagine a day that doesn't have you in it. No, it's more than that. I reject a life in which I do not lay my eyes upon you, every day. My arms upon you, my hands upon you. My mouth upon you.

Yes, yes, my Giaconda, any minute I will be arrested for the words I'm committing forever to this unworthy stationery, I will be thrown behind bars because of my love for you.

I love you more than I love myself. I feel I'm not my own when I'm away from you.

At the same time, your reciprocal modest affection for me makes of your most ardent slave a king.

You know how you keep saying You're such a dreamer, Harry. When you murmur it, it's like a caress from your lips. It's your love letter to me. A dreamer. This I freely admit. For when I dream, my beloved Sicilian princess, I dream of you.
Fervently, blindly,
Harry

Part Two

BELLAGRAND

1919–1922

When I was down beside the sea
A wooden spade they gave to me
To dig the sandy shore.

My holes were empty like a cup.
In every hole the sea came up,
Till it could come no more.
—Robert Louis Stevenson

I saw a great big, tiny house
Ten thousand miles away;
And to my view 'twas out of sight
Last night, the other day.

The walls projected inward,
The front door round the back;
Alone it stood between two more,
And the walls were whitewashed black.
—Anonymous

Chapter 8

FLAGLER'S QUEST FOR PARADISE

One

"THAT'S IT? JUST LIKE that on my way to another prison?" Harry said to Esther and Gina in the car as they headed to Boston's South Station under police escort.

"Yes," Esther said calmly. "You're being transferred to a new location for your continuing confinement. What did you expect?"

Herman didn't come to see his son off. He posted a sizable bond with the United States District Court for Massachusetts, guaranteed the house for Harry's detention and the conditions of his transfer, had Harry undergo a court-appointed evaluation and sign his release documents in the presence of a witness, hired a Pinkerton man to ensure Harry's safe travel south, and hired a round-the-clock guard in Florida to watch over his forty-one-year-old child as required. He did all that, but would not drive to Massachusetts Correctional to watch Harry walk out through the prison gates.

Harry was relieved. He knew his father had done him a service he could not repay. At the same time, to be indebted to his father for an obligation so large, a father who had shunned him, spurned him, turned his back on him, was hateful to Harry. He resented his father more, not less, in direct proportion to the degree of reprieve granted to him. He was angry, not grateful, and was benignly bitter toward his stern, well-meaning sister. But he was most hostile to the woman who carried his child. He regarded with icy stiffness her stoic demeanor, and he especially chafed at the news of the death of the most indispensable member of his wife's family: her sainted mother. Harry resented Mimoo's death with a special vehemence because her now permanent absence meant that he was left to bear the sole burden of responsibility for Mimoo's daughter. The weight of that was almost unbearable.

So as he collected his things on the morning of his departure in early January 1919, Roy, his loyal guard, asked him what in the world was wrong with him, walking as he did. "I've seen death row inmates walk faster than you."

Harry said nothing.

"It's okay, man," Roy went on. "What you worried about? You got a baby coming, it's winter time, but like a free bird you headed south …"

"Transplanted like a West Indies palm tree," said Harry.

"Away from the things of man," Roy said. "To palaces and playgrounds."

"You mean away from the *good* things of man," Harry said, pining for pulpits and principles.

"To your wife, asshole."

Harry shrugged. He didn't explain. And couldn't. "Women are trouble," was all he said.

"You're preaching to the choir, matey," Roy said, with a look of a man who was well acquainted with that trouble. "But why do they have to smell so good?"

Again Harry said nothing.

"It's only three years," Roy said. "You can do three years in Florida half asleep on the beach, can't you?"

"Three years?" said Harry. "It's an eternity. Russia had a whole *revolution* in ten days! Three years is nearly an entire presidential term of office. It's a university education."

"Well, it's seven years less than what you were looking at, man,"

Roy said, "and in a ten by ten concrete cell, too. So quit your whining and pick it up. Your wife is waiting."

Across the road Gina was leaning against the car in the cold. Esther and Rosa were by her side. Roy took one long, soft look at the forlorn but statuesque and vivid Italian woman, and turned his gaze to Harry. "You are one fucked-up dude," Roy said, shaking his head and handing Harry his satchel of belongings. "Is it even yours?"

"Fuck you."

"And farewell. See you soon, Barrington. You love it here. I know you won't be able to stay away."

Clarence drove them. In the car, they were quiet. Harry barely nodded to the kind black man, now slower and older, who had spent every day many years ago driving him back and forth to Harvard.

"What about my things in Lawrence?" Harry asked Gina. "My books, my ..." He squeezed his hands around the invisible sentiments.

"All been done," said Gina. "Already sent on ahead."

Harry turned away from the women, to the window. "So all difficulties of life have been removed. I don't have to even fold my own shirts anymore. Just like in reformatory."

"Been doing much of that, Harry?" Esther asked. "Folding your own shirts?"

"Esther, you are a wonderful woman, and you are my sister," Harry said. "But in many ways, you'll forgive me for saying this, I'm afraid you're rather like Laurence Sterne's wife Elizabeth Lumley, of whom he wrote that she was a woman of great integrity and many virtues but they all stood like quills upon the fretful porcupine."

"Sticks and stones, dear brother. Sticks and stones."

"Who in the world is Laurence Sterne?" said Gina. "And why should we care what he thought about his wife?"

The ride to Boston from Concord was an interminable seventy-five minutes.

But it was *nothing* compared to the five days Harry and the three women spent cramped together in a train sleeper compartment with a huge Pinkerton guard outside their door. Only Esther and Rosa, accompanying her mistress, chatted to each other. Gina slept, tried to get comfortable, ate, drank, alluded vaguely to some discomfort but otherwise just stared out the window. Harry drank little, ate even less. He knew his silence was like watching a stone bleed. Any day John Reed was publishing *Ten Days That Shook The World*, his eyewitness account of the Russian Revolution, while Harry was on a train with three women to a new jail!

"What do you know about this house we're going to, Harry?" Gina asked when they were past Cocoa Beach, a few hours away from their final destination in South Florida.

"I wish I could say I know nothing about it." He shrugged. "Unfortunately I know something about the man who built it."

"Have you ever seen it?"

"Not a sketch or a photograph."

Beyond the window was sun, blue skies, palm trees verdant and abundant. "It's pretty," Gina said. "Tropical. Unfamiliar. You never came here?"

"We went north to Newburyport."

"So how did your mother get this house?"

"Who knows these things?" Harry glanced at Esther and away. He didn't want to talk. But Gina had become more animated with the looming proximity of a new life.

Like a child she pressed her eager face to the window. "Tell me about the house."

"Gina," Esther said, moving closer to her sister-in-law, "my brother doesn't like to talk about these things, but our mother left an unaddressed and unsigned note in her personal effects."

"Esther, I *don't* want to discuss it," Harry said.

"I do," said Gina. "What did it say?"

"I'm paraphrasing, but it went something like, of all the meager gifts to give my son, I wish I could give him his own house, built to shelter and protect a family, with windows onto joy and onto God-created beauty, perhaps one day to shelter and protect *his* family, such a house that may he never forget the romance of life." Esther's eyes blinked slowly at Harry. "Perhaps it's this house Mother was talking about, Harry?"

"Don't know, don't care," Harry said.

"What is this romance?" asked Gina. "I already forgot."

"Funny," said Harry. "Keep joking. You know, Gina, Oscar Wilde says nothing spoils a romance faster than a sense of humor in a woman."

"And who better to pontificate about women than him."

Harry turned to Esther. "For someone who couldn't remember a lick of it," he said, "you sure managed to mangle quite a lot of it."

"He has it, Esther," Gina said.

"Has what?"

"That note." Gina didn't turn from the window. "I last saw it between the pages of a book by his bedside."

"Like the Bible?" asked Esther.

"Lenin's *What Is to Be Done?*, I believe."

Esther stared slack-jawed at Harry. "You kept Mother's note?"

"I have no idea what you're both talking about," Harry said, pressing his own dull face to the window as the train sped on. Not *romance of life*, you doltish louts, he wanted to shout. *So that he may never forget the romance of youth*, wrote his mother, Frances Barrington, the night before she died.

"Gina, would you like to hear a story about the man who built Bellagrand?" Harry said. "It's almost like a fairytale. In every way but one."

"What way is that?"

"It doesn't have a happy end."

Two

ONCE UPON A TIME into the Floridian swamps and mangroves sailed the Spanish and wrecked their fleet on the low-lying barrier islands. The gold and silver poured out of their ships and down the coast, and then the sea took it high and low, far and near. It became known as the Treasure Coast. Remnants of the riches that the Spaniards left behind can still occasionally be found under the ocean sands.

The gold remained for years in the alluvial flats on the beaches, but when the hurricanes came, they washed it away. Man came and planted palm trees and holly. Man preserved the dunes and marveled at the Blowing Rocks that looked like Badlands on the Atlantic.

Years went by, and then a man came south whose father had abandoned him because he was too poor to feed his boy. From an early age, the son learned to feed himself. The boy never received more than an eighth-grade education. He started up a salt mining company in Michigan, but when the American Civil War ended and the demand for salt dropped, he went out of business and lost his entire investment. Later he borrowed the money to lend to his friend John D. Rockefeller to start up a refinery for black gloop that spurted out of the ground and propelled engines like bullets. When Rockefeller was asked if he was the one who had come up with the purifying plan, he replied that he only wished he had the brains to think of something that clever. But it was his partner and close friend Henry Flagler who had come up with it. Their company, Standard Oil, became the most successful company in the world.

When Flagler's wife got sick, he took her to St. Augustine, Florida, to recuperate. It was there that he first glimpsed the tropical climes and starry skies and thought the seaside town would make a fine spot for a secluded summer sojourn.

Afterward, Flagler became consumed with developing South Florida. It was his vision for easy access to the tropical lands that drove him to take such an active interest in this part of the young country. Frustrated with the inadequacy of railroad access and the paucity of hotels in a place that to him not only seemed like paradise, but *was* paradise, he used his oil wealth to build and then extend his East Coast Railway, and to dredge the swamp harbor that became Miami and Coconut Grove. There was no Miami until Henry Flagler built it. When the city was incorporated in 1896, its population was 300 souls. Twenty years later it was 30,000.

Always on the lookout for investment partners, Flagler paired up with an old-moneyed New England industrialist named Herman Barrington. Their wives were friends, and so the men became friends. Flagler offered Herman an opportunity to transform the untrampled tropics into the "American Riviera."

Always on the lookout for investment opportunities, Herman readily agreed. Their real estate interests converging, Flagler and Herman developed the barrier island that became Palm Beach. In the 1880s, Herman generously invested and was generously rewarded, using the prodigious profits from Florida's real estate sales to renovate many neighborhoods around Boston, including the North End. For years, Flagler and Herman happily partnered, building yacht clubs and mansions and shopping arcades that sprang up amid the leafy palms along the Atlantic dunes. The Treasure Coast is peppered with Flagler's towns, from Cutler Bay to Jupiter Island.

Suddenly a sea change. Herman and Henry divided their business interests and went their separate ways. Flagler died in 1913, by far the wealthiest man in the United States and one of the wealthiest in the world. Herman did not attend Flagler's lavishly attended funeral.

Flagler built homes on the coastal flats between the waterway and the ocean, a few of them modest, some of them like the Louvre. He built one hotel, then another. He built one palace, then another. He lost the one wife who had brought him to Florida, married another, then another. He loved women, and for the last woman he married he built the most ostentatious home of all, Whitehall, a magnificent private dwelling, erected in the open landscaped grounds between two bodies of water, where everyone could see it.

But a decade before Whitehall, Henry Flagler built a much smaller, more humble house.

Harry stopped speaking. The train sped on. Gina waited. She turned from the window toward him. "Is that where the fairytale ends? At Bellagrand?"

"That's where the fairytale ends," he said. "At Bellagrand."

Chapter 9

THE BLUE ROOM

One

AFTER THE TRAIN DROPPED them off in Spanish City, a man named Fernando, waiting at the wheel of an Oldsmobile Tourister, took them across the rickety bridge over the Intracoastal Waterway to the strip of land where the sun both rose and set, a narrow sea-level sand barrier called Jupiter Island. Gina rode shotgun with Fernando. He was a short, cheerful-looking Cuban of indeterminate age who perhaps colored his thick black hair. He had a mustache like a con man, an old hat to go with the 'stache, was dressed neatly but like a servant, in handed-down glad rags, a halfway decent suit, and spit-shined shoes. He spoke with an accent, smiled at Gina widely with uneven teeth and understood every word she said. Except for the words she spoke to him in Italian. Those he didn't understand at all.

Harry wasn't friendly to him, but then Harry wasn't friendly to anybody lately, especially Gina. It didn't matter. They didn't come to Florida to relight the extinguished flame. He came to Florida to hide, and she came to Florida to have a baby. To her right, past the shrub and the dunes, was the Atlantic Ocean, and to the left nothing but mossy wilderness.

Or so she thought.

She could barely tell there was a driveway on the left, yet Fernando turned in and stopped the car. The entry between the trees was concealed by weeds and overgrown reeds, hidden by the dune grasses and palms, by the moss oaks with their ominous hanging webs and a creaking tall wrought-iron gate.

"Fernando," Gina said, "you made a mistake. There is nothing here."

"I don't make mistakes, señora. You will see."

Past the opened gate, the dirt road wound through the coconut palm grove. The grounds were not landscaped, but like the jungle.

At the end of the road stood Bellagrand.

Gina gaped at it from the open window of the Tourister.

"Harry," she mouthed. "I thought you said it was humble."

"Humble because you can't see it from the road," he said. "Humble compared to Whitehall."

It was a white stucco house, with white-framed windows and white marble Doric columns spanning the marble portico. The front of it faced the rising sun.

Squinting into the brightness, Gina stepped out of the car. White benches in front, white urns, elaborate vases and planters lined the white stone circular drive where the horses must have stopped once because off to the side were the mews and the stable, and every wooden board on that mews and stable was painted white. In the center of the drive was a fountain sculpture of a naked woman, demurely covering her bottom half with a draped cloth, but only pretending to cover her large stone breasts. Who was that? Her husband would know. He fancied himself a man who knew everything.

"Harry, who is the fountain a sculpture of?"

He barely glanced at it. "If it's not working, can it be properly called a fountain?"

"It is working, señor. I turn it on for you when I get you unpacked and settled."

"Who is it, Harry?"

"Aphrodite," Harry replied. "Goddess of love, beauty, sexuality. That's an interesting sculpture for my mother to have left me, don't you think?"

"Simmer down, Harry," Esther said. "She didn't leave you the sculpture. She left you the house. Now are you going to get out of the car and get yourself acquainted?"

"At the last possible minute," he replied, not looking outside.

Gina turned away from him and walked toward the house.

Stately and sprawling, with a slightly crackled grandeur of standing proud but long abandoned, Bellagrand had colonial pretensions but was really a southern mansion with Spanish overtones. Gina could not believe her eyes. The sun was blazingly strong, and she was afraid that if she blinked the house would become what she most feared: a mirage.

She needed to be helped up the steps of the portico—by Rosa. Harry, who had finally climbed out of the car, wandered off. An impressed Rosa clucked loudly, expressing verbally what Gina could not.

She overheard Esther say to Harry, "And there I was all these years thinking you got a raw deal when I received Mother's jewelry and you got nothing."

"Does it make you feel better to know for certain, dear sister," said Harry, "that I got the rawest deal of all?"

Past the African blackwood double doors that felt immovably heavy was a cavernous hall and vast rooms, nearly empty of furniture. Harry went through first, disappearing to the left. "Harry," Gina called to him, her vibrato bouncing from stone to stone, *Harry, arry, arry, eeee . . .*

He reappeared in the Great Hall. "When are you and Rosa leaving?" he inquired of Esther.

"*Marito!*" Gina said. "Don't be rude."

Esther was amused. "We haven't thought about leaving," she said. "Have we, Rosa?"

"Madam, we thought about *not* leaving," said Rosa.

"Perhaps when the child is two?" Esther suggested.

Harry looked horrified. "Impossible," he said, shaking his head. "You may come back when it's born, but you can't stay here for the next five months. We'll all go mad. You are not part of my house arrest, are you? Did I miss this condition in the fine print?"

"We'll never find them in this house," Gina said. "Let them stay."

Esther's gaze didn't waver. "Harry, we're all joking. You think I would leave my ailing father for months while I live with *you*, of all people?"

He looked slightly abashed. "*Our* father," he corrected her, but Esther leveled him with a look that said, oh, yes, sure, you haven't so much as breathed his way for fourteen years, and suddenly it's *our father*.

Gina crossed herself. Harry, Esther, and Rosa stared at her imponderably.

"You said Our Father," Gina explained. "*Padre Nostro*. I crossed myself just in case."

The three Protestant Bostonians did not soften their critical gazes at her impenetrable Catholic strangeness.

The library had a masculine feel, but was all white, except for the walnut floors and the mahogany bookshelves. Otherwise, the couches, chairs, lamps, curtains were all white. In the corner by the window stood a dark green marble round table. Harry sat down at it and said this was where he was going to read and work. He put his palms out on the marble.

"It's not marble," said Esther. "If I know anything, I know my semi-precious minerals. This is malachite."

"It's nice."

"It's from the Ural Mountains in Russia."

"That's all I need to know. It's mine."

They left him to his malachite and wandered over to the Grand Ballroom with the six crystal chandeliers each as large as Gina's former kitchen. The ballroom had ten tall windows, four doors. The floors were dark walnut. Esther said she had never seen walnut floors in any house, because walnut was prohibitively expensive to build with. They were glossy, near-black.

"What, Father's North End immigrant tenements aren't built with walnut?" asked Harry, who had caught up with them.

"Maybe you can teach Harry to dance on this floor," Esther went on, as if her brother hadn't spoken.

"He knows how," Gina said. "He just chooses not to."

They found a billiard room and a drawing room.

In the drawing room stood an old Steinway Artcase Model B grand piano. Gina didn't know how to play it, and Esther had forgotten. After they took off the white sheet, Esther pressed the E and the D on the treble clef. The E next to the middle C wasn't working. "Perhaps we can avoid the songs and scales with E in them," Esther said. "So almost all of Chopin would be out. He loved E Major."

The limestone kitchen was open to the dining and sitting areas, making it seem like one enormous room. The room spanned the entire back of the house and was visible from all the rooms in the front. At one end of the kitchen was a large area that seemed to serve no purpose except to have floor to ceiling windows and French doors overlooking the great expanse of lawn and the gleaming blue of the wide water. A white boat bobbed, tied to a long wooden dock. Gina held on to the counter. "The kitchen alone is bigger than our entire folk Victorian," she said.

"Yes," said Harry. "It is but a humble hunting lodge, as I foretold. Where's our modest Hall of Mirrors, I do wonder? Did we miss that? Oh, Fernando," he called out, "perhaps you can retire to the King's Grand Apartments upstairs?"

"Where is that, señor?"

"Just to the left of the Opera Room."

"Harry, stop it," said Gina. "He doesn't know you're teasing."

"I'm not teasing," said Harry. "I'm mocking. Big difference."

"I will not sleep upstairs, señor. I will sleep in the guest mews outside, as instructed by your father."

"He instructed my prison guard," Harry whispered to Gina.

"Stop it."

"Why else would Fernando need to position himself at the only exit?"

"Is that why you're not nice to him?"

"I'm nice. I'm precisely myself." But he wasn't.

The house smelled musty, but Gina had expected worse from a home uninhabited for nearly thirty years. They flung open the doors and the windows to air the place. She went up to Harry near the French doors that led to the lawn. "Harry, just look at all this."

He looked significantly less impressed than she.

"This may be nothing to you," she said. "But I'm not a lady of the house in a place like this. I'm the lady's maid."

"Don't sell yourself short, Gina," Harry said. "No reason you can't be both."

She turned to walk away from him. He took her wrist. He hadn't touched her since his release from the Correctional. When he touched her, she didn't pull away. "Yes?" She lowered her voice.

"One question," he said. "Would you like to take your tea in the mural drawing room or the marble one?"

Now she pulled away.

"Esther, dear," Harry said to his sister. "What, no swimming pool?"

Near the open doors, Esther pointed to the left of the flagstone patio. "You don't see?"

"Oh, yes, I see now. What, no tennis court?"

Esther pointed to the right.

"Of course. How silly of me."

"This place is a touch larger than the prison cells you've been spending so much time in," Esther said.

Harry tapped hard on his temple. "My freedom is here," he told her. "I've traded a small cell for a larger one, that's all." He shrugged dismissively. "It's got a banquet hall. So what? It's still prison."

Esther and Rosa ignored Harry and met up with Gina on the veranda. On all sides it was covered by a thin-mesh gauze net. Gina inspected the screens, wondering why they were here and if she could remove them so she could sit in the open and gaze unobstructed at the water.

"Apparently you can't remove the screens," Esther said. "Or you'll be eaten by insects. Fernando calls this the lanai. Right, Fernando?"

Fernando nodded. "Across the water is Tequesta," he said, pointing. "It's an Indian name, but Cubans live there now. That's where my family lives. We call it Spanish City. We buy everything you need there."

"Books on the revolution?" asked Harry from behind them.

"Lots of books, señor. You tell me what you like, I buy it."

"No revolutionary books for my brother, Fernando," said Esther. "He's all revolutioned out. But tomorrow we will need your help. We have to hire a housekeeper and a cook. Maybe a valet, too. And a maid for Gina."

"I don't need a valet," said Harry. "I have been putting on my own socks for forty years. I can do it for another three."

"I don't need a maid," said Gina. "I *am* the maid. I would like to buy a sewing machine, Fernando. Can we do that? And I don't need a cook. *I'll* cook. I'll make Italian food for my husband. He used to like Italian food."

"I haven't had it in so long," said Harry, "I forgot what it is."

They exchanged a faint glance of hot distant hunger.

Fernando disagreed. "You do need a cook, señora. You need somebody to shop for you. You cannot go yourself to the market, buy food, prepare, cook, clean. Look at the size of this house. It is too much for you in your condition."

"How do you think I've been living all these years?"

"You have not lived in a house like this, Gina," Esther said.

"Were you with child all those years, señora?"

"The Cuban is right," Esther said. "You are going to have to learn to live differently now. Without a sewing machine."

"But I like sewing," Gina said. "I want to make some summer dresses to wear. And I like going to the market. You must have a very good one here, Fernando. Lots of fresh vegetables and fruit, I imagine."

"Oh, yes! We have the most delicious tropical fruit. Mango, pineapples, guavas. Plantains. We have lots of bananas."

Gina flinched. Esther flinched. They stared at each other, puzzled and frowning, Esther especially, fully noting Gina's tremor. They said nothing, as if it hadn't happened. Ben was the one who had introduced them all to bananas, over twenty years ago when he first worked for the United Fruit Company and had become entranced by Central America. The bananas had been first. Then came the Panama Canal.

"Bananas, oh, wonderful!" Harry exclaimed, coming back to the kitchen. "I can't *wait*. Please, can I come with you, too, Fernando?" he asked, sitting down on the limestone floor, and smiling up at them. "I'd like to pick out my own fruit. Tell me, these bananas of which you speak, are they imported from Panama?"

"All right, enough, Harry," Gina said *sotto voce*.

"Yes, Harry," Esther said, looking at Gina even more puzzled. "Enough."

"I think the other fruit is grown locally, señor," Fernando replied. "But yes, the bananas come from Panama and Costa Rica."

"Of *course* they do."

"They get here very fast, before they ripen. The new port in Key West welcomes the ships from Panama and the new railroad that runs from there all the way up the coast brings them to us."

"How very convenient."

"Do you know," Fernando said, "that the man who built the railroad is the *same* man who also built this house? His name is Henry Flagler." He nodded, proudly as if he himself had built these things. "It is true. Don't look so surprised, señor. It is a little known fact. Local history, a special service I provide." He smiled happily.

Harry, his own mocking grin stretched from ear to ear, opened wide his hands to his flummoxed wife and sister. "Bellagrand is a gift that just *keeps* on giving, isn't it, ladies?"

Gina and Esther stood like marble columns.

"I wish you *could* come to the market with me, señor. You would be amazed."

"Believe me, I'm already plenty amazed, Fernando. As are my women. Look, you've stunned them into silence. Not an easy feat, my friend."

"Fernando, no matter how much Harry jokes," Esther said, recovering her voice, "he is not to leave this house."

"Who is joking?"

"I know my duties, Mrs. Barrington. Do not worry."

"Gia," Harry called to his wife. "What's the matter? Cat got your tongue?"

She had dropped out of the conversation entirely. She was examining the butler's pantry, impressed with its many cabinets and drawers. She opened the cabinets. White china stared out. Crystal glasses. Silverware. Serving dishes. She realized she was hungry. Maybe instead of idly chatting they could eat soon. Was there any food in this house? Or just china?

"Harry, you know the limits," Esther was telling him. "You can't leave the house for any reason. Fernando works for the Florida Department of Corrections. He knows the rules better than you. Your probation officer will visit you this Monday to introduce herself and she'll explain the rest to you. She'll be making scheduled weekly visits, but also dropping by unannounced."

"Like in the middle of the night?" Harry asked. Lightly his eyes twinkled at Esther.

Lightly her eyes twinkled back. "Don't be impossible," she said. "I know that's a Herculean feat, but can you try?"

"Fernando," Gina said, returning to the kitchen. "What can we do to help you get us settled? Because I'd like to eat soon."

Quickly Fernando excused himself to go fetch their suitcases from the Tourister. Gina motioned to Harry to go help him. Harry ignored her. She continued to verbally press him about helping Fernando, until even Esther shushed her, unperturbed that Fernando and Rosa were carrying five trunks upstairs all by themselves. That's when it occurred to Gina that she could not internalize even this simplest of all rules of etiquette: the servants served. They were paid for fetching suitcases and cooking and going to the market. Harry, raised with his father's money, simply sat on the floor. Gina began to understand a few things about her husband. He didn't get up in their Summer Street house either. He spent thirteen years sitting. Because *she* was the servant.

Slowly they made their way upstairs. Dazed, Gina stumbled around the bedrooms, six sleeping quarters, each with its own bathroom, some with adjacent sitting rooms. Each room was decorated in its own color. There was the rose room, the red room, the gold room, the green room, the lilac room, the blue room. She who had lived sharing one tiny half-in, half-out washroom with her mother, her cousin Angela, her aunt Pippa, her brother Salvo, and then her husband. *Each room with its own bathroom.* Overwhelmed, she placed her palms on her blooming belly.

Harry appeared by her side. "What's the matter? Why are you holding yourself? You don't feel well? Sit down."

"I'm fine," she said.

"Something hurt?" He looked around for a chair to place her in.

"Nothing hurts. I just touched my stomach. I feel all right."

His hand remained at her elbow.

The master suite was a series of connecting blue rooms. The bedroom itself was decorated in intricate lace-like wood trim. It had a giant white four-poster bed in the middle, mirrors everywhere, light yellow paintings of flowers and water. It had a sitting alcove by the balcony, a spiral staircase that led to the lawn below, and a library with a fireplace. Gina asked Harry if he wanted to make the library a nursery. Harry said he preferred to keep it a library. "Reading is the only joy that has not been taken from me," he said. "And now you want to take that away, too?"

"Who said you couldn't read? But the baby has to sleep somewhere."

"There are five other bedrooms. Can't it sleep in one of those?"

"No," she mimicked. "*It* can't sleep in one of those."

He rolled his eyes.

She rolled her eyes right back at him.

But she forgot all about him when she entered the sprawling bathroom, an open seafoam-blue room with two sinks, a large porcelain tub, and in the corner a shower, half enclosed by a marble wall. She had to lean against the marble wall to get her bearings. "Harry, can you believe this? There's even a place for me to sit and put on my makeup."

"Hmm," he said with an indifferent shrug. "There are too many fireplaces. There's even one in here. Why would you need a fireplace next to a bathtub? Why do you need fireplaces at all in Florida? It's a waste of money."

But when evening fell, he himself built a fire for them downstairs. Fernando found cords of wood in the horse stables.

"Seems a shame that Fernando will be staying in the barn with the horses and the wood," Harry said, sitting alone at his malachite table as Esther walked by with the crystal goblets. "Doesn't Marie Antoinette have her own private quarters near the lake? Maybe Fernando can stay there instead."

"All right, Robespierre, enough," Esther said, motioning to him. "Come eat."

Two

OUTSIDE ON THE STONE PATIO, they sat down to cold shrimp and crab, to fresh-baked bread, a cucumber salad, and strawberry shortcake. It was slightly chilly in the evening January air, but the roaring fire made it easy and comfortable to remain outside. In Boston, Rosa usually didn't eat at the same table as Esther, but here, the three women all sat together. They spent the evening planning tomorrow and the week ahead, how they would make the house smell better, get some cleaning supplies, wash the tables and chairs. Gina said she wished she had a bench to sit on, not just chairs, and maybe a hammock. They would need bathing suits to swim in, though Gina wasn't sure anyone made bathing suits for pregnant women, so perhaps she could make one, if only she had a sewing machine. They would get some fresh flowers, vases, new sheets ...

"Wonderful, now you've all become maids," Harry cut in. "Especially you, Esther. Doesn't anyone have some elevated concerns?"

"The house *is* the concern," said Gina. "The house is everything."

"On this we disagree," he said.

"Just on this?"

He took a sip of wine. "I will admit the house is in better repair than I expected. Not that I expected much. But still, being vacant for over a quarter century, I'm surprised."

"You have Father to thank for that," Esther said. "To protect your trust, he hired a building manager, who looked after the house. Every five years Father paid to have it repainted. He also paid a grounds crew and a cleaning crew twice a year."

"He kept that up for all these years?" said Harry. "Why?"

"Because if he didn't," Esther replied, "it would be worth nothing but the price of the land. Which is not insubstantial. But your wife is right, the house has value separate from the land."

Harry stared up into the bedroom balcony, the fireplace on the patio, the lights in the kitchen. "It doesn't look like a house built in 1890," he said, not looking at Esther, who wasn't looking at him either. "I can't imagine they had indoor plumbing back then. Electricity?"

"They did, they had some things." Esther paused. "Bathtubs. But you're right. Three or four years ago, around the time the war started and you served your first major stint in prison, Father decided to make major renovations to the house. You know Father can build houses, too. He wasn't to be outdone. He was going to improve on it. He put in all new plumbing, resurfaced the swimming pool, switched from coal to oil for heat, which made it easy to keep the white house from turning black. He ran new electric through it, and modernized the kitchen appliances. You can see how up to date it is."

"Father did this at the beginning of the war? Why?"

"I don't know." Esther pulled the silk shawl tighter around her shoulders. "He thought you might come to him, ask for help. He wanted it to be ready for you."

"Even after 1905?" When he and his father parted ways, Harry thought it was forever.

Esther nodded. "It's your house, placed in his trust. He took care of it for you."

"Also, you are still his son," said Gina. "Nothing you do can change that."

"Gina is right, Harry," Esther said, tightening her mouth as if disapproving of Gina's being right. "You are Father's only son. Men tend to place an importance on such things. As opposed to, say, daughters."

"No, Esther," Gina said. "Fathers adore their only girls. Believe me."

"I don't think you and I have the same father, do we?" Esther said.

"You're right, we don't," replied Gina. "Because your father is still alive."

They sat quietly in the cool evening, drinking tea, watching the fire burn out. Rosa had excused herself and gone to bed. "How are we going to live here?" Harry asked Esther. "We are Versailles-rich, but penny-paupers. How are we to buy milk? Rattles for the baby?"

Esther and Gina smiled at each other across the teak table.

"What? What are you two grinning about?"

"I'm proud of you, Harry," said Gina. "This is the first time in our marriage you've asked how we are going to pay for anything."

"I don't know what you mean."

"You've never asked before. You must've assumed it would be taken care of somehow."

"Leave it to you to turn that faint praise into a backward compliment."

"I didn't realize," Gina said, "it was ever either."

Harry spun to his sister. "Will *you* answer my question? How do we pay Fernando?"

"Fernando is taken care of," Esther said. "Father is paying for your security. After all, his word, his good name, and half a million of his dollars are on the line. He can't have you behaving how you normally do."

"Moving forward," Harry said, "is how I behave. What about for everything else? Is he going to give us a stipend?"

Esther shook her head. "Bellagrand *is* your stipend. Billingsworth has set up a line of equity for you at the local bank, against the value of the house. What that means, is you cannot withdraw from the bank more than the house is worth."

"I know how it works, Esther. I graduated from Harvard."

"Book-smart, but life-stupid," said Esther. "The way it works is, you use the house account for your living expenses, for everything from your food to your clothes, to your wife's sewing machine, to a car you might want to buy. Eventually, when Father passes, many years from now, and ownership of the house transfers to you, you will be responsible for that open account. And what that means is ..."

"Esther! I know what it means."

"I don't think you do. If you decide to sell Bellagrand ..."

"But why would we?" Gina interrupted.

"Let my sister finish, Gina."

Esther continued. "If you decide to sell it, the bank will first pay off your outstanding house account, and then issue you a check for the balance, provided there's anything left."

"Why wouldn't there be?"

"I say nothing. But the more you spend, the more frivolously you use your line of equity, the bigger your cars and your household budget, the less you will have on the other side if you ever do decide to sell."

"When you say nothing," Harry said, "you sure say quite a lot."

"Why *would* we sell?" Gina repeated.

"Wait, Gia. Esther, what happens to the open account if we don't sell?"

"Run it up and up, if you wish," Esther replied. "Every piece of food you put in your mouth is charged against the value of this home. The bank extends to you a secured line of credit and charges you interest on the money you borrow. The more you borrow, the more interest you pay. The house is how the bank knows it's going to get its money. Eventually you will have to pay the bank, either by selling the house or getting a job." Esther smiled with bitter bemusement. "So by all means, live your life, spend away. But remember, there's an end to everything."

Harry glanced inside the dimmed palatial house, built for diplomats and kings. "Not to this."

Three

THEY WERE BOTH EXHAUSTED when they finally closed the door to their blue room to get ready for the night. She unfolded the new sheets and made the bed by herself while he sat out on the balcony. She wanted the French doors open for the fresh air. He wanted them closed. She disappeared into the bathroom. When he came back inside he left the doors open for her. He sat in a chair by the fireplace leafing through a book on Spanish architecture. He glanced at the cold fireplace.

By the time she reappeared, in a thin robe, her hair loosely tied back, the fire was alight and crackling. "Why did you put on a fire in Florida?" she asked, walking past him to get her hairbrush.

"I thought you might like it. You're not too chilly with the doors open?" He glanced at the silk robe around her shoulders.

"No, I'm not cold."

He ignored her for a moment, pretending to be fascinated by the Doric columns and marble porticos, by the pillars, poles, supports and stakes. But then—

There was a glimpse of fragile roundness, a fullness, a ripeness he wasn't used to. There was a woman alone with him in the bedroom, sitting on a vast white bed, flushed, warm, his. He wasn't used to that either. Something tugged at his heart, other places. Opened. Blood rushed in. He closed the book, carefully laying it on the low table.

"Hey," he said. "Come here."

She was in the far corner, brushing out her hair.

"What?"

"Come here."

She walked up to him, stood in front of him, tired, unsmiling, her brown eyes exhausted pools of disappointed affection.

His hand reached up and touched her hip, pulled on the sashes of her robe. "Open," he whispered. "I want to see."

"See what? You've seen everything."

"I want to see the baby," he said.

She didn't protest, but neither did she put down the hairbrush. Harry thought at any moment she might hit him over the head with it. He unraveled the silk tassels and pulled her robe partly open. She stood in front of him naked like he'd never seen her before, enlarged, softened, with a swollen belly protruding in a half moon circle. His palms fanned over it. The belly felt taut, not soft, half a watermelon under velvet skin. Leaning forward, he kissed it, kissed above her belly button, kissed below the belly button, and lingered there, his hands on her hips tightening in an insistent vise. He raised his eyes. Her breasts had tripled in size, her nipples dark and large.

He groaned under his breath, as if he didn't quite want her to hear his need for her, his hands encircling her hips, moving her closer.

"How many months are you?" he asked hoarsely, gliding up and cupping her breasts. They used to fit molded into his hands. But no more. His breath was short.

"Almost five."

"Have we gotten this far before?" Pulling up in the chair, he fondled her abundantly. He kissed the underside of her breasts.

"Not this far."

His open impatient mouth closed around her hardened nipples.

She moaned, and dropped the brush. Ah. Finally.

Standing up he kissed her deeply, slipping the robe off her, pressing her bare body to his clothed body, his crazy hands wrapping around her back.

"You're completely dressed, *marito*," she whispered.

"And you're completely naked." He laid her down on their sprawling bed, stood over her, touching her ankles, looking at her. Slowly her arms lifted above her head. "You have become a different woman," he whispered, leaning over her, kissing her nipples, wishing he could undress himself without letting go of her.

"No, just a pregnant woman," she said, reaching for him, her head arching back, her eyes closing, her mouth parting, her thighs also.

He gazed at her for another mad moment, and went to close the balcony doors.

"What are you doing," she moaned. "I wanted them open."

"No, you don't," he said, kneeling on the bed between her legs. His spread-out hands palmed her thighs.

"Oh, yes, you're right." She shuddered before he laid the smallest kiss on her. She grabbed hold of his head. "Close the balcony doors, yes, yes."

"They're closed, my wife," he whispered, lowering his head and his ravenous mouth upon her, oh, the bliss, the swell, the adulation. *Tu mi hai rapito il cuore.*

Tu sei tutta bella, Harry whispered to her the words she once taught him. *Mia perfetta.*

Ho fame, she kept repeating over and over. *Ho fame.*

Me too, he whispered. O God, me too. Starving. Famished.

She cried and cried. On top of her, he had his lips on her throat so he could feel her sobbing, her nipples so red and raw, she would fly from the bed at the barest intimation of his mouth leaning down to suck them. Gina, Gina ...

Piango, piango.

Tell me what you want.

Prega non si smettere.

261

Am I ever stopping?

Into his neck, his head, his face, his heart, against his stomach, her maddening mouth was outrage in the night, and yet *pianse*, even when he was in her mouth and losing his sanity, no, it was long lost, hurled twenty years ago into the mysteries of ancient volcanoes. He perspired like never before, he *had* to open the balcony doors or they would both suffocate.

He opened the balcony doors.

They still suffocated.

Did you miss me? he whispered to her in the dark, cradled inside her. They were both wet like they lived in the womb.

I can't live without you, she whispered back, moaning. Did you miss me?

He pressed his face and his mouth between her shoulder blades in reply.

Non smettere, non smettere mai …

Am I stopping?

They lay together, panting, trying to catch a parched breath.

Gina held his face between her hands. Harry, she whispered. There is love in every room in this house.

There is love in this room.

It was a labor of love that built it, whispered Gina.

I don't want to talk about it. Please.

Look at the colors of Bellagrand. White, like a bride, like innocence, white like the sand, the distant shores, the horizon at dawn. White, for innocence, for romance, for thrall sublime.

I don't see it, and don't want to see it, he said, bending over her throat, kissing her clavicles, her nipples, her heart.

You're blind.

Not quite blind, he whispered, gazing into her face.

Her lips found his lips. He closed his eyes.

Do you know what I regret?

She lay on their bed, tremulous, listening, receiving, waiting for more.

That I have only one pair of eyes to look at you with.

She moaned and opened her enveloping arms to him.

That I have only one pair of ears to hear you with.

She curved into his grasping hands.

That I have only one pair of hands to touch you with.

She was rocking from side to side, pulling him to her, onto her, please please …

That I have only one mouth to kiss you with.

So kiss me, kiss me, put your mouth on me, adore me …

That I have only one tongue to taste you with.

He had to close the doors to the balcony again, her ecstasy echoing down the dark rippled waters.

That I have only one—

Oh Harry …

Here and there and everywhere, relentless, endless.

And still she cried.

Don't cry, *amica mia, innamorata*, he whispered, his breath heavy, his own heart opening and closing like a prayer book. *Non piangere.*

And yet … *lei piange.*

I'm sorry, he lamented to her in the moments of respite between the chaos of the hurricane. I'm sorry I'm not the man you thought I was.

You *are* the man I thought you were. I'm sorry I was weak and wrong. *Mi dispiace. Perdonami.*

It's done, it's gone. Will you forgive me for my foolishness?

I can't remember any.

I'm going to try harder. Though sometimes, like when the awful thing happened between us, I become dreadfully afraid that I am simply not equal to the task, that I will never be quite worthy of your love. This is what I fear most. And it is when I fear this that I behave the worst. Sometimes I don't know how to help us become what we both once dreamed we would be.

Never fear, *delitto mio*. We are what we dreamed. Half apart, but whole together.

Yes. Half apart, but whole together. They lay on their sides, belly to belly. Please, don't ever leave me.

I will never leave you. *Non ti lascero mai.*

Promise me.

I already did. I married you. That was my promise.

She fell asleep with Harry's palm over their baby.

He remained awake, alive, sweltering, craving her again, needing her again. But she was curled up on her side, her hands under her cheek like a child.

For a long time afterward he lay next to her, listening to her breathe, his caressing hands on her, marveling at her silken skin and the bloom of her body, at her rounded hips and the dip of her widening waist. His face was pressed into the thick mane of her wild disheveled hair.

You want to know what else I regret, he murmured to her, breathed to her when he knew she was asleep and not listening.

I regret I have only one heart to love you with.

I regret I have only one brief life to love you.

Chapter 10

Molasses

One

THEIR LAUGHTER THREATENED to disturb the ducks in the pool. They were alone on the patio, on a long wooden bench at the breakfast table, Gina perched on Harry's lap, telling him to behave, and he wasn't behaving in the least, but was still trying to explain to her things she didn't care a whit about. "Do you want me to get Fernando over here? He'll tell you."

"No! He'll arrest you for indecency. Your present morning condition is not suitable for the public." She squeezed him.

"I want him to set you right. Molasses is *not* bait for fish," he said. "Where do you get your kooky ideas from? It's human food."

As Gina had requested, Rosa and Fernando brought home a wooden bench, but Harry didn't approve of its rudimentary craftsmanship. "I should build you a proper bench," he had said. "Show you how it's really done."

Esther had laughed at that when she heard. "*You* are going to build a bench? Do you even know what a hammer is? What nails are?"

"Har-de-har-har," said Harry. "You forget, oh, mocking sibling, that you and I have the same father. And he taught me things too."

"I can't imagine you remember a single thing our father has taught you," said Esther, and Gina crossed herself again at *Our Father,* and they groaned loudly, but when they turned, there was Cuban Catholic Fernando, also crossing himself, and they groaned even louder.

Fernando had been wrong: there were no bookstores in Spanish City, but he drove the women down to Palm Beach one afternoon where they had a long lunch at the Breakers and then went shopping and even bought appropriate books for Harry in Palm Beach Gardens. So now Harry had books to read, none of them on the naughty list.

Bellagrand was slowly settled by its inhabitants. Gina and Esther opened the pool, hired a cook and a housekeeper. Emilio and Carmela, a married couple in their fifties, hardly spoke, and Gina soon discovered why. They barely spoke English. This made it difficult for Gina to tell them what to cook and what to buy. They brought home unacceptable canned goods and ketchup. They bought the wrong kind of fish. They found linens that weren't soft and loose muslin dresses for Gina that looked like burlap sacks, and then seemed silently offended when Gina wouldn't wear them. And a few days ago, after she had asked them to buy her some maple syrup, like the kind they sold at every market in Lawrence, they brought home something called blackstrap molasses, which looked like tar and tasted like (sweet) tar and for which Gina wanted to fire them, the molasses being the last straw.

"I don't want it in our house, Harry! They use it in cattlefeed."

"Who is *they*? And how do you know anything about molasses?"

"My brother works for Purity Distillers. He says it's disgusting. I don't want our baby around it."

Harry laughed. "We have over four months until the baby comes, and it probably won't be crawling the minute it leaves your womb, so we're safe for a month or so, I figure."

"Who is this *it* you keep referring to?"

Harry tickled her. "In Cuba, Fernando makes rum from molasses. He'll make some for us here. Wouldn't you like that?" He kissed her bare shoulder.

"What is this rum?" The *ron ponche* of Christmases past but a distant memory.

"Believe me, once he gives you a taste, you'll never forget."

Her arms wrapping around his neck, Gina lifted his face to hers and stared happily into his laughing eyes, blue with bliss this morning. Lowering her voice, she murmured, "Oh, but *cuore mio*, I don't need molasses from Fernando when you keep letting me taste so many delicious things."

He jumped up, nearly knocking her over, and pulled her behind him to the spiral staircase that led upstairs to their bedroom.

At the bottom of the stairs stood a flagrantly disapproving Esther, groomed and starched like a prim iron statue, in a heavy cotton twill suit and black oxfords, her arms folded.

"Your parole officer is here for your first meeting," she said. "That's where you're headed, right? To the front door?"

"Of course, Esther. Where else could we be headed?"

Like two kids caught out, they stood holding hands trying not to laugh in front of his sister.

Two

MARGARET JANKE HAD a pinched face and distrusting slits for eyes. To Harry she seemed to be preoccupied and unobservant until she said, "Mr. Barrington, I see from the selective reading material on your barely unpacked shelves that you're still interested in socialist revolutionary literature?"

Harry said nothing. Lenin's enrapturing pamphlet, newly translated and published, "The Soviets at Work" was on his malachite table. "I didn't realize—is that *also* a crime? To read?"

"Not at all. Just as long as you understand that you are not allowed to write about it, to send out letters or pamphlets about it, to contribute articles or editorials in the local paper, to send in freelance advertisements in support of it, to be in contact with anyone associated with the Socialist Party, the Communist Party, the Communist Labor Party, First International, or any other radical organizations I have not thought of and have not mentioned. You are not allowed to write

267

letters to anyone in Russia or to speak to your former comrades on the telephone. It goes without saying that you are not allowed to march, protest, or demonstrate for this or any other cause."

"If it goes without saying," Harry said, "then why are you saying it?"

"I'm simply making manifest the letter of the law under which you have gained your provisional freedom."

He made a deliberately blank face in response. "Is this what freedom looks like, Officer Janke?" he said. "Being guarded by Cubans day and night and having you in my house every Monday?"

"Yes, Mr. Barrington, this is what freedom looks like for *you*. Now, in front of me I hold a document signed by you that says you understand that you have done wrong and are sorry for your past actions. Is that true?"

"It is true that you hold this document in your hands, yes."

"The document also says," she went on, unprovoked, "that after your incarceration is over, you agree to look for gainful employment so you can materially contribute to the wellbeing of your wife and family. Do you agree with that part?"

"Who am I to argue? But tell me, Officer Janke, before I look for gainful employment, am I allowed to go swimming?"

"In your own backyard? Certainly."

"Well, the ducks are using my pool at the moment. What about at my property across the street, in the ocean?"

Janke hesitated. "If it's on your own beach frontage, then yes."

"Am I allowed to walk on the beach?"

"If it's on your own frontage …"

"So I can pace back and forth," said Harry, "across forty feet, just like I did in my jail cell at the Correctional?"

"I doubt you had forty feet there," she returned, "and it's more like a hundred and forty here, but yes."

"Gotcha. So—a matter of degree. One more question. Am I allowed to take my boat out?"

She glanced down the lawn to the dock and the newly scrubbed white boat, bobbing at anchor. "That might be all right, but only if Fernando goes with you."

"Oh?" Harry exclaimed. "So is that the condition? If Fernando comes with me, I can venture out? Just in the boat, Officer Janke, or by car also? For example, if I can go in the boat forty miles south to Palm Beach, can I go in the car three miles west to Spanish City?"

"No, you cannot travel anywhere by car."

"Can I take the boat to the market? What about to the carnival across the water? Maybe to Miami? If Fernando comes with me, may I travel there by boat? My wife and I have never been to Key West. In fact, she and I have never had a proper wedding holiday. We went to Chicago for a few days, but it rained the whole time. So if Fernando comes on the boat with us and stays with my wife and me in our little cabin, can we sail to Key West for our belated wedding holiday?"

Janke shot up and started collecting her papers.

"We're done, Mr. Barrington."

Trying not to laugh, Harry folded his arms and stretched out his legs under the table. "I thought we might be, Officer Janke. I'll see you next Monday? Perhaps we can meet at your house instead. Do you live near the water? Because Fernando can take me to you. By boat, of course."

"Good day."

"And a good day to you, too."

After she stormed out, Gina sauntered into the kitchen from the butler's pantry where she had been hiding and listening. "She is going to make your house arrest ten years if you don't stop it," she said. "Why do you torture her?"

"I can't remember the last time I had that much fun." Harry caught her by the wrist and pulled her to him, enveloping her in his arms. "Wait, I think I do remember … where were we, before the gendarme interrupted us?"

"You were spinning molasses tales about some treacly, syrupy thing you think I should put in my mouth."

"I don't understand," they heard Esther's voice from the hall talking to someone who couldn't be heard. "What if something is terribly wrong?" Silence. "What else could explain it? It's two o'clock in the afternoon, and they haven't come back downstairs. What on earth could they be doing in there?" Pause. "Until two o'clock in the *afternoon*? Impossible! It's indecent. We had plans today." Another pause. "No, something must be wrong. Fernando, Rosa, we have to break down the door." Loud banging. "Harry! Gina! Open up. Are you in there?"

Harry swung open the door, barely dressed in slacks and an unbuttoned white shirt. His hair was a mess, he was unshaven and barefoot. He looked as if he had thrown on the clothes five seconds before appearing at the door. Gina couldn't be seen.

"Esther," he said. "Can you ask Emilio to bring Gina some coffee, me some lemonade, some sandwiches, and maybe a little fruit. Also, two glasses and the remainder of the red wine from last night. We are not feeling well. We've taken to our bed. We'll come downstairs when we're feeling better. Not today, and perhaps not even tomorrow. Please, Esther, ask Emilio to keep those sandwiches coming. Leave them by the door on a tray."

Three

SHE WAS SITTING ON top of him with her starched mesh petticoat spread out in a fan over him and the bed. "Why do you like the petticoats now, *marito*?" she asked. "Our whole marriage you've been telling me how you do not care for them."

"Yes, but back then," he said, "in the days I no longer remember, you didn't wear the petticoats like you do now—with nothing underneath." He pulled down the silk chemise off her shoulders. Her breasts spilled out.

"How do you know," she murmured, "that I had anything on underneath even then?"

They both groaned. His hands reached for her, his mouth reached for her.

There was a loud knock on the bedroom door.

Harry threw a pillow over his face in frustration.

"Harry? Can I speak to you please? It's very important. Harry? Are you in there? Open the door."

"I'll be down in a few minutes, Esther!"

"How many?"

Harry rumbled Gina so her breasts shook and swayed into his face. "Fifteen," he said.

"Twenty," whispered Gina, filling his mouth with her nipples.

There was an odd commotion in the kitchen when Harry finally stumbled downstairs an hour later. Esther was on the telephone, ignoring him, Rosa was frantically cleaning the spotless limestone floor even though it wasn't her job. A local newspaper lay spread out on the table.

"What's the fuss?" Harry asked. Upstairs with Gina had been so peaceful. All he wanted was to bring her a cup of Colombian coffee (courtesy of Panama Canal, which is why Harry never touched the stuff), a sweet cake, some jam, then lie by her side and read the paper. "Rosa, hasn't Emilio made any coffee yet?"

"Where is she?" Esther said as soon as she got off the telephone and rushed toward Harry.

He backed away. "Who? Carmela?"

"Your wife! Where is she?"

"Upstairs, why—"

Esther shoved the newspaper in front of him and pointed to a small article on the front page.

Harry paled.

"HUGE MOLASSES EXPLOSION IN BOSTON'S NORTH END. 21 DEAD. 150 HURT." He read on. A two-and-a-half million gallon cast-iron tank exploded in the middle of an unseasonably warm afternoon, sending a molasses wave through the North End traveling at forty miles per hour. Buildings were crushed, trains derailed, horses and human beings submerged in the black viscous goo. It exploded without warning and poured out onto the streets in a matter of minutes. Purity and its parent company, Industrial Alcohol, which owned the molasses plant, were blaming the anarchists. The article vaguely stated "the North End," but did not detail the exact location of the damage.

"Esther," Harry said. "Call Father immediately."

"Who do you think I was just on the telephone with? He knows nothing."

"Is he all right?"

"Yes, yes. He didn't go into Boston that morning."

"Call Clarence, call Darryl, ask them to find out exactly where it happened."

"What does it matter? Doesn't Salvo work during the day? He would have been at the plant in the afternoon!" Esther started pacing the kitchen.

"Just call Clarence, Esther."

Tea and coffee forgotten, jam, cake, love.

Esther called everyone she knew. The accident had happened right across the street from Salvo's Charter Street apartment. That was one of the reasons he liked working at Purity; he rolled out of bed and was at work in minutes.

"No use scaring your wife until we know something concrete," Esther said when she replaced the receiver.

"But my God, Esther ..."

"I know. Last thing she needs. God, I pray he's all right."

"Has anyone seen or heard from him?"

"And how would I find this out?" Esther was shrill. "Maybe I could call his place of employment, see if he showed up for work?"

"No need for sarcasm, sister," said Harry. "Call Clarence back. Ask him to drive down to the North End and find a Flaminio Gallerani on Salem Street. He's a taxi driver and is always parked there, waiting for fares. Salvo and he are good friends."

"How do you know this? I thought you and Salvo haven't spoken in years?"

"I'm not deaf. I've heard my wife talking to her mother."

"How would Clarence even find this ... this Flaminio?"

"Tell him to look for the most flamboyant Italian on the block. Everybody knows him. Gina told me—"

"Gina told me what?" said Gina coming into the kitchen. "No coffee?"

The conversation ended instantly as they distracted her with rolls and preserves. They threw away the papers so she wouldn't catch sight of the bad news, and busied themselves with frantic activities.

For three miserable days, they busied themselves and threw away the newspapers. Every time the telephone rang, Esther set Olympic records dashing to it.

Gina couldn't help but notice. "Who is she expecting a call from?" she whispered to Rosa. "A paramour?"

"That must be it, though she won't tell me," said Rosa. "Come, Gina, eat. I prepared fresh fruit, some oatmeal. Emilio will make you a nice lunch when he and Carmela return from the market. You've got to start gaining some weight."

"Gaining? I barely fit into my clothes. I'm almost ready to wear the potato sacks you and Carmela bought me. I want her to buy me the cotton twill I asked for. I need to make myself a dress."

"I'm sure she's getting it today."

Each time Esther got off the telephone, she looked ashen and unwell.

"If it *is* a paramour," Gina said wisely to Rosa, "I sense trouble in paradise."

No one could find Salvo. Harry thought it was a good sign, if neither Purity, nor the nearby hospitals could locate him.

Clarence finally called with news. Unfortunately they found Flaminio. He had died of his burns from the molasses. Clarence only added to their collective panic with details of the devastation. "Like a tsunami!" Clarence told Esther. "It flowed twenty feet high, a black death tidal wave through the streets! The fire station is gone, whole avenues are gone, the horses were like flies, the dogs …"

They sat with their heads in their hands.

They *had* to tell her. Yet if they told her, they were afraid she'd lose the baby.

"It's her brother, Harry. We can't tell her."

"Esther, we have to," said Harry.

"There's nothing she can do about it."

"We don't know anything," Harry said. "We can tell her *that*, can't we?"

"No!" said Esther and Rosa.

"Now listen to me." Harry banged the table for emphasis. "I have done a lot of things that have made my wife unhappy. I'm fortunate that she places a certain *gravitas* on the institution of marriage. Calls it a sacrament or something. But this conspiracy to deceive, I think it's grounds for divorce, even in Sicily."

"She will lose her baby!" Esther said. "Is that what you want?"

"God! When did *you* become so Italian? A little restraint, please." He stood up and walked out.

One evening the three of them had come back into the kitchen after hotly discussing Gina outside only to find her on the telephone. She was speaking in Italian, and they couldn't understand a word. Watching her carefully, Harry sat and listened to her cry softly and exclaim loudly. After she hung up, she sat by them at the table.

"Why are you all staring at me like that?" she asked.

"Gina, dear, who was that you were talking to?" asked Esther in her most casual voice.

"Esther, why are you clutching the table? To my brother, why?"

Loud gasps of relief. Then they told her.

She gaped at them. "Is this what's been going on the last few days?"

They nodded. Gina rolled her eyes. "Harry, I warned you molasses was trouble, and you didn't believe me."

"I believe you now."

"You should have told me right away. I would have found him in five minutes and spared you the panic, you nervous Nellies."

"Where was he?"

Gina told them that Salvo had gone out on the town with a woman from Back Bay the night before the explosion. He was still with her the following morning, and was too hung over to go to work.

"I don't know what to say," said Harry. "Salvo's wanton ways saved his life. I really can't fathom the lesson one is supposed to learn from that."

"First, stay away from molasses," said Gina. "And second, I keep telling my brother that women are going to be either his salvation or his undoing." She smiled.

Harry smiled too. "And what does he say in reply? Why can't they be both?"

"Exactly."

Everyone relaxed. The tension left the kitchen.

"But how did you find him?" Esther asked. "I had Clarence driving around for days looking everywhere."

Smiling, Gina patted Esther's hand. "He's my brother," she said. "I know where to look for him. Wouldn't you know where to look for your brother?"

"In prison?"

"You're correct, Esther," Harry returned, happily easing into the paper he could read out in the open for the first time in days. "That's where I am."

"Stop," said Gina, pinching Harry and sidling closer to him. "Unfortunately Salvo is now out of a job."

For a moment they were silent, blinking at each other. "Is your silence fraught with meaning?" Harry shrugged. "So ask him to come down here." He patted her hand. "I don't mind."

"I asked him," Gina said. "Apparently *he* still minds."

"So I get credit for offering without actually having to do anything? Perfect."

"Harry," Esther said, "call him yourself. Don't have Gina do your dirty work. Don't be so inflexible. It's time to let bygones be bygones."

"Inflexible?" said Harry. "Bygones? Am I the one who refuses to come down here where it's safe, even though I barely escaped death by treacle?"

"Harry is right for once, Esther," Gina said, pinching him again. "Salvo is a mule. He has the nerve to tell me it's not safe *here*. He says we have hurricanes."

"It's called rain and wind." Harry returned to his *Palm Beach Gazette*. "How many serious hurricanes have there been in the last ten years? None. And how many molasses disasters in Boston? I rest my case."

Four

RIGHT AFTER THEY LEARNED that Salvo was alive and well, Esther packed up and apologetically announced she had decided to go back to Boston. "I don't feel right leaving Father for this long," she said to them on the last evening before she left. Supper was long finished and put away, Rosa had gone upstairs, and it was just the three of them in the very late evening on the stone patio. The fire had almost gone out, the wine was almost gone. It was time for everyone to head upstairs, the train was leaving at dawn the following day. Yet they sat and lingered.

The night was quiet, muggy, warm. The air smelled deeply of salt water.

"What if Father had been down in the North End?" Esther asked. "He goes there frequently during the week. He still keeps an eye on the properties he's retained. He could've been there."

"But tell me, Esther," said Harry, "what could you have done about it if he were? Carried him in your arms across Salem Street?"

Esther put her arm around her brother, kissing him on the head. "Don't worry," she said. "I promise I'll be back when the baby is born. I know you're going to miss me." She smiled. "But you have your wife. And Father has no one."

Gina poured Esther and Harry the last of the wine. They raised their glasses. After they languished for a few more quiet minutes, Gina took what she saw as the last opportunity to ask the brother and sister about some of the unspeakable things. She was afraid once Esther left, she would never find out.

"So tell me," she began haltingly, "why did Henry Flagler build this house for your mother?"

Harry glanced at his sister. "You want to take that one, Esther?"

"Not really," Esther said.

When they didn't elaborate, Gina prodded further. "Did he love her?"

"How would we know?"

"Perhaps he did," said Harry. "You said so yourself, Gia."

"Yes. This house is a labor of love. *Un travaglio d'amore.*"

"There you go."

"Was he married when he built it?"

Esther and Harry looked at each other, wine in their hands.

"Was *he* married?" Esther asked. "Yes. No? Perhaps he was married. He might've been between wife number two and wife number three. Or wife number three and wife number four. Or not. We don't know how he had time to build Bellagrand when he was busy building the 540-room Ponce De Leon Hotel in St. Augustine during the same period. Perhaps that's why it took so long," she added. "Years. He was busy doing other things."

"We don't know if *he* was married," Harry added, "but you know who definitely *was* married? Our mother. To our father."

Gina crossed herself. Harry and Esther didn't comment on it this time, looking as if they might want to make a sign of the cross themselves. "Yes," she said. "I see how that might be awkward. But did your mother know Flagler was building it for her? Or did he build it and present it?"

"Oh, she knew," said Harry.

"She helped him build it, we think," Esther said. "She was down here often."

"Esther is being polite," Harry said. "She must have moved down here. Because we barely saw her. When I was eleven or twelve, I don't think I saw her once in six months."

"You were away in boarding school," Esther said. "*I* saw her."

"You were also away in boarding school."

"Yes, but I saw her. I didn't *not* see her for six months, is what I mean. You're exaggerating."

"Maybe. It seemed a long time between mother sightings is what I mean."

"It takes a while even now to get from here to Boston by train. Back then it was easily a week each way. It was a difficult trip to make on your own."

"Yes," Harry said. "And Mother hardly made it. She stayed here."

Watching him, Gina was thoughtful. "How did she explain it to your father?" she asked. "Being gone for months at a time?"

"She was just gone."

"Harry, you're not being fair," said Esther. "She wasn't gone."

"No?"

"There's gone and there is *gone*." Esther's voice was barely audible.

Harry put down his glass. "Gia, we went sideways and I forgot your question. Oh, yes. How did she explain? I'd like to say that she probably didn't have to. Father was so busy with his work he might not have noticed she'd gone missing."

"Harry!"

"Do I jest?"

"Don't listen, Gina. Of course Father noticed. And she told her children where she was. She told us she was working on something special for us in Florida." Esther waved her hand to the darkened house. "A new summer home. Initially she and Father traveled down here together to look at investment properties. Mother stayed by the sea, while Father worked. So at first her absence seemed stamped with Father's approval."

"Yes," said Harry, "but soon Father stopped coming down here, and Mother stayed on."

"How long did this go on?" Gina swallowed. "Her, um, staying on?"

Esther and Harry sat. "A few years, right, Esther?"

"At least." Esther looked into her empty wine glass, turned it upside down.

"The cheap truth of it," Harry said, "is that Esther and I didn't *know* anything."

Esther shook her head. "You were too young. I felt something wasn't quite … in order. I kept asking Father, and he kept repeating that Mother was being delayed. That's how he put it."

"That's what they called it at the end of the last century," said Harry. "*Delayed.*"

"And then one day she was back," said Esther. "Just like that."

"After being gone almost an entire year," added Harry. "We asked her if the place was ready for us, and she said there were problems, and she had to give up on it."

"Yes, but then she took us to Cape Cod," said Esther. "Do you remember?"

"I remember," Harry said. "We went clamming on the beach at Truro."

"Yes."

"I never heard the word *Florida* spoken again," Harry said. "Not until Father came to see me in Concord."

"Me neither," said Esther. "Harry, can you believe he took her back?"

Harry's hands clenched. Gina's heart constricted.

"*Once*," Harry said, "I had found it unfathomable."

He didn't look at Gina, or at his sister. Gina hurried on before Esther thought too long or hard about it. "How many years was this before her death?"

There was no color in the exotic orchids, no sighting of the swallows, or sunset in the sky. There were no fishermen or rum-runners, no conch shells, shanty roofs, mangrove woods. There was just darkness, a flickering candle on the table, and the pungent smell of brackish water. A deepening night with dull lights across the bay.

"Six months," Esther finally replied.

"Was it that long?" said Harry. "Seemed shorter."

"The beach at Truro was in August. She died in December."

"Like I said. Barely a season between."

Gina inhaled and waited, the sadness inside her multiplying. She counted out the times the nightingale sang in the shade, the times the crickets chirped. Esther sat like a stoic, pin-straight like a gravestone, staring at the abyss of the water, and Harry was sloping forward, elbows on his knees, eyes to the ground. Gina squeezed together her intertwined fingers. Minutes passed. "How did she die?"

It was Harry who answered her. "She drowned in the Mystic River."

Dio mio, abbi pietà. Gina crossed herself, mouthed inaudibly in Italian. "Drowned ... accidentally?"

"Yes, why not?" Harry said, not glancing up.

"Yes," Esther echoed. "If you overlook the concrete slab tied in a sack around her neck."

"Or the notes she left for you and me around ours." He straightened out and put his arm around Esther. She tilted sideways, to him.

"I'm sorry, Harry," said Gina. "I'm sorry, Esther." They didn't speak. "How did your father manage?"

Esther shrugged. The shawl had slipped off her shoulder. "Who knows? He never refers to her unless he absolutely has to and never by name. I sometimes mention her in passing when we talk about other people or other events in our life, but we don't discuss it."

Gina didn't understand. That wasn't how things were done in her family. Everything was agonized over. But it occurred to her that to render judgment on the father was to judge the son as well, for she and Harry had been married nearly fourteen years and this was the first time she was hearing about the death of Frances Barrington.

"Harry never talks about his mother either," Gina said.

"Is it any wonder?" said Esther.

"What's there to talk about?" said Harry. "The less said, the better." He nudged his sister. "You and I used to talk about her sometimes."

"Yes," Esther said. "Before you wiped your life clean of your family, we would occasionally talk about our mother."

"Father told me not to come back, so I listened. I was an obedient son." Harry's arm remained steadfast around Esther. "Do you remember who couldn't shut up about Mother? Louis."

"Oh my, yes." Esther rubbed her eyes. "Until he went deaf, he continued to go on and on about her."

"What did he keep repeating?" Harry fixed his sister's shawl and squeezed her to him. "He would say, your mother's heart went done and broke."

"And who can go on living when your heart's done and broke?" Esther finished for Harry.

Gina slumped in her seat. Her eyes searched the faces of her husband and his sister. The fire had long gone out, and it was nearly dark except for a single candle flame, melting the last of the wax onto the plate on the table.

"Did she leave anything behind for you, Esther?"

A single tear ran down Esther's face. Harry drew her closer to him. "Nothing but gloom for my sister." He took a breath. "A chest of ornaments and charms. And a quote from Job."

The candlelight flared in a brief squall, and was out.

Esther spoke, her voice like wet, loose gravel. *"Wherefore is light given to him that is in misery, and life unto the bitter in soul?"*

Five

THE BIG HOUSE WITH all its noises was so strangely quiet after the two clucking, fussing women had left.

The windows were open, the French doors flung wide to the great lawn. Gina lay in the hammock under the palms. There was no breeze, the palm fronds motionless above her head. She brought with her a book about babies, but drifted off as soon as her eyes touched the words on the page.

Oh, the illusion of romance in a white house built on such desperate desire. It seemed so real. She opened her eyes to search for him.

Harry was near the waterline and the lilies. It was hot and he was shirtless. He was tanned, his ash hair bleached by the sun. He looked almost blond. He shaved only on Mondays to impress Margaret Janke; the rest of the week he sported a porcupine stubble he tickled Gina with. His gray eyes looked blue in the hazy ceaseless Florida sunshine. He was cleaning the boat, getting the hooks and the fishing lines ready. He was always outdoors, digging, hammering. He built a table for himself so he could sit and read at it. Gina couldn't believe her eyes. He had built a table! And not just any table, but a round pedestal table with a carved-out base and a mosaic top. It was intricate and stunning. Why are you so surprised? he had said, casual as all that. Do you think all I do is read and make love to my wife?

That *is* all you do, she replied.

She gave him nectar for the starved honeybees every afternoon, between the swimming and the sleeping.

But when she lay in the hammock like this and watched him, often she would cry. Could what she had learned about him explain away his initial reluctance to having children, or was that too facile? Every once in a while she would find him staring at her swollen body with uncharacteristic anxiety, with dull disquiet, and she would wonder if he perceived her differently now that she was about to become a mother. Did Harry define *mother* as someone who could abandon her children on a whim of the heart? She bought their baby silk rompers and yellow pajamas. She painted pink flowers on the walls of the baby's nursery, sewed little bonnets and napkins and swaddling clothes. She vowed to redefine motherhood for Harry into the thing it really was, the divine thing.

They put gasoline in the white boat he himself had named *Frances* and with Fernando's full approval took it out onto the Intracoastal Waterway, traveled downstream to Lake Worth, anchored it in a small estuary by the hanging palms, pretended to fish, had a picnic lunch, and purred about names for their baby. Gina suggested naming the girl like the boat. Harry balked so loudly, the herons flew away. He wouldn't consider it. She wouldn't consider a boy's name. She was convinced they were having a girl. "I have a girl feeling," she said.

Under the myrtle in the delta of the tidal woodlands, they decided on Grace, for how else to explain what was happening to them?

Gina brought bags of white and yellow purchases home to a perplexed Harry. "How can one tiny baby require such a department store of a wardrobe?" he would ask. "I have three shirts. Why does he need twenty?"

"She," Gina would correct him, the floral extravaganza of silk and pink cotton on full display.

"You know, dear wife, my enormous beauty queen, my wise and undulating princess, there is a slight possibility, a chance, however remote, that this child might be a masculine child."

"No chance," said a panting Fernando, who had carried Gina's purchases upstairs to the master bedroom. "In Cuba we are very good at predicting. We have a gift. Your señora is definitely having a girl."

"All right, well, if the oracle from Cuba proclaims it so, please, continue to buy pink bibs."

Emilio and Carmela were put on reduced schedules, because Gina wanted to gestate and hibernate with Harry in privacy, but the groundskeeper continued to work overtime mowing the back acre of their green, salt-tolerant wide-blade Seashore Paspalum grass that sloped into the water.

Margaret Janke disapproved when she saw the man sweating outside one Monday morning. She said Harry should be mowing the lawn himself, like his wife, who cleaned the house, sewed dresses, and made shrimp in garlic sauce over pappardelle.

"My wife also makes her own tomato paste," Harry said, his eyes twinkling. "I help her with that." Gina, lush and abundant in her organdy and muslin embroidered pastel ensemble, was pruning the orange trees nearby so she could listen in, and she shook her fist at him in mock outrage, grinning like a happy child.

"You should mow your own grass, Mr. Barrington," Janke repeated. "You worked in the laundry room in prison, didn't you?"

"Do you want me to mow the grass or do the laundry?"

"Both. Why not? You have time. You learned your way around the laundry room quite well. I know, I have your prison reports from MCI."

"Is this MCI? I worked the laundry room so I could buy smokes."

"Without work, man is incomplete. Man is nothing," Janke said. "Look at your wife."

"I'm looking." His eyes smiled at her. Her eyes adored on him.

"Look how many hats she wears. She is always cleaning something, cooking, fixing, sewing, mending. Now she prunes. Do you see?"

"Also shopping. She's doing quite a lot of that. Also creating human life," Harry added. "Doing a marvelous amount of that, too. As you can see."

"If you don't occupy yourself, Mr. Barrington, if you don't find some motion in your life, very soon you will find yourself weary, gloomy, fretful and vexated."

Harry stood from his mosaic table where they had been sitting, having iced tea. "Officer Janke," he said. The twinkle faded from his eyes. "Don't misquote Blaise Pascal to me. If there is one thing I know it's my French mathematicians. I am never idle, not for one minute of any day. I don't have enough hours to do all the things I want to do. I don't have enough minutes to read the books I want to read, to think about them, to write synopses of what I read in the journal I keep for that purpose. Pascal talked about man being completely at rest without passion and without study. That is not me. It's never been me. I am brimming with passion."

"For all the wrong things, Mr. Barrington."

"Also, for some of the right things, Officer Janke." A glance at the overflowing woman standing and grimly listening with shears in her hands. "But your job here is not to judge my business or my diversions."

"My job is to prepare you for the outside world, which you're going to re-enter in less than three years' time."

"No," said Harry. "Your job is to be my warden. That is all. I prepare myself. I am not weak, nor empty. I rejoice in the world. My heart is not weary. I have no gloom. I wake up every morning just after dawn and can't wait to begin my daily purpose."

"Do you feel you have purpose, Mr. Barrington?"

"Without question, Officer Janke. My purpose is not yours—to spy on an adult man in the prime of his life to make sure he doesn't wander too far from the plantation. But I will stand up for my work every day. I am preparing myself for a new life, for a new law. I recognize the life my wife and I had been living in Lawrence is done with. I understand there will come a time when other things will be required of me. So I work now at what I can, and I don't despair as I wait for the bright future."

Janke said nothing, her skeptical gaze on his affronted tanned, slender frame.

"I will not train in Bellagrand to be a parole officer," Harry said, "if I interpret your critical gaze correctly."

"You interpret it incorrectly."

"I will not be a jailer. When this brief period of isolation is over, my wife and I and our soon-to-be-born offspring will have a whole life still ahead of us. I am preparing myself now for that time. So I can be the best husband I can be, the best father I can be. What you judge as my stillness, I know is fullness, and an active interest in the world around me."

Gina stepped up to the table. "Excuse me, Harry, may I?"

With a light bow he took a step back.

"I wear many hats, you're right, Officer Janke," Gina said, metal shears open and flashing in her hands. "One of them is defending my husband. Leave him alone. You are not a philosopher. You are a warden. So come on Mondays and ward. And you are quite wrong about him. What you perceive as fruits of his idleness, are actually the fruits of his solitude. Now, is there anything else we can get you before you go?"

Six

HARRY WAS KISSING HER awake, then shaking her awake. "It's after two, Sleeping Beauty. Do you want to have lunch?"

"I can't believe I've slept so long," she muttered, needing his help to lift herself out of the hammock.

"You're like a turtle on your back," he said, rubbing her belly and hoisting her under her arms. "I can't imagine this is not going to get funnier as you get bigger."

"I can't imagine getting bigger," she said, stretching and walking to the house with him.

"That's true. You're as big as Bellagrand."

"I'm starved, is what I am. Did Emilio make lunch?"

"He didn't," said Harry, but before she could open her mouth to complain, he added, "I did."

"You *what?*"

"Oh goodness, why are you crying?"

Harry had made them a feast: shrimp and avocado salad and cucumber-and-cream-cheese sandwiches. They ate on the veranda. From across the water, Gina could hear the plaintive sounds of Spanish guitar. They ate in near silence, making the smallest of small talk.

"It's good to be alone together, live alone together."

Reaching over, Harry fondled her belly, her ample breasts, molasses-dark from the sun. "Clearly we managed to be alone together before, otherwise I'd still be in jail, and you'd be mending dresses in your Portuguese mill."

She was happy to have him be light with her, jolly. "Do you realize," she said to him, her mouth full of watermelon, "that if I hadn't hocked my wedding ring to make your bail, we wouldn't be sitting here right now? I wouldn't be pregnant, we wouldn't have Bellagrand." She shook her head, reaching for another slice. "It was terrible to give it up. But look what I have instead." She gazed at him, then reached out to caress his sandpapery cheek with her sugary hand. He said nothing.

She waited. "Why aren't you saying anything?"

"What should I say?"

"I don't know. Something. Anything. I wasn't talking to the herons on the dock."

"Indeed. I figure I'd better keep silent. A minute ago you were weeping like a willow over a cucumber inside a piece of bread. So I can't say what I want to say because you won't stop crying until May, if then, and I'll never get any peace."

"Harry! Say."

"I don't want to make you cry."

"Please, *mio diletto*," she whispered. "Make me cry."

He said he would be right back and disappeared. She waited, finishing her watermelon, looking out onto the water. When he came back, he went around to her chair and kneeled down on one knee on the limestone veranda.

"What are you ..."

He handed her a small gift-wrapped box.

Her hands dripped with watermelon juice. She didn't even open the box before she cried.

"Do you see why I wanted to say nothing?"

"Oh, Harry. What did you do?"

"I don't know. Are you going to sit and cry or are you going to open it?"

"I'm going to sit and cry," she said, sitting and crying.

After she wiped her hands, she opened the little black box. Inside, sitting in blue velvet was her two-karat diamond betrothal ring, sparkling, shining.

Open-mouthed, she stared at the ring, at him, still on his knee in front of her.

"What's happening?" she said. "Is this a magic trick? I don't understand."

"It's your ring, Gia."

"That's impossible."

"And yet."

"Harry, it's impossible! It's a sleight of hand."

"And yet …"

"I lost that ring."

"You didn't lose it."

"It's not the same ring."

"Do you want to read the inscription inside it?"

She couldn't read the inscription through the tears in her eyes. Harry had to read it to her. *Gia*, it said, *amica mia, mia bella.*

When she stopped crying long enough to listen, Harry told her that in January, before they left for Florida, he had asked his sister to go to Lawrence to the pawn shop to see if the ring was still unsold and if it was, he asked her to buy it back. "I know *you* couldn't ask my sister," he said. "But I could. And did." He wiped her face. "The man told Esther the reason the ring didn't sell was because he had raised the price beyond what anyone was willing to pay for it."

"Why would he do that? Why did he do that?"

"He did it," said Harry, "because he remembered you and thought that if anyone was going to come back for a ring like that it would be a girl like you, so he raised the price and kept it safe until you could."

Gina was weeping.

"Why did you wait so long to give it to me?"

"I wanted to wait until our anniversary in June, but you mentioned the ring, so what could I do? Besides, what if when the baby comes you won't care about rings anymore, or love, or Harry? I heard that can happen."

"*Il mio cuore*, that will never happen."

There was music in the house, from restless jazz on the radio, from Gina's attempts to play Esther's Schumann's *Traumerei*, to Fernando's Spanish-tinged guitar easing out a slow *habanera*. Fernando sat in the marble courtyard, smoked, and strummed his Cuban childhood through their palms and walkways. The sun shined morning to night, there were whooshing fans and clanging knives and slamming drawers. There was

287

life. They planted inkberry in the loamy earth, and tomatoes for later in the summer after the baby came when they could make paste again from homegrown, not market-bought tomatoes. Together they made luscious sauce, and had pasta with garlic, clams and shrimp, vegetable lasagna, capellini primavera. He drank red wine and kissed her with the opulent juice still on his lips. With his new Kodak Brownie he took photographs of her that he never developed, the film thrown into the drawer until later, the later that never came. Harry said he didn't know how Gina could show herself at the public market. He said being with her was like constantly walking through the red light district in New Orleans. She was lust on parade. She told him that was the nicest thing anyone said to her.

Late at night he would draw them a bath and build a fire in the delicate light blue bathroom. He was careful with her, and tender. He soaped her like he loved her, held her like he loved her, loved her like he loved her. Some nights there was a slight breeze through the darkness past the open windows. The room would be filled with the smell of fragrant soap, salt water, and love, like heady perfume, like opiate.

March and April dissolved into sweltering May, elusive intimacy, unabated ardor, boat-bobbing bliss.

The lemonade is made, the sugar bowl is on the table. The sun shines every day and the moon and the stars are out for us at night, she murmurs after him, like a love song.

Chapter 11

TOTAL ECLIPSE OF THE SON

One

IN THE MIDDLE OF May the newspapers started counting down to May 29, the day the esteemed weather scientists predicted the sun would be eclipsed by the moon. Not partially eclipsed either. The moon would pass between the earth and the sun, and Jupiter would become invisible even from tropical skies. For a moment, maybe longer, the world around the equator would go completely dark. Gina and Harry's neighbors to the south, Chuck and Karen, drove their fancy new car into Bellagrand from next door to introduce themselves. They were having a blowout Eclipse Bash, they announced. South Florida, just above the Tropic of Cancer, was going dark. Would Harry and Gina like to join them?

Chuck and Karen were always having blowout parties. The loud music and clamor of the crowd could be heard twice weekly around the bay, their drunken ardor audible all the way down to Lake Worth. Pleased to be invited, Harry and Gina didn't want to beg off by admitting that Harry was under house arrest.

"Thank you," said Harry, "but as you can see, my wife is about to give birth."

She looked colossal, the seams on her voile orchid-print dress tearing under the pressure of late-stage pregnancy.

"Congratulations. But surely not so soon? Not on Eclipse Day?"

"I believe it will indeed be on Eclipse Day," said Harry. "Though her good doctor disagrees."

"Doctors don't know everything, do they?" said Karen, a slim, short-haired, comfortably dressed older woman who was incongruously milk-white in the tropics. "Mine keeps telling me drinking whiskey could be bad for my health." She laughed heartily. "Yet I'm the picture of vigor." Her husband stood beside her, affably silent.

"Doctors may not know everything," said Gina, "but husbands don't know everything either."

"Yes," Harry acknowledged. "Sometimes husbands don't know everything." He paused. She elbowed him. "But the day of the birth of my first child, I know in here." He tapped his heart.

"Well, please do stop by," said Karen with a wave by the Aphrodite fountain, "if the child reconsiders arriving on party day of all days. Tell it that's just bad manners." She laughed and got into her vehicle. "What do you think of our new chariot? We picked it up a week ago."

"Beautiful!" Gina called after them. "Careful going out of the gate!"

"If he waited to arrive on a day other than one of their party days," Harry said to Gina, watching Chuck and Karen speed away in the electric blue Cadillac Phaeton jalopy, "he'd never arrive, would he?"

"*She* would never arrive," Gina corrected him. "*She*."

On May 29, 1919, Gina woke up around seven and asked Harry, who was already up and by the window, if he could see the solar eclipse from where he stood.

He said no, but the festivities underway next door made it seem as if Chuck and Karen could see something.

"They've been carousing since yesterday afternoon," said Gina. "Did you see the damage to our gate? I knew they were going too fast."

"What about the damage to their Cadillac? Gouged right down the side."

"Should we go?" she asked him. "Might be nice to go to a party. Meet new people. Take our mind off things. We've been waiting and waiting. I'm sure Fernando will let you walk next door."

"I'm not going next door. Janke hates me. This is exactly the kind of thing she's looking for. What if there's a radical at the party? No." Harry shook his head. "And take our mind off what?"

"The baby."

"We can't take our mind off the baby, Gina," said Harry, "because as I told you, you're having the baby today. It's time to keep your eyes on the prize."

"Oh, Harry," Gina said, rubbing her hot-air-balloon of a belly. "Don't be a silly sausage. I'm not even close to having the baby."

An hour later they went for a swim in the pool because it was so blistering hot out. She was sitting on the stone patio sipping a lemonade, not even bothering to dry off, looking up at the sky, and listening to Harry read to her from the paper about Arthur Eddington of the Royal Astronomical Society in Greenwich, England. Today he was wandering on an island off the coast of equatorial Africa, taking photographs of the solar eclipse because of an untested theory of a patent clerk in Switzerland named Albert Einstein.

For years, Einstein had been speculating that time and space were not absolutes but instead relative to the gravitational forces of other objects and, more important, relative to the speed with which the other objects traveled. Gravity and motion affected time and space. Only a total solar eclipse would allow Eddington to measure this theoretical deflection of light—the impact of the sun's gravity on the light of distant stars. If the sun's rays didn't bend during the eclipse the way Einstein had postulated, then his theory would be false and he would be discredited and disgraced. The world's eyes were on good old Eddington, who was taking sixteen snapshots of the sun moving out from the shadow of the moon.

"One-thirty Greenwich Mean Time," Harry said, looking up at the sky. "That's eight-thirty in the morning Bellagrand time." He looked at his watch. "That's now, Gina. Look up."

She shifted in her chair, looked up, it got darker, and suddenly she felt a tremor like a tidal wave flood through her body. Gasping, she nearly fell to the ground. It got darker still. Harry jumped up, paper falling from his lap, took one look at her, and ran to the telephone.

"Harry, get me upstairs first," Gina called after him, "but then tell the midwife to hurry."

Lucky for them Carmela and Emilio were in the kitchen. Carmela ordered Harry to remain downstairs while she took Gina up to the bedroom. Gina wanted to protest, reach for Harry, but her mouth wasn't cooperating, her body busy being swallowed up in a deluge that took away her ability to speak.

"Why so sudden?" she mouthed to Carmela. "I thought I had some time, no?"

"Señora, I think your water broke. Did you not feel it break?"

"No, I got out of the pool." She panted. "It was hot. I was perspiring." She doubled back, began inching her way downstairs. "I have to go, Carmela, I think the baby is in the pool. Help me. I left it. She slipped out."

"Señora, please come with me."

"No, I must go check. I'm here, but she's there ..."

"Señora, right here, into your bedroom. Lie down, I'll be right back."

"Carmela, ask Harry to go get her. Because ..."

"You are delusional, shh."

"How do you understand what I'm saying? How do I understand *you*? Are you speaking English?"

Why was it so dark in the room? Like it was night. What's happening? Gina looked up at her ceiling—screamed—was drowning—screamed silently like she was underwater.

The rest she doesn't remember well.

She opens her eyes, once twice, there is a man she doesn't recognize, a woman she's never seen before, someone bending over her, she tries to remember the name of the man who did this to her so she can kill him, but can't, whispers, Mimoo, Mimoo, I need my mother. It's hot and there is a piercing sound, it's wet, and in the delirium she thinks it's her. She screams but no sound comes out, she is under the ocean.

Suddenly light. The midwife, whose name escapes her, and the doctor, whose name escapes her, are smiling over her, and on her chest lies a squirming creature with a shock of hair and length in the limbs, and she almost hears something now, almost … She closes her eyes.

When she opens them again, a man stands by her side, smiling the biggest smile of them all. He bends over and kisses her deeply. Such liberties! What is his name? She can't recall. Oh, yes. Harry.

"Gia," Harry says, kissing her face, wiping her brow, beaming. "I'm sorry, but you were saying, you're going to name the baby girl—what? I can't remember the name we picked out for our daughter. Can you remind me?"

Why is he smiling like that? Like the cat that ate the canary.

Gina looks at her baby.

It's not a girl.

The May 29, 1919, universe-changing total eclipse of the sun tested and proved the theory of relativity and won Albert Einstein a Nobel prize. The eclipse that made him an instant celebrity and a household name all over the world was one of the longest on record, lasting nearly seven minutes. Gina's labor, unforeseen by everyone but Harry, lasted uncomfortably longer. The angles of a triangle no longer added up to one hundred and eighty degrees. The uneclipsed sun was low in the sky when a boy came into the world in the blue master bedroom of Bellagrand, in a mansion built for Harry's mother by a man not Harry's father. The boy warped space and time by the mass of his gravitational force and bent light around them.

Two

"IT'S A BOY!" HARRY SAID. "How can that be? Prophet Fernando told me that was impossible. So did you, the Sicilian soothsayer." He was lying on his side on the bed next to her. There was no one else in the room but the three of them.

Gina didn't answer, the baby cleaned up, wrapped up, deep in her arms. "How can I have a boy?" she whispered. "I am my mother's daughter. I only know girls. What am I going to do with a boy?"

"I don't know. What would you do with a girl? Feed her. Change her."

"What about after that?"

"I can't think past today." Harry waited for just a moment. "Well?"

"Well, what?"

"Can I hold him?"

"In a minute." She coughed. "What's wrong with my voice?"

"Maybe you strained it."

"I was loud?"

"A bit."

Evening fell. Night went by. Did they even sleep? The baby slept.

She couldn't look away from him, cradling him to her chest. She prayed for relief, for forgiveness. She prayed her thanks. She cried for her mother, she wished her mother could see him, could see her child's child, hold her child's child. Perhaps she still can. Gina lifted the baby into the air. He's here, Mimoo. Our boy is here. *Grazie, più misericordioso Dio.*

She tried to feed him. She tried to wake him, open his eyes. She couldn't sleep because she was listening to his breathing. It was too quiet, and it disquieted her.

Can I hold him?

In a minute.

I waited our whole marriage to have this child, she wanted to say. There is a good chance I will not have another. This may be the only time I will hold a baby.

Me too, Gia.

Oh, she was speaking out loud; he could hear her. She couldn't even hear her own voice.

In the morning Harry went downstairs. He called Boston, informed everyone, even Salvo, smoked a Cuban cigar, courtesy of Fernando, ate, read the paper. He came back upstairs with sweet bread and coffee.

Gina had not moved from her spot on the bed, sitting halfway up on the pillows, the baby on her chest, mother and son stomach to stomach, both almost sleeping.

Harry fell on the bed next to them, sulky like a child.

"Careful!"

"Maybe I can hold him?"

"Okay. When he wakes up." Still a rasp.

"You're going to ruin him."

"Ruin him with love?"

"He slept on your stomach all night. As if he is still inside the womb. I know it's nice there, but come on …"

"Now he is outside." Both her hands were on the baby. She couldn't eat, she couldn't drink. She opened her mouth and Harry gave her drink.

The baby was the largest the midwife had ever delivered. The baby was the largest the doctor had ever seen. There had been no complications, but the midwife had called for the doctor anyway, just in case.

"Soon he'll be too big to carry," said Harry.

"But not yet, right?"

"What are you going to do then?"

"I'll continue to carry him."

"Until he is twenty? Twenty-five?"

"Wouldn't I be a lucky mother if he let me?"

Harry gazed longingly at the dark-headed sleeping infant face down on Gina's chest. "We don't have a contingency plan for a boy," he said. "Is Grace a boy's name, too?"

"No. We will call him Anthony Alexander Barrington. After my father and brother. We'll call him Alexander."

"Um, don't I get a say in this?"

"No."

The boy stirred, started to cry.

"Perhaps he's protesting," Harry said. "Perhaps he'd like to be called Harrison."

"Harrison Barrington?" She laughed throatily. Her voice seemed to be stuck in low octaves.

"Horatio Barrington?"

"Like Britain's naval hero? You, a pacifist, want to name your son after a legendary military officer?"

"No, no, you're right, that's so wrong." He stared at her fondly. "I didn't realize, my Sicilian peasant girl, you are so well versed in British military history."

"I studied the French Revolution at Simmons. Napoleon came right after. Remember I told you how little I thought of Max Robespierre?"

"What does that have to do with …"

"He was so somber and humorless," she continued softly over the baby, coughing to clear her voice every sentence. "Not a hint of parody within. What woman could ever love him, I thought. He was so joyless in his murderous splendor."

"Um …"

"But Nelson! There was a *man* for you. Did you know he was loved by only the most beautiful woman in England? Some say in all the world."

"Like me?" Harry smiled. "*Ecco sei bella.*"

"You goose. No. Horatio Nelson and Emma Hamilton," Gina said dreamily.

"Ah, good. Another H name. How about Hamilton Barrington?"

"At least you're funny—unlike Robespierre."

"I'm not actually trying to be funny," said Harry. "I'm trying to continue the long-standing tradition of H names in the Barrington family."

"I didn't realize it was that important to you."

"Neither did I." Harry paused. "Until now."

The baby stirred, got agitated, excited. Harry stirred, got agitated, excited.

They lay the baby on his back on the bed, uncovered him from his swaddling blankets, bent over him.

After a few moments of watching the boy squirm and wail, Harry spoke. "Why does he have to look exactly like you?"

Gina kissed Harry. "He is like you in all the ways it counts, *amore mio*," she said. "But why is he crying?"

"I don't know. Maybe he wants an H name?"

"I don't think that's it."

"Maybe he wants his father to hold him?"

And finally, reluctantly, she let him.

God! A night and part of another day had gone by, and Harry at last picked up his wriggling naked son and brought him to the open window. It was so hot. Barely a salty breeze drifted off the water. The boy quieted down, lay still, blinking up at his father, and fell back to sleep. Harry sat down in his favorite rocking chair on the balcony. "My son," he whispered.

"Bring him back," Gina said.

"In a minute."

"He'll get cold."

"It's ninety-five degrees out. It's almost the temperature it was in the womb."

When she didn't speak for a few minutes, Harry glanced behind him at the bed.

She had fallen asleep, in a heap on top of the covers. Thank God. Harry refocused on the boy. The hours drifted by. "I think I'm beginning to understand why your mother won't let go of you," Harry whispered, his lips moving back and forth across the boy's sleeping head. He might have fallen asleep himself, swaddling the baby with his arms. "What should we call you, son? Whisper to me the name you'd like so your mom won't hear. What's a good name for you? Howard Barrington? Herbert Barrington? Howie? Herbie?"

"Anthony Alexander Barrington," Gina called hoarsely from the bed. "And we will call him Alexander. Bring him here." She coughed.

"Uh-oh. She's awake." Harry put his hands over his son's ears. "Now, don't you listen to that croaky Sicilian voice telling you what to do. You name yourself anything you want. What name would you like? Harvey? Hector?"

"Alexander," said Gina. "Bring him to me. He needs to eat."

"Just because only your mom can feed you, don't let that sway you," he whispered into the boy's head. "You and I can do many other things together. Fun things."

"Nothing fun yet because I have to feed him."

Slowly Harry brought the boy back to her. "Hector is a fine strong name."

"If you're Greek and on the losing side of a protracted battle, then yes. Otherwise no. Hand him over." She reached for him. "You know what's a fine strong name? Alexander." Finally he was back in her arms. She smiled kissing his head, pulling down her gown, adjusting him to her breast. "The conqueror of the world."

"My son is not a fighter," said Harry. "So he can't be a conqueror."

"He's not going to be a Hector either."

On the third day her milk had come in. Both Harry and Gina were astonished by the copious quantity of it. For the first few days the boy had been cranky and struggling at the breast. They couldn't tell if he was getting enough nourishment. They feared he wasn't. What meager sustenance he had been getting was thin and lemon in color. Suddenly a waterfall of abundant warm white milk flowed from her breasts into his mouth. The child became immediately tranquil, his appetite sated.

Harry brought his own face to Gina's breasts after a feeding.

"*Amore mio*," she whispered, "you haven't shaved in days. What are you doing?"

With his stubble he scraped her stomach lightly, where the baby had been. He licked the underside of her breasts where the sweet milk was still warm and sticky. He fondled her carefully, happily. He kissed her brown arms from her wrists to her shoulder. He kissed her full breasts.

"Don't touch the nipples, please, *mio tesoro*. I'll scream. Downstairs the servants will think you're doing unspeakable things to me."

"I'm trying to."

"Not yet."

"When can I touch all of you? Come on, undress, take off your gown."

"You can't touch me, Harry. You heard the doctor. No conjugal activity until I heal."

"I'm sure by conjugal he meant paying the bills or something. How long did he really say?"

"Four weeks."

"Four weeks! Are you insane?"

She leveled him with a look. "You were in jail longer than that, Harry."

"That was then," Harry said. "My new self is like my self of old, full of wedded abundance. Please help."

"I won't help now." She smiled. "The baby is here."

"We might need to … when is he *not* going to be here?"

"Never."

"Exactly. We might need to work around him."

Afterward, they resumed other marital prerogatives, like argument.

"How about Absalom?" Harry smiled in contentment, curling up, touching the boy's cheek. "Do you want to be Absalom, my son, my son?"

Gina stared at him puzzled from the pillows. "What in the world could *you* possibly know about Absalom, *caro*?"

"What, you think all I do is read Max Eastman?"

"Look at the books on our shelves. I *know* that's all you read."

He didn't take his eyes off his baby. "Sometimes I peek inside your little books, too."

"My little books?" She laughed, coughed. "You mean my little Bible?"

He shrugged, sidled up to the boy, cradled him. "I started reading Samuel for the battles. I kept reading for the naughtiness. There's quite a lot of it in Samuel. What about Samuel?"

"No."

"David?"

"No."

"Solomon?"

"No."

Harry thought of one last H name. "Homer!" he exclaimed. "Homer Barrington. A journeyman, a warrior, straight from the Greeks. That's good, right? Perhaps our son can also embark on an odyssey."

"Perhaps," Gina said, unwavering to the end. "But he will embark on it named Alexander."

Three

ESTHER AND ROSA STORMED the house not seven days after Alexander was born.

In the master bedroom the three women bent over the baby in genuflection. On their knees in front of the bed, they stared at him open-mouthed. They adjusted him, centered him in the middle of the four-poster bed, uncovered him, and now all four adults leaned over him, gaping, murmuring, appraising.

"What are you staring at?" Harry wanted to know. "What?"

"We're just studying him."

"Like a telescope pointed at the Alpha Centauri," Harry said. "He is perfect, isn't he?"

"He is," said Esther in wonder. "But he's not like our family. We were all born bald. Look at his black hair."

"In our family," said Gina, "we were all born with hair. That's the Sicilian way."

Esther glanced at Gina, in a peach silk robe with her wild auburn mane loosely braided. "What's wrong with your voice?"

"I don't know." Gina shrugged. "I can't seem to get it back."

Esther turned her gaze to her nephew.

"What is he doing now? What is that?"

"Nothing," said Gina. "He's yawning. It's normal."

"Why is he yawning? Does he do that often? Maybe he needs to sleep."

"He just woke up."

"Then why did he do that yawn thing?"

With amusement Harry eyed his sister. "What is happening to you?"

"Nothing," she said, trying to sound brusque. "What are you looking at?"

"You're staring at him as if he is the second coming," said Harry.

"What do you mean, the second?" said Gina.

"Esther, why are you sniffling?" Harry ran his hands through his hair. "Why does one infant make all the grown-ups around him devolve into babies?"

"Esther, pay no attention to your brother," Gina said. "Would you like to hold him?"

"May I?"

"Of course." Gina wrapped the boy in a covering, picked him up and handed him to her sister-in-law. "Any time."

"Oh, *Esther* can hold him any time?" said Harry, poking Gina in the ribs.

For a few minutes Esther didn't speak, couldn't speak, she just held the baby, trying to keep the tears away.

Harry threw up his hands.

Gina handed Esther a handkerchief. "Did you forget your handkerchief, Esther?" she said quietly, mildly, fondly. "Like me?"

"Never you mind that." Esther regained her composure. "I really think," she said, "he is the most beautiful child that's ever been born."

"It's not a matter of conjecture," said Harry. "It's simply fact."

"What are we going to name him?"

"*We?*" said Gina. "Alexander."

"What?" Esther held the infant closer.

"That's what *I* said," said Harry.

Esther shook her head, as if the matter were settled. "No one calls a child that in Boston," she said firmly.

"Are we in Boston?"

"In America, then. You're still in America, aren't you? What are you really calling him? We have to think about this seriously. Naming a child is very important."

"I agree," Gina said. "We have been given this duty by God. Man names things. And we don't have to think about it at all. We are naming him Anthony Alexander. We will call him Alexander."

"You just said that man names …"

"I meant that inclusively."

"No, no."

"Yes, yes."

Esther turned away from Gina as if shielding the infant from an intruder. "Please be serious. Harold, don't just stand there. Talk some sense into your wife while I attend to your child."

Harry opened his hands interrogatively. "Esther, why are you getting difficult with me, calling me Harold?"

"Are you not the child's father?"

"What does that have to do with anything? As if I have any say in naming him."

Rosa and Esther nearly required smelling salts.

"Esther," Gina said, taking her baby from Esther's unwilling arms. "My father was Anthony Alexander. My oldest brother was Anthony Alexander. My son will be Anthony Alexander."

"The Third?"

Gina shook her head. "They had Italian names. Antonio Alessandro. He will have the first American name."

Rosa piped up. "Have you considered other possibilities? So many wonderful names for children these days. William. Walter."

Gina's gaze shifted downward, adoring on her baby. "He is not a William or a Walter. Look at him. He is an Alexander." *Il mio bambino. Il mio figlio.*

"No use arguing, Esther," Harry said. "You're just wasting the air I have already wasted. Would you like some lunch? I'll ring for Emilio."

"Well, I'm not going to call him Alexander," Esther declared. "Never. I'll call him Xander." By her side, Rosa kept sniffling.

Harry rang the service bell. "Emilio! Come, save me! Oh my God. Will a man ever come into this house, or am I going to live out my life surrounded by wailing women?"

"A man *has* come into this house." Gina lifted the baby to Harry's face. "Your son."

"How would I know? I'm barely allowed to hold him."

"He needs his mother. Can *you* feed him?"

Harry and Gina blinked at each other with affection, intimacy, longing. "He doesn't need to be fed twenty-four hours a day, does he?" Harry asked, lowering his voice.

"Harry is right," said Esther stiffly. "You might be overfeeding him. He is too big."

"Can a boy *be* too big?" asked Gina, her voice lowered by the birth of her son. She smiled. "I don't think so."

"How much did he weigh at birth?"

"The doctor said ten-and-a-half pounds. But that has to be wrong," said Gina. "And he was twenty-four inches long. That must be wrong, too."

"All I know is he is too big. He won't fit into any of the things we brought for him." Esther turned to Rosa. "Will he, Rosa?"

"We underestimated him," Rosa said, nodding, blowing her nose.

"Let's go across the lagoon to Tequesta and buy him more clothes. Harry, can you call for Fernando? Tell him to get the car ready."

"You're leaving right now? You just got here!"

"Why dawdle, I say." She reached for Alexander. "Can he come with us?" She chuckled, nuzzling his head. "Good boy, come shopping with the girls?"

Harry and Gina exchanged a look of amazement at hearing Esther chuckle.

"I don't see why not," said Harry. "He's not under house arrest like me."

"That may be," said Gina, shaking her head. "But you can't take him out yet. He's not baptized. An unbaptized child can't leave the house. In six weeks he'll be baptized. Then he can go out."

"Fine. We'll go without him," Esther said. "We'll stay until the baptism."

Harry groaned. "I can't—I need reinforcement. Please, Gina, call Salvo, invite him to come. Tell him on my knees I shall beg for his forgiveness."

"I'm glad to hear you say this," Gina said. "Because Salvo *is* coming. He is going to be the baby's godfather."

"Salvo? Godfather?" Esther exclaimed. "Oh no—don't tell me that after naming him Alexander, you're also going to baptize this child a *Catholic*!"

With the peach folds of her silk robe, Gina blocked Alexander from Esther's view. "As opposed to what? Baptizing him into Harry's religion? Does your brother even know what religion he is?"

"Gina, I'll have you know that we've always been Methodists."

"Esther, darling," said Gina, "I guarantee you, there is not a single thing Harry can tell you about it."

"Not true," said Harry. "It's definitely a Christian religion ... right?"

Four

A WEEK LATER SALVO strolled through Bellagrand's African blackwood doors. Somehow he found his way from the train, without needing Fernando to pick him up. He didn't have a car, or a map. He asked someone for directions in Italian, received them in Spanish and walked to the house across the bridge, his earthly belongings in a duffel bag on his shoulder.

Salvo's hair was graying slightly at the temples, but it hadn't lost its thickness or its shine. He wore a white shirt, a rumpled beige suit, a brown tie, slightly askew. His perspiring olive face was covered with days of train stubble, and he had become wider than in his younger, more sinewy years. He wasn't built tall like his sister, for modeling the finest long dresses, but he had an easy carefree charm, a seductive smile. First he assessed the man or woman in front of him, then he dazzled them. The more charm needed, the more dazzling the smile.

"*Santa Madre di Dio*, it's hot here. Gia, baby girl!" He opened his arms.

She ran to him. They embraced with joy. "How did you get here, Salvo?" When he told her, she threw her hands up. "You walked? *Pazzo!*"

"What is wrong with your voice, *sorella?*"

"Never mind that." Stepping away from him, she gestured to the house. "So? What do you think?"

Salvo glanced around, trying not to whistle or look too impressed. "It's nice. A little small. Where am *I* going to sleep?" He twisted her hair, inspected her. "Gia, you're black like the Sicilian drunks who lie all day in the sun."

"Yes, the sun is merciless here," she said, wearing a light cotton housedress, her curls piled every which way. "You'll see soon enough. Would you like a tour of the house?"

"House, house. I've seen houses before. How about a tour of the child? Where is he?"

"Oh, Esther has him." She leaned to Salvo. "She never puts him down, Salvo. She's going to ruin that baby. Oh, Esther! Salvo is here."

Rosa and Esther came in from the kitchen, carrying Alexander. "Do you see how it requires two grown women to carry one baby?" she whispered to her brother.

Salvo let his duffel fall to the floor. He reached for the infant, while simultaneously assessing the two women in front of him. Gina tried not to laugh watching the cogs spin in her brother's devilish mind. Some things never changed. Salvo was terrible at hiding anything he was feeling. After a three-second appraisal, he correctly determined that Esther was going to remain forever impenetrable to his copious charms. So he wasn't going to waste a speck of his gifts on her. He turned his attention to Rosa. A toothy smile opened his face from ear to ear. Alexander stared up curiously at the new face above him.

"Alessandro," Salvo said, momentarily taking his eyes off Rosa and looking down at the nephew lying in his arms. "I'm your Uncle Salvo. *Zio Salvo*, can you say it?" He held the child to the light. "What's happening, little cowboy?" He bounced Alexander up and down. The boy's unsupported head bobbed. "You like fishing?"

The two-week-old stared.

"Hold his head, if you would, please," said Esther, prim and already disapproving.

Salvo continued bobbing him, but held his head. "I'll take you fishing, if you want."

"Maybe not yet, Salvo."

"I don't mean now, Gia. When I teach him how to hook a worm."

Gina chortled. "First *you'll* have to learn how. When was the last time you fished, *fratello*? Twenty-five years ago in Catania?" She pulled him forward. "Esther, this is my brother, Salvo. This is Esther, Harry's sister."

Holding the baby in one arm, Salvo bent theatrically and kissed her hand. "The pleasure is *all* mine," he said into her closed and critical face. "And I mean that sincerely. The pleasure is *all* mine."

Gina almost laughed out loud.

"But who is the *donna bella* by Esther's side?"

"That's Rosa, Esther's companion." Gina pulled on Salvo's shirtsleeve. "But she is not lovely."

"Thank you very much, Gina," said Rosa.

"She is not for you, Salvo, is what I meant," Gina said. "Rosa is entirely too mature."

Rosa didn't seem to agree that she was too mature for feisty, adorable, friendly, handsome Salvo.

"*Matura?*" Salvo sparkled. In Italian it meant *ripe*.

"No. Mature in English. As in, too grown up for you."

"I disagree with you, *mia sorella*," Salvo said, rolling his r's, his vowels, caressing each word on his Italian tongue. "My eyes do not lie. Rrrrosa is the verrry *picturrra* of loooveliness."

Gina dragged the blushing, giggling Rosa away into the relative privacy of the butler's pantry. "Rosa, you're a grown woman, and of course you will do as you please, but as his sister, I'm going to give you one word of *caveat emptor*. I love my brother and he has many fine qualities ..."

"Why didn't you ever tell me you had such a brother?" In the seclusion of the pantry, Rosa was busy rearranging her hair to drape more loosely around her face even as Gina kept trying to save her.

"But there is one thing my brother is especially good at ..." she continued.

"I can hardly guess what that might be." Rosa tittered.

"And that is," Gina said, "breaking the heart of every girl he's ever been with. Every single one. He's breathtakingly good at that. So approach at your own peril."

Judging by Rosa's flushed expression as she flattened out the folds of her day skirt, this only inflamed her, approaching peril be damned.

Gina rolled her eyes as they returned to the Great Hall. She could only do so much. At the end of the day, Rosa was going to have to save herself.

Harry walked in from the outside in his casual linen house clothes and stood warily next to Gina, saying nothing, watching Salvo flirt with Rosa and coo over the baby. "What's happening over there?" he asked quietly.

"What does it look like?"

"Trouble."

"Exactly."

Finally Salvo looked away from Rosa and at Harry. "Hello, Salvo," said Harry, stepping forward.

"Hello, Harry." Salvo paused a second, swallowed, and then stepped toward Harry's proffered hand. The men shook.

"How have you been?"

"Not as good as you, I see," Salvo said, appraising him, smiling lightly.

Harry shrugged. "Yes, I'm like a tree-climbing crab. All day in the sun."

Salvo agreed. "It's fantastic here. I walked four miles in the heat with such joy." He put an affectionate arm around his sister. "Hot like Belpasso, eh?"

"Much hotter." Winking at Harry, Gina kissed her brother's cheek. She was so happy to have Salvo with her. "And there are no volcanoes."

"Let's not stand here like pillars," Harry said. "Come in, Salvo, let's have a drink, relax before dinner. Gina told me you can stay for a few weeks?"

"Two at most," said Salvo.

"Wonderful."

"But now I realize," the Italian man suavely continued, "that two weeks won't be nearly enough to partake of the pleasures of this great state." He smiled widely at Rosa as they walked to the kitchen. "Perhaps a few more than two?"

"Oh, I think two weeks is plenty, *more* than enough," Esther piped up, easing the baby out of Salvo's arms, as if they were playing musical

Alexanders. "What else is there to do here besides carry the baby? Oh, and Rosa and I heard a hurricane was headed this way. Didn't we, Rosa?" Esther widened her eyes. "Very frightening. Because you know, Salvo, we're so close to the water. The tides are likely to swell. Right, Fernando?"

"No, no, do not worry, señora," Fernando said, who had joined them in the kitchen. "We are not in the path of hurricanes. The coast bends favorably for us. Not like the Keys, where it can get quite stormy." He grinned.

Salvo grinned back at him like a kid. "And who is this?"

"Fernando," said Harry.

"Fernando! I'm Salvatore. But you call me Salvo." One handshake and they were off, one speaking Italian, one Spanish, understanding nothing, and yet everything.

They had a seafood feast that night prepared by Emilio, and Fernando and Rosa both joined them on the veranda. Salvo refused to take a guest bedroom upstairs. "Neither gold nor lavender," he said. He asked instead if he could stay in the mews house with Fernando.

"Like a servant?" Esther stage-hissed as Carmela and Emilio cleared the table.

"Leave him alone, Esther," said Harry. "He's a big boy."

"You're right." Esther shook her head. "No use," she said in clipped English, "in casting pearls before swine."

Salvo remained coolly cheerful. "Have you considered the possibility, dear sister-in-law," he said, raising his wine glass to her, "that it is Fernando who may be *la perla*?"

Alexander was baptized. Salvo stayed. One week, twelve days, two weeks, a month. The house re-adjusted. Salvo and Fernando became fast friends. Salvo even tried to charm Margaret Janke, but when she asked him how much longer he was planning to stay, he couldn't get even a chuckle out of her when he told her he was thinking of never leaving. "Officer Janke, are you sure you're not in any way related to Mrs. Esther Barrington over there?" Salvo asked. "Because I am almost certain you must be."

"Is this a joke?" said Janke. "Why would I be related to Mr. Barrington's sister?"

"No reason at all, señora."

After that Gina forbid Salvo to leave the mews house on Monday mornings, just in case Janke decided to take out Salvo's mischief on Harry, who was plenty mischievous himself.

Every evening after dinner, over Esther's ignored objections, Fernando and Rosa joined the family outside, and while Alexander slumbered peacefully in one adult or another's inebriated arms, they had rum with mint, with Coke, with sugar, they had red wine with fruit in a drink called sangria, and under the palms discussed all manner of things: the menu for the next day, the path of Alexander's bright future, Salvo's uncertain future, and the best Romance language for songs of love. Salvo and Harry put away their past troubles. They shook hands, sat down to dinner, and rose the next morning as family. They raged in faltering SpanishEnglishItalian about the coming of Prohibition, like the Apocalypse. In January, 1920, a delectable nectar like rum would become illegal to procure and transport. After weeks of nightly harangues against the women's movement, their right to vote, and their subsequent cursed involvement in men's politics to the detriment of all drinking men ("And women," Gina pointed out with a minty drink between her elongated fingers), Harry told them all to rest easy, because for the past six months he had been paying Fernando to travel back to Cuba—four times—to bring back crates of the finest Havana Club rum, white, gold, and aged.

"Because let's remember, ladies and gentlemen," said Harry, "we *know* that the people on this lanai are smarter than all the fools in Washington, who decreed it was a good idea to pass the Volstead Act and ratified the Eighteenth Amendment, but forgot to insert a single mention into the new law about the *consumption* of alcohol. So we can't buy it, or sell it, or drive it from our house to Chuck's next door, who has plenty of his own, by the by, but we can store it here, and make it here, and drink it here. So fret not."

"Good man, Harry," said Salvo. "But what happens when we run out?"

Fernando slapped Salvo on the back. "*Mi amigo, por favor*, do not worry. I will teach you how to ferment your own rum." He flashed his smile.

"As long as it's not with that devil-spawn molasses," said Salvo, "I can't wait to learn."

Fernando also brought back bottles of Guayabita del Pinar, a potent Vueltabajo liqueur made from sugar and fruit of the wild guava that grew only on the River Pine in Cuba. But this Harry kept just for him and Gina. A gulp or three of this heady drink, *dolce, dolce*, and he and Gina would spend senseless hours living out in full a verse of the Canticles, *Io sono del mio diletto, e il mio diletto è mio*.

I am my beloved's, and my beloved is mine.

Five

AFTER ALEXANDER'S CHRISTENING, Salvo wasn't sure of his plans, but one thing he knew with conviction: he was never returning to the snows of Boston.

"I might get a job," he told Gina and Harry one lazy morning over *huevos rancheros* he was eating over Alexander's bobbing head. "I like the tanned summer girls." He grinned. Rosa wasn't around.

"A job doing *what*?" Harry asked incredulously. "I'm not sure what you're imagining is an actual paid position."

Salvo laughed. "Gia, is your husband right, *sorella cara*?"

"Yes," she said. "But why should that stop you from your wicked plans? Give me the baby. He needs to eat, too." She nursed him under a shawl right at the breakfast table.

Salvo found a job at a local bakery. A week later he was given a raise, because no one could bake bread as well as Salvo or increase their sales by twelve percent by virtue of his baking skills combined with his bronzed good looks and Sicilian charm. He soon realized the bakery was not a good fit for him. The blazing sun and the nearby Florida beaches with their heady accouterments were too enticing for him to spend his days in hot basements near broiling ovens. He found a job at the local docks washing the boats. That suited him better. He still worked at the bakery part-time, selling the bread he made there at the outdoor market on Saturdays, greeting the friendly and well-dressed female customers. From the musically prolific Fernando, he learned to play a little guitar, so he bought himself one, rented a tiny bungalow near the marina where he worked, and at night strummed "Rumores de la Caleta" on the Tequesta docks, like a mating call of the Italian swallows.

As the summer waned, he asked Gina for a short-term loan to finance his enrollment in a horticulture course. "I want to learn to be a landscaper," he told his family. "I'll be outside all day. It's a perfect job." He smiled happily. "I'll get hired by all the *bellissima* ladies with time and money to spare so I can make their fertile gardens blossom."

"Salvo!"

"Horticulture, Gia. Don't be cheeky. It's my next career." He raised his face to the sky. He was already black from the sun.

"Are you sure you want to loan him money for this?" Harry asked Gina. "Isn't it like being an accessory to …"

"To what, Harry?" Gina asked, smiling, nursing Alexander. "To love? To joy? To life?"

"I was thinking of something else, but all right."

Gina bent over her three-month-old son, covering him with kisses. "You're not going to be like that, are you, baby? Like your silly billy *Zio* Salvo, always searching, never finding? You're going to be a good boy, right?"

Harry took the sated child out of his mother's arms. "Don't listen to your mother, Alexander," he said, wiping his son's face and carrying him away for an afternoon stroll by the water. "Salvo is trying to remake the entire world Sicilian. What's wrong with that?" He kissed him. "Perhaps when you grow up, you can remake the entire world revolutionary."

Alexander didn't know what it was like to be laid down for a nap in a bassinet in an empty room, to not sleep in someone's arms, to be left alone. All summer long he was either with Esther and Rosa, who bathed him and swam in the pool with him and wheeled him in a

311

stroller through Spanish City, taking him out every two minutes "to check on him," or with Fernando and Salvo, who took him out on the boat and on car rides in the Tourister, with the windows down and the little boy gulping for air, unable to catch a breath in the hot Palm Beach wind. They left him lying on a blanket as they sat on the sand by the ocean, smoked and drank and played their guitars, and talked about girls, only to have Esther and Rosa snatch the boy from them on their own afternoon promenade down the dunes of Jupiter as they talked about the tantalizing but impossible Salvo.

Six

GINA THOUGHT ESTHER MIGHT be upset by Rosa and Salvo's fleeting flirtation. Nothing concrete, but Gina noticed an undertow of antagonism that flowed from Esther after a current of seemingly happy evenings with Rosa and Salvo. Not toward Salvo, mind you, but toward Gina! Perhaps Esther considered Salvo a child, beyond or below adult criticism. Gina decided Esther needed a girl-to-girl conversation. Gina had some advice for Esther, though she didn't know if she'd be brave enough to offer it unsolicited.

So one night, when the two women were sitting out front on the white marble steps by the Bellagrand fountain, holding Alexander and trying to listen for the ocean waves while the revelry continued unabated out back, Gina gulped and took a chance. "Esther, please forgive me for being presumptuous," she said. "I feel like I can speak to you frankly, but only because we've had a Cubanito and you're holding my son in your arms."

"Spit it out. Is it about Rosa?"

"Rosa? No. What about her?"

"The little game your brother is playing with her heart."

"They're just having fun, Esther. Nothing more." Her heart! Gina had warned Rosa that no heart was allowed to be involved in any dealings with Salvo. Did she listen? Of course not. And now Gina was being blamed for it.

"Fun?" Esther said. "In five minutes my able assistant is going to require an escape through a trapdoor from the sort of fun your utterly faithless brother is offering her."

"It's not about them …" There it was again, the sharpened blade lodged in Esther's manner toward her.

"What is it about, then?"

"I feel you're upset about something, Esther. I can't quite figure it out. Is it something I've done?"

Esther sat quietly, rocking Alexander back and forth. She bent, kissed the child's head, glanced at his mother, and shook her head. "No." She sighed, but through a pursed mouth, as if she were holding herself in check and didn't want to say any more. "I apologize if I've given you that impression. Everything is fine."

Gina didn't believe her. She pressed on. "Is it about your father?"

"No. But what about him?"

"That he is alone up north while we're hooting it up down here? Please, ask him to come and stay with us. There's plenty of room. We would love to have him in our house."

"First of all," said Esther, "do you think my Rosa is hooting it up? Those two bandits, Fernando and your brother maybe. But who else is a-hooting? My own brother can't get any peace from morning to night. The other day he asked me if this was really prison, why was there no curfew. And second of all, dear girl, even if I could somehow convince my father that his ill health could sustain a trip south, after what Harry and I told you about Bellagrand, do you really think he would come to the place he has spent the last thirty years blotting out of his mind?"

"Like father, like son," Gina said. "But Harry somehow managed. Perhaps Herman will, too."

"I doubt it. If ever there was a man who does not like to be reminded of unpleasant things, it's my father."

"Not just him," Gina muttered.

"Perhaps if Harry wrote to him personally," Esther said. "Invited him for the holidays. I don't know. Maybe. But I do know that neither you nor I will be able to persuade him. Harry's the only one who's got a lick of a chance. Is this what you wanted to speak to me about?"

"No." Gina blurted it out. "Esther, I think you should sell your mother's jewelry."

"What?" Esther whirled her head to Gina.

Nodding, Gina quickly went on. "I do. Not all of it. But the vast majority. I think that jewelry is like weights around your ankles. It prevents you from living your life."

"That Cubanito has gone to your head," Esther said coldly. "I'm not *trying* to live my life, you silly creature. I *am* living my life."

"I thought maybe a romance, Esther …"

"A romance!" Esther mock laughed. "For your information, I've already been married, and widowed. I'll soon be fifty. What are you talking about, a romance? It must be the drink. Oh Lord. If this isn't proof you should drink less…"

"Get rid of it, Esther," Gina said imploringly. "You don't wear any of it. What's the point? I promise you, your heart will be lighter. And other people will see that." Other men, she wanted to add, but didn't.

Esther glared at Gina with stunned iciness. "What could you *possibly* know about my heart, Gina Attaviano?"

"It's Barrington, Esther, and I know *something* about it." Gina lowered her head, not wanting to glimpse on Esther's face the remnants of love for a man long gone. She had hoped that Ben had been *le cose da bambino*, a childish thing that Esther had long put away. And yet any time someone in the house mentioned Panama, bananas, canals, ship liners, engineers, the Army Corps, Esther visibly stiffened, noticeably altered in her expression, became more brusque, more pointed, more polarizing, as if perhaps the trunk of her mother's jewels was not the only weight around her heart.

But perhaps, just perhaps, Gina looked away so that Esther couldn't accidentally glimpse on Gina's face the things that Esther should never see.

"I've always felt there was something weighing on you, Esther."

"Weighing on me," Esther repeated dully.

"Keep the things you will wear," Gina said, "and everything else be gone! Buy yourself a marble urn, or a statue for the yard, or donate to your local church, or …"

"Thank you for your advice, Gina," Esther said, giving Alexander back to her and struggling up. "I'm getting tired. That great and awful liquor went straight to my head, as clearly as to yours. I think I'll turn in." She paused. "Before I say something I will live to regret." Without another word, even goodnight, Esther pushed open the castle gate doors and disappeared inside.

Gina sat for a long time on the marble steps under the portico, listening for the ocean in front of her, for the Spanish guitar behind her, breathing in her sleeping son, the briny air.

What do we do, my sweet child, my little *bambino, il mio amato figlio*? How do we make your *zia* better? You know who makes her better? You. Every time she looks at you she softens into a pillow. Do you know why? Because there is love, she whispered over Alexander, waving her hand toward the far distance, bending to him, kissing him, caressing him, staring at him, and then there is *Love*.

Chapter 12

BIRDS OF PARADISE

One

Dear Father,
Gina, Alexander and I, and Salvo also, would be most happy if
you and Esther could join us for the Thanksgiving and Christmas
holidays. Father, I hope you're well enough to travel. The weather
here is easy, and the ocean water is always warm. No doubt,
Esther has told you. It was very enjoyable having her here, and
we missed her when she left in September. Please come and stay
as long as you like. I have repainted our boat. You would like it.
There is very good fishing down on Lake Worth.
Sincerely,
Harry

A letter came back to Harry by return post.

Dear Harry,
Thank you for your kind invitation. Yes, Esther regaled me with
many stories about her successful visit. Thank you for being such
good hosts to her. Unfortunately I'm not well enough to travel at

the moment, so we won't be able to come for Thanksgiving. But
perhaps I will feel a little better by Christmas. Please say hello to
Gina and Alexander from all of us.
Sincerely,
Father
P.S. Louis passed away two weeks ago. He said to tell you
Matthew 6:21.

And so for Christmas 1919, Esther, Herman, and Rosa took a train from Boston to the Treasure Coast to spend the holidays. Esther told Gina in advance that Herman would only be able to stay until mid-January. "We'll go back when we won't be able to buy alcohol anymore, on January 16, all right?"

"No, that's when you should stay longer," Gina told Esther. "Because Bellagrand is stockpiled to the rafters with Cuban rum."

"I hope to God you're joking," said Esther and hung up.

And soon they were at Bellagrand. Gina watched as Herman was helped out of the Tourister by Fernando. Gruffly the older man shooed everyone away, straightened up, and lifted his eyes, not to Gina or to Harry standing on the portico, waving hello, but above them, and beyond them. Esther stood by his side.

For a suspended moment Gina watched Herman, with his chin up and his shoulders stooped, gaze with anguished wonder at the white villa another man had built for his wife. Harry knocked into her slightly. "You call that easy?" he whispered. "Look at him."

"Never mind that," Gina said. "We have a boy to make him forget everything, even pain that will not be forgot."

"I would not put my last dollar on that," said Harry, heading down the stairs. "Father! Hello."

"Hello, son," Herman said, taking his eyes off the house and focusing on Harry. They shook hands. Herman patted Harry's arm. "How are you? You look well."

"Thank you. Yes, prison agrees with me."

"Yes, son, indeed it does. It'd be a shame if it didn't, you spend so much time in it."

Harry cast Gina a sideways glare.

"Herman!" she said, coming up to him with a smile, giving him a hug and a kiss. "Thank you for coming. Harry and I are so very happy to see you. Aren't we, Harry?"

"Yes, of course. How was your trip, Father?"

"Blessedly uneventful, thank you." Almost imperceptibly, Herman sighed, and forced his features to soften slightly. "Weather is pleasant here in December, isn't it? Is it always like this?"

Harry nodded with pride, as if the clement weather were his doing. "One of the best things about this area."

"What's it now, about seventy?"

"Seventy-nine according to the thermometer."

"Very impressive. Is it too hot to sleep?"

"No, it gets cooler at night. It's breezy between the two waters. We leave all the windows open. You'll see."

"Does the salt air corrode everything inside the house, the pots, the metal fixtures?"

"Not yet," Harry said.

"I see it's quite windy. Are the waves impossible to swim in?"

"Usually no. The waves are mild. Mild enough even for Alexander to go swimming with his mother. Even though she knows I don't approve."

"The boy loves it, Herman," Gina said. "And so will you. Come in, please. No use standing on the doorstep like delivery boys. Esther, how are you? You haven't said a word."

When they looked over at Esther, she was dabbing her eyes.

"What's the matter with you?" Herman frowned.

Harry waved it away. "Pay her no mind, Father. You will unfortunately witness a certain inexplicable mawkishness when it comes to the women who enter this house. The best remedy is to ignore them. Really. Come in, please."

Herman started through the doors. "Yes, but *why*, Esther?"

"He's right, Father," Esther replied. "It's best to ignore me."

Once inside, Herman barely glanced around. He wasn't easily

318

impressed. "Are you going to have any room for me, son? Gina told us all the rooms in your shack are filled with liquor."

"Indeed they are," Harry said. "But don't worry, we made the cupboard under the stairs like a mansion for you."

"Are you thirsty, Herman?" Gina pointed to a filled glass pitcher. "Would you like some lemonade? I make it myself."

"I'm fine for now. What happened to your voice, Gina? You don't sound like yourself."

Ruefully she smiled. "Your grandson happened to my voice. I strained it, and it's never recovered."

Harry leaned into her from behind, whispering, "But now you sound like you're always *nuda nel letto* …"

"*Marito*, shh!"

"Speaking of this grandson …" Herman said, walking toward the sunlit kitchen. "Is he a phantom?"

"No, he's sleeping." Gina caught up with him.

Herman looked disappointed. "In his bed?"

"Oh no, Father," Harry said. "The child doesn't know what the term *his bed* means." Arching his brows at Gina, he prodded her forward. "Go introduce him to Alexander. Though I doubt Salvo will part with him. I'll go take Father's trunk upstairs."

"He'll have to part with him now," Esther said, walking purposefully outside. "*We're* here."

On the green grass of the great lawn, Herman met Salvo reclining in a chaise lounge under full sun. On his bare chest lay a sleeping form covered from head to toe with cotton blankets. The men shook hands. "How are you, Mr. Barrington? Sorry I can't get up to greet you, but I've got …" Salvo nodded toward the baby on his chest.

"No need to apologize. And please do call me Herman."

Esther stepped forward. "Salvo, I can't believe you're keeping him in the sun like that," she said, swiping the child and all his blankets off her brother-in-law. "He'll get heat stroke."

"He's completely covered," said Salvo. "*I'll* get heat stroke."

"Then why aren't you sitting in the shade?"

"And hello to you too, dear Esther," Salvo said with a smile. "Nice to see you again. Back so soon?"

"I've been gone three months."

"And one week."

Separating them by walking between them with a tray of lemonade and glasses, Gina elbowed Salvo in the stomach. "Herman, here's some lemonade for you. Are you hungry?"

"Not yet, but thank you." He downed the lemonade in two gulps. And yet not five minutes earlier he had been saying he wasn't thirsty. Gina called for Emilio to get lunch on the table. Esther was trying to wake up Alexander with little success.

Herman stepped toward the house. "Esther, let the poor child rest. I know how he feels." He smiled at Gina. "If you would be so kind as to point me to my cupboard under the stairs, I'm going to go freshen up." He glanced at the large, covered shape in Esther's arms. "I'm sure he is a fine boy," said Herman.

Gina left Alexander with Esther for a few hours while she went Christmas shopping with Fernando and Rosa. As soon as Alexander sensed he was being left without his mother, he began to cry. Esther rocked him, cajoled and carried him through the vast downstairs rooms, but he continued to express his ardent displeasure. Besides Carmela there was no one to help her.

Herman came in from the outside, where he was relaxing by the pool, his gray head shaking.

"Why the ruckus?"

Esther showed him the wailing baby.

"No, I know *who's* making the ruckus. I hear that. What does he want?" Herman squinted his eyes and flinched because the boy really was making a lot of noise. He stood at the open French doors for a moment and then walked in, leaning on his cane. His rheumatoid arthritis made his movements slow, his breathing labored. Exertion was difficult.

"I don't know."

"Where is his mother?"

"Out shopping."

"Where's Rosa?"

"With her. So is Fernando."

"Where's the child's father?"

"You mean your son? Trying to catch your dinner."

"Where's the man you don't care for?"

"With the child's father."

Herman studied the screaming boy. "Maybe he's hungry."

"She fed him right before she left," Esther said. "He's not supposed to eat again until she returns."

"Clearly she is wrong. Do you hear the hollering? He is starved."

"Father, I don't think so. In any case, we've got nothing for him. He is on milk only."

"Milk only! How old is he? School-age?"

"Six months."

"So go get him some milk."

"Not that kind of milk."

"Oh." Herman stood by the breakfast table, cautiously. Esther circled the kitchen jostling the boy up and down. "Esther, what the devil are you doing?"

"What? I'm rocking him. Movement helps."

"That isn't movement, you'll shake his stuffing out. Besides he's been on a blue streak for half an hour. Has it been helping?"

"Think how bad it would be if I weren't doing it."

"It could hardly be worse. Try something else."

"Like what?" She patted the baby's back in brisk movements.

"Why are you walloping him?"

"I'm trying to get him to burp."

"Maybe he needs changing?"

"I changed him."

"Would he like to go for a walk?"

"I don't know, do I?" Esther sounded slightly hysterical, as if at any moment she herself might start hollering.

Herman took another step inside the house and sat in the wingback chair by the French doors that led to the lanai. "Give him here," he said.

"Father, he needs to be walked, you can't just sit …"

"Give him here, will you."

Gingerly, Esther handed Alexander to Herman. The exchange took an excruciatingly long time because the big boy wriggled so frantically that both father and daughter were terrified of dropping him. "Isn't he a squirmer," Herman said. "What in heaven's name is the matter?" he asked the boy, finally getting a firm hold of him. "Shh. Why are you making such a fuss?" He held the baby close to his chest, upright. "There, there. It's fine. Nothing to cry about. Wait until you grow up. Then you'll have something to cry about. At your age there's just sleep and milk. How bad can that be? Shh. By the way, that about describes my life, too. So there you have it. You and I are even. Do you see me hollering like I'm being murdered? Exactly. Shh. Calm down. No need to cry. What did you say your name was? Alexander? Shh, Alexander. Shh. Who is Alexander?" he asked Esther.

"Her father. Alessandro." She stood solicitously close, hovering, fretting.

"I thought the child was Anthony?"

"Anthony Alexander."

"Ah."

The boy fell quiet. Esther stopped fretting. Herman stopped talking. Alexander looked into his grandfather's face, reached up, grabbed a good hold of Herman's cheek and lip, moved from side to side to get comfortable, and then put his head down on Herman's shoulder. His hand remained partly in Herman's mouth. Herman settled back, reclined, got comfortable himself. Esther stood quietly by his side. "Do you want me to take him?" she asked.

"Oh, now that I've got him quiet, you want to take him?" asked Herman, his voice muffled by Alexander's chubby fingers. "Some caretaker you are. Go do something else. But quietly. I'll sit here a minute. Don't leave me too long, though."

The kitchen was dappled in afternoon sunlight streaking across the limestone floor and the oak tables. Herman sat facing the green lawn, beyond it the sparkling water shimmering like a mirage.

Esther backed out of the room, whispering that she would be right back, and when she was out in the hall, she put her hand over her mouth to stifle her deep and lingering cry of anguish, of longing, of happiness, all in one tormented silent O.

When she looked in on them half an hour later, she found them in the same position. They were both asleep.

Two

THEY SAT OUTSIDE on the lanai and had dinner. Herman said they would go inside if it got too cold for him, but it never did. Not even the night breezes from the Waterway drove him inside the four walls.

There was nothing sweeter to Gina than listening to Fernando teach her brother how to strum chords and to accompany himself as he sang. Fernando was supremely musical, supremely gifted, but he informed them that Salvo was hunting for a wrong vocation. "Because, señora, your brother has singing skills like I've never seen. He is like, what do they call it?"

"A prodigy?" offered Harry.

"A genius," declared Fernando in front of the unabashedly pleased Salvo. "He has nearly perfect pitch. Do you know how rare that is?"

"I don't even know *what* that is," Gina said.

"It's not the only thing that's rare," muttered Esther.

"Well, never mind," Fernando said. "It's amazing. Salvo, if horticulture doesn't work out, you can always become a troubadour. You will have to go to Miami for work, but you will be handsomely rewarded for your commute."

"*Amigo*," exclaimed Salvo, "*that's* your big dream for me? You want me to be a busker?"

"Sounds about right," Esther said under her breath.

"What can be better than being a singer?"

"A singer on the streets?"

"Better than the flower lessons you've been taking."

Salvo started to hem and haw.

"*Madre di Dio!*" Gina exclaimed. "You're still in the thick of it. You're not already done with it, are you?"

"Yes, we want our money back," said Harry.

Esther snorted. "Kiss it goodbye. You'll never see a penny return on that investment."

"Listen, all of you," Salvo said, "*Sorella mia*, stop the overreaction. Gardening is not for me because I realized I don't want to be dirty all day. What lady is going to like me if I'm on the ground digging dirt, have messy hands, sweat in the sun?" He gleamed. "No, ladies like it when I'm fresh and clean, and I wear silk suits and drive fancy cars, like the drunks next door. I want a nice house too, not the garage I live in. I want to treat the ladies like they deserve to be treated, like princesses."

Esther was about to stiffly disapprove before she was stared into silence by Herman. "These are admirable goals, Salvo," Herman said.

"Thank you, sir."

"How do you intend to accomplish them?"

"I was thinking of taking another course."

Everyone groaned loudly.

"Stop it, all of you. *Basta*. Hear me out before you mock me."

"Why can't we mock you first?" Esther asked.

"Salvo," said Harry, "is this going to cost me more money?"

"Just listen to me, *prego*. I have a great idea."

They complained, poured more drinks, toasted the night and the guitar and the family and Alexander sleeping in Harry's arms, and then listened.

"I want to take a real estate course."

"To do what?" asked Harry.

"To learn how to sell real estate."

"What do you know about real estate?"

"Nothing. That's why I want to take a course."

"His logic *is* impeccable, Harry," said Herman.

"Herman, how can a *pazzo* have logic?" Gina said. "Logic implies sanity."

"Not necessarily," said Salvo. "And, *sorella*, either defend me or keep quiet." They had been drinking sangria for hours, and were on their seventh toast and third helpings of *tres leches* cake, before the profiteroles and ice cream were brought out.

"Harry," said Esther, "can you believe your ears? Father thinks it's a marvelous idea."

"Well, look," said Herman. "Don't go overboard. I wouldn't go so far as to call it *marvelous*. Salvo, I don't know how many of these ideas you come up with each week …"

"Twenty-seven," said Gina.

"*Sorella!* What did I ask you?"

"What I'm saying is," Herman continued, "that of all the places in America to take a real estate course, Palm Beach is one of the best. The houses are spiking in value and flying off the market."

"Exactly!" Salvo moved so close to Herman he was almost sitting in the old man's lap. "And I get a commission every time they fly. Sell or buy. Soon I'll be flying myself, like the Wright Brothers."

"It doesn't sound stable," Esther said. "Market rises, falls, people stop buying houses, and then what?"

"Then on to the next adventure." Salvo grinned. "Maybe I'll learn how to drive a boat. Or become that street singer Fernando was talking about. But for now, real estate is where the money is, and where Salvo wants to be."

"Gina, dear," said Herman, "this would be a wise investment on your part. Because if Salvo is out of a job, guess where he'll be living. With you."

Gina raised a glass of sweet sangria to her family. "Then it's settled," she said. "I will not lend him a penny. For nothing would make me happier than to have him live with me again." Live with all of you, she thought but didn't say.

It was Herman, to Gina's great surprise, who quoted from Nathaniel Hawthorne. "*The ideas of people in general are not raised higher than the roofs of their houses*," Herman said. "*All their interests extend over the earth's surface in a layer of that thickness. Only the meeting-house steeple reaches out of their sphere.*"

"I like that, Herman," said an approving Gina. "And I agree with you. Nothing for me rises above this house and all that's in it." She gazed at her husband holding her huge and sprawled-out sleeping boy.

"I don't agree at all, Father," said Harry.

"Of course not, son," said Herman, winking at Gina. "You're the objection-maker." He turned his attention to Harry. "All right, I'm ready." He took a swallow of wine. "Tell me why you don't agree."

"Because there are ten things you're overlooking."

And fueled by wine, off they went, communicating the only way they knew how—adversarially.

Palm Beach has magic and majesty in it. It has the world in the palm of its hand. It has lakes and seas and extreme weather, dramatic skies and comforting breezes. It has beautiful people, dressing in finery, clicking their high heels, twirling their parasols. You're the lady of the house now, Gina. Carmela's work is no longer your work. You pay someone to do what used to be your work. Now you walk with us down Worth Avenue in tony Palm Beach, you peek through the shop windows at wide-brim silk hats and velvet buckles, you walk in and buy them, just like that. No more taking in sewing to make an extra few dollars so you can afford a pair of used gloves that other beautiful people have discarded. You are the beautiful people now. You discard. You don't sew, you don't launder. You don't make your own bed or breakfast. You sit and let someone else bring you the fruits of Henry Flagler's labors.

They would leave Harry at home with Fernando, and Gina would drive the rest of the clan south to Palm Beach. They stopped at the Breakers, for it was a magnificent hotel, even Herman had to admit it. After a leisurely lunch one afternoon, they walked half a mile under the tall palms to Whitehall, Salvo carrying a heavy Alexander. Herman said he wanted to see Henry Flagler's Taj Mahal of Palm Beach, wanted to see the seventy-three room house Flagler built for the last woman in his life. Herman stood in the front driveway and appraised the marble house. He refused to go in, even for afternoon tea, even for a quick drink, and on the way back home said only, "I'm glad I finally got to see the house that man built for the woman he preferred to the woman I couldn't discard."

* * *

Herman forgot to go back home. December, January, February flew by. He and Esther got into the daily habit of taking Alexander with them in the early mornings for a walk on the beach, even though it meant that Esther had to carry the squirming giant the entire way. When she dared put him down, he would eat the sand and crawl toward the ocean like a laughing black-haired squid. Esther said she had never been so fit in her life as she was after months of carrying her restless nephew. Sometimes Gina and Harry joined them for their morning constitutional, and sometimes even Salvo, if he hadn't been out too late the night before. Esther grudgingly admitted to Gina that when Salvo and Harry came to the beach, they made it easier—because they took turns carrying Alexander. Three generations walked along the ocean spanning the divided cultures. Salvo loved to carry Alexander and was ceaselessly patient with him, throwing him up into the air, swinging him upside down, hoisting him onto his shoulders, dangling him above the foam of the waves. Even Esther could disapprove of the Sicilian man only so much in the humid mornings. After watching Esther watching Salvo, Gina nudged Harry. "*Marito*, look at your sister's face."

Harry looked. "I see nothing."

"Look at the way she is looking at my brother play with our son. I told you she'd warm to him eventually."

"No, she liked Alexander right from the start."

"*Ilare!*" She squeezed his arm. "Do you see? No one can stay indifferent to Salvo for long. Not you, or your father, or even your hard-to-please sister."

"Don't be so sure," Harry said. "I think you underestimate her. Look, she's about to engage Salvo in a discussion. What could those two be possibly chatting about?"

A curious Gina hurried from her husband's side to her father-in-law's. She gave Herman her arm and sped him along, straining to hear Esther and Salvo over the crash of the high tide and the warm wind. Harry sidled up to them, a mischievous grin already wide on his tanned and rested face. Gina strolled between father and son.

"You seem to enjoy your nephew, Salvo," she heard Esther saying.

He nodded. "Well, he *is* my nephew, Esther. You quite enjoy him yourself."

"Indeed I do," she said. "I haven't been fortunate enough to have children of my own." There was a deliberate pause from Esther, like an inhale. "Have you been this fortunate?"

"I am blessed in many ways," Salvo replied.

"Blessed with children?"

He nodded. "Blessed even with children." Grinning he spun around to glance back at Gina, who shook her fist at him. *Stop it!*

What? mouthed Salvo. Alexander rode facing forward on his shoulders, pulling his hair.

"Gina," Herman said, "do you think this talk they're having is going to end like hell in a handbasket?"

"Yes—for Esther."

"I thought so."

Next to her Harry laughed soundlessly. When Gina glared at him, he whispered, *told you*.

"Children as in … *plural?*" Esther asked Salvo.

"Yes, yes. But all girls," Salvo added wistfully, patting Alexander's chubby bouncing leg. "Haven't been lucky enough to have a boy. Right, Harry?" Salvo turned around. "You feel lucky to have a son, don't you? Like all fathers." He tutted. "I keep trying, but with no success."

"Yes, Salvo," Harry replied. "I don't know about *all* fathers, but I'm pleased with my son. But, don't let me interrupt your conversation. By all means—continue."

Esther pressed on. "*All* girls? How many, um, girls do you have?"

"That's a good question," Salvo said pensively.

"I thought it was a simple question."

"Esther," Herman said, "stop grilling the poor man. He's not steak."

"No, no, Father, please let her," said Harry. Gina pulled a blond hair out of his tanned forearm and groused at him. He had to cover his mouth to keep from laughing out loud.

"Harry is right, it's fine, Herman," Salvo called back, now holding Alexander upside down by one ankle as they ambled down the beach. "I don't mind. What was your question again, Esther?"

"How many children do you have?" she said sharply.

Salvo counted off by bending *all* the fingers on his left hand. "I'd say five," he said and, after a considered pause, added, "Five that I *know* of."

Esther gasped. Even Gina nearly laughed.

"Where are they?" Esther asked. "These babies, your children, your daughters?" She used her most demanding tone.

Salvo shrugged. "I don't know. With their mothers, I presume. I *hope*."

"*Mothers?*" Esther put a hand on her heart.

"Yes. Is this upsetting you, Esther? I hear something in your voice. You've gone so pale. Or am I being overly sensitive?"

"*Mothers?*"

"The children have mothers, yes. Why does that surprise you?"

"Mothers as in *plural?*"

"Yes, yes, five girls, five mothers."

Nearly falling over, Esther spun around only to see Harry bent in half by laughter. She stormed away from them as they continued to laugh behind her.

Gina pinched Salvo hard. Alexander threw his arms out to his mother. "How is she *ever* going to like you," Gina said, "when you torture her like this?" She hoisted the boy onto her hip.

"You're right I might have to try something else to make her like me." He winked at Gina.

"Salvo!"

"What?" He was all innocence.

They both turned, and there was Harry staring at them unblinking. "That's my sister you two are slandering."

"Salvo! Harry is right," Gina said, with a mock frown. "How can you even joke about a thing like that?"

While they bantered, Herman caught up with Esther. "Do you know why he torments you?"

"It's not funny, Father."

"I know."

"Then why are you laughing?"

"Answer me, do you know why?"

"No, why?"

"Because he can," said Herman. "You make it too easy for him. It's not even fair. It's like shooting fish in a barrel."

"But who jokes about things like that?" Esther said, her voice high-pitched.

"He knows you judge him, so he toys with you." Herman nodded. "Believe me, I know something about this."

Esther fell quiet.

"Daughter, if we sat in judgment of every person who didn't behave to the standards of the house across the road, we'd be too busy to eat, wouldn't we?"

"There *are* no standards in the house across the road."

"Well, no, you're right, not back then." Herman regrouped. "But these days, except for Gina, who is above reproach"—he continued through Esther's scornful exhale—"we have your brother, who is doing God knows what, while pretending he's a changed man. We have Salvo attempting to make all of South Florida Italian, and infuriating well-born women from Boston, turning them into shrews. Fernando is smuggling mansionfuls of liquor from his native land, hoping not to get arrested for committing a felony. Carmela is a terrible housekeeper, who speaks English but pretends she doesn't, and Emilio is a mediocre cook at best. Gina is heads above him. When she prepares the food, I actually look forward to dinner. Rosa has behaved so badly that she won't even come to the beach with us because Salvo is here. And you, my dear, sit and tsk all day. You'll wear out a hole in your cheek, Esther, where your tongue is."

"And where did I learn to render judgment on everything and everyone, I wonder?"

Now Herman looked chastised. "Well," he said, "perhaps the children should strive to be better than their parents."

"Was Mother critical, too?" Esther asked after they had walked a while by each other's side.

Herman was quiet as the tide got lower. "Her problem was just the opposite," he said at last, staring straight ahead. "She wasn't critical enough. She loved everyone, accepted everyone. She had no protection of any kind against life."

Three

"ESTHER, CAN WE PLEASE TALK about something other than your salacious interest in Salvo's romantic endeavors?"

"I have no interest in them whatsoever, salacious or otherwise."

Herman and Esther strolled down the street. Esther took his arm, to touch him, not to burden him with her weight. Today it was just the three of them, Herman, Esther, and Alexander. Fernando had dropped them off at the Breakers for breakfast, and afterward they ambled past the fancy shops, Herman pushing the carriage along Worth Avenue.

"Instead of talking about procreation that doesn't concern us, can we talk instead about how studiously your brother is hiding his reading matter?"

"What's he reading?"

"*Ten Days That Shook The World* by John Reed for one."

"I haven't noticed. But he can read what he likes, no?"

"Then why does he hide it?"

Alexander started to fuss, so they stopped for a moment while Esther adjusted his blankets and gave him back the rattling teddy bear he had dropped. "You're a good boy," she murmured, kissing him on the head. "You're a very good boy." She straightened up. Her seventy-three-year-old father, who had been pushing the carriage because keeping both hands on the rails made it easier for him, resumed walking, his pace ever so slow. "Are you asking because you know, Father, or because you're fishing?"

"Both," Herman replied. "I'm asking because I know, but I'm fishing to see if you know."

"I don't know anything," said Esther. "I ignore Harry completely when he is in his strange other world, and pay attention to him only when he is engaged in ours."

"Good," Herman said. "His lovely and gracious wife may be wise to adopt the same approach."

"I don't know why you're so taken with her," Esther said, adjusting her hat to protect her face from the sun. "What else is he reading?"

"*In the Penal Colony* by Kafka."

Esther smiled. "Harry is so funny."

"But do you know what he's pretending to read?"

"What?"

"*A Letter to my Father.*"

Esther laughed. "He is hilarious. Did you know that Kafka's father was also named Herman?"

"I didn't. Laugh now, but what are we going to do in 1922 when his house arrest is over?"

"Let's not count those chickens yet. Have you seen how scrupulously Janke observes him? It's almost as if she wants to catch him breaking parole. Do you hear him on Mondays? He's taken to calling her Inspector Javert." Esther looked amused. "To her face!"

Herman laughed. "Your brother's always had a knife-like quality to his sense of humor."

"My brother, but *your* son." She patted her father with deep filial affection as they ambled down a pristine tropical street, gazing inside the window displays of *nouveau* art and fancy shoes. "You worry too much. He'll be fine. Look where they're living. You don't think Bellagrand will get under his skin like it has got under Salvo's? And Gina's?" Esther nudged him. "And even yours a little."

Pushing Alexander, Herman pulled ahead slightly, away from Esther's fond teasing. "Yes, sure, it got under my skin," he said. "Like chiggers."

"Harry, have you had a chance to read John Reed's new book?" Herman asked casually after a few days had passed. They had been having a perfectly congenial lunch of shrimp *ceviche*, fresh bread, and mango with ice cream.

"Why would I, Father?" said Harry. "My prison guard—I mean, my parole officer, the honorable Margaret Javert, prefers I don't read such things."

"Perhaps she is right. I, for one, found the book quite harmless. Should I advise her that it's all right for you to read it, if you wish?"

"Herman, you've read *Ten Days That Shook The World*?" Gina asked with surprise.

"Yes, dear girl, why not?" he said cheerfully. "In your very house. I found a copy in your library, lying around, collecting dust. I'd heard so much about it in the papers, I thought I'd give it a go. I confess, it was curious to find it here. It was published barely a year ago."

Silence fell over the table. "I don't understand what's going on," a perplexed Gina finally said. "What am I missing?"

"Nothing, Gia," Harry said, reaching out to take her hand. "Father is just being Father. Doing to me what Salvo was doing to my sister." He turned to Herman. "Okay, fine. Yes, I read it. It can't be a surprise that I read my friend John Reed's book. Did you see, he had it signed to me? I was honored to receive it."

"Hmm," Herman said. "I would keep this small detail away from your corrections officer, if I were you. I think that a lack of correspondence between you and CPUSA members is one of the conditions of your current situation."

"Yes," Harry said, letting go of Gina's hand and staring into his bowl of melted ice cream. "Which is why I didn't tell her."

"Wise."

Harry chewed his lip. "So what did you think of the book, Father?"

"I thought it was swell." Herman shrugged. "Why not? The man is clearly enraptured by guns and rifles and shootings and mass police action, and mobs on the streets. It would have been great as a play without words. Just a lot of movement and noise, no dialogue, very little narrative."

"I thought there was quite a bit of narrative," Harry said. "Why do you say there wasn't?"

"Why? Because his book ably showed me what it was like to live through violence on the streets. It didn't do so well to explain why there should have been violence in the first place."

"I don't know what you mean."

"A sixth of the country is trying to brutally oppress and murder the other five-sixths of the country, who do not like whatever this thing

Bolshevism is, and want no part of it, or of being murdered. Someone thinks this brute force is a good idea. But no one will tell me why."

"Do you really need John Reed to tell you why?"

"I wouldn't have minded at least gleaning what this thing was that was worth slaughtering people on the streets over, so yes."

"He is writing a new book about that very subject. He's writing it now."

"Interesting. I don't want to know how you know this," Herman said. "Funny thing though—lots of people keep telling me our current way of living should be overturned. Many governments in Europe, and even our government, live under threat of this overthrow, if you judge by the demonstrations on the streets, of which, of course, you're no longer part, though I assume you read all about them in the papers. But I, for one, along with a million others, am still waiting for an answer as to why such an overthrow is needed."

"I don't see how other people's failures to inform you of this are John Reed's fault."

"Oh, it's his fault also," Herman said. "When I read a book on the French Revolution, I want to know the meaning beyond the guillotine. When I read a book on the American Revolution, I want to know something other than Washington crossing the Delaware on Christmas Day. I want to know what he was crossing the river for. Why is that so unreasonable? Why did Caesar cross the Rubicon? Does anyone need to know?"

"Father, you can't really tell me you don't know what *Bolshevism* is!" Exasperated, Harry looked at Gina. But she was studying him puzzled, almost troubled, taken aback at his sudden intensity about a seemingly casual conversation on a languorous afternoon when they all should have been having a nap.

"No," Herman said, "I don't know what it is. Mr. Reed refuses to tell me. He writes that the question of what Bolshevism is cannot be answered on the pages of his book. I've never read anything stranger. They're revolting, rebelling, fighting, overthrowing, all of it is glorious, valiant, vehement. Why then am I left in the dark as to why all this valiant glory is taking place? Is that deliberate?"

"Of course not!"

"Well, then, perhaps John Reed himself doesn't know." Herman sat back with satisfaction. "For he tells me so many other things in his book, both trivial and profound, I should think that if he knew the answer, he would tell it to me. No?"

"It's a book about his experience in Petrograd during the Russian Revolution, Father," Harry said, impatient and defensive. "It's not an encyclopedia."

"I should hope not," Herman said. "It wouldn't be very comprehensive and educational if it were." He paused, scraping up and enjoying the last of his mango and ice cream. "Son, let's take your oldest friend Ben as an example of what I'm trying to say."

Everyone visibly stiffened. Herman's only reaction to the inexplicable discomfort of the rest of his family was his knitted-together eyebrows. Then, a little more uncertainly, he continued with his point. "Uh—if Ben Shaw were Panama's John Reed, and he wrote a book about the monumental undertaking that was the building of the canal, in many ways, metaphorical and literal, like a revolution in itself in the way it upended and detonated what was, and then proceeded to build what was to be, do you think that Ben would be able to answer the question of why he endeavored to spend fifteen years of his life building the canal in the first place?"

"I don't know," Harry said coldly. "Would that he were here to be asked."

"We don't need him to be here," said Herman. "We know the answer. He's told us often enough. Hasn't he, Esther? He expounded his reasons to us at our Sunday dinner table for years. We were sick to death of his reasons. We knew them by heart! And then he went to Panama. His book would definitely answer my question. Because he knows why."

Esther said nothing. Gina said nothing.

Harry smirked. "The Panama Canal is hardly Bolshevism, Father," he said, moist with condescension.

"Indeed it's not. But no matter how small or large your undertaking, shouldn't you be able to give at least one reason why you're undertaking it?" Herman pushed away his chair and got up. "Well, thank you for a lovely lunch, ladies, Harry. This lively conversation has exhausted me. I haven't been so animated in years, and I'm grateful for that, but now, like my bonny grandson, I need a nap. I'm going to go and partake of one."

Herman said the warm air was easy on his old bones. His rheumatoid arthritis got better. He swam in the ocean, fished in the freshly painted boat that was now called *Gia* not *Frances*. He even went with Gina to buy fresh fruit at the market, to Esther's great shock, who said she did not realize her father knew what a market was. He stayed for six months, stayed long enough to see Alexander take his first step, say his first word, and see the blue balloons on the boy's first birthday. He left only when it got unbearably hot.

Four

SIX MONTHS LATER, a few weeks before Christmas 1920, Herman arrived once again, strolling through the tremendous marbled foyer of Bellagrand. His breathing had become more labored, he was thinner, he looked more worn-out. He hugged Gina, firmly shook Harry's hand, took one fond look at him and frowned. "What's the matter? Why so grim? Did Emma Goldman get deported again?"

"Oh, it's not you, Herman," Gina hastened to say when Harry didn't reply. "John Reed died recently."

Herman searched Harry's face. "I didn't realize you two were that close."

"A brilliant man. A visionary," Harry said. "He was only thirty-two! I can't believe it. Died of typhus, in Petrograd. Who dies of typhus?"

"Well, John Reed for one." Herman looked around. "Perhaps if he hadn't galloped off to Russia he'd be thirty-two and alive. Where's …" He didn't finish. A boy ran in, dark-haired and brown-eyed, inordinately tall for his age. He was almost nineteen months, but he looked four. He hopped in like he was riding an invisible horse, stopped, stared at the adults, at the smiling Esther, at gleaming Rosa, his gaze stopping on Herman. His face broke into a grin.

"Alexander, do you remember who this is?" Gina asked.

Alexander nodded.

"This is Daddy's father, your grandfather," Gina said, keeping her hand on her son's shoulder, bending down to him. "Grandpa."

"Mama, let go," Alexander said, pulling away from his mother. For a few moments he stood, stared, appraised, considered.

"What's the matter, Alexander?" said Herman, a happy smile on his lined face. "Cat got your tongue?"

"No cat," Alexander said. "Frogs. Come?" He extended his hand.

"Let's go," Herman said, taking the boy's soft little hand into his giant weathered one. "Will we have to walk far?" The boy slowed down so Herman could keep up with him.

"No." He pointed. "Water."

"Water, eh? Well, are you sure they're frogs, Alexander? How do you know they're not baby alligators near the water?"

Alexander quickly turned around and glanced at his mother.

"He is joking with you, son," Gina said. "Like Daddy does. Gators, Grandpa meant. In Florida, we say gators, Herman."

The boy looked up at his tall, gray, slightly stooped grandfather. "No, no," he said, pulling on Herman's hand. "Frogs. No gators. Me show."

They walked on.

"What's that?" Alexander pointed to Herman's cane.

"My walking stick. To help me walk."

"Oh," the boy said. "Me want."

"Maybe we can make you one."

"Yes. Make now."

"Later, okay? I can make lots of things."

"Oh?"

"A table. Chairs. A bench. A shed. A house."

"House!" Alexander laughed.

"I'm not joking."

"Me build house," the boy instantly said.

"Okay. I'll teach you how. But can we have lunch first?"

Shaking his head, Alexander looked keenly disappointed.

"We'll need a hammer, you and I," said Herman, "if we're going to build a fort for the gators."

"What's hammer?"

"Your father hasn't let you handle a hammer yet? Well, perhaps that's wise."

"What's hammer?"

"I'll show you," Herman said, squeezing the boy's hand. "Oh, your dad used to be very good with a hammer when he was a little guy like you."

"Me not little. Me big."

"Yes, you are quite tall. Maybe you and I can go to a store to get some tools."

"What's tools?"

"Hammers, pliers, a saw, a wrench."

Alexander shook his head. "Me get bananas, cookies."

"Yes, those are called girl stores," said Herman. "When you grow up, you'll have to learn to stay *far* away from those. You and I are going to go to a man store, Alexander. Okay?"

The boy vigorously nodded, not letting go of his grandfather's hand. "Now. No frogs. Go now."

"Maybe a little lunch? Your grandpa is starved."

"No lunch."

"Please?" Herman said.

They walked outside into the blinding sunshine.

Alexander showed Herman the pond and the frogs under the lilies, the palm trees he and his mother had planted, the lemon trees, the grove of oranges. He showed Herman the dock with the boat and the fishing lines.

"Is that your fishing line?"

Alexander nodded. "Me fish. Daddy fish. Gampa fish?"

"I eat fish. And I like to fish. Your dad and I went out on the boat quite often when I was here last. You were too little. But perhaps this time, all three of us can go?"

"*Zio* Salvo go too."

"How could I forget." He rumpled Alexander's hair. "Of course *Zio* Salvo go too."

Gina called them in for lunch, and both old man and little boy looked reluctant as they trudged up the slope to the lanai.

After lunch, Alexander had a tremendous temper tantrum. "No nap, fish! No nap, fish!" Alexander kept yelling and kicking his legs as he was carried upstairs by Gina. But after the nap that never happened and before dinner, Alexander, Herman, and Harry sat on the dock in the warm December setting sun, legs dangling, and threw their lines in the water. They didn't succeed in catching a fish that day, but they succeeded the next, and the one after that.

Herman bought Alexander a hammer.

Alexander stopped having naps in the afternoon.

"What are you two looking at?" Gina asked. Herman and Esther's backs were to her. Since they both paid attention to little else but Alexander and his activities, Gina assumed her son was being extra special.

"We are trying to figure out what he is doing," Esther said, moving slightly away from her father's shoulder, to let Gina take a peek. Alexander was rolling multi-edged stones from one end of the grass to the other.

Gina watched him. "Clearly he is building a fort."

"Alexander, stop that!" That was Harry, from his mosaic table by the dock, where a moment ago he had been engrossed in Sabatini's *Scaramouche*, a romance set during the French Revolution. Fiction was the only thing Janke heartily approved of. She deemed fiction "fangless, because it was so far-fetched."

"Janke's not wrong there, Harry, about it being far-fetched," Gina had said. "How else to explain that in *Scaramouche*, Robespierre plays the part of a romantic action hero?"

"Alexander! What did I say? Stop it."

"Yes, Daddy."

"But you're not stopping!"

"Me no finish!"

"Not, me no finish," Harry yelled. "You finish."

"Okay!"

"I think," said Gina, watching her son, "he is trying to build two forts on opposite sides of the lawn and then have a battle."

"A battle with what?" Herman asked.

Gina shrugged. "Anything. Everything. Two carrots. Two bananas. The hammer you bought him."

"I didn't know he was a fighter," said Herman with unconcealed pride. "But clearly your son is a builder."

"And a fighter," said Esther with unconcealed adoration.

"Alexander! Did you stop?" This time Harry didn't even look up from *Scaramouche*.

"Yes, Daddy."

Gina knew how much Harry was enjoying a book by how much he kept quoting from it. *He was born with a … sense that the world was mad.* And by how little attention he paid to everything else.

Gina called to her oblivious husband. "Harry, *tesoro*. Can you please look up from Robespierre? Your son is about to take off in the boat."

Alexander chortling, trying to untie the rope at the dock hook, Harry dropping his book, running down to the dock, Herman, Esther, Gina laughing, Harry scooping up Alexander, swinging him upside down by his feet, pretending to throw him into the water, Alexander laughing, laughing, *more, more, Daddy, more, more.*

Five

THE ONLY THING THAT marred the idyll was the occasional rumble between Herman and Harry, like the South Florida weather with its distant but daily sound of afternoon thunder. Gina had mentioned this to Esther, about the way the two men kept bickering about all manner of things petty and small, and Esther laughed. "Darling, that's not bickering. That's them getting along like wood and matches. If they're arguing, it means all is well with the world. It's when they don't talk that you've got to worry."

Gina wasn't convinced. "It doesn't seem like they're sorting *out* their differences. It's more as if they're showcasing them. Neither gives an inch."

Esther nodded. "Harry is his father's son through and through. The more he doesn't give in, the more proud Father is."

"I don't think Harry knows that," said Gina. "I'm fairly certain he doesn't."

"Yes," Esther said, "Harry's always been the last one to see the truth of anything."

"Maybe we should ask Salvo, our new expert on all things real estate, to have Bellagrand appraised," Herman said one fine evening after a late lobster dinner when they were sitting outside on the screened-in lanai while Alexander, unmindful of the evening flies by the pond, was attempting to find a wooden stick for himself so he could walk like his grandfather. "The bank had estimated the house's value when they extended you the line of credit, Harry, but that was a couple of years ago. Prices have been booming. Perhaps Salvo can update us, tell us something concrete."

"I'm sure he can, Herman," Gina said when Harry didn't immediately answer. "He'll be here tomorrow for Sunday dinner. We'll ask him."

Harry grunted. "How's Salvo going to help?" This seemed to be directed at Herman, though Gina could not say for sure. "There is nothing concrete about the price of a house."

"Come again?"

"Never mind."

"What do you mean, son?" said Herman. "This house has value. That value is expressed in price. How can anything be more concrete than that?"

"You know what the word *price* is short for? *Caprice*."

"Oh, here we go," muttered Gina, motioning to Esther to help her clear the table. They had sent Carmela home early.

"I don't follow," Herman said, sitting up straighter in his chair.

"Prices are arbitrary," Harry said. "They can be set high to make maximum profit for the owner of this house."

"Which is you."

Harry shrugged. "I'm indifferent to that, Father, as you know. The house is like a widget. The workers who made this widget can't afford to buy it. *That* I'm not indifferent to."

"Well, yes. Many people can't buy boats or diamond rings. What does that prove? That we shouldn't have boats or diamond rings?"

Gina hid the hand with her ring on it. Harry blinked. "No, but it proves that price is set arbitrarily."

Herman chuckled. "Are you saying that nothing has intrinsic value?"

"Not at all. Things you can't put a price on have intrinsic value. Like babies. Things you *can* put a price on have arbitrary value. Like houses."

Who was going to disagree with him there? thought Gina. Except in her mind, both things had value.

"Have you ever seen a profit and loss statement for a business, Harry?" Herman asked. "In Salvo's restaurants perhaps? I think you're confused about your terms."

"I'm not at all."

"Oh, I'm *certain* of it," said Herman. "You're confusing prices with costs. They're not synonymous."

"I know. The cost of this house is X. The price of this house is a capricious Y."

Herman took a cheerful last sip of his Mojito and motioned to Gina for one more. "If prices are arbitrary, then, by your logic, wages are also arbitrary."

"Aren't they?"

"Are they? Why did Wood Mill pay your wife X amount of dollars per week? Why not pay her half of X? Or a quarter of X?"

"Precisely! Why not twice X? Or three times X?"

"But why so low, son?" Herman asked with amusement. "Why not pay Gina twenty times X to work in the mending room?"

"Exactly. And you know *someone* is getting twenty times X, just not Gina."

Herman turned to Gina. "Gina, why didn't your brother pay the pizza baker twenty times X?"

Gina was making the rum and mint drinks by the high table. "Ask your son, Herman, not me," she replied. "He paid the pizza baker twenty times X."

"And where did that bring you?"

"To bankruptcy."

"Precisely. Because Harry separated prices from costs by making one arbitrary and the other not. To pay the baker twenty times X, he would've had to raise the price of the pizza to twenty times X."

"But that would have run us out of business in five minutes."

Herman nodded. "What was it that I was saying about prices expressing the intrinsic value of things?"

"Father, you're drifting away from my original point about Bellagrand," Harry said, as Gina watched his rigid features. "You can't charge twenty times X …"

"Don't be stuck on twenty. It can be two. Or three hundred and two. Why can't it be any number at all?" Herman asked. "If you think the price of a widget is arbitrary, then the wage to make that widget can be arbitrary."

"Two different things."

"Relating to exactly the same thing," Herman said. "The cost per unit of widget. In fine-tuning the balance between price and cost, only the fluctuating market can tell you if you're charging too much. Do you know how? No one will buy it, and you'll be out of business." He nodded to Gina to thank her for the Mojito she brought over to him. "Ask four million dollars for this house. Or forty million. See if someone will bite."

"Or I can ask fifty dollars and everyone will bite," said Harry.

"But then how are you going to pay your electrician and your mason twenty times X as you wish? The mason's salary and the price of the house are inextricably related. Almost like the gravitational force in physics. The heavier the thing is, the more it's forced into the ground. Make it lighter and you'll have to put weights on it to keep it from flying into the sky."

"Father," Harry said, "none of this is my point."

"Fine," Herman said agreeably. "Let's take Bellagrand as your point."

"I'm saying that the gap between the rich and poor is widening because capitalism is inequitable and inefficient, and one of the things that's expressed in is price. But now, in contrast, let's look at Russia. To concentrate the power in the hands of one party devoted single-mindedly to preserving the fundamental rights of man and extending his happiness, that's what I'm whole-heartedly advocating."

There was a baffled silence.

Harry amended. "I mean not anymore. I *had* been advocating it. I meant to say devil-advocating. I'm reformed now, Father, Gina, please don't worry. I won't let you down." He forced a smile. "I'm still the objection-maker, though. You're all right with that, aren't you?"

Less agreeably Herman tapped the table. "If we're just advocating and objection-making, you won't mind if I advocate right back?"

"When do you ever not? Please go ahead."

"Two things. You said something about happiness. Shall we allow that in Russia it might be too early to tell? Because from where I'm sitting, the Russian peasant's two greatest joys, outside of his own body, are the market and the church. And your Vladimir Ilyich Lenin seems to be devoting his life to depriving the peasant of these two foundations."

"It's not the *only* thing he's doing," Harry said.

Troubled, Gina glanced at Esther, but Harry's sister was unperturbed, as if she'd heard it all before.

"Oh?" said Herman. "Because it sure seems like it is. From where I'm sitting. But the second thing. You say the market is wasteful and inefficient. Let me ask you—the suit you're wearing, how did it get on your body? The threads that made it, the yarn that spun it, the looms and the mills, and the cotton or wool that made the yarn, the fields that the cotton grew on, tell me, how did you just happen to put this suit on your body this morning? Or for that matter, how did you, when you were an urban man living in a building in a big town or a man of leisure like now, living in a small town, happen to get up in the morning and cut yourself a piece of bread and put it into your mouth? Did you get up extra early and ride out west to Iowa to your own wheat field? Did you thresh it today, mill it, bleach it, make flour from it, combine it with an egg from your handy and nearby chicken, milk your cow and churn your butter and then bake it in your self-made kiln? And if not, then how did this bread that appeared miraculously at your doorstep get to you?"

"Salvo made it."

Gina and Esther laughed.

"And then he brought it to my doorstep," Harry added, smiling himself.

"Where did he get the grain?" Herman asked. "We know Salvo didn't grow it, so how did it get to him? By train? That other men built? The roads, the railroads, the cars, the threshers, the grain elevators all built by other men? Last night you slept in a bed with white sheets, and you had running water that came through a pipe. Where did these sheets come from? How did the pipe make its way into your house? For that matter, how did the water?"

Harry listened to him. "Father, I'm getting weary. What does any of this have to do with what *I'm* talking about, with what John Reed was talking about and fighting for?" Harry paused. "And dying for?"

Herman stretched back, crossing his arms behind his head. "I don't know what your John Reed died for. Nothing, I should think. He got sick and died. But I'm answering your original complaint. You said capitalism was wasteful and inefficient. I found your argument faulty and explained to you how the free market is the emperor of efficiency."

"Yes, but everything you mention was built on the backs of slogging workers! *That's* always been my only point."

"Who pays the workers?"

"This entire American civilization is built on Mimoo's back and Gina's back, while all the profits go into the pockets of people who don't work on the railroad tracks."

"Profits into the pockets of people like Henry Flagler?" Herman spoke the name almost without flinching or pausing. "What profit did Flagler see from this house? He built it over thirty years ago, invested his own money, used the finest materials, as you can see by the slate under your feet and the marble in your bathroom, paid the architects and the electricians their wages, and then—what? The house cost money, Harry. Flagler, I, we reached into our pockets plenty, and sometimes we didn't make a nickel." Herman smiled warmly. "In fact, the only one who appears to have reaped *any* profit from Flagler's very private capital expenditure is *you*." Herman sat back. "Must gall you a little, doesn't it, my son?"

Harry stood up from the table, exasperated by his father's good humor. "I just want Gina and Fernando to be paid better. Is that so unreasonable?"

"Without capital first and revenue second, there are no wages. Gina can't get paid. Neither can Fernando."

"The state also has capital." Harry went to pour himself a whiskey from the bar.

"Where does the state get money from?"

A balky Harry didn't answer.

"I'm asking, Harry," persisted Herman. "Where does the state get the money to build something like Bellagrand?"

"The same place Flagler got it from."

"Savings, then? Returns on risky ventures all over the Eastern seaboard?"

"Why not?"

"In other words, *profits*?"

"It wouldn't be profits, Father, if the state held the purse strings." Harry downed his whiskey and poured another. "Rather, it would be profits that were distributed evenly among the people who built this house."

"Well, first of all, to build this house back in 1890, workers had to be paid then, yet there is no profit on the house to this day. But let's say Flagler sold it instead of just giving it to Mrs. X." No one at the table acknowledged who this Mrs. X might have been. "Let's say he needed the money, and he sold it. If the profits from that sale were distributed between the painters and the door hangers, where would the capital to build Whitehall after Bellagrand come from?"

"How is that my concern? Who cares about Whitehall?"

"Not me by any stretch," Herman said, "but salaried workers built Whitehall, too. Where did the capital to build Bellagrand come from? If Flagler gave away the profits he made on the railroads and the oil, there would be no Bellagrand. No reinvestment, or construction, or development. There would be no Palm Beach, no St. Augustine, no Miami, no Port of Key West. No wages, no profits, no business. No investment equals no future."

"You're just arguing yourself into a corner here," Harry said.

"*I'm* arguing myself into a corner?"

"Yes! There would be plenty of other money."

"From where?"

"Russia has money," Harry said. "They're doing right now, this moment, what you say can't be done. *They're* doing it."

"Harry, Russia repudiated *all* of its foreign debt. They called it illegitimate. Imagine if any other government or business was run like that. That's one way they have capital. The other way is, they have taken over, by force, what private businesses have built with private funds. They appropriated property and real estate—land, farms, factories—that belonged to the Russian people, the same way they appropriated borrowed foreign money and called it their own. There's another word for what they did both in Russia and abroad." Herman stared pointedly at Harry. "It escapes me right now."

"Say what you like, Father, against Russia," Harry said, "but private capital is a poisonous thing, Bellagrand notwithstanding and besides the point."

"We started with Bellagrand," Herman said gently, "and now it's besides the point?"

"Russia is still in the middle of a civil war! After they're victorious and the rest of the world has left them alone, let's watch them awhile and see what happens. Let's reserve our judgment until we see their grand experiment played out. They have capital now, however acquired, they own the means of production. Let's watch them industrialize, collectivize, organize. Until we see what happens to the Russian economy under the new command structure, nothing you can say, no fake facts you can throw at me will make me believe otherwise. I know what the truth is going to be. The question is, why don't you?"

Herman struggled up from the table. "Dear boy," he said. "But without the capitalists to demonize, who would you rob?"

And to Gina he uttered a worrying quote before he kissed her hand goodnight and headed upstairs: "*No man for any considerable period can wear one face to himself and another to the multitude, without finally getting bewildered as to which may be the true.*"

"What did your father mean by that, Harry?" Gina asked later as they got into bed.

"I think he was talking about himself, Gia."

She shook her head. "He must believe you're hiding something."

"I'm an open book. Come here. I'll show you what my page is open to."

Yet despite all the objection-making and paternal concern Herman had for Harry's future, like birds of winter that flew south to stay, they all lived together in the great big house and fished and ate and swam and went to Spanish City. Herman, Alexander, and Harry built benches together and gardens, swimming platforms, koi ponds and toy chests. The adults took the child to Alligator Joe's gator farm on the Jungle Trail, where they had a lunch of oysters while Alligator Joe showed the fearless, fascinated Alexander his largest gators. In the mornings, Herman went off with Salvo and Alexander to show houses and to get a glimpse of how the other beautiful people lived. Afterward they met up with Gina and Esther and drove down to Palm Beach where they sat outside at the Breakers and had lunch in the briny air by the ocean. Herman and Salvo took Alexander swimming in the barely there waves of the Atlantic, while Gina and Esther sat and watched until it started to rain. Alexander showed Herman and Harry and Salvo how to catch a tree-climbing crab. He climbed a moss oak himself, and Salvo had to go get him, though he did offer the rescue duties to Esther, who politely declined, because she was wearing a skirt, she said, and it wouldn't be proper.

For Alexander's second birthday, they had soft-shell crabs, shrimp and steak shish-kebabs, and a strawberry cake with whipped cream. Herman taught Alexander how to build a fire and how to swim in the large pool on that lit-up birthday night. Herman stood close to him in the water, hands outstretched, and Alexander kept pushing him away, yelling, I can do it Gampa, I can *do* it.

"Do you want to hear my Rose Hawthorne thought for the day?" Gina said to Harry. They were sitting on the evening patio, in a wooden swing, intertwined around each other, drinking Cuban rum and Coke, watching Herman and Alexander frolic under the stars and the lights. Slowly a sloop drifted by, adorned with festive sparkles, festive people. The music pounded out the beats of Gina's calm and blissful heart. *In the morning, in the evening, ain't we got fun …*

"Oh, the Rose sayings are back, are they?" Harry smiled. "I wondered when they would rear their heads. Dad! Catch him!" He jumped up, hands outstretched. Alexander had vaulted off the diving board into the deep end without a flotation device.

Everything was fine. He sat back down.

Gina nuzzled him with kisses.

"What's that for?"

"You just called him Dad. I could cry."

Harry stared unblinking at the two shadows, large and small, in the pool's limpid waters. "What's the Rose quote?"

"*Our creator would never have made such lovely days and have given us the deep hearts to enjoy them, above and beyond all thought, unless we were meant to be immortal.*"

Alexander cried for two days after Herman left in June to go back to Boston.

Chapter 13

THE WISDOM OF ALEXANDER POPE

One

IN THE FALL OF 1921, a few weeks before he and Esther were scheduled to return south for the winter, Herman called to speak to Harry. But Harry was out on the boat with Salvo, and so it was Gina who talked to her father-in-law for a few minutes and then gave the telephone to a jumping-jack Alexander.

"Gampa, where you?"

"What a good question, dear one. Where are *you?*"

Alexander giggled. "Here. You come soon?"

"Another good question. I would like to very much."

"Mama says you come soon."

"I'm going to try, sunshine boy."

"Me growing gators, Gampa!"

"That is exciting. *Real* gators?"

Alexander laughed. "Silly Gampa. Of *course.*"

"Wonderful. What are you going to do with them when they've grown?"

"Have gator farm like Alligator Joe."

"Marvelous."

"We sell them. We be Alligator Alexander and Gampa."

"Grand idea! But I want to be Alligator Gampa. You can be just plain Alexander."

The boy laughed. "Bye! I love you!"

Herman tried to say something else, but Alexander had already dropped the earpiece and bounced like a ball outside.

"Sorry, Herman," Gina said, picking up the receiver. "We're still working on our manners. Do you want me to give Harry a message?"

There was a pause. "I called to say hello, that's all," said Herman. "Tell Harry, the world is young."

When Harry and Salvo returned with their tremendous fish catch, both in long dirty boots, perspiring, brown, happy, and Gina told Harry while he was still in the boat that Herman had called, he dropped the netting with the fish, jumped to the dock, and without another word hurried to the house.

Gina ran after him. "Harry, wait! Not in your boots! Please. He sounded okay. He didn't say it was urgent."

"Do you know how many times in my life my father has called me *just* to say hello?" Harry said, dialing the Barrington number. "Once. This time."

No one picked up at the house. When Harry finally got hold of Esther hours later, Herman had already died.

Two

THE HUSBAND AND WIFE sat outside in the sunny late October morning. Harry drank his coffee, the fingers holding the cup slightly unsteady. Alexander was nearby, digging a large hole with a small spade. Gina was watching her son. Harry was reading the paper.

"Can you believe it?" he said. "Big Bill skipped bail."

She turned her gaze to Harry. "Bail? I thought he was in prison for twenty years."

"No, he was out pending appeal. Which was denied. So he ran."

"Ran where?"

"Russia, of course! Where else, Canada?"

"Oh, good riddance." Gina pointed. "Harry, look at your son." The boy was running back and forth, a pail on his head, the spade held out in front of him. He was making odd noises, too, like the spade was popping.

"Alexander, what are you doing?"

"Me shoot bad guys, Daddy!"

Harry and Gina exchanged a look. "Why is there a pail on your head?"

"It my helmet, silly bunnies!"

Harry got up from the table, walked down to the water, took the pail off Alexander, straightened out his white-and-blue sailor suit, kissed him. "Don't get too messy, bud. Your mother just dressed you for the day. Where did you learn to do that?"

"What?"

"Run and shoot your spade with a pail on your head."

"Me don't know," the boy said.

"Did you see a picture?"

"What picture?"

"How do you know what a gun is?"

"*Zio* Salvo took me to house. There was one on wall."

"One what?"

"*Zio* Salvo said long rifle. It was *so* big, Daddy!"

Harry waved him away.

"Tell your brother I don't want Alexander going with him to show houses anymore," he said to Gina when he came back to the table. "It's ridiculous to take a child with you to strangers' homes. A rifle is the least of what you could accidentally see."

"Oh, it's fine. Alexander loves going. Salvo says the little guy is good for business." She changed the subject. "We should get ready and head down to the Seminole Courthouse. Appeal Janke's decision. She is being completely unreasonable."

He shook his head. "I'm not appealing it."

"Harry, be serious."

"I am. I don't want to rock the boat. I'm so close to the end, Gina.

Four months to go." He was firm. "No. *You* go. Besides, someone has to stay with Alexander."

"Harry, don't joke. Salvo will stay with him."

Harry raised his eyebrows, nodding toward Alexander, the pail back on his head. The boy was flat down in the grass, dragging his torso and legs behind him, shooting from the ground.

"How is *that* Salvo's doing?" Gina wanted to know. "I've never in my life seen my brother drag his body along the ground. Alexander! Stop it! You're getting filthy!"

"No matter," Harry continued. "I'll stay. Otherwise, what will he think, both his parents gone? He's never been without us. Even if she let us go, we'd have to take him with us. And then what? I'm sure everyone's going back to the house after the burial." He shook his head. "I'm not doing it to him. He's not old enough."

"Harry …"

"Gina, you heard Janke. We did ask. She said no. Specifically no to Boston."

"It's immoral of her," Gina said. "She let you go to the church for the baptism."

"Yes, twenty minutes' drive. Not quite the same as returning to Boston."

"*Marito*! You can't *not* go to your father's funeral."

Harry opened his hands to say, *this is how things are.* "You can be my emissary. Represent us both. Tell everyone I'm stuck here for four more months."

She wanted to ask what he meant by *stuck*—on the grass under the palm trees. She wanted to ask what he meant by four *more* months. As in, *only* four? "It's your father."

"I don't want to risk an appeal for nothing."

"It's not nothing." She frowned at him.

"I mean, to appeal and fail. Or, to go and have a problem." He shook his head. "I'm so close. And you heard her—reluctant though she was, she's going to recommend reduced probation because I've been good."

"You want me to go to your father's funeral by myself?" Gina was aghast.

"Or don't go, if you don't feel comfortable. Stay here. Everyone will understand." But he didn't look at her when he said it, didn't look up from the paper. "Can you believe, though, about Big Bill? To Russia!"

Gina was not sure everyone would understand.

Tentatively, she tried again. "Harry ... you don't want to talk about it?"

"I do. I wonder how he did it, evaded the authorities. That's not easy."

"I mean ... about your father."

Harry didn't raise his eyes from the newspaper. "Isn't it obvious," he said, his voice breaking, "that I *don't* want to talk about it?"

Gina couldn't imagine both of them not showing up. She went by herself.

Three

IN BOSTON, ESTHER, looking older for her grief, greeted Gina at the door, glanced down the walkway to Clarence's car, back to Gina, and said, "He didn't come?"

"Janke—" was the only word Gina managed to utter, before Esther abruptly turned on her heels and walked away from her down the hall. After that she didn't bring up Harry's absence.

On the day of the funeral, with Rosa and Gina flanking her, Esther was impeccably composed in black crepe. A veil covered her face. She walked stiffly, barely spoke, but kept herself together through the funeral service and burial, through the condolences and speeches. The repast was organized and catered at Herman's house, just as Harry had surmised. "My father would've wanted that," Esther said. "All his friends and family—*most* of his friends and family—coming to his home to have a bash in his honor. I don't know how we'll fit everyone. There must be four hundred people attending."

At the packed church Gina was alarmed to see Ben sitting in one of the back pews. She stumbled, tripping over the edge of the carpet, and walked right past him, her face to the altar, not looking left or right. She hadn't expected to see him. On one side of him sat his mother, Ellen Shaw, whom Gina had not seen in many years, and on the other, a Spanish-looking woman, no doubt his wife.

At the end of the service, an unusually fidgety Gina stood on the condolence line next to Esther, dreading the inevitable encounter, but thanking God that with the number of people in front and behind, it would be blessedly brief.

They were waiting for the pallbearers to carry the casket to the hearse for the drive to the cemetery when Ben, his mother, and the Spanish woman stepped up to Esther.

She spent longer with Ben than with anyone else. He hugged her, patted her back, kissed her. They talked quietly to each other. He held her hands. Ben was salt-and-pepper gray now. He looked older, a little stockier. But he smiled the same, was animated as before. He was still Ben. He pulled forward the woman next to him, then his mother. Gina continued to stare straight ahead, only in the periphery of her rapidly blinking gaze noting the nodding, the handshaking, the quiet introductions. She tightened her mouth in what she hoped was a polite and indifferent smile.

Ben was in front of her. He opened his mouth to say something, and she blurted, "Thank you!" before he could speak.

"Um—you're welcome?"

"I'm sorry for your loss." But that wasn't the proper response.

"No, I'm sorry for *your* loss," said Ben.

Mercifully he moved down the line to Harry's three imposing cousins, their wives, and their four or five dozen half-grown children. The Spanish woman walked by Gina with a nod. She was uncomfortably pregnant.

Ellen Shaw stepped in front of her. "Gina! What a surprise. It has been such a long time."

She shook Ellen's hand. "I'm sorry for your loss," Gina repeated. "Thank you. Thank you for coming."

Ellen was gray, little, round, frailer than Gina remembered her, less forceful. "You look well." Ellen smiled. "Ravishing as ever. Florida is good to you? How is Harry?"

"Oh, fine. Well, no. He's upset, of course, and regrets he can't be—he's with—"

"Mother!" Ben called, coming toward them and taking his mother by the arm. "A condolence line is not a receiving line. I trust you are aware of the difference?" He pulled Ellen away from Gina with a fleeting apologetic glance.

"When did *he* come back?" Gina whispered, leaning into Esther. She felt she had to say something.

"Last July," Esther replied, leaning away.

It had been many years since Gina saw him last. Here, at the white-steepled Methodist church in Barrington, in a rush of people, all of them adult and grown, men, women, black suits, black dresses, black hats and bags, dark umbrellas, white flowers, everything was proper, proper. Yet just a blink away—Harry, Ben, and Gina stand on Essex Street together, also in a rush of people. She dresses in what she can to look flirty and pretty, to be the kind of young girl that those two boys might notice, especially the other one, the one who doesn't speak, who just stares at her with his colorless eyes to make her imagine all manner of stormy seas under the placid glass. They hawk bananas and hand out flyers to promote ditch digging in Central America, and she serves lemonade with too much sugar so that when those Boston boys drink it, they'll think it's sweet, and will like it because she made it.

Another blink away—they teeter on blades, just Ben and Gina. They glide in white circles deep in the valley of Fairyland.

It had been seven years since the black-ice night ponds. Six years since his hat came off for the farewell bow at the foot of her Lawrence porch. Twenty-two years since the sickly sweet lemonade, summer laughing, flyers for Panama.

Gina fixed her lipstick, tucked in the loose strands of her pulled-back hair, adjusted her crepe black hat, straightened her spine and, blinking rapidly, climbed into the black limousine with Esther to take them to Herman's house.

During the repast, she avoided Ben. But not handily enough. With a drink in one hand and the Spanish woman on the other arm, he finally strolled across the stone patio to Esther and Gina, sitting away from the crowd. Everyone else was eating, drinking, talking, socializing. Esther wanted no part of it. And Gina was happy to sit by her sister-in-law's side, to keep her company. She didn't know anyone, and no one knew her, except for Ellen, who had left early, and Harry's cousins, who'd heard of her, but had never met her. She might as well have been Esther's lady-in-waiting, like Rosa. When people approached and offered condolences, Esther nodded, and Gina patted her back. Would you like a handkerchief, Esther? No, thank you. A drink? No, thank you. Something to eat? No, thank you. When the people moved on, Gina moved her hand away from Esther's back and stopped with the questions.

The afternoon waned and cooled, the guests slowly filtered out.

Now it was Ben's turn to socialize with them. Gina put on her blank face, her formal smile when she saw them approaching. It was October, the blazing month, and for a few days in Boston before the snows, the crisp chill air was filled with the pungent smell of decaying sugar maple leaves and summers past.

After the soft repeat of sympathy, Ben said—to Esther? To Gina?— "I wanted to introduce you properly to my wife." He prodded the woman forward and smiled. "This is Ingersol."

Esther and Gina sprang up like wooden string dolls. They shook hands and nodded, smiled without prodding, turned their heads this way and that, said how do you do, and so nice to meet you, how do you like Boston, yes, isn't it pretty, this time of year especially so.

Ingersol was pregnant again, "our fourth," she happily informed the two women in heavily accented English. They were hoping for a boy this time. Who said this—Ben, Ingersol? She liked Boston, she said, but could never live here. "I don't know how you live with the cold and the snow."

The marionette's head that was Gina's nodded up and down. "You are so right. I live in Florida now. It's sunny, and salty, warm, so much better."

But sometimes, there's magic in it.

Did Gina just say that? The puppet blinked, the ice-covered Walden Pond blocking her eyes. They had walked too far and got lost in the woods, holding hands, the skates on their feet, gliding across the ice to the distant shore, perhaps a way out.

Another blink. The puppet nodded her wooden head. All her American life Gina divided people into two kinds: those who loved Boston and those who did not. She was disappointed and yet pleased Ben had married a girl who was the latter. It made Gina think less of his wife. What a blessing.

"Magic in what?" asked a puzzled Ingersol. Ben said nothing.

Oh, disaster! "Sometimes in the snow," Gina stammered.

Ingersol was pretty, in a soft sort of way. Nondescriptly attractive. Everything was right, but forgettable. Except for the large stomach— that was unforgettable. A pale and weakened Esther eased herself back down into the patio chair. While Ben chatted to her, Gina remained standing, making small talk with Ben's wife about the weather and the pumpkin fair on the Boston Common and the season for clams (through May). Presently Ben joined the conversation.

"But not oysters?" he asked.

"No." The string for Gina's mouth went up, went down. "Oysters now. Oysters only in months with an R in them."

They laughed, both Ingersol and Ben, at how the puppet on a string could know that, they counted out the months of the year, and delighted some more, and even the marionette bobbed her head, as if she were also laughing. It was Harry who had told Gina this, and he had learned it from his mother. Frances Barrington had been such a good hostess. She always knew what to serve and when. Like oysters. The puppet wondered if there were any oysters in the Mystic River in half-frozen December. Did oysters get that far, swim into rivers like salmon, trying to find their way home? Oh, what was she thinking about! What was wrong with her? This was excruciating.

Ingersol excused herself to go to the powder room. Ben and Gina were left alone, standing two feet in front of a sitting Esther. Gina tightened her mouth and without meeting his eyes smiled like he was the postman. After all, Esther was watching.

"What happened to your voice?" he asked. "You sound hoarse."

She fake coughed to fake clear it. She couldn't tell him she had torn her vocal cords giving birth. "Just a touch under the weather," she said.

"So Harry didn't come?"

"He's under house arrest until February. So no."

"Yes, yes, of course. But it's been good otherwise?"

"Yes, okay, oh, fine. Why not, no, it's been good. Great, actually. What about you?"

"Very good. Can't complain."

"Exactly. Can't complain." Gina was afraid even to ask a question. "So are you back for a visit, or ..." She searched for other words. The only ones that came into her head were *per sempre*. Forever.

Ben smirked. "Ingersol prays every day it's just for a visit. How do you say just for now in Italian?"

"*Solo per ora.*"

"*Solo per ora,*" he repeated. "We'll see. A year ago I was invited to be a guest lecturer at Harvard. It's a big honor. I couldn't refuse."

"Oh, yes. Big honor. Harvard? Congratulations. Lecturer in what?"

"The only thing I know. Civil engineering."

Gina said nothing. She was stuck on canals, and rocks, and explosions. The detonating things in her head were so loud. She couldn't look into his face.

"Go ahead, say it," said Ben.

Oh, no! Her eyes darted back and forth across his jacket. "Say what?"

"Do we need another canal somewhere?"

Ah. "No. Or yes? Of course we do."

She didn't ask, but Ben told her anyway. "I have a three-year commitment. But don't tell the wife. She thinks we're here for only one more semester."

"The Spanish don't understand the Italians, don't worry," said Gina. "But your wife, she can tell time, no?"

Ben laughed. "Only by the sun."

"So. No worries then. No sun in Boston until the spring."

"Right." His voice was almost even. "No sun in the winter."

Gina was poured out like water. How was she even breathing? She glanced around for a back of a chair to grab onto. "I'm not used to these heels," she said, swaying. "I'm having trouble standing in them. I've been barefoot for so long."

"I heard you had a child."

"Yes. A son."

"Congratulations. I have three girls."

"I heard. Your wife said. Congratulations, too."

"Is he here with you?"

Head jerk from side to side. "He's too little. Plenty of time for funerals in his future."

"What's his name?"

"Alexander."

"Alessandro," said Ben. "Is he a good boy?"

"Very good." Please, to change the subject! "Your mother seems well."

"And why not? Women have the vote, men can't drink, we're not at war …"

"And her son is back."

Ben smiled. "That, too. How is *your* mother?"

Tears sprang to the puppet's eyes. Ben leaned forward, said *what?*—and Ingersol came back, sparing the puppet a weeping response.

Putting his hand on his wife's back, Ben stepped away. "You all right, Inge?"

"Yes, of course, I'm fine, darling." She smiled at Gina and down at Esther. "I do not know if you two have children, but at the end, it is so difficult to move around. I do not know what I do without Benny."

Benny. Gina smiled like it was drawn on.

Leaning down, Ben kissed Esther on the cheek, rumpled her shoulder a little. "Buck up, Est. Hey, come on now. What did I say?"

"You said buck up."

"Are you bucking? Up?"

Esther almost smiled.

"Herman would've been proud of you," Ben continued. "Look how many people came. Seems like all of Boston is here. You've sent him off so well. Like he deserved. He was a great man. You've outdone yourself." Ben kissed her temple. "Also the food is excellent. Better than at your wedding."

Esther laughed. "That's what I shoot for. That the funerals are more memorable than the weddings."

Ben laughed with her. "Like I said. Outdone yourself." He motioned to the food station. "We're going to get some more before we go."

Esther patted his arm. "All you want, Ben."

"But then we'll head out, all right? Ingersol is tired."

"Of course."

"I'll see you next week. I'll stop by on Friday after my seminar. Do you want me to bring some more of that apple cake from Crimson's you said you liked?"

"That'll be fine."

After Ben and Ingersol walked away, Gina sat down by Esther's side and downed the drink that was next to her. It was strong and revolting, and not even hers. Suddenly she stood, excused herself to Esther, and hurried inside the big house, tripping over her skirt, running down the grand hallway and into the parlor room. She stood at the bay window by the side curtain watching Ben's back as he helped his wife into the car. He had another car now, a nicer one. Shiny. Cream colored. After he shut Ingersol's door, he straightened up and turned to glance back at the house. His eyes searched the windows, as if looking for her. Not knowing what to do, Gina hid herself halfway behind the sheer white curtain. But Ben saw her. He smiled and lifted his hand in a wave. She lifted hers. He walked around the hood of his car, got in, and drove away. Gina fanned her trembling palm against the glass pane. *Addio, il mio ex amante.*

Four

AFTER THE GUESTS HAD LEFT, and the servants all gone to bed, Gina and Esther sat in Herman's study, and to commemorate him sipped his finest brandy out of his crystal goblets. Except for the honeyed wild-guava juice from Cuban rivers and the diluted Mojitos, Gina hated the taste of hard liquor. She drank tonight to keep Esther company.

Esther had been tense, silent, clipped with everyone, especially Gina, but even with Rosa. Well, who wouldn't be, Gina reasoned, on the day you buried your father. Esther had never moved out of her childhood home, not even when she married Elmore. They had lived here with Herman until Elmore left with the Red Cross during the war.

The house was quiet except for the crackling of the wood on the fire. Finally Esther spoke. "Once this liquor is gone, it's gone," she said. "Father bought this bottle on the day I was born, his first child. He told me we would open it when I turned eighteen, and then we would drink from it to commemorate other momentous events in my life." She lifted up the bottle to show Gina how full it still was. "We drank on my eighteenth birthday. We drank when Harry got engaged to Alice. When I got married. We had several drinks when your son was born. And one week ago my father sat where you are sitting tonight, and he and I drank quite a lot of it. He said to me, no use saving it, Esther. Might as well enjoy the finest brandy that money can buy." She lifted the bottle higher. "And yet look how full it still is."

Gina bowed her head. "Herman's advice is spot on. Long ago my mother bought herself a dinner service for four of good china. She said we would use it on special occasions. She had the set for twenty years. We ate off it exactly once."

"When was that?"

Gina paused. "When I brought Harry home after we got married."

"Fascinating," Esther said. "So in your house that was seen as cause for celebration."

Gina wanted to kick herself. She swallowed. "What a long time ago these things were. Seems like someone else's life in many ways."

"Many things were a long time ago," said Esther. "Then again, some of the things you did a long time ago are continuing to cost me dearly in the present, aren't they." It wasn't a question.

Kick. Herself. And hard. Thinly Gina smiled. "You must be tired, Esther. Can I help you upstairs? It's been such a difficult day. I remember when my father d—"

"It's *so* glib of you to dismiss the past as the past," Esther interrupted. "But how far away can it be, really, when at my father's funeral, which is *today*, the son he gave life to *yesterday* is not *present*? Pray do tell."

"Oh, Esther," said Gina, "that has nothing to do with me. He's not free to come and go. I begged him to talk to Janke again. But you know what a militant she is. She wasn't going to let him return to Boston, of all places."

"How hard did he try?"

"He tried." Gina chewed her lip. "I begged him to try again."

"Did you?" Esther paused. "Like you begged him to marry you?"

"What?" Gina's hands became unsteady. She hoped it was because of the brandy. "Of course not. I didn't beg—" No, there was no use defending *that*. Carefully she placed her goblet on the small table near her chair. No point holding it. What if she dropped it accidentally? Then where would they be? "Esther, what's the matter? Why would you want to talk about *that*, today of all days?"

"Because my brother isn't here, today of all days."

"It's awful. I'm sorry. I know how you feel ..."

"Do you? Do you really have *any* idea? Somehow, I don't believe you do."

"Of course, Esther." Gina frowned slightly as she stared at her sister-in-law. "You know I lost my father, too. And I wasn't nearing fifty. I was only fourteen. I was still a child."

"Yes, Gina, you keep reminding me you were only a child when many things happened," Esther said. "Many things that all have *you* as the common denominator, things that changed the course of my life, my father's life, my brother's life." Esther took a breath. "And Ben's life."

"Ben?" Gina wanted to sprint from the room. Oh no. *That's* what this was about. "Esther, don't blame me for Ben. Please." Gina stared to the left of Esther's face. "Blame me for your brother, fine, but ..."

"He went to Panama to get away from you."

"What?" What was happening? Color drained from Gina's face. All she could do was shake her head.

Esther nodded hers. "Yes. Oh, yes. Do you want me to count how many times you made him run for his life? Three." To Gina's horror, Esther held up one finger. "The first time was back in 1900. After he found out about Harry helping you in secret with Salvo's restaurants. He up and left."

Gina was shaking her head so vigorously, she was becoming dizzy. "Esther, I was fifteen—I had no idea about anything."

"Oh, you had an idea about some things."

"He was always going to go." Flyers! Lemonade! Signatures! Petitions!

"Was he? How do *you* know? I thought you had no idea about anything?"

"I know because he used to talk about nothing but Panama."

"To whom? To you? To an immigrant Sicilian *bambina* who didn't speak four words of English?"

"Please, Esther ..."

Esther held up two fingers. "Two—the year you and Harry snuck out of the house for your secret nuptials. Have you noticed—everything my brother did with you was in secret? Everything. Yes, don't even get me started on Harry and you. But Ben had come back to Boston to be his best man—for his actual wedding, the real wedding—and he didn't want to return to Panama. He was having work trouble. I was very close to persuading him to stay for good. But the minute he found out about you and Harry and your rendezvous with the justice of the peace, he was off." Esther's voice was measured, contained. She was speaking deliberately and clearly. She was loud and ice-cold. She was frightening.

Gina opened her hands. "Esther, I didn't even see Ben when Harry and I got married. I hadn't seen Ben at that point in five years."

"Ben couldn't face Harry—because of you. No one could after what happened. But Ben couldn't fake it, couldn't be friends with Harry like before. Because of you."

Gina stared sideways into her cognac glass. She wished she liked the drink more, so she could have a ladleful not a thimble, to not hear quite so well, to become diffuse like a vapor, to vanish. That's what she wanted. To vanish.

How fresh the burns still were. But Gina had her own wounds to deal with, her own sharp disappointments. She thought Bellagrand had healed them, made the ragged things smooth like satin. Certainly for her. Who could remember old burns when every morning she woke up, and the breeze came through her balcony doors, and the sun rose on the ocean, on her marble house? There was no mud, only marble. There was no pain when she spent her days on the lawn playing bricks and mortar, and hide-and-seek. She had a boat named *Gia*, her own dock, two ovens. She mastered the culinary arts of her home country and her adopted country, she drank heady wine and never lost all the baby weight, she was dark like a Sicilian urchin running around in sackcloth, barefoot and in bliss, and her husband whispered to her in the night and at noontime, *tu sei tutta bella. Mi amica, tu sei tutta bella.* Harry had learned well the Song of Songs in the Romance language. All his edges had been silked off. He wasn't sandpaper. He was glorious. He read, ate her food, swam, fixed boats, planted trees, built playhouses for Alexander, and loved her. *Bellagrand.*

All the other Bs in her life she had almost forgotten. Belpasso. Boston. Ben.

What Esther brought to the surface tonight was the other Gina— not the current one, who wanted nothing more, all apologies to her beloved papa, but to forget where she came from.

"Please, Esther," she said. "I'm sorry. Forgive me for your brother. But you see us now, you've seen us in Bellagrand. Your brother and I … from the beginning, Harry and I had a great love."

"Do you even *know* what love is?"

Gina sat up straighter, terrified not so much by the incongruous question, but by Esther's brutal intensity. "What are you talking about?" she asked tremulously, shaking from distress. "Of course I do—"

Esther held up three fingers.

Groaning, Gina put up her palms as if in surrender. "Please, Esther," she whispered. "*Ferma!*"

"You used him," Esther said, slamming her empty goblet on the wooden table. "You used Ben when you were young, when you say you didn't know any better, and you used him again when you were older and knew very well what you were doing. You took him and wrung him out. To escape *you*, he had to run for the third time from this continent."

Esther's hands were in balls, her long polished nails digging into her clenched palms. "In 1914," she said, "when the cursed canal finally opened, I was so happy when he came back! We were always close, and I needed him so much when Elmore left for Europe, and when my poor husband got sick and died. I don't know why he had to die. He was a decent man and deserved a longer life. But through everything, Ben was so good to me. As always. So comforting. Suddenly, with barely a notice, he up and left again—back to Panama. Wouldn't even stay for Christmas. I begged him to stay. I thought he was done with Panama for good. He had promised me he wouldn't leave again. And yet, he fled! And it wasn't until today, when I saw him with you, that I finally realized why. He fled *you*."

The tips of Gina's fingers were numb. It was unbearably loud in Herman's dark and quiet study. "No, Esther."

"Once—when you were supposedly a child—you used him to get *to* Harry," Esther said in a gutted voice. "Did you also use him to get *back* at Harry? When my brother was in prison, reading books, becoming a radical, you were left alone. You were relatively young. Considered yourself quite fetching, didn't you? Oh, yes, the Sicilian swoon! Gina this and Gina that. And your husband was never with you. Thought the universe owed you a little bit, didn't you?"

"None of what you're saying is true. God owes me nothing. It is *I* who …"

"So you chewed him up, and when you were done, you spat him out like stale gum. Him, the best man I know!" Esther cried.

Gina squeezed her hands together in entreaty, in prayer. "Esther, what are you talking about? How could I have used Ben for anything? Harry didn't *stay* home, did he? If what you say is true, then my efforts were futile, no?"

"Yes, your efforts *were* futile," Esther said. "Because your charms are limited, and they didn't work on my brother. But what I say is true."

"No. It's not true."

"If it weren't for you, Ben never would've left."

"But he was meant to go! The Panama Canal needed to be built."

"Not in 1915 it didn't!"

Gina slumped against the chair. She would have gotten up and fled herself, except she knew her flaccid legs would betray her.

Esther, her eyes glazed over by half-a-century-old brandy, leaned forward, narrowed her gaze at Gina, bitter pupils pinpointed like tips of swords, like her words, which she almost didn't slur. "You wouldn't look at him," Esther whispered agonizingly. "You *couldn't* look at him! He kept trying to catch your eye when his wife stepped away. And you wouldn't oblige him. He tilted his head! And you wouldn't return his gaze. You looked at his tie! At his shirt, at the grass, at your glass, at anything, but his face. There was *nothing* friendly about your talk with him this afternoon. That's not how friends behave. That's how old lovers behave. He carries a torch with your name on it, and you looked away because you couldn't bear to see him waving it still burning into your shameless face."

"Esther, you've had too much to drink." Gina was gasping.

"That changes nothing."

"You're wrong."

Esther shook her head. "About this? Never."

"I'm sorry you're upset with me. But today is the day your father was buried. Why do you bring up these other things?"

"Because my brother is not here! My father's only son is not here!" Esther cried. Gina cried.

Feeling that she owed Esther something, a word, a hint of confession, a breath of honesty, Gina lowered her head in heavy remorse. "Esther," she quietly said, "supposing for one moment that what you're accusing me of is true, wouldn't you then have your answer as to why your brother isn't here?"

Esther was dry heaving. "That's supposed to make me feel *better*?" she said in a voice filled with shards of glass. "That's supposed to make me *understand*, make me forgive you, perhaps? That you broke not only Ben's heart, not only my heart, my father's heart, and Alice's heart, but that you also broke my brother's heart?"

"Esther, don't say that!"

"The instant you came off that boat, the second your life intersected with ours, you have caused all of us *nothing* but misery!"

Gina was dry heaving herself. "Esther, how can you say that ... what about Alexander, what about Bellagrand ..."

Esther wept. "Yes, yes, yes. I know how bitterly my heart is divided. You give Alexander with one hand, but what do you take away with the other? After my mother died, my brother and my father were all I had. You destroyed that, our small family, our broken but bonded unit. You have rent apart my father and my brother for most of their adult life—and mine. You separated father and son. Think about that. You took my father's Alexander away from him! And now it's too late. All the years, they're gone, gone. You divided this house, just so you could have what you want. And *then*! because that wasn't *enough* for you, you took Ben!" Esther covered her face, screamed into her palms. "I don't know how I can look at you, how I can talk to you. You have ruined me. Look at me."

Gina couldn't speak. *Esther,* she mouthed, repenting at the ineffable altar of someone else's suffering, *please forgive me* ...

"You took him from my life, and from Harry's life. Has Harry ever had a friend like Ben? No. Never. And you, like a feeble-minded child, advised me to sell my mother's jewelry. You said you understood things. Oh my God. You understand *nothing*!" Esther threw up her hands, and brought them down like a mortally wounded bird falling inconsolable from the sky. "Don't you *understand* that Ben is the love of my life?" she said. "I have loved him since I was fifteen years old, since the day Harry first brought him home. He put a smile on my face then, and he has never stopped. Secret, yes, unrequited, yes, but my deepest longing, the deepest desire of my heart. And you've killed that for me, too. My family, my brother, my beloved. What's left, Gina Attaviano?" said Esther wretchedly. "Would you like my house? Rosa? What else is there for you to take from me, to cart away in your fancy suitcase bought with my dead mother's money?"

That's how it ended, the forlorn day Harry's father was buried. Esther sat collapsed and alone in a chair by the fire, bereaved, hollowed out, with Gina unable to find a word of solace for her husband's sister except *mi dispiace*.

Five

HARRY WAS ON THE GRASS by the pool when Fernando brought her home from the train station. Incongruously he was teaching Alexander how to box. At first Gina thought they were dancing, but no. Arms flying out, they were circling each other, one tiny, one large, like two shirtless warriors, skinny and dark, Alexander especially. She'd been gone two weeks, and yet the boy seemed older, taller. He leaped in lion strides to his mother. "Mama, Mama, where you went? Me missed you." Harry wasn't far behind.

"I went to Boston on Mommy business," she said, squeezing his tanned skinny body, kissing his face. "I brought you back a model of a sloop. Maybe you and your dad can build it?"

"Maybe." He wriggled out of her arms. "Daddy teach me to box. Watch, Mama." He put up his fists.

"Hold on, buddy," said Harry, his steadying hand on the boy's head. "Let me talk to your mom for a minute." They hugged, they kissed. He poured her some lemonade. "I tried to make it like yours," he said, "but mine is not sweet enough, though I had dropped a pound of sugar into it. How much sugar do you put in it?"

"More," she said.

"Well?" He studied her face. "How was it?"

After five days on the train, Gina hoped her face was unreadable, a wan blank. "Not good." She paused. "Did you call your sister?"

"Yes. She didn't come to the telephone."

"Mmm."

"What? Rosa said she wasn't feeling well."

"Quite." What equivocation! But what else could Gina say? She couldn't speak about what had passed between her and Esther.

Harry scooted his chair closer to hers. "Why do *you* look upset?" His hands rested on her legs. "Something happen?"

"I'm not upset, *amore mio*. I'm exhausted. Happy to be back." Tilting her head to the sun, she closed her eyes.

He was quiet. "Anyone I know at the funeral?"

She didn't look at him. "Probably everyone you know."

Silence from Harry.

"Yes, Ben was there." Is that what he had been waiting for? "With his very pregnant wife. Baby number four. Hoping for a boy, I think."

"Ah." Gina heard the chair scrape against the patio as he got up. "He brought his wife? Esther must have been pleased."

"Esther was upset at many things at your father's funeral, mostly the two obvious ones. You should try calling her again."

"I've called her twice a day for a week. Rosa keeps saying she is not well enough to come to the telephone. Did anything happen?" He paused. "I mean anything else?"

Still bleeding from her saber-toothed evening with Esther, Gina shook her head. She feared that every word out of Esther's twisted mouth had been true. There was no part of it she could relate to Harry. Except, "You should have come, *marito*."

"I'm not allowed to leave this house. Why does everyone keep forgetting that?" He stopped speaking, and when she opened her eyes, he was gone, already down by the docks with Alexander. Slowly she walked down to her men. She was tired, whole-body tired, but she wanted to be awake, go swimming, catch a fish. Silently she stood.

"Watch and learn, Alexander." Harry was circling his son. "Jab is this. A hook is that. Come on, show me you know the difference."

Alexander rushed up to his father and jabbed him in the ribs with his little fist. "That was a hook, Dad," he said.

Harry rubbed his sore side. "No, son. That was an uppercut." He ruffled the boy's hair. "I'm going to need ten minutes to recuperate."

"Okay. Me look at my baby gators."

Harry and Gina sat on the bench by the dock, staring at the water and at Alexander, immersed in the reptile pond up to his elbows.

"I sort of wish he was joking, don't you?" said Gina.

"Wait until they're no longer baby gators."

"*Divertente. Grazie.*" She smiled the benign smile of the one being comforted. "I didn't know you knew how to box, *caro*."

"Roy taught me. You learn some crazy shit in prison."

She could imagine.

"Do you want to take the boat out?" he asked.

"Yes, very much. After a bath and a nap."

"I can help you with both of those." His hands reached for her arms, for her neck.

They mulled over what to do with their son in the middle of his napless afternoon. "When's the reading of the will?" Gina asked.

Harry shrugged. "I don't know. Two weeks. But what does it have to do with me?"

"What do you mean?"

He placed his hand on her hand, leaned over and kissed her fondly. "I love you. In two weeks, you will know what I mean. Alexander! Hey, bud, would you like to have a nap? Mom and Dad are going to have one." He kissed her again. "A sleepless one."

Esther did not call before, during, or after the reading of the will. It was opened and read, and the details of it appeared in *The Boston Globe*, which was delivered by subscription a full week later. Aside from the *Palm Beach Gazette*, that's how they had read the news for three years. On a seven-day delay. Herman Barrington left half of his estate to Esther, as well as his main property in Barrington, his secondary property in Newburyport, all his cars, his two boats, and all his material possessions. One quarter he bequeathed to the cardiac unit at Boston Memorial Hospital, which had kept him alive an additional decade, gave it in memory of Elmore Lassiter, Esther's husband and a cardiologist. The rest he distributed between the various charities supported by Esther's foundation. Herman stipulated that until such time as the boy didn't need it anymore, Esther would provide for Alexander's education, and only his education. To Harry he left nothing. He didn't even mention a son by name, as if he didn't have one. The only reference that might have alluded to Harry was the cryptic coda: "*Blessed are those who expect nothing, for they shall never be disappointed. That is the ninth beatitude.*"

"Is that for you?" Gina asked. "The last part?"

Without reply Harry poured himself the last of the fresh-squeezed orange juice.

"It is!" she exclaimed, remembering. "It's from before. When we first met, you and"—she decided not to say Ben's name out loud—"how you bickered over the meaning of those words. Oh, Harry." What had she done? What had they done?

He smiled. His gray eyes were clear, not occluded. He seemed at ease, perhaps at false ease, but she couldn't be sure. "Gia, I'm not upset," he said, "precisely because of Alexander Pope and his ninth beatitude." He took out a knife to cut some more oranges. "I know my father." It was a while before he spoke again. She watched him use the hand juicer to squeeze out the orange halves. "I expected nothing. I deserved nothing. I'm not disappointed."

"Why do you say you deserved nothing? You're his only son."

Harry waved her away. "You are so Sicilian."

"This isn't Sicilian. This is fathers and sons." She stood away from the counter, and from him.

"Not this father and son." He was busy with the oranges, as if he weren't paying attention.

"But I don't understand." She started pacing the kitchen. "You were getting along so well. He was happy." She wrung her hands.

He eyed her affectionately, his own hands covered with pulp. "Gia … you're so adorably overwrought."

"What about your legacy?"

"What legacy? The business our family had built and my father expanded was given to Uncle Hank's sons. They're in charge of it now. How do you think my father felt about that? That his brother had sons who carried on with the century-old family business, while he had a son who sat in prison? He and I couldn't even talk about it. Oh, sure, we talked of other things. Sheds and chairs, Alexander's gators and boats. John Reed. This house. But that's all secondary, isn't it, to the heart of the matter. Which is—I turned my back on my father. That's how he felt, and there is no getting around that. He behaved exactly as I thought he would." Harry nodded. "I respect him for that. I would've been ashamed to receive profit from the fruits of his lifelong labors, after I had been so dismissive of his work." He sounded nonchalant and remorseless. Gina wanted to call Esther and demand to know why she didn't hold her brother to account for anything. Why was a woman the only one blamed, never the man?

"My father knew my apathy to his money," Harry went on, "and then my antipathy. I always let him know it." He threw away the scraped-out orange halves. "I'm hungry. Can you make us some eggs? Maybe a frittata?"

Dejected, she trudged to the cabinet to get out the pans. "Will your sister help you?"

"She won't even take my calls."

"You should have gone to the funeral, Harry," Gina repeated, a refrain of shame.

"I think it was too late to change the will by then, don't you?" Harry said. "Father was already dead."

"That's not funny."

They stood without moving. They stared into each other's faces.

From across the kitchen Harry spoke to her. "Gina, you pay a price for where you stand. I keep telling you, but you refuse to listen. You and I made our bed long ago. We picked our place. We said we would not live my life, nor your life, but a new life."

"We certainly didn't live your life." She lowered her head. "Until now." Though they had lived plenty of hers. "But you grew up with something that I never had."

"Which is?"

Gina tried to define it. What was it that his rejected wealth gave him—in one word? "Freedom," she said.

"You mean slavery," he said.

One of them had to move out from the impasse. It was always her. "I guess it depends where you stand when you cast that vote."

"I suppose so."

She knew he said it to end the discussion, not to give her opinion weight. Frowning, she stepped back into the ring. "But Harry, slavery is what you called my having to work every day to pay the rent and feed us. Remember that?"

He frowned in response, back in the ring himself. "So?"

"How can both opposites be defined by you as one and the same? I worked to eat. You refused that life. But you didn't have to work at all, except at what you wished. And you refused that life, too. How can both be slavery? Besides these two choices, what else is there?"

He stood and was silent, except for a sharp, knowing shrug. Why did Gina feel it wasn't because he didn't have an answer, but because he had an answer he didn't want to share with her?

She waited for him to speak, and when he didn't, she opened her mouth and spoke. "Until recently I didn't even know what it was that you took completely for granted. What you had turned your back on."

"My back may have been turned, but what was my face looking at?" He pointed to her.

"I don't know if we had thought it through." Her shoulders slumped.

"I want to say two things in response. One, I hope you didn't marry me for my money."

"I would have been a fool to."

"Indeed. And two, don't fret so much. We have not been left with nothing. This isn't like before." He opened his hands to the lawn and the sky and the gleaming waters. "We have everything we need. This is where we stand, the price of our marriage. To live in paradise by the sea. And soon I'll be free."

"Yes," she whispered, gulping for air. Why did her throat suddenly constrict, why did she find it hard to breathe? Free or in slavery?

Chapter 14

SPANISH CITY

One

"HARRY BARRINGTON, I CAN'T believe I'm saying this, but I'm proud of you."

"I can't believe you're saying it either. Would you like some wine to celebrate?"

"I'm working, so no. But you go ahead."

"You want me to drink alone? Nice. Do they allow you to have orange juice on the job?" He poured her a glass. "We have the groves right here, out back."

She drank and praised it. "Delicious. So fresh. I'm going to be truthful, Mr. Barrington. I didn't think you'd be able to do it."

"Grow oranges? It's not that difficult."

"Stick it out. Keep to the program. Behave yourself. Alter your thinking."

"Perhaps less truthful might be a better approach?"

"I really thought you were going to fail. I expected you to fail."

"Um—I'm sorry I let you down?"

"You surprised me."

"Pleasantly, I hope."

"No question. I'm sure your family is relieved."

"I hope so. I don't think they wanted me to fail."

"Oh, I didn't *want* you to fail. I just expected you would."

"O ye of little faith." He smiled.

"Well, never mind that. Here we are. The moment you've been working for. And you really have worked hard. You were exemplary. You were upfront with me, you broke no laws."

"That you *know* of." He kept a straight face.

"You were always here, where you were supposed to be, and even when I made unannounced visits, you welcomed me."

"You were the entirety of my social circle, Officer Janke. Frequently your visits were the highlight of my week."

"Sometimes I can't tell if you're joking with me, Mr. Barrington."

"I would never joke about a thing like that."

"Well, good. Because I enjoyed getting to know you, and getting to know your family."

"And they you. My brother-in-law Salvatore especially."

"Really?" Janke leaned forward and lowered her voice. "I must admit something to you—I've never liked him. But please don't say anything."

"I would never."

"He seems shifty to me."

"You don't say."

"Unlike you. With you, what I see is what I get. I wasn't so sure in the beginning. But I am now." She closed her book. "There are many decisions before you," she said. "Big decisions. After all, now that you can go anywhere, and do anything, you have to decide where you want to go and what you want to do."

"You are right, that is a big decision indeed."

"But a rewarding one. On the one hand you can be like that brother-in-law of yours, jumping like a bean from one rock to another …"

"Yes."

"Or you can be like your father—a rock until the end, for other people to jump on."

"People other than me."

"Or you can be somewhere in between."

"A new thing perhaps?" Harry smiled.

"Yes! A new thing." She got up to leave. "Just remember: without work, man has no meaning. Life has no meaning." She collected her papers. "So what's the first thing you're going to do as a free man?"

He rolled his eyes. "Apparently I have plans to take my wife and son to the market. For three years they've been telling me what I've been missing."

"They're right, it's wonderful. You'll enjoy it. If you go next week, it'll be better. A carnival is rolling into town for a few days. Your son will like that."

"Perhaps we'll go again. Because I don't think that boy can wait for anything."

They both glanced outside on the lawn, where mother and son were playing volleyball, or as it was called in the Barrington house, go-in-the-bushes-and-get-the-ball.

"Please be careful. Keep to yourself. Stay away from trouble. Probation doesn't mean you can do what you like."

"Of course not."

"Probation means you are no longer bound by the walls of this house. You can go where you please. Except to Communist Party headquarters."

"And who'd want to go there?"

"Exactly." They shook hands. "You're going to do well," said Janke. "Whatever you choose to take up, I'm certain you will be very successful at it."

"Why, because of the way I've navigated the terms of my prison sentence, Officer Janke?"

"Precisely, Mr. Barrington. You learned to live inside the box. That's very important for all adult men to learn. Just look at your brother-in-law for the other example."

"He's not an adult yet, that's why. Goodbye, Inspector Javert."

"You've called me that several times over the years, Mr. Barrington. You do know that's not my name, correct?"

"Yes, Margaret," said a smiling Harry. He opened the heavy front door to let her out. "I hate to admit it, but I'm going to miss you. Your little pronouncements, your hectoring nature, your prim coda. I don't meet someone like you every day."

"Well, perhaps then, we can arrange for you to keep seeing me, Jean Valjean." She walked down the marble steps, with a jaunty backward wave.

Harry laughed. "So you *are* human!" he exclaimed. "All these years, I wasn't sure."

And so for the first time in three years, the three of them piled into their Packard. Gina drove them across the water to Tequesta, where they parked and strolled among the friendly folk, while Alexander ran ahead through the market in the waterside park. They could barely keep up. At the produce stalls, the vendors all knew him; they gave him mangoes, and candy, and cakes, and toys. He returned to his parents with arms full of things, which he dumped at their feet.

"Is this how it always is?" Harry asked. "He just sprints by and they give him things?"

"Well, just look at him," Gina said, a vision herself, elegant and chestnut-haired in her flowing frock, her lady's silk hat, her arm through Harry's.

"I know what he looks like. But why do *they* care?"

Gina squeezed Harry's arm. "You don't want other people to notice your boy, *mio amore*?"

"I don't know why they would, that's all. Alexander! Not so far ahead! Stay close."

With amusement Gina notes Harry's peevish expression. Alexander hugs a woman Harry doesn't know. Harry frowns. This woman, like the boy is *her* boy, gives him a truck and crayons and a chocolate bar. Harry frowns. He asks if there is anyone, anyone at all, whom Alexander doesn't instantly take to. Gina replies there is not. She can't drum into him the concept of strangers. Harry says churlishly that to Alexander every stranger is a friend whose name he doesn't yet know.

"I find it delightful," she says.

"You would," says Harry. "Because you put him on a purple pedestal the day he was born, and since that day, the rest of us live at his feet."

"And this upsets you why?"

"Look!"

Alexander runs and jumps into the arms of a flashy man in a smart suit. Harry frowns, opens his mouth, is about to yell when—

"Oh, hello, Salvo."

It was Salvo's jewelry-adorned neck Alexander was hanging off like a marmoset. In 1922, Salvo had become almost unrecognizable. Having made wagonloads of money off his real estate commissions, enough for three cars, a brand-new house, a boat, and a minority interest in the recently opened Cuban–Italian restaurant, Salvo walked around the Tequesta grounds like he was part owner of the entire town, not just a little dive off the docks. He didn't look or act like the man who merely supplied the money and the expertise in making pizza, while someone else counted the profits and rolled the dough. He looked like a man in control of everything, including his destiny.

Gina bought Alexander and herself some ice cream. The men abstained. The four of them strolled under the moss oaks along the overgrown tropical paths near the marina.

"So how does it feel, my brother?" Salvo asked Harry, slapping his back. "To be free to walk among us, hordes and commoners?"

"Overrated."

Salvo laughed.

"Come on, Alexander, get down," Harry said. "You're dripping ice cream on Uncle Salvo's nice suit."

"I don't mind." Salvo abundantly kissed his sticky nephew. "Right, crackerjack? You're the only boy related to me by blood. Drip your messes on me. I carry two extra white shirts in my car for just this purpose."

Alexander stuck his ice cream cone into Salvo's cheek, laughed and kissed the cheek through the creamy spot of ice cream. "Do you want me to do that to you, too, Daddy?"

"No, thank you, son."

Gina's smile didn't leave her face as she watched the three men she loved most.

The sky is cloudless blue, the sun super bright, even in February. It's all so simple, so easy. Gina walks on and watches it all, a watercolor onto which rain is falling.

Two

JANKE WAS GONE from their life a month before Harry broached things.

They were down by the dock around his mosaic table, eating waffles and strawberries, the quiet water balmy and beautiful. Fernando was somewhere unseen playing "La Bruja" on his Spanish guitar. He played it for Gina because he knew she liked it. Now that Harry was a free man, Fernando came off Herman's security payroll, but Harry and Gina decided to keep him on as their driver (and troubadour), and invited him to live in the mews rent-free. Gina was so relieved when Fernando agreed. Alexander loved him and his Spanish strings. She didn't want one more person to vanish unmarked from her boy's life. Although Esther hadn't made it through Christmas before she called to speak to Alexander. "I told you, she wouldn't be able to stay angry for long," Harry said. "She can't be apart from that boy. He is our secret weapon."

Do we need a weapon? Gina wanted to ask.

Having finished his breakfast, Harry was threading worms on hooks, ready to go fishing with Alexander. "So what do you think?" he asked her. "What should we do?"

"We?" She smiled. "Salvo promised to come for lunch. I'm going to make quesadillas and mend half of Alexander's wardrobe. We swim. We live. Just like before."

"I meant us. What is our plan for life, for you and me, for Alexander?"

"Do we have to have a plan?"

"That's like asking do we have to have a future."

"Well, *mio marito*," Gina said, "you were telling Janke for three years how you were getting yourself ready for this moment, so that when it came you'd be ready." She smiled at him lovingly. "Are you ready?"

"Are you?"

A moment drifted by. "Let's open a bookstore," she said. "The town is sorely in need of one."

"*That* town is in need of a bookstore?" Harry made a face. "Do they even know how to read?"

"Oh, nice," she said. "Since when did you become such a bourgeois snob? I thought you were one of the people. Go be one of them. Sell them oranges and books."

"You want *me* to open and run a business." He sounded incredulous.

"A *bookstore*, Harry. The best kind of business besides a pizza joint." Harry shook his head.

"You'd rather work for someone else?"

"That also doesn't please me. I don't like to take orders."

"Everyone has to take orders from someone, *amore mio*. Even the communists take orders."

"I can't be a communist, I'm on probation." They stared at each other. "I'm joking." He strummed the fishing lines like guitar strings. "Where's your sense of humor?"

"I don't know why you're against a bookstore," Gina said. "It'll just be you and me. You won't have to hire anyone else, so you won't exploit them. Just me." She smiled. "And I want to be exploited."

"Okay, it's still the middle of the morning. Don't get naughty. Though ..." He put down the hooks and the lines, leaned over and kissed her, kissed her so deeply that the small metal chair tipped backward. She yelped.

"But back to the bookstore," he said, straightening her out, "if we're even a little bit successful, we'll have to hire someone else, won't we?"

"Oh, Harry, *caro mio*. We'll make absolutely sure we're not successful. We'll vow right now not to make a single dollar in profit on our little shop of books."

He carried his fishing lines to the dock. "I won't be taunted by you."

She followed him. "I'm not taunting, *delitto*. I'm teasing."

"Well, all your teasing dreams are premised on our staying in Bellagrand."

When he glanced back at her, she had paled.

"I'm not taunting, *delitta*," he said. "I'm teasing."

They stopped talking about eveything but Alexander and what food to eat. March windswept silently into April. Ever warmer, the days remained blessedly dry. She wondered what Harry was waiting for, until one morning she overheard him on the telephone with his sister, saying, "Well, *how* soon? It's been months. What's taking so long?" There was silence while Esther spoke. "How long is this damn probate going to last?"

He was waiting for the deed to be transferred from the trust into his own name. Gina watched his back as she cut up the lemons for lemonade. But why? What did *that* matter to how they lived?

After he got off the telephone, she wanted to ask, but he became buried in a newspaper. She glanced at what he was so absorbed in. The Germans and the Russians had made a secret deal flouting the Versailles Treaty and the League of Nations. Both foreign ministers said it was just an economic development agreement. Everyone knew it was code for a military alliance.

"Why are you asking Esther about the probate?"

"Just curious." He wouldn't lift his head.

She wanted to swipe the paper from him. For days on end he wouldn't get his nose out of it. He read it like other people read the Bible.

"What do you want me to tell you?" he said, pushing her elbow slightly away from his head. "Right now I might want to be left alone." The Allied nations were uniting against Russia: no diplomatic recognition until it paid off the debt it repudiated four years earlier.

"Did they leave you alone in prison?" Gina asked, nudging him, standing close, leaning over him, resenting the damn news.

"I always enjoy your apt comparisons."

"What about all your lofty interlocutions to Janke? Were they just for show?"

"No. What interlocutions? Oh. Work? Yes, I was trying to manage her."

"Like you're managing me right now?"

"Not very well, am I?"

"Why probate? What do you care? You said you didn't. So why?"

He said nothing. He was engrossed in Russia's war debt. Perhaps he hadn't even heard her.

"Harry!"

"Oh no ..." He put his hands on the paper, and finally looked up at her with weary, affectionate eyes. "Gina," he said mildly. "Let's make a bargain. I can finish my paper, and then I'll take you to lunch in town, and we'll have a proper conversation. Where would you like to go? The Breakers? Would you like to drive down to Palm Beach?"

"Alexander is showing houses with Salvo this afternoon," she said, "but Salvo has plans at three so he has to drop him off. Maybe Palm Beach another time? When we can make a whole day of it."

"Okay. Today we'll go to Seaside. Now, may I finish the one little article that I've been trying to finish for the last twenty minutes?"

He took her to an early lunch on the harbor at Seaside, a local popular seafood joint.

She made small talk. Did you see that the herons have just given birth to their young?

He replied that he saw them.

Did you like the dolphins at dawn this morning? They finally reappeared in the ocean. Summer is close.

Yes, he said. It was nice to walk so early in the morning on the empty beach and see them frolic.

But finally, not small talk.

"You know," he said, "with the probate almost over, the papers we've been waiting for are finally being drawn up. They're going to be with us next week. The papers for the beneficiary transfer. We'll go to the bank together. I've asked Jenkins to put both our names on the deed. So that Bellagrand can belong fully and equally to both of us."

"That's good. Who is Jenkins?"

"Trevor Jenkins, the bank manager."

"Oh."

He took her hand. "Does that make you happy?"

What was the correct response? "Yes, Harry, *il mio unico delitto*," she said. "It does."

She was waiting, waiting, waiting …

"What if I told you I wanted to go back to university to finish my doctorate?" he asked over the shrimp *ceviche* appetizer.

There it was. Gina looked thoughtfully into her soda. "I didn't know there was a university in Jupiter," she said. "I thought the closest one was in Miami."

"Not Miami. Cambridge."

She wanted to focus on him, but could not. Her vision had blurred. She continued to stare into her soda. "Harvard?"

"Gia, look at me."

Somehow she looked. He took her hand, as if he were proposing marriage. Only the kneeling was missing. "What if I told you I wanted to move back to Boston?"

She couldn't speak for a moment because she couldn't catch a breath, as if her lungs had deflated. And there she had thought it was a choice of *vocation* that had been at issue! Alas. She had mischaracterized the thorny subject by one crucial letter.

He continued to hold her hands across the white tablecloth. "Don't get upset. Hear me out first."

"Hear you out, then get upset?"

"What if we moved back and bought a mansion in Beacon Hill? You've always wanted to live there. Where the fancy people live." Harry smiled. "Alexander could play on the Boston Common every day."

She pulled her hands away. She used all her Protestant training not to rip them away. "I dreamed about Beacon Hill," she said, careful not to raise her voice, "long ago. Before I had laid my eyes on Bellagrand. You know I don't want to live anywhere else."

"Come on," said Harry. "You've always been a city girl." He tilted his head, full of easy charm. "You'd be so beautiful in your day frocks and court shoes, your pillbox hats and long silk gloves. You could join the Daughters of the Revolution. You could get a job at the Boston

Library in Back Bay. Give historic tours of Beacon Hill. Tell me you wouldn't want that." He spoke as if dreaming the dream for her.

"Oh, so I'd work."

"No, no. You could go back to school, too. Get your degree from Simmons. I know how much you once wanted that. I can give that back to you, what I took from you. Maybe you could become a teacher."

She tried not to move a facial muscle. "What would we live on?"

Raising his hand, he pointed across the shining waters. "Same thing we're living on now. Bellagrand."

She was mute.

"We'd have two houses?"

"We'd sell this one."

Her throat hardened like concrete. She could barely shake her head. She still couldn't breathe.

"Sell it," he continued, as if not seeing her distress, "and with the money we'd make from it, we'd move back to Boston and live like royalty on Mt. Vernon Street."

All her effort went toward shallow panting. "The deed is not even in our names yet," she managed to croak. "The ink is still in the inkwell for our signatures. And you already want to sell it?"

"If it's to return to Boston like conquerors."

She tried to take a gulp of air, but couldn't.

Harry grabbed her trembling hands. "Listen to me, my beloved wife. I want you to have the urban life you dreamed of."

She tried to pull away, but he wouldn't let her. "I have the life I want."

"Do you have any idea how much this house must be worth? We haven't had it properly appraised, as my father advised. But we'll do it now. Salvo can help us. When Flagler built it, it was worth a pretty penny. But now? Gia, my father was right, we could be sitting on a field of gold!"

"Is it a potter's field?" She wouldn't raise her eyes to him.

"A what?"

"Never mind." She admired his enthusiasm, but why was it invariably that his excitement meant a diminished life in her? Why did a numbness pour over her, like a coldly moving lava? Why was she terrorized instead of enthralled? She shook her head. "Harold, I don't want to sell Bellagrand."

He let go of her, sat back. "Did you just call me *Harold*?"

"That's your name, isn't it? I'm not changing your name, am I?" Like I had changed mine. Even God wouldn't recognize me, wouldn't find me anymore.

"You want to continue living here, as we have been?"

"That's all I want."

"But *I* want to go back to Boston," he said. "I want to get my doctorate at Harvard. And Gina—I'd like to be closer to my sister. She is the only family I have left."

"I want to be close to my brother," Gina said. "He's the only family *I* have left." She couldn't tell Harry that she and Esther were not on speaking terms and might never be again. What had transpired between them felt unfixable.

"I know she's been difficult with you. She's reeling. It's hard for her without my father in the house. And she desperately misses Alexander. Your brother is a vagabond. He moved here on a whim, he'll move back on a whim. Come on, be reasonable. My sister is never leaving Boston, and we're all she has. She wants us close. Alexander especially."

"Alexander only."

"Okay."

"Alexander also benefits from being close to his *zio*." Cucumber sandwiches, seafood salad, crab soup, barely eaten, barely looked at. "Esther can come stay with us here whenever she wants," Gina said. "As before."

"It's not the same. You're not listening to what I'm saying."

"*You're* not listening to what *I'm* saying."

"But we already lived your way for more than three years, Gia. Can't we now try my way?"

"We lived your way for fourteen years." Did she really need to remind him of it?

He mock laughed. "*Lawrence* was my way?"

"Of course," she replied calmly. "Who else's? Mine?"

"Okay, okay. But can't we now live the *other* life you wanted?"

She shook her head.

"I am a Bostonian," Harry said. "Maybe *you* can be transplanted like a mangrove, but not me."

"I'm not a mangrove," Gina said. "I'm an immigrant. I have already transplanted myself. I've already remade myself into something new. An American."

"I'm an American, but I'm not going to be a Floridian. This is always going to feel second best to me. It's never going to feel like home. Why can't you understand that?"

Gina looked out across the water. Somewhere on the other shore stood their house. If she squinted, she could almost make out its white stucco walls.

"Why sell it?" she asked. "Why can't we just continue borrowing against it, as we've been doing?"

"How can we be free with a noose like that around our necks?"

"Bellagrand is not a noose," Gina said. "She is freedom." She looked away. She didn't want him to see her expression—as if she didn't know him. How could he feel so starkly different than she did about Bellagrand?

"Allow me to disagree with you," he said, "having just done time inside her fortress walls. Besides, do you remember what Esther told us? Eventually we'd have to pay back the money or sell the house. We won't be able to keep borrowing indefinitely."

"If it keeps rising in value, we could." She would rather do that than sell. Or the worst: sell *and* move.

"Rising in value? One of these days remind me to give you my lecture about capitalism." Harry gestured to the waiter for the bill. "Nothing in it goes up without eventually crashing down."

Gina pulled herself up from the table. "That's not what you said to Esther in the beginning when she told you there was an end to everything."

Harry took her by the elbow. "Gia, who knew, but my sister was right. There is an end to everything."

They paid and left in silence.

Three

A DAY TICKED BY. And then another.

"Don't you love it here?" They were in their bed late at night, both fragile and naked.

He shrugged, his tone conciliatory. "I like it here. I like it because you like it. But you like it more than I do. I don't like the hot sun as much as you. I don't enjoy the beach as you do. I will never think of Jupiter as home. I'm not a country boy. And Alexander is not one either. Even if he is, I don't *want* him to be one. I want him to grow up to be cosmopolitan and suave."

"Like you?"

He squeezed her. "Yes, father wants son to grow up to be like him. Stop the presses."

"As your father wanted you to be like him?"

He breathed in deeply before speaking. "Gia, what does Florida have to do with who we are? What is Alexander going to grow up as? There is nothing for him to do here. For him or for me," he added.

"Flagler found something to do. He changed the world here."

"By building a few houses?"

"Why are you being derisive? Yes, like your father in Boston, by building a few houses, like this one, and then a railroad, and St. Augustine, and Palm Beach, and Miami. By spending the last ten years of his life building an impossible bridge to Key West, a bridge that spans nearly a hundred and fifty miles over water, to make it the closest U.S. port to the Panama Canal."

Harry visibly tensed. She regretted ticking off Flagler's list of accomplishments starting and ending with the worst. But why did he have to be so dismissive?

"Well, the railroad and the canal are already built," Harry said. "Nothing more for me to do on that score. But I'm not just talking about me." His arms were off her body. He lay in his corner of the bed. She lay in hers. "I'm talking about our *son*, Gia. What is he going to do in Florida? All he does is build dwellings for frogs and birds and gators. All he does is fish and swim, and run around the tennis court. I know it seems fun now, when he is little. But what kind of life is that for him in the long run? Alexander is too good for Florida. You know it. He can be anything he wants."

"Clearly you haven't asked your son what he wants to be."

He turned his head to stare at her with blank incredulity. "Have I asked a three-year-old what he wants to be when he grows up? Um, no, we haven't had that particular father and son talk yet."

"You should go ahead and ask him. Because he is all set."

Harry crept over and hugged her, as if she had told the funniest joke. "Gina! This place is a dead end for a smart boy like him. He can grow up to be mayor. Governor. President. Everyone who meets him—much to my irritation, I admit—sees what a remarkable child he is. Don't thwart your son's essential nature. Let him grow up in a place where his greatest talents, his greatest potential will be realized."

Gina tried not to cry. "There is nothing but beauty here."

"Those who visit Attica think there's beauty in it also. But I've been in exile."

I don't want to sell the house, Gina kept repeating like a poem, like an omen.

But we must, he kept repeating, if we're to have the kind of life we want.

"I don't want another life. Only this one."

"Is that true?"

Yes, her heart cried, while her lips stayed silent. "To live your life facing away from the truth is to live out your life in hell."

"The truth isn't in Bellagrand!"

"It is."

"Where's my sophisticated Simmons girl?" Harry whispered in the dark. "The young girl of velvet and chignon is now a woman in full bloom. Don't you want to wear white gloves while strolling on Beacon Street?"

"Instead of a sundress on Fiesta Avenue?" She paused, changed tactics. "What would your mother want? She left you this house. What do you think her wish would be?"

"Who can say?"

"*You* can say. Read again the note from her you have by your bedside. *Such a house that may he never forget the romance of youth.*"

"By virtue of her rejection of her one and only life, she denied herself the right to have a say about anything."

The next morning Harry called Alexander back as he and Gina strolled down the beach, arm in arm, all three of them barefoot so they could wade in the surf. "Son," said Harry, "what do you want to be when you grow up?"

"A builder," the boy replied. "Like Gampa."

Gina kicked through the foamy water without comment.

"That's it, a builder?" said Harry. "Nothing else? You don't have a choice number two?"

"If I can't be a builder, a soldier."

"A soldier!" Harry tried to catch Gina's eye, but she was having none of it. "Why a soldier, son?"

Alexander kept trying to run off into the tidal current. "Dad, let go. I don't know why. So I can carry a gun? I don't know, Dad. I. Just. Don't. Know."

"You put him up to this," Harry said, catching up to her and pushing her into the waves.

"As if that boy is remotely susceptible to being put up to anything."

Gina remained baldly unpersuaded. Harry worked on her. He went into town with Alexander, bought her a white hat. He took her out on their boat, dropped anchor, and spoon-fed her half melted ice cream. He soothed her with stories of the bright and clement future, soothed her with fine words and long kisses. Soothed her with his languorous kisses most of all. He really upped his game.

Gina retreated into Bellagrand and into herself—watching Alexander play with his frogs and crabs while she navigated her own murky koi ponds. What was best for her dancing boxer boy? She wasn't sure it was Boston. But she also wasn't sure it wasn't Boston.

Harry was convinced a busy city was the answer. "Every day he could play soccer on the Common," he kept saying. "He could learn how to play hockey, like me. Perhaps he could learn to ice skate—like you?"

Gina steadfastly ignored him.

"He would learn independence," Harry continued. "He would go to the best schools. He would go to Harvard, like every Barrington before him. Perhaps I could be his professor, if things go the way I plan. What a wealth of experience, what a rounded childhood. You can't think only of yourself, Gina. You have to think of Alexander."

"What in the world do you mean? He's almost all I think about. I still don't want to sell the house."

"Treat it as the one sacrifice you must make," Harry said to her on another long afternoon over their too-strong sangria. There was rum in it, and fruit, and sugar, and wine. Soon all talk would cease, and other discourses would begin. For now they languished with sangria coursing through their blood.

"I don't want to sell the house."

"We'll get another vacation home, closer to Boston. We'll get a place on Cape Cod, as my sister recently did." He smiled, grabbing her, lifting her out of her chair, pretending he was going to dance with her on their veranda with the dim sailboats in the dusky distance.

"The water in Cape Cod is cold," Gina said, unmoved, though touched. "It's not here." *Nothing* was like here.

Round and round they waltzed around Bellagrand. *Dance with me, come with me, leave with me, sell with me* ... He cajoled and ministered while she meandered through glutinous mud.

"For thirty years the house rose in value," Gina said. "Value that you told your father, may he rest in peace, was arbitrary. Doesn't seem quite so arbitrary now, does it? If we keep the house, it will continue to grow in value. But if we sell it, what will we do in Boston when the money runs out?"

"If we sell it, the money will *never* run out." Harry assured her. "But we can't keep one house here and another in Boston. We can't keep running two large households. That's profligate. My way we're set for life, angel. We sell, we take the money, we put it in the bank and live off the interest. My way, no more mills, sewing machines, cleaning other people's houses. Your way, we continue to owe the bank money instead, paying for two homes instead of one. Your way, we are broke in ten years. My way, never."

"Live off the interest," was all Gina said in response. "A fine way for a former communist to speak."

Harry blinked, and fell quiet while he regrouped. But he couldn't quite circle around to a rolling wagon of command-economy persuasion. All he had was the rickety carriage of the free market.

"In Boston," he said, going a step further, a leap deeper, "if we're by some outside chance running low, I easily can get other work. In fact I'm counting on it. I'll have my doctorate. I intend to teach again. But what am I going to do here?"

When Gina said nothing, he took it as an opening. "I mean, just think about it. If we stay, what am I going to do? You heard Janke. Man without work has no meaning. And there is no work here for a man like me. Please. Just think about it from my point of view. My solution has everything going for it. Alexander, me, you, Esther. It has something in it for all of us. Your way has something in it only for you."

Your way has everything in it except Bellagrand. Did she say it to Harry or plead it to God?

"You can't have your feet in two states, in two lives," Harry said. "Bellagrand will buy you your Boston life. You will finally be the thing you once dreamed of, Harold Barrington's society wife. Everybody will call you Jane Barrington."

"And God won't know who I am, if I change my name." Gina's voice was faint.

"You already changed your name, my Simmons college girl. Long before me."

She didn't want to tell him she had changed it only for him. There was no profit in those confessions now.

Gina wavered. Gina swayed. He caught her swooning, and romanced her, and said things and did things to weaken her resolve, to dissipate her fear.

He kept appealing to the fundamental passion in her, to her most elemental longing of how to remake herself from a *povera contadina* to a lady of the manor. It *was* seductive, the way he spoke of it, to live on Beacon Hill. A woman of means with an adorable, perfectly mannered child, a handsome, old-moneyed husband, shiny patent shoes and alligator bags, made from other alligators, of course, not her son's.

She could have lunch with her fancy girlfriends at the Harvard Club, and on the weekends throw lavish parties and charity events, just like Alice once used to. She could be a patron of a church, or a park. She could walk Alexander to school and back, holding his hand on Charles Street. She could go dancing and shopping, buy the finest makeup and the latest flouncy skirts. Women's fashion had become so light, so appealing, so sensual. Who wouldn't be seduced by that, who wouldn't be swayed?

Gina played the ivory keys as she ambled through her house, trying to remember Schumann's melancholy "Traumerei." She sat at the piano and imagined leaving it all, giving it up, this material permanent thing with walls and windows, bartering it for a few unseen shekels in the bank. But the shekels would mean Beacon Hill and Harvard and fancy friends. It would mean restaurants, and opera, and society balls. She lay down on the glossy walnut floor. Once a house, but soon just invisible money behind a bank vault with a wheel for a lock. Now: grass, ocean, frogs, palms, a boat. Life. Soon: Boston, trains, noise, Alexander playing soccer. Also life …

There was romance in both, a desire for both. But the absence of one filled her womb with numb dread, as she imagined herself without this house in her future, without this view, or the sandy barefoot walk on the beach in the early mornings when the dolphins dived near the shore, deepest serenity, Fernando and his Spanish strings plucking "Rosario de mi Madre," while she sat outside in the night, sipping Bellinis and appletinis. *Esta será la última cita de los dos … this will be the last time for us both.*

Even that part was already behind her. Esther wasn't returning, nor Rosa. Herman was gone. Salvo, busier than ever, was never here. They had just lived it, and already it was receding into the rosy dimness before her eyes.

Gina wandered through the cavernous rooms and remembered going to one of Emma Goldman's lectures, back in 1908. Harry had long stopped going with her. She had gone with Angela. Emma's talk was called, "What I believe." In it she spoke about property. *"Property is not only a hindrance to human well-being,"* she had said, *"but an obstacle, a deadly barrier, to all progress. Property condemns millions of people to be mere nonentities, living corpses, machines of flesh and blood, who pile up mountains of wealth for others and pay for it with a gray, dull, and wretched existence for themselves."*

Am I that other? Gina wondered as she wandered, touching her plaster walls, her marble sinks, her blackwood doors. The windows were open and the salty breeze so fine in the late afternoon. She hadn't thought of Emma and her property rights in years. Emma Goldman had been deported to Russia on the *Buford* two years earlier. How did the anarchist and the communists get along on the *Soviet Ark*? She bet Harry would know. She wanted to ask him, but she didn't care. Now, recalling her idol while standing in the middle of Bellagrand, Gina felt that Emma Goldman was wrong. Their existence wasn't dank upheaval. It was shining grace.

What did Harry feel as he advocated selling? Did keeping Bellagrand mean to him that he was selling out his deepest principles? Gina was afraid of his answer.

"Gina, you have to decide what you want," Harry said. "We can't just keep riding the ocean waves and eating *ceviche*."

"You and I want different things," she said in a pinched voice.

"But we don't! You want the urban swell, too. You've always wanted it. And you're still the same girl I married, the same impetuous, wild, smart, full-of-life girl. Come on, Gia," he whispered into her neck, into her heart, between her breasts. "Don't you want to be young again, flamboyant, bedazzling? Don't you want to be *yourself*?"

The broken voice of Frances Barrington faded, whispering not crying about the *romance of youth*, and her own father's voice faded, too, admonishing her to *never forget where she came from*. Gina shut her heart to the dread, denied the ghost of premonitory terror within her, and agreed to move back to Boston.

Four

BEFORE SHE COULD CHANGE her mind, Harry called Salvo and asked him to put the house on the market. Gina told Harry she would give it two months. If it didn't sell in two months, she would know it wasn't supposed to leave their hands.

Bellagrand sold in a span of one post-lunch lull. Salvo brought the man in a suit at the hazy hour of three when everyone else was having a siesta. The man, Jon Turner, said he had a wife, but didn't consult her. After a tour of the house, he didn't even haggle. Salvo asked a price; Turner agreed to pay it before he walked down the front steps to the naked Aphrodite.

Gina balked. They sold too low, she said. That's why it went so quickly.

Harry disagreed. "We asked a fair price. My father had estimated this house to be worth a hundred thousand dollars. We were just offered double that."

"That's *my* point," she said. "In three years it has doubled in price. In three more years, it'll be worth half a million."

"We're not going to be here to see it. What if the housing market plummets? We won't be here to see that either."

Salvo smirked. "Harry, how often you say the zaniest things. This area is the most lucrative property market in the United States." He and Alexander were sucking the juice out of their oranges by holding the wedges to their lips and racing to see who could do it the fastest. They were making a big mess in the kitchen.

"Yes, yes," Harry said impatiently. "It's good now, a seller's market. It won't last."

"The market is very stable," said Salvo, mouth full of pulp.

"If by stable you mean volatile, Salvo, then yes," Harry said. "If we're forced to sell later, in a buyer's market, we'll lose money instead of make money. How is that smart?"

"My question is, is it smart to sell now?" asked Gina.

"Very, *very* stupid," said Trevor Jenkins, the Tequesta National Bank manager, who stood at their front door not two mornings later, admiring the blackwood. The bank manager was making a house call. Gina was impressed.

"*You're* Mr. Jenkins? Nice to finally meet you."

"What do you mean, Mrs. Barrington? We've met. You come into my bank twice a week. You signed the deed in my office."

"Of course." Gina had no recollection of him. "Won't you come in? Would you like some lemonade? I made it fresh this morning. We grow our own lemons."

Harry strode into the Great Hall and shook Jenkins's hand. "Mr. Jenkins, come try my fresh-squeezed orange juice instead." He smiled. "I should go into business for myself, it's *that* good. Right, Gia?"

"Right, Harry." A little slower, she followed both men into the kitchen, where Salvo was on the floor with Alexander, who was building an impossibly tall wall of wooden blocks, a termite building a mound a hundred times its own size. He had to get up on the table to finish the top of it.

"Salvo, get the boy off the table," said Harry, getting down a glass. "What do you think of our home, Mr. Jenkins?"

In Salvo's arms, Alexander was adding the last of the blocks to his tall tower.

Jenkins loudly fawned over the spaciousness, the light colors of the white and limestone kitchen, the lawn, even over Alexander.

"Tell him the child doesn't come with the house," Gina whispered to Harry as he poured the orange juice for the bank manager. Jenkins drank and then buttered up Harry over the orange juice.

"All right, Mr. Jenkins," Harry said. "Thank you. But now tell us—to what do we owe your unexpected visit?"

Jenkins wiped his mouth. "May I speak freely?" He glanced at Alexander and glared at Salvo, who smiled widely and took a mocking bow.

"Of course," Harry said.

"With all due respect, Mr. and Mrs. Barrington, I think Mr. Attaviano over there has advised you poorly. Very poorly. This is *not* the time to sell. Certainly not for what you've agreed to." He stuck out his clammy hand to Gina, shook hers softly and moistly. "Mrs. Barrington, you are one of our best customers."

"Thank you, Mr. Jenkins," said Gina.

Harry smirked.

"Yes, most certainly we would hate to lose your business to a Boston bank, but because of my own personal regard for your family, I'd like to give you a bit of invaluable advice, explain a few things. May I sit down?" He plonked himself down at the table near Alexander's blocks. They rattled. Now it was Alexander's turn to glare at the bank manager. Gina perched near him, but Harry continued to stand.

"Salvo," Harry said, picking up Alexander and handing him over. "Please, take Alexander swimming. I want to hear uninterrupted what Mr. Jenkins has to say. Don't worry, son, we won't touch your Egyptian pyramid. Now scoot."

"It's going to be a sweltering day," Jenkins said when the uncle and nephew had left. "You're lucky, your boy can spend all day in the pool." He smiled unctuously. "Won't be able to do that in Boston, will he? Quite cold there last week. I read it in the papers. June 15 was fifty-two degrees and raining."

"Tell us what you've come here to tell us, Mr. Jenkins," Harry said, formal, clipped, dressed in a sharp suit, Boston-sharp, not Bellagrand casual. "We don't have all day. The Turners are waiting for an answer."

"I fervently advise for that answer to be no," Jenkins said. "And I will tell you why." He coughed. "You have vastly underpriced your house in current market conditions. Oh, I'm not saying that's not what your house is worth. What I'm saying is, it's not what your house and all the other houses on the coast from Miami to Daytona are valued at. The houses here are in extraordinary demand. You're selling both too short and too soon." Jenkins nodded, wiping his brow. "But I'm not advising you to sell slightly higher. Just the opposite. I'm advising you to wait."

Gina glanced up at Harry triumphantly, but her triumph disappeared into his closed face. For some reason he wasn't buying what Jenkins was selling.

"In 1919," Jenkins told them, "a man bought undeveloped ocean frontage about fifteen miles south of here for a quarter an acre. That's twenty-five *cents* an acre, sir and madam. He just sold it for over a million dollars. Did you not read about it? It was all over the papers."

"We must have missed it," Harry said grimly.

"From twenty-five cents in 1919 to a million dollars in 1922. A tiny Miami lot that was bought six years ago for twenty-five dollars just sold for a hundred and fifty thousand dollars. Have you not heard that the *Miami Herald* has become the heaviest newspaper in the *world* because of its real estate advertisements? You have one of the rarest lots in the area, a house with two water frontages, both of them private beachheads. You have over two acres of property, a well-built, modernized house. I guarantee you, *guarantee* you," Jenkins repeated for emphasis, "your house will be worth five million dollars in two years' time. At *least*." He nodded into Gina's astonished face. "And to prove to you how certain I am of the upward trajectory of your one-of-a-kind home, I have already dropped the rate on your line of credit from six percent to three, and I will also forego all interest payments for the next twelve months. That's right. I will also," he quickly added, judging from Harry's face that he wasn't quite closing, "extend your equity line from its current outdated appraisal value, which is what Mr. Attaviano is trying to forfeit your house for, to eighty percent of what I *know* your house will be valued at by, say, 1925. I will give you three million dollars in credit right now, to use as your personal bank account. Oh, and Mrs. Barrington, just so your brother doesn't suffer because I'm advising you *not* to sell your home, I will pay him his commission on the lost sale out of the bank's regulatory fees."

Gina excitedly looked up at a silent Harry. Did she just hear Jenkins correctly? Did he just say …

"So let me understand," Harry said. "You will lend us—"

"Against the value of your home, naturally."

"Naturally. You will lend us three million dollars, halve our interest rate, waive all interest payments for one year, and pay Salvo's fat commission on a non-existent sale out of your own end." Harry made a skeptical but incredulous face. "Why would you do this?"

"You are one of our finest customers," repeated Jenkins. "I would like it to stay that way. Perhaps I forgot to mention," he added, "but we're in an unprecedented boom, Mr. Barrington."

"Did you say unsustainable?" said Harry, his voice dry.

"No, no." Jenkins slowed down his speech. "I said un-pre-ce-den-ted."

"Oh. Thank you for speaking slower."

"You're welcome, sir. I will do anything to keep your business and to keep you from making a lifelong mistake. It's your choice, of course."

"Thank you."

"Talk it over between yourselves. May I have a glass of your lemonade while I wait, madam? Your son looked to be enjoying it very much."

Harry grabbed for the lemonade pitcher. "We don't need to talk it over, Mr. Jenkins," he said, quickly pouring the bank manager a short glass.

"We don't?" said Gina.

"The lemonade is wonderfully sweet, madam. Your son is right." He smiled at Gina.

"We don't need to talk it over," Harry said, "because we agreed to sell this house to Jon Turner. His offer is already extravagant. Your way, Mr. Jenkins, forgive me for saying so, is how people lose their life savings. By being greedy, by wanting more. Nothing is ever enough. Well, we don't need more. The sale price is more than enough for us."

Gina raised her hands to stop him from speaking. "Harry … wait …"

"Mr. Jenkins, you don't have a crystal ball, do you?" Harry went on. "You can't see the future? Because that would be quite a trick if you could. But you can't promise me, can you, that the housing market won't sustain a bust." He downed a glass of his own orange juice. "You can't sign your name to *that* piece of paper, can you? The point of the market, as you well know, is that it fluctuates. Well, just try to imagine our life, Mr. Jenkins," Harry coolly continued, "if on the largesse you've extended us, my wife and I mortgage our new life in Boston. We buy a house, a boat or two, fine clothes, some automobiles. Maybe even a Rolls Royce. Why not? We've got your three million dollars. We're like my son in a candy store. And what happens if the market collapses and we are into your bank for a million, possibly even two? Where would we get the money from to repay you?"

"Well, you would sell your home, of course, Mr. Barrington," Jenkins said condescendingly.

"Would I, Mr. Jenkins?" Now it was Harry's turn to be condescending. "And what happens if I can't sell my home? What if there are no buyers? What if what we owe you is more than what the house is worth? Have you considered *that* possibility?"

Jenkins laughed. "There are people sleeping on the beaches, waiting for a house in this area to become available! I don't know what you're talking about."

"I'm talking about a housing bust."

"Why would there be a housing bust?"

Harry glanced interrogatively at the sullen and unwilling Gina.

"What you're saying makes no sense," Jenkins continued. "I will admit the market sometimes corrects itself slightly. But it doesn't fall off a cliff."

"I understand." Harry shook his head. "It's a risk my wife and I are simply not willing to take. Right, Gina?"

What could she say? Did she have a crystal ball? Could she see the future? Salvo impeccably dressed in silk! The house receiving an offer from the first buyer! Jenkins extending them a three million dollar line of credit, nearly the gross national product of Sicily. It didn't seem, with what was in front of her, as if Harry could ever be right. And yet, living on borrowed money was anathema to her. Life was unpredictable. There was fear in her heart of everything.

"You're right, Harry," Gina said, in an uncertain whisper.

Harry extended his hand to the perspiring and perplexed bank manager. "Thank you so much for making the trip to see us, Mr. Jenkins. I'm sorry it was for nothing." The three of them stared outside to the lawn where Alexander was showing Salvo how to catch a wading secretive bittern. "It's true, the boy likes it here very much," Harry said. "But he is a young boy, and soon he will start school. He needs a different life. This will be a great house for another family. I won't keep you a moment longer."

After they showed an unhappy Jenkins out, they stood on the porch over the bleached stone drive and smelled the ocean air from across the road. Gina kept her mind deliberately blank and her face placid. Harry took her hand. He told her that in the spring, he used to stand on the front step of his house in Barrington and inhale for the wind wafting in from the mighty Atlantic ten miles away. The briny easterly breezes foretold that summer was just around the corner.

Five

WE STAYED IN VALHALLA long enough, Gina quietly cried as she showed the movers how to pack and mark her crates and boxes. That's how well off they had become. She didn't pack her own things anymore. She hired men to do it for her.

Anticipation of imminent change overcame other misgivings, like the night sweats she began having as they got closer to leaving. Eldorado was what she carried inside her, she said to calm herself down. Anywhere they went, as long as they went together, they would find their Eldorado again. She said that, yes, but she would wake up in the night, gasping, unable to go back to sleep. What is it, Harry would ask. What are you dreaming about? She couldn't remember. She saw herself sitting in an empty room behind a table.

"Well, that doesn't sound very scary," he purred to comfort her. "You sit behind a table three times a day when you eat. Who's in the room with you?"

"No one. Like I'm waiting for someone dreadful to arrive."

"Where am I? Where is Alexander?"

"That's the thing." She would cry, her face in her hands. "I don't know. I sit at this table, and I don't know where anyone is. It feels as if everyone's gone."

"And then what happens?"

"What happens? I wake up. Like this."

"Why don't you stay asleep a little longer so you can find out where you are? That way you won't be afraid anymore."

"I can't," Gina said. "I feel such a black terror, I can't."

He held her close, rubbed her back, kissed her hair, murmured to her. "Tables can be very scary, my love. I understand. Shh."

They packed up their things and sold their cars. Two taxis came to take them to the train. Fernando stayed composed as he held Alexander. "My little man, you're going to do great in Boston. Are you kidding? You are going to have so much fun. Big cities are fun, *mi amigo*. You'll see. You will love it like I love Miami. In the big city, everything happens at once."

On the train north, Harry took hold of Gina's hand. "Are you all right?"

"I'm all right." She forced a smile.

"Don't you feel it's the absolute right move?"

Nodding, she pressed her lips into the back of Alexander's head and stared out the window, with him on her lap, as the train gained speed, rolling between the two waters, palm trees gleaming, sun shining, people already on their boats, two boys flying a kite, the bromeliads, the cypress swamps, the American jungle frontier receding from view. Salvo had wept when they said goodbye the night before. She had asked him to sing, but he couldn't, his voice kept breaking. She asked him to sing her favorite song from *Tosca*, "E Lucevan Le Stelle." Usually he sang it to pierce the heart, his beautiful multi-octave tenor carrying to Tequesta across the water, as if he himself were Tosca's doomed lover. But not last night. He was out of pitch, up and down the whole song, and couldn't finish when he got to *svani per sempre*. *Vanished forever*. Gina hadn't seen her brother cry since Sicily, since their father died. She couldn't think about it now as she held Alexander, who was banging very loudly on the window, trying to get the attention of the ladies in their boats below the moving train. Why had Salvo been upset? Was it because his adored *nipote* was leaving? Or was there an omen in his sorrow? Did he fear that he might never see his sister and her family again? He wouldn't answer when she had asked him. You'll come for Christmas, Salvo, she said, full of hollow assurances, and we'll be back to visit, we're just a few states up north, we're not in another country.

Like Russia.

Like Panama.

"I know you thought it was Shangri-la," Harry said on the train, throwing his arm around her, kissing her, kissing Alexander. "Now Beacon Hill will replace it. Son, please, don't bang so loud on the glass.

The conductor says you're going to break it. And the girls can't hear you anyway."

Gina didn't want to correct her American-bred husband; after all, he had graduated summa from Harvard, and she didn't even graduate from lowly Simmons. So she didn't mention that Shangri-la was an imaginary fantasia, a place that existed only in Mozart's sheet music and in the mind of the heart. It wasn't real. Whereas, there was nothing imaginary about Bellagrand, except that now it was wholly in the past, and nothing made that clearer than the first-class compartment on a train that clanged its way north and away from what was and would never be again to things that weren't yet but were about to be very soon. The train was the moment of dizzy suspension between two worlds. It was the ocean liner from Naples to Boston. It was the train from Boston to Lawrence. It was the train from Boston to Spanish City. How pretty it had looked to her years ago, before Alexander was born. How full of untapped promise. There had been a carnival on the outskirts, she had watched it from above, from her train window. She searched for it now, the Ferris wheel, the arcades. She remembered Alexander sitting on the carousel, on a white horse, clutching the reins and the pole, a toddler horseman, spinning around the circle of joy with the happy beat beat beat of the lilting music.

How to bring up the Blaise Pascal quote Gina had found transcribed as the last entry in Harry's open and disjointed journal, written out in his precise careful hand. She had read it while they were packing to go.

Our nature consists in motion; complete rest is death ... Nothing is so insufferable to man as to be completely at rest, without passions, without business, without diversion, without study. He then feels his nothingness, his forlornness, his insufficiency, his dependence, his weakness, his emptiness. There will immediately arise from the depth of his heart weariness, gloom, sadness, fretfulness, vexation, despair.

Inspector Javert could not have been right, could she?

Shangri-la.

Are there carnivals in Boston, she asked him, her voice fading, like that of Frances Barrington, like that of Alessandro Attaviano.

Every day, baby, Harry said, there will be a carnival.

Part Three

THE MAN WITHOUT A COUNTRY
1922–1929

The rain was pouring down,
The moon was shining bright,
And everything that you could see
Was hidden out of sight.
—**Anonymous**

Whither is fled the visionary gleam?
Where is it now, the glory and the dream?
—**Wordsworth**

Chapter 15

ISADORA AND SERGEI

One

THEY RENTED A GRAND old brownstone on Mt. Vernon, the finest of all fine streets in Beacon Hill, just a few doors down from Henry Cabot Lodge's house. The home they found was spacious, if a touch musty, but the kitchen was renovated, and the light-hued walls and rugs reflected electricity usage instead of coal, which made all things dank and dark with its by-product soot. The house had light. It wasn't *white*, like the other house. Some of the walls between rooms had been knocked down, giving the illusion of space. Harry and Gina wanted to buy, but the owners weren't selling. It had been his wife's family homestead since the early 1800s, the weary husband explained. They weren't living in it now because it was too cold for them in the winters, so they had moved to South Florida, of all places. They wanted a quiet respectable family to take care of their prized Beacon Hill property. The Barringtons, with a professorial, Boston Brahmin husband and only one child, seemed ideal.

Harry told Gina not to worry. They would move in and take their time to look for the perfect house to buy.

They had left Bellagrand in early August, during the muggiest of muggy weather, but in Boston things weren't much cooler. Boston was airless and stifling, and, as Gina pointed out to a less than receptive Harry, the warmest of oceans was no longer twenty yards across the road.

Esther's reunion with Alexander was an extended tearful embrace. For as long as Salvo had cried saying goodbye, Esther now cried saying hello. "I'm so happy you're here," she kept saying to a delighted but confounded boy. She offered to take Alexander to her newly bought summer cottage in Truro, to give Harry and Gina a month to themselves—to look for a house, buy furniture, apply to Harvard, settle in, make friends, hire help, and all without worrying about what to do with a child in the city. Rosa and I will take him clamming, Esther said. The fishermen would love to show him how to do it. Alexander didn't know what clamming was, but was thrilled nonetheless. Gina and Esther were formal with each other, as if they had just met.

"Alexander, I was going to give you lunch," Esther said, carrying him away to the nearby car with Clarence waiting, "but you are very heavy. What are they feeding you?"

"I'm big for my age, Mama says."

"Your mother is right. Maybe no lunch for you today then? You look as if you've had plenty to eat."

"Aunty Esther, I'm starving. *Zio* Salvo always feeds me a lot."

"Does he? Well, then, I'll have to feed you even more. Did he feed you ice cream?"

"Two scoops and fudge."

"I know a place where they'll give you three scoops, fudge, and whipped cream. Let's go there now." Esther didn't look back as they sped down Mt. Vernon.

Gina and Harry spent the month overheated and buying new furniture. They had left everything behind, even Harry's favorite malachite table, even the mosaic table he had made himself.

They engaged a charmless but highly recommended real estate agent, who did not wear silk suits or cart small boys around, but who did take Harry and Gina to look at the available properties in the area. Houses were expensive, and nothing was as beautifully located as the sprawling brownstone they had rented. They decided to stay put. Gina found Alexander a playgroup on Byron Street that all the pre-school-age Beacon Hill children attended. It would be good for Alexander to play with other children, and she could make friends with the Beacon Hill mothers.

But in September, when she started taking him, she discovered that the women who brought the children were not the mothers but the nannies. The mothers were at recitals and conservatory meetings, having fundraising lunches, buying art for the Boston Museum, and opening hospital wings. Gina wanted to make friends, but knew socializing with nannies wasn't appropriate. She looked up her old friend Verity, who had lived in Back Bay, but learned to her disappointment that Verity was back in Lawrence with her husband and seven children. Seven! She had more than enough for a volleyball team. Gina kept meaning to visit her.

A few blocks down Mt. Vernon on Louisburg Square lived a beautiful, vivacious woman named Meredith, wife of a financier and a mother of two, one of them a boy Alexander's age. She had the potential to be a friend, and Gina made a determined effort to find common ground with the stylish and well-connected woman. She seemed to grasp well the intricacies of the social calendar and the duties expected of a Beacon Hill wife.

The first thing Meredith did was advise Gina to hire a full-time nanny, without which, the young woman said, it was much more difficult to keep to a proper schedule. Big money needed to be spent to make Boston more modern, more literary, more progressive. The symphonies, the concerts and the lavish dinners were not going to organize themselves. Gina ignored Meredith's principal piece of advice as long as she could, changing the subject, even laughing it away. "You're so funny, Meredith," Gina would say.

"But I'm not trying to be funny, Jane," Meredith would reply.

"I know. That's why you're funny."

Gina suggested activities she and Meredith could do together with their children, like walking in the Public Garden, or going to the Freedom Docks, parts of which were being converted into an immigrant museum. Meredith would think for a moment. "You mean the two of us, with the children and the nanny?"

"I was thinking without the nanny."

"Without the nanny? But what if the children need something?"

Gina shifted from foot to foot at Meredith's front door. "What could they need? Like an ice cream?"

"Well, I don't know, do I? But I know they need things because Gemma is always fetching one thing or another."

Gina pulled on Meredith's sleeve. "Come on. It's a beautiful afternoon." Alexander stood almost quietly by her side, holding a soccer ball, every once in a while whispering, "Mom, let's go, Mom, let's go, letsgoletsgo—MOM."

"Darling," Meredith said with a disapproving glance at both mother and son, "you simply *must* hire a nanny. It'll make your life *so* much easier."

"My life is not very hard," Gina said. "All I do is play with my boy."

"That's what I mean," said Meredith, arching her perfect eyebrows.

It took a month for Gina to ease Meredith into the Public Garden for a "quick" walk, fitted in grudgingly before pre-opera cocktails, an invitation to which Gina and Harry had politely declined.

"Why are we going to the Public Garden?" Meredith grumbled. "It's not Sunday. I'll walk with you there on Sunday. That's when all the mothers walk their children, after church and brunch on Sunday afternoon."

"We can go then, too," Gina said. "But today Alexander and Walter want to play ball."

"Darling, please don't tell me you still haven't followed my advice to hire someone. Good help is the one true measure of a respectable home."

"I have a housekeeper, if that's what you mean. She is very good."

"That's not what I mean," Meredith said, her eyes flicking to Alexander, who was running ahead with Walter and his tag-along toddler sister, Mabel.

Gina nodded. "Trouble is, Meredith," she said, "it took me a really long time to have my one child, and I don't want someone else to take care of him. *I* want to take care of him."

"But that's just not how it's done, darling," Meredith said. "It's simply not done. Where *are* you from?"

"Sicily."

"Sicily? Really! You must tell Edward. He'll be fascinated. He studied the African cultures at Brown. He'd love to talk to you about it. When are you free for dinner?"

"Sometimes Harry's sister takes Alexander on the weekends. Maybe then?"

Harry found Edward an unacceptable bore, and the four of them didn't get together as often as Gina would have liked.

It was a shame, because Gina really wanted to establish a friendship.

Harry would try to make her feel better. "What can I tell you? Maybe she can get herself a more scintillating husband. If I hear one more word about the taxidermy of gazelles, I'll taxidermy him. And you—hire a nanny and you'll fit right in. The ladies of the house do not cook their own meals."

"Or look after their own children."

Harry would shrug. "Now, in Florida you stepped all over Emilio's toes by meddling in his kitchen—"

"You mean *my* kitchen."

"He was a good sport about it. But here, it's not done. The housekeepers will gossip. Their ladies will gossip. And then the men will gossip about me."

"Better that than another word about antelopes," she said.

He laughed, catching her in an embrace. "Quite right. But do you really want to socialize with people who need a lesson in geography with their cocktails? You keep trying to explain to them that Sicily is not part of Africa. They're not grasping it, though."

"Perhaps it's the language barrier," Gina said. "It's like Babel."

While Gina settled into their new life, Harry settled into his. He took a long time to apply to Harvard's doctoral program. They had moved too late for him to attend the fall semester, but he made plans to start in the spring, researching a number of dissertation topics in the meantime.

Their first fall in Boston, he was even-tempered and happy, except for one early morning in October, 1922, when he fumed more than usual after glancing at the newspaper.

"Did you see the way they treated her?" he said. "It's shameful. Just shameful."

"Who?"

"I thought you'd seen the papers."

Gina usually got up before Harry and glanced over the news as she made breakfast and got ready for the day. "Obviously not carefully. What happened?"

Harry threw the paper down in disgust and went upstairs. Gina flicked through the front pages. She found nothing there, but buried in the arts section was a short article on Isadora Duncan's dance performance the night before at the Boston Theater. The mayor of Boston banned Duncan from performing in Boston ever again after she bared her breasts to the public and yelled, "Life is not real here!"

There was something else, too. She had held up a flowing red scarf and proclaimed that red was the color of life and vigor. "This is red," Isadora Duncan shouted. "And so am I!"

"Do you think the mayor is being unreasonable?" Gina asked Harry when he returned downstairs.

"Unreasonable? He's abhorrent. Where is Alexander? I'm going to the Athenaeum. I want to say goodbye."

"Still asleep," Gina said. "You can go and wake him." She studied her husband thoughtfully. "I didn't realize you were such an aficionado of Isadora. We should've gone to see her perform."

"Hardly aficionado. Besides, all the tickets were sold out. But the woman comes to our city on tour and the officials treat her with contempt."

Gina stirred her coffee. "Isn't she now a Russian citizen?"

"What does *that* have to do with anything? The mayor is scaremongering."

"Maybe. But what do you care?"

"I don't. I just think it's shameful." He bent to her for a kiss. "I'll go wake him. I promised him I'd take him to a soccer game later today. Where are you going to be?"

"Nowhere." She paused. "I was thinking of going to Lawrence to visit Verity."

He laughed. "Yes, okay, but on the off chance you don't go, where can we meet up? I feel I'm close to choosing a new topic. I want to play with Alexander, but I also can't wait to talk to you about it."

Harry spent almost a year deciding on his dissertation and thesis. He couldn't find a topic worthy of his interest. Every morning he left the house all dressed up, as if he were going to work at the bank, and walked up the street to the Athenaeum, just past City Hall, where they had been married. The Athenaeum was the oldest library in the United States, with entry by special membership only. It was not open to the general public. Access to it was one of the perks of belonging to the exclusive Beacon Hill Club. Harry loved going to the Athenaeum not just because the stacks were private, but because the depth of the library's research materials was profound. He said he had never worked so hard in his life at anything. He spent long days there. Initially he had wanted to choose a topic involving Russian literature or poetry, but Gina talked him out of it. She thought he should stay away from all things Russian. Kenneth Femmer, Harry's probation officer, wouldn't approve, she said. Harry agreed.

After a fall and spring of studying, reading, researching, and talking to Gina about his plans, when it came time to apply to Harvard, Harry demurred. A week or two later, he told her he would not be comfortable going there and was thinking of applying instead to another university to get his doctoral degree.

Gina was taken aback. "I thought the whole point was to go to Harvard, your alma mater. Isn't that what you told me in Jupiter?"

"That's just it," he said. "That's precisely the part I don't enjoy anymore. I didn't know I was going to feel this way, but I have too many bad memories of being poorly treated by the economics chair, and by my peers—the people I thought were my friends—and also by the students. Their sense of entitlement is matched only by their arrogance. I'm just not comfortable with the thought of returning." He shrugged. "Live and learn. I find the place repulsive, to be perfectly honest. I hope never to set foot on that campus again."

She didn't know what to say. She said nothing.

"It's not a problem, Gia. I'm allowed to go to a university other than Harvard while I'm on probation."

"I said nothing."

"I just want a different intellectual environment. I want new friends, and respect. A fresh start. I'll clear it with Femmer. I'm sure it won't be a problem for me to go to Medford."

"What's in Medford?"

"Tufts."

"That's where you want to go?"

"Very much. The school has an excellent reputation."

Gina tried to calculate the distance in her head. "I think it's too far."

"Too far from what? It's not even as far as Barrington."

"You don't go to Barrington." He hadn't been there once since they moved to Boston.

"It's not even as far as Lawrence," he said.

She hadn't been there once since they moved to Boston.

"I'll take the car," he said. "It won't be bad. I won't be gone long. I'll try not to have too many seminars at night."

"*Too* many? How about none? And Harry, we don't have a car."

He smiled broadly. "We'll have to buy one then, won't we?"

Harry applied to Tufts and was accepted. His probation was ending in early 1924, a year early. Harry was glad. He had no relationship with Ken Femmer, an elderly gentleman forty years on the job. He often talked about how much he missed Margaret Janke.

"Because that's what you want," Gina said. "Avid rapport with the guards who watch over you." But what she was really thinking was: the only thing Harry said he missed about the Florida life was Margaret Janke.

They bought a fancy car, a powerful and expensive black Mercedes. They had to rent a space for it, because Boston was now so full of cars that there was nowhere to park on the streets. They found a carriage house, where, barely twenty years earlier, wealthy Bostonians had kept their horses.

Two

BOSTON IS A REMARKABLE CITY. Gina was always exceptionally fond of it. Being in a city—with shops and pavements and parks and people—made for a different daily existence than seeing nothing but water and sky every day, palms and frogs, mangroves and moss oaks, leisure boats, orchids. Not better. Different.

In Boston she would enjoy dressing up her family in their finery and walking through the Public Garden on Sunday afternoons when everyone was out with their children and parasols, smiling, nodding, chatting amiably with one another. The vendors sold ice cream and drinks on Charles Street, and the Park Avenue Hotel served a delicious Sunday brunch. Gina would almost not miss Emilio and his comparatively pedestrian preparations. Alexander would run ahead of them, and she and Harry would walk arm in arm, Harry tipping his hat every five minutes, Gina nodding and smiling.

"We are so well trained," Harry said.

"Like puppets," said Gina. "Tip, nod, smile, move onward, tip, nod, smile."

"And yell—Alexander, not too far!"

"Alexander, not too far!"

Tip, nod, smile.

The one thing they couldn't find common ground on was what church service to attend. In Tequesta, it had been all about the Catholics, and Harry, in any case, wasn't allowed to leave the house even for weekly worship. So it didn't matter what Harry wanted, because every Sunday Gina took Alexander with Fernando and a frequently hungover, yet repentant Salvo to St. Domingo Ibanez. But in Boston, the only Catholic church Gina wanted to attend was St. Leonard's in the North End, and Harry had no interest in going there. If he would attend anything, he said, it would be the Congregational Park Avenue Church. Gina tried attending it. Once. But everything in the service, from the beginning to the non-Eucharist end, was alien to her. "Why don't they read 'Our Father'?" she asked Harry as they were leaving.

"I don't know."

"Seems odd not to read the Lord's Prayer."

"I don't know why they don't."

"Yes, you said. But why wasn't there a Eucharist?"

"They don't do that."

"But why?"

"I don't know."

"Yes, you said."

So every Sunday, Harry would stay home and catch up on his work, and Gina would take Alexander to St. Leonard's.

Sometimes Esther would come to Beacon Hill on Sunday afternoons to have dinner with them. She was polite, complimented Gina on the house, the furniture, ate like a bird, but ate whatever Italian preparation Gina put in front of her and praised it, played with Alexander, took him to the park, talked to her brother, and then made her leave before Alexander's bedtime. Civilized and casual. Gina and Harry didn't once go up to Barrington to have dinner at Harry's father's house that now belonged to Esther.

Gina asked Harry why they didn't go, and at first he said that Esther's coming to them was more convenient, which Gina couldn't argue with, but which also didn't answer her question. When prodded, Harry admitted he no longer felt comfortable in Barrington. So she stopped prodding, and they never went. Every other Friday afternoon, Esther would have Clarence drive her down to Boston, and they would pick up Alexander and take him back to Barrington for the weekend.

This allowed Gina and Harry to spend time alone, to get dressed up and go dancing, to listen to jazz, to go to dinner at their new friends' houses. The dancing was enjoyable, more so than the dinners, which Gina would find burdensome, though she couldn't pinpoint why. In anticipation of the evenings, she would go shopping on Newbury Street, where she would buy beautiful dresses, silk skirts, suede shoes, crepe hats, white gloves. She had her curly, unruly, slightly graying hair colored and styled. Dressed in smart evening garb, off she and Harry would trot, perhaps to Meredith and Edward's, or to dine with Barnaby, who had just lost his wife to an undisclosed illness and sorely needed some companionship, or to William and Nancy's, a fetching young couple, who lived in a house overlooking the Boston Common on Beacon Street, where kings and ambassadors had lived. Gina enjoyed walking downhill to them, though she liked the slog back uphill at the end of the night somewhat less.

But this was the thing: the gatherings and dinners inside the plush and well-appointed homes were less successful in reality than in her mental renditions. The problem was Harry. He would act like such a stick in the mud. While everyone else would buzz with talk about libraries and parks and fall fairs, about industry and economy and politics and the stock market, about who and how much and where and what was good and why and what was going to be good in two months, Harry would sit and palm his glass of wine. When he was asked by the men at the table what he thought of the rising value of real estate, the farm prices, the factory overproduction, Harding's sudden death, Coolidge's ascension, or the civil war in Russia, he would mumble—literally mumble—some non-response and turn the subject around to the questioner. He did not argue, did not object, did not engage. He was no longer the objection-maker; he was the furniture. His doltish lack of participation would occasionally prick Gina into a squall of an unwanted argument instead of half-sober love at the end of an evening.

"Most couples have jealous fights after a night of drinking," Harry said late one evening as they were climbing, panting, up steep Charles Street and Gina was goading him to bicker with her. "Not us."

"I'm not fighting, Harry. I'm striving for understanding."

"Are you? What's not to understand? I'm not interested in the things they talk about. I have no opinion."

"But, darling, tonight Edward, instead of his usual savannah harangues, brought up the recent Scopes trial and William Jennings Bryan. You love this subject."

"Hardly love. It piqued my interest for five minutes when Scopes was first arrested."

"You were thinking of reading a seminar on it. And yet you said nothing."

"Tonight I had nothing to say about it. Bryan and Darrow went at it in court, like the mortal enemies that they were. It's what we were all expecting. Bryan gave it his all and died of a brain hemorrhage five days later. Darrow's fine oratorical skills weren't enough. Scopes was convicted in a kangaroo court despite them. Fined one hundred dollars. What's to discuss?"

"You could've said all *that*."

"What's the point? They think Darrow is a hero."

"I thought you liked persuading those who disagree with you to come around to your opinion?"

"I no longer care what anyone thinks or believes."

That was it. There was a supercilious whiff to his dismissal of friendly conversation with others. It was as if he deemed them to be little more than ants arguing.

"Last week Meredith brought up the Teapot Dome scandal," Gina said, "and I know how fond you are of discussing bribery and conspiracy in high places at oil companies."

"Not last week," said Harry, "and not with a woman. What am I going to do? Argue with a woman in her own home at a dinner she had her kindly cook prepare for me? That is not what I do, Gina."

"I understand. But Barnaby, who so wants to be your friend, was desperately trying to drag you into a discussion about Chrysler's new $1500 car, which you said you might want, and the reduced working hours at U.S. Steel, and you—"

"And I refused to be dragged in?" Harry nodded. "I'm not interested. I'm studying unrelated things at Tufts. My dissertation is on Thermopylae."

"I know." She paused. She had something to say about that, too. "That's not unrelated. It's metaphorically significant."

"Only to you. I'm interested in the actual history."

"How is that going by the way?" It seemed as if he had spent years on the dissertation, and it still wasn't done.

"It's coming along." He shrugged it off. "Admittedly slowly. I'm trying to get it right. The subject is complex. Did I tell you the amazing thing the Greek king Leonidas said to Xerxes at the hot gates to the pass when the Persian demanded the surrender of Sparta's weapons?"

"You told me," Gina said. "Leonidas said, *come and take them*."

"Isn't that incredible?"

"You know what's incredible?" She was irritated and out of breath. "That a man who spent twenty years of his life advocating and demonstrating against military action of any kind, even going to prison for his beliefs, Wilson's whitest dove if you will, would write his doctoral paper on the bloodiest, most brutal battle of them all."

"I am interested in many things, Gina," Harry said. There was that loftiness again. "Why does that surprise you?"

"Yes, many things. Not Clarence Darrow, or Chrysler, or even Theodore Dreiser."

"Other things."

Was it her imagination or had Harry become disengaged from their daily life? He was studying so much at home and at the Athenaeum, reading, writing, muttering under his breath, driving to and from Tufts, busy, busy, busy with everything but her. *The scarlet flowers of passion seem to grow in the same meadow as the poppies of oblivion.*

Who said that? Was it that wisecracker Oscar Wilde again?

They stopped speaking as they climbed their way to Mt. Vernon.

Yes, Boston is a marvelous town. Everything a town should have, Boston has in abundance. It's a walking town, which means it's intimate, despite being large. It's technologically advanced. It's aesthetically beautiful. It sits on a mighty ocean and perches on the banks of a winding, not too wide river. It has universities and libraries and parks. It has shopping and nightlife, restaurants and opera. It is populated with beautiful, bountiful people, people who are sensible and polite, well-dressed and well-mannered.

There is no other city Gina would rather live in. And she lives in the most beautiful part of Boston, perched on a hill overlooking a park and the city skyline. The salty smells of the nearby ocean fly in on the wings of breezes. What could be better? She dresses elegantly, like a lady, and everyone sees it. Her son is stunning, and everyone sees that, and admires *her* for having a boy such as he. What a successful mother, what an accomplished woman she must be to have a tall, handsome, well-behaved boy. Alexander's greatness is Gina's reflected glory.

Her husband is bookish, scholarly, erudite, and amiable (mostly), studying (and studying and studying) to be a doctor of letters, so he can become that most respected of things, a professor. After all those years of toiling for pennies, she doesn't have to work. What a blessing. She joins a reading club, a parents' club, a park conservatory committee. She becomes a charter member of the Daughters of Boston, fundraising for all the right causes. She volunteers at the Boston Library on Copley Square. She buys a sewing machine and makes dresses and skirts, which she donates to the local branch of St. Vincent's. She volunteers at St. Vincent's. As before, in Lawrence, working at St. Vincent's eventually starts to overwhelm the hours of her day, because there is so much to be done. But she manages. She takes Alexander with her everywhere. They are rarely apart, except when he is at school or when Harry plays soccer with him at the park.

Alexander hasn't suffered as she had feared. He has blossomed. He loves his weekends with his aunty; he has made friends in Barrington—a boy named Teddy, a girl named Belinda. Esther jokes that she has trouble calling him in for tea because the three of them are always out in the yard, in the woods, by the creek. Esther's laughing face sometimes clouds at that point, as if she wants to add *like Harry and Ben* to that sentence, but of course doesn't, and Harry is long gone anyway, in another room.

Gina reads and cooks and shops and cleans. When Alexander is old enough to attend kindergarten, she busies herself until the hours have passed and it's time to go get him. When he starts grade school at Park Street Kids on Brimmer Street, she walks him there each morning, hand in hand, and then busies herself until it is time to pick him up again. She dedicates herself to the full-time tasks of household maintenance and child-rearing, to being a good and loving wife. If someone asked her to describe herself, Gina, without pause, would say, I am Jane Barrington, and I am Alexander's mother.

But she is also Harry's wife.

The Russian civil war over, the Union of Soviet Socialist Republics named, Lenin dead of cerebral hemorrhage, *The Great Gatsby* all the rage.

Alexander four, five, six, rifles out of sticks, frogs as bombs, cannons not soccer balls. Everything he holds in his hands he makes into a weapon.

1923, 1924, 1925. Like seconds, the years tick tock by.

Why would Isadora Duncan's words come back to haunt her at the oddest times? Why would Gina remember that peculiar woman, a sensualist who lost her children to a tragedy, who danced with abandon through Boston on her last tour of the United States, who married Sergei Esenin, a Russian poet eighteen years her junior, who left her and then hanged himself? "Life is not real here!"

Goodbye my friend, goodbye, Esenin wrote in his own blood before he died. *There is nothing new in dying, but living also is no newer.*

Life is not real here.

Chapter 16

BATTERY WAGNER

One

"ALEXANDER, DID I EVER tell you the story of a man named Samuel Sebastiani?"

"No. Tell me now."

They were ambling through the Public Garden. It was summer, 1926. Gina took his hand. Alexander let her. At seven he was still young enough not to be embarrassed by his mother. She wore a wide white hat with a purple silk ribbon. He wore a light skimmer cap, which made his hair appear almost black. They made quite a picture shimmering together down the floral paths. Maybe they would have time to get some ice cream before she had to be back to start dinner.

"Samuel was born in Italy."

"Just like you."

"Yes. But in Tuscany."

"That's not like you."

"Right. In Tuscany his family grew grapes, and made wine. He came to America when he was eighteen. He was penniless."

"That's not like you either. You were fourteen."

"Right. Samuel went to San Francisco."

"That's not like …"

"Alexander." Gina put an affectionate hand on the boy's shoulder. "You don't have to point out every difference between my story and Samuel's. It's not a game of spot the difference. It's a listening game."

"Oh! How do you play?"

"I talk, you listen."

"Oh."

"Now then. Where was I?"

"He was penniless in San Francisco."

"Precisely. He worked for three years in a quarry in Sonoma, cutting up cobblestones."

Alexander raised his hand.

"You don't have to raise your hand, *mio figlio*. What is it?"

"What's a quarry?"

Gina fought the impulse to cover him with kisses in public. "It's a big dusty pit in the ground which is mined for rocks and stones."

"Oh."

Like the granite quarry your father and I meandered to, alone for five minutes, me in a sheer pink froth, like bubblegum, him in a suit, our whole life in front of us, feeling happier than we had the right to feel, wanting nothing more than to be together. Quarry also means prey. I hope that doesn't apply here, to me and your dad.

"In 1896," she continued, after the barest of pauses, "Samuel bought a wagon with four horses, loaded up this wagon with cobblestones and carted them to San Francisco, where he began supplying the city with much needed building material. A few years went by. He made money. Lots of money. He made enough money to buy the quarry."

"He must have been rich."

She nodded. "He saved his pennies. He did well. The stones from his quarry were used to build the city hall in Sonoma."

"What's city hall?"

She pointed far across the sloping expanse of the Boston Common to the shining gold dome on top of Beacon Hill. "*That's* our city hall. A big government building. In which your father and I got married, by the way. Not important. By 1904, Samuel had saved enough to buy some

425

land to grow grapes. And he bought and bought, and grew and grew, just like his family did in Tuscany. He made the grapes into wine. He built the Sonoma Valley, which is where the wine industry was born in the United States."

Alexander was quiet. Gina waited. "Well?"

"You and Dad got married in a government building?"

"*Madre di Dio!* That's all you have to say?"

"What is wine?"

"Something adults can't drink anymore. It's a delicious adult beverage."

"Why can't you drink it?"

Gina smiled. "Too much of it makes you silly in the head. Our government decided it didn't want us to get silly in the head. So they outlawed wine."

"What's outlaw wine?"

Gina laughed.

"Mom …" Alexander furrowed his brow. "What does it have to do with me?"

"Every story has something to do with you, son."

"You keep saying that. But how does this one?"

"Well, think about it, and you tell me."

He thought about it. "I never want to get married, yuck, but if I ever did, I want to get married in a church, like Aunty Esther."

Gina shook her exasperated head. "No, *cuore mio*. Samuel is the kind of man I want you to be. If the good Lord gives you five stones, make ten from them. If he gives you fifty, make a hundred. He gives you one? You make two. Work like Samuel. Turn your stones into wine, Alexander. Do you understand?"

"You want me to dig for stones?"

"No …"

"Drive a wagon?"

"No."

"Make horses into wine?"

"No—" The sun was going straight to her head. "Why must you be so literal?"

"What's literal?"

Both Gina and Alexander stopped speaking. Across Charles Street on the Boston Common, they heard a distant booming voice. They waited for the cars to pass. They crossed the road. There was a crowd assembled on the grass.

But the voice! It sounded troublingly familiar. A needle went into Gina's heart. They stepped closer, Gina holding Alexander tightly by the hand. "Don't be afraid, son," she said. "They're a little boisterous."

"I'm not afraid," he said calmly.

She pushed on, standing on tiptoe, trying to see the speaker.

"It sounds like Dad, doesn't it, Mom?"

Gina gripped Alexander's hand.

"Mom, let go. Ouch."

"Sorry."

The voice was so intense! But that's not how Harry spoke. He was measured, thoughtful, evenly calibrated. It was rare for Gina to hear his unmodulated voice. Yet here it was, and in public. She paid no attention to the content as she pushed through the crowd, muttering to the old men and young women, pardon me, excuse me, dragging Alexander behind her.

The crowd was lapping up the speaker's words. All around her they hooted and clapped. Some booed, shouted things, but everyone was engaged, fired up.

Finally, Gina and Alexander stepped forward into the open area in front of the speaker. It can't be him, she thought, paling, her entire Beacon Hill world fading, washing away in the highest tide, just like that, before her eyes.

"Long LIVE the proletariat as it goes forth to renew the WHOLE world! Long LIVE the working men and women of all lands! By the strength of their HANDS they built up the WEALTH of nations! They now LABOR to create new LIFE! Long LIVE Socialism, the religion of the FUTURE! Greetings to the fighters, to the WORKERS of all lands! Have faith in the victory of TRUTH, the victory of JUSTICE! Long LIVE humanity, fraternally united in the great ideals of equality and freedom!"

"Look, it's Dad," said Alexander.

Two

HARRY GLANCED AT THEM standing below the crudely made construction, a wooden crate, his boxy pulpit. He barely paused to acknowledge them. A blink for her, a blink for the boy, his attention redirected to the crowd.

"What's Dad yelling about?" Alexander asked Gina.

"I don't know, son." An icy numbness flooded her. She shivered, still clutching the child's hand. "I'm not sure it's Dad."

"Dad!" Alexander waved.

Harry waved back.

Alexander turned his face to his mother. "It's Dad."

Gina pushed her way out of the crowd and on shaking legs hurried home with Alexander. Her mind was empty of thought. Her heart was empty of feeling. It was as if she had been anesthetized, body and soul.

Alexander got busy reading and trying to start a fire by rubbing together two rocks he had brought home. Gina got busy making ravioli with pesto sauce.

The front door opened, closed.

Harry stood in the kitchen.

She thought her voice might fail her, like her body, paralyzed. But no.

"How was your day at Tufts, dear?" she asked. "Your dissertation going well? Almost done?"

He said nothing.

She said nothing.

"Don't be upset."

"You don't think I should be upset?"

"I didn't say that. I'm asking you not to be."

"I shouldn't be?"

"I didn't say that."

"There's a lot you're not saying, Harry. Reticent as a mute. What's the matter? Gave it your all on top of the apple crate?"

"Remember what I told you about Oscar Wilde and women with a sense of humor?"

428

She wiped her hands on a dishrag. "Do I seem to you as if I'm remotely joking?"

"Don't be upset."

"Oh. Okay, then. I won't be. That was simple, wasn't it?"

They ate dinner, the three of them, as always.

"Dad, why were you shouting this afternoon?"

"I wasn't shouting, son. I was passionately speaking about things I believe in."

Alexander swallowed his ravioli. "Sounded like shouting to me."

"Maybe next time you can come with me. Hold my notes, my pens, my bag of pamphlets."

"When? Because I'm going to Aunty Esther's on Friday."

Gina sprang up. "*Tesoro*, if you're done eating, go to your room and finish your reading or making your fire. Please."

"I'm not done eating."

"I hear talking but not a lot of eating," said Gina. She didn't sit down. She could barely hold her tongue.

Finally, after the water torture of artificial civility, they were alone downstairs.

"What are you doing, Harry?" They were in the drawing room with the door shut, standing far apart, the length of the couch between them. Gina didn't know where to look. She couldn't look at her husband.

"What I've always done."

She could barely get the words out. "I thought you were done persuading other people. Isn't that what you told me?"

"I've finished with trying to persuade the bourgeoisie we live amongst," he said. "I'm not interested in winning over *their* hearts and minds. I'm with your Emma on this. *What others consider success, the acquisition of wealth, power, social status, I consider the most dismal of failures.*"

The disappointment must have shown brutally on her face. He took a step away, his back pressed against the bookshelf.

"Don't be cross because you can't remake me into the man you want me to be," he said. "You can't even remake yourself into the woman you want to be."

429

"In this also, you are wrong," Gina said. "I am how I wish to be. I have remade myself like this." She swallowed, her throat dry. "I thought you were done with it all."

"Why would you think that?"

"Because that's what you told me. It was in the past. Nothing more than the foolishness of our youth."

"Is that what it was to you? Foolishness?" Now he looked disappointed in her.

"No. It was youth." It took a titanic effort not to throw at him the empty glass she was holding. She waved her hands across the great unknown, to the great beyond. Most things in the universe were completely beyond her understanding. "Since 1919, when your father saved you from ten years in prison," Gina said, "you've been promising all of us you were finished with the things that put you there."

"And you believed me?"

"I did," she said. "Not your father. You couldn't hide it from him. He knew! All along he knew. He kept trying to warn me. He said as much. I didn't listen. But tell me, were you *ever* planning to show me the face you've been hiding?"

Harry thought about it—or pretended to think about it. "I don't know," he admitted. "You were so happy. I didn't want to ruin things."

"Ruin things," she repeated. "What was I happy with? Fraud?"

"Happy with me. And I wasn't deceiving you. Not really. You were content to look the other way."

"I was oblivious," said a demoralized Gina. "That's not the same. I wasn't looking the other way." But even now she couldn't look directly at him.

"I guess," Harry said, as if he didn't believe it. As if even he didn't believe he had kept himself *that* well hidden. As if he wanted to chide her for not paying closer attention. He walked around to her side of the couch. She stood quietly, her shoulders slumped. She was vanquished. He took her hands in his. "Gia … listen to me," he murmured. "It is only right that idealists like us, who have stopped believing in God, should seek some other way to make out of earth a heaven, out of men and women earthly angels—selfless, altruistic, hard-working, resolute, strong."

She pulled her hands away from him. "I don't fit into your model of the perfect socialist, Harry," she said. "I'm not an idealist like you. You have me all wrong. I have not stopped believing in God."

He shook his head, persisted. "You *are* an idealist."

Vehemently Gina denied it. "Not me. Idealists see the world as it is, find it wanting, and then strive to remake it into how they think it should be."

"Yes!" he exclaimed, as if they were in full agreement.

"That's not me," said Gina. "That's *never* been me. I'm all for improvement of course ..." She paused. "Like a Christian. Knowing I will fail, I strive to be better. I struggle to be good. But what I'm not is an idealist. I see the world for what it is, but think a little better of it."

"Like me?" he smiled. "You see me for what I am, what I always was, what you fell in love with, and accept me anyway?"

She wanted to whisper *yes*, but couldn't.

He stopped smiling. "So what do you call that, then? What do you call yourself?"

"A romantic," Gina replied.

They stood apart as if at separate fronts. He was unrepentant, acting as if he had done nothing wrong, and it was she who had transgressed.

"How did you manage to do this and go to school?" She blanched. "Is this why the degree has been taking so long?"

He said nothing in response, but seemed to be chewing over the truth.

"Is this why you decided on Tufts instead of your alma mater, the place that educated your family going back ten generations? Because it would be easier to keep this heady deception going?"

"No." He spoke coldly. "I chose Tufts because I wouldn't be dragged to be lynched into the square where your Panamanian ditch digger is teaching. Why didn't you tell me he was at Harvard?"

For a moment Gina was speechless. "What does that have to do with *this*?" Now it was she who became unrepentant. "What does it have to do with *you*? You are using Ben to lie to me? You aren't getting an engineering doctorate, are you?"

"Still."

"Still nothing! It should've taken you a year to finish. You could've been done in nine months and never had to lay eyes on him."

"I was starting from the beginning. You mean two years. And is that what you hoped for? That I'd never run into him?"

"I didn't hope for anything. I didn't think about it."

His stance, his glance, remained accusing. "I don't believe you."

"Be that as it may."

"Well, just imagine my tidy humiliation," said Harry, "when I accidentally bumped into him on my second or third day there, taking a stroll in the Yard. He was quite surprised, too."

"To see you?"

Harry smirked dismissively. "That you didn't tell me he was there. He lectures there now. They've offered him tenure. He decided to accept. The gall of that man! Do you know he actually said to me that if there was anything I needed, anything at all, not to hesitate to ask him. Imagine!"

She covered her face. Not out of shame. To stop herself from screaming.

"What does Ben have to do with what I saw you doing this afternoon?" An awful realization struck Gina. "Tell me, are you or are you not attending Tufts?"

Harry was silent. "No," he finally said. "I'm not."

"You never attended?" She grabbed on to the chair for strength.

"I never attended."

"And the Athenaeum …"

"Oh, I go there to work. It's remarkable there. I am left in peace. I get so much done."

"What work are you talking about!" Anger made her ramrod straight. "You've been lying to me, to your son, to your sister for years. Getting your doctorate, Thermopylae, the Greeks, King Leonidas, all complete bullshit! You lied to me about leaving your radicalism behind, about what you do each and every God-given day when you're away from this house—and you bring up Ben at Harvard?" Her chest was closing up. Panic. She couldn't take a breath deep enough to continue speaking.

432

"Stop shouting! We're not in Sicily. Do you want Alexander to hear you?"

She lowered her voice. He was so good with words, wielding them like a hammer over her anvil. "What else besides your communism are you hiding from me?"

"Don't be absurd." He tapped his heart. "Communism is my only mistress. I've joined the Workers Party." That was the current moniker of the Communist Party of the United States of America, forced to go underground by the Red Scare of 1919, the year Alexander was born. What a momentous year 1919 had been.

"But what have you been doing with yourself?" She pushed breath through her closing lungs. "Three years of what, Harry?"

"Three years of revolution in secret, Gina. Even you couldn't know. Three years of translating Soviet pamphlets into English. That's how good my Russian is now," he said proudly. "I learned while I was in prison and I've put it to good use."

"Translating."

"Yes. I'm the Boston editor-at-large of the *Daily Worker*," he said. "I co-write and edit many of the longer articles we publish. And like Ben's mother, Ellen, many moons ago, I'm starting a new organization. It's called the League of Struggle for the Emancipation of the Working Class. I've just finished a month-long study on unemployment and how to fight it."

"You find no irony in that?"

"I won't be baited by you."

"No?"

"No. You want to know what I've been doing with my time? I'll tell you. I've been extraordinarily busy. I'm proud to say I helped James Cannon with the research for his monumental piece, 'The Fifth Year of the Russian Revolution', one of the most influential pamphlets the Workers Party has produced."

She stood without words. He stood and counted off his accomplishments on his fingers.

"After Lenin died, I wrote a ten-thousand-word piece on his life and work. I was the one who wrote the famous letter from the Communist International to the Mexican Communist Party that's been recently quoted by all the newspapers in America. I edit the arts section, and co-edited the *Poems for Workers* anthology. I'm very proud of that one. And I publicly advocate for the Workers Party, what it stands for and why everyone should join, which is what you saw me doing today."

"Are you done?"

"No," he said. "My point is that in the three years prior to *these* three years, I was doing fuck all. Lollygagging in a beach bungalow. But these past three years, I've been *alive!*"

Her knees would not give way. She was made dense by incomprehension, like a block of concrete.

"And I did it without anyone knowing," he continued, all his feathers up. "Not just you, but, more importantly, Femmer. My goal was to work, but to keep it underground. Now that he's out of my life, we don't have to worry."

"How proud you must be. The way you were carrying on today in a public place, it's only a matter of time before they catch up with you. The Red Scare hasn't passed." It's right here on Mt. Vernon Street, she wanted to add. "You think there won't be a crackdown? That you can just keep living like this?"

He nodded.

"And the promise you made me in the beach bungalow?" Gina asked. "When you said you would do right by me, by Alexander, that you would stick by your family?"

"I *am* sticking by my family," he said. "I am devoted and true. The question is," he added, "whether my family is devoted and true to me."

Gina squeezed the glass she was holding so tightly that it shattered in her hand and cut her fingers and palm before falling to the floor. Harry stepped forward to help her, but she flung out her arms to block him, drops of crimson blood flying between them.

"You were going to get your degree," she said, her voice breaking. "You were going to get a respectable job, become a professor, become *something.*"

"Why are you overreacting like this?" he exclaimed. "What's changed? I'm still the same man I always was."

"But I thought you were going to be a new man!" She could barely speak. "What's your plan? Yelling, protesting on Boston streets? Translating Soviet propaganda for the *Daily Worker*? Is that your permanent strategy? Writing articles on the differences between Leninism and Trotskyism? Are they even paying you?" She saw his face and laughed bitterly. "I thought so. You're about to turn fifty. Are you just going to keep doing this? Little by little tearing down everything?"

"Not little by little," he said. "The strike-breaking and the union-destroying actions of the American democracy continue unabated. They must be stopped. Passaic, New Jersey is in a struggle against starvation wages—"

"Oh God! Stop it! Stop speaking!"

"Stop shouting!"

"Who's going to save you this time, Harry?" she whispered, wrapping the hem of her skirt around her injured hand. "Who is left to save you?"

"I don't need anyone to save me. I don't need saving."

But who is going to save *me*, Gina wanted to ask as she crept out of the room like the war-wounded. Who is going to save your son?

Three

GINA WAS NUMB for two days, the shock wearing off slowly, her hand scabbing over, her heart too, but once the fog in her head cleared and the wound healed, she started to make quiet plans to leave with Alexander and go to Tequesta to stay with Salvo until she figured things out. In her outward life she still met with Meredith and her other friends, helped at St. Vincent's, cooked dinner, picked up Alexander from school and did homework with him, even entertained Esther on Sundays. Inside she gnawed on the bone of how best to leave. She suspected that if she informed Harry of her plans he might not let her go, or worse, he might prevent her from taking Alexander, because he knew that without her boy she would and could never go anywhere permanently. But how could she swipe Alexander from his father without a goodbye?

It was impossible.

Weeks passed as she watched her son happy in his life, watched him having fun with his father, watched Harry at home, the same as always: dry-witted, modestly affectionate, calm, serious of purpose, affable, parentally straight. After seething in secret, she soon began questioning the wisdom of her intended actions. She began wondering if Harry had been right, if she might not have overreacted. Was she really going to hold him to the promises made to Janke when he was under house arrest? At the same time, whenever Harry left the house in the morning, Gina was filled with churning dread until he returned. She was afraid he would be apprehended on the street like a common criminal, and she would have to explain *that* to Alexander. Neither of her alternatives was easy: taking the boy to Florida for a little time apart, or staying in Boston and seeing Harry, a Barrington no less, a first Bostonian, a citizen of Beacon Hill, behind bars for being a communist? Neither she nor Alexander would be able to show their faces anywhere in the city, not the school or the park, or the shops on Charles Street and Newbury, where everyone knew them by name.

She stopped sleeping in their marital bed. Two weeks, then three she stayed in one of the guest rooms. Harry did not come in, beg her to come back, ask what she was doing. At night he would read and work at his round table by the window, and when he got tired, he would go to bed. In the morning, he would come down to breakfast, in his suit, ready for his day, have some bread, eggs, a sip of tea, and be on his way.

All day he was gone from her house. All night she was gone from his bed.

Once, Alexander asked him what he was going to do that day, and after brief eye contact with Gina, he said, "I'm writing a long article, son, on how American imperialism is the greatest menace of the capitalist world."

"What's menace?"

"Alexander," said Gina, "let your father go. Can't you see he is late?"

How easy she had been to deceive! Three years to get his doctorate! He fed her his lies, and she swallowed them like a sheep, with nary a bleat. She was being punished for her sins. Absolutely. This is what it must have been like to be Alice twenty years ago. Harry had been five minutes away from finishing his doctorate—and then he crashed into Gina at the narrow pass through the Harvard gates. While Alice was busy planning their wedding, their trip to the volcanoes of Europe, Harry was under crisp white sheets with Gina, all their weapons surrendered. Blissfully oblivious, Alice prepared for the future, not knowing that the life she was living was a mirage and the man she loved an illusion.

Gina felt like that now.

That's why she never pried. She closed her heart, her eyes, pretended it all was fine. He was right. She didn't want to know. Because in the bitter light, she had only two options. Leave. Or stay.

In this manner of purgatory, the summer passed. Cape Cod with Esther, Cub Scouts, clamming.

Gina continued to live, paralyzed, motionless, frozen in place.

She knew what kind of a mother she was, but what kind of a woman was she? What kind of a wife? She cooked for him, and cleaned for him, but refused to touch him, refused to lie down with him. Eventually she would force his hand and he would leave her, to get elsewhere what she no longer offered him, what he no longer took from her.

Whom could she talk to about this? Why did *his* communism isolate *her* from other people? Why did the philosophy of brotherhood, of collective ethic, of fraternal community, alienate *her* from the rest of the world more successfully than any solitary confinement? Perhaps she could contribute an article about *that* to the *Daily Worker*, for free, of course, because they clearly had no money to pay her. Communism as the greatest force of alienation in the modern world.

Whom could she turn to?

Esther? She and Esther were like a divorced couple. Courteous for the sake of the child they both cared for, and nothing more, even when they got together at Esther's summer home in Truro. Gina carried herself as if always on the verge of leaving. Meredith? The woman who couldn't understand why Walter and Alexander might want to play ball after school in the park? Meredith and the others talked about clothes and museums, not marital problems. Gina was the wife of a man who preached the coming end of Boston's easy life to the residents of Boston! Her current friends would be aghast if she were to tell them the truth about her husband, the civil man who sat in their parlor rooms on Saturday nights and kept his objection simmer on low while all around him the political waters heatedly boiled over.

Her old friend Verity, with a team of children in a noisy home? To talk to Verity, Gina would have to go to Lawrence.

She couldn't talk frankly to Salvo. His only advice would be to leave Harry instantly.

Ben?

Oh, God help her.

Rose Hawthorne was not well, and in any case, now lived in New York. Gina had not seen Rose since their return. No short day trip to Concord to ask Rose for a dose of wisdom.

Her options narrowing, Gina returned to Harry's bed. He was as fervent and intimate as ever. "I'm so glad you are with me," he whispered. "That you've finally realized it's just a tempest in a teapot."

She cried.

Afterward, this was their pillow talk.

"Gia, we still *refuse* to recognize the Soviet Union!"

"Perhaps we think it'll go away if we ignore it."

"Russia is not going anywhere. It's not capitalism, Gia. It doesn't eat itself."

"Maybe they hope it will. Eat itself."

"Who is this *they*?" He was too agitated to hold her in his arms. "This is coming from the American Federation of Labor, no less! Did you read the *Globe* today?"

Gina pulled the blanket over her body, trying to get warm. She nearly pulled it over her head.

"They're such cowards." Harry pounded the bed. "Fucking Green." William Green had become the new head of the American Federation of Labor after Sam Gompers died.

"Shh!" She didn't want her son waking up, overhearing. His bedroom was next to theirs. What if, God forbid, he ever started to talk like that? She was teaching him to be a proper Bostonian, always polite.

"Who are they afraid of? Have you been reading the lies they write?" Harry was on his side next to her, drumming on her back, uncovered, but warmed by his convictions. "'We believe in the people's right to freely choose their government through constitutional means. We oppose revolution of all kind.' Oh, I'm sure!"

"You don't think Green means it?" Gina stared at the window. The curtains were drawn. No balcony double doors to open here, no warm night air.

"The AFL is a bunch of mealy-mouthed hypocrites. This country was made by revolution! We wouldn't have a country right now if brave people back then thought the way Green thinks."

"Yes," said Gina, "but maybe now they like their country the way it is."

"Because they're cowards." He kissed her shoulder. "I'm glad we're talking again, I'm glad you're in our bed, but don't side with cowards, Gina."

"I'm not siding, I'm repeating. The AFL denounces the communist idea. It's emphatically against violent means to change our government."

"How can they stand emphatically against anything when they have no spine?" Harry exclaimed. "Invertebrates cannot stand for or against anything."

"Perhaps you're right," she murmured into the pillow, the way some people murmur sweet nothings like I love you.

"Oh, being governed by the unenlightened," he said, covering himself as he sidled up to embrace her. "What a burden."

Four

THAT SUMMER OF 1926, Rose Hawthorne died. She was seventy-five. Her body was brought up north and was buried with the Hawthornes and the Peabodys in Concord. Gina didn't attend the funeral. She read about it in the paper, tears falling on the newsprint.

From Rose's long-dead father in the obituary finally came the counsel Gina had been desperately seeking. "*It is but for a moment, comparatively, that anything looks strange or startling—a truth that has the bitter and the sweet in it,*" Nathaniel Hawthorne wrote.

Her new life with its unwelcome truth soon began to resemble her old life without any truth in it. The old: a transformed Harry was going to be a doctor and a professor. The new: Harry was not going to be a doctor, nor a professor. The impossible within mere months began to seem so normal as to be banal.

And then there was an actual tempest.

Five

AFTERWARD, MANY SAID that the seeds of the ruin of South Florida had been planted long before. The year to reap them was 1926. There had been rumblings since early 1925, articles that cropped up here and there, editorial pieces warning of the imminent collapse. A boom based on nothing but wild speculation could not continue indefinitely. The market could not sustain itself if the price of the thing being bought and sold had no relation to its intrinsic value. It was as if Herman were speaking from the grave. Anyone could sell you an umbrella in the rain, but you'd be a fool if you bought it for a thousand dollars. That the umbrella was not worth a thousand dollars was obvious to an *eejit*.

So it was with the housing market in South Florida. The land, except for its proximity to the ocean, had little intrinsic value, and the houses and their attached prices were built not on reality, but literally on sand. There had been a railroad embargo of some kind, a traffic jam that paralyzed the region, and a ship that had capsized, or so Gina had vaguely remembered reading.

In September 1926, she talked to Salvo, and everything was normal, and then a few days later she read about a hurricane, on page seven. Suddenly, reports of the hurricane's aftermath moved up to page one, after it emerged that Miami had sustained the kind of damage no one had ever seen, except in the 1906 San Francisco earthquake. When Gina called Salvo to make sure he was all right, there was no answer.

"The telephone lines are probably out," said Harry when he heard. "That happens after a storm. There's nothing to worry about. Tequesta is a hundred miles north of Miami. Try again tomorrow."

But there wasn't a tomorrow. The Boston papers reported frightening details: a hurricane had swept from Miami across the bottom third of Florida to the Gulf of Mexico and Sanibel Island, destroying a swathe of civilization in its wake. The pictures told the story. Where once were houses, now there was driftwood washing out to sea.

Gina couldn't reach Salvo or Fernando, or Carmela, or their old neighbors Chuck and Karen. The telephones lines are down, Harry kept saying. Don't worry. You know your brother. Don't you remember the molasses explosion? We were all frantic for days and he was sleeping it off at his *amata's* house. This is just like him, not to contact you. And anyway, he can't. There is no telephone.

After Gina endured a sleepless week, the telephone at the Tequesta City Hall started working. It was picked up by a harassed staffer who had no information and hung up, but not before saying, "Don't you know what's happened? We can't find nobody."

Gina did not believe in coincidence. She had been thinking too long and hard about taking Alexander and fleeing to Tequesta to stay with her brother.

What if something terrible had happened? They could have been there, they surely would have been, had Gina left as she had first planned. She saw this as a warning, and a lesson. There but for the grace of God would she and, more importantly, Alexander have been. It convinced her that she had been right not to walk out on her marriage.

Was she warned, or saved?

And if saved, then for what?

This justification of her choice was trumped by her unyielding anxiety over Salvo's silence. She was angry at him at first. He knew how worried she would be.

Except …

Days turned into weeks, and bodies kept being found in the rubble. There was still no word from him, of him.

Fernando called. Gina broke down in tears when she picked up the telephone and heard his voice. He had been in the hospital for weeks with a concussion and broken ribs. He still sounded dazed, not at all like his old self. He had no news of Salvo. That was worse than anything.

Gina vaguely remembered the last conversation she had had with her brother. Such a mundane chat, yet how she obsessed over every recalled word, trying to find clues. He said something about driving somewhere. She had a dim recollection of a place …

She got out an atlas, found Florida, pored over the towns near Tequesta, Palm Beach, Fort Lauderdale, Miami.

There it was! Coral Gables! What an odd name. That's where Salvo had said he was headed. Just south of Miami Beach, across from Key Biscayne.

Gina called the Miami health authorities, the Miami police department, the Miami hospitals. There was no news of him.

Fernando was getting weary of fielding Gina's numbing questions. Nothing was being accomplished by telephone. Finally in October, she left Alexander and Harry and took a train to Miami to look for her brother. Harry said he would have no problem taking care of his son. If he needed help, Esther was just a telephone call away.

Will you be back for Thanksgiving? Harry asked her when he took her to South Station.

She wanted to say yes. But she didn't know. She wanted to say she would come back when she found her brother. She couldn't say that either. What she said was, Yes, God willing.

He rolled his eyes, and that was how they left it.

Alexander had been surprised to find his mother packing.

"Who is Salvo?" he asked, watching her tie her suitcase closed.

She straightened up. "What do you mean, *caro*? Salvo is my brother. *Zio* Salvo. You remember him, don't you?"

Alexander shrugged. "I didn't know you had a brother, Mom," he said. "I thought, like me, you were an only child."

"Why would you think that? I'm always talking about *Zio* Salvo."

"I thought he was *your zio*."

"You don't remember Salvo?"

"I don't remember last week."

"You don't remember Florida?"

"Mama, I was just a baby then. No, I don't remember."

She studied her son as she always did—intensely.

As he always did under her unblinking stare, he rolled his eyes like his father and turned to his own things. She continued to watch him.

What if it wasn't me God was trying to save? She reached out to touch his black hair, but he had moved away, spread out on her bedroom floor with his toy soldiers. And if the good Lord was saving Alexander, what was he saving him *for*?

Six

TO GIVE HARRY A break and some time to himself, Esther cared for Alexander every weekend after Gina left for Florida. One Saturday afternoon after she had picked him up at home, where he had been languishing alone, she took his hand and, instead of depositing him into a waiting car with Clarence at the wheel, told him they were going for a walk on the Common.

"The Common? Aunty Esther, I live near the Common. I play there every day."

"Do you ever see the sights?"

"What sights? The silly flowers?"

"Don't be fresh. I know you've never seen what I'm about to show you."

"I'm not being fresh. I'm telling the truth, is all."

"Well, I want you to meet a good friend of mine. His mother is not feeling well, and I have a few books I'd like to give her."

"I don't see any books."

"They're in the car. I have many, and they're heavy. You and I will go for a little walk with my friend and then we'll drive him to his mother's house. You don't mind walking, do you? It's warm." She tied the outdated bonnet she insisted on wearing below her chin. "For November, this is wonderful. Sixty degrees. Just like Jupiter, right?"

"Where?"

"Never mind." She patted his shoulder. "We're not going to get another day like this."

"Who is your friend?"

"You'll see."

On Beacon Street, right in front of the State House, they stood and waited by the wrought-iron gates. Finally, a waving man carrying a package strolled up to them, in a suit and tie and hat, a serious, upright man with dark eyes. "I'm sorry I'm late, Est. Been waiting long?"

"No, just a few minutes."

They had been waiting a half-hour! Alexander squinted up at his aunty, wondering why she was fibbing.

The man and Esther seemed to know each other well. If Alexander hadn't known they were friends, he would have guessed they were family. His aunt was as familiar with her friend as she was with Alexander. She stood close to him, gave him a kiss on the cheek, squeezed his arm, smiled into his face, exchanged a few words, and then bent down to Alexander, whose hand she was still holding.

"Alexander, this is my old friend Ben Shaw."

"I'm not so old, Esther, speak for yourself." Ben extended his hand to the boy. Alexander shook it, appraising him. "Very nice to meet you, Alexander."

"You too, Mr. Shaw."

"Please don't call me Mr. Shaw. I've known your father and your Aunt Esther almost my whole life. Call me Ben."

"Don't, Ben," said Esther. "We're trying to teach the boy manners. If he calls you Ben, he'll start calling his teachers Ben, and then where will we be?"

Ben leaned down to Alexander. "You're not going to do that, are you?"

Alexander looked into the man's friendly face and shook his head. "I don't have any teachers named Ben."

"Very good! Like your father, indeed." Smiling, Ben patted his head. "I have something for you. A small gift." He handed Alexander the shopping bag he carried. "Your aunt told me you like to play war?"

Alexander glanced inside the bag and then quickly looked to his aunt, to check if it was all right to accept gifts from this person.

She nudged him. "Go ahead, darling boy," she said. "Ben brought you a gift. What do we say when we receive gifts?"

"Thank you," said Alexander, instantly reaching into the bag. He pulled out a replica hunting knife in a black leather holster with a star on it, and a replica Colt revolver, heavy and silver with the same star on its barrel. "Thank you very much!" The revolver was the most amazing thing he had ever seen. The knife was good, too. But the revolver ... he spun the cylinder. "Where did you get this?"

"A good friend of ours lives in Texas, and she did us a favor when I asked her to help me get a gift for a boy who enjoys weapons."

"Tell her thank you very much from me," Alexander said.

"I will. I wish I could give it to my own children, but I have four girls. They're not as interested in knives and guns as you."

"I'm glad you have girls," Alexander said. "What is this star?"

"That's the Texas star," Ben said. "The Lone Star."

"This gun looks so real," said Alexander, turning the revolver over in his hands, weighing it. The knife was already tucked under his arm. "Are there any bullets?"

Esther and Ben smiled at him. "It's not a real gun, Alexander," Ben said.

"All right. Are there any fake bullets?"

"Alexander," Esther said, "let's make a pact. We'll keep the gifts at my house, and you can play with them when you come to visit me. We don't want to upset your father."

Alexander looked sorely disappointed. He was prepared to sleep with the Colt and the knife under his pillow. "I guess, but ... no, you're right." He sighed. "My dad doesn't like weapons."

"Shall we walk a bit?" Ben said. "Or should we play with your new toys?"

445

"Do you want to play?" Alexander asked eagerly. "You can have the knife."

"You want me to bring a knife to a gun fight?" Ben tutted. "That's not going to end well for me."

"Well, that depends," Alexander said. "How good are you with a knife?"

Ben laughed. "Good point. But let's walk instead. Maybe we'll play later, if we have time."

They started strolling down the path on the Boston Common that ran alongside Beacon Street, Alexander jumping and skipping between the adults. "Teddy is going to be so jealous, he'll die!" Alexander exclaimed, not taking his eyes off the revolver.

"Maybe you can let him have the knife when you play."

"Nah, never," said Alexander. "He won't give it back." He studied Ben. "What do you do, Mr. Shaw?" he asked. "Are you a soldier?"

"I am not, no," said Ben.

"Alexander, Ben is an engineer for the United States Army Corps."

"Not anymore, Esther. Now I just teach."

"Yes, at *Harvard*. Ben built the Panama Canal!" Esther exclaimed.

"Esther!" Ben shook his head. "Your aunt is prone to exaggeration."

Alexander did not know his aunty to be prone to this.

"I didn't build it," Ben continued. "I did help dig it."

"Don't listen to him, Alexander. He designed it, planned it, fought for it, built it. His name is written in historical lights."

"Esther!"

"You work for the Army, Mr. Shaw? Are you sure you're not a soldier?"

"No," said Ben, "but I'm *related* to a soldier. Does that count?"

"Oh, yes!" Alexander paused. "Are *we* … related?" he asked wistfully. He wanted to be related to a soldier.

"We might as well be." Ben smiled. "Your father and I used to be very good friends when we were just a little older than you. For many years we were friends."

"What about now?"

"I haven't seen him in a few years."

"He was home this morning. Then he had to go out."

"Where did he go?"

"To the university, I think. Or the library. He's writing songs for an operetta," Alexander said. "That means a short opera, and it's called 'The Last Revolution.' He is also studying to be a doctor. He doesn't like weapons, but he is studying Greek wars. Do you know about them?"

"Not very much." Ben smiled. "Your father always liked books more than anyone I know. He is very smart. Do you like books?"

"Hmm." Alexander didn't want to lie. "I like playing more."

"Well, who doesn't?"

"My dad," Alexander replied. "He likes books more. Though sometimes he likes baseball. Do you know my mother, too?"

Esther knocked into him, apologizing for her carelessness.

"Yes," Ben said tersely. "I also knew your mother. How is she?"

"She is good. But there was a hurricane and her brother is missing. I didn't know she had a brother. She went to find him, I think."

Esther looked down at Alexander in dismay. "Alexander, you don't remember your Uncle Salvo?"

"No, Aunty Esther. Mama asked me that. I was little."

"Ah. And now?"

"Now I'm big," said the seven-year-old boy. "Where are we going?"

"Ben wants to show you a memorial to his uncle."

"Who is your uncle?"

"My Uncle Robert was a colonel in Ulysses Grant's army during the Civil War. You said you liked soldiers. I thought you might like to learn a little bit about my uncle."

Alexander became doubly excited. He loved stories about soldiers. He didn't hear enough of them at home. Out of the hundreds of books they owned, the only two he could find about soldiers were *The Red Badge of Courage*, which Alexander liked very much, and *The Man Without a Country*, which his mother told him his father had loved when he was a young man. Alexander read that book, but with puzzlement. Because his father had liked it, *he* tried to like it, but there was nothing about the story he found remotely appealing. If he was perfectly honest about it, it was gloomy and not a good soldier story at all—most of all because it was about a sour-cabbage-bucket of a man named Philip Nolan who didn't want to be a soldier! Who didn't even want to be an American. Alexander couldn't understand why his father would like that book.

He hoped this man's uncle had a better story.

"What do you and your dad do together, Alexander? You don't play war ..."

"No. He takes me places."

"What kind of places? Parks?"

"Yes, sometimes. We kick the football around. He throws a baseball with me. We joined a father–son softball team. But it's only in spring. He took me to a Bruins hockey game last week. I really liked that. He's been taking me with him everywhere. Mom is strict sometimes. Dad doesn't care when I go to bed or what I have for breakfast." Alexander chuckled. "Sometimes I hardly have breakfast at all, and he doesn't make any fuss about it."

"I'm sure," said Esther, with a disgruntled headshake. "Where else has he been taking you?"

"I don't know. Around Boston. We hand out pieces of paper. And sometimes he talks to people, almost shouts."

"What pieces of paper, Alexander?" said Esther. "What people? Your father doesn't shout."

"I call it shouting. He says he talks about things he believes in. Something about workers. Maybe money."

"These pieces of paper ..."

"Workers of the World Unite," Alexander said. "Or something like that."

He couldn't miss the frowns that ghosted across the adult faces.

"Oh, and the other day, the police came!" Alexander said, ready to let out the things he had been keeping inside. "They told the people listening to Dad to go away, and then they told Dad to go away. But we didn't, so they said they would arrest him if he didn't go away in *five seconds*, and he said, my son is with me, and they said they would arrest me too!" Alexander looked like he felt—deeply let down. "Dad and I left, but he didn't want to." He paused, watching the silent exchange between the adults. "Aunty Esther? What's arrest?"

"When the police tell you to do something, you have to do it, or they put handcuffs on you and take you to the police station where they accuse you of committing a crime."

"But Dad was just talking."

"Do you do anything else with your father besides getting almost arrested?" Ben asked.

Alexander laughed. "Last year he and Mama taught me how to ice skate right here on Frog Pond—"

"Oh, look," Ben interrupted, walking ahead. "Here we are."

How strange adults are, Alexander thought. Why ask a question if you don't want to hear the answer? He clutched his revolver tightly just in case he had said something upsetting, and this nice man decided to take his presents back.

The three of them stood silently in front of a dark bronze relief of a man on a horse, with foot soldiers around him.

"Is that your uncle?"

"That's my uncle. Colonel Robert Gould Shaw."

"Do you see him much?"

"He died before I was born, Alexander," Ben said. "But he was a great man. I would've liked to have known him."

"I would like to know my *Zio* Salvo," said Alexander. "But I don't think he is a soldier."

"No," said Esther. "But your uncle is the best singer I've ever heard. He is funny. And all the girls adore him." She kissed Alexander on the head and whispered, "As they will you, someday."

"Ugh! Aunty Esther …" An embarrassed Alexander moved away from his aunt toward Ben. The three of them stared at the monument. "Why is *your* uncle great, Mr. Shaw?"

"Because he was a real hero."

"Really?" Alexander paid attention. "What did he do?"

"He led a platoon of Negro men to battle against the Confederate army," said Ben. "His was the only platoon of Negroes in the entire North. No one wanted to lead them. But my uncle did. They fought and ate and slept side by side in Virginia and North Carolina. No one else would do that. But my uncle did. When other commanders asked him how he could do that, he said because he knew with absolute certainty that all his soldiers were better men than he was because they were braver. He was convinced, he said, that God would prefer his foot soldiers over him."

Alexander shook his head. "God doesn't play favorites like Mr. Duncan, does he?" Mr. Duncan was Alexander's grammar teacher, and did not care for Alexander at all.

"My uncle thought God did."

They ambled around the monument while Ben continued to talk.

"In 1897, a couple of years before your mother came to America, this monument was unveiled. Your father and I stood where you stand right now for its dedication. We were not yet twenty. William James said of my uncle that he was a blue-eyed child of fortune, upon whose happy youth every divinity had smiled." Ben smiled himself. He took Alexander's hand, the one that wasn't holding the revolver, and squeezed it. "In that way, he was a little bit like you, wasn't he?"

Alexander was perplexed. Why did this man who seemed so familiar with Esther, so casual with her, not at all full of restrictive manners, look down on him, a boy he barely knew, with such fondness, and why would he say things that made no sense? "I don't have blue eyes," Alexander said. He pointed at one of his caramel-colored eyes. "See?"

"I was being figurative. As William James was. I don't think my uncle had blue eyes either."

Alexander tried not to frown. Why were adults so hard to understand? Why couldn't they just say what they meant? "Was he old?"

"He was twenty-five," Ben replied. "Is that old?"

Alexander nodded. "Very."

Smiling lightly, Ben continued. "He and his men were defending Fort Wagner in South Carolina. But they were outnumbered and outgunned."

"They had guns? Like this one?" Alexander cradled his trophy.

"Yes. Except they were real. And bigger."

"What kind of guns?"

"Well, I don't know. Muskets probably. Rifles. Cannons."

"A cannon is not a gun."

"You're right. They had lots of weapons and were using them all."

"I like weapons …" Alexander said dreamily. "Tell me about the battle."

"He led the charge, but was killed—"

"How?"

"He was shot."

"Soon after starting?"

"Very soon. I told you, they were vastly outnumbered."

Alexander was disappointed. He wanted the battle to last longer. Like Gettysburg. That one lasted three terrible days.

"After hand-to-hand fighting, his infantry men were killed, too."

"Hand-to-hand?"

"With knives, like yours. With bayonets."

"How many?"

"How many what?"

"How many soldiers died?"

"Everybody, Alexander," said Ben. "Everybody died."

"Oh," said Alexander, lowering his head. That wasn't very good. "Like the Alamo."

"Yes. Like the Alamo. Which is why I thought you might enjoy the Lone Star revolver. The Confederate general in charge of the opposing army was so angry that my uncle was leading a charge against the South with *black* men, he refused to return my uncle's body to my grandparents, and instead had him buried in a common grave with the fallen Negroes."

Alexander was surprised. "So he isn't buried here?"

"No, it's just a monument."

The boy whistled. "Your grandfather must have been mad."

"On the contrary," Ben said. "My grandfather said that his son could have no greater honor than to be buried with his men, 'no holier place' in which to lie."

Alexander clapped his gun into his palm. This was a much better story than the Philip Nolan one. "That must have *really* upset the Confederate general. What was his name?"

"I don't remember."

"Wasn't it General Hagood, Ben?" Esther cut in.

"How do *you* know that, Est?"

She shrugged. "You may have told me once. Or I read it."

Alexander placed his warm palm on the cool monument. "General Ha*bad* is more like it," he said.

Ben laughed. "Indeed, Alexander. Indeed."

After they dropped Ben and the books off at his mother's, Alexander was quiet on the short drive to Barrington, clutching his revolver and hunting knife, looking out the window.

Esther broke the silence. "What did you think?"

"Of what?"

"Of my friend Ben."

"He was nice," Alexander said. "He was very nice to bring me gifts. I like his uncle."

When Alexander told his father about the afternoon with Ben, Harry showed little interest in the story of Ben and Esther and Robert Gould Shaw. But later that evening Alexander overheard him on the telephone talking sharply to Aunty Esther about weapons and colonels and the evils of war. After that Alexander didn't see Aunty Esther's friend again, though he would ask and ask and ask to spend another afternoon with him, to hear more of his war stories. Perhaps he could ask his mother to intercede on his behalf when she returned home. He couldn't wait to tell her about Battery Wagner.

Chapter 17

PRINZ VALDEMAR

One

"PRACTICALLY NO DANGER of summer storms," the brochures had proclaimed since 1912, luring tourists and residents to South Florida. Everyone believed it. No one had been evacuated leading up to the storm they were now calling the Great Miami Hurricane. True, the National Weather Bureau had issued a warning for a severe storm off the Caribbean, but the warning fell not so much on deaf ears as uncomprehending ones. The brochures clearly stated in bold print there was *practically* no danger of summer storms.

So on September 17, 1926, everyone remained in their homes. On September 18, there were hardly any homes left. Fifty thousand people homeless, four hundred people dead. Thousands missing, Gina's brother included.

The seventy-mile-an-hour winds came with the rain in the dead of night, but by sunrise Miami stood largely intact. At dawn the relieved Miamians poured into the streets and onto the bridges to see the mighty ocean swell. You see? they collectively said. Look how calm it is. It came and went. We were right. There was noise, but hardly any danger.

What they didn't know was that they were standing in the hurricane's very eye. Forty minutes later, the rear of the eyewall hit Miami. The winds swirled to a hundred and twenty-five miles an hour. The ocean rose fifteen feet in a surge. The mayor later said of Miami Beach that his barrier island town, separated from the mainland by a narrow causeway, was on all four sides "isolated in a sea of raving white water."

The property destruction was stupefying. "Madam, everyone and everything in Miami Beach washed out to sea," was how one sailor put it when Gina stood at the dry docks that had been mutilated by high winds. Along the length of Collins Avenue, the grandiose hotels and fancy vacation homes appeared to sit two or three stories closer to the ground. The sandy beach had washed into every grand marble lobby. There was no electricity, and the only running water was from the ocean tides. The abandoned hotels were being used as hospitals.

"But my brother wasn't in Miami Beach," Gina said to the sailor with hope. "He had gone to Coral Gables."

The sailor took off his hat and crossed himself. "I'm very sorry," he said. "But Coral Gables was landfall."

It took her a long time to find a taxi to take her down to Coral Gables to file a missing persons report, to search for Salvo amid the ruins. In the Bay of Biscayne, an enormous ship, nearly two hundred and fifty feet long, lay on its side, blocking entry in and out of Miami Harbor.

"That's from the hurricane?" Gina asked one of the marine workers.

"No," he said. "That's *Prinz Valdemar*. Ten months ago, in January, it was sailing into the harbor to become a floating hotel for the tourists, when it tipped and sank in the harbor, blocking all trade by sea."

"Why did it sink?"

"No one knows. It's a mystery."

"Was there a hurricane?"

"I told you, there was nothing. Just a ship, suddenly on its side, like a blockade of our city. We were planning to tow it to a nearby marina when this storm hit."

"Now what are you going to do with it?"

"No one knows. Who cares?"

Gina found a room at a small hotel inland. She stayed a week, talking to the police and the sailors and the salvage crews, every day looking through the rolls of the missing, walking the ruined streets in hopes of catching a glimpse of Salvo, a word of Salvo.

Finally she called Fernando, who drove down to Miami to meet her and take her to Tequesta. Fernando had stopped coloring his hair and was now completely gray. He looked beaten up, too, troubled, shaken. There was barely a smile for her, as they embraced, both of them trying not to cry. He moved slowly and with effort. By the uncommon grimness of his demeanor, Gina reckoned the old Cuban was making peace with the worst.

Not she!

The only small talk they managed was when he first opened the car door for her and glanced at her frame in its short-sleeved cotton flapper dress. "You have gotten so thin, my señora. I've never seen you like this. You are not sick, are you? Do they not feed you up in Boston?"

In the car they spoke of the devastation. "We weren't as badly hit as Miami," Fernando told her. "Still, I was hurt, as you can see. I'm still hurt. I thought it was terrible for us. But now that I've seen Miami ..." He trailed off. "We were barely touched by comparison."

Yet in Tequesta the palm fronds were on the ground, the fences, the houses.

Salvo's bank account had not been touched. Jenkins, as weaselly and sweaty as before, told Gina there had been no withdrawals, no deposits, no checks cashed since September 16, 1926, the day before the day before the hurricane. Aside from the lack of activity, Gina was startled, though she tried not to show it, by how little money remained in Salvo's name. The real estate market had been booming all the years he was a sales agent, yet the commissions didn't make it into his savings account. When she mentioned this to Jenkins in the most non-confrontational of terms (what was she afraid of? That Jenkins embezzled from her brother?), the man smirked. "Mr. Attaviano may not be savings-rich, Mrs. Barrington, but he was life-rich. Tremendously so. Your brother spent his money as fast as he could earn it, God bless him. And he earned quite a lot. He spent quite a lot. He drove a very expensive Duesenberg."

That Gina knew. Just days earlier, the recovery crews had found Salvo's luxury fire-engine-red Model A sunk in the waters off Key Biscayne, dredged it from a canal near Coral Gables. Salvo wasn't in it.

"Yes, he lived well, Mrs. Barrington. Have you been to his home?"

Gina had indeed been to his home. Fernando had taken her there first. Salvo had built himself a beautiful white hacienda with a red-tile roof on the Tequesta side of Hobe Sound, practically overlooking Bellagrand. Not much remained of his home. The tile roof had been blown off and lay like brick lava all around the yard. The house stood empty, like a shell from which the clam had fled. The windows had been blown out, the doors torn off, the porch was in splinters. Debris and garbage were spread all over the grass front yard. The fence was gone. Gina couldn't breathe, that panic rising again, as she surveyed the damage.

Fernando asked if she wanted to drive across the bridge to see Bellagrand. He was certain it hadn't been badly damaged. He had seen the gate from the road, still in one piece, and he wanted her to be sure, to be comforted. Gina looked at him as if he were offering her a trip into the portals of Hades.

"Why would I go there, Fernando? Why would I torment myself? Don't you know it would bring me nothing but heartache?"

She turned her back to the well-meaning Cuban so he wouldn't see her cry. But the smell of the ocean, the demolished houses, the absence of her brother, became too much for her. She broke down. She wished she hadn't come.

Salvo: a goat shepherd, a lumberjack, a rag collector, a street sweeper, a bread-maker, a singer, a seller, a lover, living in a custom-built Spanish revival house, driving a flame-red Duesenberg and wearing silk suits. *I'm going to Miami, mia sorella Gia*, he had crooned to her in a cheerful singsong on the telephone the day before the day the eyewall came. *There is a girl in Coral Gables … it sounds like a song, doesn't it? A girl in Coral Gables, I'm going to drive down, take her out to dinner, buy her pretty flowers, go dancing on the town. Her name is Stella. A bellissima name. A bellissima girl. Tonight I'll be hers and she'll be mine. Stella.*

Salvo, *melted into air, into thin air.* Doubled over, Gina wiped the tears from her face.

Fernando helplessly stood patting her curved and hollow back.

After a few futile weeks in Miami, Gina returned to the National Bank to check on Salvo's account. There had been nothing taken, nothing added. Before she left she asked Jenkins how much her old home was currently worth.

Jenkins hemmed and hawed. He told her there had been too much inventory before the hurricane. There was also a traffic jam on the railroads and a subsequent embargo by many companies that couldn't move their products into the region. Unreasonably bad press didn't help matters. The prices had been driven down.

"But won't they go up now?" Gina asked. "There seem to be so few intact properties left." She swallowed. She didn't mention Bellagrand by name.

"One would hope home values will indeed go up, Mrs. Barrington. But you know, we have been at a historic high—"

She interrupted him. She didn't want to know about then. She wanted to know about now.

"Your old home?" Jenkins leafed through his catalog of inventory. Or pretended to leaf. "I should think that if the new owners were determined sellers and it was priced correctly, I could find a firm buyer within three months for …" He mulled over a figure. "Fifty thousand dollars."

"What?"

"Yes, yes. At least."

"Did you say *fifty thousand?*"

Jenkins closed his book. "Have you seen the property destruction around these parts, Mrs. Barrington? You did survey it with your own eyes, am I correct?"

"Hurricanes make the value of homes fall from four million to fifty thousand in two months?"

"Who said anything about four million?"

"You did, Mr. Jenkins," said Gina. "To me and my husband. You stood in our kitchen in 1922 and offered us a three million dollar line of equity against the value of our home. Do you remember?"

He gestured airily. "Markets rise and fall, everything goes through a cycle of growth and decline. We are in a fallow period, I admit. A house is a long-term investment, Mrs. Barrington. You can't sweat every price drop."

"This is not a price drop, Mr. Jenkins," she said weakly. "I don't know what you call this. A price nullification?"

"On the plus side," he said, "if you wanted a house now, it's a buyer's market. Very good time to buy."

"I should say. You're giving them away for free."

"Hardly—"

"Let me ask you a question. Say we had taken you up on your offer and accepted your generous line of equity … what would happen to it right now? What would happen to us?"

"You're not your brother, are you?" Jenkins chuckled. "You weren't going to use up all three million dollars worth of credit, were you?"

"Let's say we were. Let's say we did."

He clapped his hands together. "But you didn't. So … *that* disaster was averted. All there is to it. We've got plenty of other disasters around here. Now … is there anything else I can help you with?"

Gina backed away from him and stumbled onto the street where Fernando was waiting to take her back to Miami.

"What's the matter, señora? You're completely white."

"Nothing, Fernando. Let's go."

"Did you close his account?"

Gina sighed. "I can't just yet, *mi amigo*. One more week. I'll look for him one more week."

They drove to Salvo's house and sat outside for a few minutes, not looking at the abandoned dwelling.

"What do you think?" she whispered. "Do you fear he is not coming back?"

Fernando cried. "He was the best friend I ever had," he said. "He was like my brother."

In silence he drove her back to Miami and dropped her off at her small hotel. He told her that if she wished it, he would come again in a week so they could try once more.

She drew him to her, embraced him.

"It's okay, dear Fernando. You've done all you can. I'll leave you be."

"I don't know what's worse," he replied. "Us trying again, or us not trying again."

"Clearly us not trying again is much worse," said Gina to her faithful servant and her brother's friend.

From her hotel lobby Gina called Harry to tell him what was happening. They talked a long time, longer than they had in months. They reached a rapprochement, were united again. The cross she carried was too heavy for her, and he helped her carry it. He comforted her. He told her how sorry he was about her brother. He was good to her. They chatted the next day, and the next. Gina told Harry about the housing market. How narrowly, they both agreed, they had avoided the blackest doom. They congratulated each other on their prescience and wisdom, chuckled a little, figuratively patted each other on the back. Imagine if they had been seduced by Jenkins's promises and took his multi-million dollar loan!

"It is too terrible to contemplate," said Gina.

The next time they spoke, Harry told her he was so unnerved by their conversations that he was considering selling their super-charged Mercedes. They didn't need such an expensive car. In fact, he said, they didn't need a car at all. Better to live more simply. Look what had happened in Jupiter, in Miami. That could happen to them.

"But there are no hurricanes in Boston," said Gina.

Harry brought up moving to a smaller home. Their Mt. Vernon place felt entirely too big for the three of them. What did they need with six bedrooms, two dining rooms, two sets of staircases, servants' quarters? It was absurd to have something that extravagant. It was unseemly, he said. He was looking out for them. They should talk about it when she got back.

She agreed they would talk about it when she got back.

Gina might have remained in Miami until she found her brother, which is to say indefinitely, but a week before Thanksgiving, the hotel front desk manager knocked on her door to tell her to come to the lobby for a call from her sister-in-law.

"It's time for you to come back," Esther said. "Because they've arrested your husband and son."

"What are you talking about?" Gina leaned on the counter for support.

"Why didn't you tell me he's been up to no good again? Why did I have to hear about it from Alexander? This is something I deserve to know about, don't you think?"

"How could I tell you, Esther, when I didn't know myself until five minutes ago? What happened?"

"Harry fomented a revolutionary uprising, what else?"

"What does Alexander have to do with any of that?" She tried not to shout.

"Who do you think the boy is with, while you're on holiday in Florida?"

"I'm not on holiday, Esther. I'm searching for my vanished brother."

"Welcome to the club, sister."

Gina was left with no choice but to return to Boston immediately, her only show of faith: not closing Salvo's bank account. It had remained untouched since the day before a strong wind and heavy rain swept away South Florida and washed him far away.

Two

HARRY AND ALEXANDER were waiting for her at South Station. Having Alexander to cling to stopped her from discussing volatile issues with Harry. She was grateful she had held her tongue about things like the arrest, legal trouble, the threat of prison, because Alexander, still in the crook of her arm, said, "Mom, we moved."

"Moved what?"

"Not what. Where. We moved to Spruce Street."

Gina stopped in her tracks. Harry, carrying her suitcase, pulled her along. "Come on, don't dawdle, let's hail a taxi."

"Where's the car?"

"I told you. I sold it."

"No," she said slowly, "you didn't tell me you sold it. You told me you were *thinking* of selling it. You asked me if I thought it was a good idea. I hemmed and hawed. I suppose you also told me we were moving?"

"I would have told you, but I found the place on Spruce so quickly, and five other people were looking at it. I was afraid we'd lose it if I waited another second. I took a chance. I know you'll like it. It's better this way."

"It has no furniture, Mom," said Alexander.

"Where's the furniture?"

"I sold it," said Harry. "It was too big to fit into our new home."

The apartment was on the fifth floor of a narrow walk-up on a narrow street. Just like the one the Attavianos had stayed in when they arrived by sea from Sicily a quarter-century earlier.

"Not quite," Harry said. "That one was a tenement in the North End ghetto. This one is on the Boston Common in Beacon Hill. A world of difference, wouldn't you say?"

Gina didn't think there was a world of difference. She didn't think there was a daylight of difference between them.

She put down her gloves, her bag, her hat and walked around, or took "a tour," as Alexander called it. It took two minutes. The place had one washroom, two bedrooms, a kitchen, a living room, a dining room. One fireplace. The rooms were small, dark, sooty, as if steam heat hadn't come yet to the fifth floor. The boxes were still unpacked, waiting for her.

"So what do you think?" Harry kept asking, in remarkably good humor.

Gina was less enthusiastic. "Where is the rest of it?"

"That's all there is, Mom," said Alexander. "There is no other part to it, like a room where we dance."

"You were never much of a dancer, son," Harry said. "You used the ballroom to stage fake gun battles. You can do that on the Common. It's right across the street."

"On the Common there are no frogs," Alexander said sullenly.

"Were there frogs in the ballroom? And what do you mean, there are no frogs on the Common? Why is the pond called Frog Pond?" Harry took Alexander over to the window to show him the patch of black water they could see across the street, through a stone gate.

"I don't see any frogs."

"All right, enough." Setting him down, Harry lightly pushed the boy away. "Go and get ready for bed. Let me talk to your mother."

She was searching through the kitchen cabinets for pots, for vases, for spoons.

Alexander hugged her. "Don't worry, Mom," he said. "It takes no time at all to find things. Dad sold most of it."

"I sold the things we don't need," Harry said. "I kept our bed"—he arched his brows—"Alexander's bed. The sofa."

"You should have kept the malachite table," said Gina, pointing to the window where an ugly old pedestal table stood romantically placed. "You'd have enough to make bail for a year."

"I keep telling you and telling you about women who think they're funny."

"A few more moves and we'll be right back in the North End," Gina said, glancing around the cramped space. "Fitting to come around in such a circle, no?"

"I don't think you understand the definition of a circle. For you, a circle would be ending up in Sicily. For me, in Barrington. Do you see how it works?"

Oh, she saw how it worked.

"Are we low on money?" she asked carefully.

"Of course not."

"Is that why we moved?"

"Of course not. We have *more* than enough. We moved because I don't want to waste our money foolishly. I didn't think you'd want that either."

"I don't want that."

"Good. Then we both want the same thing."

Where was she going to go now? Salvo was gone.

What a thankless affair Thanksgiving was.

Three

"CAN YOU TRY not to be upset with me all the livelong day?" said Harry as she was angrily cleaning up one night in December after Alexander had gone to bed.

"I'm not thinking of you at this precise moment," said Gina. "My brother is gone."

"I'm very sorry," he said. "I'm so sorry—"

"But perhaps if you stopped dragging our son to your violent uprisings advocating for peace, you could make me less upset."

"I'm not advocating for peace. I'm advocating for revolution."

"That right there is the gist of why I continue to be upset."

She spent her time hiding from everyone else: her friends, her sister-in-law. How could she bear it? All she wanted to do was scream. She and Harry had reached a truce, a moment of kinship, a respite from disagreement when they had commended each other for selling Bellagrand and not ruining their life with Jenkins's fake millions. How short-lived that truce had been. Like joy. Like everything.

"When did you become so ideologically inflexible?" she asked when she found him buried in Russian books near the window while she, like an asylum patient, wiped and re-wiped the same wooden coffee table trying to make it shine.

"What do you mean? This is how I've always been."

She showed him her skeptical face, but wondered was it true? Had he always been like this, and she had never noticed?

"Did you know that my sister has been taking our son on excursions around Boston with our old friend Ben?"

Gina did know, but she didn't want to talk about it. Why would Esther do that? Why would she introduce Alexander to Ben? What was the point? To make trouble? But there were so many other details turning Gina's insides upside down that this inexplicable mystery had remained unsolved. She didn't ask Esther about it. She didn't care to.

"Alexander invited him over for dinner," Harry said.

"Oh. When is he coming?"

"You're joking, right?"

"I am, yes."

"Well, stop it. You're not funny."

"But there is so much to joke about. I see how you've handled things while I was searching for my brother. Leaving our seven-year-old son alone in the house. Getting yourself and him arrested, being charged with a felony. It's all so humorous."

Harry was dismissive. "I'm not concerned. The war is over. I'll get a good lawyer before my hearing next month. It'll be fine."

"And then what? You'll stop?"

"Stop what? My life's work? No. That won't happen."

Gina threw down her useless rag, grabbed her own book, and headed for the bedroom. "You might want to put that lawyer on a retainer then," she said.

She perched on the bed by Alexander's side. He was under heavy blankets, covered up, cosy. Was he sleeping? He opened his eyes and stared at her, unblinking in the dim light from the street.

"How long have you been watching me, Mom?"

"Coming on eight years, *caro*."

He sat up and hugged her. "Don't be sad about your brother. Please. Promise me you won't be sad anymore?"

She wiped her face behind his back so he wouldn't see. "Okay, sunshine, *mio amore, mio amato figlio*." She held him close, kissed his head, but he was the one patting her back, as if to say, there, there.

"You helped your dad while I was gone?" She caressed his cheek. "And you were a good boy for Aunty Esther?"

"Of course," he said. "Don't tell Dad, but …" Alexander lowered his voice. "Aunty Esther's friend Ben got me a revolver, Mom! A *revolver*!"

"Yes, she told me. Keep it in Barrington."

"I know. I will. But do you know what Dad and I did while you were gone? He taught me how to play hockey!"

"He did?"

"Yes. We weren't just getting arrested, you know. Though that was interesting. But I already knew how to skate, and then Dad bought us two hockey sticks and a puck and we went to Matthews Arena. It was so much fun! You have to come and watch. He says I'm good. I should join the hockey team when I go to grammar school. I can be as good as the Canadians."

"Oh, better than the Canadians, I would hope."

"The Bruins are playing again next week. Do you want to come to a game with us? It can be violent. Sometimes there is blood. Will you be all right with that?"

"I'll manage."

"Do you know what Dad told me?"

"No, *il mio cuore*." She brushed the hair out of his face. "What did your dad tell you?"

"He told me that the Swedes are going to be the team to beat in the 1928 Olympic Games. He said they're almost as good as the Canadians."

"Then they must be really good." She eased him down, covered him up. "Go to sleep. I don't know why you're still awake."

"Because you came into my room and stared at me until I woke up and talked to you."

She leaned over him. "Who is my beloved?"

"Me, me," he said. "But Mom, don't be upset at Dad about the arrest. He was great, shouting at the police. He was brave. He wasn't afraid of them at all." Smiling, remembering, Alexander pulled the blankets up to his neck. "He was like a soldier."

Four

NOT LIKING THE GIST of what Harry had been shouting about, the police told the crowd to disperse. Harry told the crowd not to listen. He yelled to them that strength in numbers was on their side. It was for this he was arrested and detained with Alexander. After he was forcibly taken into custody, he was charged not only with seditionary speech and disturbing the peace, but also with resisting the police. He found himself an excellent lawyer who was an underground member of the United Front. The lawyer took him on, but a few weeks later dropped him with no explanation, returning the entire retainer along with a terse letter.

When Harry confronted him—by going to the man's residence, no less—the lawyer told him that, in professional circles, defending Harold Barrington was tantamount to displaying his party card on his lapel. The lawyer had already lost six clients, and his firm received another dozen angry letters threatening to take their business elsewhere. The lawyer would lose his practice if he continued to defend Harry. Despite their communist ties, he couldn't do it. He was sorry. He was wearing a custom-tailored evening coat and gold cufflinks when Harry called on him. His shoes were newly shined. His residence was a spacious mansion off Newbury Street, larger even than Harry's former abode.

After weeks of searching, Harry admitted to Gina that he was facing difficulties he had not anticipated. Little did he know, he said, how hard it would be to find a lawyer whose socialist virtues were sturdy enough to withstand the shallow anxieties of the bourgeoisie.

Gina, doggedly wiping the table, dusting the shelves, told him to keep at it.

Harry tried. Everywhere he went, he was refused as a client. It was the last thing they needed, they all said, the kind of trouble he invited.

"When did you become so circumspect?" Harry asked accusingly of the seventh man who had turned him down.

"I have a good life," the lawyer said. "Why would I risk it? Find someone whose life is in shambles—like yours."

"My life is not in shambles," said Harry, taken aback.

"Really? You come to my door under cover of night. Why don't you come to my office during working hours?"

"I don't want to upset your bosses. I don't want them to put pressure on you to say no."

"But eventually they'll know I'm defending you, won't they? Someone will see your name and mine joined together on the court docket?"

"It's not just standing up for *me*," Harry said. "It's standing up for the rights of man."

"I might believe that at the gentlemen's club," the man said, stepping back inside his front door. "But I don't believe it in my paycheck."

Five

IT WAS GINA who finally came to Harry's aid. She took the train to Cambridge, went to the Engineering Hall at Harvard's graduate school campus, and asked to see Ben Shaw.

He was neither unhappy, nor entirely surprised to see her. He left his office and together they stepped out into the frigid air. It was January, a bad month to be in Boston.

"We don't have to walk, Ben. We can stay in the vestibule," she said, covering up her shivering with her words.

"No, let's walk for a bit."

"At least it's not snowing."

"Yes. But snow makes everything new," he said.

She responded not even with a breath as they crossed Cambridge Street and entered Harvard Yard.

"So, I heard about your outing with Esther and Alexander," Gina said, diverting.

"Hardly an outing. We were across the street from your house." Ben paused. "Harry wasn't happy?"

She shook her head. "Not with you, or Esther, or Alexander—and certainly not with me, even though I was fifteen hundred miles away."

"Perhaps if you were nearby, it wouldn't have happened."

"That's exactly what Harry said."

They walked silently for a few moments.

"I thought your contract was for three years," she said. "You decided to stay?"

Ben shrugged. "Harvard tenure is not small bait. Ingersol got used to living here. In the winter she leaves me for four months and goes back to Colon with our daughters."

"She leaves you for Christmas?"

"Not very sporting of her, is it?"

"I should say. She's in Panama now?"

"Until March."

Gina hoped this wouldn't backfire on her, visiting Ben while his wife and children were away.

"So what's going on, Gia—Gina?" He quickly corrected himself. "Is everything all right?"

She told Ben about the trouble that had brought her to Harvard. "Harry is out of options, Ben. I'm sorry to bother you with it. He has spent nearly two months trying to hire someone, but he can't find anyone to represent him, and his hearing date is next week. We've postponed twice already, but that's all the Christmas charity we're allowed. Come seven days from now, he must be in court. What's he going to do—represent himself?"

"Does he know you're here? Because I told him to come to me if he needed anything."

She shook her head. "You know his pride would never allow it."

"That's what I thought." Ben fell quiet. "He couldn't find *anyone* to take his case, no matter how much he offered?"

"It's the prospect of career suicide that's scaring off the lawyers. We'd have to keep paying them for life if they lost their jobs because of him and then couldn't find other work. It would be like the protection racket of *Cosa Nostra*."

He laughed. "You always make such apt comparisons. But what makes you think a canal builder and Harvard professor would know a lawyer greedy enough or unscrupulous enough to take on a case like this, regardless of what it would do to his reputation?"

"A man who parts mountains?" She smiled. "Who else could I possibly turn to?"

Ben nodded. He looked grateful to be asked. "I see Harry's conundrum. What is he yelling to the man on the street, to the lady in the wheelchair at the Haymarket? If he wants someone to represent him, he must find a man who either knows nothing about him or who desperately needs the money. Preferably both." He gave Gina the name of James Domarind. "He graduated from Boston College. Read in biological sciences, but when his mother died, he wanted nothing more to do with medicine or test tubes. So he came here to Harvard Law. He took an engineering course with me to satisfy his graduation requirement."

"What makes you think he can help us?"

"Because he was still in his first year when he started handing out laminated business cards. I thought that spoke of his audacity. I have one here in my wallet. I was impressed." Ben produced the card and handed it to Gina. "He works out of a tiny office on Boylston. His practice is concentrated on family law, but I figure this might fall under that."

"Yes," said Gina. "Trying to keep a family together."

"Exactly." Ben paused as if weighing his next words.

Now that Gina had a name, she wanted to say goodbye and rush off, lest someone saw her here, someone who knew Harry. But Ben wanted to tell her something.

"You know I went to see him a few weeks ago," he said. "He was here in Cambridge, rabble-rousing. He was determined, despite the cold. And he got a pretty good crowd response."

"Did he see you?"

Ben shook his head. "I was in the back. I wanted to say hello afterward, but ..." He sighed. "He didn't look ready to hear from me."

"So what did you think?"

"Of what?"

"Of Harry. Becoming like Eugene Debs. Proselytizing on street corners."

Ben didn't reply at first. "Something's happened to him," he finally said. "He was always fascinating, and he still is. But he used to be good-humored, easy-going, calm. Now all I heard was disdain. A little boring to listen to, if I'm being frank. Even if you agree with him, all you want is for him to shut up. He speaks in such platitudes. Business is bad, profit is bad, money is bad, materialism, the hunt for wealth. It's hard for people to support, even college students, and as you know, they will support anything. He used to be witty. Poke fun at himself."

"Not anymore. Not in a long time." She lowered her head. Not since they had come back to Boston.

"Well, his grimness is rather off-putting. The system's not working, he keeps saying. Yet most of the people he says this to are working!"

"Not your Harvard crowd." She sped up.

"Students, yes, but others? Bankers, small business owners, hotel managers, accountants, engineers. Professors. Boston is thriving, investing, rebuilding. Everyone has a new car, a cottage in the country, silver bicycles, leather sofas. We send our children to private schools. We go to the Cape for Christmas and August. We dance. The only minus for the rest of us are the liquor laws. Prohibition and Harry—two things that dampen our spirits and both for the same reason: they're joyless."

Gina wanted to laugh, but didn't. She couldn't agree—she couldn't side with Ben, of all people, against her husband, whom she was, after all, trying to help—but she couldn't whole-heartedly disagree either.

"Was there ever joy in the revolution?" she asked.

"It doesn't matter," Ben said. "It's just my observation. Advise him to lighten up, if he can. His current predicament we will fix. I guarantee Domarind will take the work. He'll be perfect for this."

"Why do you think so?"

"Because his only scruple is himself. Beyond that, he cares not a whit for the affects of man. Harry will doubtless tell you, and doubtless has, that the seat of capitalist conscience is not in the heart but in the pocketbook."

"Oh," said Gina, "he's told me."

"Capitalism is a system that coins profit out of the misery of millions."

"This also I've heard."

"The irony will be," said Ben, stopping Gina at the train station on Harvard Square and taking off his hat to say goodbye, "that it is this very system that will keep Harry out of jail. Because James Domarind is about to coin some profit out of your husband's misery."

Six

BEN WAS RIGHT. DOMARIND, a large, ungainly man with a pot belly and thinning hair that he kept meticulously flattened in a comb-over to the right, did not ask about the revolution or dialectical materialism or the command economy. When Gina and Harry went to see him in his one-room, seedy, stale-smelling office above a fancy shoe shop on Boylston, he examined the police report assiduously. He talked about every last detail of it with Harry, while Gina sat silently trying hard not to think about what lovely finds there might be downstairs. She had glimpsed a pair of green suede buckled pumps. Maybe they had her size? Could she excuse herself, say she would be right back?

Domarind wore a suit that had been pressed a week or two earlier, and his shoes, which he clearly had *not* bought downstairs, looked distantly shined, at best. The desk was piled three-feet high with papers and manila files.

The first thing Harry said to him after they had been introduced was, "Everyone is afraid, Mr. Domarind, because the Russian Revolution has sounded the death knell of the old order."

"Perhaps that is why they're trying so hard to throw you in jail, Mr. Barrington," Domarind replied. "They'd like to stay alive a little longer."

After he read the complaint against Harry and listened to the long story of Harry's side, he asked, "Is that all? Any other incidents I should know about?"

"That's all," said Harry.

Domarind chewed on his pencil. He wasn't looking at Harry or at Gina, only at the files in front of him. "Here's the thing," he said. "After you called a few days ago, I wanted to get better acquainted with the man I would be meeting, so I took the liberty of asking the Boston police if they had any other reports on you." He coughed. "I was quite surprised, as you can imagine, by the, um, extensive record of your activities that I received from the police, from the DA's office, and from the District Court—activities stretching back nearly fifteen years and to another city."

"That's all bygones," said Gina, her mind off the shoes. "It's old news."

Domarind nodded. "Absolutely, Mrs. Barrington. That may be. Except …" He coughed again. Still no eye contact. "What is *not* old news is the little incident in 1923, while Mr. Barrington was on probation for a major felony under the Espionage Act, when he was accused of distributing seditionary—"

"No, that can't be right," Gina interrupted. "Harry's had no violations since we returned to Boston."

Harry said nothing.

"Harry?"

"It was just a bullshit thing!" Harry exclaimed.

Gina wobbled in her chair.

"Oh I agree," said Domarind. "Except the terms of your probation clearly stated that you could not violate the terms of it even to litter." He opened his hands in question. "So tell me—how did you keep yourself out of jail?"

Gina could tell Harry was reluctant to confess. "I paid off two of the cops to bury the charge," he said at last. "I don't remember, but they might have taken long sabbaticals to Barbados or St. Croix right at the time of my hearing, and without them, there was no case."

"Well done." Domarind nodded approvingly. "A tropical vacation for two, and no case. What there is, unfortunately, is a file a block long. And the prosecutor has found it. He didn't even have to look that hard."

"What does this mean?" asked Gina.

"What this means," Domarind replied, "is your husband's straightforward case for disruption of the peace has gotten a touch more complicated. Had he stayed away from trouble, the 1923 incident would be swept under the rug. But now, it's a serious and felonious prior. You're currently already being charged with a felony under the Espionage Act for advocating the overthrow of the U.S. government."

"I wasn't advocating. I was recommending."

"After committing a felony by violating probation, you decided to recommend that a mob of civilians take up arms against the United States government? In other words, revolution?"

"Don't worry," Harry said. "I'll be going easy on the revolution from now on."

Green suede shoes forgotten forever, Gina sat swallowed up by the din of the roaring ocean. It felt as if a roof had just blown off her house. The eyewall was behind her the whole time, and she didn't even know it.

She heard Domarind say he would do what he could. He watched Harry write a check for his retainer.

They started for home in silence. Eventually Harry spoke. "I'm delivering papers in the morning. For a little money."

"That's where we are? We need paper delivery money?"

"Just a little extra. For incidentals."

"What paper? The *Globe*?"

He hemmed for a moment. "The *Daily Worker*."

"The *Daily Worker*," she echoed. "You're facing felony charges of sedition, insurrection, possibly treason, and you're selling the Communist Party rag to prove to them that they have no case against you?"

"Not a good case. I do believe that freedom of the press is still a protected right. Look, I'm asking you not to worry. Please. It's not how it was. In the last few years the Workers Party has regrouped. We've moved away from advocating open overthrow. It's a difference in emphasis. We're now focusing on recruiting new members, not campaigning for immediate change. It's less volatile. Everything is fine. So don't fret so much, okay?" He kissed her. "I'm going to the library."

She went home and cleaned the little apartment obsessively until it was time to pick up Alexander from school.

* * *

Domarind asked for one postponement after another until he got a judge he knew to be overworked and close to retirement. The lawyer cited the First Amendment and the Fourth in support of his argument that the case against his client should be dismissed. Miraculously the judge agreed. The case was dismissed. "You're welcome," Domarind said on the steps of the courthouse. "But Harry, you heard the venerable Judge Dockery. You must keep away from the public square. Tempers are high over this communist thing."

"Of course. You're right."

Two months later Harry was arrested again, this time for inciting indirect violence in a piece he had written for the *Daily Worker*.

"I didn't incite violence," Harry told Domarind. He had gone alone this time.

"Did you or did you not quote Berkman and Goldman?"

"Yes, but …"

"Did you or did you not say that all significant change can only be brought about by force?"

"I *quoted* them! *I* didn't say it."

"Harry, please. It doesn't fool even your wife, who, I see, is not by your side today."

"She is busy with our son."

"It won't fool the court."

"Get me the judge you got me last time."

"Unfortunately Dockery's been transferred to Boise."

"Boise … as in Idaho?"

"Is there another one?"

"Is that code for something?"

"Dockery has retired, Harry, yes."

"So find me a socialist judge!"

"Because they abound here in Boston."

"You know they do. Max Eastman didn't serve time for his First Amendment violations in *The Masses*. Who was *his* lawyer?"

The gauntlet was not picked up. "Was Max Eastman on probation?"

"*I'm* not on probation!"

"Of course you are. Dockery had dismissed your last case without prejudice."

"Right. I thought that meant it couldn't be reopened."

"A little knowledge is a dangerous thing, Harry. You should've listened more closely. It means just the opposite. Without prejudice means they can reopen at any time if there's another violation. Which there now is. Reopen the old one, move forward with the new one. Plus the felony probation violation, plus a mile-long record. Charges pile up and up."

"Okay, small mistake on my part. So what do we do now?"

Domarind looked weary. "When you go to the hearing, make sure your wife is not busy with your son, but is by your side. It doesn't look good if you're married, and you go alone. It looks really bad, actually."

"I understand."

"Everywhere you go, take her with you. Do you understand? Whenever you utter a single word in public, make sure she is standing by your side, holding your arm, looking like an elegant Beacon Hill princess."

"I got it the first time, Domarind."

Gina agreed to stay close, but before they got to the next hearing date, they were all arrested: Harry, Gina, and Alexander. They had been in Washington DC, protesting in front of the White House. Harry refused to leave Lafayette Park, and Gina and Alexander, staying close, were collateral damage.

"It's not in the same jurisdiction," Harry said to Domarind. "How can it be considered a mark against me?"

"Tell that to Frank and Jesse James."

"I don't believe the law got to either one of them," Harry grumbled.

Domarind blinked. "Oh, right, I forgot. Okay, so you'll be the smartest person in Liberty Jail," he said. "Is that what you want? You can have the last word on this."

"Clearly I don't want to be in jail."

"It's not that clear, Harry. And what about your wife?"

"Under no circumstances does my wife go to jail."

* * *

After months of legal machinations, Domarind persuaded the District Attorney to accept a plea bargain. Harry got a two-year suspended sentence, six months probation, and four hundred hours of community service on a park-cleaning crew. He appealed only the community service, saying it would be impossible for him to work and serve the four hundred hours. When he was asked what he did for a living, Harry said he took care of his son while his wife worked at the Boston Library and at St. Vincent de Paul's. Citing Alexander's interests, the judge reduced the community service to a hundred hours, to be completed on the weekends when his wife was home. No one checked to see if Gina actually worked at the library or volunteered at St. Vincent's.

"You're lying in court now, Harry?" Gina said, as they walked home. "Isn't there a name for that?"

"I have to edit and condense Bertrand Russell's *Practice and Theory of Bolshevism* for a feature we're running over the next eight weeks. I can't be sweeping up garbage."

Not three months later, Harry got himself arrested again, this time for nothing more than standing with a sign and yelling slogans. The sign said, "Workers of the World Unite!"

Domarind took the city of Boston to the cleaners, making his loud and heady argument on the pin of the First Amendment—the Espionage Act, Sedition Act, and *Schenck v. the United States* be damned. The country wasn't at war. And the point of the First Amendment wasn't protecting speech you agreed with, Domarind yelled from his own apple crate of the lawyer's box, but speech you *didn't* agree with. There was no revolution this time, nor treason. All Harry was doing was displaying the innocent words of the Third International. Harry and Gina fervently hoped that no one in court actually knew what the Third International or Comintern was: an apparatus of Soviet control over the international communist movement. *Unite* was such a good word. It wasn't incendiary! It had many positive connotations. In fact, the very States of America were *United*!

The Boston judge slapped Domarind with contempt of court and denied the motion to dismiss. Domarind took Harry's case to the

District Appeals Court, and then to the Federal Court of Appeals for the District of Massachusetts. The Supreme Court was next, and Domarind was fired up like a kiln. But the Federal Court overturned the original conviction, backing away from sedition and stipulating that just because Harry was on probation did not mean that his First Amendment rights could be trampled on.

Gina breathed a momentary sigh of relief.

Seven

THEY STOPPED RECEIVING INVITATIONS to dinner and to social events like weddings and engagements. How short-lived her white-gloved existence had been, Gina thought, as she walked Alexander to Park Street School every morning.

The lunches with Meredith became sporadic and then stopped altogether. Meredith cited other obligations and duties, but during one such cancelled afternoon when Gina was walking down Beacon Street, she saw Meredith sitting outside a cafe, drinking tea with another Beacon Hill matron, and laughing. Gina walked by with her head raised, smiling as if she were the one having fun.

When she told Harry about it, he laughed. Good riddance, he said. Who needs them? I never liked them.

Their weekends were open, their Saturday nights free.

And then one morning, as Gina was walking up Beacon Street after dropping off Alexander, she saw two female acquaintances coming toward her, still some distance away, chatting with each other, and watched dumbfounded as they, without breaking their stride, crossed the street to avoid the discomfort of acknowledging or even passing her.

"You imagined it," Harry said. "You are blowing it out of all proportion."

It happened again and again. It happened with casual ease and across all spectrums: young and old, rich and working class, men and women—all ostracized her. At Alexander's school, the other mothers stopped speaking to her. Oh, they nodded when she said hello, some even smiled, and then they hurried along as if they were so very busy or they had remembered a vital thing they had to attend to at that precise moment. It was as if she wore a scarlet letter on her chest, or maybe four. W of C. Wife of a Communist.

You're imagining it, Harry said. Don't be paranoid.

She devised a test. For a month she did not speak to anyone at Alexander's school. And in that time no one initiated a conversation with her, not even about the Boston weather.

Alexander was no longer invited to other children's houses; there were no more birthday parties, First Communions, cookie-making afternoons, no more games in the park. In May 1928, when she sent out twelve invitations for his ninth birthday, all twelve came back with regrets. So they took Alexander and his friends from Barrington, Teddy and Belinda, camping in the White Mountains instead. They had a great time. And Harry remained unperturbed. "Did you *want* to be friends with them?"

"I wanted to be friends with someone," said Gina. She missed the social gatherings, her evenings dancing, the charity fundraisers, the hospital functions.

Harry looked at her disapprovingly when she continued to complain. "Have all our desires truly become so empty of meaning?"

Was Gina imagining it, or were Harry's crowds dwindling, too?

Ben was right. Harry was a gifted orator, a fine rhetorical speaker, but he was losing his crowds. The system must be fundamentally rebuilt, he insisted. Okay, but most people didn't want that, not even in the park on Saturday. So he got out of Boston: to Medford, Gloucester, Lexington, Arlington Heights. Gina and Alexander went with him, hoping to spare him arrest. For some reason his unsoftened rhetoric provoked the police less if his stylish wife and engaging child were by his side.

Soon the out-of-town crowds, too, lost their enthusiasm. Was it any wonder? Harry would tell his audience they had to suffer before they had what they needed. But he couldn't answer their shouted questions about how long the suffering would last.

"You're alienating your audience," Gina told him after one especially unsuccessful outing. *Just* his audience, right?

"I don't care," he said. "I know it's hard hearing what I have to say. They'll come around."

Gina bit her tongue. "Alexander! Off the swings. I know it's hard hearing what I have to say. But the bus is waiting."

"The good times will end," Harry shouted in another homily on a Saturday morning on the Common in Watertown. "And then what? Yes, it's good now. But it won't be good like this always. Look at Miami. Do you see what happened there? That's going to happen everywhere. What are you going to do when the money is gone? Where will you turn? Who will help you?"

"It's a cycle," someone yelled back. Someone always yelled back. "Your way, the good times will end for good."

"No economic boom can last forever," Harry roared. "If history taught us anything, it's that."

"Your way, we'll never have an economic boom again."

"Not true. It's the end of injustice! The end of economic slavery! The end of war! You will reap the benefits of your hard work. You won't go hungry."

"I won't be free either." The heckler wouldn't stop.

"What would you rather have, bread or freedom?"

"Man cannot live by bread alone!" someone else shouted out, a woman. They were joining in now, emboldened. Gina stood on tiptoe, to spot the woman who had said that. It almost sounded like her own voice, like something she might say.

Harry paused for an answer. "What will you do when the bread is gone?" he yelled.

"Throw yourself off the rock you stand on," the woman shouted back. "Show us how the state will help you then."

"I can throw myself off the rock till Kingdom come," Harry said, "but you'll still be out of work with no one to turn to. Who can you count on when all the jobs leave this city? You'll have no one to turn to but yourselves. Is that the kind of country you want to live in? That's not the America I believe in!"

"To the sewers," a man shouted, clearly with some rhetorical powers of his own, "and you'll take millions down with you! Your way we will live under the sword. Who wants that?"

"You'll have bread!"

"We'd rather be dead than live under the sword. We'd rather starve."

Hear, hear, the restive crowd murmured. *Hear, hear.*

He wasn't getting through to them.

"Harry," Gina said on the bus back home, her arms around a sleeping Alexander, "do you know why you're not getting through?" She wished she could sleep anywhere, like her peaceful boy.

"They're not ready to receive my message," he said wearily.

"No. Because yours are totalitarian dreams. That's not the model for America. This isn't the country for it." To soften her words, she added, "Perhaps another country. Perhaps Russia."

"Yes!" he exclaimed, as if the thought hadn't occurred to him before she said it that summer evening on public transit.

"I'm being *ironic*," Gina said, brow furrowing. "How is the Soviet Union being held together? They've been decimated by their civil war. They pulled out of the Great War only to lose millions on their own soil. Russia is coming apart. How long will it be held together by the sword?"

"However long it takes."

"Oh, Harry," said Gina, so disappointed. "Even your utopian dreams have become Mussolini-like in their execution."

"Which is to say *what?*"

"You're fascist even in your daydreams, Harry."

"You understand nothing, Gina." He rubbed his perspiring face.

"Perhaps you can explain it better in Roxbury next Saturday. Because the people don't seem to understand you either." She nuzzled Alexander's head and turned to the window.

"What hope is there, if I'm not getting through even to my own wife?"

Pointed silence was her only answer. He changed the subject. "Where have I heard the phrase *Man does not live by bread alone?*" he asked. "They keep shouting it at me during my orations, and I have no response. I feel like I need to have one."

Benevolently Gina smiled. "There's so much you don't know. And you don't even know you don't know it. You want a proper reply to that?"

"Yes."

"Next time you say: that's right, man *doesn't* live by bread alone, but by every word that proceeds from the mouth of God."

Harry groaned. "Oh no. It's from the *Bible*?"

"From Christ's forty days in the desert. From His chat with the devil about miracles and why He refused to perform them."

"How is that possible? Everything I say you turn against me."

"Shout back," continued Gina, mild as the weather, "that Christ is the bread of life. *Cristo è il pane della vita*."

"Oh dear God. Stop it."

She stopped.

"The hopes which inspire Communism," Harry said, "are, in the main, as admirable as those instilled by the Sermon on the Mount."

"So tell that to your people, Harry," said Gina. "Don't hold back. Begin with that next week in Roxbury before you ease into the suffering."

Eight

ON A FRIDAY MORNING in late September, 1929, Gina picked up the telephone receiver to call Esther to find out if she was fetching Alexander from home or from school and discovered that the line was dead.

She didn't know what to do. Why would the telephone be broken? She sifted through the papers in Harry's desk to find the address of the telephone company, but couldn't find any of their bills. She looked for the checkbook, but couldn't find that either.

Harry had already gone out; she no longer asked where, because she didn't want to know, and he no longer told her, because he said he wanted to protect her from knowing. Alexander was in school. Gina had nothing but time. She had planned to go to St. Vincent's. Instead she put on her coat and hat and went to the bank.

Afterward she might have stumbled in the opposite direction from home, toward the water, the docks, the ships, distant lands, somewhere far.

Somewhere else.

Anywhere else.

She was Miami, a once tropical paradise, isolated in a sea of raving white water. The railroads jammed and embargoed on the left, the *Prinz Valdemar* lying beached and sunk in her harbor on the right, precluding the arrival of rebuilding materials and any departure of battered tourists. No way out, by rail or by sea. Just Gina, Alexander, and Harry, bankrupt and trapped with the unquenchable, indestructible Mediterranean fruit fly.

Chapter 18

WHITE TERRORISTS ASK FOR MERCY

One

SHE WAS HUNCHED OVER on the floor in the kitchen, her head in her hands. Harry was standing over her trying to explain what he couldn't explain, like on a Saturday in Roxbury.

"There's less money than I'd hoped there would be."

"When you say less, you mean no money. Right? Because that's what there is. Nothing."

"Not nothing."

"*Nothing.*"

There was nothing to say.

"Where is it?"

"What?"

"Where is our money?"

"Where do you think? We spent it."

"On what?"

"On living. You don't have shoes? You don't have dresses? I don't have books?"

"That's all we have," she said. "And I don't have many dresses or shoes anymore. Three years ago I donated most of them to St. Vincent's on consignment. Where is our money?"

"Boston is expensive. Now do you see why I wanted to move from the Mt. Vernon house? It drained our resources. We never should've lived there. We should've rented a smaller place from the start."

She couldn't look at him. What was she going to do when Alexander came out of his room for dinner? No dinner and his mother on the floor. For the sake of her son, she had to get herself together. "We lived like kings and queens in Jupiter," she said, struggling to her feet, refusing his proffered hand. "We wanted for nothing. We ran a real house, not a hovel you rented us on Mt. Vernon. We had servants. We paid a rum-runner to smuggle all the liquor out of Cuba into our cellars. We had two cars. We had a boat. We spent barely twenty thousand dollars on that blissful, astonishing life."

"I thought it was more," he said.

"No. We came to Boston with enough for forty years of fine living. I know what we came here with. And you're telling me that seven years later we don't have enough to pay the June telephone bill? In September?"

"I *know*." He was sheepish. "I can't believe how fast the money has gone. I almost wish you were still taking care of it, like you did in Lawrence, and at Bellagrand. It was so much easier."

"Easier!"

"Yes. Why are you looking at me like that?"

"Because I don't know who you are," she said. "I don't know who I sleep next to every night."

"Please don't wring your hands like that. You're going to break something. You're scaring me."

"I'm scaring *you? Dio mio!*" she cried. "*Dio mio!* Is there nothing left to be exalted?" To despair was a sin, but Gina couldn't help it—she was losing all hope.

"My struggle against inequality is left."

"There is no more money left for your inequality!"

"There's always some somewhere."

Gina shook her head.

"Don't worry about the rent, I told you. And Esther will take care of Alexander."

Gina didn't dare lift her eyes lest Harry see the boiling scorn in them. "How dismissive you are of her money," she said, "and yet how sure of it. You rely on it the instant you reject it. You do understand that someone out there must make money so you can be a communist."

"Who would that be? My sister? She wants for nothing. She hasn't worked a day in her life."

"Your sister," Gina said, "spends her days volunteering at hospitals around Boston and raising money for the poor, for charitable food pantries and clothes bins. She and Rosa take dinner to the local home for the terminally ill every Sunday. She spends hours reading to people who are about to die. The only privilege your son has comes through her largesse. His bikes, his hockey skates, his shoes, clothes, books, his private school all come from her." Gina couldn't get far enough from him. The ten plagues had well and truly descended on Egypt if she was now defending Esther to Harry.

"I don't want another material thing."

"It's always wise, Harry, not to want what you don't have."

"Don't be flippant, Gina. Why can't you trust me? It'll turn out all right. It always works out, and this will, too."

"How?"

"I don't know. But it will. I promise you. It'll work out."

"Where is it? Where is our money?"

"I don't know where it is."

"Yes, you do."

He was silent.

Gina wanted him to tell her, to not be afraid to say the words out loud. The helpful bank manager had already informed her of the sacks of cash that had been carried out in wheelbarrows for the bail bondsmen, the court fees, the penalties, the legal costs. Bribe money to pay off the police and the lowly assistants at the DA's office, who would inexplicably lose files, evidence, names of material witnesses. Domarind. It all added up—and how. Oh, and let's not forget the barrelfuls of dollars that went to the Boston offices of the *Daily Worker* and to the Workers Party.

That's where their money had gone. The communists had coined quite a profit from her misery.

"It's Domarind," Harry said. "He's a vulture. He's a shyster. A thief. He overcharges me for every minute he spends on my case. Every time he goes to court to file a five-minute motion, it costs me a hundred dollars. He is merciless with his fees. He's terrible. Who recommended him? We couldn't have done worse if the person who referred him hated me and wanted to cause me nothing but harm."

"What are you talking about? Domarind has kept you out of jail for three years."

"Is it my fault he overcharges me?"

She stumbled back against the kitchen table, tripping over the sash of her beige housedress. She almost fell. She didn't understand the words that came out of his mouth. It was as if she had reverted to the language of her childhood. Everything he said sounded like gibberish. Why, just now he had said something so *irrational* as to make her doubt she'd heard it right. For a moment Gina thought Harry said it wasn't his fault that all the Bellagrand money had gone to his lawyer.

Her face must have been a sight.

"Okay, okay," he said, with a conciliatory tilt of his head. "I admit, a little bit did go to the CPUSA. Membership dues, small contributions, donations to the *Daily Worker*. It's an operational issue. Printing costs, ink, newsprint, distribution—they're all expensive. It's like the local parish, Gia. Didn't your mother tithe at St. Mary's? Don't you tithe at St. Leonard's? It's all right for you to give to the Catholic Church, but not all right for me to give to the Communists?"

She slammed her hands over her ears to stop herself from hearing him. For one agonized second she thought, *if I throw myself from the window, I will stop hearing him forever.*

"What happens now?" she whispered. "The host has been bled dry. Now what?"

"Bear with me a few more weeks. I'm working on a plan."

How far was it to the window?

"Why can't you trust me? Everything will work out fine."

486

Why could she still hear him while her palms squeezed her head in such a vise?

The following day she was supposed to take Alexander to school, but at six in the morning he and she were all the way over in the North End, at St. Leonard's. Mass was long over, and yet there she remained in the pew on her knees, her head bent, her hands clasped together.

"Mom, what are you doing?" Alexander whispered.

"I'm praying."

"I know that. You've been kneeling a long time."

Why do I suspect it hasn't been long enough.

"What do you keep praying for, Mama? We have to go. I'm going to be late again. I was late four times already."

I'm praying for you, *mio figlio*. That's all I ever pray for now. Only you.

"Is he talking back?"

"Who?"

"God."

"I don't know, *caro*. I'm trying to listen, but all I keep hearing is *you*."

Alexander thought for a moment. "That's because Jesus has nowhere else to be," he whispered, "but *I* have a math test first period, Mom. We have a really long walk …"

"We'll take a taxi."

She dragged herself up, and took him by the hand.

"Well? Did he answer you?"

Her arm around Alexander, she searched Salem Street in vain for a taxi. Her poor faithful Flaminio would've taken her to Park Street for free. "Yes," Gina replied to Alexander. "With his silence, perhaps he did."

"It's good when God is silent?" Alexander looked at his mother as if she weren't right in the head.

"Of course, *mio bambino*. It means things aren't so bad yet that he must answer you. It means he's busy taking care of those who need him more."

Two

WEEKS THAT FELT LIKE YEARS passed in leaden silence. The telephone remained disconnected. Gina hoped her sister-in-law would volunteer to take care of the unpaid balance when she discovered she couldn't get in touch with Alexander. But it didn't happen. Their standing arrangement simply continued. Every other Friday, Esther drove in from Barrington, picked up the boy after school and took him back with her for the weekend. They didn't need to speak because they lived together three days out of every fourteen.

Gina's self-imposed balloon of denial about all things was soon punctured by a letter she received from James Domarind.

> *Dear Mrs. Barrington,*
> *I have been trying to get in touch with you by telephone for the*
> *last three weeks, to no avail. I am writing to you because it is*
> *of the utmost importance that you call me immediately and*
> *schedule an appointment to come and see me as soon as possible.*
> *There are grave complications in your husband's ongoing legal*
> *proceedings that profoundly concern you, and which I must*
> *discuss with you at your earliest convenience.*
> *Yours sincerely,*
> *James Domarind, Esq.*
> *PS As a side matter, my secretary informs me that your*
> *husband's last four checks for my retainer, for June, July, August,*
> *and September, have been returned by your bank for insufficient*
> *funds. I'm sure this is an oversight on his part, but I respectfully*
> *request that you please bring payment with you when you arrive*
> *for your appointment.*

Gina wished she could close her eyes, wake up, and have it be morning the next day.

Or perhaps a day farther up the road.

But how far?

She couldn't say.

No use wishing for that, she decided. Every tomorrow only leads to the end. And that would be upon her soon enough. This felt different from other crises, other problems, other hardships. There was something final about these waning Indian summer days. As if there was no way out.

Gina did not call Domarind, did not make an appointment to see him. She couldn't pay him, so what was the point? If they had no money for the telephone bill, Harry's lawyer was not going to extract a nickel from her purse.

A few days after the receipt of the hateful letter, on the morning of an unseasonably warm Tuesday, there was a knock on her door. Harry had already gone out; he couldn't bear to stay with her in their cramped apartment. When she opened the door in her tattered housedress, there stood James Domarind, panting from walking up five flights of stairs. He tipped his hat.

"Good morning, Mrs. Barrington."

"Good morning, Mr. Domarind." She tried to calm her pounding heart. "To what do I owe the pleasure of your visit?"

"No pleasure in this, Mrs. Barrington. But you haven't responded to my entreaty for your presence in my office. I had no choice but to call on you in person."

"I apologize," she said. "I have not received any letters from you."

Quietly he stood on the landing. "Why are you lying to me?"

"I'm not."

"The last letter I sent, I sent certified. You signed for it yourself. I have your signature in my hands."

She stepped out into the stairwell. "Yes, yes, I now recall receiving something." She held the door almost closed behind her. "But you're my husband's lawyer. I passed on the letter to him. I don't know what he did with it. He'll be home later this afternoon. Would you like to come back then?"

Domarind shook his thick, slick head. "It's you I came to see," he said. "You're the one I need to speak to."

With reluctance, she allowed him inside, cursing herself for not finding the words to keep him out. She asked him to wait and hurried to change into a rust-colored autumn walking dress with a pleated flare, a drop-down waist and velvet side ties. She pulled back her hair into a monastic bun. She pinched her cheeks to make them look less ashen.

She would've offered him coffee, but she didn't have any. She would've offered him a baked good, but it had been a long time since she made anything sweet, bought anything sweet.

He must have seen her discomfort, because he took pity on her. "I don't need anything," he said. "I didn't come here to eat. This isn't a party. You are in trouble, Mrs. Barrington."

They sat across from each other in the living room. She sat by the window in Harry's hard chair. Domarind sat on the soft couch. When she needed to turn away from his tough, uncompromising face, which was all the time, she would look to the right and see the Common through a dazzling backdrop of leafy flame. She wondered if today was Harry's apple crate day. Or was he teasing out the subtle nuances between Leninism and Trotskyism in a ten-thousand-word feature for the *Daily Worker*? She looked away from the park. She didn't know where to look, what to do. She stared into her hands.

"I'll be brief and I'll be blunt," Domarind said, "because you are out of time. Have you heard of the Immigration Act of 1903?"

"Vaguely, why?"

"The Immigration Act of 1917?"

"I suppose."

"The Immigration and Sedition Act of 1918?"

"Mr. Domarind ..."

"I will explain." He produced a piece of paper from his pocket and unfolded it. "In 1903, the government stipulated that four classes of undesirables be forbidden entry into the United States. Anarchists, epileptics, beggars, and importers of prostitutes." He coughed, as if for emphasis. "But anarchists *first*, Mrs. Barrington."

"Mr. Domarind, the law does not apply to me. Frankly, I don't know why you're bringing it up. I am not requesting entry into the United States. In case you're not aware of it, I am already *in* the United States. Boston, to be specific. Sitting in front of you."

He continued. "The 1903 Act was amended in 1917 after all the trouble during the Great War, trouble with which I am aware you're personally acquainted. Then—and this is the part that concerns you—the law was amended for the third and final time, and came to be called the Immigration Act of 1918. The new law has greatly increased the powers of the Department of Justice and the Department of Immigration to deport any and all undesirables by simple administrative fiat without any due process niceties such as deportation hearings."

"Mr. Domarind, this has nothing to do with me."

"It has everything to do with you, I'm afraid. Under the provisions of the Act, all aliens who are either themselves members or are affiliated with any members, organizations, groups, or persons who disseminate, circulate, propagate, print, display, or advocate, among other things, the overthrow of the government of the United States by force, or any other kind of sabotage can and will be deported."

"I am not an alien," Gina whispered.

"We'll get to that. Aside from your damaging affiliation with your husband, who is a vociferous and unrepentant member of the Communist Party of the United States, you yourself retain a paid membership in the Free Society, do you not? You have a lifetime subscription to *Mother Earth*. These are expenses, Mrs. Barrington, that won't be easily explained to the Department of Justice once they've noted that you cannot pay your telephone or your legal bills."

"My husband is full of words," she said. "He is not full of action. And I will cancel my membership in the Free Society, if it pleases you." She had forgotten about that. Harry must have been renewing her dues.

"Too late for that," said the brisk lawyer. "You know your husband's record better than I do; I don't have to review it for you. The number of times he has been arrested for obstructing recruitment stations, for violent assault, for incitement to violence, for disturbing the peace, for endangering a minor—your son—and for advocating the overthrow of our government by *any* means necessary and establishing a communist dictatorship here in the United States such as they have in the Soviet Union beggars belief."

"If you don't have to review it, then why do you, Mr. Domarind?" said Gina. "And if you're not up to the job ..."

"There isn't a lawyer in this country who is up to the job, madam. And if there were, you'd have no money to pay for him anyway. You think a public defender will do better for your husband?" Domarind sighed. "Look, the purpose of my visit is not to discuss Harry. It's about you. You are going to have to wash your hands of him, if you are to save yourself."

Gina braced for the coming blow.

"Because they are going to deport you."

She tried to take a deep breath. She couldn't even manage a shallow one. "That's not possible. I'm an American citizen."

"I'm getting to that," said Domarind, taking out a handkerchief and wiping his brow, even though it was cool in the room. "You are an American citizen because you married Harold Barrington. Isn't that correct? Well, your husband was stripped of his citizenship in 1928. So guess what happens to you?"

"No, he wasn't. That's a lie."

"Not only is it *not* a lie, but he himself agreed to it as part of his last plea bargain. You weren't in court for that particular hearing? I don't blame you. Been to one, been to them all, I say. Nonetheless, as one of the conditions of his release, your husband's citizenship was revoked. He told the court he had no desire to be a citizen of any country that oppressed its people like the United States."

"He was hot under the collar," Gina muttered.

"Perhaps. But did that preclude his understanding of the judge's order? Because he was clearly told that as a non-citizen, any transgression could get him deported. He and you have been living at the mercy of the Justice Department. So what does he do? Instead of lying low, behaving himself, he has gone on an underground rampage of disseminating, by any and all means available to him, Soviet cables to the CPUSA."

"That can't be, Mr. Domarind."

"But it is, Mrs. Barrington. He was told what would happen, and he flipped them off."

"It's a mistake. It's …"

"I will allow that he didn't think it through. But he knew what it would mean. He just didn't know what it would mean for you. Or for your son." Domarind paused. "Or did he?"

At the mention of Alexander, it went dark for a moment in the apartment, as if night had fallen in the middle of the morning. Gina may have fainted, sitting up straight and narrow. When she came to, she was slumped in the chair, Domarind was still sitting on the couch, the fired-up trees were outside her window, and Harry was standing in the open doorway, a paper bag in his hands.

The three of them eyed each other. Gina tried to collect herself. Harry shut the door. "Why are you here?" he said. "Why are you upsetting my wife? I told you last week, I'll pay you soon."

Domarind stood up. "I don't believe you. But that's not why I'm here."

"Then why are you here?"

"Because I've been telling you for three years to consider how your actions will inevitably affect your family. You refused to listen. And you haven't been truthful with your wife. She doesn't even know what's been happening."

"Get out."

"I heard it straight from the DA four days ago: you are going to be deported. I told you what would happen if you broke the law one more time. You ignored me. As always."

"I said get out."

"The United States is about to latch its doors." Domarind turned his attention to Gina. "Either Italy or the Soviet Union, Mrs. Barrington. But I'll tell you right now, Italy is not as welcoming as it used to be. Mussolini has cracked down on all anarchists living in his country, and when I say cracked down, I don't mean cracked down like our friendly justice system cracks down, giving your husband twelve chances, thirteen, and then three more. Oh no. Mussolini is putting the anarchists against the wall and shooting them in the town square. Just read the papers. Trust me, even if you could, you don't want to go to Italy."

"I'm not an anarchist," said Gina.

"Domarind, get out," said Harry. "There will be a deportation hearing."

"I wish just once, Harry, you would pay mind to someone other than yourself. I told you, the DA told you, the judge told you, there are *no* deportation hearings for you. A court-ordered signature is all that's required. And if you will forgive me, as of today, I am going to respectfully bow out as your legal counsel."

"You are the legal *enemy*, that's why. You've never helped me."

"That's right," said Domarind. "It's all my fault. Well, blah blah. The only thing J. Edgar hears is that you continue to actively support the Soviet Union against the United States. In your book it's freedom. In his it's treason. And on this one, he has the last word, not you. So pack your bags." Domarind turned to Gina. "Gina," he said imploringly, "you've got one chance to save your son. Leave him with his aunt—"

"Domarind! Get the fuck out!"

"You heard my husband—out!" Gina yelled. "Get out, get out, get out!"

She pushed him with her hands, shoved him across the apartment, out onto the landing, and slammed the door so hard behind him that the wooden jamb splintered and broke.

Panting, she turned to Harry.

Three

SHE SAID NOTHING. The pit of black dread made her mute. And he was never one for words, not unless someone was being oppressed. He took two sandwiches and a canister of soup out of the paper bag he'd been holding. "I got this from Trinity Church," he said, as if they had just finished playing cards. "They were giving it away."

"Nice to know you can count on the Church in time of trouble."

"This isn't a time of trouble, my darling," said Harry. "This is a time of opportunity."

She watched him from across the room. "Why didn't you tell me you renounced your citizenship?" she said quietly. She put her hands on her chest. Something was wrong with her. She couldn't get out a full breath without pain.

"I didn't want you to worry," he said. "Look at how you get. That's why I don't tell you half of what's going on. You get so anxious, and most of the time everything works out."

"Is this going to work out?"

He wasn't stressed. He was joyous, animated. "Gia," he said, coming around the dining table to get close to her. "Don't misconstrue what life is offering us. It's not closing a door. It's opening our future."

"Harry, did you know we faced deportation if there was one more charge against you? Have you known this since last year?" Known and rolled on anyway, pulpits, pamphlets, promises?

"I knew they were threatening it," he said, nonchalantly. "Now listen to me …" Catching her by the hand, he wrapped his arm around her waist, as if they were dancing. "Come with me." Kissing the inside of her wrist, he pulled her toward the open bedroom door.

She yanked away. "Have you gone *insane*? There is no peace inside me."

"You're wrong, there's always peace inside," he whispered, trying to catch her mouth in a kiss, but settling for her wrists and palms. "I know this for a fact. Even when there is a squall outside. Like now."

Unseduced, she pulled away. When he reached for her again, she feinted this way, that. He took one step forward, she took two steps back.

"Did you know you were putting our family into this kind of danger, and did it anyway?"

He lowered his arms to his sides. They stood without speaking.

"Well, they finally heard you, Philip Nolan," Gina said. "My dear man without a country. You've been wishing to never hear of the United States again. Now they're about to see to it."

Harry chewed his lip, rolled his head from side to side. "If we want, I have a man who can fix it. Fix it better than Domarind."

"Who will pay this man?"

"Maybe Esther. You don't think she'll pay to keep Alexander here?"

Gina raised her chin. "Still falling back on your father's money," she said with scorn. "Nothing is ever real, even this, because you think there will always be a way out."

"That's just the thing, though!" He lurched forward. "I don't want a way out. I want a way *in*." His hands flew toward the window. "To the Soviet Union."

"You're delusional." Blood had drained from her white hands.

"It's my strongest desire. You know that. I've never wanted anything more in my life."

"Anything?"

He caught her again, both hands on her waist, drawing her near, ignoring her horror-struck face. "You are my love, and my life. Have you been walking the streets for months, as I have? Have you recited the arguments for and against, as I have?"

"For and against staying with you? Leaving you? Running screaming? Oh, yes, Harry. I have."

"Stop it," he said, letting go of her, cooling down. "Stop being cruel to me when I'm trying hard to be loving."

"You should have told me about your secret desires," she said. "Shared some of these musings with me. With me, Margaret Janke, Kenneth Femmer, your father, the parole board, the District Attorney."

"Russia, Gina! Beyond the shadow of my name and my station. Where no one knows me, or us. Not like Boston, where you can't walk down the block to buy a newspaper without some idiot judging you. In Russia, we can be like everybody else."

"Who is we?"

"You, me. Alexander."

"You want *Alexander* to go to the Soviet Union?" Gina mock laughed.

"Why are you laughing? We can't leave him here."

"We can't?"

That's when he backed away from her. That's when he lost his good humor. *Finally.*

"Are you joking again? Because—"

496

"Do I look to you like I'm joking?"

"Gina! You want to leave our son in America while we move to the Soviet Union?"

"I don't want to move to the Soviet Union!"

"But there's a chance we will have to." He paused. "A good chance."

"You just told me you know a man who can fix it."

"I lied! We can't fix it, okay? They are going to deport us."

"What have you done?" She was shaking. "Not Alexander. They're not going to deport *him*."

"Can you hear yourself right now?"

"Are you hearing *yourself*? It's the Soviet Union!"

"It's our son!"

"I know!" she cried. "You should have thought of *him* on your streets of daydreams!"

"I did think of him! It didn't occur to me for a moment we would leave him."

"We can't take him to Russia, Harry!"

Harry's mouth dropped open. His eyes drained of color. He stared at her uncomprehendingly. "You want to *abandon* Alexander?"

"I didn't say that!"

"Then what *did* you say? Because that's what I heard."

"I don't want him to go to the Soviet Union," she breathed out.

"It's because of him that I want us to go more than anything. Him, most of all. Do you want him to grow up soft like me? Do you want impossible expectations to suffocate him, too?"

"You want him to go to the Soviet Union so no one will *expect* anything of him?" She laughed. Cackled.

"In Russia," Harry said, "Alexander won't have anything to fall back on except himself. He will be forever free of my father's name, and of my father's money."

"You want that for him? To have nothing?"

"Not nothing!" Harry yelled. "To have *himself*. That's more important than power, or status, or wealth, or God. It's more important than anything."

497

"If you want him to have nothing," Gina said, "you've done a splendid job of making that happen here. Why would he need to go all the way to Russia?"

"Because his parents are going."

"Get another lawyer, Harry," she said, gasping again. "Save us. Stop us."

"Save us for what? We have no money. I can't write a word for a newspaper without the DA practically threatening me with execution!"

"So what? You weren't making any money at your Red newspaper!"

"We can't live here anymore. And besides, here our son will always be a Barrington. Have you not walked down the street lately? It's an abomination. I can't get milk at the grocery store without nasty looks being thrown my way."

"Harry, please!" She folded her hands in prayer. "I have dragged Alexander with us everywhere, to bail you out, to stand by your side, to talk to your lawyers, to join you in court, to proclaim our solidarity. We have gone with you everywhere—but you can't be serious about Russia."

"Since 1917," he said, nodding. "And in Russia we will work for *ourselves*."

"We could have worked for *ourselves* in Spanish City," she said. "We could have sold the books you love, grown oranges."

"In Russia we will change the way man thinks."

Gina would not allow herself to be cheated out of words as she was out of choices. She would use all the English at her disposal to prove to him he was mad.

"Have you not read what Emma Goldman wrote after she came back from Russia?" she asked. "She published a scathing book about what's going on there."

Harry dismissed it with a twirl of his hand. "First of all, they were fighting for survival when she was there. She was thrust into Russia during the civil war. That was unfortunate. It's better now."

"She wrote there was no freedom."

"Is there freedom here?"

"Yes! You've lived your whole life here and never worked," Gina said. "You've stood in the park in the afternoon and shouted at the passersby about what a terrible country America is. You think you can do that in Russia?"

"I wouldn't *want* to do that in Russia. And we're broke because I'm not free to say what I think, to do as I please."

"We're broke because you haven't worked and you've spent your mother's money and your father's money!"

"You think *you're* free? Gina, they've taken away one of your most fundamental rights—the right to drink what you like. Your freedom to imbibe spirits as a free woman has been snatched from you by the busybodies in Washington, because they decided you don't have the right to your own body."

"It's detestable. But it's going to be repealed."

"Yes, but you do understand the concept of a man in a suit taking away from you power over your own life?"

"Harry! Emma Goldman says in Russia the Communists have taken away *everything*! Yes, Prohibition is a great example of the corruption of the meaning of government. But in Russia that corrupted power is unchecked. There wouldn't even be the possibility of a repeal. They've taken away the people's right to get together with their friends, to print things, to make copies of the things they've printed, to disseminate them on the street corner the way Goldman had distributed *Mother Earth*. They've taken away the right to speak your mind in public. You're no longer allowed to use Marx's dialectical method to arrive at the truth."

"Because Lenin believed they had already arrived at it," Harry said. "They were fighting a civil war. How many times do I have to say it? It's better now. Where have you been reading this propaganda?"

"Emma Goldman," said Gina. "She is not in Russia anymore. She is writing her propaganda from Germany."

"So she was free to leave?"

"It wasn't so good that she stayed. Read her book, Harry."

"I don't want to read her damn book! I've been reading all my life. I don't want to read anymore. I want to go and *do*."

"Go and *do* in the Soviet Union?"

"Yes! I want to live the way I want, *my* way. I want Alexander to learn to live *his* way."

"This isn't about Alexander. Stop it. This is about *you*."

"And him. I want him to have a new consciousness. I want him to be a new man."

"Yes," said Gina. "But will he be a free man? Will he be able to choose his own work, will he keep the product of that work for himself? I don't care if he is a shoemaker or a poet, Harry, but what I *do* care about is this: will he live in bondage? Will he be a serf?"

"Stop echoing the anarchists, Gina. Think for yourself. This whole freedom thing, it's so bourgeois. It's how the Americans brainwash you—by making you believe it's the greatest good."

"Isn't it?"

"No! Equality is the greatest good. Justice. Community."

Gina stared at him, baffled. She tried again. "Big Bill Haywood, your old employer and friend. Do you know where he is?"

"In the Soviet Union."

"Well, no," Gina said. "He is dead. What, you didn't hear? Yes, he died last year. Probably right around the time you were renouncing your American citizenship—and mine. Drank himself to death in a tiny room in Moscow, utterly marginalized after Lenin's death. He had been petitioning the U.S. since 1925 to allow him to return home."

Harry glared at her with open hostility. Gina welcomed it. At least now he reflected what she was feeling. They had stopped moving in their antagonistic *pas de deux*. "What's your point?"

"Begging them to let him come *home*!" she said. "But he had skipped out on a twenty-year sentence, so the Americans were not amenable to having him back."

"What's—your—fucking—*point*!"

"All your old colleagues who went to Russia are coming back with horror stories! That's my point. Are you going to listen to them?"

"No! We are going to forge our own story."

She was breathing hard, thinking hard. "They killed the Tsar," she said.

"It's supposition. No one knows for sure."

"They *shot* the Tsar," she repeated slower, as if he hadn't heard her properly, "and his entire family. They shot them in the middle of the night, in a small room, smaller than this one, with machine guns."

"Conjecture. You don't know."

"Harry Barrington, if that's how the Bolsheviks treat royalty, what do you think is going to happen to *you*?"

"Emma Goldman was fine. Big Bill was fine."

"She ran for Germany, and he drank himself to death! He spent his whole life advocating for radical change and after he saw what it looked like he killed himself!"

"Right there, that's how you know we're going to be fine," Harry said, a picture of fake calm. "Because I hate the Germans, and you don't drink."

They backed away into their separate corners, to get their breath back between rounds. Shaking, she took a drink of water. He took off his suit jacket, his tie, unbuttoned his shirt. He was perspiring.

"What's *wrong* with you?" Harry asked her from his corner. "The Soviet Union is the one thing you've decided to become a skeptic about?"

"Yes."

"Your whole life you've judged everything through rose-colored glasses. The difficulties between us, Lawrence, your immigrant roots, your hard-scrabble existence, my father, your brother. You've put a shine on it all. For thirty years you've lulled me with your peachy vision. But right here is where you draw the line?"

Gina didn't know what to say. Was he right? No, he wasn't. He wasn't right. "Yes. This is where I draw the line. I should have drawn it at Bellagrand. Live and learn. Everybody has to draw it somewhere, and this is where I draw mine."

"You mean draw it exactly between what I want and what you want."

Her fists stiffened, her jaw stiffened. "What do you mean?" she asked quietly, trying to keep the Sicilian in, though inside her, the volcano was spitting steam. "All I've done is walk the line behind you in everything."

"Not this."

"In everything else."

"You most certainly have not."

She stepped out from her corner, around the couch, walked closer to him. Took long strides toward him.

"You wanted to read, become *smart*, find your way?" she said, mocking him. "You didn't want to work for penny wages? So *I* did. I was used to it, I reasoned. You already gave up so much. No point in your giving up the things you love most—reading and dreaming. *I* gave you that!"

"If you really wanted that for me, you would have let me stay in prison."

"I told you to stay!" That was shouting, straight from Belpasso. Red in the face, breathless and loud. "I gave you that choice, Harry! Me or the *Buford*! Me or prison. All you had to do was say the word. One word! And you would have had what you wanted." She was too close to him now, and they had nowhere to go.

"I knew you didn't mean it."

"I meant it! And still do—go now! Get out! No one is going to stop you from your heart's desire, least of all me. Go!" Steam was coming out of her mouth, her ears, her very pores. She flailed at him, hit him with her arms, hit him with desperate blows to his head, his shoulders.

He grabbed her wrists. "And what are you going to do?"

"Don't worry about me!" She tried to yank away. He wouldn't let her go. They struggled, in the middle of their living room, in the middle of the morning, with the sun outside, the Boston Common, trolleys screeching to a stop under their windows. "What are you afraid of?" she panted. "*Vada con Dio*. Who's stopping you? Go to Russia. Go with God."

"If I go, I take Alexander with me. He's not staying with you."

She screamed in desperation. And still he wouldn't let go of her.

"What I *want*," he said, gasping for air himself, "what I want *most* in the world is what I've always wanted. For you and me to be one. For us to share the same dream, you, me, our boy."

"Let go of me."

He let go. She fell away.

"I admit," he said, "Back then, I didn't want to go to Russia by myself. Or now. I want us to go together. As a family."

"No."

"All I want is for my life to have meaning."

"Dream a different dream." She was rubbing her wrists, hyperventilating, not looking at him.

He stepped toward her.

She staggered away. "Leave me alone."

"I didn't want to work with my father because I don't want to build the same old tired things! I want to build something that has never been built!" He was bowed over in his overwrought intensity, unable to continue.

Like Panama. Gina straightened up. Her heart raced, but she appraised him coldly, despite his impassioned cry for understanding. Her eyes glazed over. She reached back in memory, recalling another time when she had this very discussion about the crux of all life: What was the price you were willing to pay for the thing you wanted most in the world?

Her eyes on him softened. *She* was once what he wanted most.

She searched again for the words that might convince him. "John Reed, Max Eastman. Have you read them since they've come back from the Soviet Union? It's not just me, Harry. Everyone has become a skeptic, everyone has metamorphosized into a non-believer, has changed his opinion, his allegiance."

"They're wrong," Harry said. "Besides, I'm hardly going to take their word for it."

"Why not? You took their word for everything before."

He shook his head. "I didn't. I approved of them because they agreed with *me*. Not because I agreed with *them*. Now they're no longer useful to me."

She stood in front of him, shoulders down, arms hanging. "Am I still useful to you?"

He opened his hands. "What am I without you?" he whispered. "What am I without Alexander?"

She opened her own hands in reply.

"I can't go without you," Harry said. "The Soviets won't let me enter without my family. I've been in touch with them through Comintern." He bowed his head with remorse. "I'm sorry. After I lost my citizenship I had to start planning for our future. They'll take us, but only if we're together. Like Big Bill, they don't want my allegiance to be divided. Me there, my family here."

"*Would* your allegiance be divided?" Gina asked. "Or …" Her voice cracked. "Would it be wholly with them?"

"Of course it would be divided. In any case, *they* think so."

"You can always divorce me, to placate them."

"I don't want to divorce you, what are you saying? They don't want a single man. Families are the bedrock of the new Soviet society. All the generations, the young and the old, become reborn."

Confusion reigned in Gina's head. "It sounds so much like evangelization. It even uses the same language."

"Why are we arguing?" he asked. "This is who you married. This is who I was thirty years ago. This is who I am now. Did you think it was all posturing?"

He stepped so close, his chest was almost touching her breasts. She stood like a pillar in front of him, letting him touch her, letting him caress her.

"It was for me," she said quietly.

"What was for you?" He stroked her arms.

"Posturing."

"What are you talking about?"

"Don't you see?" She stepped away from his caress. Divided again. "How blind you are. How eternally blind. I don't care about any of it. I never did."

"You did once."

Gina shook her head. "I never did. You have fundamentally misunderstood *me*."

"Unlike other men, perhaps, who might have understood you better?"

Her hands flew to her heart. She cried out in anguish. "There are no other men! There was only you. From the moment I stepped

504

off the boat, my heart was only yours. I was just a silly girl and you dismissed me, and I spent five years reforming myself for you. I finished high school for you and learned to work for you and read stupid books I had no interest in for you. I learned to talk politics and anarchy and socialism, I learned to read Russian, so I could read Bakunin, I read Marx, I pretended to be a feminist, not to care about religion or children—all for *you!*" She sobbed from the depths of her despairing soul. "I wore silk gloves because I loved them, yes, but mostly because in wearing them I made myself into the kind of woman I thought you could love. Into the kind of woman your family might accept. Because I thought that was what you wanted. A woman of your own kind."

"It *was* what I wanted," Harry said in a stunned voice.

"I *know!* So I gave you what you wanted. You wanted progressive? I gave you a modern version of the girl I never wanted to be. I wanted to run the restaurant with my brother and mother, have a house, have a baby with you, five babies! I might have dreamed about being a Harvard professor's wife, but I didn't want to march on the streets or be a Wobbly. I didn't want Angela to die, or for you to be in prison, I didn't want the unions or the syndicalists. All of it horrified me!"

"*You're* horrifying me," he said. "What *did* you want?"

"Nothing." Gina wept. "Just you. I loved you. That's it. From the moment I met you, I loved you. I stood with you. I went to Simmons College for you and adopted a radical air for you. I pretended to be interested in other boys, so you would think I believed in free love, because that's what the socialists believed, that's what Emma believed."

"It was the least attractive thing about her sermons," Harry said.

"You say that now, because I'm your wife. *Love has the magic power to make of a beggar a king.* Remember? How you liked waking up next to the woman who believed in free love on the beach in Revere."

"Who wouldn't? A medfly could've woken up in love next to you."

They couldn't look at each other, remembering the ocean sands in Hampton when their entire life lay open before them.

"Please, Harry," she whispered, her breaking voice catching on every letter. "Don't ask me to go to Russia with you. Don't ask Alexander to go to Russia with you."

"Gia," he said, "I will never leave my son behind. Never."

"Me neither."

"So why are you saying you want to leave him?"

"Because I don't want us to go!"

"You can live only one life. We all have to choose. Like before. Either Boston or Bellagrand. One or the other. You can't have both."

Bitterness flowed through her on the dry banks of her empty rivers. "And now, as my ultimate punishment," said Gina, "I will have neither."

Hours passed. The day was at a standstill. Alexander, the object of their agony, would be home soon. Unfed, unquenched, unresolved, Harry and Gina undressed and in bed tried to feed and quench and resolve themselves. They always had that to fall back on, the white rumpled sheets of their mutual ardor. When Harry wasn't at the Athenaeum translating Joseph Stalin's "Theory and Practice of Leninism," but home instead, he still reached for her with wanton desire, he still whispered to her the breathless words she longed to hear, he still took from her the remains of her Sicilian passion. "*Man is yet poor and desolate, if love passes him by*," Harry whispered, kissing her open lips. "*And if it stays, the poorest hovel is radiant with warmth, with life and color ...*"

"Emma Goldman is slightly better than Green," murmured Gina, her eyes closed, inviting his *languide carezze*. "But do we have to adopt the last part so literally?"

"*Man is utterly helpless before love*," he whispered into her damp throat, embracing her with his body, on top of her, holding her face between his hands. "Utterly helpless before *you*. *Tu mi hai rapito il cuore*. Isn't that what you used to whisper to me?"

Spent, they lay naked, exhausted, counting down the minutes until their boy bounded up from the street.

Harry was on his back, eyes closed. "It has been so long since you've whispered to me in Italian," he said. "I cannot remember the last time."

That was true. The Italian verbal caresses had vanished. Gina was on her side, eyes open, staring at him. "What if you're wrong about Russia, Harry?"

He sighed. His eyes still closed, he reached for her, stroked her back, leaned over her, kissed her face, held her to him, cradling her. "I'm not going to be wrong."

"The price you pay for being wrong is too high." She didn't want to say it. She didn't want to pay it. She didn't want to admit to him how afraid she was for Alexander.

"What are you afraid of?"

"That people smarter than you will turn out to be right."

"Who do you know that's smarter than me?"

"Max Eastman."

"Don't listen to him. The man has been in a bad mood for ten years."

She jumped up, went to her dresser, pulled out a newspaper article she had clipped and saved, came back to bed, and lay down, squinting at the page. Soon she might need glasses.

"*The universe of dialectical materialism,*" Gina read out loud, "*is a pantheistic god masquerading as matter and permitting itself forms of conduct equal to if not surpassing the cannibals at Carthage.*"

"Eastman wrote that?" Harry smirked. "He's really left the collective, hasn't he?"

"Yes, *after* he went to Russia he left the collective."

Harry shrugged, mock disappointed. "He used to be such a good socialist."

"Listen to this—"

He took the article out of her hands and threw it on the floor. "Is he back in the States?"

"Yes."

"So he spouts crazy things like what you've just read, and yet, alive and well, he has returned to America?"

"Yes."

"Cannibals at Carthage indeed." Harry laughed. "What do you think will happen to us?"

"I don't know. They'll throw us in prison?"

"Darling, why would they throw *us* in prison? Just think about what you're saying."

"What about the stories of brutal suppression?"

507

"All lies."

"All of it, lies? Have you read any of the letters Max sent back home? The Bolsheviks permit no departure, no matter how slight, from Bolshevism." She snickered. "*No socialists allowed* should be their motto."

"Even *you* have bought into the propaganda, Gina," Harry said. "I thought you were smarter than that."

"I'm not smarter than Max Eastman," she said. "The man who went to Russia to live the utopian dream now writes that in order to aspire to such a dream we must set aside all of our moral principles and advocate instead for fratricide. *Fratricide*, Harry! He is not saying prison. Oh no. He is saying murder. Cain killing Abel because killing Abel is now the right thing to do."

"Gina, Gina, my love. Please." Harry rubbed his face. "Don't you see? The people who *are* in jail in Russia, they call themselves 'socialists' now, but not five minutes ago, the guns were still warm in their hands as they fought the Bolsheviks to the death in the civil war. That's what Max observed. Civil war, Gia, not fratricide! Those people aren't socialists. They are White terrorists. I wrote about them not too long ago for the *Daily Worker*. I know all about them. They simply use that term now, 'socialists,' to receive mercy. They are pitiful."

"Do you mean they are deserving of our pity?" she asked. "What if you become one of those people?" Or me? Or Alexander. She couldn't speak her son's name aloud.

"We're not going to Soviet Russia to fight *against* the Bolsheviks!" Harry exclaimed. "Why would we do something so stupid? Why even go?"

"Good question."

"We are going to support them. To help them."

She fell back on the pillow. "It's like you read the paper, but you don't *read* the paper."

"I don't know what you mean." Her provocation made him move away from her. They were too naked and unprotected, lying so close to one another.

"The *Globe* every week prints stories about the counter-revolutionaries that fester in Soviet political prisons," she said.

"It's capitalist propaganda. I don't read the *Globe*."

"I know, I know. You read the *Daily Worker*. Soviet propaganda."

"I don't read it. I write it."

"Harry, Max Eastman, the man who hired you for *The Masses*, the once ardent communist, now writes that the word 'capitalism' has been maligned, has been made deliberately sinister. He says it is nothing more than an abstract noun. Yet this uncoordinated impersonal entity has been transformed into the devil. It is but wordplay, he writes, to make a mortal enemy out of fog."

"Gina, I don't want to hear about Max anymore! He's a turncoat."

"You revered him."

"Until he started to betray us, yes. And you should stop reading the *Globe*. Don't be so unduly influenced. You must read critically. God! What else are they going to say? They don't even recognize the Soviet Union. They're never going to say it's going swell over there."

"Well, why not? If it is, why not?"

"Because that would endanger their whole belief system. You heard Domarind. Who wants to hear the death-knell sound for their own way of life?"

"You think that's what it is? The Americans are afraid of how great things are in Russia?"

"You should read Walter Duranty if you really want the truth about what's going on there," said Harry. "It's true, a handful of counter-revolutionaries were arrested in a country of a hundred and fifty million people. There are now about five hundred of them in prison. Does that sound like a lot to you when tens of thousands are imprisoned here for speaking against that fog you call capitalism? And do you know where those five hundred are housed? Many of them are in *Solovki*, which is an ancient former monastery. Do you know where that is? On an island in the middle of the White Sea. Stunning surroundings, an excellent climate. Read Maxim Gorky, too. He wrote an essay about this so-called prison that I've recently translated." Harry sat up in bed, eager, excited. "Health and good food is their daily regimen. That's how the Soviets treat their enemies. I'm not making this up. The prisoners, French, German, Italian, write letters home. Maxim Gorky saw the island with his own eyes. They have walks twice a day in a grove of fruit trees."

"Like orange groves?"

"Almost!" Harry laughed. "They have milk, tea, sugar, cigarettes, soup, meat, potatoes. Gia, they eat better than we do."

"The poor I used to feed in the basement of Holy Lazarus eat better than we do."

He patted her fondly. "They fish, they have lively conversations over tea and jam. There are no locks on the doors or windows."

"Did you say *Solovki* is an island in the middle of the White Sea? Probably no need for locks then. Escape sounds unlikely."

"It doesn't *sound* like prison is what I mean. It's more like the Cub Scout camp we sent Alexander to."

"So not like prison at all?" she said.

"Exactly!"

"So just like Bellagrand?"

The breath was taken out of him for a moment. "I can see," he said tersely, getting out of bed, "that you *refuse* to have a serious conversation. I'm telling you truths that should comfort you, and you make nonsensical analogies. Why even bother talking? Where was I?"

"I believe you were telling me how well we are going to live in a Soviet prison."

"No! I was telling you how a civilized country treats its handful of political prisoners. Which is not going to be us. Unless you plan to go there to agitate."

"Because that's me," she said. "An agitator."

"You still get *my* blood up and boiling," Harry said. "You agitate me, the calmest of men, into a temper."

She opened her arms to him. He looked at her for a moment, and then came back to her. They held each other close, not moving.

"Communism is the future," he crooned into her ear, like a love song. "Remember how you were taken with Ben"—Harry paused, deliberately—"when he kept spouting that Panama was the future? Can you allow *me*, your *husband*, the tiniest measure of the support you once accorded him?"

Ben.

It was with Ben that Gina had spoken about desire and sacrifice fifteen years ago.

"It's time, my wife," said Harry. "We've been talking about going since the October Revolution, when the idea became a reality. When the impossible was made possible."

"Sort of like *the Word was made flesh?*"

"I guess." As if he had no idea what she was talking about. She didn't explain. "It's time for us to go man the barricades."

"There you go again," she said, "inserting the language of war into the peacetime relations of men."

"Gina! *Basta!*"

"You *basta,*" she whispered.

It was a standoff in their marital tango.

Alexander was walking home from school. Domarind was back in his office. The Justice Department was readying the deportation papers. There was nothing more to say. Gina got dressed, pinned up her hair, put on her warm walkabout coat and hat.

"Get up," she said. "Alexander is almost home. Don't forget to take him to his hockey practice at four."

"Where are *you* going? I was going to read."

"You can read at the rink. I'm going out," she said. "I want to clear my head, and I need to think."

"When you come back will you have an answer for me?"

She promised him she would.

"I want to know just one thing," Gina said before she left. "Are you and I going to beg for mercy?"

"Never," said Harry. "We are never going to be like those White terrorists."

Chapter 19

PSALM 91

One

CAMBRIDGE WITH HARVARD as its jewel is most beautiful in the fall. Gina had always thought so. The inflamed vermilion beauty stopped her heart. It took the breath from her lungs, brought her hand to her chest. She felt this especially keenly today as she got off the bus on Oxford Street and tarried a little, ambling slowly toward the Science Center. Past the white fence the Japanese lanterns glowed in the distance with the promise of later, when they would be the only light in the darkness, but now, the maples, ash, oak, and willow—syrupy sugar, fire, gold, and yellow—were all in a blaze. Her chin raised, her shoulders squared, she walked. Perhaps Harvard was especially poignant to her because she suspected she might be seeing it for the last time. Just as when they knew they were leaving Belpasso, every broken-down hut, every crumbling fence, the dirt roads, the deepest blue of the sea past the calamitous Etna looming above their city, made her and Salvo cry. They said they hoped to God the place they were sailing to would have a tenth of the beauty before their eyes.

And it did. America did.

On the second floor of the Science Center, she knocked hesitantly on Ben's office door and waited. The door opened. He stood in front of her in a double-breasted suit, well-groomed but slightly creased, as if appearances were less important than the textbooks and essays piled on his desk or the young man in a tweed jacket, looking anxious and pale, sitting in the student's chair, fretting.

"Gina, how are you? Is everything all right?"

"Yes, of course, I don't mean to intrude …" Her mouth twisted. "Do you have a moment?"

Ben glanced at the nervous student.

She stepped back. "Another time, perhaps. Please. Go ahead."

"Can you wait?" he asked. "I have him, then two more."

"I'll wait."

"You're sure? It might be …"

"However long. I'll be in the Yard."

"I'll find you," he said. "Enjoy the autumn day. There'll be a blizzard for the next three months."

"Oh, I'm sure of it."

Forty minutes later, Ben found her sitting on the steps of the Memorial Church, wrapped in her wool coat.

"Sorry it took so long. Academic consults take forever. Are you cold?"

"Not at all." Then why was she shivering? "I'm glad you could get away."

"I have a lecture at six." He sat down on the marble steps next to her. "Did you get tired of walking?"

"I didn't walk. I just sat here. Taking in the view." Together they looked out onto Harvard Yard, with Widener Library rising past the magenta maples, the golden oaks. It was nearing dusk. The lanterns would be lit soon. Her heart hurt.

"You know," Ben said, "this is where I used to sit and wait for your husband to finish class."

"I know. He told me." Gina and Ben sat together watching the people—young like they had been—rushing to dinner with friends, to write their essays, to evening class, to life.

Ben gave her his hand to help her off the stairs. "Let's walk a bit," he said. "To keep warm." They didn't touch each other as they meandered under the sparse brilliant canopy of the last bloom of fall. She didn't put her arm through his. This wasn't Concord in 1914. No pumpkin fair awaited them through the historic archways at the end of today.

She made some small talk: the recent events (the Dow Jones Industrial average hitting an all-time high of 381); Ben's teaching schedule ("no time to engineer the sorely needed expansion of Mass Avenue with four courses to teach"); Alexander's hockey abilities (prodigious); the weather (fickle); Ingersol (fine); Esther (fine); Harry (silence).

"So what's going on, Gina? How can I help? Is he in trouble again? I heard he fired Domarind."

She took a deep breath. She told him of her meeting with the erstwhile counsel, and the rest. They had spent all their money on legal fees, court costs, other things. *What* the other things were was more than Gina cared to confess to Ben. There was nothing left, she said, and Justice and State were fed up to *here*. They didn't want Harry in federal prison. All they wanted was for him to leave. Which was good, because that's all he wanted. "I fear we haven't got much choice," she finished, but interrogatively as if she were expecting Ben to refute, or assent.

"So let him go," said Ben. "You stay. Stay with Alexander."

Gina felt small like a child when she shook her head.

"You're not *seriously* thinking of going to the Soviet Union? Is this devil's advocacy?"

She didn't reply. Not because she didn't want to. Because she couldn't say the impossible words out loud. *We lost our American citizenship. We are going to be deported.*

She told him, finally, reluctantly.

He stopped walking. "This is absolutely awful," he said. "Does Esther know?"

"I don't want to say anything to her until we're certain what's happening. Please don't say anything. Please. Promise me."

"Okay." But he didn't sound convincing.

They resumed their anguished roam in the afternoon crowd.

"Please, Ben. I know you and Esther talk. She can't know. Not until we're sure."

"She can help, Gina."

"No. She will only make things worse. Believe me."

"How can she make things any worse?"

"Because Alexander makes her lose all reason. She will offer to keep him."

Ben nodded.

"Don't nod, Ben! She can't have him. If we must go, he comes with us. Neither Harry nor I can have it any other way, *will* have it any other way. We will not leave him behind. Esther won't understand, but you do, don't you?"

Ben said nothing. They wandered around the whole of Widener before he spoke again. The grass between the criss-crossing paths was blanketed with decaying leaves.

"She can help you stay here."

"Please … you don't understand, and I can't explain."

"Fine." He pulled his coat closed. "So what's your question for *me*?"

Gina lowered her troubled head. Her choices were so narrow, it was like threading twine into the head of a pin. "Every decision in life can't be this painful," she said.

"No. Only the most difficult ones." Ben paused. "Please let Esther help you, Gina. It's not too late. She will use her father's connections to keep Harry here."

"It *is* too late," Gina said quietly. "Harry wants to go to Russia. Can she help with that?"

"She is his sister. Maybe she can talk him out of it."

"I can't talk him out of strong tea too late at night. But she's going to talk him out of *this*?"

"Gina!" Ben adjusted his hat and for a moment stopped speaking. After he collected himself and spoke, his voice was calmer. "Forget Harry for a moment. Do you think your father would have wanted you to leave America, to go to *Russia*?"

She deflected away from the honest reply. Which was no. "Perhaps. I don't know. He approved of all sorts of progressive ideas. Russia still feels like the future to me. Unknowable, that's true …"

"Is there any other kind of future?"

"No, you're right. I suppose not. Should I maybe find a fortune-teller to help me?" She smiled at him, tilting her head, trying to lure him into a smile in reply. Instead he curtly glanced at his watch. He was losing patience with her.

"I need some advice from you, Ben," Gina said quickly. "A word of wisdom. I need you to be my Rose Hawthorne."

"I'll be whatever you need," he said with an unsuppressed sigh. "What's your question?"

"Do you remember when you and I talked about Panama?"

"Which time?"

"Fifteen years ago."

"Oh, okay. Yes, of course. That conversation is top of mind." Now he smiled, if barely.

"I asked you then, if the heart of your only life was worth the sacrifice of going to Panama. Was your youth worth the risk, the threat, the danger, to do this impossible thing? And truly, it was impossible. A fifty-mile canal through mountains, one end at lower sea level than the other. And to do it in such a way that it permanently solved a grave international problem. The death, the disease, the expense, the sheer mechanical lunacy of it, do you remember the arguments and anger that flowed between men on this subject?"

"Too well. I teach a graduate-level course on it. Next class is tonight at six o'clock, if you'd like to pop in, have a listen."

"What I'm asking is"—she regrouped—"don't you think that in many ways, your past dilemma mirrors my own current mess, the life-and-death question before Harry and me? Well, before me, really, because Harry is not wavering. He made up his mind a long time ago." Gina nudged Ben. "A little bit like you with Panama."

They both reluctantly acknowledged the truth of this.

"So, the humans involved are just as intractable," she went on, "and the issue of the future of the Soviet Union is as complex and uncertain as Panama. To build or not to build? To go or not to go? Will this fledgling thing that's barely off the ground grow wings, or will it continue to be a bottom-dweller? Will it be a success, like Panama? Will it be worth it? You told me back then to ask you these questions in fifteen years because you couldn't answer me when the canal first opened. So here I am, Ben. Little did I know how desperately I would need your answer. Was Panama worth the risk and the sacrifice?"

"In the case of Panama," Ben said, "the answer is an unequivocal yes. I haven't lost my life to accident or disease, I've benefited from my association with the canal, both personally and professionally, and quite apart from me, it has transformed the world."

"Perhaps in a few years I'll be able to say the same thing about the Soviet Union."

"Transformed the world for the *better*," Ben amended.

"Perhaps Russia will, too. Harry thinks so. He has faith."

"Like in God?"

She nodded. "Man has to replace God with something."

Ben stayed silent.

She knocked into him lightly. "Why are you so quiet?"

"I don't know if I'm on Harry's side, Gina."

"Okay, but if you separate yourself from the personal ..."

"This isn't personal. This has to do solely with the question you put before me. Men are always looking for the bright hope that changes imperfect humanity into a perfect brotherhood, a society of inequality into one of economic equals. It's especially true of modern man. But the Soviet Union is no longer an abstraction, or as some economist once called it, 'a social myth to mull over at the dinner table.' It's a real and tangible thing."

"Just like your Panama after it left the planning stage and entered the building stage."

Ben allowed the similarity, but unhappily. "The question isn't about the future," he said. "It's about the here and now. With Panama, we knew how long the canal would take to build, and we knew when we could hope to see the effect of it on maritime travel and international trade. How long do we plan to wait with the Soviet

Union? Have they given themselves a benchmark, a barometer? Look at what the Soviets are doing now, taking farms away from the Ukrainians at the point of a Tommy gun. My question is, if, despite Stalin's best efforts, communism doesn't flourish, erasing the need for government by such and such a date, will the Bolsheviks admit they've failed? Will they give the country back to the Tsars and the farms back to the farmers?"

"Well, no, clearly not to the Tsars, since they've killed them all." Gina didn't know if they had killed all the Ukrainians.

"So what's Harry's answer? How long are they giving themselves to succeed?"

"As long as it takes, I suppose." She squinted at him. Had Ben, too, been reading Max Eastman?

"And if it doesn't happen in your lifetime," Ben said, "how will you know if you've done the right thing? Panama didn't purport to be the answer to all the world's problems. Panama was a practical solution to a narrow, concrete dilemma. Personally, I'm wary about global programs that are dependent on fundamentally altering mankind."

"Why do you say it won't happen in our lifetime?" she asked. "Look at what Duranty wrote after returning from the Soviet Union. He is very optimistic."

"Gina, are you arguing from a strongly held conviction, or just arguing? When you discuss this with Harry, what side are you on?"

She didn't want to admit to Ben how many words she had used to try to change her husband's mind. *All* the words. "I suppose on his side." She stared at her feet.

"Okay. Sometimes you must pay a heavy price for where you stand. Harry must have said this to you once or twice. So then, what advice could you possibly want from me?"

She smiled. "Yes, Gina. Go. Of course it's worth it."

Ben nodded. "Yes, Gina. Go. Of course it's worth it."

"You're just saying that. You don't mean it."

He laughed. "I told you back then, even when I could touch the immense change that was about to fall upon the globe, to ask me in fifteen years. Even when I was very sure, I told you I wasn't sure."

"But I'm asking you to give me an answer now," Gina said. "Is it worth it? To go and build communism in the Soviet Union the way you went and built the canal in Panama?"

"I don't know," Ben said. "Are you willing to sacrifice your life for it?"

She was mute.

"I suppose you'd have to know the answer to one question," he continued.

"What's that?"

"At what price communism?"

They wandered along the shadowy leafy paths between Weld and Grays. She knew it was time to head to Johnston Gate and out, but she didn't want to.

"I could ask you the same question," she said. "At what price Panama?"

"Ah," said Ben. "Clearly when I was young, I believed the answer was: the ultimate price."

Was Harry willing to pay the ultimate price? Except it wasn't just his head and hers he was staking on the tip of a sword. It was Alexander's. Gina couldn't stop shivering.

They were almost at the brick and iron gate that led out to Peabody Street, the gate she had blocked twenty-five years earlier to trap Harry into love, into herself. *Love never fails. But whether there be prophecies, they will fail.* The future was unknowable. Only love was knowable.

L'amore tollera ogni cosa, crede ogni cosa, spera ogni cosa, sopporta ogni cosa.

"He is my husband, Ben," Gina said. "He and Alexander are the only family I have left. He fully believes. And I have to believe in him. I hope he is proven right, as you were. That his leap of faith on Bolshevism will turn out to be as sound as your leap of faith about Panama."

"And what if it isn't?"

They stared at each other, at a loss for words.

"We'll have to cross that canal when we get to it," she said at last.

They had come to the end of the walk, the end of the conversation, the end. Awkwardly they moved off the path to the grass, to let the hurrying noisy students pass. She had to rush back home. He had to rush to prepare for his evening lecture. It was time to part.

"Thank you for today," she said. "I really needed it."

"You're welcome."

She stood motionlessly without touching him. Then she moved forward, opened her arms, and embraced him. She held her purse. He held his umbrella. She lowered her voice before she spoke into the collar of his coat. It was long ago what had passed like a song between them. They had lived many lives since then. And yet she couldn't leave without acknowledging their *gioia effimera condivisa*.

"I never forget you, Ben," she said. "I never have. I never will."

He squeezed her in reply, in a shudder, as if surprised by her intimate words. Holding her, his voice breaking, he spoke. "I thought Panama was the adventure of my lifetime," he said into her hair. "But I was wrong. It wasn't Panama. It was you."

"Please don't say that." A whisper. She tried to move away, but he wouldn't let her.

"Nothing in my life compares to the fleeting moments of glory I spent with you." Now he let her go.

"You don't mean that. Please."

Silently he gazed upon her as they remained too close to each other, their coats touching, on the edge of Harvard Yard under the Japanese lanterns.

She shook her head and stepped away, regret and repentance falling across her face. "It left us, Ben," she said. "The maples, the willows, the ice skating."

"It didn't leave us. We left it. I couldn't build the canal now. I couldn't part mountains and stanch eruptions of liquid clay. I don't have the old vim anymore."

"Sometimes I feel my life is a slide on an eruption of clay."

"A glacier of mud."

"Marble and mud. That's what Rose had told me."

Ben nodded. "She also told you to make the best of everything."

"Is going to Russia making the best of it?"

"No," he said. "Don't go, Gia. That's my true advice. Please don't go."

She looked away, unable to bear the expression on his face, anxiety, other things.

"So what do you think?" He tilted his head to catch her eye one last time. "Have I set you straight?"

"I believe it's too soon to know, *mio amico*," Gina said, holding out her hand in farewell. "Ask me again in fifteen years."

Removing his hat and lowering his head, Ben brought her hand to his lips. He kissed it through her frayed silk glove, then pulled off the grey glove, turned her hand upward and kissed the bare skin inside her palm. Both he and she trembled slightly. They did not speak again. He bowed before he put on his hat and walked away, his squared, dark silhouette blending in with other men and disappearing out of view. At the edge of Massachusetts Avenue, she climbed aboard a bus. She cried all the way home.

Two

THE BLOOD DRAINED from Esther's heart when over a month later she finally learned from Ben about Harry's plan to move to the Soviet Union. She, a lady, who wore court shoes and long gloves, who never left the house unless completely put together, arrived at her brother's doorstep on a Saturday morning unmade-up, unmanicured, manic-eyed and without her hat. The only thing that saved them from a scandalous scene was Alexander. "Aunty Esther!" he said, kissing her and showing her his skates. "Why didn't you come yesterday? I waited all evening for you."

"I'm sorry, dear one. I had a small emergency. I tried to call but ..."

"Yes, our telephone is out," he said. "Please take me back with you right now. Because Teddy is playing a must-win hockey game at the pond this afternoon and I swore to him I'd be there."

"Darling," Esther said, "it's been over forty degrees this past week. The ice on the pond is not safe. The last thing you want to do is skate on it."

"I'm not skating. I'm cheering. Please? I promised."

"Son," said Harry, intervening, "why would you promise Teddy something you can't control?" He and Gina were at attention in the living room, Harry pretending to casually glance inside a newspaper, Gina not even pretending, standing stiffly in the farthest corner. She looked so elegant. She would have made a fine first Boston lady. A skeletal Boston lady. Esther couldn't help but notice that Harry's wife for the last of her Beacon Hill years had become the thinnest woman in the room.

"Dad, by that definition, no one would ever promise anyone anything!" Alexander looked beseechingly at Esther. "Please," he whispered intensely.

"But I'm right, son," said Harry. "You should never promise what you can't control."

How did Esther continue smiling through the pointless talk? Somehow she managed—for her nephew. "We'll see," she said to him. "Let me talk to your mother and father first, darling."

"But we'll go right after?"

"I'll try. I can't promise."

He squeezed her hand, blessedly oblivious to her deathly pallor and stricken expression. "If you take me with you," he whispered, "I will sit for your dumb Christmas portrait."

Leaning forward, she pressed her mouth to the top of his black head. He was growing so tall. Soon he would have to bend to her for a kiss. "Go play in the park for a few minutes. Get yourself some ice cream." She fumbled in her bag for some change. Her fingers felt like swollen sausages; they couldn't grasp the coins. "Here you go. Now let me talk to your mother and father."

Alexander ran from the apartment, leaving the three grown-ups in a Mexican standoff.

"I don't know where to begin," Esther said. She saw from her brother's closed expression that he would be impervious to persuasion. He had the look of someone who was being accosted by a cat, or a bird.

"What is the matter, Esther? You seem distraught."

"Please tell me what I've heard is wrong. Please tell me you are not seriously thinking of taking your family to"—how did she even speak?—"the Soviet Union."

Frowning, Harry hesitated. "Where did you hear that?" He glared at Gina. "I thought you and I agreed not to say anything?"

Gina opened her hands and shook her head.

"Esther?"

In the mute polka dance of strangled allegiances that followed, Gina looked away from Harry and at Esther, who was staring at her sister-in-law, staring at her piercingly and yet pleadingly, as if to say, *Gina! I know you have been visiting Ben, trying to help my brother, and for reasons known only to you, you have not told Harry of this, and for reasons known only to him, my brother, despite living thirty minutes away from his oldest friend, has not been in touch with Ben in seven years. Ben has not been in touch with Harry either, though he is clearly not averse to helping him—or is it helping you? I know this, you know this, and I have said nothing. I will say nothing now, if you heed the silent scream inside my throat, if you heed your own conscience. Tell me what you want me to say to my brother.* All of it was in Esther's unyielding gaze.

Gina furtively caught Esther's eye, and melted away. She lowered her head.

Esther turned to Harry. "Ask your wife," she said, "how I might know of this."

"Gina has no idea, Esther," Harry said. "Perhaps through our former lawyer, Mr. Domarind?"

"Not through him."

"Look," he said, "I don't know what's going on between you two right now, just as I don't know what's been going on between you for years. It's not important. However you found out, Esther, it *is* true, we *are* going to the Soviet Union."

Esther squeezed together the bones of her fingers, as if she wanted them to break. "Were you *ever* going to tell me? Or were you just going to vanish into thin air?"

"Don't be silly," Harry said. "We were going to talk to you this week."

"As you talked to Alice a full week before your wedding date to inform her that you had married someone else—oh, wait."

"Not someone else, but my wife, and Alexander's mother—"

Both women groaned at the sound of the same word: *Alexander.*

Harry's gaze grew cold. "Esther, I know you must be upset, but there's no need …"

"Upset!"

"Why are you going on like this?" he asked. "We're not saying *you* have to come with us."

Esther couldn't get the words out, they were so painful. It was as if they were tearing apart her throat as she tried to speak. Desperately her eyes darted from Harry to Gina, her hands clenched together in agonized supplication. "Gina," she said hoarsely, her breaking voice just above a whisper, "what about our … *Alexander?*" Sadness seeped from her eyes.

"What about him?" Harry asked.

"He's got his whole life ahead of him!"

"Exactly. We have to think about Alexander."

Esther shook her head. And kept shaking it. "He's just a boy. He doesn't know anything. He can't make this decision. You're making it for him."

"That's what parents do. They make decisions for their children. That's why we are the parents. And they are the children."

"But it's wrong, Harry. You will ruin his life. It's so wrong."

"Obviously we disagree."

Digging her nails into the palms of her hands to contain her terror through physical pain, Esther took a small, shaking step toward Gina. "Please," she said to the pale woman standing next to Harry like a salt pillar. "Gina! I've reconsidered all my previous positions. Imagine what a shifting of the sands this is for me. Please forget everything hurtful or hostile I've ever said to you, and forgive me. But *please*—don't do this. Your son is your ladder to the stars. He deserves better than this."

"We disagree, Esther," Harry said.

Gina's lips were as white as her skin.

"I have helped you before," Esther said. "You know I will do anything to help you stay here."

"Yes, you helped us," Harry said. "But you *wanted* to help us. We didn't ask for your help."

"Your wife did," Esther said. "She asked for my help."

"That was without my approval."

"This will be, too."

"This? There is no *this*. There's nothing to be done."

"There's always something to be done."

"Do you see, Gia?" Harry turned to his wife. "And you think *I'm* the one who always falls back on Father's money."

"Please, Gina." Esther had to ignore Harry to keep a hold on herself. "Don't do this. Don't destroy your son's life."

"Esther!" Harry raised his voice. "That's not how Gina and I feel about the Soviet Union. We are going to live in Moscow. We are starting a new life. Everything will be fine."

"If you go, you will never be able to come back," Esther said, addressing only the mute woman before her. "Because of my brother, you've lost your American citizenship. Oh Gina! You're no longer an American, no longer an Italian. What will you be? What will Alexander be?"

"Russian," Harry said.

"Let her speak, Harry!"

"We've told you, Russian," Harry repeated.

"But he is not Russian." Esther's voice was failing. "He is a Barrington. He is not a Pavlov, or a Smirnov, or a Litvinov. He is a Massachusetts Barrington. Gina, your son's ancestors built this country and this city you say you love."

"All right, enough," said Harry. "He is his own boy. He is not a slave. He is not bound by the Barrington heritage. Russia needs young men like him. He is coming with us to help the Soviet Union. They need us a lot more over there, Esther, than the city of Boston needs us."

"Because you've been getting yourself arrested every five minutes! How much will the Soviet Union need you if you say vile things against it every Saturday afternoon?"

"Well, we're never going to find out. Right, Gina?"

"Gina, I *beg* you …"

"Esther, our mind is made up," Harry said. "The visas have been applied for, the citizenship signed away, the bank account liquidated.

It's really just a matter of nuance," he went on, "but we've been given the choice of leaving voluntarily or being deported. We took the first option, but because of that, we have to pay for our own passage." He shrugged. "Gina wanted it this way. Right, darling? If we were deported, true, the government would foot the bill for our relocation, but then it would be very hard to return if …"

"You will never return," Esther said.

"But because Gina insisted on this option," Harry continued, "we are a little short of cash …"

"I will not give you a penny to go to Russia."

Harry glared at Gina, almost smugly. "What did I tell you? I told you she wouldn't help us."

"Not with this."

"Well, never mind. We don't need your money. We'll be fine."

"I will do *anything* to help you stay here," Esther said. "I will pay anyone any amount. You owed money to Domarind? I've already taken care of that. Your legal fees? Your apartment? Your debts? I will hire you the best lawyer in the United States to fix this. I will buy you a house."

"No, Esther," Harry said. "That's not the kind of help we need."

Esther turned to Gina. "I will buy you back Bellagrand!"

The pillar that was Gina swayed.

"Esther, stop! What are you trying to do, bribe us?"

"Not you," Esther said. "Your wife."

"My wife will not be bribed."

Gina said nothing.

"Gina?" said Harry.

"Gina?" said Esther.

Gina said nothing.

"Gina, please!" Esther cried. "Let him go! If he wants to go so badly, let him. You and Alexander stay here."

A trembling Gina hung her head.

"Esther, we told you," Harry said. "We are all going to the Soviet Union."

"Gina, listen to me. I will take care of everything for you. The citizenship thing, I'll fix it—"

"No!" Harry became red in the face.

"You will never have to worry …"

"You're barking up the wrong tree, Esther. A loan for the passage is all we need."

"I will never give you a cent for that."

"Did you come here to tell us you *won't* help us?" Harry scoffed. "Why even come?"

"I came here …" Esther couldn't finish. "I will not be an accomplice to the end of …" She stepped toward the silent Gina. "You're a *mother*!" she cried in a whisper. "You are *so* lucky. You've been blessed with motherhood. Think of your son!"

Another sway from Gina before Harry's indignation reached full-bore. "Don't speak to her that way, Esther," he said. "Don't talk to her about things you don't understand."

"You think *I* don't understand what's happening?"

"I don't think you do."

"*She* doesn't understand what's happening!"

"Don't say *she*! She's standing in front of you!"

"Or maybe she understands exactly what's happening!" Esther was breathless. "Gina, please!"

Harry raised his hand. "Enough. Leave her alone. You always were a suck-up, Esther. Always wanted Father's money. And now that you have all of it, you won't help us even a little."

"I didn't want his money, you imbecile! I wanted him to think about me one-quarter of the time he spent thinking about you—his whole life!" Incensed, she addressed only the trembling woman in front of her. "Are you going to tell me, Gina, that fathers and sons have a special bond? Is that why you're going to ruin Alexander's life? Because *now* you can't separate father from son? Do you think you can make up for the past? Do you think Harry even *knows* what a father–son bond is?" Esther laughed. "They hadn't spoken since the Russo–Japanese War! If it weren't for Alexander, Father would have died and Harry never would have called him. What kind of a special bond does it require for a son not to come to his father's funeral?"

"He threw me away," Harry said. "He turned his back on me. I will never turn my back on my own son."

"You're turning your back on him by trying to kill him!" Esther yelled. "And Father didn't throw *you* away. You threw *us* away. For *her*!"

"Don't talk to my wife that way!"

"I wasn't talking to her, I was talking to you!" Esther clenched her hands into fists, upbringing be damned. "My brother is a fool," she said to Gina, her frantic, desperate voice hardening. "But *you* are deluded. You think he will love you if you go with him to the Soviet Union?"

"Esther, that's enough!"

"No, it clearly isn't!" Esther lost all composure. "You think because you became an anarchist, my brother married you? Because you spouted inanities about social conditions and market value? Don't you understand *anything*?" She uttered a wrenching cry. "Gina, you will *always* come a distant second to whatever it is he wants first. I know something about this. You've been with him twenty-five years. Haven't you understood that yet? He went to prison, and didn't care that he left you behind. He promised you a life of plenty and then wasted the only inheritance from our dead mother paying his lawyers so he could spend Saturdays on a soapbox instead of playing hockey with his son and taking you dancing. Look at where you're living! God knows what else he spent Mother's money on. And now that he's run out of options, taken away your citizenship, forced your family into an impossible corner, he has somehow convinced you that life will be sweeter in the Soviet Union." A mirthless laugh. "And you believe him?"

"Yes," Harry said, "she does."

Esther slapped Gina across the face.

"Esther! My God!"

"What kind of a mother are you?" Tears rolled down Esther's face. Tears rolled down Gina's. She hadn't lifted a hand to defend herself. "What's wrong with you? This is abuse, this is malicious negligence. *You* should be in jail—for endangering the life of a minor. You are a *terrible* mother!"

"Who are you comparing her to?" Harry yelled, yanking his sister away from Gina. "*Our* mother? This mother doesn't desert her own children!"

Esther gulped to keep herself from retching. She felt physically sick. "How can I not get through to you, brother?" she whispered. She implored the speechless Gina. "How can I not get through to *you*, a woman, a mother?"

"Get out, Esther," said Harry. "We've had enough."

What happened to our life, Harry, Esther wanted to say. What happened to our family? There were four of us once, and we had such a full and good life. And one by one everyone has up and flown from me, through sadness, illness, death, lack of love—and now you. You're the only family I have left. You, your wife, my beloved boy. Once you leave, I will have nothing. You're going to a dreadful place, yes, but you're also leaving *me*, and that feels so wrong. How can you not understand that? Do I have to even say it?

She didn't.

She couldn't.

She picked up her purse, her hands shaking, her fingers numb, picked up her purse, but not her hat, because she had forgotten to bring one. Very carefully, so as not to trip or faint, she walked across the empty living room, her heels tapping out the uneven rhythm of growing distance on the wood floor, opened the front door, and was gone.

Outside, she slumped against the gate until she felt able to cross Beacon Street to the Public Garden where Alexander was kicking a ball with some friends.

She called for him. He ran to her.

"Are we going?"

"No, I'm sorry," Esther said. "You have to stay here. But I have to go."

He looked disappointed. "I promised Teddy."

"I know. Teddy and Belinda will understand."

"Can I come next weekend?"

She pushed the hair from his forehead with the tips of her thin unsteady fingers. "I think you're about to embark on quite an adventure. So I don't know about next weekend."

"Dad says not before Christmas."

"Oh. Well, if you're right, maybe I'll see you for the holidays then." She opened her arms. "Come, give your aunty a hug." He was such a good boy, Esther thought, letting her embrace him, even though his friends were watching. She held him to her, eyes shut tight, *Please please please, don't let him see me break down.* She kissed his head, and took a deep breath.

"Alexander," she said, stepping away, still holding his hands. "I'm going to tell you a little prayer, a short psalm. Will you promise you'll try to memorize it?" She even managed a carved-on smile.

He rolled his eyes mightily. "Mom is always trying to get me to remember this or that."

"She is right to. Now listen: *Thou shall not be afraid for the terror by night, nor for the arrow that flieth by day, nor for the pestilence that walketh in darkness, nor for the destruction that wasteth by noonday, a thousand shall fall at your side, and ten thousand at your right hand, but it shall not come near thee.*"

Alexander stared into his aunt's wretched face. "You want me to remember *all* of that?"

"Yes. Can you try?"

He must have noticed the despair graying her features. He frowned. "Okay, Aunty Esther. Don't get so worked up. I'll try. I promise. Later, though. My friends are waiting."

"Yes, of course. Later. Moses wrote that prayer to help himself during his forty years in the wilderness. Repeat it to yourself, until it is written on your heart."

Alexander chuckled. "Is that where you think I'm going, Aunty Esther? To forty years in the wilderness?"

"Of course not! It's just a metaphor. A figure of speech."

"Which part? The forty years, or the wilderness?"

Esther didn't reply right away. "I'm hoping both."

"After the wilderness, what did Moses find?"

"The promised land." She was barely audible.

"That's funny. That's where Dad says we're going now. The promised land."

"Live how you wish, Alexander," Esther said. "Your grandfather would be so proud of you. You are a Barrington. A child of privilege, a child of liberty. The advantage of being born a Barrington is that you have the freedom to choose your path in life."

Alexander grinned. "Like my father before me, right?"

"Yes, my dearest heart," said Esther, glancing around for a bench to fall on. "Just like your father before you."

"Aunty Esther," Alexander said, lowering his voice, "can you please tell my parents I really want a dog for Christmas?"

"A *live* dog?"

He gave her a funny look. "Yes, silly. Of course a live one."

"I thought maybe a stuffed toy?"

"I'm too old for toys." He smiled. "Except for the *toys* I leave at your house."

"Of course. I'll be sure to put in a good word for you."

"My second request is a Colt I can keep in my own house."

"You know your father will never allow that."

"I know. But you could tell them if I'm going to grow up to be a soldier, I need to keep a gun in my house."

"A *real* Colt?"

The boy stared at her, arching his eyebrows.

"Of course. I'll be sure to let them know."

"My third wish is for a big red sled. Like everybody else has in Boston but me."

She tapped on her temple. "Got it all right here. Dog, Colt, sled." Reaching out, she patted his smooth cheek.

He smiled, and ran from her, calling back, "Goodbye, Aunty Esther!"

It was a rare mild day in Boston in December, dry and fine, and the sun was out. She watched him approach his friends, his aunt already forgotten. *Goodbye, my darling boy.* She cast her eyes away from the bonfire in the day, from the conflagration of all that was most precious to her heart. Everything burned down.

She turned on her fine court heels, out of habit reached up to adjust her non-existent hat, her fingers fumbling for the invisible ribbons under her chin, and stumbled out, with blind eyes searching for Clarence, for the car parked somewhere on Tremont Street.

Harry and Gina left Boston with Alexander two weeks before Christmas. The American Communist Party and Gina's bartered diamond ring paid for the passage to the Soviet Union. They never saw or spoke to Esther again.

Chapter 20

HARRY'S FAVORITE BOOK

WHEN HE WAS PACKING, Alexander found *The Man Without a Country*, a book he hadn't read in a couple of years. It had been collecting dust on his shelf. Taking a break from the chore of deciding which of his few things he would take with him, Alexander perched on the bed, opened the slim volume and began to read. It took him no more than forty minutes to devour the story of Philip Nolan and his unfortunate exile. He lost himself in the book, and as he closed it, he heard his parents shouting at him from down the hall. The suitcases had to be packed and ready in two hours. Was he even close?

"I'm almost done!" he shouted, continuing to sit on the bed. When he heard his father's footsteps, he jumped up and pretended he had been working hard.

"Alexander, your room looks just as it did this morning," Harry said. "Which is to say unpacked."

"No, no," said Alexander. "It's an illusion. I'm almost ready. I just have to get dressed, and find my Boy Scout tie, and then I can go, I think."

"You think so?" Harry looked around. "In ninety minutes, whatever is not in your suitcase is not coming with you. It's that simple."

Alexander picked up the short story he had just read. "Dad, look at this book I found. Wasn't this your favorite? Mom told me it was." He showed it to his father. "Dad, it's the saddest story. This man hates

America, and as punishment he is exiled and when he wants to come back, he can't."

Harry took the book out of Alexander's hands and threw it emphatically in the trash. It made a loud thud as it hit the metal container. "It's nonsense, Alexander. Tripe and utter nonsense. I was a child when I read it. Little did I know how vapid it was. You're not taking it with you. Get back to your packing. Please. Your mother will blame *me* if you're not ready. Have you looked under your bed for your tie?"

Alexander stared into the bin where *The Man Without a Country* lay broken-spined and discarded. "I don't normally keep clothes under my bed, Dad," he said. "Do you?"

"Well, then, find it, clever clogs. Eighty-five minutes." Harry walked out of the room, his shoes making a stern tap-tap on the wooden floor.

Alexander studied the *National Geographic* map of the United States his mother had hung in his room to help him with his lessons. Turning to the mirror, he theatrically clenched his fist, furrowed his brow, deepened his voice, tried to make himself look as intense and fierce as he imagined Philip Nolan might have looked, and whispered, his clenched hand shaking, the other pointing to the reflected map of America, "*You see? I have a country!*"

Chapter 21

THE SNAKE AND THE FALCON

"GIA, LOOK! ARE YOU looking?" Harry's excitement was infectious. "You have to admit they're amazing. I've never seen anything like these Alps. This is just—look how close we are! We can almost touch them."

He was right. They could almost touch them. The train raced its way along the side of the carved-out mountain, perilously plunging into tunnels, nearly grazing the rocky cliffs. Alexander said it was like a roller coaster ride on Revere Beach during the summer fair. Which is better, she asked, but he didn't reply.

In the valleys outside Gina's window were farms, and fields, and women working. One woman, struggling uphill, carried her son on her hip and a large metal bucket. Both looked too heavy for her, because she was so small, but somehow she balanced, she managed. Gina watched Alexander watching the woman, her little boy, her bucket. He was tall now, and big, but it wasn't so long ago that she had carried him everywhere on her hip the way that woman was carrying her own son.

"Dad is right, Mom. It is beautiful here. What country are we in now? Austria?"

Gina's eyes didn't leave Alexander, sitting across from her by his father's side.

I've seen this beauty, she wanted to say. I've lived with beauty my whole life. I grew up at the foot of Etna. We were born and raised looking out at the peak of that majestic, fearsome volcano. When

Salvo, Alessandro, and I climbed the hills, we could see all the way down to the blue Catania. We swam all year round in the Ionian Sea. I know what beauty is. I've seen *donne contadine* carry their children. There is no reason to romanticize it. It was easier for me to raise my son in Boston than it was for my mother to raise me and my brothers on the outskirts of Belpasso in a hut with no running water. Many years ago we sailed to America because my father wanted to give me and my brothers a chance at something more than carrying buckets of water and milk uphill along with our hip-sized children. He who cut hair and made violins, though he himself had never played the violin, the barber of Belpasso, the greatest man I've ever known, the love of my young life, he wanted us to study, to learn, to become successful, to become anything we wanted. Even me, a girl, his only daughter. He wanted me not to be defined by my sex or my children. Gina studied her son, sitting next to his occupied father, forehead pressed against the glass, gazing at the mountains. And yet—here I am, defined by my one child. I am defined more by the one child I have than my father's mother was by the twelve children she had. My motherhood is undiluted by quantity.

They were moving down the mountain. Soon the Alps would be behind them, the way America was, the way Italy was. They would leave Austria, be in Hungary, then Poland, they would switch trains, push east and north past Warsaw, be in Moscow in two days, three? Moscow. To think. Her fingers trembling, Gina glanced across at Harry. The image-maker, the pulpit-maker, the objection-maker. His objection had been first to her youth, then to her anarchy, then to her love. To the ties she imposed on him, to the conventions of a normal life she forced on him, to the baby she desperately wanted from him, at whatever the cost. He objected to her desire to live as a normal woman, not as a revolutionary. He objected to it all. He didn't want the upper-class life any more than he wanted the ghetto of Lawrence or the mansions of heaven or the whiteout of Bellagrand, their one brief shining moment in the blinding sun.

Alexander coughed. Instantly Gina blinked, came to. "Why are you coughing?"

"I am a child, Mother. A human being. I got a piece of bread stuck in my human child throat. I coughed to clear it."

"Come here, let me feel your forehead."

"Leave him alone, Gina. He's fine."

"I said come here. Are you sick?"

Dutifully he came and squeezed in between her and the window. "I'm fine. I coughed." But because he was Alexander, he coughed again, dramatically hacking and doubling over. "Just kidding, Mom," he said when she grabbed him by the shoulders and started pounding his back. "I'm fine. You've got to learn to relax. Otherwise you'll soon be just like Dad."

They both looked across at Harry, now sitting by himself, reading, making notes in those Cyrillic hieroglyphs he had been studying. He looked over at them, somber and unsmiling. "What is it?" he said. "I'm practicing Russian. Which is what you should be doing instead of clowning around, coughing, reminiscing like silly children."

"But I am a silly child, Dad."

"Stop it." Harry looked down into his books. Gina and Alexander turned back to each other, and to their mountains. She gave the boy some chocolate, and he nibbled on it, not taking his eyes from the river streaming through the valley, from the bare trees in brown contrast against the sky. She stroked his black hair. He would need another haircut soon. His hair grew too fast. Like him.

"Are you excited, son?"

"About what? Oh." He paused. "*That.*" He sucked on the last of the chocolate. "Sure. Why not? Aren't you?"

"Sure. Why not?"

"Hey, Mom, did we bring any money for this adventure?" he asked. "Dad told me we won't need any in Moscow. But he was joking, right?"

"I wasn't joking, son," Harry said. "We didn't bring any money because we don't need any money. The Soviet government will set us up, and then I will find work. We'll be fine. That's the whole point. We are not going to be defined by how much we have—"

"But by how much we don't?"

"Don't be fresh."

"Sorry." He nudged his mother. "Is that true, Mom?"

"Yes, don't be fresh."

Gina did not want to catch Alexander's eye when he posed his question, when he turned to her searching her face for the truth. Putting her arm around him, she drew him to her and put a palm over his face. She jostled him a bit, distracted him, and soon they turned their gazes once again to the countryside beyond their windows, watching the Danube flow past them … hours … days … through Belgrade, through Budapest.

"Mom, what was that thing you used to sing to me? I can't remember. But you used to do this thing, when you held me like this. You would say words and kiss me between them."

"I kiss you all the time." To prove it, she kissed him. "What words?"

"I don't know. Something sing-songy. For bedtime."

"How did it go?"

"Are you listening? I don't know. Something like …" He tried to remember. "My bubby rubby bug. My hip, my bubbiness, my bug, my bug, my bug."

She laughed. "Yup, that's it."

"Mom!"

"What? You got it. Exactly right."

He tickled her to get her to stop teasing him. "How did it really go?"

She took his head in her hands. "My bubby rubby bug—" She kissed him.

"Mom!" He tried to get free, but she wouldn't let him. "Are you going to tell me, or are you just going to sit here and joke?"

She pretended to think about it. "I'm going to sit here and joke."

He continued to tickle her.

She continued to laugh.

"You two are so loud, I can't hear myself think," Harry said, putting down his books and getting up. "How long are these childish games going to continue?"

They pretended to quiet down. Harry stepped out of the compartment to stretch his legs.

As soon as the door closed behind him, Gina spoke. "Don't worry, son," she said in a low voice, rushing through her words. "Don't tell your dad, but I brought a little something with us. A small nest egg. Just in case. You know? For a rainy day."

Alexander studied her face. "I thought we were broke. That's what Dad said. That's one of the reasons we had to leave, he said. We had nothing left."

"Well, he's right." She swallowed, dry-mouthed. "Still, though. A few extra dollars to exchange for rubles might come in handy, in case we need something."

"Where did you get it? Did it come with you from Italy?"

"From Italy? When I was fourteen?" She ruffled his black head. "No, rubby bug. I didn't bring it from Italy. From there we truly came with nothing. What money we had saved, we spent on my father's funeral. Your grandfather's. The one you are named after."

"I know who I'm named after, Mom," Alexander said. "Where did you get the money from then, if we have no money?"

"From a secret place."

"What place?"

"A green valley surrounded by mountains," Gina said. "An isolated, forever happy land far away from the troubles of the outside world. A mythical kingdom."

"If it's mythical, how is the money real?"

After she found out what Harry had really been up to behind her back, and she started to make plans to take Alexander to Florida, Gina had gone to the bank. Back then, there was still plenty of money, although less than she had expected. After she returned from Miami and discovered that Harry had moved them to a smaller place and sold their furniture, she intended to re-deposit it, but never got the chance.

Hundreds of parchment notes, crisp, clean, recently minted. A stash so slim it was barely a bump in the smallest pocket of her purse on the train seat next to her, barely a dent sewn carefully into the silken lining.

And although she had initially felt slight remorse for holding onto it instead of paying their rent or their phone bill, once she discovered what Harry had wasted their money on, she regretted only one thing—not that she had taken it, but that she hadn't taken more. Better her family to have kept it than the Workers Party. And the money wouldn't have made much difference to Harry in the end. One more tithe to the *Daily Worker*, one more payment to Domarind. What hubris to think that her tidy sum could have tamped down his lofty dreams.

Blinking, she smiled at her son. She touched his face. She pressed her fingers to his mouth in a shh. "I saved it instead of spending it, in case *you* might need it."

Alexander giggled. "What do I need money for, Mom? I'm a child."

"You're not always going to be a child, are you?"

"You better not tell Dad. Ever. He won't forgive you for keeping secrets."

"Perhaps," she said, having never been forgiven. "I'm hoping we won't need it. But if we do, or if God forbid something happens to me, there is enough to take care of things for you."

He frowned. "What do you mean, if something happens to you?"

She half-smiled. "I'm not getting any younger, Alexander."

"Hmm. I suppose not. But, Mom, no one gets any younger."

"You're right about that."

"Dad is not worried."

"Dad is never worried about anything."

"Are *you* worried? About moving to Russia?"

She smiled. "No, *mio caro figlio*. I'm not worried either." She kissed him. "My *lovely, living boy*," she said, kissing him between each word. "*My hope*"—kiss—"*my happiness*"—kiss—"*my love, my life, my joy*." Kiss, kiss, kiss.

"That's it, *that's* the lullaby!"

"You're telling me? I *know*."

Harry returned, sat down.

"You two have settled down, I hope?"

"Dad," Alexander said, "did you say the Soviet Union is a socialist utopia?"

"Yes, son." He opened his Russian books, took out his notepad, his pen.

"Did you know that in Greek, the word utopia comes from *ou*, meaning *no* and *topos*, meaning *place*?"

"The English word is a homonym, Alexander, don't think you're so clever. The first syllable, if rendered as *eu*, means *good*."

"Like I was saying. A good place that doesn't exist."

"It exists. I'm not going to talk about it anymore to win over you or your mother. Very soon, you will see for yourselves. Now say, *menya zovut Aleksandr*."

"*Menya zovut Aleksandr*," the boy dutifully repeated, and then, leaning to his mother and lowering his voice, whispered, "Tell me the number in Russian, see if I will understand. It's good practice for me. How much?"

"How much what?" said Harry.

"Nothing, Dad. Mom is teaching me how to count in Russian. Tell me, Mom," he whispered.

She was silent, struggling, ambivalent. "*Dvatsat tysach dollarov*," she finally whispered back.

Alexander gasped.

"What's wrong?" Harry looked up. "What did you see, son?"

"Nothing, Dad, nothing." He sat, his mouth agape, his astonished eyes unblinking.

"That's how you know you are fluent in Russian," Gina said. "If you can understand spoken numbers. It's one of the most difficult things to grasp in a foreign language. I know how hard it was for me in English."

Alexander slumped against the cloth seats. He glanced at his unaware and busy father, avoided catching his mother's eye, and turned to the window, placing his forehead on the December glass. "What are we headed to," he whispered, "if that's for the *just in case*?"

Gina didn't answer.

Soon Harry and Gina closed their eyes. Night fell. Only Alexander remained awake, catching the shadows of the mountains, the black peaks, the leafless trees, the needle spires, all fading from view. Teddy's house, where his family lived, Teddy's big house in Barrington, with a mother, a father, two sisters, and two grandparents, cost three thousand dollars. A Rolls-Royce his Aunty Esther once told Alexander she was thinking of buying cost twelve thousand dollars. And here was his mother, headed to *utopia*, with over six Teddy mansions or nearly two aunty Rolls-Royces stuffed in her back pocket, for the *just in case*.

For reasons he didn't understand and didn't want to, Alexander shivered, even though he and his mother were sitting close and were both covered by an itchy wool blanket. He hoped his mother was just being cautious. She had a tendency to be like that, just as she fussed over his coughing. Perhaps girls who came from volcanic Sicilian villages whose fathers were barbers and violin makers, who once had nothing, tended to be more careful about relocations. But Alexander felt queasy now that he saw the world through the prism of the troubling greenbacks. It was as if the money had tainted something inside him, had stained his anticipation of the bright future. Instead of excitement he began to feel dread.

Then why are we going, he wanted to ask, but his mother was sleeping. Perhaps the answer was the same as the one she had given him a while back, after his father was arrested, and she was arrested, too, because she had been by his side. Alexander had stayed on his own in their apartment until he thought to call Aunt Esther to come and get him. Thank goodness the telephone was still working then. His mother had returned home after four days, but wouldn't bail out his father. When Harry had finally come home after a month in jail, she was as livid with him as if the wounds were still freshly bleeding. Why do we stay? Alexander asked her that night, after their terrible fighting had subsided, a violent squall dispersing into scattered showers.

And she said, I stay because I love him. I stay because he is my family. Because you deserve to have a father. Everywhere he goes, I go. He is the ship, Alexander. We are just passengers. *Condividiamo l'amarezza.*

What if the ship goes down?

We go down, too. When I am dead and opened, his mother had said, the bitter tears still wet in her eyes, you will find your father lying on my heart.

Tonight on the train she said to Harry before she slept, "Let's hope Macbeth was wrong, husband. *All our yesterdays have lighted fools the way to dusty death.*"

542

"Who is Macbeth?" Alexander asked.

Harry waved away his mother's stab at an answer.

"Instead of teaching our son Shakespearean overdramatized nonsense, why don't you tell him *why* we're going. Tell him instead about Maxim Gorky's greatest prose poem, 'The Snake and the Falcon.'"

"Ah, dear Maxim again," Gina said. "He of the lyrical descriptions of peaceful Arctic retreats for enemies of Bolshevism." She folded her hands on her lap. "You know it so much better, Harry. Why don't *you* tell it?"

Harry got up and squeezed in between Gina and Alexander. Putting his arms around his wife and son, kissing one, then the other, he told Alexander a story. "The snake doesn't understand the falcon. 'Why don't you rest here in the dark, in the good slimy moisture?' the snake sibilates. 'Why soar to the heavens? Don't you know the dangers lurking there, the stress and storm awaiting you, the hunter's gun that will bring you down and destroy your life?' But the falcon ignores the serpent. It spreads its mighty wings and soars through the skies, its triumphant song resounding 'cross the heavens. One day the falcon is brought down, blood streaming from its heart, and the snake slithers to him and hisses: 'You fool. I warned you. I told you to stay where I am, in the dark, in the good warm moisture, where no one could find you and harm you.' With its last breath, the falcon replies: 'I have soared through the skies, I have scaled dazzling heights, I have beheld the light, I have lived, I have lived!'"

"That's all I wanted my life entire," Alexander's now sleeping mother had said. "To be the falcon, and not the serpent."

Alexander could barely make out the churches in the open valleys between the hills, the low lights, the spires and the evergreens, all shadow, but for the white crosses lit up by the dim evening lamps. The train raced on, not stopping in the small towns near the hills, towns much like the ones a young girl named Gina Attaviano left behind when she first sailed across the ocean. *That sea I loved*, Alexander whispered, reaching for the faint fading memory of Spanish carnivals and merry carousels, *and once or twice, I touched at isles of paradise.*

Epilogue

1936

"WHERE HAVE YOU BEEN? God!" Harold paces frantically through the kitchen. "You and your mother have been gone for days! Are you going to answer me? I've been worried *sick*. I was out of my mind. I didn't know what to think."

Gina is already inside, crumpled, lying down.

"Is your mother all right? She looks ..."

"She's fine, Dad, just tired."

"I thought the worst. Why would you do that to me? I thought the *worst*."

"And what would that be? Please—tell me."

"Don't start again. My God!" Other than this Harold doesn't answer, can't answer.

Father and son eventually calm down enough to sit at a wobbly table in the communal kitchen.

Alexander looks awful, and knows it. He is unshaven, haggard, exhausted. But his white-with-anxiety father doesn't look great either. He looks as if he hasn't shaved or eaten since his wife and son left.

Alexander agonizes over whether or not to tell his father the truth. Had they succeeded, had his mother succeeded in getting him inside the American consulate, he and his father would not be having this one-sided quarrel. It had felt wrong to Alexander to just up and go without a word to his father, not so much as a note on a scrap of paper.

545

As if there had been no life before the bleak day they took the train from Leningrad to Moscow, no happy summer in Krasnaya Polyana, no hockey on Frog Pond, no fishing, no love. His mother had said, you can write him a long letter *full* of words when you're out. But he isn't out. He's trying to figure out if there is still a need for words.

In the end Alexander says nothing. He doesn't have the heart to tell his father they have been to Moscow, with his mother's single desperate failed mission to save her son betraying everything his father has held most dear. Alexander knows what his mother has sacrificed with her plea to the Americans. He fears that the three of them have become duly marked, an endangered species, foreigners, spies, saboteurs, traitors. It's best his father doesn't know. He has the most to lose, so vocally the Soviets' most ardent defender all these years.

Alexander is afraid for his mother. He doesn't want Harold to lose his temper again. His mother is helpless these days and can't take Harold's anger. Alexander is not helpless, but he can't take it either. He doesn't want them to have another ugly scene. Lord knows there have been enough of them. Alexander lies to protect his mother and to comfort his father. He lies to give them a fraction of peace on what might be the last calm night, the last calm day. On some level he has to admit he feels relieved. It had felt so wrong to flee, to leave his father behind, oblivious and unknowing. It had felt like abandonment. Like betrayal.

"You're not leaving him behind!" his mother told him, crying, trying to persuade him. "You're leaving him with me. That's his place, and it's my place, too. With him. *I'm* not going. Only you. I made my life. Not you. Your father made his life. Not you." Sobs filled the long gaps between her words.

And although Alexander is sandpapered raw with anxiety for what's ahead, he is grateful to see his father again.

He tells Harold he took his mother to Pulkovo, to a sanatorium, to dry her out.

"You took her for three days to Pulkovo?" Harold repeats it slowly as if he doesn't believe it. "To dry her out?"

"They wouldn't take her."

"No?" He scrutinizes Alexander.

"They said she wasn't sick enough."

"If your mother is not sick, the word has no meaning."

Alexander says nothing. He doesn't understand how his once perfect mother could have fallen so deep into the liquid abyss of the bottomless bottle.

"So it wasn't a success?"

All Alexander hears is his mother pleading, screaming, crying into the closed face of the consulate guard, as he keeps trying to pull her away, *Please please please help him, we have money, a place to live, help him, help him, help him—*

"No, Dad. It was a complete failure."

Silence. Then from Harold, an echo of Alexander's own heart, only broken: "What a shame."

Alexander stares at his father in troubled confusion. Harold's hands are shaking, his lips are trembling. Alexander can see his father struggling with disbelief, with anguished suspicion. Yet his father's tortured, exhausted gaze is softened, as his mother's is softened, by the wellspring of devotion for their only child. Harold's entire lined countenance seems to grow younger as he gazes at his son, mines his son's face so intensely, as if, Alexander doesn't know what, as if Harold is trying to carve the boy's features into the marble of his memory.

"What is it, Dad?"

"Nothing." Harold blinks, but doesn't look away. "You don't look well."

"I know. We were on the trains too long."

"Pulkovo is only a few hours away," Harold says quietly. "Really, how long could it have been?"

Without a pause: "We were stopped forever between stations."

"Ah. Perhaps they were fixing the railroad."

"Or building it."

Lightly they both nod, no rueful smiles between them.

"Where did you sleep for two nights?"

"On a park bench."

His father reels away from the table. "You and your *mother* slept on a bench?" Old before his time, Harold lowers his head and stares elsewhere for understanding, for truth, for illusion. "*Everything is mud,*" he whispers.

Alexander forces himself to clear his throat. Reaching out, he puts his hand over his father's, pats him gently. "Dad, it's fine. We're making the best of it. She is not as sick as we feared. That's good, right? Listen, I'm sorry, but … is there any food? I'm starving."

Harold leaps up, grateful to be spurred into feeble action. He throws some wood inside the stove and in a few minutes is frying up some potatoes with onions. Alexander can't wait. Standing by his father's side, he eats straight from the pan, the potatoes half raw, laden with salt and pepper. He *inhales* the food, swallows it almost without chewing.

"There is never enough food, never."

"It's terrible to be hungry," agrees Harold.

"I can't wait until the Red Army takes me. They feed their soldiers well."

"Please, God, don't joke. Now is *not* the time."

Alexander swears. "I'm such an idiot. Did I eat all there is?"

Harold shakes his head. "No, I ate earlier. Eat, son, eat."

They stand in the silent kitchen. His back stooped, Harold steps away, watching his son scrape clean the cast-iron pan with a wooden spoon. Eventually he takes the empty pan away. "It'll get better. Sit. I'll make you some tea. I just got a second job. Nights and weekends. I'll be making a few extra rubles."

"What are you doing?"

"Carpentry, believe it or not. Benches, tables." Harold smiles. "I *know*. Don't look so shocked. Amazing, though, isn't it? The past always catches up with us."

"Doesn't it just. Grandpa would be proud of you."

"You think so?" Harold shakes his head. "Why do I doubt it?"

Alexander rattles the rickety table. "Perhaps they can find you a spirit level at your new job?" He smiles.

"Hey, my table is perfectly level," says Harold. "This floor is uneven." His mouth twists. "In any case," he quickly carries on speaking, "we'll have extra for food. You know my friend Slava? He says he can get us white bread. And for a hundred rubles, even some meat. We'll save. Maybe for your seventeenth birthday next month we'll have enough to celebrate with a half-kilo of pork. Would you like that?"

Alexander says nothing for a few moments.

"How much would you need? To get food."

Harold shrugs. "I don't know, two hundred? For pork, some bread. And chocolate." He smacks his lips. "It's been such a long time since I've had chocolate. Never thought I'd miss it as I do. I'm drooling just thinking about it."

Alexander watches his father, affection etched on his young face. Reaching into the inner breast pocket of his parka, he peels off a few bills from the hidden stash inside.

"Here." He slides four hundred rubles across the table as if he's playing poker. Years ago, when they were still living in Moscow, desperately hungry, they had changed half of his mother's money into rubles on the black market. They spent nearly all of them on food.

Harold stares at the money as if he's never seen rubles before. "Where did you get this?"

"When Mom was still working at the Leningrad library," Alexander says, "I would make her give it to me, so she wouldn't spend it unwisely." Father and son look away from each other. They both can't bear to think about what's been happening to their wife and mother. "So take it and buy us some food from Slava. Not in May, but now. I need food now. Get it, but hurry back, and we'll have a feast. Get some *kvas* to drink. Get some butter, too. We'll eat like kings. I'll wake Mom when you come back. She'll be happy to have a little butter with her white bread."

Slowly, Harold reaches for the money. "I understand nothing," he says. "I can't save fifty rubles, but you can take four hundred from your barely working mother?"

"Mom and I don't have bills to pay, Dad," Alexander says. "You do."

"You're sitting in front of me with more money than I make in six months. What's going on?"

I don't know what's going on, Alexander thinks. "What don't you understand?"

"I'll tell you what I don't understand. Why didn't you use it to buy yourself food? Why are you coming back ravenous with a fistful of rubles?"

Alexander squeezes his father's hand that's clutching the money. "We didn't want to eat without you," he says. "Now will you stop asking questions and go? You go, and I'll wait."

Harold gets up. He puts on his coat and hat, and before leaving the kitchen where Alexander sits, shadowed, solemn, studying the grain of the square table, he walks over to his son, leans to him, pats his stubbled cheek, and kisses his black head. "You're a good boy, bud."

"I know. And you're a good dad. But you'd be a better one if you brought back some grub."

In the crooked doorway, Harold glances back. "I just want to say ..."

Alexander tensely waits.

Tears spring to Harold's eyes. Alexander looks away.

Black moments tick by.

"I don't know where you went. You don't want to tell me. That's fine. But I hope you and your mother didn't do anything stupid to put you in danger. I told you how careful you must be. You saw what happened to Mario and Viktor."

Alexander turns toward the darkened window. "How can I not be in danger, Dad?" One of the glass panes is cracked, and the cold April wind is whistling through. "I'm the man without a country."

Harold nearly doesn't continue; his legs won't hold him. "*You* are your country now!" He opens wide his hands, then makes a shape like a barricade. "Build walls around you, a fortress. Arm yourself. Protect yourself. Find a way to keep yourself."

For a moment they stare wordlessly at one another.

"Son, promise me you'll find a way."

"I want to be ignorant of all mysteries, but free," Alexander says.

Harold leaves to get his family butter and bread from the black market with the rubles his wife had stockpiled, just in case.

Like a statue Alexander fruitlessly remains, palms down, into the long night.

What did his father say to him in Russian just before he left? Quoting his mother quoting Isaiah. Я начертал тебя на ладонях своих; стены твои всегда предо тною. *I have engraved you on the palms of my hands. Your walls are ever before me.*

Alexander waits and waits. He falls asleep in the chair, his head pressed into the rocking wooden table.

Paullina Simons

Six Days in Leningrad

a memoir

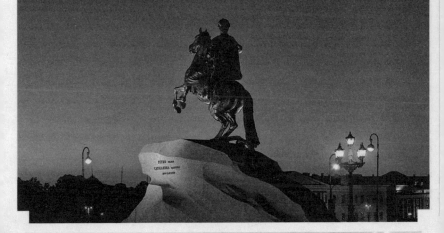

Six Days in Leningrad

PAULLINA SIMONS

The never-before-told story of the journey behind
The Bronze Horseman

Available now as an ebook

From the author of the celebrated, internationally bestselling Bronze Horseman saga comes a glimpse into the private life of its much loved creator, and the real story behind the epic novels. Paullina Simons gives us a work of non-fiction as captivating and heart-wrenching as the lives of Tatiana and Alexander.

Only a few chapters into writing her first story set in Russia, her mother country, Paullina Simons travelled to Leningrad (now St Petersburg) with her beloved Papa. What began as a research trip turned into six days that forever changed her life, the course of her family, and the novel that became *The Bronze Horseman*.

After a quarter-century away from her native land, Paullina and her father found a world trapped in yesteryear, with crumbling stucco buildings, entire families living in seven-square-meter communal apartments, and barren fields bombed so badly that nothing would grow there even fifty years later.

And yet there were the spectacular white nights, the warm hospitality of family friends and, of course, the pelmeni and caviar. At times poignant, at times inspiring and funny, this is both a fascinating glimpse into the inspiration behind the epic saga, and a touching story of a family's history, a father and a daughter, and the fate of a nation.

Read on for an exclusive extract …

Before: The Texas Life

Kevin and i got to our new house at 8:20 in the morning and not a moment too soon because the moving truck was already parked in front of the driveway. We had to drive on the grass to go around it. We had barely opened the garage doors when the moving guys started laying down their moving blankets and getting out their wheeling carts. The next thing we knew, they were moving stuff into the house.

Into a house, I might add, that wasn't ready yet. The builder's cleaning crew had just arrived. The cleaning women were in the kitchen, scrubbing. The movers started piling boxes onto the carpet that had not been vacuumed since the day it was installed. So, in other words, *never*.

I asked the women to please vacuum the rooms before they continued with their other tasks so that the movers could pile the boxes onto clean carpets. You would have thought I had asked them to carry heavy objects on their backs upstairs in 100-degree heat. First the diminutive ladies huffed and puffed, and then they said they spoke no Inglés. Phil, my building manager, explained to me that the women worked at their own pace and according to their own schedule. I looked at him as if *he* were not speaking Inglés to me and finally said, "Phil, I don't know if you've noticed, but we're moving in. Please ask them to vacuum the floor in the bedroom and the living room."

"Problem is," Phil said, "Most of them don't speak any English."

"Could you find one that does?"

My two young sons, Misha, three, and Kevie, one, zigzagged in front of the movers. I think they were trying to trip them. Misha was crying, "I don't want to go to Burger King for breakfast, I don't want to go to Burger King for breakfast!" Natasha, eleven, was wisely reading, perched on top of a book box, ignoring everyone and everything.

The babysitter cajoled him, but in the meantime, the one-year-old had toddled off to the pool. The dogs barked non-stop. They either wanted to be let in, be let out or be shot.

My husband ran in and said, "Please go to the garage and talk to the movers. They need one of us there at all times to tell them where things are going."

"But I labeled all the rooms!" I protested.

"Well, they don't know where to go," Kevin said.

The pool guy knocked on the back porch door. "Hey, guys? Is this a bad time to show you how to use the pool equipment?"

One-year-old Kevie ran in from the pool, draped himself around his father's leg and wouldn't let go until dad picked him up. The babysitter pried him off with difficulty. The dogs continued to bark. Three-year-old Misha continued to scream about Burger King. Apparently, he wanted to stay right here at the new house.

Our builder walked in. "Well, good morning! We needed just a couple of more days with this house, but that's okay, we'll make it work! Hey, do you have a couple of minutes to go over the change orders? I have your closing contract. I need both you and Kevin to sign."

One of the moving guys stuck his head in and said pointedly, "Mrs. Simons, could we see you in the garage, please?"

The phone rang.

How could that be? I didn't think we'd unpacked a phone yet.

Open boxes were on the kitchen counter.

The front door bell rang. It was the guy from Home Depot. He had brought the barbecue. Where would I like it?

Another delivery truck stopped in front of the house. This one was unloading a dryer and a television.

Another truck pulled up, this one with my office desk. The two desk guys steadfastly refused to take the desk upstairs, "because we're not insured for damage." They asked if maybe the moving guys could move my desk upstairs.

The moving guys said they *certainly* weren't insured to move the desk upstairs. So I told the desk guys that either they moved the desk upstairs or else they could take it right back to the warehouse.

They moved the desk upstairs.

"*Mrs. Simons!*"

In the garage, the four large moving guys stood with their arms folded and impatiently told me they were having a problem with the cleaning ladies who really needed to stay out of their way. "We cannot do our job, *Mrs.* Simons." Again punctuating my marital status.

The dogs were still barking. My sons were now running around in the street as the babysitter ran after them trying to corral them into the minivan.

Pressing my fingers into my temples, I looked at my watch. It was 8:45 AM.

The phone rang again. It was my father. "Hey, Papa," I said weakly.

"Are you excited about our trip?" he asked.

"Huh?"

"Our trip to Russia? It's not a small thing, you know, you going back for the first time in twenty-five years. Are you thinking about it?"

"Oh, absolutely, Papa. I'm thinking about it right now."

THE BRONZE HORSEMAN

WE HAD BEEN PLANNING our trip to Russia for a year. Ever since the summer of 1997 when I told my family that my fourth novel *The Bronze Horseman* was going to be a love story set in WWII Russia during the siege of Leningrad. I said I couldn't write a story so detailed and sprawling, if only in my mind, without seeing Russia with my own eyes.

My family had listened to me very carefully, and my 90-year-old grandfather said, "Plina, I hope I'm not going to be turning over in my grave reading the lies you're going to write in your book about Russia."

"I hope not, Dedushka," I said. "Though you're not dead."

Going to St. Petersburg was not an option before the summer of 1998. The logistics of the trip were too overwhelming. How would I get a non-Russian-speaking husband and three non-Russian-speaking kids, one of them barely walking, to Russia? And what would they do there? Either my husband would be watching the kids full-time in a foreign country — and not just any foreign country, but Russia! — or we would be watching them together, and I wouldn't be doing any research.

I didn't need to go all the way to Russia to take care of my kids. I could stay home in Texas and do it. Kevin and I considered leaving them and going just the two of us, but in the end decided that was a bad idea. Leave the kids with a babysitter for ten days? Too much; for them, for us.

Still, thoughts of Russia would not go away. Also, there was no book. Eighteen months earlier there had been a nebulous vision of two young lovers walking in deserted Leningrad on the eve of a brutal war, but a vision does not an epic story make. How could I not go to Russia?

I finally said to Kevin that it looked like I would have to go on my own. He didn't love the idea, my going to a "place like Russia" by myself. He said I should bring my sister.

I ran the idea by my father. "Kevin thinks I should take Liza to Russia with me," I said.

My father was quiet on the phone for what seemed like an hour, smoking and thinking, and then said, "I could come with you to Russia."

I had not thought of that.

A girlfriend of mine said, "Oh, that's neat! When was the last time you and your dad took a trip together?"

"Never."

That had been nine months ago. And little by little the trip took shape. My father told me, "Paullina, I'm retiring at the end of May. We have to go before I retire." My father is the director of Russian Services for Radio Liberty/Radio Free Europe. Working has defined and consumed him. Working is and has been his life. And with good reason. His team of writers translated western news, both political and cultural, into Russian and then broadcast it over short waves to Eastern Europe and the Soviet Union. They broadcast to Russia 24/7 with 12 hours of original programming every day. For twenty-five years. I believe that four people were responsible for bringing down the Berlin Wall and Communism during 1989-91: Ronald Reagan, Margaret Thatcher, Pope John Paul II, and my father.

We couldn't find a convenient time for both of us to go. Finally my father postponed his retirement a few months and we settled on July 1998. It was the perfect time to go, my father told me, because we would stand a chance of having some nice weather. Also the nights would be white. "That's a sight to see. You do remember white nights, Plina?"

"Not much, Papa."

What would be the shortest time I could go to Russia, and not traumatize my kids? I figured a day to travel there, a day to travel back, and then six days in St. Petersburg. But I vacillated, procrastinated, mulled.

Truth was, I didn't want to go.

In 1973 There Were Sharks

I WAS BORN IN St. Petersburg when it was still called Leningrad and came to America when I was ten. We left Leningrad one fall day and lived in Rome while we waited for our entry visa to the United States.

Those were blissful months. Every Thursday my mother gave me a few lire to go to the movies by myself *and* buy a bag of potato chips. That bag was worth three movies. I'd never eaten anything so delicious in Russia. The movies were all in Italian, of which I spoke exactly three phrases: *bella bambina*, *bruta bambina* and *mandjare per favore*. Cute baby, ugly baby, and food please. It was two more phrases than I spoke in English.

We spent my tenth birthday in Rome. My parents asked me what I wanted, and I said, gum. I got gum. Also some strawberry Italian gelato and then we went to the American movies. We saw *The Man for All Seasons*. I liked the gum better than the movie. I didn't understand a word of it, but at the end, a man had his head cut off.

We came to America two days before Thanksgiving 1973. Our first big American meal was turkey and mashed potatoes and something called cranberry jelly. We celebrated in Connecticut, in the home of a young man we met briefly in Vienna and who invited us to his house for the holidays. We gave thanks for our amazing luck, for getting out of Russia, for coming to America. After all, America was every Russian's beckoning light. America seemed like heaven. True, first you had to die, but *then*, you had—America! The death was leaving Russia. Because once you had left you could never go back.

America was life after death.

That Thanksgiving when everyone else at the table was done with their meal, my father walked around the table and finished all the food that the Americans had left behind on their plates. People of a certain age born in Leningrad do not leave food on their plates.

Our second American meal was the lasagna our landlady brought up to our apartment in Woodside, Queens. Don't ask me how this is, but during our stay in Rome, *Italy*, I had not tasted tomato sauce once. I had not had lasagna. I had not had pizza. I did not know tomato sauce until our Italian landlady knocked on our door in Woodside.

In America there was Juicy Fruit gum, and chocolate ice cream, which I had never had, and something called Coca Cola, which I also had never had. And television. I found a children's cartoon: *Looney Tunes*. I had never seen anything like it in Leningrad. In Russia, we had black and white war movies, black and white news. There was some animated programming, but it looked like war movies, though less interesting.

War movies and news. The Olympics. Which was the single most exciting thing on Soviet television, but unfortunately the Olympics came only once every four years.

Suddenly, in my life there was *Looney Tunes*! Bugs Bunny! Elmer Fudd. Porky Pig! Our first TV set was black and white, but the cartoons were straight out of someone else's Technicolor dream. The bunny blew up a pig and a hunter, ran away, blew up a cave and fell off a cliff, all in eight minutes.

The war movies in Russia were set in gray tents and starred two gray men who talked non-stop until there was a battle, followed by more dialogue, all concluding in a blaze, more dialogue and eventual victory for Mother Russia. The movies lasted, it seemed to me, as long as the war itself.

In Queens, after eight minutes, the *Looney Tunes* bunny disappeared and was suddenly replaced by a lady selling towels made of paper. Towels made of *paper*? The cartoon was over, so I turned off the TV, utterly disappointed.

It took me many weeks and the force of inertia to discover that the cartoon did not end but was merely interrupted by the lady selling towels made of paper. Imagine my happiness!

I used to read in Russia, and who could blame me? What else was there to do? Now that I had Bugs Bunny, all reading vanished for a good four or five years.

In school I would occasionally be asked to talk to the other students about my experience of life in the Soviet Union. That's how it was put: "Your *experience* of life in the Soviet Union." I wanted to say even then that it wasn't my *experience* of life, it actually *was* my life, but I didn't. I did give my broken-English little talk: about the communal apartment, the small rooms, the cockroaches falling on my bed while I slept, about the bed bugs and the smell of decomposing skunk they made when I accidentally squished them, about the lack of food, the lack of stores, the lack of my father.

When I was asked, "How did it feel living with that kind of deprivation?" I would shrug and say, "I didn't know it was deprivation. I thought it was just life."

My American friends grew up with Coca Cola and Jesus Christ.

I grew up with hot black tea and the astronaut Yuri Gagarin—the first man in space.

Kevin watched *I Dream of Jeannie* and *Star Trek*.

I watched Gagarin's funeral, and a one-hundred-and-twenty part film called *Liberation* — burning tents and dark winter nights —which they rebroadcast every December because Decembers near the Arctic circle just weren't bleak enough.

I'd never seen a palm tree, I'd never seen an ocean, I'd never heard a church service, and had never read *Charlotte's Web*. I read *The Three Musketeers*, *Les Misérables* and a Russian writer named Mikhail Zoschenko. By the time I was ten I had read all of Anton Chekhov and Jules Verne, but what I wanted, though I did not know it, was Nancy Drew and Laura Ingalls Wilder.

What was baseball? What was peanut butter? I didn't know. I knew what soccer was, what mushroom barley soup was, what perch was.

And who was this Jesus Christ?

I, who had not grown up with Christmas carols, pageants, cookies, decorations and a divine baby in a cave, had no idea what Jesus had to do with Christmas. My first Christmas Eve in New York my parents went out, leaving me, I thought, alone and joyfully watching Bonanza, except to my great consternation, Michael Landon on whom I had quite the crush, was replaced on Channel 11 by nothing but a log burning on the fire and instrumental musak playing in the darkened background. My Pavlovian reaction to learning that the pre-emption of Bonanza was all about something called Christmas, was less than spiritually positive, as you can imagine.

While my husband was vacationing near Lake George, I was learning how to swim in the icy Black Sea.

Kevin knew Atlantic Ocean beaches? I knew the dirty sand on the Gulf of Finland. It was enough for me when I was a child. I spent ten summers of my life in a tiny Russian fishing village called Shepelevo near the Gulf of Finland, and it was all I needed. My childhood summers in that village is the treasure I carry with me through life.

But I didn't want to go back there.

I lived ten years of my life in a communal apartment, nine families sharing 13 rooms, two kitchens, two bathrooms.

Didn't want to go back there either.

My father was arrested when I was four and spent the next five years of his life—and mine—in a Soviet prison, in a Soviet labor camp, in exile.

I lived alone. With my silent mother.

Not interested in reliving any part of that.

There was no romanticizing our life in Russia. In leaving, we had all died and gone to heaven. If it weren't for my stupid book, why on earth would I want to go back?

The Bronze Horseman

PAULLINA SIMONS

A magnificent epic of love, war and Russia …

Leningrad 1941: the white nights of summer when the sun hardly sets on the beautiful palaces and stately avenues that still speak of a different age, when the city was known as St Petersburg. Two sisters, Tatiana and Dasha, share the same bed, living in one room with their brother and parents.

On 22 June 1941, Hitler invades Russia and Tatiana meets a brash young officer named Alexander. For the Metanovs, for Leningrad and for Tatiana, life will never be the same again. With bombs falling, the city under siege and the Russian winter closing in, Tatiana and Alexander are drawn to each other in an impossible love. It is a love that could tear Tatiana's family apart, a love that carries a secret that could mean death for anyone who hears it.

Mesmerizing from the very first page to the final, breathtaking end, *The Bronze Horseman* brings alive the story of two indomitable, heroic spirits and their great love that triumphs over the devastation of a country at war.